THE COMPLETE DEADLAND SAGA

RACHEL AUKES

WAYPOINT BOOKS

Series by Rachel Aukes

The Deadland Saga

Bounty Hunter

Waymaker Wars

Space Troopers

Flight of the Javelin

Fringe Series

WAYPOINT BOOKS

For Brian, always.

100 Days in Deadland

Part One of the Deadland Saga

PART ONE
LIMBO

THE FIRST CIRCLE OF HELL

ONE

I paused on the way to my two o'clock meeting, and watched the woman standing outside the restroom with her forehead against the wall, clawing at the paint. After a long moment, I hesitantly reached out. "Excuse me, are you all right?"

At the sound of my voice, Melanie from Accounting turned her head. Her skin had a sickly jaundiced pallor to it, her eyes glazed over. She stared, swaying from side to side in a stilted trance-like manner.

I winced. "Christ, you look like shit."

She groaned, the jerky motion causing the line of drool hanging from her mouth to swing from side to side. She cocked her head as though trying to figure me out.

I took a cautious step back, not wanting to catch whatever bug was taking my coworkers and half of the Midwest by storm today. Ever since lunch, people had started complaining of indigestion. The cafeteria's daily special had been known to bring on afternoon bouts of heartburn, but this was crazy. "You had the taco salad, too, huh?"

The door to the women's restroom swung open and a blur ran past us, startling me and knocking Melanie out of her stupor. Her lips curled in a snarl. Then she lunged at me, her jaws snapping.

"Shit!" Lucky for me, she moved slowly and I sidestepped to the left, leaving her to stumble clumsily onto her stomach. My papers fluttered to the floor while she floundered around. I threw out my hands. "What the fuck, Mel!"

She glared up at me, this time vocalizing a guttural growl that sent shivers up my neck. She jerkily dragged herself up. Fear crept into my nerves. I edged around her, careful to keep my distance, and pulled the bathroom door open and jumped inside.

I put all my weight into pushing the door closed, but Melanie was over twice my size. She heaved the door open, tumbled inside, and took me down. The air whooshed from my lungs. She pressed against me, her jaws snapping like she wanted to swear-to-God *eat* me.

Holy fuck, I'd been scared in my life before, but this went beyond terror. When folks talk about fight or flight instincts, it's really fight *and* flight instincts. Everything I'd learned from self-defense classes was forgotten as I held my forearm against her neck while kicking and pushing with everything I had to get out from under her.

My arm shook under the weight. With a surge, I rolled her off me and shoved away. She grabbed at me, her fingers snagging my shirt and taking most of a sleeve with her with a loud rip. With nothing left to pull, the back of her head collided into the wall with a solid smack.

The bathroom door opened, and a high-pitched shriek pierced the air.

"Help!" I yelled while kicking away from Melanie, my Doc Martens squeaking across the floor, but whoever had opened the door had already disappeared.

A staccato pounding erupted from one of the bathroom stalls, matching the beating of my heart.

Knocking her head against the wall didn't slow down Melanie in the least. If anything, she was more pissed off than ever, now crawling at me like a clumsy, rabid dog. Out of the corner of my eye, I caught the yellow "caution: wet floor" sign propped in the corner. I grabbed it and swung just as she closed the distance, nailing her across the cheek.

Snarling, she charged and I swung again, this time breaking her nose. Thick brown blood sprayed out with every snort and hiss. She came back at me like I hadn't even hit her. With no time to swing, I shoved the hinged end of the plastic sign forward as hard as I could, karate-chopping her in the throat. The force knocked her back just enough for me to get solidly onto the balls of my feet.

Having her windpipe crushed put an end to the animal sounds and stopped her from spraying any more blood. Yet, even though she clearly couldn't breathe, she came at me again like she didn't even need air.

Terror froze my muscles.

My instructor had said a throat chop would take down an assailant in mere seconds. Yet, it had done nothing to stop a desk jockey from Accounting.

With the pounding and growling escalating from the bathroom stall a few feet away, I started swinging the sign relentlessly at Melanie's head. My heart pounded and my breaths came in gulps, yet Melanie kept on coming at me.

When she moved to pounce, I slammed the sign into her temple, causing her to misjudge her attack, and she head butted the wall instead. She turned around. Her forehead was a bloody mess, and she still didn't seem fazed.

"What the hell?" I asked breathlessly and swung again. The now-bloody sign's corner nailed her in the eye, knocking an eyeball out of its socket. Another hit made her eyeball swing until it finally flew free and bounced off the wall. I swung again and again and again, my blows echoed by whoever was pounding on the stall door.

Bones crunched, and Melanie collapsed face-forward onto the floor.

More of that gelatinous coffee-colored blood trickled from her head and pooled on the floor. I hit her with the sign one more time to make sure she wasn't playing possum, and I was about to kick her when the stall door swung open and Julie, the new girl, tumbled onto the floor. She looked up at me with that same sickly, *ravenous* look.

"Agh!" I smacked her in the face with the sign, and ran out of the bathroom, throwing the sign at her before I yanked the door open.

And I found myself in utter chaos.

I flattened against the wall in the corner where I'd come across Melanie earlier. Copies of my meeting agenda still littered the floor. Cubicle city was generally a quiet place except for the white noise piped in, but now people were running, shouting, and screaming. The pounding of work shoes across hollow floors echoed around me. Over a nearby cubicle wall, I watched as one man tackled another to the ground, his mouth clamping onto his victim's throat. The other man screamed. Red dots splattered the beige fabric walls.

I'd like to think that it was because I was in shock that I didn't run to help. But to be honest, I was scared shitless. Still watching the wall where the men went down, I ducked and crabbed down the hall, trying to ignore the anguished screams, focused only on avoiding the crazies. When the man's screams abruptly stopped, something in my brain kicked me into gear, and I took off running toward my cubicle.

A hand reached out for me, and I twisted away. The work alarms blared. Phones were ringing everywhere. There were more screams and shouts in every direction. Some were begging for help, others were crying.

"Calm down! It will be okay!" a woman yelled from her desk. The next second, bloodied hands grabbed her and yanked her down as she let out an earsplitting scream.

Someone ran into me and I jumped back to find Alan from my team. He looked behind him before looking at me, his eyes wide. "This shit's fucked up. I'm outta here," he said under his breath as he headed past me.

Biting my lip, I glanced down the direction of my cube a dozen long feet away, where my bag and car keys waited in a drawer, and then turned back to Alan. "Wait up," I called out. "I'm coming, too."

He kept moving, and I sprinted to catch up. He slowed down, looking to the right, and I tugged him to the left. "This way."

We ran in the opposite direction of the mass exodus heading toward the main elevators. Alan hit the down button at the rarely used back bay of elevators. While we waited, a terrifying image shot through my mind of Melanie jumping out from the small six-by-six compartment.

Just as the elevator dinged, I grabbed Alan's elbow and tugged. "Stairs."

"Why?" he asked but followed me around the corner to the back stairs.

There were several others already heading down the steps. Alan pushed ahead of me, and I stayed at his back as he shoved past others, followed by a chorus of "hey" and "watch it."

We were only on floor eight, so we made it down the stairs fairly quickly. I paused at the third floor landing when I saw two men tackle a third man. One bit a chunk out of the guy's face while the other went for the screamer's throat. My adrenaline had already taken over, and my feet kept moving despite my shock. A gunshot rang out somewhere on the first floor. It was kind of like watching disasters on TV. It's so horrendously surreal that it doesn't fully register in the brain as reality. The whole Prima Insurance building had turned into the set of a slasher film, and unwillingness to face reality was the only reason I hadn't frozen.

Alan flung open the large glass doors. I rushed outside, shading my eyes against the afternoon sun, and scanned the parking lot. Some spaces were empty, some cars were tearing out of the lot, but most were still peacefully parked, waiting for their owners.

Gunfire erupted somewhere in the distance.

"Where's your car?" I asked breathlessly.

He turned around and looked at me like he'd forgotten I was still there. "Uh." He looked around. "Over there." He pointed to Lot C and took off toward it.

We were panting, but we sprinted all the way to his car, making wide arcs around other people running to their cars. It was a warm spring day, and my clothes clung to my sweaty skin.

Alan was an early-morning person, so his small Mitsubishi was parked only a few cars down the second row. He fumbled with his keys before holding out the fob. The lights flashed, and I yanked open the passenger door.

I swept the papers and CDs off the seat with a brisk move and fell onto the hot black leather. I had my door locked before Alan had the key in the ignition. The engine roared to life, and he squealed the tires in reverse, throwing me against the dash.

I hastily fastened my seatbelt and held on.

"What the hell is going on around here?" he muttered, throwing the car into gear and squealing the tires again.

I swallowed. "No idea."

For the past two weeks, there'd been talk about a fast-spreading epidemic in South America that had been quickly moving northward, though I hadn't worried. The Midwest was a long distance from South America, and we'd closed our borders to Mexico over a week ago. And most of the military stood between us and them to make sure the borders stayed closed.

Strange. The epidemic in South America was said to cause violent symptoms, exactly like what I'd seen today.

Maybe I should've worried.

Today had started as a typical Thursday. I'd listened to the radio on the commute to work. There'd been more talk on the growing epidemic, but local news overshadowed talks of the epidemic. At Prima, gossip ran wild all morning about last night's attacks on joggers and walkers in nearly every southern state west of the Mississippi. Several paranoid employees had called in sick today.

Then, two cooks in the cafeteria got into some kind a brawl just before lunch. One left in an ambulance, and the other had been taken away in handcuffs. The news was reporting similar attacks across the Midwest and Western United States. With all that, would Prima close for the day? Hell, no.

Several worried employees had already left for home to pick up their kids from school. And now, not even three hours after lunch, half of the office was going ape-shit crazy on each other. Whatever was going on, it felt like I was caught in the middle of Ground Zero for some seriously screwed up shit.

I focused on breathing in and out. I reached for the radio and fumbled with the knob. I wrung my shaking hands, wiped them on my black pants, but they kept shaking.

Alan cranked up the volume, and I noticed his hands were shaking even worse.

"Reports are coming in from Kansas City, Des Moines, and Minneapolis of a fast-spreading pandemic. Seek shelter immediately and avoid contact with anyone infected. The infected will display violent tendencies and attack without provocation. They do not respond to reason," an unfamiliar even-toned woman reported. *"If you or a loved one is infected, you should quarantine yourself immediately so as not to spread the virus. Do not go to the hospitals as they are at full capacity. Stay tuned for more information."*

"That's it?" Alan asked. "That's all those idiots have to say about this thing? Nothing like how it's transmitted, or what we can do to protect ourselves?"

"Give it time," I said. The news last night had shown footage of random people attacking others without provocation, but I'd assumed the attacks were the result of some new illegal drug gone bad. The idea of a pandemic made my jaw clench.

My dad was a doctor. My mom was a nurse.

My parents, early-retiree snowbirds, lived in a southern suburb of Des Moines. With me as their only child, they kept their house in town for the warmer months while moving to Arizona every winter. I prayed that they were safe at home, that they didn't think to go help out at the hospital. I had to believe they saw the news this morning and knew better than to get caught in the middle of some off-the-charts violent pandemic.

I wanted to call them to make sure they were all right, but my phone was tucked into my bag, which was still sitting in a drawer at my cubicle. I looked over at Alan. "Can I use your phone?"

He felt his pockets and then frantically swerved around a fender bender before shooting through a red light. Sirens blared as a police car sped past us.

"I think it's still on my desk," Alan replied in between panting breaths.

"This is crazy," I said. "Everyone's gone crazy."

"It's got to be a terrorist attack," he said. "Chemical warfare or something that's making people go nuts. It's like they're jacked up on serious shit like bath salts or something. Damn it!" He swerved again. "This traffic is insane." He turned to me, his glasses slipping down his sweaty nose. "You live on the north side, right?"

I nodded. "Yeah, why?"

"I'm way out on the east side. Mind if we hit your place until the roads open up?" His voice cracked and he wiped his face.

"Sure." I scrutinized him. "Are you okay?"

He grabbed the wheel with both hands. "No, I'm not okay! What about today would make you think that I'm okay? That anything's okay? It's World War III out there. No, it's worse than that. It's like the end of the world out there!"

I got it, I really did. The proverbial shit had hit the fan, and the rational part of my mind had decided to curl up in the fetal position. "We got out early," I said with as much confidence as I could muster. "Hopefully we can beat the worst of the traffic."

As though on cue, a car veered in front of us and rammed into the concrete separating the lanes. "Watch out!" I shouted as Alan cranked the wheel, nearly sideswiping the vehicle. I could've sworn the driver looked in the same bad way that Melanie had. The SUV behind us wasn't so lucky because it rammed into the jackknifed car and started a domino-effect pile-up behind us.

Alan and I stared at each other, and he stepped on the gas.

In the background, the radio station had switched to interviewing people outside one of the hospitals.

"I thought the kid was lost. I bent down to help, and the little bugger bit me! Can you believe that? The kid damn near took my thumb clean off! He went nuts, like he had rabies or something. And now they won't let me into the hospital. They've got barricades in front of the doors, and cops are in full riot gear, just standing around everywhere. I'm stuck outside bleeding, and no one is telling us what's going on. We have a right to know!"

"You think you got it bad?" another male voice chimed in. *"You should've been downtown. This old bum attacked a woman. I saw it all. He was stumbling around all drunk-like, and then he just attacked. He went straight for that poor gal's throat like he thought he was a vampire or something. A couple guys tried to pull him off her, but he wouldn't let go. I jumped in to help, and he tore a chunk out of my arm. He wouldn't stop.*

Some guy had to shoot him. Can you believe it? It was insane, man. What's the world coming to?"

My heart felt like it was going to jump out of my chest, and I found myself on the verge of hyperventilating. I punched in another radio station, only to find the same barrage of stories. No one had any useful information, just more of those horrific tales. I leaned back, tried to tune out the radio, and focused on the traffic outside. With every mile, the number of vehicles on the side of the road increased. Some cars were in pileups, others looked like they had stopped haphazardly, as though their drivers had decided to simply stop driving.

I sucked in a deep breath. "I think I killed Melanie," I said quietly.

"Melanie Carlson?"

"What?" I glanced at Alan. "Oh. No. The other Melanie."

"Oh." He frowned. "Did she try to hurt you?"

"Of course she tried to hurt me. She tried to *eat* me."

Alan was quiet for a time. "I bet she could eat a lot."

I belted out a laugh. Not because it was funny but because my adrenaline high was coming down, and with it, my shock. Alan laughed, too, though the stress was getting to him. He wiped his sweaty forehead with his arm and kept driving.

I'd killed someone today. The truth really hit me just then, and I let my head fall against the headrest. I hadn't even thought about the repercussions. Would I go to jail, even though it was an open-and-shut case of self-defense? I closed my eyes and rubbed my temples. I'd lose my job. That was a given. How the hell would I pay the bills?

And then there was Melanie. That poor woman's final minutes were in a bathroom of all places.

"No, no, no, *no*," Alan chanted.

Startled, I glanced up to find a massive pileup of cars dead ahead. Vehicles were mashed together, filling up every inch of open space in the four lanes in front of us. An ambulance and two police cars were on scene but no tow trucks yet. Concrete prevented us from getting into the lanes of oncoming traffic, and a deep ditch prevented escape off to the right.

"Can you turn around? Take the last exit?" I asked.

He was staring in the rear-view mirror. "I don't think so. It's getting pretty crowded back there. Maybe we can find a way around this mess."

Doubtful, I scanned the wreck as we drew closer. People were running away, but not everyone. One cop was handcuffing a man who kept twisting his neck, trying to bite him. Several others were standing by cars, helping free the drivers and passengers. I narrowed my eyes.

Hell. They weren't helping free the people still in cars. "Oh, God," I whispered.

"What is it?" Alan asked.

"We have to get out of here," I said, staring at the crazies attacking the people in cars. It was like the entire world decided to go cannibal at the same time.

He frowned, pointing ahead. "Exactly how do you think we are going to get past this mess?"

"I mean *now*, Alan."

A man jumped out of his car and started firing his pistol into the mob. The sound must've finally registered what was underway because Alan's eyes widened, and he yanked the car around. Something slammed into our car and an explosive force threw me against the seat. Dazed, I blinked to see that we were now facing another direction.

Powder from the airbags sent dust flurries in the air. I shoved at the deflating white bag. The driver of the car that had t-boned us was still hidden behind his airbags. I glanced back at the horde of crazies to find them looking in our direction.

I unlatched my seatbelt and tugged on Alan's arm. "C'mon. We need to get out of here."

He muttered something, and shook his head as though to clear it.

"Stupid idiot!"

I looked outside to see the other driver climb groggily out of his car, shaking his fist. He stepped up to Alan's door, and pounded on the window. "Moron! What were you thinking turning around in the middle of the road like that?" he yelled.

"Fuck off!" Alan growled right back.

Alan was not a large man. He was my height and had maybe thirty pounds on me. To see him yelling at a pissed off guy only added fire to a tinderbox. Then I saw them coming our way. "Uh, Alan?"

"What!"

I pointed at several crazies with pallid skin stumbling toward us, their jaundiced sights homed in on the man standing outside our car. Their faces and chests were blood-soaked, and a few sported violent injuries of their own. One hobbled along with a broken leg. Another was missing an arm. Still another looked like half her throat had been ripped out. They moved slowly and jerkily but were relentlessly closing the distance. Alan looked and gasped.

The man outside continued to yell until he realized Alan was no longer paying any attention to him. He followed Alan's gaze. He cried out and took off running back to his car but was too late. All of the crazies attacked him at once. The driver screamed. It was an awful, blood-curdling scream, but I couldn't see what was happening under the pile of writhing flesh and gushing blood. Not that I wanted to.

I glanced at Alan, and then opened the door and ran.

<h1 style="text-align: center">Two</h1>

Tires squealed as cars rammed into the bottleneck. Gunshots rang though the air. With Alan at my back, we sprinted away from the crazies and into the oncoming traffic.

I headed straight for the midnight blue eighteen-wheeler just rolling in, with an American flag painted on its trailer, dwarfing the vehicles around it. Even though the truck was still moving, I jumped up on the driver's side step, pulled on the locked door handle, and pounded on the window. "Please let me in!"

The driver scowled. His eyes were covered by aviator-style sunglasses, and I couldn't see if he was watching me, the crazies, or something else. His lower lip bulged with chew, and with a wave of his hand he motioned me away.

I tried the handle again. No luck. I risked a quick glance behind me to see that, sure enough, the group of crazies that had been huddled around a small truck was now headed this way. I swung back to the truck driver. "Please!"

After a long second, the window opened, and the barrel of a shotgun pressed against my chest.

I didn't fall back. I didn't jump to the side. Instead, I stood there as though waiting for him to shoot me. "I've got nowhere else to go," I said weakly.

He scowled even more, causing lines in his five o'clock shadow. He kept the shotgun level at my chest. "You bit?"

I gave my head a fervent shake. "No." Then I frowned, confused. "Why?"

He seemed satisfied with my answer, though he also didn't seem in the mood to elaborate. He cranked his head around mine and nodded toward Alan, who was hanging on right behind me. "How about you? You don't look so good."

I glanced back to find a sweaty, pale Alan.

"I'm f-fine," Alan replied with a stutter. When the trucker didn't respond, Alan threw up his hands. "I was just in a freaking car accident, man!"

The crazies were less than thirty feet away and quickly closing in. I snapped my gaze back to the trucker, pleading. "Mister, *please*!"

He moved his head slightly to check out the crazies closing in. He spit off to my right and pulled in his gun. "If you want to live, you'd better climb in."

I heard the *pop* of the door unlocking, and I stepped to the side to open it. "Thank you, thank you, thank you," I murmured as I crawled over him, knocking his cap askew, on my way to the passenger seat. Once there, I fastened the seatbelt as fast as I could in case the trucker changed his mind and tried to shove me out. Alan came in right behind me, only he collapsed in the cab behind us. The driver slammed the door shut, set the gun between him and the door, and grabbed the long shifter. Air shot from the brakes.

A crazy rammed the door and clawed at the now-closed window. The truck lurched forward, and the man in a bloodied business suit tumbled off the truck.

"Damn zeds," the driver muttered, his hat still crooked.

"Zeds?" I frowned, recognizing the term. "You don't mean..."

He pointed outside where several crazies stood literally dead ahead of us. "You know damn well what they are."

What the trucker had said made perfect sense, but it shouldn't be possible. Yet, not only did one of the infected try to eat me less than an hour ago, they moved like zeds—zombies—clumsily and relentlessly. No different from the crazies in front of us now. With no regard to their well-being, they kept shambling toward the truck barreling down the road on its way to meet them.

"I guess you're right," I said softly as the realization of fiction becoming reality hammered at the tension headache already pounding behind my forehead.

The driver stepped on the gas, and I sucked in a breath. The heavy rig rammed through the group of crazies like a bowling ball, only these pins left behind goo and flecks of skin.

"Holy shit," I muttered as the trucker ran over zeds like they were nothing more than small speed bumps. The windshield wipers smeared brown streaks across the glass. He kept picking up speed, setting us up for a bull's-eye approach to the roadblock. I braced my legs against the dash the instant before he rammed into a small car jackknifed between an SUV and a minivan. Something heavy slammed against the back of my seat, followed by a muffled moan.

I looked back to find Alan crumpled on the floor. "You okay?"

"*Nnnh, yeah.*"

The truck shoved the car to the side with metal-on-metal screeching. As we carved our way through the wreckage, the rig knocked around the sedan the zeds had swarmed earlier. The driver, still strapped inside, reached out to us with his only remaining arm. Even though he no longer had a face, the man watched us with unblinking eyes while his mouth opened and closed.

I shivered and turned away.

Once we broke through the bottleneck and put distance between us and the zeds, the road opened up. In the distance, a few cars entered from the next ramp, but most of the traffic was headed in the opposite direction.

I grinned. "Hot damn! We got through!"

In response, the trucker glared. "I'd be surprised if I didn't bust something," he growled out. "She's not made for this sort of abuse."

I glanced in the side mirror to see a line of vehicles following us, though the zeds were closing in on the cars on both sides. The woman in a convertible never stood a chance. I snapped my gaze straight ahead to the open highway. After a moment, I found my voice again. "What you did back there...thanks. I mean it. You saved our lives."

He grumbled something under his breath.

The open road looked like freedom, and for the first time since getting mauled by Melanie I let myself relax. I felt halfway in control again even though I knew it was a false feeling. Too much had changed since this morning. I loved routines. I hated chaos.

Five days a week I sat in a small mushroom-colored cubicle in a sea of mushroom-colored cubicles, at the same desk I'd sat at for over five years since college. I was an actuary, which my parents thought was a pretty big deal, but really it just meant I ran a lot of reports and analyzed spreadsheets.

Two years ago, I'd saved up enough money to make a decent down payment on a fixer-upper in the Gussdale district, and most of my free time went to renovating the old bungalow. Well, to that, and flying. My Piper Cub was the one splurge I'd allowed myself after college. Dad had been a pilot, and I got my pilot's license the same week I got my driver's license. I rubbed my bare arm where the Cub logo tattoo—a fuzzy teddy bear—looked up at me.

After today, I'd probably never get the chance to log another hour in the Cub. The entire world had fallen apart before my eyes. After running a finger wistfully over the teddy bear, I looked out the window.

Startled, I pointed to the sign. "My exit is the next one coming up."

A small nod was the only acknowledgement I got before the trucker picked up a soda can from a cup holder and spit in it.

Another grunt from the back seat reminded me that I wasn't the only passenger. I turned around. Alan was lying on the floor, his face covered by his arm. "How are you holding up back there?"

No response. I frowned. He hadn't hit the back of my seat *that* hard. "Alan?"

Still nothing.

"Alan," I said louder.

Alan looked at me then. His tongue was hanging out as though he was panting. His eyes had yellowed, and his features morphed from confused to dull. Then he moaned.

"Oh, shit." I unlatched my seatbelt. The trucker was watching me, and he caught on fast.

"You've got to be fucking kidding me," he said, taking his foot off the gas and reaching for his shotgun.

My intent was to grab Alan and toss him out of the truck before he went crazy. It seemed like there was a short window when Melanie had been out of it before going into raging attack mode. But I didn't get the chance.

I was halfway to Alan when the shotgun went off.

The next split-second was a blur. The shot blasted my eardrums. Alan's face literally split in half. Brownish blood and brain matter sprayed the cabin and me, and Alan's body slammed against the back wall. I may have yelled, but I couldn't hear it if I had. The only sound in my world at that moment was a loud, throbbing, constant ringing.

Even though I thought I'd just recovered from shock, it was amazing how quickly I was thrown right back into it. I stared at Alan's crumpled body in a daze. Dark liquid spread out from his head. I felt the truck come to a stop.

The trucker leveled the gun on me and said something.

"What?" I asked, his words nowhere near as loud as the ringing in my ears.

"I said...one good reason...blow your brains out."

It took a moment for his words to make sense in my head. Then I watched him, numbly, for a moment. "I can't."

A flash of genuine surprise crossed his face, but the expression was lost all too quickly to anger. "I asked if you were bit, goddammit."

"I'm *not* bit," I said, before shaking my head.

He motioned to Alan. "And him?"

"I thought Alan was just freaked out from everything."

The driver sat there and scrutinized me for what seemed like an eternity. "Are you cut? Did you get any blood in your mouth or eyes?"

I looked down at my clothes damp with Alan's blood. With my black clothes, the dark blood blended in but the flecks of skin and brain dotted my shirt. "I'm okay."

"You sure?"

"Pretty sure."

"You better be more than 'pretty sure,' Cash. Because this thing spreads through contact. Blood-to-blood, saliva-to-blood. If you got it, you're going to be like your boyfriend before long."

I didn't answer.

He motioned over my shoulder. "Get out."

I looked out the window. I was still at least three miles from home. I thought of my tiny bungalow in a neighborhood full of tiny houses. How many neighbors were already sick? With my car still back at the office, where could I go?

Outside was already turning into a war zone...

A man boarding up windows on his house just off the interstate.

Two people running down a street.

The occasional pops of gunfire becoming constant echoes of *rat-tat-tat*.

A shape stumbling around a tree.

How many zeds stood between me and home?

The only thing I knew was that I would never even make it to my front door, let alone to my parents' house on the other side of town. It was both a miracle and luck that I'd already made it this far. Out there, on foot, I didn't stand a chance.

Operating on autopilot, I opened the door but couldn't make my legs obey. I lowered my head, and the tears came. It wasn't an act. I didn't want to cry, I *never* cried, but the tears just kept coming. My shoulders shook from exhaustion as much as from adrenaline and hopelessness.

Silence filled the cab for what seemed like an eternity, before I heard a heavy sigh. "I know I'm going to regret this. If you start looking sick, I swear to God I won't hesitate to fill your brain with buckshot. If you're not sick, I'll give you one day." He held up a finger. "One day. Then you're on your own. Got it?"

Sniffling, I nodded vigorously. "You won't regret it, I swear."

"I already do," he grumbled.

I went to pull the door shut; he nudged me with the barrel. "Nuh, uh," he said. "Get rid of your boyfriend first. And be quick about it. He's stinking up my cabin."

I looked back and winced. "He's not my boyfriend," I said weakly before my gag reflex kicked in. I twisted and reached out the door just in time to throw up the pepperoni pizza I'd had for lunch. After several heaves, I was able to sit up again. Taking a deep breath, I glanced at the trucker. He was watching me carefully, but at least he didn't mistake my retching for getting "sick" and shoot me.

I wiped my chin and headed to the back of the cab. Fortunately, Alan was slouched over, his face hidden in his lap, which made it a bit easier to pretend that this wasn't someone I'd worked alongside every weekday. Dark, brownish blood and brain bits were splattered *everywhere*. Dazedly, I noticed the blood around Alan seemed darker and more congealed than it should have been, but I was no expert. My parents would know that kind of detail. I nudged him with my toe to make sure he was really dead, as though a shotgun blast to the head hadn't been convincing enough. *No response.* Some of the tension in my spine released.

Once I could breathe without gagging, I glanced around. A stack of folded bedding sat neatly in the corner, and I grabbed the top sheet already speckled with dark spots. Breathing through my mouth, I knelt by Alan and none-too-gracefully rolled him into the sheet. Frowning, I noticed his pants had been ripped, and I nudged the material aside to see a jagged wound in the shape of a human mouth.

"He was bit," I said, taking a long breath to keep from throwing up. "In the calf."

"Figured something like that was the case," the trucker replied.

I continued wrapping Alan in the sheet, trying to distance myself by imagining this was anything but a human body, but my subconscious kept reminding me. Once he was fully wrapped, I tugged and dragged him to the door and had meant to lower him gently to the ground, but he was heavier than me and the position was awkward. The sheet-wrapped body slipped right out of my hands and landed on the concrete shoulder of the interstate with a solid thud.

I stared at the body. While Alan deserved better than to be left at the side of the road to rot, I really, *really* didn't want to leave the safety of the truck and risk being left behind. Biting my lip, I turned back to the trucker.

He shifted the truck back into gear. "You're cleaning up the rest of this mess when we get to my place."

I collapsed onto the seat and slammed the door shut just as the truck moved forward. I let out a breath and stared outside, focusing on nothing in particular as the trucker drove and weaved around cars. As we left the city behind, traffic shrunk to nil. Other than a couple small military convoys and state troopers, few vehicles were heading into town, and those vehicles were speeding down the interstate, as though they were in a hurry to get to Des Moines.

No doubt they were trying to get to their families.

While I'm abandoning mine.

I sat in a numb trance, my head resting on the headrest. *Stay safe, mom and dad. I'm coming back. I promise.*

The radio was on, but the CB radio was louder, with truckers constantly reporting in status of the interstates. All the talk was of zeds and blocked roads. Every couple minutes I found the trucker eying me.

"I still feel okay," I said each time I caught him looking at me.

Seemingly assured that I wasn't going to go zed on him, he put on a Bluetooth and reported in on the CB. "This is Clutch dead-heading at yard stick 153 on I-80 reporting in. Avoid I-80 eastbound near Des Moines. Just passed through a bad 10-50 with zeds rubber necking the area. Over."

"10-4, Clutch. This is Dog Man. Heading west from The Windy. How's the big road westbound outside city limits? Over."

"Hammer lane for now, Dog Man. But I wouldn't count on it staying that way. Two Rivers has been overrun. Zed city. Over."

Zed city. I thought of my parents, and the rock in my gut grew into a boulder, and I hugged myself. They'd be so worried right now, unable to get a hold of me.

They were okay, safe at home. They *had* to be okay.

"Same with The Windy," the other driver said. *"Also heard The Circle*

and The Gateway are zed city, too. Whatever this thing is, it's spreading hard and fast. I saw a guy get nearly decapitated and he was back on his feet in two minutes joining up with the other nut jobs. Have three beavers on board, and hoping to make the Big Miss by dark. Over."

"Picked up a seat cover myself. Watch your six, Dog Man. Clutch over and out."

Clutch removed his Bluetooth, clicked off the CB, and turned the radio back up.

He shot me a look, then returned his focus to the road. I noticed he wasn't as old as I'd first assumed—mid-forties, maybe. And he was big and tough and scary. He'd straightened his cap, hiding more of his brown crew cut. He wore nothing fancy, just old jeans and a T-shirt, with tattoos covering his arms. His clothes were clean, whereas I looked like I'd just escaped a war zone.

Which was too damn near the truth.

Clutch nodded toward the red cooler at my feet. "Grab me a beer, Cash." Then he tacked on, "Grab something for yourself if you're thirsty."

I didn't care that his last sentence came out more like a gripe than an offer. I reached in and pulled out a beer and a bottle of water from the ice. "My name's Mia. You go by Clutch?" I asked. "Or, at least that's your CB handle, right?"

He didn't reply.

I handed him the can and opened the plastic bottle. The water was cold and oh so good. After throwing up, my throat was raw and my mouth tasted awful. The water soothed and I swooshed it around my teeth. I drank the entire bottle before opening my eyes. "So," I said, drawing out the word. "Where are we headed?"

"My place."

Three long tones beeped on the radio.

"About time," he said as he cranked up the volume.

"*This is the Emergency Broadcast System. This is not a test. Repeat, this is not a test.*"

Three more tones sounded before a man's voice came on. "*This is Doctor Jon Meriden, managing director of the Center for the Disease Control. A state of emergency has been declared for the continental United States. An epidemic is now affecting the Midwest and quickly spreading. Houston and Kansas City are considered the worst locations and should be avoided. Cases of the virus have been reported in all major cities in the United States, southern Canada, and all of South and Central America.*

Any borders that remained opened as of this morning have now been closed. Cases are also being reported at Hong Kong International Airport.

The virus has been confirmed to be a member of the Marburgvirus *family. Scientists are working hard to identify the new virus, and it is believed to have originated in South America. However, due to its symptoms and the mannerisms of the infected, we've assigned the layman term* zombiism *to the superbug.*

Symptoms include slow and awkward movement, jaundice, and severe violent propensities. We strongly urge you to distance yourself from anyone displaying these symptoms. If you come into contact with someone displaying any of these symptoms, the CDC recommends quarantining yourself. If you are infected, symptoms will begin to appear anywhere from minutes up to an hour, depending on severity of initial infection. The more severe the initial infection, the quicker you will succumb to the virus. Treatment is not available at this time.

We have traced the entry of the virus into the United States to several dozen contaminated shipments of produce from Mexico. At this time, we recommend you do not eat any fresh produce imported within the past three days.

The superbug is transmitted through contact with bodily fluid of an infected person. The slang term 'zed' is trending across the Internet and radio. Should you hear this term, it simply refers to an infected person or persons.

Due to the ease of the virus' transmission, all public transportation and air travel have been suspended until further notice. Travel is not advisable and is considered unsafe. If you must leave your current location, expect delays and likely increases in lawlessness. Emergency responders may be overwhelmed. Please be patient and remain where you are. Gather emergency supplies should you need to evacuate to a temporary location. Do not panic.

All military units have been assigned to contain the spread. All inactive and retired military personnel have been reactivated and should immediately report to the nearest base for assignment. Martial law is now in effect. Stay inside, stay safe, and help will be on the way.

We will report on all channels every thirty minutes. For more information, go to www.emergency.cdc.gov online."

Three tones sounded once more, and the radio resumed to what sounded like a national talk show sharing more information about the "zombie outbreak" and how to protect against zeds.

"How are you feeling?"

I glanced over at the man next to me. His hands were tight on the wheel as he watched me.

"Fine." I realized he was asking about symptoms rather than my emotional well-being. "Really, I'm still okay." Terror had long since given way to hopelessness. "The world's seriously fucked, isn't it," I stated quietly.

"Yeah." He spit into the soda can. "We're all fucked."

THREE

When we pulled into Clutch's driveway, I wouldn't have been surprised to see a sign that read: *Abandon all hope, all ye who enter here.*

Not that the farm wasn't lovely. Fields and woodlands went on for miles and miles. Just above a valley, a long gravel lane led us through several acres of woods, with flowers blooming along both sides. The lane opened up to a classic farm setup: a two-story white farmhouse standing boldly alone with three sheds as backdrop. A tabby cat lounged under a tree, watching me.

Clutch pulled up along the largest shed and cut the engine. The whole scene was idyllic...and very, very isolated. I was alone with a stranger who'd killed Alan and run down several zeds like they were nothing.

Sure, I'd killed Melanie, so I guess I wasn't any different. But, what if he changed his mind about letting me stay for the night and killed me? Almost as bad, what if he wanted "favors" in exchange for shelter? I'd been terrified of being alone in this mess, but I suddenly wondered if being alone wasn't the safer option.

"What's up, Cash? You're looking at me like I'm about to dismember you."

Startled, I realized Clutch had taken off his sunglasses and was now watching me. His piercing hazel eyes seemed to see too far into me.

I blinked a few times. "Just feeling like a fish out of water. That's all,"

I replied in a rush, opening the door and jumping outside. In the fresh air, I stretched my tight muscles as I stood before the sun dipping low in the sky. The weather was beautiful, a spring evening with a gentle breeze.

Clutch walked toward the house, and I followed. "I wouldn't have guessed you for living on a farm," I said.

"Why?"

"With you being a truck driver—"

"I'm from a fourth-generation farming family on this land. I just drive truck in the off season for extra income."

He unlocked the porch door, but instead of opening it, he turned around and studied me for several long moments.

Any confidence I'd built bled away under his scrutiny.

"Stay here," he ordered. He didn't wait for an answer before disappearing inside, leaving me to wait. The peaceful chirping of crickets was the only sound besides the ringing in my ears, and I realized that the same isolation I feared about this place was the key quality that made it all the safer. The farm was in the middle of nowhere, far from any city. The yard was big enough to see zeds coming from the woods on any side, and the trees concealed us from the roads.

Clutch returned with an armful of rags, some rubber gloves, a garbage bag, and a couple spray bottles. "There better not be a spot left in the cab when I check it out."

I nodded dutifully, taking the supplies.

"There's a light in the cab. Just be sure to turn it off when you're finished. I want to keep everything fully charged in this cluster fuck."

"Light off when I'm done," I replied with a robot-like tone.

He grunted before turning back into the house.

With a sigh, I headed back to the truck and started scrubbing away every last drop and bit of Alan.

———

Four hours later, I peeled off the yellow gloves covered in brown goo and chemicals. With a sigh, I dropped them into the garbage bag and tied it shut. Even with the industrial-strength stain remover, Alan's blood had been a bitch to scrub away, and I wouldn't know if I got everything until daylight. I'd been desperately motivated to do a good job. I only hoped it was good enough that Clutch wouldn't make me leave before the National Guard got the whole zed thing under control and I could return home.

I sprayed every surface in the cab with one more round of disinfectant before turning off the light and stepping outside and groaned. I was flat-out exhausted. My arms were numb. My lower back hurt. My thigh muscles ached. Every inch of my body throbbed.

Despite the stench, I'd kept the truck doors closed while I cleaned in case any zeds showed up. After taking several deep breaths of fresh night air, I sprayed my grimy body with disinfectant, knowing it probably didn't do any good, but figured it also couldn't hurt.

The half-moon was fully overhead now, sharing just enough of its light for me to hurry to the house without tripping over anything. I was half surprised to find the porch door unlocked. Looking down at my Doc Martens, I suspected the black leather was as grimy as I felt. But, there was no way in hell I could scrub them until tomorrow when—hopefully —I could feel my fingertips again. Stepping inside, I took off my boots and left them on the unlit porch.

A savory, meaty smell wafted forth, and my stomach growled. It was late, and I'd lost whatever had been left of my lunch after Alan died. I hustled forward, only to be blocked at the mudroom by a towering Clutch. He was wearing different clothes, and his hair was still wet. Gray peppered his stubble. Lines marked skin that had seen a lot of the outdoors.

He was handsome in a hard way. Maybe it was his eyes. There was an intensity in his gaze. Even without his tattoos, he would've had an aura of power.

Or, maybe it was because he had a pistol leveled on me.

My eyes widened as I met his gaze.

He grimaced. "Relax. If I was going to kill you, I would've done it outside where you wouldn't make a mess."

I chortled. Like that made me feel any better.

It was then I noticed that he was also holding a rag and a small bottle of gun oil. "You were cleaning your gun."

He looked me up and down before narrowing his eyes. "Take off your clothes."

I pulled together the collar of my utterly destroyed shirt. "What?"

"I don't mean it that way. Jesus." He ran the back of his hand over his face. He laid his weapon on the washer, reached behind him, and pulled out a garbage bag. "You're covered in zed sludge, and I don't know how contagious that shit is. Everything's got to go. I'll burn it tomorrow."

He held open the garbage bag. I shot him a hard glare while I unbuttoned what was left of my shirt.

He sighed. "Don't worry. I won't look. You're not my type, anyway. Too scrawny."

"Scrawny?" I asked but received no response.

Clutch kept his word, looking over my head while I stripped out of my disgusting clothes. I stopped at my bra and underwear. "Nothing soaked through."

He glanced down and grimaced, like he wasn't enjoying himself. I scowled. I wasn't that hard on the eyes, and I was petite, most certainly *not* scrawny.

"Turn around," he ordered. "I have to check."

I gingerly spun and felt his eyes on my back. I shivered, more self-conscious than I'd ever been in my life. If I'd known how this day was going to turn out, I wouldn't have worn a thong. Then again, I would've done many things differently.

"I think they're savable," Clutch drawled out in a rough voice. "Throw both in the wash when you're done with your shower."

Turning back to face him, I covered my chest as best I could with my arms, though thankfully Clutch was busy looking anywhere but at me.

"The shower's upstairs. Second door on your left. I set out something you can wear for tonight. Dinner will be ready by the time you're done."

"Got it," I said and hustled past him.

"Oh, and Cash..."

I paused.

"Be sure to scrub good and hard," he called out behind me. "You've got bits of your boyfriend's brain in your hair."

Bile rose in my throat, and I bolted up the stairs, taking them two at a time. Once in the bathroom, I took deep breaths, refusing to look in the mirror. When I had control of myself again, I pulled off my remaining clothes in a rush, cranked on the shower, and hopped in before it was warm.

The cold water that ran down the drain was brown at first, with little flecks of things I didn't want to think about. I set the water as hot as I could stand, grabbed the washcloth, and started scrubbing. Clutch clearly wasn't married, because the shower/tub combo only had a bar of soap and a bottle of generic shampoo.

I washed my hair three times before I felt relatively confident that it was clean. And, I scrubbed at my skin until it was red, standing under the spray until it was lukewarm.

Stepping out, I grabbed the towel left out on top of a thin stack of clothes, and dried myself off. I caught my breath when I looked into the mirror. Dark circles underlined my bloodshot eyes. Fresh bruises marred my chest courtesy of Melanie. I looked like shit, plain and simple.

Picking up the clothes he'd left, I found a pair of white long john bottoms and a gray T-shirt with ARMY across the front. Both were huge on me. The shirt nearly went to my knees, and the bottoms slid down every time I moved. Sifting through the well-stocked medicine cabinet, I found a couple large safety pins and tightened the long johns around my waist.

I couldn't find a brush, so it took ten painful minutes to finger-comb through my snarled, unconditioned mess. Finally, my strands began to resemble hair again, with its bold red streaks interlaced with the black. Reaching for the dental floss, I pulled out a long strand and used it to tie my hair back before it snarled all over again.

Glancing down at the discarded pile of underwear, I grimaced. I really didn't want to touch anything that I'd worn today. I probably should've tossed it, but I went ahead and wrapped the towel around the tiny pile of undergarments and carried everything down to the washer in the mudroom.

I walked past the kitchen on my way to the mudroom, and saw Clutch pulling plates from a cabinet. His back was to me, though I had no doubt he knew I was there. His back was broad, like he worked out every day. He was well over twice my size. Part of me felt safer, part of me worried how easily he could overpower me.

My stomach growled loudly, and I hustled to the mudroom. After stuffing my dirty clothes in the washer along with Clutch's clothes that were already in the tub, I went double-duty with the detergent, and started it up.

When I returned to the kitchen, he handed me a cold beer, silverware, and a plate covered with a huge steak, a baked potato, and steak sauce poured over the entire thing. He motioned to the living room. "I eat in there." He grabbed his own beer and dinner, and I followed him, taking the couch when he claimed the recliner.

I dug in before opening the beer. I was thirsty, but I was even hungrier. With the plate on my lap, I sawed at the T-bone, cutting off the next piece while chewing on a piece twice the size I should've cut. "This is really good."

My words were muffled as I chewed loudly, but Clutch seemed to make them out. "It sucks wasting a good T-bone on the stove, but I don't know how long the grid will stay up. Figured I may as well clean out the freezer now."

I swallowed, the steak going down painfully hard in my suddenly constricted throat. I cracked opened the beer and took a long swig. I hadn't even thought about losing electricity. What else would give out? Water? Phone lines?

Stores would be closed, which meant no fresh food. My sudden reality made me set my fork down. "How long do you think it will be until the military makes it safe again?"

His left brow rose. "I think it's already too late. The outbreak spread too fast and too hard. If we didn't get out when we did today, I doubt we'd be talking tonight. You better start getting used to this way of life."

"But the military—"

"Doesn't stand a chance against millions of zeds," he interrupted. "It's a numbers game. The zeds are spreading too fast. There's no way our guys can keep them in check. Not without nuking every populated area. And that would also take out any survivors."

The next bite tasted like cardboard. And the one after that. If nearly everyone turned into a zed, there wouldn't be anyone left to fight them. Even soldiers weren't impervious to a zed's bite if they were caught unaware or without ammo.

If I hadn't hitched a ride with Clutch, I'd still be in Des Moines, surrounded by zeds right now. Out here, miles from any town, I was relatively safe. More important, I wasn't in this alone. I looked up. "I have skills." *Not really.* "I can help." *I have no idea how.* "Give me one more day, and I'll prove it."

He shook his head and held up a finger. "The deal's for one day."

"An extra pair of eyes and an extra pair of hands can't hurt. I can help," I added.

"Do you know how to fire a gun? String a snare?"

"I can learn."

"It would take you months to become proficient, even if you had the aptitude for it." He leaned back. "You'll only slow me down and eat my food."

"Then I'll go out and get us more food."

"First time I take you with me, you'll get bit, and then I'll have to put you down."

"I'll be careful." I jutted out my chin. "Besides, I killed a zed today."

"Really?" The corners of his mouth curled upward. "And exactly how did you manage that?"

I thought for a moment. *With sheer luck and a miracle.* "With a 'wet floor' sign."

He looked confused at first, then smirked, but shook it off. "You'll be a drain. You'll use up more resources than you could possibly bring in."

"I'll go get us whatever we need. If something happens to me, then you'll be on your own again. It's a no-lose situation for you."

He rubbed his eyes. "Not good enough. I'm not set up here to take in strays." He looked up, his gaze hard with resolve. "The deal was for one day. Come tomorrow, you're on your own. I'll get you to a car, but then we're done."

I wanted to argue. God, I wanted to beg him to change his mind. Instead, I looked down at my plate and gave a tight nod.

Clutch turned on the TV, and flipped through channels. It looked like nearly all the channels were offline. Only one news channel remained, and the reporter was giving updates on the major cities. With the TV as a backdrop, we finished the meal in silence.

When Clutch stood, I came to my feet. "Here," I said, reaching for his plate. "I'll clean up."

He probably thought I was trying to show him how I could help, and he'd be right. He eyed me for a moment before holding out his plate. "I'll secure outside. When you're done, there are a couple plastic jugs I set out. Fill them with water."

"But you're out in the country," I said. "Don't you have well water?"

"I do," he said. "But the pumps still need electricity. I have a manual pump outside that will still work if the power goes out, but that's no reason to not be prepared in case it's too dangerous to leave the house."

"Oh." I headed toward the kitchen and paused. I debated for a moment before asking, "Do you have a phone? I'd like to call my parents. They're still in Des Moines."

A flash of sympathy flashed on his face, and he pulled out a cell phone and set it on the side table. "I tried to make a call earlier but couldn't get through. Phone lines are probably still choked." The look on my face must've bothered him, because he added on, "But go ahead and give it a shot."

"Thanks."

He left without another word, and I went about cleaning up. After filling the five-gallon jugs, I sat on the couch and watched the cell phone still resting on the side table. I'd been putting off the call, afraid of having my worst fears confirmed. After cracking my knuckles, I grabbed the phone and punched in my parents' number.

Call Failed.

Next, I tried to send a text message.

Message failed.

"Damn it," I muttered, tossing the phone on the cushion next to me and leaning back, covering my eyes.

"No luck?"

I jumped at Clutch's voice. "Service is still swamped. I'll try again in the morning."

He turned away.

"Need help with anything else?" I scanned the room, and my eyes fell on the windows. "I could help you board up the windows."

He followed my gaze. "I'll get to those tomorrow. I'm far enough out of town that as long as we keep dark and quiet, we should be okay for tonight. From what I've seen, zeds operate with minimal physical acuity. It won't take much to defend this place against a few who find their way near the house."

"I can help in the morning," I offered hopefully. "Many hands make light work, you know."

He watched me. "Get some sleep, Cash. You'll need your strength for tomorrow."

He turned and headed up the stairs. He didn't say I was staying. But he also didn't say I was leaving, and I clung onto that tiny splinter of hope.

"Why do you call me Cash?" I asked as I followed him upstairs.

"You were dressed like Johnny Cash when you jumped onto my truck."

"Oh." I thought for a moment "I guess I do wear black a lot." I glanced down at the oversized T-shirt and long johns. "But not always."

Clutch showed me to the guest bedroom containing only an old dresser and a full-sized bed. No pictures hung on the wall. The bedding was flannel and, though dated, looked enticingly comfortable.

I pulled back the comforter and found myself shoved onto my stomach. Clutch's weight bore down on me from behind. My face pressed against the mattress. I tried to fend him off, but he managed to pull my arms behind my back, and I heard the zip of a plastic cord as it tightened around my wrists.

"Fucking asshole!" I yelled out, kicking, while he all too easily did the same to my ankles.

"You keep going on like that, Cash," he murmured from behind me. "We're going to have zeds from a twenty-mile radius upon us."

I quieted, kicking at him as he backed away. No matter what he had planned, I refused to go down without a fight. "*Asshole,*" I muttered.

Clutch pulled the comforter out from under me. I tried to roll off the bed, but he pulled me back and then, surprisingly, covered me with the blankets. He positioned the pillow under my head.

Frowning I looked up at him. "What are you doing?" My voice cracked.

"I don't want to wake up to find a zed loose in my house," he said before walking to the door, where he paused. "If you don't turn, I won't have to kill you in the morning."

Then he turned out the light and left me alone in the dark.

Four

I bolted awake at the sound of a thunderous gunshot. My wrists and ankles were free, the plastic ties lying in broken pieces beside me. I jumped to my feet, and every muscle in my body protested. With a wince, I made my way to the window. The sun had not yet peeked above the trees bordering the backyard, but in the glimmer of morning light I caught sight of Clutch dragging a body and disappearing around the side of a smaller shed.

A zed? Someone else?

I scanned for more signs but found nothing. The yard stood empty except for a large vegetable garden that had been tilled for spring planting and three, twenty-foot cylinders of propane sitting side-by-side. Beyond the yard stood acres and acres of woodland, making it impossible to see if there were more intruders out there.

The birds had started singing their morning songs again, which meant my hearing hadn't been permanently damaged by the shotgun blast yesterday. The birds chirped like the world was peaceful, but they lied. The world was deadly and vicious. And, instead of getting ready for work, I was about to head out and fight for my life.

I rubbed the pink scrapes that marred my wrists where I'd wriggled to pull free last night, but the plastic hadn't stretched. I wanted to crawl back into bed and pretend that it was Wednesday—not Friday—the day before the world I knew ended. But, I needed an early start if I was going to find a safe place before dark. After a quick stop at the bathroom, I headed downstairs to find Clutch sitting in his recliner, decked out in camos, eating eggs, and watching the news.

"Breakfast is in the kitchen," he said without taking his eyes off the TV.

I wanted to strangle him for what he'd done to me last night. But while I'd lain in bed, working at my restraints, I'd realized he was protecting himself. To be honest, I would have done the same if I'd been in his place had I thought of it. This whole time I'd been thinking of how bad *I* had it, never once thinking of how bad he had it. Clutch had allowed two strangers—one infected—into his truck and brought one of those strangers into his home. Before I'd fallen asleep, I'd made the vow to myself to let go any remaining anger.

I'd enough to deal with the way it was.

I stepped into the kitchen to find fried eggs, bacon, and toast already on a plate. After having a huge steak dinner, I was surprised that my stomach was already growling. Then again, running for your life burns a lot more calories than punching keys on a computer.

I took my seat on the couch and dug in while watching some national news channel. The reporter looked ragged, like he hadn't slept or been home since yesterday. A map of the United States was behind him with red Xs over every major city. The map then expanded to the world, showing parts of Europe and much of Asia in red.

"The infected are considered dead by all medical definitions, but yet they continue to move...and feed," the reporter said. *"For lack of a better term, they are undead. Their bodily functions, such as heart rate and blood pressure are nonexistent. Their blood has congealed and they will not bleed out, which the CDC believes accounts for their stiff gaits.*

If you must come into contact with the infected, use extreme caution. Destroying the brain stem is the only known method of killing an infected. Due to lack of blood flow, the brain seems to be their only critical organ. A bullet directly through any other normally vital organ, such as the heart, has proven ineffective. However, they can be incapacitated by decapitation or removal of limbs, but they will continue to pose some risk even incapacitated.

The high fever that sets in before the virus takes over seems to destroy most brain activity, which means they can be outsmarted if you do not panic. The infected are violent and hungry and do not seem to require rest. The CDC believes that their insatiable hunger is caused by the superbug altering the hypothalamus in a way to promote transmission of the virus. While a bite is the fastest way to transmit the virus, any direct contact with infected saliva or blood may lead to infection. Even a small open wound, such as a scratch or blister, carries risk of infection. The CDC does not believe the infection can be transmitted by mosquitoes or through contact with animals bitten by the infected, but that doesn't rule out the possibility of infection through those means.

We have reason to believe the virus originated from a new biologically engineered pesticide where the cells were coated with silica. When the pesticide was combined with a specific cleaning agent, the cells were shown to mutate.

There is no cure. Infection rate is believed to be at or near one hundred percent. Once infected, the virus will take control of your body, and you will either die or turn violent. This was all the information we received before we lost contact with the CDC."

Clutch tossed me his cell phone. "Phone service seems to be unclogged," he said while the reporter started reading off a paper he'd just been handed.

I stared at the phone's screen and already knew why the phone lines were no longer clogged. There weren't enough people left to make calls. No one left to go to work or school. Ah, but the schools would be closed today, anyway. "Today's Good Friday."

"So?"

I shrugged. "No reason, I guess." I swallowed and redialed the number I called nearly every day of my adult life. I tried not to think about how my parents could've been calling my phone over and over and not getting an answer. And if they hadn't been trying to call...I tried not to think about that at all.

After the fourth ring, the call went to voicemail. My heart panged.

Hi. You've reached the Ryans. We can't come to the phone right now, but if you leave a message, we'll return your call as soon as possible.

I took a deep breath and tried to sound cheerful. "Hey, Mom and Dad. I hope you're okay. I wanted to let you know that I'm out of town and safe. And I'll see you soon." I went to hang up, then added, "I love you."

I also sent a text message to them before I opened my email through the phone's web browser. Nothing but the usual spam. I sent off a quick email, filling my parents in on where I was and assuring them I was safe. I left out the parts about Melanie and Alan and sleeping tied up the night before.

With that done, I handed the phone back to Clutch. "Thanks."

He gave me an almost gentle look before he reached behind him and plugged the phone back into its charger.

I thought back to the gunshot this morning. "Any zeds pass through the area yet?"

He paused. "Just one."

Something in the way he spoke made me look up. "You knew him, didn't you?"

After a moment, he gave a tight nod.

"Sorry," I said, not knowing what else to say.

After that, the news reporter's voice was the only sound as I finished my breakfast. The military had set up roadblocks and bombed bridges, but I suspected Clutch was right. They were facing a losing battle at containing the zeds.

The reporter ran through a list of every major city considered no longer viable, which was government-speak for saying the military had pulled out and the city had been overrun by zeds. He could've saved ten minutes by saying nowhere was safe, because there didn't seem a city left unaffected in the States. Contact had even been lost with Hawaii and was spotty with Europe and Asia. The northern parts of Canada and Alaska seemed to be the only places still keeping ahead of the outbreak, and I imagined masses of survivors were heading north already.

Clutch got to his feet, and I moved into action, taking his plate and heading into the kitchen to clean up. He disappeared down the hall, reemerging once I'd finished, with knives and guns strapped to his chest, waist, and thighs. Yesterday, I would've been terrified. Today, I felt protected. He may be dumping me off, but at least I'd be safe as long as I was still with him.

Which wouldn't be for much longer.

A sense of doom weighed me down as I laced up my stained Docs, tucking the long johns into the boots. I tied the oversized shirt at my waist so it wouldn't get in the way in case I had to run.

Coming to full height at over a half-foot above me, Clutch nodded, and I followed him silently out of the house and toward the big rig. Every step I took dripped dread onto my veins. When we reached the truck, he opened the passenger door and climbed up and inside. I waited under the sunshine, leaning against the tin building, while he spent the next several minutes examining the cab. Done, he hopped out and looked me up and down.

My muscles tensed, and I held my breath. Clutch would send me off on my own soon. While I wanted to make sure my parents were safe, I couldn't imagine how I'd possibly get to them without getting myself killed. I'd barely gotten out of town yesterday. To head back to the city after a day of those things infecting others...I shivered.

"We need to get you gloves if you're going to help hang boards over the windows. Those hands of yours will get all sliced up otherwise."

It took me a long moment before his words sank in, and my clenched jaw inched open. Without thinking, I squealed and hugged him. "Thank you!"

I let go about the time he pushed me away.

I held out my hands. "I won't let you down. I swear it."

"It's just for another two days," he said, holding up two fingers. "As I told you before, I don't have the supplies to take in an orphan. Then you'll be on your own. Got it?"

I nodded, hoping, praying that I'd be able to convince him otherwise within two days. "Deal."

"Okay, Cash," he drawled. "Let's get this place secure."

———

Three days later...

Clutch and I got along just fine. His clothes were huge on me, but it was nothing that an extra hole in one of his tactical belts couldn't fix. He liked things quiet. When he did talk, he barked out military jargon and acronyms I didn't know. I felt the nervous need to fill the silence. Even with a bad shoulder, he was a hell of a lot stronger than me. Without caffeine, headaches shortened my temper. When Clutch ran out of chewing tobacco two days ago, he got cranky.

But I never complained. Not once, even though more than once I had to walk away to cool down.

After all, Clutch was the only thing that stood between me and a world full of zeds.

"When the power goes out, we can't count on the generator. It's damn fussy and works only some of the time, and when it works it's noisy as all hell," Clutch said while we worked on setting up an early warning system around the perimeter. "As soon as we use up the perishables in the freezer, we're going to have to ration."

I strung another tin can on the wire. "I'll start inventorying food and supplies tonight, and I can start planting in the garden in a couple weeks. My mom and I had just picked up supplies for expanding her herb garden last weekend."

I swallowed a lump, remembering that had been the last time I'd been with my mother. Focusing on surviving kept me busy enough to not dwell on Mom and Dad, but I still thought about them. Often.

"We'll have to make a run into town for seeds."

"Oh. Okay." Until the outbreak, I'd never realized how dependent I'd been on stores for everything. While we could set up the farm for long-term survival, there were some bare essentials, such as seeds, that we needed from town to get us started. Once we had a garden, we could prep our own seeds for next year, though I had a lot to learn.

Not that I could even think of everything I'd yet to learn without stressing. Surviving each day was enough of a struggle. "How about all those bags of seed in your shed? Can we use those?"

"The seed corn and soybeans?"

"Yeah."

"We can, but we won't want to depend on them. Seed corn is bland. It doesn't taste anything like sweet corn, but it would provide some basic nutrition at least. Soybeans are a solid option. But no matter what we plant, we're going to have to go old school and plant by hand. The tractors and combine make too much noise."

I nodded in acceptance. Funny thing, before all this, I'd always been the leader with both coworkers and with friends. Now, I found that I could follow just as easily. Strange how quickly people can change.

Clutch's life before the outbreak had been completely different from mine. He knew his stuff. He'd served two tours in Afghanistan and became a doomsday prepper when the economy turned to shit a few years back. I had complete trust in him, even though I'd known him for only a few days. To be honest, I trusted him more than I had anyone in my life, maybe even more than my parents.

I still couldn't reach them, though I continued to send them an email every day. The email became my journal, proof that I still existed. I'd never gotten a reply, so I could only hope that they were hunkered down somewhere safe without access to the Internet. I knew it was a weak hope, but I held onto it nonetheless.

The last news channel had gone offline yesterday, leaving nothing on the TV. We'd scanned radio stations every few hours. Nothing was left on FM, and only random updates were sent through AM, and most of those came from folks holed up like us. No one reported anything on Des Moines, and I had to assume that whatever was left of the military had pulled out. Each night, I prayed for my parents' safety, even though in the pit of my stomach I suspected I'd never see them again.

"That should cover everything for now." Clutch came to his feet after tying the last wire. "I'm heading out."

Taken aback, I stood. "What for?"

"The chaos should have settled down enough by now. I need to scout the area to see what we're up against. And I need to start stocking up our supplies before looters clear out the town."

"I'll go with you," I said right away.

"No."

"I can stay in the truck and watch for zeds. It can't hurt to have an extra pair of eyes."

His lips thinned before he released a drawn-out sigh. "Let's get you some gear."

Feeling a surge of anxious excitement, I headed back to the house with Clutch.

"Come on," he said, and I followed him into the room he'd disappeared to every day. A metal desk sat in the center and a bookcase filled with books, magazines, and boxes covered much of one wall in the small room.

It looked like Clutch had an extensive library of manuals covering the spectrum from survival and first aid to gardening and canning. There was an entire section on organic farming. "Nice library," I said.

"I like to be prepared." He pulled out a book and then twisted on something. A loud click sounded, and he pulled the *entire* bookcase out. Behind it was an even smaller room, lined with metal cabinets and a rack of least a dozen guns, knives, and other weapons.

My jaw dropped. "Holy shit, Clutch. You've got a hidden room."

"Gramps had this room put in way back during the Depression. He'd always said a person needed to be prepared for the worst." He motioned me to come closer. "Give me your belt."

I pulled it off, and held up my pants—an old pair of Clutch's cargos —while he slid a sheath and holster onto the canvas strap.

He handed it back to me. I was still fastening the belt when he held out a knife. "This tanto is yours to keep. It's a good blade, so take care of it. This should be your go-to weapon in close quarters, especially in dealing with zeds."

I slid it into a black plastic sheath, which he then snapped shut.

"Have you ever fired a gun?"

"Sure. I had a BB gun when I was a kid."

He gave me the same exasperated look I'd seen many times over the past few days. "I'll take that as a 'no'." He held up a gun and stepped through the basics of loading the cartridge and firing it. He dumped bullets into my left hand and handed me the pistol in the other.

I looked at the gun in my hand, the gun rack, then at the gun in his holster. "Why's mine so much smaller than yours?"

"That's because mine's a Glock and yours is a .22. Yours is a great starter pistol because it doesn't have much recoil. Show me you can use it well, and I'll let you try my 9mm."

Dropping the extra ammo into a cargo pocket, I repeated everything he'd shown me to make sure I understood.

"We can't afford to attract attention, so only go for your pistol as a last resort. And whatever you do, don't fire unless your target is less than eight feet away. Save your bullets. The .22 is a baby and will just piss them off from any distance greater than that."

"Thanks." I holstered the gun.

"Be careful. If you're bit, you'll turn. There are no second chances out there. Got it?"

"Yes."

"Good. Let's go."

He locked up, grabbed a small backpack of extra gear, and we headed to the shed where his black 4x4 super cab pickup truck waited. He topped off the gas tank at one of two large cylindrical fuel tanks set up behind the shed. We were strapped in and heading down the lane in no time.

Clutch drove slowly down the gravel road, turning left, then left again. He continued until he'd made a full square loop around the house. The next time, he went one road farther out, and repeated the process. He slowed down near each of the three farmhouses we passed but never stopped. I saw no signs of zeds, but I also saw no people. Cattle still grazed in the fields. Everything looked deceptively normal, completely different than how busy Des Moines had been a few days earlier.

"We'll check each one out later," he said, moving on. We continued the scouting mission, me watching for zeds and Clutch watching for I-don't-know-what until we pulled onto a paved road, and he came to stop.

"What if there are people still living there?" I asked.

"Then we leave them be. I'm not taking in any more strays."

I had thought about that, too. And, though I knew it was selfish, I didn't want to have another mouth to feed. We had a good thing going, and another person would only throw a wrench into that dynamic. I also felt guilty thinking that way, knowing we were equipped to help others. "At least we'll know who's in the area. We only clear out the places that have been abandoned. Mark the others as off-limits." I thought for a moment. "What now?"

He turned right. "Let's check out town."

I swallowed. It had been over three days, but it felt like an hour ago now that we were back on the road. "Are you sure it's not too dangerous?"

"We have to know what we're dealing with. Today will be a quick recon. Just to the edge of town. I need to hit two stores before they're looted...if we're not too late already."

We drove for several miles without seeing a single car or zed. Only one house, with its windows boarded, showed signs of survivors. As Clutch didn't know them, he quickly laid down the law that we'd avoid that particular farm for now.

My anxiety climbed when we passed a sign that read: *Fox Hills, 3 miles.*

I focused on breathing normally while scanning for zeds.

He stopped the truck at a roadblock. Cars and debris were piled across the road.

"Who do you think did that?" I asked.

"National Guard," he replied. "I heard it on the CB during the outbreak. When they saw that zeds prefer to stick to flat surfaces, they blocked all the roads to contain the spread as much as they could."

Clutch pulled the truck into the steep ditch, and I held on, waiting for the truck to tip over. It sure felt close, but once past the roadblock, he climbed back onto the road, nearly getting stuck in the mud at the bottom.

Just on the other side of the roadblock was a sign indicating that we'd just entered Fox Hills' city limits. It wasn't a huge town. According to the sign, 5,613 souls lived here. But the idea of 5,613 zeds lumbering around was downright petrifying.

We came to the Wal-Mart first, a new monolith standing alone on the outskirts of town. A couple dozen cars sat in the parking lot like the store was still open, and I wondered where the drivers to those cars were. "I need some things if we're stopping."

His brows furrowed. "What do you need?"

"Some clothes that fit would be good. A sports bra." The lacey bra I'd been wearing was pretty but worthless for the work I'd been doing the last few days. "And..." I bit my lip. "I'm going to need some, uh, feminine products within a couple weeks."

"I'll see what we can find," he said, wrinkling his nose. "You definitely need gear. My clothes are too loose on you. Too easy for a zed to grab. Same with your hair."

"My hair?" I twirled a handful of the long, silky strands.

"A zed could grab it and pull you down."

"Oh," I said quietly, and disappointment flared. "I suppose I could cut it."

I heard another engine and jerked my head to find the source. A red SUV came tearing around the corner of the Wal-Mart, and one of the cardboard boxes stacked on top tumbled off. As it approached and slowed, I gripped the arm rest. Inside, I could see three occupants. A male driver, a woman in the passenger seat, and a teenage boy leaning forward between the two front seats. Clutch stopped, and they pulled up alongside. The man was favoring his bloody arm, while the woman, who I assumed to be his wife, cried in the seat next to him. She was pale and bleeding profusely from her cheek and neck. *Bitten.*

"They're neighbors," Clutch said before rolling down the window. "Good people. They live a few miles west of me."

The man leaned against his steering wheel as he rolled down his window.

"Frank," Clutch said with a slight tilt of his head.

"Clutch," the man replied, and I cocked my head. Everyone called him Clutch?

Clutch nodded toward the Wal-Mart. "How's the pickings?"

"I bet there's plenty in there," Frank said. "But we just grabbed what we could off the back of a truck behind the building. There are zeds everywhere. Even in the unloading area."

Clutch nodded. "You bit?"

The other man grimaced, and then looked at his wife and son. "Afraid so. We both are. We needed food and underestimated the bastards. They just never *stop.*"

My jaw tightened. Clutch and I were about to do the same thing, maybe even to the same store, and I wondered how many zeds were where we were headed.

"Sorry to hear that," Clutch said before nodding toward the backseat. "And your boy?"

"Jasen's too fast," the man replied with a proud smile in his son's direction. "The zeds can't get close to him."

I looked from the teenager to his parents and back again. Wet streaks lined his cheeks, and his eyes were red. Oh, the poor kid knew exactly what was in store for his parents.

"He's not safe with you, you know," Clutch said in a low voice.

Frank lowered his head. "I know." He gave a long look at his wife. "We're just going to get these supplies home for Jasen before..."

Silence filled the air.

Frank's wife leaned forward. "Please, Clutch," she said, sobbing and oblivious to her injury. "Please look after our son. He's just a boy."

"I'm not a boy, Mom," the teenager replied. "I can take care of myself. I'll be all right."

Clutch didn't speak for the longest time. When he did, his words sounded like they were weighted down. "Jase, how about you come on over and climb in my truck."

Jase's mother gasped. "Oh, thank you! Jasen's a good boy. He's strong and smart and you won't be sorry. God bless you, Clutch."

Frank's face instantly lifted. "You're a good man. I wish I could—"

"Don't worry about it," Clutch interrupted.

"I'm not leaving you guys," Jasen broke in from the backseat.

"Jasen," his father said, sounding exhausted. "You've got to go."

"Not until you get sick. The guy on the radio said that he heard that not everyone got sick," he replied.

"That's just a rumor, Jase," his father said.

"Besides, Betsy's still at home," Jasen said. "I'm not leaving her locked in the house to starve to death."

"Betsy?" I asked.

"The dog," Frank replied with a sigh.

"Your parents are going to get sick, Jase," Clutch replied. "Soon."

"I know," he replied, the words barely above a whisper. "I can't abandon them now. They need me."

"Go with Clutch, Jasen," his mother pleaded to her son. "You'll be safe."

"I'm not leaving you like this, Mom."

Clutch sighed. "We're burning daylight. The offer stands, Jase. You know where I live. Come on by anytime. I'll be home in a few hours. Just be careful to not attract any attention."

Jasen nodded before sinking back into the shadowed seat.

"No, Jasen," his mother said. "You go with Clutch."

Clutch rolled up the window and pulled away, and we could hear Jasen's mother piteous cries for us to stop.

"He's going to die, staying with them like that," I said.

"Probably," Clutch replied. "But it's his choice. If he left with us, that regret of abandoning his parents would fester and eat him up inside. If he makes it through the day, maybe we'll see him again."

"Maybe," I mused, wondering what it would be like to have to take in a kid. Clutch already complained about the amount of food I ate. A teenage boy could easily eat twice my share. If Clutch suspected there wasn't enough to go around, would someone have to leave? The thought sat like a rock in my stomach, because I suspected if Clutch had to choose, he'd choose the son of a friend over an unskilled girl he didn't even know four days ago.

"So everyone calls you Clutch?" I asked, forcing myself to change the subject. "I thought that was just your CB handle."

"It came from a tractor incident back in grade school," he replied.

My brows rose. "What happened?"

"Don't ask."

I smacked the leather and smirked. "You're killing me here."

"Well," he drawled out. "When I was just learning how to drive the tractor, I hit the gas instead of the brakes, and drove *into* my dad's shed."

I burst out laughing. "I bet your dad wasn't happy."

"No. No, he wasn't."

I caught a movement that had been nearly hidden by a minivan, and I sobered. "Look," I said, pointing at the blonde woman coming around the minivan.

Dark stains marred the front of her shirt and her mouth. Her arms, what was left of them, swung limply with each step. Then I saw the boy hobbling behind her, dragging his left leg. He couldn't have been more than three or four. He was also covered in blood. He followed her like she was his mother, though according to the news, zeds retained minimal cognitive functions, let alone memories.

I shivered at the thought of a kid getting attacked. What kind of monster would go for a kid?

"You can't think of them as people anymore," Clutch said, and I found him watching me. "That kid would kill you the first chance he got. Any of them out there would. They're the enemy. Out here, you either have to kill them or be killed."

"I know," I said as Clutch drove past a row of new houses. A garbage can sat at the end of each driveway waiting for a pickup that would never come, a stark reminder that civilization had just *stopped*. "But knowing it is easier than seeing it."

"You'd better come to terms with it quick because we're stopping up here."

I looked out the window to see Clutch pull up to a row of old brick buildings. He stopped in front of a pharmacy, wedged between a barber shop and a clothing store. The sign overhead read Gedden's Drug. The store was small and easy to miss. The glass window next to the door was intact. Through it, I could see decently lit aisles, and everything looked quiet and nothing appeared out of place. A Closed sign hung on the glass door, and I hoped they'd locked up before any zeds got inside.

"No telling how many are wandering around outside so we'll have to be careful," Clutch said, and I followed his gaze to the end of the block, where another zed limped across the street. Tires squealed, and a truck lurched around the corner, barreling right over the zed. Someone let out a whoop, and the truck tore past us.

Clutch gripped his gun. Neither of us moved until they'd turned another corner.

"Trouble?" I asked.

"Don't know." He drove us around the store and down an alley alongside the building to the lower-level back entrance off the street. It only had one door, and it was closed. The small parking lot backed up to the river.

I grimaced. Two cars sat in spaces marked Employee Parking. At least the door to the pharmacy was still intact. "Looks like we may have a couple helpful smiles in the aisles," I said, nodding toward the cars. "At least it doesn't look like anyone else has been here yet."

"Looters think short-term. The idiots will go for things like cash, booze, and electronics. The smarter ones will go for food, drugs, and ammo first. I'm surprised no addicts have hit this store yet for pain killers, so we need to treat this run as our only shot. The more drugs we can load up on now could save our lives when winter hits."

That's what I respected about Clutch. He was always thinking ahead. Not just a day ahead, but months and years ahead. Being a prepper, he already had a full year's supply of food tucked away in his basement. Well, six to eight month's supply now that he had me hanging around. The basement was lined with shelves, and every shelf was filled with food, water, and supplies.

His need to be prepared started with something he'd seen in the military, but I was thankful for his worst-case-scenario mindset now. "So what's the plan?"

"I go in and check it out. You keep watch out here. Keep the doors locked and stay low. If that truck comes around again, lay on the horn, and we'll cut our losses. If everything's good, when I give you the all-clear, follow me in. Once inside, get to the pharmacy and load up on every antibiotic and any other drug you can find for sickness and injuries. When in doubt, throw it in the cart. What we can't use ourselves, we can barter with. We won't be coming back. I'll hit the aisles for painkillers, Imodium, and other supplies. If anything happens, you run straight to the truck and lock yourself inside. I got a key and can unlock it from the outside. Got it?"

I nodded, though the entire time my mind was locked on the potential for caffeine. Clutch had to be the only trucker in the world who didn't drink coffee. My life had done a one-eighty, and while I'd fallen into a new routine more easily than I'd expected, my brain hadn't. It still craved its daily fix, and reminded me with a headache every morning.

Clutch checked the door, and it didn't open. With the butt of his rifle, he broke the glass, unlocked the door, and disappeared inside.

Silence put every single one of my nerves on edge. I scanned the open lot, watched the door, and then repeated the process. After a couple minutes, my leg started to shake with nervous adrenaline. No zeds showed up in the alley or from another building. After five minutes, I was convinced we'd arrived without being noticed. After five and half minutes, I opened the door and stepped onto the pavement.

Come on, Clutch. Where are you?

I had taken four steps closer to the building, still looking out for zeds or looters, when the back door opened, and Clutch held up his hand. *All-clear.*

I closed the distance in a heartbeat. "Any problems?"

"Nothing I couldn't handle."

I followed him into the building and up the stairs. He hopped over a bundle, and I stopped cold. A body wearing a white lab coat lay crumpled on the steps. The dark gore around its head looked fresh. Even though it had only been days since the zeds came out, I was surprised how quickly I was becoming desensitized to the sight of dead bodies.

I glanced up at Clutch. "Your doing?"

He looked over his shoulder and shot me a quick nod before continuing on. With my teeth clenched tight, I took a cautious step over the body, part of me afraid that it would twist around and bite me in the ankle, just like Alan had been. As soon as I cleared the body, I rushed up the remaining steps to meet up with Clutch at the top.

"I took out two zeds, so the place should be cleared, but be careful. They're slow, which makes them quiet." He motioned to the left. "Pharmacy's that way."

I nodded and watched Clutch head off in the opposite direction. I nervously edged toward the counter with PHARMACY written in all caps above it. Clutch was counting on me. This was my first chance to show him I could help him in the field. When I approached the pharmacy, another fear hit me as I stared at the rows and rows of drugs. How the hell would I know what to take?

I grabbed two red shopping baskets and jumped over the counter. Nearest to the counter, I recognized a few of the names, such as *Prednisone* and *Amoxicillin,* so I assumed that this was where the most common stuff was kept and used my arm to slide everything into the cart. From there, everything looked to be arranged alphabetically, so I just grabbed anything that sounded or looked remotely useful, leaving little behind for the next looters.

When two baskets were overfilled, I climbed back over the counter to track down Clutch. I heard him rustle off to my side. I smiled, turned, and lifted my baskets. "Look what—"

A zed tumbled from the top shelf of the aisle and landed in a heap in front of me. It clumsily climbed to its feet. It still wore a smock with the name LAURA on a pin. A chunk was missing from its neck, but it looked otherwise uninjured. Except for the jaundice and hungry stare fixed on me.

"Clutch!" I dropped the baskets. The zed staggered toward me, and I reached for the knife, but it didn't budge. I realized it was still snapped into its sheath, and I fidgeted with getting the tanto free. The zed was almost upon me. I instinctively shoved it back. Its mouth snapped at me. I finally pulled the blade free. The tip of another blade suddenly protruded from its mouth, and I stumbled back.

The blade disappeared. The zed collapsed, revealing the man behind it glaring at me.

"You bit?" Clutch asked.

I shook my head.

He picked up at least a dozen shopping bags, sliding them up his arms and shoulders, watching me. "Let's go."

Still holding onto the knife, I grabbed the baskets and hustled around the zed.

Clutch moved fast. He was back to the stairs and down the steps by the time I reached him. I'd expected him to head straight to the truck and half expected him to leave me behind. But he stood at the door, waiting for me.

Outside, he checked around and under the truck. He didn't speak, just opened my door and then climbed in on his side. I dropped the baskets in the backseat and was in the front seat by the time he revved the engine. He tore out of the parking lot and turned in the direction of the farm.

The tension was palpable in the cab.

"She dropped down from the top shelf. She must've hidden up there to get away when she was attacked, and stayed until I walked by—"

The steering wheel creaked under Clutch's grip. I didn't speak another word the rest of the way back to the farm. Unease roiled through me as he pulled up to the house and slammed on the brakes. I grabbed the baskets, tossing in bottles and boxes that had spilled out on the rough ride back. Once outside, I closed the door and stood for a moment. When I turned and looked at Clutch, he was looking straight ahead, both hands on the wheel.

I knocked on the window.

He moved, and the window rolled down.

"I messed up," I said. "You told me to be careful and I wasn't. You told me to run, and I didn't. I should've been ready."

"No, Cash," Clutch graveled out. "I was the one who messed up. I knew you weren't ready, but I let you come along. You're not ready, and you'll never be ready."

And then he drove off, leaving me standing under quiet, gray clouds.

Part Two
Lust

The Second Circle of Hell

FIVE

Clutch didn't return to the farm.

I paced the yard for over an hour, checking traps and alarms, waiting for him. At first, I'd been afraid that he'd send me packing and I'd be on my own. But then my fear morphed into something much more useful.

Anger.

I wasn't mad at Clutch.

He'd been right all along.

I was mad at myself for not being stronger, for not being prepared. Even if he let me stay, I had to be able to depend on myself to get out of trouble, and right now I couldn't.

I headed straight back to the house, grabbed the kitchen shears, and walked upstairs. I put the garbage can in the bathroom sink. I stared in the mirror for a long second. Then I sucked in a deep breath, lifted the shears, and chopped off a twenty-four-inch chunk of hair.

Then, I cut a second chunk.

I cut until there was nothing left to cut.

It had taken me years to grow my hair to the length it'd been. I'd always considered it my best feature. Yet, now, without all that hair, my head felt light and free. *Empowering*. After running a hand through the dark stubble, I nodded to myself and headed back outside.

I marched to the smallest tin shed for supplies before picking out a solid tree in the middle of the open backyard and sprayed the outline of a zed on its trunk. Then I hammered the sandbag I'd stuffed with rags about where a head would go.

I took out my knife and put everything I had in my swing, completely missing the bag and impaling the tree instead.

"Damn it," I muttered, examining the tanto blade to make sure I hadn't damaged it. Taking a deep breath, I focused on the bag and swung very slowly, this time hitting the bag nearly dead center.

I'd never had any kind of training with weapons except for pepper spray, so it was improv based on what I'd seen on TV and what I knew about zeds. Slashing would be a waste of energy since to kill a zed its brain had to be destroyed. I knew better than to throw the knife because, if I threw my knife, I'd no longer have it to take down the next zed lurking around the corner. I had neither the strength nor the weapon to decapitate. And so I focused on stabbing.

I spent the next five hours trying to figure out how to kill a zed using nothing but my knife. I grunted as I thrust and stabbed at the bag, the entire time Clutch's words *you're not ready* echoed in my ears. But he was wrong about one thing.

"I *will* be ready." I said out loud before every strike.

The poor tree suffered. I missed the bag as often as I hit it. I almost sliced myself wide open once. After that, I became more conscious of every movement. With short breaks to rehydrate, another two hours of stabbing, with sweat drenching my skin, I finally discovered my rhythm. Stabbing became a semi-natural extension of my body, though I knew I'd be foolish to assume I was an expert yet. The tree didn't move or bite.

Zeds were a different story.

An engine rumbled in the distance. I sheathed my blade, grabbed the canteen, and took a long drink of water before setting off toward the house to meet Clutch at the driveway. As the engine noise grew louder, I slowed. Whatever was coming down the drive wasn't nearly as hearty sounding as Clutch's throaty truck.

Setting down the canteen, I pulled out my pistol and moved cautiously toward the drive. A familiar red SUV emerged from the tree line. Several boxes were still on top, and it looked like the back was piled full of clothes and bags. The SUV stopped abruptly in front of the house, and two boxes tumbled onto the ground. I warily holstered the .22 when I saw the driver.

He didn't look so good.

Frank's teenage son sat, shoulders slumped, with both hands gripping the wheel. The kid stared at the house. He was covered in blood, though most of it was crimson, not thick and brown like that of zeds. The painful realization hit me that, with Clutch gone, the responsibility fell on me to prevent the kid from turning.

I waited. After a moment, he wiped his eyes and then opened the door and stepped out. He was a tall kid for his age, about the same height as Clutch. But, where Clutch was filled out with muscle, Frank's lanky son was still very much a boy.

"You're Jase, right?" I asked. "Call me...." I'd first thought to give him my real name but realized that Mia Ryan no longer existed. Who I'd been died four days ago during the outbreak. "Call me Cash."

He held out his bloodied hand, noticed it, and pulled it back. He simply nodded instead. "Where's Clutch?" he asked.

"He'll be back later." I took in a deep breath before speaking my next words. "I hate to ask this, but I have to." I paused. "Are you bit?"

He looked down and shook his head. "No," he croaked, and he cleared his throat. "I'm not bit."

"That's a lot of blood for not being bit," I countered.

He shook his head harder this time. "It's Betsy's." His voice cracked again, and he glanced back in the truck, running a filthy hand through already mussed sandy blond hair.

The poor kid looked like he was about to break. I wanted to make Jase take off his shirt to prove he hadn't been bitten, but instead I kept one hand near my pistol and put the other hand on his shoulder. "Well, let's get you cleaned up then."

He wiped his nose and then nodded, taking a few steps with me toward the house. Then he stopped and pulled away. "Wait. I can't leave Betsy..."

Frowning, I watched as he went around to the other side of the SUV. He returned, carrying what looked to be a small collie. Much of the fur on her back was matted with blood, and her eyes were glazed over. Whenever Jase moved, she whimpered.

I grimaced. Betsy looked in bad shape. With the amount of blood on her fur and covering Jase's shirt, I doubted even a vet could help.

When we reached the house, I didn't open the door. "Listen, Jase. You know how contagious zed blood is. You and Betsy can come into the mudroom, but you can't come inside, not until you're both cleaned up and in the clear. Got it?"

Jase nodded and sniffled again.

"All right." I opened the door and he stepped inside, cradling the dog to his chest.

Inside the mudroom, I rummaged through the cabinets until I found where Clutch kept his rags and cleaning towels. I grabbed the thickest one in the pile and made a nest on the floor. Jase carefully set Betsy down on the towel, but she still yelped at the movement, her back legs kicking out. He collapsed next to her, keeping a hand on her, and making small cooing sounds.

I left them, locking the door behind me. It took some time, but I found a disposable plastic bowl that would work. I returned to Jase a few minutes later to find him petting Betsy. The motions seemed as soothing to him as it was for the dog. I set down the plastic bowl full of water near Betsy, but I doubted she'd drink. Her eyes had closed, her breathing labored.

I put a glass of water on a shelf near Jase before taking a seat across from them. The news had said that dogs didn't turn, that bites were simply fatal, but I kept a close watch on both the collie and the teen, anyway. I'd left the .22 in its holster but had it ready.

"Mom turned first," Jase said softly. "Dad told me to leave the room, but I stayed and watched. He shot her. Right in the head. He had to shoot her twice before she quit moving. God, the blood…" He sucked in a breath. "Then Dad, he turned the rifle on himself, but he just couldn't do it." He rested his head on the wall behind him. "We're Catholic, ya know. He couldn't do it. He shot Mom because it wasn't murder since zeds don't have souls. But he had to be able to get back to Mom."

I stayed silent. I didn't voice my thought that Frank had been selfish. No boy should be asked to kill his own father.

As Jase spoke, his voice became stronger. "So he handed the rifle to me. He hated himself for it. I could tell. But I didn't mind. He was my dad, ya know? He raised me good." His voice cracked and it took him a couple breaths to continue. "It was my turn to take care of him. But, then he started to turn…and then I…"

He looked at me then. "I couldn't do it. When he looked at me, I thought that he was still in there, somewhere, but then he came at me. I stumbled back and tripped. Dad—no, he wasn't Dad anymore—when he *growled* at me, I knew he was gone."

Jase's gaze went to the collie, her breaths had become weak and shallow. "Betsy was yapping, and then she jumped at him. Can you imagine a twenty-three pound fur ball flying through the air?" He chuckled, and then put his head in his lap. "He picked her up, just like he did every day to let her kiss him. Except this time, he bit into her. God," he cried out. "He just kept biting and biting. Betsy was crying out so loud. I raised the rifle and started shooting. I shot at him until the mag was empty, but he didn't even slow down. So I ran at him. I used the butt of the rifle to nail him in the head. I don't know how many times I hit him before he finally let her go."

Jase sighed. When he spoke again, the words were just a whisper. "At least Dad's with Mom now."

I found my lip trembling. "I'm sorry about your parents."

"It's my fault. If I'd shot him when I should have, Betsy wouldn't have been bitten. She'd be fine now. She jumped in to save me. *It's my fault.*"

"No," I scolded. "We all make our own choices. You waited because you loved him. Betsy attacked because she loved you. Don't drown out her bravery with your regret. Honor her by holding memories of her bravery."

He sniffled and scratched behind the dog's ears. "You're a good girl, aren't you, Betsy Baby."

The dog showed no reaction, and Jase leaned forward and hugged onto her.

My vision blurred, and I looked away, while the boy said good-bye to his dog.

After several minutes, when I was confident that Betsy wasn't coming back, I climbed to my feet and stepped outside to give the kid space. From inside, I could hear Jase sobbing.

I walked out to the small shed, grabbed a shovel, and picked out a patch of grass under a shade tree. It took me over forty minutes to dig a hole that would hold a twenty-three pound bundle.

By the time I returned, I was pleasantly surprised to discover a boy, not a zed. Jase's face was red and blotchy, but he'd stopped crying. His hand rested on Betsy. His eyes held a faraway look that I'd seen in Clutch's gaze every now and then. It was a look of someone who'd been to hell and didn't get out in one piece.

Something tugged Jase back, because his eyes slowly focused on me. He opened his mouth to speak but closed it.

"I have a nice spot picked out back," I said, breaking the silence.

With thin lips, he carefully wrapped the collie into the towel and followed me. He clutched his precious package against him and kissed her before setting her down gently in the center of the hole. I intentionally moved slowly and dropped the first shovel of dirt carefully onto the bloodied towel. Jase clasped his hands together and his lips moved as he recited prayers.

"I didn't bury them," he said aloud. "Mom and Dad. I-I couldn't do it."

I paused. "I'll see that they get a proper burial."

He swallowed visibly, and then nodded.

I went back to shoveling. The hole filled in quickly, until a small mound of black soil was all that remained of Betsy. Leaning on the shovel, I looked at Jase. He was clearly exhausted. The poor kid should be at school, hanging with his friends, not burying his family. We had about an hour before the sunset. "I'm going to get started on dinner," I said. "Take all the time you need."

With that, I left Jase to mourn. If he hadn't turned yet, I figured the odds were low that he would. I returned the shovel to the shed, and headed back inside, locking the front door behind me, just to play it safe. Jase knocked just a few minutes later. I grabbed a garbage bag and went out to meet him. He'd already kicked off his tennis shoes. I held open the bag. "Anything with blood on it goes. Leave the shoes outside." Though I had my doubts, I added, "We'll see if we can scrub them clean tomorrow."

"I packed clothes. They're still outside," Jase said in a daze.

"You can grab them in the morning," I said, still holding out the bag.

In went his T-shirt, then his jeans and socks, and I looked him over for bites. Other than some bruises and a few scratches, he looked unharmed. But the scratches worried me.

When he went to pull his boxers off, I stopped him. "If there's no blood on them, toss them into the washer in the mudroom on your way in. The shower is on the second floor. I'll grab some clothes for you, and set them outside the bathroom door for you."

"Thanks, Cash," he said and I moved to let him in.

"And be sure to scrub good and hard." After a moment, it hit me that I'd just echoed words Clutch had told me the first night.

While Jase showered, I set three steaks under the broiler, skipping the sides. I was simply too hungry and too tired to go to the effort. I jogged upstairs and stopped outside Clutch's bedroom door. I reached for the handle but paused. I'd never been in there, and it felt almost like I'd breach some unspoken rule by stepping inside.

Instead, I turned and headed into my room and grabbed a pair of long johns and a T-shirt from my pile. They'd fit Jase better than they fit me and would get him through the night. Dropping the clothes at the bathroom door, I hustled back downstairs and finished cooking the steaks.

I wrapped Clutch's steak in tinfoil and set it in the refrigerator. Each of the remaining steaks went on a plate. Just like Clutch had done, I drizzled steak sauce over each steak and grabbed a bag of potato chips.

Jase came down the stairs. "I'm not very hungry tonight."

I dumped some chips on both plates, and handed him a plate. "Eat. You need to keep your energy up."

He followed me like a lost puppy into the living room, much like I'd felt four days earlier. I took an edge of the couch and motioned for Jase to sit. I wolfed my steak down while he pecked at his. After cleaning off my plate, I grabbed a beer. I'd almost grabbed two but changed my mind and poured a glass of water instead for Jase. After a quick stop in Clutch's office for something I'd need later, I scanned through the TV and radio stations but came across nothing but static.

Clutch had left his phone at home, and I sent an email to my parents. Even though I suspected no one was left to read them, I kept writing them. I needed to send the email as much as I hoped my parents read them. By the time I sent the email, Jase had finished his dinner. He looked out of place, and I wondered if I'd looked that insecure when Clutch took me in. "Let's get you to bed," I said, coming to my feet.

That it wasn't yet nine and Jase didn't object was a clear sign the kid was beat. He followed me up to my room. Instead of turning on the light, I said, "Now that the sun has set, don't use lights upstairs. We don't have the windows upstairs boarded, and the light is too easy to see from a distance."

"Okay," Jase said as he felt out the dark room.

Even though he didn't act sick, I knew what I needed to do. I pulled out the zip ties I'd picked up in the office. "Listen, Jase..."

He turned around, noticed the plastic. His eyes widened and he took a step back.

I sighed. "I wish I didn't have to do this, but it's a necessary precaution until we have this whole zed virus figured out. If you turn, and I'm asleep, well, you see what I'm saying. We both know you're bigger and probably stronger than me. If you fight, I won't be able to get these on you. So I'm asking you...please let me tie your ankles and wrists. It's only for tonight and it's just a minor discomfort. Come morning, if you're healthy, the ties will come off. Will you do that for me, Jase?"

After a moment, he nodded and then took small steps toward me. He gave me his back, and I strung the restraint around his wrists, careful to not make them too tight but making sure they would do the trick. I went to the bed and pulled back the blankets. Jase laid down in an almost robotic manner, and I pulled the strap around his ankles.

Stepping back, I tried to smile. "I know it's not comfortable, but it's only for one night. Try not to think about it."

"It's okay," he said, rolling to his side. "I get it."

I patted his back. "You're a good kid, Jase."

"I'm not a kid," he muttered.

Sadness pricked at my heart. "No, you're not." *Not after today.*

I locked his door, and headed downstairs. I cleaned the mudroom and headed back inside, leaving the SUV and everything inside for tomorrow. At eleven, after a hot shower, I locked the door, figuring I'd hear Clutch drive in. I curled up on the sofa and passed out within seconds.

I was dreaming of cans rattling when something niggled at my subconscious, a warning percolating to the surface.

Cans rattling...

I shot awake.

The sound of tin banging against tin continued. I jumped up from the sofa and grabbed my belt with the .22 and knife strapped on and was ready to go. That the cans still rattled was an ominous sign that a shitload of zeds was passing through.

Once I pinpointed the direction the sound was coming from, I opened the window. From the outside, the window was completely covered by wood two-by-sixes, except for small sniper holes covered by plywood sliders.

With a clear night sky and a full moon, the yard was brighter than the living room, and I sighed in relief. Only one adult zed. It was hard to make out any more details in the dark at this distance. Sure enough, the dumb bastard had snagged the tripwire and was now dragging a line of cans as it lumbered across the yard.

I don't know if zeds retained some hint of humanity and they sought out houses or if it was a predatory instinct. Whatever it was had the zed heading straight toward the house as it sniffed at the air. I scanned the yard for more, but saw no others.

I glanced at the .22 in my hand. My heart hammered a warning: *don't go out there.*

I headed into Clutch's gun room and used only a flashlight to not screw with my night vision. I shone the light over the guns, settling on a cluster of hunting-style rifles and shotguns that looked less complicated than the black military-style rifles. I grabbed the rifle in the middle that looked the most straightforward but also big enough to get the job done.

Holding the flashlight in my mouth, I checked the weapon, burning precious time since I really had no idea what I was doing. Once I verified that its magazine was loaded, I turned off the light and headed back to the window.

Careful to be silent, I slid the barrel through the sniper hole and took aim. The zed was less than a hundred feet away and lumbering through an open area, spotlighted by the moon.

I pulled the trigger.

Nothing. Not even a click.

Mentally cursing, I pulled the rifle back and looked at it. *Stupid safety*. I slid the black switch and aimed again. My first shot clipped the zed's neck and nearly knocked it down, but it kept coming. The recoil kicked my collarbone, sending white pain shooting through my shoulder. It took me a moment to fix my aim.

"Cash?" Jase called out from upstairs.

"Just a zed passing through," I said. "Go back to sleep, Jase."

I took a deep breath. The second shot took out the zed.

Silence filled the night.

My collarbone pulsed from the recoil.

I knelt against the window, watching, waiting for more zeds to show up at the sound of the shots.

After my knees hurt and my tired eyes could no longer focus, I closed the sniper hole, switched the safety back on, and collapsed on the sofa.

My grip on the rifle never relaxed as I faded off to sleep.

———

I awoke the next morning to find Clutch watching me. He was in his recliner, eating steak sandwiched between two biscuits. He was wearing the same clothes from yesterday, and he looked utterly exhausted.

"You cut your hair," he said, rubbing his shoulder.

I sat up and ruffled my hair, and found that it was sticking up *everywhere*. After a couple attempts at trying to tamp it down, I gave up. "Your warning system works," I said. "A zed snagged on it last night."

Clutch nodded like he'd already seen the corpse. "You okay?"

"Yeah." I reached for the rifle but realized it was gone. I glanced around, but it was nowhere in sight. I paused and remembered the most important thing. "Jase is staying with us now."

"I know," he replied with his mouth full. "I saw the SUV outside."

I came to my feet. "I should go check on him."

Clutch swallowed. "Already did. He's not sick, so I cut him loose, and he's out cold."

I let out a deep breath and closed my eyes. "Thank God."

"You did good."

I swallowed and faced Clutch. "About yesterday, I'm sorry. I—"

"Do we have any eggs left?" he cut in, coming to his feet. He stretched his back, and his joints cracked and popped.

I frowned. "Yeah, I think so. Why?"

"I'm hungry. If you wouldn't mind cooking up a couple for me, that'd be great."

I thought about pressing Clutch to talk more, but then I simply replied with a "sure" and headed for the kitchen to fry up several of our last dozen eggs. I stood there, thinking about Clutch. He was the sort to shove things deep down. If he didn't want to talk about something, it was impressive how quickly he could change the subject. I imagined he'd done that his whole life. I already knew about the bad dreams—I heard the muffled sounds and curses he let out in his sleep. Twice I'd stopped outside his closed bedroom door. Once I touched the handle. But I hadn't entered. Not yet, anyway.

I slid eggs on each plate, and I paused by the mudroom. Inside the door was a pile of military and hunting gear. Lots of OD—olive drab—with tags still attached.

I headed back to the living room and handed a plate to Clutch. He glanced up with his bloodshot eyes.

"Where'd you find all the military stuff?" I asked, taking my seat.

"There's a surplus store in town, and it hadn't been hit yet."

I raised a brow. "I figured that would be a hot place for looters."

"Me, too. Surprisingly, it wasn't even locked. Most of its gear was still there."

"Any zeds?" I asked.

He shrugged. "Nothing I couldn't handle."

The room was quiet, except for the clanging of forks on plates.

"You were right yesterday," I said quietly.

Clutch paused for a second before taking another bite.

"You're right," I said louder. "I'm not ready yet. But I will be. I swear it. The way I see it, there's two types of people left in this world: survivors and victims. And I sure as hell plan on being a survivor. All I ask is that you give me a chance."

He gave a hint of a smile, but the dark circles under his eyes overshadowed any other expression.

"Why don't you get some sleep," I offered. "I can work on whatever you need today. Once Jase is up, I can start getting him up to speed."

We sat in silence for a moment, before he nodded. "Move everything from the back of the truck to the office and sort it. I grabbed whatever shit I could, but there's got to be a lot more to grab at the surplus warehouse out of town."

"You bet," I answered, popping to my feet.

He nodded, rubbed his stubble, and then stood and moved slowly and stiffly up the stairs. He paused. "Be careful out there, Cash. Zeds will start drifting through these parts in bigger numbers soon. I saw three on this road yesterday."

"I'll keep on the look-out."

Ten minutes later, I had rubber gloves on and checked out the SUV, while keeping a constant watch for zeds. Fortunately, the vehicle had leather seats, making it easier to clean. Jase had put Betsy on the passenger floor mat, so I threw it out. After scrubbing down everything with bleach and disinfectant, I grabbed a wheelbarrow and went to the backyard to where I'd killed the zed last night.

With most of his head gone, it was impossible to tell its age, but by the filthy coveralls and flannel shirt, I'd guessed it had been a nearby farmer. Spring winds buffeted me today, but at least the zed was downwind so I didn't have to smell its rankness. After dumping the body into the fire pit and tossing the rubber gloves on top, I poured some gasoline over the corpse and felt pride when I tossed the lit match. I hadn't freaked out. I'd protected the house. For the first time since this cluster fuck started, I felt like I had a shot at surviving in this new world.

I ran a hand through my short hair. Already I was glad I'd cut it, for more reasons than to eliminate the risk of zeds grabbing at it. The winds would've turned it into a snarled mess by now, and I no longer had to deal with the hassle of hair in my eyes.

After the fire charred the zed, I cleaned out the SUV, dumping everything into the mudroom. From there, I headed to the truck. When Clutch said he'd loaded up everything he could, he wasn't exaggerating. Both the bed and backseat were piled full of tan, green, and black gear.

It bothered me that he had put himself in danger. He had gone on a looting run, with no lookout, no backup, because he couldn't count on me. *Never again.*

On my tenth or so trip, Jase joined me. He was still wearing the long johns and T-shirt from last night. He was moving slowly, looking around like a lost lamb. He'd pulled out a pair of jeans and a T-shirt from a bag I'd carried in from his SUV.

"Hold up," I called out and closed the distance and handed him the armful of duffels and other things. "Take this to the office. It's past the kitchen and to your right. Then, once you change into your clothes, help me unload the rest of the truck."

"My shoes—"

"Are now melted rubber," I said. "Go through the gear in the office. There might be some boots to fit you. Otherwise, we'll grab shoes from your house."

At the mention of his house, his face fell. Jase was quite a bit taller than me, but in his face, he was still a boy, a boy who'd seen far too much. I hadn't really thought about how bad he'd had it since yesterday. I grabbed the armful back from him and set it on top of a box. "Let me see your wrists."

He held them out. There were some faint pink lines, but it was obvious he hadn't struggled.

"I'm sorry about having to do that. You know that, right?"

He nodded. "Yeah, I know."

"Did you have breakfast yet?"

He shrugged.

I cocked my head. "What did you have?"

He jutted out his chin. "I had some chips."

I rolled my eyes. "C'mon. I'll make you something. You're going to need your energy. I plan to keep you busy."

He muttered something but obeyed. I washed up and cooked up the rest of the eggs and toast. It was already ten in the morning. I figured it would get him through until lunch at least. "Clutch was out all night and is sleeping in, so keep it down. Once you change clothes, you can help me finish unloading."

He slid the eggs between the slices of toast and squeezed the sandwich together. "Sure thing, Cash."

I ruffled his hair, and he wrinkled his nose.

I smiled. "I think we'll get along all right."

Several dozen trips later, Jase and I had filled the small space of the office with surplus gear and had sorted out the groceries, toilet paper, and other odds and ends from the SUV.

We spent the next two hours quietly sorting all the gear into piles. Clothing by size, bags by type, cots, and everything else in piles of similar items. I even made a pile of my own stuff. Cargo pants with large pockets, button-down camo shirts made of not-so-soft hearty canvas, black sports bras, olive drab tank tops, a heavy-duty rain jacket, a thick winter coat, a tactical belt, and two pair of boots. My old Doc Martens had held up great so far, but the abuse was already starting to show.

I changed in the mudroom. It felt good to wear something in my size. The knife and gun sat more comfortably against my waist on the smaller belt. For the first time in a long time, I felt a genuine smile.

I went back to find Jase, and he started chuckling. "You look like G. I. Jane."

"Looks who's talking. You look pretty badass yourself. OD looks good on you." He'd already changed out of his clothes and into fatigues, changing his look from high schooler to soldier in the blink of an eye. He still had a youthful face, but the clothes infused him with confidence that I hadn't seen this morning.

"Dad always thought I'd join the ROTC," he said, and the smile dropped from his face. His next words were barely a whisper. "I-I don't think I can go back there."

I sobered. "Clutch and I will take care of it. Let me know anything else you want from your house, and I'll see that we pick it up."

After a stalled silence, he mumbled, "Thanks."

I motioned him up. "Let's grab some fresh air."

Jase followed me outside. It wasn't yet time for lunch, so we walked the perimeter, checking Clutch's simple yet effective early-warning systems.

"You're lucky you found Clutch," Jase said as we walked.

"It wasn't just luck," I replied.

"What do you mean?"

I kneeled, checking a tripwire. When I stood, I faced Jase. "My mom always hated that I didn't go to church." I smiled, remembering how she scolded me. Then I sobered. "I was never what you call a true believer so once I moved into my own place, I quit going through the motions. I don't know why I'm still here when so many good people aren't, but I think there had to be something more at play than just luck when Clutch pulled up and took me in when I needed help the most."

"You're saying it's a miracle or destiny or something like that why Clutch saved you?"

"Is that any different than luck?" I scanned the yard one more time and then headed over to my tree.

I pulled out my blade and began practicing. Jase sat off to the side, watching me but more often watching the mound of dirt a couple trees down. There was nothing I could say. He needed time, and I hoped that with time, he'd heal.

"Can I get weapons, too?" he asked while I stabbed.

"Ask Clutch," I replied. I'd give him weapons if I could, but it wasn't my place. Every weapon here belonged to Clutch, except for the two he'd given me. If and how he distributed his weapons was up to him. "Now, keep an eye out for zeds."

The rhythm came easier today, like my body remembered the motions from last night. Muscles in my biceps and thighs reminded me that I needed to get in better shape. And I worked at doing exactly that.

After about an hour into my workout, I had to tape up the sandbag because it'd been thoroughly shredded. With the bag wrapped in silver, I went back at it.

"Put your left leg forward a bit more. You'll be less likely to be knocked off balance."

I jumped to find Clutch behind me. He'd shaved and had changed clothes, though he wore as many guns and knives as usual.

I turned back to the tree and spread out my feet. After a few awkward stabs, the wider stance put more strength into each thrust.

Jase clapped. "Looking good, Cash."

"Now come at me," Clutch said.

My eyes widened, and I held up the tanto. "With a knife?"

He chuckled. "I've been watching you. I'm not worried."

My attack was hesitant, and he scowled. "Damn it, Cash. You can do better than that."

My next attack wasn't much better, but as I got more and more aggressive, Clutch had to work at avoiding me.

"Better," he said. "But you need to remember that evasion should always be your first choice. If you're forced into an attack, defensive maneuvers are more important than taking the offensive. Zeds will come at you with their teeth and hands. Looters and common criminals will be worse because they can think and use weapons."

The next time I attacked, Clutch swung out, and I barely jumped out of the way in time. I was thrown off balance, and he knocked me down with a kick from behind.

"You're relying too much on your weapon. Put it away, and focus on your body. You need to be able to protect yourself using just your hands and whatever is readily available."

I sheathed the blade and spent the next hour alternating between getting my ass handed to me and watching Jase get his ass handed to him by a seasoned military vet. I was on the ground more than I was on my feet. Clutch was relentless. Once, I nearly got the upper hand with a self-defense kick to his knee, but he jumped back before my foot connected. In return, I got a well-placed hit to my solar plexus.

I collapsed to the ground next to Jase and sucked in air.

Clutch took a seat on the grass next to us and rubbed his shoulder. "Tomorrow we'll head a few miles out and practice shooting."

"I can shoot," Jase quickly offered up.

"What's your weapon?" Clutch countered.

"I'm a decent shot with a rifle. I've hunted both deer and ducks before."

"Well then, we'll see what you can do," Clutch said.

I laid back on the soft grass, staring up at the clouds. Lying there, I realized that even though Clutch was no longer on active duty, he'd never really left the military. He was a Ranger—he had to be one of the best in my mind—and I think that was how he defined himself. Though I suspected his nightmares came from the tours he'd served. Driving the truck, farming, those were just jobs. Clutch was a soldier. He worked out every day as though he were still in the military. And now he expected the same from Jase and me.

Every part of me felt bruised, while Clutch wasn't even breathing heavily, though I knew his joints ached at the end of each long day. Cracking my neck, I glanced at Clutch who was cleaning his nails with his knife. I noticed his nose had a bump from where it had been broken.

Under his gruff exterior, I could tell he was fiercely protective of me and now Jase. Clutch would've made a great father, that was, if he could've tamed his militant ways. Then I realized, for all I knew, he was a father. "You have any kids? A wife? Girlfriend, maybe?"

The knife paused, and he looked at me. "Why?"

I shrugged. "Just curious."

"Clutch had a hottie around for a while," Jase chimed in. "I saw you two in town a few times. She was blonde, curvy, and..." he whistled.

After a minute, Clutch sighed. "I never found someone I wanted to settle down with."

A wide grin spread over my face. "See? Sharing isn't so hard now, is it?"

He smirked before looking up to the sky. "Looks like a storm will be rolling in later." He pulled himself up, held out a hand, and helped me to my feet. "Not too many folks know about the warehouse for Doyle's military surplus store, but someone will come across it soon enough. It's too close to Camp Fox for it to be missed. I want to get a truckload or two while we still can." He glanced at Jase and me for a moment. "I could use a lookout."

My brows rose with hope. "I'm in."

He turned to Jase. "Think you can hold down the fort?"

Jase jumped to his feet. "You can count on me, sir."

"I'd better show you what to do in case anyone or thing shows up." They started to head off, and Clutch paused, turning to me. "Meet at the truck in fifteen."

"Wilco," I replied with a grin and a salute. Knowing this was my second chance, I took off at a jog to get ready.

Fifteen minutes later, I leaned against Clutch's truck, holding on to a two-foot-long bolt cutter. When Clutch appeared with weapons and the backpack he always carried, I nodded toward the house. "Do you think he'll be okay?"

"Kids are resilient. Give it time. He'll get there."

We climbed in and headed down a different gravel road than we'd driven down the day before. Fields of black, waiting to be planted, went on for miles and miles.

"Where's this surplus warehouse?"

"It's southeast of town. At an old farmers' co-op," he replied.

We drove along for a while, past several farmhouses. I saw only one zed wandering in the fields, but I think I saw another one standing at the window inside one of the houses we passed.

The winds had started to pick up, almost whistling through the truck. Then I saw something. "*Wait,*" I said.

Clutch slowed. "What is it?"

I pointed to the big galvanized corn bins. "I thought I saw someone."

"Zed?"

I shook my head. "A woman, I think. She was running too fast, but she must be running from something."

Neither of us missed the two men sprinting toward the bins next, also far too fast to be lumbering zeds.

Clutch's jaw clenched. "Sonofabitch."

A woman's scream pierced the air, and I gasped, cranking my neck to try to see anything.

"Fuck." He yanked the truck into the driveway, throwing me against the door. He reached for the shotgun. "Stay here and stay low. Whatever you hear, do *not* let yourself be seen."

"Okay," I said, frowning.

"Is the safety off the .22?"

I pulled out the pistol and checked. "Yes." I also unsnapped my knife's sheath.

"Stay out of sight." He gave me one last look and then jumped out of the truck and flattened against the side of the bin.

I moved the seat back as far as it could go and crouched on the floor, holding the gun in one hand, and the bolt cutter in the other. The driver's window faced the bin, but from my low vantage point, all I could see was metal and sky.

Shouts and gunfire erupted, and I tried to make myself invisible. Then...silence.

A minute later, Clutch opened the door and I jumped up. "What happened?"

"I took down both tangos, and I'm going to check out the other buildings in case they weren't alone. Stay put."

"And the woman?"

He grimaced, and then slammed the door.

I retook my position on the floor and waited. Was she dead? Whatever it was couldn't have been good because Clutch had looked enraged. I wanted to go check on the woman, to see if I could help, but I didn't want to break my word to Clutch even more.

After three minutes ticked by, my muscles began to cramp. The door snapped open behind me, and before I could turn, an arm wrapped around my neck and yanked me from the truck. I tried to yell out but couldn't breathe. I struggled but was only pulled harder against my assailant.

"Well, well, well. What do we have here," an unfamiliar male voice whispered in my ear. His breath reeked of booze and his body stank of sweat.

I swung the bolt cutter behind me, and he cursed. His grip relaxed enough so I could suck in air. I twisted around and swung again. But, this time he was ready. He caught the bolt cutter and wrenched it from my hand. I went to punch him, but he grabbed my wrist and jerked me tight against him as though we were slow dancing. He chuckled. Shivers covered my skin. The winds howled around us.

I looked up into the face of a man with a half-grown beard and greasy hair. He pulled me even tighter against him while he licked my cheek, and I winced. "Oh, we're going to have fun, you and me."

He threw me to the ground and fell on top of me. My face was shoved into the dirt. Panic blurred my vision. He was too busy grabbing at my pants to notice that I still had the pistol. I couldn't get onto my back, but when he yanked on my cargos, I was able to aim it under my armpit. I fired, and he cursed, jumping back. "Wha?!"

I spun onto my back and fired three more shots. The first shot had only startled him. My next three hit him solidly in the chest and stomach. It was different than in the movies. There was no blood spray, only three red dots growing on his shirt. He looked down and frowned as though he hadn't felt any pain.

He looked up and his face turned red. "Fucking bitch!" he yelled, spittle flying from his mouth. He tackled me, punching me in the face, and—blinded by white and black stars—I pummeled his head with the gun handle. I kept pounding his temple until he fell lax. With a grunt, I kicked him off me.

I pulled myself up into a sitting position, gasping and spitting blood, unable to see through the stars. Every inch of my face hurt. He'd very nearly knocked me out. As my tunnel vision slowly widened, I could see Clutch running toward me. When he got close, he looked at me and then at the guy who was already starting to come back to consciousness. I struggled to aim my gun, but Clutch was in the way. He kicked the man in the gut and then fired two shots at my attacker's head.

Clutch knelt by me. "You okay?"

I came to my knees, spit out some more blood, and ran my tongue over the nasty cut on my lip. "I need a bigger gun."

He belted out a single laugh, helped me to my feet, and held me up until the wooziness passed.

I rubbed my cheek. "Damn, that guy hit like a sledgehammer."

"He's had plenty of practice."

I looked up at him, but he was scanning the area.

"The woman..." I said.

"They hurt her. Bad."

Shivers crawled over my skin. There were too many victims of the zeds already. Adding more unnecessary victims poured acid onto my emotions. I looked over at the guy Clutch had put down. "I'm glad you killed him."

"Some folks need to die."

A flurry of movement caught my eye, and I turned to see another man run toward a truck in the distance. "Clutch!" I yelled, wincing at the sharp pain in my cut lip.

Clutch turned, a look of unadulterated fury washed over his face, and he bolted after the man.

The guy was a couple hundred feet away. My .22 was worthless at this distance, so I ran for the truck, jumped in the driver's seat, and gunned the engine, kicking up pebbles.

Clutch was closing the distance, but he was still too far away. The man had already climbed into a dusty blue minivan. Clutch kept running even as the vehicle cranked around and sped directly toward him.

Clutch stopped, took aim, and fired at the windshield. Buckshot fractured the glass. The minivan was going to hit him head-on, but he fired again. I was on my way to T-bone the van, but I wasn't going to get there in time.

At the last second, Clutch dove to the side.

I floored it to intersect the van, but it sped away, spinning out on the gravel road before straightening and tearing away from us.

I stopped, got out, and ran toward Clutch.

He was already on his feet, checking the shotgun.

"Are you okay?"

"Fucker got away." He grimaced. "I didn't recognize him, but he knows that there's someone else out here now. We'll have to be on our guard."

"If we hurry, we might be able to chase him down."

He shook his head. "It'll draw too much attention. We'll find him again."

I nodded tightly, and then looked at the bin and started walking.

"Cash, you don't need to see that. I'll take care of it."

I kept walking. The girl wasn't far away, just out of the line of sight from the truck. She was covered in dried blood and bruises, making it impossible to tell her age, but she looked young. Probably hadn't even graduated from high school yet. Could've been one of Jase's classmates, even. Her nose was broken and one arm was bent at an unnatural angle. All the skin had been scraped from her knees.

She was nearly naked, her skin sallow. The wind flapped the tatters of clothing left on her. Her poor body looked like she'd been abused and broken since the virus outbreak started. She belonged in a hospital. Now, without doctors and medical technology, there was nothing that could be done. She lay there, one eye swollen shut, staring into nothingness. It was a blank stare. I thought she'd already died, but then she blinked.

I realized that it was only her spirit that had already died.

A tear trickled down her cheek. I came down on a knee and wiped the tear away with my thumb. I found it hard to breathe, like a fist had wrapped around my heart.

She tried to speak. Her pale, broken lips moved but no sound came out.

I pointed the pistol at her temple. "I'm sorry." They were the only words I could manage to get out without choking.

She closed her eye and gave a weak smile.

I held the .22 as close as I could get it without touching and pulled the trigger. The blast made me jump, and I let out a sob.

I came back to my feet, staring at the girl, her destroyed features now relaxed.

Finally, she'd found peace.

Tears streamed down my cheeks.

I knew Clutch stood at my back. I had a protector, something this girl had never had. The first raindrops landed on her, creating shiny trails through the blood and grime. I turned my face to the sky to let the cool rain wash away my tears. But the rain could wash away neither the sins nor the memories of what had taken place here today.

Part Three
Hunger

The Third Circle of Hell

Six

"I agree," Clutch said as we shoveled mud into the hole where Jase's parents now rested. "Zed sludge is the foulest odor in the world."

I would've chuckled except I was still too focused on breathing through my mouth, my bandana doing little to block the stench. The mud stuck to our shovels, making the process tedious, but we both agreed that Jase needed to know that his parents had received a proper burial.

"I'll finish up here. You want to finish loading the truck?" Clutch asked.

"Gladly," I said and jogged away before Clutch could change his mind. I sucked in fresh air, though hints of decay still saturated the air.

Jase had made one hell of a mess in the living room. Frank's wife hadn't been too nasty, just a zed corpse with a headshot in the earliest stages of bloating. But Frank could've been an extra in a horror film. His head had been nothing but pulp, and from his chest up, he'd been covered in dried blood and sticky brown goo. The blood, if I had to guess, was canine.

Propped outside the front door sat bags and boxes filled with everything we'd found useful in the house. I grabbed the other two rifles Jase had told Clutch about and slid them behind the front seat before loading the remaining food from the cabinets and supplies into the back of Clutch's black pickup truck.

This morning, Jase had also asked for us to grab his Xbox, and

Clutch snorted out a "hell, no" before going off about how we were about to find ourselves in the dark ages. I grabbed the Xbox, anyway.

By the time I'd loaded the last bag, Clutch was headed my way.

He tugged down his bandana and didn't look happy. "Ready to hit the next stop?"

I swallowed and gave a tight nod.

Neither one of us spoke on the drive to the corn bin where we buried the girl. We strung the bodies of her assailants together with a tie strap and propped them against the corn bin.

Finished, I pulled out a can of red spray paint I'd found at Jase's house and painted large letters on the bin above the men: *R-A-P-I-S-T-S*.

I stared at the letters for a couple minutes. With no law enforcement, it seemed fitting to somehow note these men's crimes. When I tossed the can on the ground, Clutch gave me a nod and headed back to the truck.

We drove around for an hour, scanning for the minivan, and only saw a zed here and there. The bastard was either long gone or had gone to ground, and neither option did us any good. I felt like our duty wouldn't be done be until we could find the fourth rapist. Only then would the poor girl finally be avenged.

All in all, taking care of corpses took us five hours. We sat in the truck and ate the sandwiches I'd made this morning.

"Check out the warehouse next?" I asked between bites. I had the bolt cutters along, and Clutch had been hankering to get his hands onto all the surplus gear.

He nodded while he chewed.

Not even a minute later, thunder rolled, and the damn rain picked up again. I watched heavy drops pelt the windshield. "It'll be tough watching for zeds in this."

"Agreed. We'll try again tomorrow," he grumbled as he wiped his hands on his pants.

"At least the storms should keep other looters away, too," I offered.

He grunted. "We can only hope." And he started the truck.

By the time we'd returned to the farm, the rain had become relentless. Jase stepped out from his cover under a nearby shrub. With the rain parka, he blended seamlessly into the foliage around him. He unlocked the heavy chain and pushed at the gate. Metal screeched as he shoved it open. Something clanged, and the gate broke free from its rollers and swung out at an odd angle.

"Damn it. I knew we were going to have problems with that piece of shit gate," Clutch muttered before gunning the engine through the open space. Once through, he jumped out of the truck and I followed.

It took all our strength to right the gate. The wind pushed against us and the hail pelted our heads. Once the gate was back in place, we tied it to the barbed wire fence we'd reinforced with chain link on each side. It wasn't pretty but it would at least hold the gate and slow down anyone—alive or otherwise—trying to get onto the farm.

A thunderous boom shook the ground. A crack echoed through the air, followed by a large branch off an old maple tree slamming into the ditch behind us.

"C'mon!" Clutch yelled out, his voice a whisper over the wind. "We need to get inside. Now!"

We ran to the truck. Even though there was a backseat, Jase and I both tumbled onto the front bucket seat.

The truck lurched forward, buffeted by the wind that seemed to come at us from every direction. "This one's going to be bad," Clutch muttered.

Going to be? Spring storms in the Midwest were known to get nasty. But, maybe because I'd lived in a city where buildings tempered the winds, I didn't remember a storm this bad in a long time.

Hail bombarded the truck, the noise deafening. When we reached the shed, both Jase and I tumbled out to slide open the large door. The hail hurt, and the wind had become vicious. The sky had turned an ominous green. We started pulling the door shut while Clutch drove the truck into the shed. Once in, he jumped out and helped slide the large door closed.

Hail sounded like an atrocious muddle of drums on the shed's metal roof.

Then the screaming winds mysteriously stilled and the hail stopped.

We all stood and looked up as if we could see through a metal roof. Chills crawled over my skin.

"This can't be good," Jase said.

"We should get to the cellar," I said. I headed to the side door to make a break for the house, but Clutch stopped me.

"No time. This way."

Jase and I hustled behind Clutch through the winding stacks of seed corn waiting to be planted and to the far corner of the shed. He moved aside a couple empty pallets to reveal an earthen-colored tarp. He lifted the tarp and opened a round steel hatch.

"Cool! A bomb shelter," Jase said from behind me.

"I wouldn't call it that," Clutch said, getting down on his hands and knees and pulling out a lantern. He pressed a button, the light clicked on, and he handed it to me.

The winds picked up again, howling like banshees, touting impending doom.

Holding the lantern in one hand, I gingerly climbed down the ladder into the dark hole. The small light lit up the dismally small space below. It couldn't have been more than a five-by-five-foot hole, with the walls taken up by shelves of food, water, and a shotgun vacuum-sealed in plastic. A small square fan covered what I assumed to be the only air vent in the bunker.

Jase landed right behind me. "Cozy."

The walls were rough concrete, but it still smelled of dank earth. "What is this place, Clutch?" I asked.

"My TEOTWAWKI hole," he replied after locking the door above us. "Made it myself."

Sudden silence boomed in the small space.

"The End Of The World As We Know It," I clarified to Jase when he shot me a confused glance. Clutch had used the acronym the day I met him, back when I could still rely on the Internet to get my answers.

"I built it to support one person for fourteen days. But it's tornado-proof, so we'll be safe for tonight. There's no way anyone or anything is going to get in here without a blow torch and several hours of extra time." He tore open a plastic bag and pulled out a metallic sheet. "I have only one blanket, so we'll have to share."

As I sat next to Jase and dried my pistol, I wondered what would await us in the shed when we went to open the hatch in the morning.

———

"We could set up a fenced-in pasture out back," I offered while we sat around a huge breakfast feast, cleaning out the last of the food from the freezer and refrigerator. Since the storm had blown the power out, the mood was somber. My final bite of steak marked the beginning of rationing. Clutch said we'd get used to being hungry. I wasn't so sure.

More so, it was an eerie feeling to know that there was no one left to bring the power grid back up. Even though Clutch had a generator, he'd made it clear that it was for winter use only. It was old and loud and would only attract attention. It also used diesel fuel, and he had only a couple hundred gallons left in the diesel tank out back that had been used for his farm equipment before the outbreak.

No more TV, radio, or ice. No more Internet. No more email to my parents.

"Livestock will attract zeds," Clutch countered, bringing my attention back. "Besides, that's too much meat for the three of us. It'll go bad too quick."

"Not if we find goats," I said.

"Have you seen any goats around?" Clutch said.

"What if we smoked the meat?" I asked.

"Mm, I love jerky," Jase added. "Can we try it, Clutch?"

He scowled. "That means we'd have to keep a watch on the fire. If it puts out smoke that can be seen over the trees, then we can't use it. The smell of smoked meat may also pose a risk. It could attract attention."

"We'll make sure it's good and sealed," I said. "Any risk whatsoever and we won't use it."

He watched me for a moment. "And you know how to make a smokehouse?"

I shrugged, and then smirked. "No, but I bet you have something in your library."

He sighed. "See what you can find. But I check over anything you build before you start a fire in it."

"Deal," I said, and Jase gave me a high-five.

"Don't you first need to build that chicken coop you've been talking about?" Clutch added.

I'd planned a pen out of chicken wire and two-by-fours to be connected to the smaller shed so that zeds, wildlife, and raiders couldn't easily get to the chickens. It wouldn't be pretty, but it would do the job. "I saw chickens at a farm a couple miles that way." I pointed. "I'll pick them up today and put them in the shed until I'm done with the coop. They won't last long on their own."

"That's the Pierson's," Jase added. "They're nice. Moved in just a couple years ago."

"We'll stop on our way back from Home Depot if there's time," Clutch replied. "If we don't get that roof patched, we're going to have serious problems, no thanks to all these rains."

While we'd huddled together in our underground tomb, a twister had blown through. We'd been fortunate. The machine shed and two smaller surrounding sheds were left untouched except for some dents and bent corners courtesy of wind damage. The storm had uprooted one tree and split another in the backyard, but we decided to leave them where they fell since they provided decent obstacles for zeds.

One of the wood covers had snapped off a ground-floor window—a quick repair. The only real damage was to the roof of the house. When we checked out the roof the next morning, all Clutch said was, "I've been meaning to get that roof redone one of these years."

"And the surplus," I added. If Clutch thought there was some badass stuff tucked away in the warehouse, it was going to be Christmas for us. I was keeping my fingers crossed for a Jeep.

"It's going to be a busy day," Clutch said.

"I'll stay back and guard the house," Jase offered.

"Negative. You're both coming. Home Depot is big. If I knew where I could get shingles anywhere else, I would, believe me. I need extra eyes and ears there."

"But who's going to protect the farm when we're gone?" he asked.

"We'll lock the gate up good and tight before we go. That should cover us for a few hours," Clutch replied. "And you can carry in today's water before you gear up."

Jase slumped.

I gave him a reassuring pat. With the power out, we had to get our water from the manual pump outside.

A thump against the outside wall sent us all to our feet. "I'll check it out from the living room," I whispered, pulling out my pistol. Clutch had upgraded my .22 to a Glock 9mm after the run-in with the rapists, and the weight felt good in my grip.

"I'll take upstairs," Jase whispered before taking the stairs three steps at a time.

Clutch nodded and reached for his rifle.

I headed toward the source of the sound and paused, waiting for the next thump. When it came, I took the window on my left and slid open the peephole. The yard looked clear under the overcast sky, though with the peephole, I couldn't see anything against the walls.

I turned to Clutch who was now behind me and shrugged. When I turned around to look outside again, I found a jaundiced face staring back at me. I jumped. "Shit!"

"*Ahhnn.*" The zed pounded on the wood and began to chant the meaningless sound over and over as though it was saying, "Let me in." The window frame vibrated under the pressure.

"Cash?" Clutch asked.

I lifted my pistol, held it just inside the sniper hole, and fired. The pounding stopped and daylight shone through the hole once again.

Jase came running down the stairs a moment later. "The yard's clear. That was the only one I could see."

"It never should've gotten this close to the house. We need to take shorter breaks with the three of us together," Clutch said. "No more than fifteen minutes without anyone on guard every three hours."

"That gives us less time to plan and report status," I said.

"We should use treadmills," Jase said.

"What?" Clutch and I asked at the same time.

Jase gave us a wide grin. "Treadmills. We should surround the house with them. Any zed who comes up to the house will step onto a treadmill and will just keep walking and walking. Then we don't have to stand guard at all."

"Exactly how are you going to power a hundred treadmills?" Clutch asked.

Jase shrugged. "Solar power, maybe."

"Oh, solar power. Of course. I'll pick some up on my next grocery trip," I said drily.

Jase flipped me the bird. "Jeez, can't you guys take a joke?"

I smiled, though Jase had a point. It was too hard to find humor in a world that had given up.

Clutch sighed. "C'mon. Let's hit the road."

Jase's smile dropped. "I'll grab my stuff."

As we headed out to repair the gate, the weather reflected Jase's mood. The sun refused to shine, giving reign to a gray mist instead. I felt sorry for the kid. Going into Fox Hills would bring back a lifetime of memories for him. Where he went to school, where his mom picked up groceries—everything we'd drive by would be a stark reminder of what he'd lost.

With the gate back in place and operational, Jase sulked in the backseat while Clutch drove down the gravel road. Jase feigned nonchalance, but in the side mirror I noticed that he stiffened as we drove by the empty ranch house he grew up in. It looked deceptively welcoming, the scene of death hidden within its red brick walls. My overactive imagination feared that Jase's parents somehow had come back again and dug out of their graves. Fortunately, the house disappeared behind us with no sign of zeds, those related to Jase or otherwise.

Another mile down the road, Jase and I got out to move a small tree that had fallen across the gravel. Broken branches littered the gravel, and one low part over a culvert showed signs that the road had been underwater a few hours earlier.

A bloated zed lay floundering under the shallow rapids of a rushing creek beyond the culvert. Trapped under a log, its arms flapped clumsily at the water.

"I don't get it," Jase said from the backseat. "That thing's probably been underwater all night. How can it still be alive?"

"They're not alive, they're just...echoes of life," I answered honestly. It's what I told myself every day so that I no longer thought of them as people. When the time came to kill—not in self-defense like when Melanie had attacked me—if I believed that they still felt or thought, I wasn't quite sure I could go through with it.

When we reached Fox Hills, we had to lay down plywood in the muddy ditch to get around the roadblock. From there, Clutch drove down Main Street, straight through the center of town. The store we needed was on the opposite side of town, and rather than burn precious gas, he'd made the call to risk driving through the more populated areas of town. It also gave us a chance to see how many zeds we'd have to deal with if we were to start looting houses.

Last night's storm had wreaked havoc on Fox Hills. Plastic trash bins that had lined driveways the day of the outbreak were now strewn about. Garbage was scattered *everywhere*. Diapers, magazines, and milk cartons littered every open space, looking like the aftermath of a wild party. Every now and then we saw a zed with its head shoved in a garbage bag, going after an easy meal.

"They'll eat *anything*," Jase said.

"Yeah," I replied, though we all already knew their favorite meal.

Clutch drove around trees that had been ripped from the ground, and their branches crunched under the truck's tires along with garbage. A tree had smashed a convertible. A Honda and a Chevy were slammed together like bumper cars. Every now and then, we saw a zed lying motionless on the ground, which meant they must've taken serious blows to the head during the storm. But the storm hadn't taken out nearly enough. More zeds than I'd seen last time wandered aimlessly outside, open doors and broken windows the only hints as to where they'd come from, though I suspected most of the zeds still lumbered around inside their homes.

I held the pistol on my lap. I had the tanto, but it was still in its sheath. My real confidence builder was the crowbar I'd found in one of Clutch's sheds. Whenever we left the farm, I carried the crowbar since the knife was short and required me to get awfully close and personal to do any damage. The crowbar, on the other hand, was a power driver of cold iron.

At the sound of the truck's engine, zeds turned and lumbered in our direction, sniffing at the air, but as we put distance between us and them, they soon lost focus and returned back to their eerie shuffling.

"Hey, you!" Jase yelled, opening his window. "Over here!"

Several zeds emerged from the shadows, coming at us. At the way their expressions changed when they homed in on us, I could imagine their mouths watering at the sight of three healthy people.

"Fuck, kid. Are you calling every zed to us?" Clutch spat out, stepping on the gas.

"What are you doing, Jase?" I asked.

He kept waving, not answering our questions, but after a moment, he slumped back in his seat. "I saw someone. A lady. But she darted around the corner of that house over there."

"We ain't a search-and-rescue, kid," Clutch said, then added more softly, "Roll up the window."

"But we have to help others if we can," Jase countered.

"She didn't want our help," I said. I'd seen her, too. She looked in her late fifties or early sixties, and she'd been carrying a baseball bat. We'd made eye contact just before she ran. Was it bad that I was glad that she'd run away rather than toward us? Any orphan we took in was another mouth to feed.

I was pretty sure I saw another couple—a man and a woman— watching us through shuttered windows from a small starter home. I didn't mention them to Jase. I figured if they needed help bad enough, they'd run to us.

It wasn't our job to play hero.

Selfish? Hell, yeah.

But honest. And necessary to survive. After all, I was only human.

Besides, after seeing what had happened to the girl at the corn bin, I realized that laws and scruples were no longer viable in this new world. Now, people scared me as badly as zeds.

What I saw next made me burst out laughing.

The guys turned to me, and I pointed. "Look. A zed kabob." Off to my right, a zed had somehow gotten itself skewered onto a still-upright parking meter, with the thick round top of the meter embedded in its ribcage. Its arms and legs flailed uselessly like it was trying to air-swim. The guys didn't find it funny, and we continued on.

A stoplight was down in one intersection, and we had to turn around and find a detour. Two more detours past smashed cars and fallen power lines, and we were back on Main Street. I carefully noted every obstruction on a small notepad.

It took us twenty-three minutes to drive six miles through town and to our destination. Home Depot was a new massive store on the outskirts, sidled up against an old elementary school of all things. A wood privacy fence went out from behind the school to enclose what I assumed to be the playground.

A sense of bad omen settled into my stomach. I turned in my seat to face Jase. "When the outbreak hit, when did they let out the schools?"

He shrugged. "I don't think they officially closed, but I know some parents picked up their kids, anyway. It all happened so fast. At the high school, some of the teachers let us out early, and I drove my bike home. But those who rode buses...I-I don't know how they got home."

I grimaced. "I'm guessing school is still in session."

"You have a bike?" Clutch asked.

Jase nodded. "Mom and Dad got me a kickass Suzuki for my birthday. I've been practicing up for motocross. I'm going—I mean, I was going to race at the county fair this summer."

I could hear the enthusiasm in Jase's voice bleed out as he spoke.

"The bike's at your house now?" Clutch asked.

"Yeah, why?"

"Because a bike is the perfect vehicle for us to scout the farm and surrounding area. We'll pick it up on our way back. Don't worry. You'll get plenty of motocross practice in." He sighed as he turned into the large parking lot. "Add the bike to our ever-growing to-do list."

Jase gave a low whistle. "That's a lot of cars."

"Are you sure there's nowhere else that might have roofing supplies?" I asked.

Clutch grimaced. "'Fraid not."

He pulled into an open area toward the back of the parking lot. If zeds came at us, the one thing we had on them was speed. Having the truck at a distance from the store could be a lifesaver when it came to putting space between us and hungry zeds.

We checked our gear and weapons. We left the Kevlar vests at home since they were heavy and zeds tended to go for the face or extremities. With the black Kevlar helmets and gloves, we looked like Special Forces, but I felt nothing like an experienced soldier.

Clutch looked at both of us. "All right, we've got to be smart about this. No fuck-ups. We get what we need, then we're out of there. The other supplies in there aren't worth the risk, not until we know the place is cleared out. We go in silent and we stick together. We know zeds hunt off their senses, so we move slow and silent. Always keep a direct line to the exit. If either of you screw up, I might decide to leave your ass behind. Got it?"

Both Jase and I nodded.

Clutch left the keys in the ignition in case we needed to make a quick getaway, or, worse, in case he didn't leave the store with us. "Let's do this. Exactly as I taught you. Follow my lead. Silence from here on out," he said and opened the door.

I gripped the crowbar. We moved as a trio of dark-colored shapes slowly through the parking lot. I'd expected that we'd have to take out a couple zeds in the parking lot, but nothing emerged from around the cars. Not a good sign. Because the owners of those cars had to be somewhere.

We flattened against the wall on either side of the wide glass entrance, and Clutch bent around to scan the area. He frowned and led us down the sidewalk to the exit door. He scanned the interior longer this time before finally nodding. Forcing myself to breathe, I stepped next to Clutch, holding the crowbar up. The sliding door didn't automatically open. Just as we'd expected, the power grid for the entire area was down. Clutch pulled at the door while I stood ready to knock back any zed that may attack. Jase stood at our backs, a rifle slung on his back and a long wood-handled axe in his hands.

Clutch pried the door open just enough for us to squeeze through one at a time. Clutch went in first. Once through, he crouched and flattened himself against one of the checkout counters. He held his machete out while he checked the area behind him.

When he gave us the *all-clear*, I went in next, moving exactly as Clutch had done. When Jase reached me, he tapped my left shoulder. *Ready.* I did the same to Clutch's shoulder, just like how he'd made us practice.

Clutch moved to the edge of the counter and looked left and right. After making a quick hand motion, he crossed the aisle, keeping slow and low, until he flattened against the other side. I moved but abruptly pulled back when I saw a zed in the aisle, sniffing at the air. Taking a breath, I waited until it faced the other direction, and I crossed the aisle. Jase followed.

We continued this process, avoiding zeds and following Clutch, as we moved deep into the belly of the store. For the number of cars outside, there were surprisingly few zeds meandering around, which made me wonder exactly where all the drivers to those cars had gone.

Clutch clearly frequented this store because he led us to the aisle we needed without any wrong turns or detours except to bypass zeds. I opened the duffel, and he slid in several heavy stacks of shingles. Jase stayed at my back and scanned the entire time.

"Uh, guys?" Jase whispered.

I glanced up to see a zed come around the corner and into our aisle. It'd been badly gnawed. One of its arms was nothing but white bone and stringy sinew. We didn't move, hoping it wouldn't see us.

We weren't that lucky.

It only took a couple seconds for the zed to sniff the air and home in on us. It moaned and stumbled toward us. *It's like a fucking bloodhound*, I thought to myself. Clutch stood, walked right up to it, and swung, his machete taking off the top of the zed's head with a single powerful slice. The zed collapsed, and he caught the body just before it hit the floor and laid it down quietly.

He returned and grabbed the duffel as though nothing happened. On our way out, we nearly walked into a small group of zeds and were forced to backtrack. As we neared another aisle, Jase nudged me. "Look," he whispered and pointed at a glass display case.

My mouth opened, and I tugged Clutch and then pointed.

He saw the display case, looked around, and then headed toward it. On proud display behind the glass was a little piece of heaven. Small camping axes, knives of all sizes, and the Cadillac—black machetes. While Clutch's arsenal of rifles and pistols was impressive, he had few blades, with the exception of a machete and a wood axe, his blades were knives.

He felt around the back of the display case, then around the edges. When the glass didn't slide open, he grabbed Jase's axe.

"It's locked. Get ready to move fast," Clutch whispered. "Know what you want, and grab it. Don't try for everything. We head straight to the truck two seconds after this breaks."

He stood, laid an empty duffel against the glass, and then brought down the heavy end of the axe. Even with the fabric, the sound of breaking glass echoed through the store.

Clutch grabbed a couple small axes in one swoop, and then got out of the way. Jase and I were smaller and could reach in at the same time. We both went for the machetes, and then I grabbed an axe, sliding both into my belt.

"Let's go," Clutch said aloud, and we headed down the aisle.

We made it two rows over before we hit a roadblock of a half dozen zeds. We turned to the left and ran. Jase pulled ahead, though Clutch was quick. I struggled to keep up, my shorter legs a clear detriment in outrunning zeds.

The guys came to a screeching halt in front of me. The zeds had discovered the opened door, and had flocked toward it, moaning as they pressed through. That was, until they saw us, and their moans grew in volume as they changed direction en masse toward us.

A quick glance at the entrance door proved no better option.

Clutch looked around. "There's a door to the lumberyard on the side." He took off at a run. We followed, weaving around stray zeds. Clutch kicked the door open, and we burst outside.

I sucked in a breath.

At least fifty zeds turned our way. They must've fled outside when the outbreak happened, only to be corralled in the lumberyard. The herd moaned and came at us. We ran toward the front gate, only to find it locked with a big ass padlock.

"Oh, shit," Jase said. "We're so dead."

We couldn't go back inside because we'd already drawn the attention of every indoor zed. The herd closed in. Some were wearing orange vests with nametags, others in casual jeans and T-shirts.

"We need to get to higher ground. Stay with me," Clutch called out and led the charge.

He ran toward the herd, and then cut to the left to dodge outstretched arms. Jase was insanely fast and moved ahead of Clutch in no time. By the time I reached the corner, the herd had blocked off the aisle the guys had taken, and I cut to the right, jumping over a stack of hoses. A zed stood in my way, and I swung the crowbar, smashing its head and knocking him to the side. I kept running, dodging zeds, swinging only when I had to, until I found the guys again.

Jase was climbing the lumber stacks on long shelves lining the back wall. Clutch had climbed into a forklift and was headed straight toward me. I ran to the side as Clutch skewered the closest zed. He jumped off the still-moving forklift and quickly caught up to me. "Get your ass in gear, Cash!"

With one final surge, I flung the crowbar onto the second shelf before leaping for a stack of two-by-fours. I'd been working out, but one week of strength-building didn't cut it. I awkwardly held on to the end of a two-by-four and prayed it wouldn't give. When it didn't move, I swung, trying to get my leg over the edge. A zed grabbed onto my foot, and I kicked out. Its grip relaxed, and I used its head to step off, pushing myself onto the shelf.

Clutch had also leapt onto the shelf, though he made it look easy.

Gasping for air, I got back on my feet, and followed Clutch. I grabbed on to a metal shelf post, and pulled myself up to the next level. A gloved hand reached out from above, and I grabbed on, letting Clutch pull me up to the stack he and Jase were on. I hugged on to him as soon as I felt the solid surface under my knees.

Still on a knee, Clutch pulled back and looked me over. "You all right?"

I nodded. "Yeah, thanks."

"Come and get us, you stinky zed bastards!" Jase yelled out, flipping the zed the bird. Jase was on his knees, panting, looking over the edge.

"Jesus," I said. "You're a freaking mutant, Jase. I've never seen anyone run that fast."

He grinned. "State 100-meter and 400-meter relays. Twice. Not to mention Fox Hills' varsity football team's best tight end."

I couldn't help but smile. Until I looked over the side. The zeds gathered below, looking up, reaching and groaning, as though begging us to come back down. Some tried to climb, but they fell back after the first step.

We'd use up all our ammo to clear out the herd below. And who knew how many more the noise would draw out. Already, the zeds from inside the store were filtering outside to join the soggy herd surrounding us. Why were there so many here? It had taken Alan nearly an hour to turn. That should've given most of these folks time to get home and turn there. Though, I remember the news had said that the worse the injury, the faster they turned. Many of the zeds below had serious bites.

And they looked ravenous.

I glanced at Clutch, who seemed to be thinking the same thing.

"C'mon," he said. "Let's get to the top."

I poked my head out and looked up. There were three more shelves to climb. The fact that I was scared of heights did nothing to help my nerves. Jase took the lead. He climbed like a monkey, amped up on pure adrenaline. Clutch went next. Even with the heavy duffel and being laden with weapons, he climbed like he carried little extra weight. I double-checked my weapons to make sure they were secure, and I started to pull myself up the side. It was like climbing a rope on a jungle gym, except the bars were unforgiving, and if I fell, I'd get eaten.

At each level, Clutch helped pull me up, and we took a few minutes to rest, although I think it was mostly for my benefit. If it hadn't been for the gloves, my hands would've been raw. Even with the gloves, I felt blisters forming.

Once we reached the top, I lay down on the stack of thick plywood and panted. Clutch scanned the area, and I pulled myself up to gauge the situation. Large shelves holding stacks of wood, blocks, and boxes lined the three walls. We had plenty of horizontal movement up here, but getting to the ground without becoming zed-food would be a challenge.

Clutch set down the duffel. "You two stay here. I'm going to check things out."

I pulled myself up as Clutch leapt onto the next shelf over. He moved slowly but with a gracefulness that belied his size as he leapt from one shelf to the next. I looked out over the wall to see open countryside. A zed shambled along here and there, but otherwise, it was wide-open. The problem was we were a good twenty feet up, without any ladder or rope to get down the wall.

"We're so dead," Jase said at my side. "We're going to die, aren't we?"

I punched him in the arm. "I don't ever want to hear you say those words again. Clutch will figure out something."

"Yes, ma'am," he replied quietly.

We sat in silence after that. When Clutch finally returned, Jase didn't complain, not once.

"Find anything promising?" I asked.

Clutch pulled off his helmet and ran a hand through his hair. "It's a hell of a jump, but the roof of the elementary school looks like our only shot. Our other option is to wait it out and hope these guys move on."

"You think they'll move on?" I asked.

"No chance in hell," Clutch quickly replied.

I slid my gloves back on. "I guess we'd better get going then."

The shelf we needed was four over from the one we were on, and I moved more cautiously than Clutch. Once I reached the shelf, I looked over at the school. "For once, I wish you were exaggerating," I grumbled. When he'd said it was going to be a big jump, he should've said it was going to be an Olympian feat. Not only was the roof nearly a good five feet lower, there was what looked like an eight-foot gap between the shelf and the roof. If I didn't make the roof, the fall would likely kill me.

To make matters worse, a lone zed was stuck in the alley, blocked on one side by the playground fence and the other by a car. It was on the ground, its legs mangled as though it had been caught between the car and the fence at some point, and it had dragged itself around in circles, if the brown trail was any indication.

"Oh, Jesus—"

My glare cut off Jase's words and he clamped his mouth shut.

"If I go first," Clutch said. "One of you will have to throw me the duffel."

I almost chuckled at the absurdity. There was no way I could throw a fifty-pound bag two feet, let alone fifteen. "I'll go first," I said. "I'll catch." What I meant was, *I'll use my body to block the bag's momentum and hopefully not die upon impact.*

He nodded, and I backed up to the edge of the shelf overlooking the lumberyard. If I thought about it, I knew I'd freak, so I didn't wait. I took three big breaths before sprinting forward. At the other edge, I kicked off into a scary-as-shit long-jump. Just when I thought I'd never reach the edge of the roof, I landed on the flat surface, falling forward instantly. The air whooshed from my lungs, and my teeth snapped shut painfully when I hit my chin. I slid down a couple feet before coming to a stop on the abrasive shingles.

I rolled over and coughed and wheezed.

"You okay?" Clutch called out, and I held up my thumb.

Once I could breathe again, I pulled myself up and inched my way back up to the peak. "Throw me the bag."

Clutch held up the bag, and I held out my arms and swallowed. Jase stood off to the side, watching with wide eyes. Clutch swung the duffel in a wide arc and released it with a grunt. I stood there and waited for the smack-down, and Clutch's aim was dead-on. The duffel hit me square in the stomach, and I fell backward, holding it to me. I slid several feet down the roof, but the duffel's canvas helped slow my descent. By the time I sat up, I found Clutch on the roof with me.

"Nice catch."

I coughed and handed him the duffel. "I don't think I have tits anymore."

He gave that deep rumble of a chuckle, heaved the bag onto his back, and winced.

"Your shoulder?"

He rubbed it. "Yeah. Twisted it when I threw the duffel."

He reached out with his other hand and helped me to my feet. We looked over at Jase. He stood there, frozen. The zed in the alley was groaning, reaching up.

I motioned him over with one hand while still holding my bruised ribs with my other. "You can do it, monkey boy."

He looked down once more and then slowly backed up. With a half-crouch, he rocked back and forth before kicking off. He easily closed the distance and landed solidly on the roof. But his footing gave way, and he kicked out and went tumbling down the side. He grabbed at the roof but kept sliding until he disappeared over the edge.

"Jase!"

Clutch and I moved cautiously down the angled roof to the edge. Jase was on the ground, holding onto his ankle. Instead of the parking lot side, Jase had fallen into the playground. *Shit.* I scanned the enclosed area but saw no movement.

Jase winced. "My ankle. I think it's broken."

"Can you stand?" Clutch asked.

Jase grunted, was able to get to his feet, but he favored his right leg.

"Good. Now, do you see a door in the fence? Or, is there anything around you can use to climb back up here?"

As Jase looked around, I scanned the privacy fence, but found only a gate at one end, and it had a large, shiny padlock on it.

"There's nothing down here," Jase said, holding up his hands in defeat.

"Jase, do you see any zeds around?" I asked.

"Not out here. I see some inside, though. Oh, God. They see me."

"Bloody hell," I muttered. "I'll handle this."

Clutch eyed me. "Cash..."

"He's injured. I'm not. You can pull me up once we get Jase to safety." Before I had a chance to think about how dumb the idea was, I shimmied down, holding onto the edge until I had to let go. The drop sent shockwaves up my shins, but I landed without twisting anything.

"Godammit, Cash," Clutch said from above.

I also heard a small pounding behind me. I turned to see children watching us through a classroom window. They were young, one of the earlier grades, and they were no longer alive. They watched us hungrily, smacking their small hands against the glass.

I hooked my fingers together to make a step. "Climb up, and be quick about it."

Jase didn't argue. With a grunt, he stepped into my cupped hands with his good leg. I lifted his weight as high as I could, using my legs. Clutch reached down from the roof. It wasn't quite enough. Jase stepped onto my shoulder, and then his weight vanished. I looked up to see his legs disappear onto the roof.

Clutch reappeared an instant later. "Now get your ass up here, Cash."

I jogged around the playground, looking for a jump rope but finding only rubber balls and jungle gyms. I fidgeted with the padlock at the gate, but I had nothing to pick the lock with, not that I even knew how to pick a lock. I tried to jump up to grab the top of the privacy fence, but it was too high. With a sigh, I looked at the windows, each filled with hungry, hollow little faces.

"Is there any rope in the truck?" I asked.

Clutch thought for a moment. "I've got tie straps." He moved. "I'll come down, and you can go grab them."

I held up my hand. "No. Then you'll be stuck down here. Go for the truck."

Glass shattered, and I jerked around to find a teacher stepping through the now-broken window. I pulled out my new machete. "Get Jase to the truck. I'll catch up."

"We're not leaving," Clutch yelled back.

I swung the machete, nearly decapitating a teacher with its hands and forearms covered with little bites. "Go. Hurry!" I wasn't used to the blade, so my aim was off. The second swing killed it. Small zeds tumbled out of the window. A gunshot rang out. A boy in jeans and a sports jersey dropped. Another shot. A girl with pigtails dropped. Several more shots and the rest of the zed kids dropped. The ones still held inside were pounding harder on the glass now, in a frenzy to get out.

I looked up at Clutch to find him reloading. "The shots will draw more zeds to the school," I yelled up. "Take Jase and get to the truck before the parking lot fills up."

"No," Clutch replied.

I watched him. More glass behind me shattered. "I won't let you die for me." After a quick glance at the newcomers, I went for the only door that I knew would be unlocked.

"Cash!"

I pushed open the glass door with my left hand, and swung the machete at the first zed with my right. The kid went right down. The hallway was not nearly as congested as the classrooms, which I noticed nearly all had their doors closed.

I jogged down the hallway, shoving zed kids out of my way, thankful for the thick gloves and jacket I'd worn. A zed could bite through it eventually, but at least it'd have to work at it.

I turned the corner into the main hallway and froze. A couple dozen three- and four-foot tall zeds with three adult zeds turned to face me. One growled, and the groans began. They lurched forward.

I spun around to backtrack, but the hall had filled in behind me as well, with a zed wearing a tag reading HALL MONITOR leading the group. I lunged for the double door to my left and jumped inside. After making sure the door was shut tight, I spun on my heel.

"Fuck me."

I'd found the school cafeteria. Food trays were scattered across the floors. The buffet line had been ravaged. Several bodies, with most of their skin and muscle gone, were sprawled on the floor, covered in writhing maggots. And now, the large room was full of food-stained, bloodied zeds, and every single one of the bastards were focused on me.

They staggered toward me with outreached arms, and I jumped up onto a table, then onto the next table, sliding through spaghetti sauce that I knew wasn't really spaghetti sauce.

I slid the machete in my belt and leapt, grabbing the fluorescent light hanging from the ceiling. Surprisingly, it held. Miraculously, my adrenaline helped me pull myself up, safely out of reach of the small arms. But larger arms connected to zeds in lunch lady uniforms reached perilously close.

"I'm not going to die," I muttered and punched up at the ceiling. The white panel moved, and I realized this was one of those drop-down ceilings that allowed space for wiring and cables.

Gripping the metal frame, I swung and kicked up, knocking out another white panel, catching my foot on the frame. Using the strength of my legs, I was able to pull myself up and above the frame.

A sea of jaundiced dead faces looked up at me, growling, reaching, and chomping. I moved carefully and slowly onto the next frame, careful to distribute my weight over two rows of metal framing. I had no idea how much weight these ceilings were meant to hold, but they sure as hell couldn't have been built for human travel.

I crawled over one panel to the next, pausing every few panels to catch my breath. My directions were jumbled in the darkness. I had no idea if I was heading toward the parking lot, back to the playground, or if I was going in circles. I lifted the edge of the panel to find that I was still in the cafeteria. Zeds stood under the opening I'd made in the ceiling in the opposite side of the room, still looking up, sniffing the air, reaching, mouths opening and closing like baby birds.

A crack of light filtered in through the corner I'd lifted and lit up the wall of concrete blocks in front of me. *Shit.* The ceiling ended where the wall separated the cafeteria from the hallway. My arms and legs were already shaking. I had to figure out something or else I'd fall right down into the cafeteria again. Except this time, I'd never have the strength to get back up here.

But there was nothing up here except space, wiring, and...air ducts. My attention shot to the large duct leading straight through the center of the cafeteria and through the concrete wall. Many smaller ducts ran off it like a spider's legs. Ducts looked so much bigger in the movies, but I prayed that this one would be big enough. It *had* to be.

I made my way toward the metal duct. Sweat burned my eyes and tickled my neck as rivulets ran down to soak my shirt. By the time I reached the duct, I was exhausted and clumsy, nearly tumbling off the ceiling grid twice. I moved alongside the duct until I found where one section ended and another began. Both were held together by screws. I pulled out my tanto and used the tip to unscrew the first screw, and then the next. It was a painfully slow process to take out the six screws on the sides I could reach.

I pushed against the duct but it didn't budge. Trading my knife for the axe, I pulled back a few measly inches and swung. The metal clanged and dented, echoed by moaning and shuffling below. A couple dozen hits later, the duct broke open. I slid the axe inside and shoved myself through. Sharp metal from the axe's damage dug into me, but I continued to squeeze into the tiny boxed-in darkness until I filled up the area of the duct.

I sneezed in the dust-laden air, causing the zeds below to echo with moans. Using my elbows, I pulled myself forward. I could see nothing except light filtered in from vents every eight feet or so.

At each vent, I paused and looked down. The hallway was filled with shoulder-to-shoulder zeds sniffing the air. When the duct split into three pathways, I decided to head left over the hallway, hoping it would bring me to the front doors. I followed the duct, through several more intersections.

I sobbed out in exhausted frustration. My cramped muscles burned. My helmet clanged against the metal, but there was no space to take it off and leave it behind. When I finally reached a vent where I could see the front doors, I rested my head against the vent and nearly cried.

The glass doors were blocked by zeds.

Biting back a whimper, I backed up about ten feet until I came to an intersection and I took the first right. This duct led to a room with a couple office-style desks. It wasn't a classroom, which gave me some hope.

Seeing no movement below, I fidgeted with the vent until I figured out how to remove it, and it dropped, landing on the floor with an echoing clang. Something moaned, and a shadow moved. A female, wearing khakis and a blue blouse with dark stains, stepped on the vent and looked around.

"Can't I get a fucking break?" I muttered.

Moving slowly, I reached out of the duct with the axe. The zed looked up right as I swung. The axe caught it in the forehead, and it tumbled back, taking the axe with it.

I grabbed my machete and waited for another one, but none came. I breathed in and out and waited. Dropping down feet first into a room with possible zeds was not my idea of a good time.

Careful to not bang my helmet on the metal, I lowered my head out of the vent to scan the room. It was an office with two desks and glass walls. The principal's office was just on the other side of the glass wall to the right, and it was still occupied by a zed in a tailored skirt suit. She rocked on her feet, looking out the window.

The other glass walls faced two angles of the hallway, giving full views of the zed near the front doors. At least both doors were closed, but I had no idea if they were locked or would hold back the weight of zeds pushing against them.

I'd be in a fishbowl the moment I dropped.

Like the principal's office, the fourth wall had a nice wide window overlooking the school parking lot. I could make out only one zed, and it was trapped inside a car. Maybe the zeds who'd escaped the Home Depot had followed Clutch's truck when he left with Jase.

God, I hated maybes.

Unless the window was heavily tinted, the sun had nearly set, which meant I'd been crawling around this place for at least eight hours. I wasn't the least bit surprised, not with how exhausted and thirsty I was. I even wondered if I'd be able to stand once I got out of this duct. My stomach had quit growling hours ago. My throat was parched, and my clothes were soaked.

I pulled my head back in, and shimmied forward over the opening so that I could back up and drop feet first into the room. I would've preferred to go head first to see around, but the opening was too tight, and there would be nothing to grab onto to keep me from breaking my neck from the drop.

After sliding the machete back into my belt, I squeezed through as quietly and motionlessly as I could to not draw attention. About halfway through, I heard a pounding on the glass. I shoved myself through the rest of the way, and I finally popped through, dropping onto the floor.

The moment I landed, every zed, including the principal, clambered to get to me. Putting a foot on the dead zed's chest, I grabbed the axe handle and yanked it free. I ran to the window, swung the axe, and the glass shattered apart. The hallway door behind me cracked. I saw a handbag under the desk. I grabbed it and jumped on the desk and through the window.

I had no time to barricade the window, and I started running through the parking lot. Clutch's truck was long gone, which I'd expected. They would've been idiots to wait around to get overtaken by zeds for the slightest chance that I'd survived.

Three zeds came out from around a minivan in front of me. I stopped, dropped the purse, and pulled out my Glock. Three shots. Three went down.

Slinging the bag over my shoulder, I ran to the car where I'd seen the zeds and ducked behind the trunk. I dumped out the contents of the large purple purse, and sifted through the pile of crap that had tumbled out until I found the one thing I needed. Coming up on a knee, I held up the car key, and hit the unlock button. Lights flashed and chirped on a car parked near the front door.

Five zeds had already emerged through the broken glass window. It wouldn't take long for the parking lot to be flooded. With the Glock in one hand, the key ring dangling off my pinky, and the axe in another, I ran toward the car.

The zeds staggered toward me, but I was faster. With a cursory look through the car's windows, I yanked open the car door and climbed inside.

Dropping the axe on the passenger seat and the gun on my lap, I slid the key into the ignition. The engine started with pop music blaring from the speakers, and I shoved the gear into reverse. The car barreled over the zeds coming around behind and struggled as it dragged itself over the bodies.

I needed a tank. I got a fucking Prius.

Zeds stumbled at the car, and I swung the car around, shifted gears, and peeled out. I took off my helmet and threw it onto the seat next to me and turned off the CD player before picking up speed. I barreled right down Main Street, taking out another four zeds on my way through. The Prius was no truck and one of the zeds clung onto the hood for several blocks before I finally managed to throw him off.

The compact car wasn't made for demolition, but I was counting on its gas mileage. It showed a near-empty tank of gas (who the fuck drives on an empty tank?), but being a Prius, the computer indicated it had plenty to get me back to the farm. I sped straight back through town the way we'd come this morning, and nearly ran into a Humvee at the second detour. It was full of people, including the couple I'd seen this morning.

The blond guy manning the .30 cal machine gun on top waved me down. He might've been a soldier, or he might've been friends with the bastard raiders from earlier. I stepped on the gas, and the tires actually squealed as I sped away.

The Humvee followed for several blocks before slowing and breaking away. I checked the rearview mirror all the way back to the farm to make sure I wasn't followed. When I reached the lane, I found the gate closed but unlocked, and I frowned.

This wasn't like Clutch. He never made mistakes like this.

I didn't have the strength, but somehow I managed to slide the gate open and then closed and locked it. As I drove down the lane, I scanned the trees for raiders and zeds, but my eyes could barely focus. My body was way past its limits. I prayed that the farm was still safe because I wasn't sure I could defend it.

When I pulled into view of the house, I cried out with relief. Clutch stood at the truck, holding two rifles and a shitload of ammo. He set everything down. "Cash!" he yelled, jogging toward me.

I got out of the Prius, and stumbled to my knees. Adrenaline had abandoned me, leaving me utterly without strength. But then Clutch was there, picking me up.

"You're safe now," he murmured as he carried me into the house.

Sighing, I rested my head against his chest and listened to his steady breathing. I laid my hand over his pounding heart. It felt good to feel something alive again. I'd killed children today. Even though they were zeds, they still wore the guise of innocence. And still, I found killing was easy.

It's the living with yourself afterward that's tough.

Part Four
Greed

The Fourth Circle of Hell

Seven

Exhaustion claimed me, and I sank deeper into Clutch's safe arms. Saying nothing, he carried me into the house and rather than bringing me to the sofa where I'd slept since Jase came to live here, he carried me upstairs.

"Cash! We were so freaking worried!" Jase yelled out through the open door of his bedroom.

Without pausing at Jase's room, Clutch carried me straight into his bedroom. I barely stayed awake while he helped me out of my sweat- and dust-drenched layers, leaving me in only my sports bra and underwear.

He left, returning moments later with wet washcloths. He ran the cloths gently over my skin, likely checking me for bites and injuries more than cleaning me, but I didn't care. His touch felt good.

Finished, he helped me crawl under the blankets of his king-sized bed, and tucked them around me. I groaned at the protective comfort of the blankets and pulled them tighter to me. "So good to be home."

Clutch grunted before disappearing again, and the next thing I knew he was nudging me awake. I grumbled as he lifted my head up and held a glass of water to my lips. My hands wrapped around his fingers on the glass while I clumsily slurped at the contents. The cool water drenched the dust and debris lodged in my raw throat and I coughed. Once I could breathe again, I gulped down the rest. He wiped water from my chin before he lowered my head back to the pillow and stepped away.

At the door he paused. "I never should've left you behind," he said, his voice a rough whisper.

I shook my head. "I made you go."

"No. You didn't." Then he walked away, closing the door behind him, leaving behind only silence.

"Clutch," I called out with a cough, but he never returned. At first I fought to stay awake so I could talk some sense into him, but all too quickly I surrendered to a dreamless sleep.

I slept through most of the next day, though I remember Clutch checking on me several times. Each time, his calloused hand brushed across my forehead and he made me drink water before letting me doze off again. One time, he wouldn't leave until I'd eaten a protein bar. I grumbled, he grumbled, and I ate it. Then I fell back asleep.

Nightmares of children that were no longer children yanked me back to consciousness. Luckily, instead of the moans of zeds, I came awake to the sound of stacking plates and the smell of warm food.

Every muscle in my body griped when I climbed out of bed. After a full-body stretch, I forced myself through fifty sit-ups and fifty push-ups to get my blood pumping. My body hated me for it, but I pushed through it. Finished, I headed across the hall to the bedroom I'd given up to Jase when he moved in, and grabbed fresh clothes from a drawer I'd kept in the dresser.

Without power, we had no water pressure for a shower the three of us shared. I sighed in relief when I found four buckets of clean water waiting next to the tub. I poured them into the tub, stripped, and settled into the biting cold water, trying to scrub away the memories from yesterday, with little success.

Not having warm water tended to speed up the cleaning process. Shivering, I jogged down the steps to find Clutch cooking dinner on the tabletop propane grill we'd moved into the kitchen after the power went out. He gave me a small nod before turning his attention back to the food. I grabbed a spoon and reached into the pot, but he grabbed my wrist. "Nuh-uh. You have to wait like the rest of us."

I pouted and then smirked. "Hurry up. I'm starving," I ordered and headed into the living room, the only light from a small lantern.

"Hey, Cash," Jase called from the sofa.

I nodded toward his left foot propped up on a chair, a thick wrapping around his ankle. "How's the leg?"

He rubbed his ankle. "It's just a sprain. Clutch says the swelling will be down enough in another day or two that I can start putting some weight on it again." He looked up. "Wow, you slept for like twenty-four hours straight."

"She needed it," Clutch said before handing Jase and me each a bowl.

I grabbed a seat next to Jase and dug into tonight's specialty—a steaming mix of mystery meat, beans, and rice.

Clutch returned with his own bowl and a warm beer.

"So tell me about the school. Were there more zeds inside?" Jase asked.

I paused before taking a bite. "Yeah."

"What was it like? I bet it was scary," he continued.

I kept chewing. The memories were bad enough for me. No one else needed to have them haunting their conscience.

Clutch gave me a knowing look but said nothing. He finished his dinner and beer before I was even halfway through mine. He came to his feet. "I should get back outside."

I looked up. "Have you been covering both Jase's and my shifts?"

He didn't reply, but the dark circles under his eyes told me enough. He looked beat, and I'd bet he hadn't slept once in the past two days.

"I'll cover all of tonight," I said. "You're on bed rest, effective immediately."

He raised a brow. "You're ordering me around now?"

I smiled. Then nodded.

A smirk tugged at his lips before he relented. "Wake me when you need a break. Don't overdo it because, at sunrise, we need to start hitting the farms around here hard and fast. A vehicle drove by slow yesterday, which I'd bet are looters scanning this area."

"Shit," I muttered. While I'd expected looters to sniff around this area sometime, I'd also hoped that they'd take their own sweet time before doing so. There were literally hundreds of miles of roads in the area. Why couldn't they leave our four-mile stretch alone?

"We need everything we can get and fast," Clutch added. "And, I'm out of beer and almost out of whiskey."

I grimaced. "I can't believe you'd drink warm beer."

"Warm beer is better than no beer."

"Point taken." I shooed him away. "Now go. Hit the sack. You're even grumpier when you're tired."

He grunted and cracked his neck. "Be careful out there. I saw a group of zeds pass through the field yesterday. We've been lucky they've mostly avoided the woods so far."

"I wonder why they haven't hit the woods more," I said. After all, if I was a predator, they'd be a prime spot.

"I'm thinking they prefer taking easier routes since they can't get around as easily as us," Clutch replied before disappearing up the stairs.

So far, most zeds we'd seen had stuck to open flatlands like roads, yards, and fields. But a few had stumbled through the woods already, so they certainly didn't have an allergy to shrubbery.

I would've eaten faster, but my stomach was cramping from going nearly two days on only a protein bar, and I had to pace myself. At least I was wide awake. A near-coma was exactly what my body had needed. My muscles were amped. I wished it was morning already so that we could get started on looting the nearby farms. We'd been forced to put it off while we fortified the farm against looters. But we *needed* food and supplies. Even though winter was at least eight months away, we needed to hoard anything we could to prepare.

Running into zeds or looters was a chance we had to take.

"You were lucky you got back to the farm when you did," Jase mumbled with a mouth full of food. "Clutch was packing up to head back into town for you. I wanted to come, but he said I had to stay back and hold down the fort."

"He was an idiot," I said. When I'd seen Clutch loading weapons into the truck, I'd already figured he wasn't heading out for another solo looting run. Going anywhere after dark was a suicide run, especially to a particular elementary school. Clutch could've gotten himself killed for the infinitesimal chance that I was still alive. It was a fucking miracle I'd gotten back to the house when I did. If he'd gone into town to look for me...if he hadn't returned...

With a shiver, I came to my feet and headed into the kitchen to clean up, all the time praying that those thoughts would never become reality.

After I had my weapons strapped on, I stopped by the living room. "You need help getting upstairs?" I asked.

Jase looked up from the book he'd been reading and shook his head. "Nah. I'll hang down here for a bit. I'm tired of being in bed." He thumped the book down. "I hate being cooped up like this."

"You'll be back on your feet before you know it." I gave him a quick wave and then headed outside. The sun had set, and I walked the perimeter around the house first. I'd always hated night-watch. Now, I had a whole new perspective. Even in the dark where zeds could lurk, I found the open space and fresh air a vast improvement over the school's cramped air ducts.

The walk down the long lane, with trees lining both sides, seemed easier tonight. Sure, a zed could shuffle out from the darkness at any moment, but the idea didn't terrify me as much as it had less than two days ago.

There was hardly a breeze, with every sound lingering in the air. My natural warning system of crickets chirping and frogs croaking was in full effect tonight. Insects and animals tended to go silent when zeds were around.

At the end of the lane, the gate stood solidly fastened to the barbed wire and chain link fence doubled up on both sides. I double-checked the locks. It was the only opening in the fence lining Clutch's property along the roadside. We'd reinforced the old fence with reams of chain link we'd taken from Jase's farm, but we needed much more to make it strong enough to hold back zeds and to build a secondary fence around the house.

A single human could climb easily over the fence or come through the woods, but with the deep ditches for Iowa winters, vehicles could enter the farm only through the gate. And, except for a couple trails, the woods surrounding the house served as a barrier against vehicles on three sides.

But the woods wouldn't hold back zeds, not for long. Clutch owned a few hundred acres and with a fence only along the roadside, the other three sides were wide-open fields. If the zeds passed through in large groups, we'd have some serious problems on our hands.

I leaned on the metal gate, staring out at the star-studded sky. The stars were so much brighter here than in Des Moines...or at least when too many city lights clouded the nights. I guess the stars would shine just as brightly everywhere now.

A clear night and smooth air: it would've been a perfect night for a flight. God, I missed watching the sun set from the air.

Even more, I missed my parents. They lived in a residential area not far from downtown. Mom had diabetes and needed daily insulin shots. If they were still in town, they'd be surrounded by hundreds of thousands of zeds by now. The first week, I mentioned the idea of heading into Des Moines for them, but Clutch had said it was too dangerous. After seeing Fox Hills, a town point five percent the size of the Des Moines area filled with zeds, I couldn't argue his logic.

My only regret was that I'd never even gotten the chance to say good-bye.

A rhythmic scraping sound off to my left drew my attention. Careful to avoid Clutch's booby traps, I made my way down the fence line until the zed came into sight. A green John Deere hat hung crookedly on its head. It had been an older man, with short white hair peeking out from under the hat. Its facial features were impossible to make out since decay had already started to set in. It dragged one leg, its boot grating the gravel with each step in a monotonous rhythm.

Step.

Scrape.

Step.

Scrape.

The signature sound of a zed.

Once I made sure it didn't have any friends, I stepped up to the fence. "Hey, fucktard."

The zed lifted its head, and sniffed in my direction. Even with yellowish pupils, it seemed to see fine because it moaned and shuffled its way straight toward me, stumbling while walking down the ditch. When it finally regained its footing and dragged itself up to the fence, I pulled out my machete.

When it reached for me, I swung. Its head lobbed off and bounced on the ground. Its fingers had tangled in the fence, and I kicked the body, sending it backward into the ditch. Its hat had fallen off and landed near the head.

I leaned over the fence and watched the head for a good ten minutes. The fucking thing just kept watching me, moving its mouth. I narrowed my eyes but couldn't see any kind of humanity left in its gaze. Its eyes were truly devoid of *anything*.

After scanning the area one more time, I climbed over the fence, looked at the head, and then brought the heel of my foot down. Its front teeth shattered. I stomped again and again until the skull crushed inward and the mouth finally stilled.

I picked up the hat and tossed it onto the body. The smell would be worse tomorrow, when I could safely move the zed's body farther away and cover it with dirt since we'd decided to quit burning the zeds we took down. It was too much work and the smoke could be seen and smelled from too far away.

The crickets resumed their chirping. The stars still shone brightly, happy in their places so far away from a world consumed by death. And so I climbed back over the fence and continued my patrol.

I rehydrated every hour. At four a.m., I headed into the house to check on the guys. Jase was sleeping soundly on the couch, a paperback copy of the *SAS Survival Handbook* sprawled open across his chest. I gently tugged it from under his hand, dog-eared the page, and set it on the floor. I tiptoed up the stairs and paused outside Clutch's room. Muffled grunts came from the other side. Every night was the same. A couple hours after he fell asleep, the nightmares would come.

Every other night, I listened, waiting for him to wake or fall back into a restful sleep.

Tonight, I turned the knob and entered.

Clutch lay in the middle of the bed, the sheets tossed around him. His skin gleamed with sweat. He grunted and jerked, lost within his dream.

Careful to not disturb him, I sat down on the edge of the mattress. I reached out and laid my palm on his chest. His blade swung out.

I sucked in a breath.

He stopped just before slicing my throat ear to ear. Blinking, his eyes grew wide. "Jesus." He fell back onto the mattress, pulling the knife away. "Fuck, Cash. I could've killed you."

I let out the breath I'd been holding. "You were having a bad dream." Again.

He rolled onto his side, facing away from me. "It was nothing."

I slid up on the bed, sitting with my back against the headboard. "Tell me about it."

"Everything all right outside?" he asked instead.

I sighed, disappointed. "Just one. No problems."

"What time is it?" he asked, sounding all too tired himself.

"Four."

He sat up. "I can take over the patrol now."

"No," I replied, not moving. "I'm wide awake."

He lay for a moment before sighing. "What are you doing?"

"I'm staying until you fall asleep."

After several long seconds, he gave me his back. "Have it your way."

I rested my head against the headboard and sat there in silence, waiting. I remembered when I'd had bad dreams as a kid, my dad would stay with me until I fell asleep. His presence chased away the imaginary monsters. I had no idea if it would help Clutch. His monsters were bigger and badder, but I couldn't let him go on every night facing them alone.

After Clutch's breathing became deep and regular, I crept from his room, grabbed another protein bar, and headed back outside. I had time to make another pass around the farm before the sky morphed from black to purple to orange. The world, for once, was at peace, and I savored watching the sun rise over the horizon.

Clutch emerged from the house looking refreshed, and we were ready to hit the road before the sun was fully over the horizon, with dew still creating sparkles on the grass. Jase limped outside to see us off, leaning on a tall stick for support, and armed to the teeth.

"I swear it, guys," Jase said. "It doesn't hurt bad. Take your time. I'll cover the place today."

Clutch nodded at Jase's stick. "Then why are you still using your crutch?"

Jase pursed his lips.

Clutch narrowed his eyes. "The only way you're staying behind is if you can shimmy up on the roof. That way, you can scan while you start replacing the busted shingles."

Jase grinned. "Heck, yeah, I can do that."

"Be sure to bring plenty of ammo with you. Watching for looters and zeds is more important than patching the roof," Clutch added. He started to turn, then paused. "Oh, and use a mallet. I don't want you drawing every zed in a ten-mile radius."

Jase gave an enthusiastic nod. "You bet!" He grabbed his stick and hopped back into the house.

I smirked. "You were planning on letting him stay behind all along."

He shrugged. "Ready?"

I held out my hand. "After you."

With a fleeting smile, he headed toward the truck, and I followed.

On our drive, we came across a group of zeds feasting on a cow while the rest of the herd huddled together in the far corner of the pasture. I gripped my rifle tighter.

"We need to conserve our ammo," Clutch said as though reading my thoughts. "They're still a ways from the farm. Maybe they'll keep moving on."

"We should at least cut the fence," I said. "Give the rest of the cattle a chance."

He sighed before slowing to a stop. "We won't be able to save all the livestock. The zeds will get to all of it eventually."

"I know, but at least we can help these few."

He jumped out and opened the back door and pulled out a bolt cutter. I got out and held my rifle at the ready. The fence was a simple barbed-wire, taking Clutch no more than four quick snips to open up a section for the cattle to escape should they find the gap. We were back on the road seconds later.

We saw a couple dozen more zeds, mostly alone or in pairs, walking aimlessly on roads and through fields. As we entered an older residential part of Fox Hills—what Jase named Chow Town after the Home Depot experience—the area was eerily quiet. With no people or cars, nothing moved except for the occasional zed.

"Where is everyone?" I asked softly.

Clutch didn't reply, just kept on driving.

When he pulled in between two zeds meandering on the pavement and into the parking lot, I let out a sigh of relief. Mabel's Garden Center was nothing near the size of Home Depot, meaning that there shouldn't have been nearly as many people there when the outbreak hit.

Hopefully.

Still, my stomach was in knots.

I kept my fingers crossed that the remaining zeds in the area had already moved on to find food elsewhere. Clutch backed the truck up to the front doors, so we could load and then get away quickly. We moved silently from the truck, knowing that even though the area seemed relatively clear, zeds lurked everywhere.

He looked at me. "You can stay outside and stand guard if you want. I can cover the greenhouse."

I pulled out the small axe and shook my head. "No. Let's stick to the plan."

We opened our doors at the same time. I scalped the first zed with a quick strike to its temple, and it fell lifelessly to the ground. I turned to see Clutch standing over a dead zed.

We walked up to the front glass doors and looked inside. A cashier still hovered at his cash register. With an axe in one hand and the machete in another, Clutch rapped on the glass, and the zed turned around. Its empty gaze leveled hungrily on us, and it stumbled forward. Another one emerged from an aisle. It had been an older woman, still wearing gardening gloves, and she'd been badly chewed upon. A third, another employee, headed toward the doors.

We waited until all three were at the doors, before counting down...*three, two, one.* I yanked the door open and jumped back. Clutch swung the axe and then swung the machete. One of the zeds refused to go down after a glancing blow, but my axe to its forehead finished the job.

We dragged the bodies out of our way, and scanned the rest of the place, finding only one more zed trapped under a collapsed shelf.

We wasted no time in grabbing all the heirloom seeds, fertilizer, and fencing we could find. If we could plant enough crops, we could get through the winter and have plenty of seeds for next year. We might even be able to take in another survivor or two, which we desperately needed. Defending an entire farm with only three people was exhausting work.

We were heading back to the front doors to close up the greenhouse when we saw them. All four men wore military fatigues—much like ours —and had automatic rifles slung over their shoulders. With shaved heads, the men looked all the same: white, dirty, and mean.

And they were currently in the back of Clutch's truck, stealing our loot.

Clutch threw me a quick glance, then whispered, "Stay inside, and be ready to run in case this goes to shit."

"Be careful." I pulled the rifle off my shoulder and leaned against the door, aiming at the men busy moving things from our truck to theirs.

Clutch fired a shot into the air, and they froze like skittish deer, one of them dropping his stolen cargo. They scrambled to raise their rifles as Clutch took a couple steps forward, keeping his Glock leveled on them.

The cleanest looking of the men relaxed and grinned. "Clutch! It's good to see a familiar face."

Clutch narrowed his eyes. "What are you doing here, Sean?"

One of the other men stepped forward. "You're taking things that don't belong to you."

"And it belongs to you?" Clutch countered. "I knew Mabel, and she's lying dead inside."

"It doesn't matter, Clutch. It's the rules," Sean said. "All supplies must go through the Fox Hills militia for reallocation. We divvy them out to citizens based on need."

Clutch chuckled, though there was no humor in the sound. "Based on *whose* need? Yours or theirs?"

"You'll turn over the truck, the supplies, and that girl with you," another man called out, pointing at me.

"Good luck with that," Clutch said before turning back to Sean. "Where's the government order establishing a militia?"

"There's no government anymore," Sean replied.

"Camp Fox has fallen?"

Sean stammered. "We—we're working in collaboration with the National Guard. We're helping them out."

"And who's in charge of this little militia?" Clutch asked.

"Doyle," one of the men said. "And he'll kick your ass for getting in our way."

"Let me see the government order from Camp Fox instating Doyle as head of the militia," Clutch said. "Until then, you're all just bandits. And, I'll shoot any man who tries to take *anything* of mine."

The men kept their fully automatic rifles raised.

"But Clutch..." Sean pleaded

"You going to shoot me, boy?" Clutch guffawed at the man who looked about my age. "You might get in a lucky shot or two, but I guaran-fucking-tee that I'm taking every last one of your sorry asses with me. And I don't give a flying fuck that you've sold seed corn to me before, Sean."

"Let's just kill this asshole and be done with it," one of the men said, and I leveled the rifle to aim dead center in the middle of his forehead.

"Dibs on the girl," the third man added.

"Fuck you," I called out, keeping my aim steady.

"Soon, girly," the man with the toothy grin said.

Sean patted the air. "There's going to be no shooting today. We're leaving." The men around him raised an uproar. Sean snapped around to his compatriots. "We're leaving! This place is going to be crawling with zeds soon enough the way it is." Sean turned to Clutch, looking exasperated. "You can keep this stuff from today, just because we have a history. But the militia is in charge around here. You'd be best to join up or get out of our way. And your little girl over there needs to be moved in with the other civilians at our camp for protection. The rules have changed. I'd watch your back if I were you."

With that final warning, they climbed into their truck. One of the men in the truck bed fired several shots into the sky. They whooped and one flipped us off as they sped away, kicking up rocks.

"Assholes," I muttered, coming around to stand by Clutch.

"Sean was right." He looked at me. "We're going to have to watch our backs. They've seen us. Sean knows where I live. And they know I won't play along with their games. That makes me an enemy. As for you..." He looked me up and down.

I shivered, even though the sun shone brightly in the sky. "Then we'd best avoid them."

He locked the lift gate and headed to the driver's side. "These guys are nothing but Doyle's dogs, using the façade of a militia to take what they want."

"Who's this Doyle guy?" I asked. "Someone to worry about?"

"He's a cocky asshole who's owned the surplus store for decades. He's also one hell of a survivalist. Armageddon would've been a wet dream for him."

————

We spent the next two weeks converting the farmhouse into a fortress and planting gardens, all the while killing any zeds that made the mistake of stumbling too close to the farm. We set up a sniper's nest not far from the gate to watch for Doyle's Dogs—what we'd nicknamed the self-proclaimed militia.

Jase turned out to be a great asset. Even though he slept until ten every morning, once awake, he was boundless energy, and his ankle healed quickly. Between the two of us, we could lift nearly as much as Clutch could.

We covered the first floor windows with chain link fence to hold back zeds and fastened strips of fencing up to the second floor windows, giving us a way to get inside in case the front door was blocked. We even boarded up the front door, leaving the only entrance in and out through the cellar door, which could be better secured from the inside. We rein-forced the gate at the end of the drive so that intruders with anything less than a tank or heavy bolt cutters would have a tough time cutting the chains to get through.

Using the fertilizer we'd picked up at the greenhouse, Clutch intro-duced Jase and me to the art of setting explosive booby traps, multiplying the reliability of our existing perimeter protection tenfold.

But the three of us worked together only when absolutely necessary. Most of the time, we rotated shifts to have one person on guard duty. No more zeds passed through the yard, but more and more were showing up on the roads and in the fields. Only Clutch scouted the woods. Jase and I were neither gutsy enough nor good enough yet to go deep into the acres of tangled trees alone, though Clutch regularly reminded me that I needed to get familiar with those woods sometime. If the Dogs came at us, hiding in the woods could make the difference between life and death.

We figured that, at the speed zeds shambled along, it would take only a few months before they started spreading outward from Des Moines in a mass exodus. The four or five thousand zeds in Fox Hills were another story. We had to be ready for them *now*.

One thing that bothered me was that we hadn't seen signs of any more uninfected humans. Clutch had said that they'd hide out as long as they could, but it had been three weeks since the outbreak. Most would've run out of food by now and would be forced to loot. Not hearing any other traffic made me wonder exactly how few of us remained.

The hours not spent on fortifying the farm were spent training for self-defense and killing. My strength and skills improved quickly, though I had a long ways to go. I could now do fifty diamond pushups without stopping. And, my caffeine headaches had finally gone away. Jase was already in good shape from playing in sports. Even with his still-healing ankle, he could run up to windows, check out a house, and be on his way back to the truck before zeds had a clue he was there.

Where Jase was our designated runner, I learned I had a natural affinity for being a sniper. Clutch, of course, was our diplomat should any Dogs show up. He excelled at hand-to-hand combat and could handle any weapon. He was also our strategist. Building on our areas of specialty, Clutch began to lay out plans—for both offense and defense. We were transforming from three individuals into a team.

Hoo-fucking-rah.

Clutch gave both Jase and me our own rifles. They were matching M24s with all the accessories. I hadn't even heard of an M24 before the outbreak. Now, I spent hours practicing dry shooting, disassembling, and cleaning until I could use it in complete blackness. I could load the cartridges blindfolded.

Only when I'd perfected dry shooting—aligning my body position, sight picture, breathing, and trigger squeeze—did Clutch let me fire a real round. Rather than setting up a shooting range, Clutch had taken me several miles out until we'd come across zeds. At each outing, I was only allowed to use one cartridge to conserve ammo, which meant that I had to make every shot count.

The only differences between dry and real shooting were the noise and the recoil, both of which I'd been expecting and was ready for. It was during that first time, when I took out three zeds back-to-back at a hundred yards, that I saw the rare glimpse of pride in Clutch's eyes.

Back at the farm, I'd studied the art of learning my surroundings. I trained myself to look and listen while remaining focused on something else.

I could stab the sandbag head every time, better than Jase, and I'd even dodged a couple of Clutch's moves. But I was nowhere near Clutch's class. He could still take me down any time he wanted. I gained a worship-like appreciation for Army Rangers after seeing what he was capable of.

"Every corner poses a risk," he said after knocking me on my butt. Again.

"Silence is my friend," I replied, coming to my feet.

"What is your best weapon?" He lashed out.

I dove to the side. "I am."

"What is your second best weapon?"

"Anything I can use to shoot, stab, blow up, strike, or throw."

Clutch moved, and I found myself in a choke-hold.

"OODA?" he asked, loosening his hold somewhat.

"Observe. Orient. Decide…" I pushed back into him, but he anticipated my move and pushed forward, and I elbowed him in the stomach. He relaxed his grip, and I twisted away. "Act."

He stepped back a safe distance and crossed his arms over his chest. "And your mantra?"

I smiled. He'd given me an assignment the night before to come up with one rule, which I could meditate on to prep for any mission, to keep from getting too nervous. His was *Hit 'em hard and hit 'em often.* I wanted something that spoke more to my own internal muse. "Get 'em where I want 'em."

"Meaning?"

"To never be stupid. Never let them get me where they can overpower me or take me down. Turn my opponent's actions to my advantage."

Clutch nodded. "That'll do." He looked around the yard. "That's enough for today."

I tugged off my leather gloves. Clutch was adamant that we wore gloves any time we worked or trained so that they became like a second skin. They made me clumsy at first, but I preferred them now, even with the rifle. If they could keep me from getting a cut that could get infected, or worse, a zed bite, they were priceless.

Walking back to the house, I scanned the yard. Jase would be at the end of the lane right now, checking the gate. He ran six laps a day down the long lane to scout for zeds and raiders. He'd turned into a regular grunt. Even though we all were decked out in military gear, Jase took the style to heart. He practiced running, crawling, and combat like he was at boot camp. I'd even found him trying out different types of mud to camouflage his face the other day.

But I also knew what he did at the end of the lane. He'd pause at the gate, and stare wistfully down the road, in the direction of his old home. It was a hard reminder of what he'd lost.

Keeping busy helped me to not think about my parents.

I kept very, very busy.

We remained vigilant, day and night, watching for intruders, especially for Doyle's Dogs. At night, we took three-hour rotations, to give each of us a solid six-hour sleeping break. With the physical labor, I could fall asleep the second my head hit the pillow on the sofa. I'd gotten into a routine and was pulling my own weight next to the guys. We needed more people, but the simple fact was, aside from Doyle's Dogs and possibly Camp Fox, we'd come across no one else in some time. Even the house with boarded windows now appeared abandoned, with its front door broken wide open.

As for our house, even if zeds could get inside, which I doubted, Clutch had jerry-rigged the stairs with C4 that he could blow at a moment's notice. I never knew C4 was even legal, so I had no idea how he had come to own it. Fifty foot of paracord was placed next to each upstairs window in case the house was overrun. In the cellar, we'd built a fake wall in front of the shelves to hide our food just in case looters managed to break in.

In the gardens, Jase stood watch while I planted, and then we rotated every hour. We'd planted nearly all the seeds we'd taken from the greenhouse. We'd even planted a few herbs so we wouldn't be doomed with overly bland food all winter, though salt was already missed.

Even with all the food in the cellar, we only had enough food to get us into the winter. We had to grow a hell of a lot of food if we wanted to survive. The fields weren't safe—too much open space, and we couldn't eat the corn or soybean seed as it had all been treated with pesticides and herbicides. So we planned to plant by hand seed corn and soybeans in rows closest to the farm since he had all the seed already on hand.

Clutch estimated that we'd converted the backyard into one and a half acres of garden. Within a year, living off the land would become our only source of food. It was terrifying yet empowering.

After the quick seven-step process—which had to be done in order—of getting into the house without setting off a trap, Clutch headed to the kitchen and I turned on the small battery-powered radio and began my routine during every break of slowly scanning both radio bands. Like every other day, FM was quiet. AM had a couple of transmissions, but they must've been too far away because static drowned out the voices. As I continued to scan stations, Clutch said, "Wait. Go back."

I tuned the knob, and turned up the volume. The man spoke in a slow monotone, which was why I'd gone right past the station the first time.

"...militia now controls the towns in southern Iowa and some in northern Missouri. I drove near Des Moines two days ago. Had to see it for myself. The rumors are true. It's scorched. The military dropped H6s on it at least a week ago since there were only a few fires left burning."

I suddenly found it hard to breathe, and I fell back on my butt. Des Moines...bombed? *Mom. Dad.* While I'd known their odds were hopeless, knowing with certainty...I pressed my hand to my heart.

Clutch handed me a glass of water. He placed a hand on my shoulder. "Maybe they got out."

His words were clumsy and rushed, and I knew he didn't believe them. "Yeah, maybe," I lied right back, breathless. The finality of the situation forced me to finally admit to myself that I'd been clinging to a strand of false hope for too long. Jaw clenched, I tried not to think about my parents, focusing instead on the stranger's words.

"...I heard all major cities have been bombed to contain the spread, and any intact military units have pulled back. Though, it's safe to assume there's not much government or military left. At least one National Guard base is taking in survivors in Iowa, and that's Camp Fox. Camp Dodge was destroyed along with Des Moines. I don't have status on any Iowa units at this time.

During the American Revolution, the active forces in the field against the tyranny never amounted to more than three percent of the colonists. We are the three percenters of today. We are the militia, and we will survive this war. We will defeat the zed scourge and rebuild. I'm wired into stations across the country and will broadcast every day at 0900. This is Hawkeye broadcasting on AM 1340. Be safe and know that you're not alone. Three percenters, unite!"

Silence came from the speakers, and I sat and stared at the radio.

"Any news?" Jase asked, walking into the living room, sweaty from his run.

"Des Moines was bombed," Clutch said in a low, rumbly voice.

Jase smiled. "Hopefully they cleared out all the zeds so they won't be heading this direction."

I tossed him a glare and then turned away.

"Oh," Jase said after a moment. "Damn, Cash. I'm sorry. I forgot—"

"It's time we head out," Clutch said.

I turned back to see him standing and motioning me to get up. My limbs felt like they'd been filled with lead, but I dragged myself to my feet.

"Where are we going?" Jase asked.

"To check out the Pierson farm and pick up those chickens Cash has been wanting," Clutch said.

"If they're even still alive," I mumbled.

Clutch ignored me. "But you're staying back and guarding the house. We'll be back within three hours."

Jase looked relieved that he didn't have to go. "You got it, boss."

"Whenever we're away from my farm, we're at risk of being overtaken," Clutch said to me. "So we'll clear the house and buildings first. Then, if everything's clear, we'll grab the chickens, food, and supplies."

"Do you think it's safe?" I asked.

"I haven't seen any of the Dogs on this road yet. Maybe it's because they're giving me this road as long as I stay off the others."

I nodded, but I also knew any time he used the word "maybe", he didn't mean it. Besides, the men we'd come across at the greenhouse seemed too greedy to give up a few miles along one quiet gravel road.

I grabbed my helmet and gear before rustling around for a couple duffels Clutch had gotten from his surplus run. This time, I packed a bottle of water and a protein bar in my jacket, a lesson I learned after finding myself empty-handed at the elementary school. Clutch was already downstairs, geared up and eating a protein bar. We needed the chickens. Having fresh food would be a much-needed morale boost for all three of us.

In the truck, I asked, "How many lived there?" Up until now, we'd only grabbed anything off farms that didn't require entering buildings, waiting for numbers to thin out. That was before we realized that zeds just kept on going.

We all knew we should've started cleaning out the nearby houses earlier, knowing that it was just a matter of time before the Dogs raided the area. But by the same token, they could've been watching us already, waiting for the time we left the safety of the farm to come after us or the supplies on the farm.

We had to be careful. We didn't yet know which farmhouses hid infected inside. The only way to tell was to check them out. Chances were, occupants—infected or otherwise—would likely be hostile. I gripped the machete.

"Two. The Piersons were a young couple. Just starting out," he replied, as we reversed the seven steps to get out of the house and headed for the truck.

Clutch drove slowly enough to not kick up any dust on the gravel road while I scanned for zeds and looters.

A creek meandered down the end of Clutch's property line. With all the rains, the Fox River had flooded, filling its tributaries, this creek being one. The ground had given way not far from the road, and I saw why we hadn't seen more than a few zeds for a couple days. "It's better than a mousetrap," I said, watching the zeds trapped in the mud.

They moved in dull, slow motions that only served to have the mud pull them in deeper. One zed was naked, with mud smeared over his bloated body. All the zeds were bloated, looking as though they'd ingested twice their body weight with polluted water. A pair had been pulled so deep that they'd become stuck under the dirty water, their mouths opening and closing like fish.

"Stop," I said.

Clutch pulled to a stop and watched me.

"Once everything dries up, they could break free," I said.

He looked outside, thought for a moment, and then nodded.

I opened the door, lifted my rifle, and took aim. The naked zed went down. I fired again. Fourteen shots. Twelve dead zeds. I needed to work on my aim.

"Happy now?" he asked when I settled back in.

I smiled. Twelve fewer zeds to trespass onto the farm. "Very."

The Pierson farm was only another mile down the road, just past a farmhouse much in need of a new paint job. "Since it's so close, we can check out this one next," I mentioned as we drove past.

"Earl's," he replied. "A bit of a hermit, so he may have ridden out the outbreak. If he's not around, we may be able to pick up an extra gun or two."

A new green combine sat next to a machine shed. I thought back to the zed I'd decapitated a couple weeks back. "Was Earl a tall, skinny guy? Wore a John Deere hat?"

Clutch narrowed an eye at me. "Yeah, why?"

"We don't have to worry about him anymore."

He was quiet for a moment. "I guess we'll check out his place next, then."

He stopped before turning into the Pierson's driveway, while we scanned their farm, but it looked quiet and untouched. But we knew that wasn't the case.

We knew at least Tom Pierson was home. The house was close enough to the road that on two different drive-bys we clearly saw a man staring blankly out the window. Close enough for the man inside to see us and start thumping bloody fists against the glass. I suspected the only reason he hadn't broken the glass yet was because zeds seemed to have a limited ability to retain focus.

Even though he wasn't standing in the window now, we knew better than to believe the house was safe. We had at least one zed waiting inside. The question was, where was Tom's wife? She could be in the house, or she could be lurking around the chicken shed. Or, if she was lucky, she got away.

I'd already learned that very few people tended to get lucky in this world.

Thunder boomed in the distance, startling me.

"You okay?" Clutch asked.

I nodded. "Sounds like another storm's coming."

Clutch parked the truck behind the Pierson's Ford truck and cut the engine. The garage door had been left open, and the driver's door was left ajar.

"We'll clear out the house first since we know Tom's in there. Then the yard," Clutch rumbled in his rough voice. "Be ready."

We moved with slow, silent steps into the attached garage. Putting my back to Clutch's, we scanned the two stalls. He checked out both vehicles. I bent down to check under the vehicles. When I came to my feet, I gave him the sign for *okay*.

We stopped at the door leading from the garage to the house. Streaks of dried blood marred the paint. Clutch reached for the handle and turned it slowly. The hinges protested with a small creak. He looked inside and then took a step in. I immediately followed, checking behind the door and then taking the side of the door opposite from Clutch.

Even wearing a Kevlar helmet with the face shield down, the stench of decay and excrement was overpowering, and I forced myself to breathe through my mouth. No zed had emerged yet, which meant that maybe it hadn't heard the door open.

Or maybe it just moved slowly.

A zed that I assumed had once been Tom Pierson ambled around the corner right when Clutch took a step forward. It saw us and gave a guttural hiss. I was closer. I swung, cleaving the top section of its head clean off. Some brown goo hemorrhaged from the wound, but not nearly as much as had come from Alan's head in the back of Clutch's rig. It seemed like the longer they'd been infected, the less "wet" they were...and a hell of a lot more smelly. I gagged and tried to block the stench that made me think of what moldy cottage cheese, rotten eggs, and putrid ground beef blended together would smell like.

Clutch kneeled by the body, and lifted its shirt. "Looks like someone unloaded a small caliber into him. If I had to guess, I'd say it was done after he turned." Then Clutch stood, stepped over the body, and moved into the next room.

I followed, hoping the smell would improve. It didn't. The living room was a mess. Broken glass and suitcases littered the floor. On the coffee table sat a purse with several hundred dollars scattered about. It looked like the guy's wife was planning an escape. Too bad money couldn't have helped her. I noticed the pistol then. It was a .22, similar to my first pistol. I picked it up and checked the cartridge. *Empty*. I frowned and slid the .22 into the back of my belt. "I don't think she got out."

Clutch's lips thinned and he nodded before moving through the room and into the hallway. He took the stairs with silent steps, and I had to concentrate to be as quiet. Upstairs, there were no signs of struggle, though there were clear signs that someone had been in a hurry to pack. Drawers were pulled open, clothes draped the bed.

But no dark stains or bodies.

I checked under the bed while Clutch checked the closet. We repeated the process with the next three rooms. "Clear," I said, though fear nagged at me. Where had she gone? Had she managed to flee the house before she turned?

We headed back down the stairs and finished off the rest of the ground floor. When we came to the last closed door, I groaned when I saw the blood on the handle. "It had to be the basement, didn't it."

I reached over and pulled out the flashlight from Clutch's belt, and clicked it on. He motioned *three-two-one* before opening the door. Pitch black and vile stench greeted us. Beneath the smell of decay that haunted the entire house, the basement also smelled of wet earth and mildew.

With no windows to let in light, I realized that this must be a cellar like the one at Clutch's house. I shone the light down the stairs to reveal dried blood stains on the steps but no movement. I glanced at Clutch. With a shrug, he called out, "Any zed-fucks down there?"

Something clanked, and then something grunted. The sounds of moaning, shuffling, and banging continued.

"Come out, come out, wherever you are," I sang, shining the light across the floor to draw it out. There'd been plenty of blood, and I suspected this was where Tom's wife escaped after being attacked. Dark water covered at least a third of the floor, and I realized that without power, sump pumps could no longer do their jobs.

At the edge of the water, the light fell on a horribly damaged carcass of something small that had tufts of yellow fur still attached. I cringed. "Ah, geez. She ate the cat."

A shape fell forward, and I jumped.

"And there's the missus," Clutch said drily.

Mrs. Pierson must've been brutally attacked by the man she'd trusted most in the world. Bites spanned the zed's neck, hands, and arms. Scratches covered its face, but I suspected those were from the cat fighting for its life. The zed stumbled forward, reaching for the light with each step. Clutch pulled out his Glock but didn't fire.

The zed kicked the first stair step. Bumped into it again. The third time, it fell forward.

"How about that," I said. "They can't climb stairs."

As it dragged itself up, it started the process over again.

"But they never get tired," Clutch replied. "I bet if it kept at it long enough, it'd get lucky and fall *up* the stairs." He fired the gun, and the zed fell backward, its hand making a small splash in the standing water.

"Let's make this quick," he muttered, taking the first step.

I kept the light in front of us, moving it to scan the sides. It was an unsettling feeling, entering the literal bowels of the house, not knowing what else could be down here. At the foot of the stairs, Clutch motioned for the flashlight. He took it and shone it across the basement. I held the machete in front of me.

Fortunately, the basement was wide open, with no doors or rooms, let alone shelves or boxes. In fact, the only things down there were two corpses, one zed and one tabby housecat. "There's nothing down here. Maybe they've always had flooding issues with it," I said, thinking aloud.

"Good," he muttered. "Let's get out of here."

He wasted no time hustling back up the stairs.

"Don't like dark basements?" I asked when he shut the basement door behind us.

"Not one bit."

I chortled.

"What?"

"I never would've guessed you to be afraid of anything."

After a moment, he shrugged. "I'm only human."

The thought of Clutch getting hurt—or worse—quickly sobered me. "Yeah. Guess so."

With the house clear, we moved quickly through to inventory food and supplies to load later. The Piersons weren't very good planners. They had little to offer, so we went ahead and loaded everything we found into one suitcase. I was about to open the refrigerator when Clutch pressed his hand over mine. "Before you do that, I'd hold my breath if I were you."

I bit my lip. "Oh. Good call."

Clutch stepped back as I sucked in a breath and opened the refrigerator. And I was glad I did. Milk, leftovers, and raw meat filled the shelves. I moved quickly, grabbing only the items I was hoping to find. Aluminum cans.

I pulled out the twelve-pack of light beer and the four cans of soda and slammed the door shut. I lifted the beer and smiled. I made the mistake of inhaling to brag about my find, and gagged from the lingering stench from the refrigerator.

Clutch smirked and opened the door to the garage.

I pushed past him and sucked in fresh air. He came out behind me and dropped the suitcase into the back of the truck. He pulled out an old wire carrier he'd found somewhere along the way. "Let's wrap this up."

I put the twelve-pack and soda in the back and followed. We'd only burned a half hour clearing the house, leaving us plenty of time for the only other building on the farm. It looked like an old hog house that had been converted to store machinery. A large caged-in chicken area had been built onto the side with a door leading into the old shed. The door was closed, likely blown shut in the storms. Four chickens and one rooster pecked at the grass. Their feathers were matted, and they were scrawny. They had to be near starving, with nothing to eat but what they could find in the twenty-by-twenty area of grass fenced in for their home.

They seemed agitated, ruffling their feathers and chattering away. I realized why when I saw the furred shape nearly hidden in the shadow of the tractor. It was big, maybe a wolf, and I nudged Clutch and pointed.

"Looks like we're not the only ones eying these chickens."

He took several steps toward the beast and waved his hands. "Shoo. Get out of here."

It growled, showing its teeth.

Clutch stomped closer. "Sorry, bud. But we need these chickens as bad as you."

It kept growling even as it backed up with every step Clutch took forward, until it turned and ran off. It was actually a mutt, big but skinny. Probably some farm dog in the area. I felt a bit bad that he'd probably suffered as badly as any of us had since the outbreak, going from an easy diet of dog food to having to fend for himself. But I didn't feel bad enough to toss him a chicken. Clutch was right. We needed them.

Other than the dog, there was nothing to scare up around the building. Only a tractor and lawn mower sat in the shed, making it easy enough to check for zeds.

Inside the building stood a chicken coop made out of plywood, probably used to protect the chickens at night and during cold weather. I knocked on the door and listened for any movement. When I heard none, I opened the door, with Clutch at my back. Inside was hay and wooden roosts. Eight white-feathered bodies lay dead across the floor, likely from starvation or thirst, if the empty water and food bowls were any sign. A few eggs rested undisturbed in the nest boxes, but I left those, unwilling to test their level of rottenness.

There was another door across from us, and I opened this one without worry, having already seen where it led from the outside. "Hey, chickies," I said, taking a step onto the grass.

They came running to me, clucking happy little welcomes, and I grinned. "They're tame."

"Get them loaded up," Clutch said from the doorway. "I'm going to check out the fuel situation, and see if the vehicles have anything worthwhile."

"I'll take it from here." I didn't even look up. I was too busy enjoying being the center of chicken attention.

"And be careful," he warned.

I was sweating by the time I got three of the five chickens loaded into the carrier. Just because they were friendly creatures that couldn't fly didn't make them easy to catch.

Taking a break, I grabbed the three large bags of chicken feed from inside the building and tossed them in the truck next to the portable fuel tank, which Clutch was finishing siphoning gas into from the Piersons' two cars.

Finished, he disconnected the portable pump's cables from his truck battery, and slid the pump handle behind the tank. He'd used the portable tank for his tractors in the fields, but it hadn't taken him long to dump the diesel from the tank so we could use it for gasoline.

Clutch eyed the two chickens still milling in their fenced area and raised an eyebrow.

I shrugged. "They needed a break."

He smirked, leaning on the truck.

I went back to work getting the last two chickens into the carrier. I must've worn them out because I caught both in less than five minutes, only falling on my ass once. The scraggly chickens didn't look pleased to be cramped in a little cage, but I figured I'd earn their forgiveness by giving them a dry home with plenty of food and water.

I turned to find Clutch with his head in his hands. "What's wrong?"

He looked up, laughing. "I've never seen anyone work so hard to catch chickens before."

I lifted the cage. "Want me to release them and you take a shot?"

He cleared his throat. "You know, they're starving. You could've put a bit of feed in the kennel, and they would've practically run into it."

I wanted to snap back some smart remark, but he was right so I flipped him the bird instead.

A boom sounded in the distance, and Clutch's face fell.

Confused, I looked around. "That didn't sound like thunder."

His brow furrowed. He stepped back and snapped his head in the direction of the farm. "That was an explosion."

Shock blasted through me.

"The gate," he said before taking off at a run toward the truck. I walked as quickly as I could, without risking injuring the caged fowl. He had the engine going by the time I set the carrier in the back. I hopped in the front, and he tore out the driveway and sped out of the driveway and onto the road. I grabbed my rifle and Clutch pulled out his Blaser—a heavy, impressive rifle with an even more impressive scope.

I opened my window and leveled my rifle on the frame as he slowed. As we approached the farm, we found the gate collapsed and a Jeep on the other side with a blown axle. The bloodied driver slumped over the steering wheel must've taken shrapnel. Two other men with shaved heads were outside the Jeep, walking down the lane toward the house. One was clutching his bloody arm. The other held his rifle in front of him. He must've heard our approach, because he snapped around. His eyes widened, and he nudged the guy next to him and aimed his rifle at the truck.

"Follow my lead," Clutch said. He drove over the fallen gate and pulled off to the right of the lane where no booby traps had been set and stopped. "This is private property!" he yelled out. "Stop where you are and lower your weapons, or you will be shot."

They didn't lower their weapons. "This area is in the jurisdiction of the Fox Hills militia!" the injured man yelled back. "You have to pay tribute to stay on these lands."

Clutch fired, and I startled. The injured man fell to the ground and didn't move.

The other raider's eyes widened. "You killed him, you fucking bastard!"

"This is your one and only chance," Clutch said. "Drop your weapon. Leave in the next ten seconds and live. If you or any of your buddies comes near my place again, you will be shot on sight."

"But you can't. I'm with the militia!" He glanced from his dead buddy and back to Clutch.

"Seven," Clutch said.

"But, but my Jeep is busted!" He pointed to the sky. "It's going to be dark soon. There's zeds out there."

"Five."

The guy paused, then dropped his rifle like it was on fire and ran toward the road. Once he passed the truck, he yelled, "Doyle will kill you for this!"

Clutch got out of the truck and aimed.

I froze.

The guy went down with one echoing shot.

In shock, I stepped out of the truck as Jase came running from the woods. "I was watching them the whole time. I wasn't going to let them get to the house, I swear," he said, breathless.

"I know," I said, squeezing Jase's shoulder.

He grimaced and took a step back. "Dang, you stink like a zed that took a shit bath."

Another shot fired, and we yanked around to see Clutch standing beside the Jeep, the driver now sporting a gunshot to the head. Clutch looked up. "Let's get this mess cleaned up."

"Do you think they'll know these guys were here?" Jase asked.

"Oh, they'll know all right." Clutch looked outward. "Doyle started the war today."

PART FIVE
WRATH

THE FIFTH CIRCLE OF HELL

Eight

Two weeks later

J ase slammed his machete through the forehead of the first zed, while I split the skull of the second one right down the middle. I stood back and let Jase take down the third, wielding his machete like a broadsword.

"I'm getting sick of Doyle's Dogs throwing zeds at us," he muttered as he wiped his blade on the grass.

For the past three days, a garbage truck had driven down this road and dumped hungry zeds over the gate. On the first day, they dropped one. The next day it was two. Today, they were up to three. Tomorrow, it'd be four.

Eventually, it'd be a truckload.

They were toying with us, plain and simple. With every assault, they were saying, surrender or we'll kill you.

"C'mon. They're giving us practice," I said, tugging a dead zed to the ditch. "What else is there to do on a Friday night besides killing zeds?"

Jase paused while dragging another zed and cocked his head. "Is it Friday?"

I shrugged. "No idea. Doesn't matter, I guess. We should be heading in for the night."

"Yeah. The fabulous dinner I made is getting cold," he said with a sly grin.

I looked down the road where the green garbage truck disappeared in the distance. After today's dump, the truck sported several new bullet holes, courtesy of Clutch, who was just coming down from his sniper's nest in the tree. But the bullet holes weren't enough. We needed to disable that damn truck. And soon.

Clutch checked his Blaser. "I should've taken care of those Dogs back at the greenhouse. Then they wouldn't have known about this place."

I didn't need to voice my agreement. Clutch was right. If we'd killed Sean and his buddies—without getting ourselves killed in the process—we could go about our business and no one would be the wiser. For the past few days, Clutch had been beating himself up about letting Sean get away and outing our location.

But it wasn't his fault any more than it was mine. They'd caught us off guard and now we were dealing with the repercussions.

We headed back to the Jeep. It had taken the guys two full days, but they had the Dogs' Rubicon running again. Jase had even added his own brand of style by painting "Zom-B-Gone" across the back.

The Jeep could get through anything the truck could, but it was smaller and faster to get in and out of, unlike the efficient Prius, which the guys bitched about every time they climbed in. And so the Jeep had joined Jase's motorcycle as a scouting vehicle around the farm.

Jase claimed driving rights and I snagged the passenger seat, leaving Clutch to hop in the back. When Jase gunned the engine, I grabbed onto the windshield. "Do you even have a driver's license?"

"Of course," Jase replied indignantly, and then shrugged. "Well, basically. I've got a school permit. But I've been driving tractors for most my life."

I would've snapped back a witty remark, but my stomach growled. "What's for dinner tonight, Jase? I hope it's take-out from Pizza Hut. I could really go for a Cheese Lover's with extra cheese."

"I'd take Red Lobster," Clutch added. "All-you-can-eat shrimp."

"It's better," Jase said. "Tonight you get my specialty: Spam and rice."

I let out a dramatic sigh with a hand fluttering to my chest. "My favorite."

"Stop the Jeep," Clutch ordered, and Jase slammed the brakes.

"What's up?" I asked.

Clutch held up a finger. "Sh."

I heard it then. The hearty growl of a big engine heading down the road.

"Son of a bitch," I muttered. "They're coming back already?"

"Sounds different." Clutch said. "Get back to the gate, but be careful. Don't get made into a target."

"Did I mention that I'm getting sick of this shit?" Jase muttered as he whipped the Jeep around.

I picked my M24 off the floor and checked the cartridge. Jase parked at our usual spot just before the last curve in the lane leading to the gate, and Clutch took off running for his sniper's nest. Now that we were out of sight, I hopped out and flattened against a large tree, Jase took a tree on the opposite side of the lane.

A deep-throated engine purred nearby, and I poked my head around the tree to see a desert-tan Humvee parked at the gate. A single soldier climbed out of the passenger side. Another soldier stood behind a .30 cal mounted on the vehicle, leaving who knew how many more men with rifles hidden inside.

The soldier standing outside the Humvee held his rifle in the air before putting it back on the seat and then closing the door. He said something to the gunner, who took a step back from the .30 cal.

The soldier walked up to the gate. "This is Captain Masden with the United States National Guard," he called out. "I'm unarmed and have come here to talk."

This was one of those times I wished we had ear pieces so I could check in with Clutch. I wanted to ask him what to do, but I couldn't risk him leaving his spot in the tree. He was our best and last defense.

Masden checked out the pile of zeds in the ditch before looking up and scanning the tree line. "I know you're out there. I give you my word that my men will not fire unless you shoot first."

I glanced over at Jase and held up my hand. *Stay put*. He didn't look happy, but he readjusted his rifle to get a better view of the gate.

I propped my matching M24 against the tree so I could get to it easily in case things went to hell. "Don't cross the gate. I'm coming out." I waited a second before taking that first step around the tree. Knowing Clutch had me covered gave me the confidence I needed to walk up to the gate and into the view of the soldiers, even though I had no doubt each and every one of them had me in their sights.

Masden was attractive and well built, with tan skin and blond hair. Fatigues fit him nicely. The last time I'd seen him, it had been in Fox Hills, and he'd been behind the Humvee's .30 cal.

When he saw me, his eyes widened slightly in surprise.

I walked warily up to the gate and stopped just on the other side from the soldier.

He held out his hand. "I'm Captain Tyler Masden. But you can call me Tyler."

I shook his hand. "I'm Cash."

His lips twitched. "Cash?"

I took a breath. "What brings you here, Tyler?"

He smiled. His grin was warm, inviting, and hinted at a flirtatious personality. "I represent Camp Fox. We try to locate all survivors, and either bring them to the Camp for safety or see how we can help. Someone mentioned that there was a small camp of survivors out here." His smile fell. "It's also my responsibility to make sure some level of law is still obeyed."

I narrowed my eyes. "Meaning?"

He sighed. "I received a report of insurgents in this vicinity. My source said there were folks stealing from other survivors."

"You're looking in the wrong place for thieves," I said. "We've had supplies stolen from us, but we've never taken anything from a survivor."

His brows lifted. "Did you see who did it?"

"Of course," I said. "They held us at gunpoint. It was Doyle's Dogs. The so-called militia. And they've hit us more than once."

Tyler shook his head. "We send them out with supplies to help survivors, not to steal from them."

I cocked my head. "And you believe that?"

He lowered his head and rubbed his temples. "Honestly, I don't know what to believe anymore when it comes to the militia."

I felt sorry for him. His intentions seemed genuine, but we still had a problem to deal with. "If the Dogs are working with you, then you clearly have a communication problem or you're lying to me."

He sighed. His eyes narrowed and he smiled. "I've seen you before."

"In Chow Town," I said. "It looked like you were picking up survivors."

"Chow Town." He gave a tight chuckle. "That's a good name for it. Yeah, I've been through there quite a few times." Then he slowly shook his head. "Dang, I wish you would've stopped."

"I'd had a long day," I said.

"Too bad. I wanted to meet you. And, I could've offered you Camp Fox's hospitality."

My breath hardened. "The Dogs wanted to lock me up with the other women for my own 'safety'," I said with air quotes. "If you're offering the same kind of hospitality as the militia, I'm not interested."

Tyler's jaw tightened. "The reserve militia was formed to kill zeds and rescue survivors. They have clear orders to send over any survivors to Camp Fox. They don't have the authority to house any survivors except for the minutemen and their families."

Even Tyler didn't sound like he believed his own words.

When I didn't speak, he continued. "Listen, I know they may be a bit unorthodox, but they're keeping the zeds clear of the Camp. And they've brought in eighty-seven survivors already. Maybe you misunderstood them."

"Maybe not," I said.

He glanced at the pile of zeds in the ditch, and then took a step closer and leaned on the gate. "It looks like you're having your own share of problems with zeds. If you're not ready to relocate to the Camp, I could have Doyle send over a squad every day or so to help clear the area."

I belted out a laugh, and Tyler frowned. "What's so funny?"

I pointed to the pile. "Those zeds are courtesy of Doyle."

He stepped back. "What are you talking about?"

I leaned on the gate. "Dogs come by in a garbage truck every day and dump zeds over our gate because we refused to pay tribute to the militia. We had no problem keeping zeds out of this area until the Dogs started importing them."

Tyler cursed. Then he reached up and his thumb brushed against my cheek, startling me. "Come to the Camp. Doyle has no authority there. You'll be safe from him and the militia." He motioned toward the tree line. "All of your friends here can come, too. Out here, alone, it's too dangerous. I've heard about entire herds of zeds moving through Missouri right now. At the Camp we're rebuilding the way things used to be."

I stood and watched him for a moment. "How long do you think Camp Fox is safe from Doyle?"

"Doyle reports into Lieutenant Colonel Lendt, and we've treated the militia fairly. I might not agree with Doyle's methods, let alone like the guy, but he's been effective in eliminating zeds. Even if he did try something incredibly stupid," he replied. "He has only eighteen men, most of them farmers or desk jockeys. We have over fifty trained troops holding down a base with a fortified perimeter. No one would be dumb enough to go up against Camp Fox."

From what I'd seen of the Dogs so far, I figured they'd be exactly that kind of dumb once they got enough numbers. The Camp would be Eden for the militia.

"Well," Tyler drawled. "I'm going to have a talk with Doyle. I'll make sure these attacks stop. Still, I'm glad I found out about your camp."

I cocked my head.

He grinned. "Because I got to meet you."

I couldn't help but smile in return.

He leaned on the fence, closer to me. "How about I come back in three days, just to check in?"

"Yeah," I said. "Sure."

"How many of you are here?"

I narrowed my eyes and tensed. "Why does that matter?"

He held up his hands. "Relax. I'm not scoping out the place. I'm only asking so that I can bring back some MREs when I return. That's all."

"There are several of us here," I replied simply. "Any food would be appreciated, and we could really use some 9mm rounds if you've got extra."

"I'll see what I can scrounge up." He paused and glanced back at the Humvee before looking back to me. "The offer stands. If you or anyone here wants to relocate to the Camp, you just let me know. You'd like it there."

I nodded. "Thanks. I'll mention it to the others." I didn't mention that the others had been listening the entire time.

He reached into his pocket, smiled, and handed me a candy bar. "See you three days from now."

———

Three days later

Clutch was crankier than usual while we scouted the woods. "I don't trust them to not take control of us or our resources."

"I don't either," I said. "But Tyler offered to bring us supplies."

"Feels like bribery." He shook his head. "We can't count on them for help. We take care of ourselves."

"But we can't turn down any food or supplies," I said.

"He's working with the Dogs."

"But he doesn't trust them." I shrugged. "Not completely, anyway."

"He was flirting with you."

I stopped and looked at Clutch. After a moment, I put a hand dramatically over my heart. "My, oh my. Is big bad Clutch jealous?"

He scowled.

I laughed. "Tyler's too pretty and not nearly grumpy enough to hold my attention."

Clutch narrowed his eyes. "What—"

A pained howl sounded beyond the trees, yanking our attention back to the woods.

"That sounds close," I said.

Clutch took the lead and jogged us through the trees, keeping our weapons ready for any zeds that could be skulking around.

More cries followed, and we closed in on the pitiful sounds.

At the edge of the woods, three zeds tore at a fallen tree trunk. A fourth zed, several feet away, chewed on something with golden fur.

A tiny shriek shot out from inside the log, and I gave Clutch a quick glance. He gave a nod, and we moved in. One of the zeds saw us right away. It came to its feet with a moan, bringing the attention of the other two at the log.

Clutch swung first. He took the zed's head clean off. My swing went wide and landed in the shoulder of the second. I stepped back and swung again, this time my machete lodged into the skull. I kicked up, planting my boot against its chest, and yanked the blade free. I pulled my weapon up just as the third zed reached for me, but Clutch decapitated it, just like he'd done the first, before slamming his machete through both heads on the ground.

The fourth zed looked up and snarled, its mouth covered in fresh blood. Bites and scratches covered its face, chest, and arms, enough that would have caused serious injuries in a human. It went after Clutch, and I stepped around it and took off half its head from behind. It fell, dropping the carcass it'd been feeding on.

I edged closer to the hollow tree trunk and got down on my knees. I rested my weapon against the trunk, and Clutch stood guard.

I leaned down to find the source of the whimpering inside.

Pups.

They were much smaller than the animal the zeds had been feeding on. She'd likely been their mother and had sacrificed herself defending her den. Two pups were already dead, one struggled to breathe. Without obvious injuries, I suspected they'd been crushed when the zeds dug at them in a frenzy. The fourth pup in the far back corner continued to whimper. I reached in. It cried louder and nipped at my gloved fingers.

I gently blanketed the pup with my hand. It was cornered and began to wiggle fervently. Wrapping my fingers around it, I picked it up as gently as possible and pulled it free. She screeched in my hand as I examined her, and then I pulled her against my chest. "Shh. It's going to be okay, sweetie," I murmured.

She couldn't have weighed more than a couple pounds. After a moment, the pup's shrieks turned into whimpers before it finally quieted but continued to shake.

Clutch came up behind me.

"There's another one in there, but he's hurt pretty bad," I said, while stroking the pup's fur with my thumb.

He took a deep breath, bent down, and reached in with both his hands. When he stood, his hands were empty. "It's taken care of."

I gave him a tight smile and held up the pup. "She's definitely a mutt, but she's cute in a mutty sort of way."

He chuckled. "It's not a mutt. It's a mangy coyote."

A coyote? "Oh. Well, it's a she."

He shook his head. "Coyote are wild. They're not domesticated like dogs."

"But she'll die if we leave her behind."

"That's nature, Cash."

"There's been enough death already," I said quietly.

After a moment, he scowled. "Let me see it."

I reluctantly held her out.

He picked her up by the scruff of her neck, looked her over, and then handed her back. "It doesn't look injured or sick. But it's young, not even weaned yet. It'll probably die, no matter what we do. I don't know much about coyotes except that they're a nuisance."

The pup snuggled into my arm and I scratched her oversized ears. "I'll take care of her."

"I can't believe you're bringing a coyote home," Clutch said.

I shot him a smile. "We're all leftovers in this world. She's no different." I carried her in one hand, grabbed my machete in my other hand, and started heading back into the woods. "I think she'll fit in nicely."

Clutch caught up and we walked in silence through the woods. Once we reached the yard, I lifted the pup. "What should we call her?"

"Ugly."

"Har, har." I smiled. "Jase is going to love her."

By the time we crossed the yard and reached the house, the pup had nearly chewed a hole through my glove. Jase rode up on his bike and pointed, his head cocked. "What kind of dog is that?"

"Coyote," Clutch replied.

Jase raised a brow. "A coyote? For real?"

"She's yours if you want her," I offered.

His eyes widened. "Really?"

"Yeah, really."

He held out his hands, and I handed the pup over. "Hey, little Mutt," he murmured, scratching her back.

I smiled. As soon as I held the pup, I'd hoped she could help fill the void for Jase. "Hopefully, she'll take to the powdered milk," I said. "And you'll need to make up a little bed or kennel for her."

"Yeah, yeah," he said and headed off into the house.

"Make sure it doesn't have fleas before you bring it inside," Clutch called out, but Jase was already gone.

Clutch tried to give me one of his hard looks but failed. When his lips curled upward, I knew he'd also seen the light in Jase's eyes.

There were too few moments like that to brush them off.

"Let's check the gate," he growled. "The kid's going to be worthless the rest of the day."

I tried not to grin as I jumped in the Jeep, and Clutch shrugged off the backpack of extra gear he always carried now and drove us down the lane. About midway there, we heard the now-familiar sound of the garbage truck.

"Those sonsabitches just won't quit," he muttered before gunning the engine. "Get ready."

I lifted my rifle.

He stopped at the bend in the lane, and we got out and took cover behind the trees.

The garbage truck had stopped and was in progress of backing up. Either someone different was driving today or Sean was drunk off his ass, because the truck nearly backed straight into the ditch.

It would've been a lot easier for us if it had. But the driver overcorrected at the last moment and nearly went into the ditch on the other side. The back of the truck smashed into the gate, and the dump box opened. The box needed a couple more feet of space behind the truck to rotate. Terrible metal-on-metal screeching sounds ensued as the box tangled in the gate, lifting it, until something broke, and both the box and gate slammed to the ground, taking several feet of the barbed wire fence with it.

One zed caught between the box and gate was cut in half. The remaining five zeds began to crawl over it and onto the ground.

"You got to be fucking kidding me," Clutch cursed. "You got the zeds?"

My first shot went through a zed's eye. "Yeah," I said.

"Good." Clutch walked straight toward the truck that was now trying to pull away, but it was locked onto the gate. It wasn't an ordinary garbage truck. They'd welded metal over the wheels so we couldn't shoot the tires. Same with the windshield and windows. With the exception of a few peepholes, everything had been covered by sheets of metal. Otherwise we would've shot them the first time they'd invaded our territory.

Its tires spun, trying to break free, and the collapsed gate protested.

I took down the next four zeds with easy back-to-back shots as they tried to drag themselves to their feet. One final shot took down the half of zed still caught between the gate and truck.

Clutch came to a stop less than a dozen feet from the truck. Its engine and wheels suddenly calmed. A barrel poked through the slot in the driver's side window, but Clutch fired first. His shot was close enough to hit or scare the driver because the barrel disappeared back inside the cab, and the truck engine roared. The gate moved several feet with the truck.

Clutch jogged up to the window, stuck the barrel of his rifle through and started firing.

I sprinted toward Clutch, holding my rifle ready. He quit firing by the time I reached the truck. Everything had stilled, with only the sound of the truck's engine going.

I reached for the door handle and looked up to Clutch. He took a step back, aimed, then nodded. I flung the door open and jumped back, pulling up my rifle. But the two men inside didn't move. Blood had splattered the interior. The driver was slumped over the wheel, and the passenger was lying back, sprawled across the vinyl seat. Neither was Sean.

Clutch took a step closer and fired two shots, one into each man.

A couple months ago, I would've found that action heartless. Now, I would've done it myself if he hadn't shot first. These Dogs had attacked my home and the only people left in the world that I cared about. There wasn't much I wouldn't do. The only thing that scared me was how quickly and easily I'd slid into a ruthless way of thinking.

Jase came tearing down the lane on his bike. He jumped off and jogged toward us, holding his rifle. "What the heck happened here?"

"We won this round," I said since Clutch was busy examining the mangled gate.

The pouch attached to Jase's belt wiggled and whimpered. I cocked my head. A furry head with big ears poked out and looked around before disappearing back inside the pouch.

"It's okay, Mutt," Jase said, patting the pouch. "Just taking care of bad guys."

"The gate's fucked," Clutch said, walking up to us. He sighed and then kicked the gravel. "Godammit. I've had enough of this shit."

"Without their truck and two men down, it should take them some time to regroup," I said.

"Doesn't matter," Clutch said. "The game's changed. This is the second time I've killed Doyle's men. He'll up the ante next. I need to see what we're up against."

My brows furrowed. "What do you mean?"

"I mean," he turned to me, "that I need to see what kind of numbers and firepower Doyle's got at his disposal."

My jaw dropped. "Going to see Doyle is suicide."

Of all the shitty timing, the Humvee pulled up outside the gate. When Tyler stepped out, I kept an eye on Clutch to make sure he wasn't going to gun down the newcomers. He didn't shoot. Instead, he stomped forward to meet Tyler at the gate. I followed, not trusting the situation.

"What happened here?" Tyler asked as we approached.

While I knew Clutch had been in the military, it surprised me when he saluted Tyler.

Tyler's brows lifted, and he saluted back.

"Captain," Clutch said. "You can't control your own goddamn militia."

"They attacked again?"

"Every fucking day." Clutch pointed at the truck. "Take a look. It's pretty clear who the aggressor was here. We're being forced to defend our home against the militia."

Tyler walked alongside the truck, pausing at the open cab and again at the zeds, before returning to the gate by us. He leaned toward me. "Are you okay?"

I nodded. "No thanks to the Dogs."

Tyler looked at Clutch. "You have my word. I'll do my best so that this won't happen again."

"That's what you said last time," Clutch said. "No. *I'll* make sure they won't bother us again."

Tyler ran a hand through his hair. "Those two minutemen lying dead in that truck were sworn in. Attacking the militia is the same as attacking Camp Fox. Even though this was a clear case of self-defense, I can't let you go after Doyle on your own. We have to go through the proper channels."

My hands flung to my hips. "So the Dogs have get-out-of-jail cards to kill, steal, and rape?"

"I'm not saying that," Tyler replied quickly. "You have to understand. It's a tricky situation."

Clutch paced, stopped, and paced some more. "If you want to help, take us to Doyle."

"I don't think that's a good idea," Tyler cautioned.

Clutch spun on his heel and pointed at Tyler. "I'm going to see Doyle with or without your help, Captain. You can either take me to him or stay out of my way. Doesn't matter."

Tyler frowned and stared at the truck for several agonizing moments. Finally, he spoke. "I was going to see Doyle today, anyway. You can ride along." He held up a finger. "But I have to take the lead. Doyle can be a bit...difficult."

"Difficult?" I asked. "You said he reported to this Lendt guy."

"He does, but Lendt's offered him some leniency as long as the militia delivers results," Tyler said before motioning toward the Humvee. A soldier stepped out from the back, followed by a teenager in jeans and a T-shirt carrying a cardboard box.

"Eddy!" Jase called out, coming out from where he'd taken cover behind a shrub.

The new kid nearly dropped the box in his rush. Tyler grabbed the box, and Eddy hurdled a collapsed part of the fence. "Jase!"

While the two teenagers slapped each other's shoulders and bantered, Tyler set the box on the gate. "MREs. Enough to feed six for one week."

Clutch took the box, set it on the ground next to him, and rummaged through it. "How about ammo?"

Tyler shook his head. "I can't authorize the transfer of ammo. Even if I could, Camp Fox is an armory, not a munitions site. We barely have enough for ourselves."

Clutch's lips tightened. He headed back to the Jeep and grabbed his backpack. "Let's go meet Doyle."

Tyler didn't look pleased, but he motioned to the young, clean-cut man behind him, who walked up to us. "I'll leave Corporal Smith behind to help bury the minutemen and guard the place."

"How do I know I can trust your man?" Clutch countered.

I put a hand on Clutch's forearm and looked at Tyler. "If he stays, he's not allowed in the house, and he does what Jase says. Aside from the MREs, you haven't exactly proven that we can trust Camp Fox."

Clutch's jaw was clenched, but he nodded. He turned to Jase. "You get all that?"

Jase looked up from where he and Eddy were playing with Mutt. "Yeah. Want me to start working on the gate?"

"No," Clutch said. "That truck isn't going anywhere. It's a better barricade than the gate was right now. We'll get it fixed tomorrow. Just keep an eye out."

"Can I stay, Captain?" Eddy asked.

"Eddy and I were in the same class. We played football together," Jase added, and then stuck out his chest. "Of course, I could outrun Eddy any day of the week."

Eddy razzed Jase right back while Tyler smiled. "You both stay out of trouble. We'll be back in a couple hours. Smitty has a radio, so have him call me if you need anything." The corporal jumped the fence and Clutch gave him a once-over as he walked over to the two boys.

"Let my mom know I'm all right, okay, Captain?" Eddy asked.

Tyler gave him a thumbs up before turning back to us, and he looked at my M24. "You won't need your rifles on this trip."

I clutched it harder as I climbed over the gate. "I always need my rifle."

He opened his mouth to speak but shut it. He waved at the Humvee. "Nick, Griz, Tack, you're with me."

Clutch hopped the fence, his Blaser in tow. He brushed past Tyler, and opened the back door of the Humvee. I climbed in, followed by Clutch who sidled next to me.

Tyler took the front passenger seat, and I noticed another soldier behind the steering wheel. In the rear of the vehicle, I found two more soldiers: a black man at the .30 cal and a younger, lanky white man who, after seeing us, closed his eyes and leaned his back against the side. Even though neither looked aggressive, I was glad Clutch had sat next to me.

"Meet some of my team," Tyler motioned to the other men. "Tack and Griz are handling the .30, and Nick's our fine driver. Guys, meet Cash and..." Tyler turned in his seat to face Clutch. "I didn't get your name and rank."

"Seibert, Joseph. Sergeant First Class," Clutch replied.

"With what unit, Sarge?" Tyler countered quickly.

"75th Ranger Regiment."

"Hoorah," the soldier manning the .30 cal called out.

Tyler nodded to the man who spoke. "Griz back there is a Ranger, too."

"Hoorah," Clutch replied, lifting a fist in the air.

"Being with the Rangers, I'm guessing you saw some action, then," Tyler said.

Clutch gave a tight nod. "OEF-A. Two tours."

Tyler whistled. "Two tours in Afghanistan? Yeah, that counts as action. Have you thought about joining up at Camp Fox? We could use a soldier with your experience."

"How long do you think the Camp will be safe, Captain?" Clutch asked. "All those people confined in one place are going to attract zeds. And, all that heavy equipment is going to attract no-gooders. I'll support your efforts, but I've got my own people to protect. I can't relocate my people to Camp Fox until I know you can maintain a defensible position."

"I could order you to relocate to the Camp, Sarge," Tyler said. "All troops, including retired and inactive, were recalled to service when the outbreak started. And all remaining able-bodied men were called in for the reserve militia."

Clutch jutted out his chin. "Too bad I didn't get the memo."

Tyler pursed his lips. "I'll let that slide for now. I don't want to force you, but we need you. There may come a time when I'll have to order you back to duty, and that time could come soon."

Clutch's lips thinned and the tension thickened the air. "Yes, sir."

"If the militia is tied to Camp Fox, why do you let them do whatever they want?" I asked.

"What they did wasn't right," Tyler replied. "I'll make sure we get to the bottom of it, though it won't matter much longer. The militia is just a temporary structure until order can be restored." Then he gave me one of those warm smiles. "Have you thought more about moving to the Camp? As you saw, one of your folks has a classmate there."

"Jase can make his own decisions. But I go where Clutch goes." Feeling a hard gaze on me, I turned and found Clutch scrutinizing me. Did he want me with him? Did he want me to go to the Camp? It drove me nuts that I couldn't make out his expression.

"Well, there's a lot of folks counting on our help at the Camp, and Sarge could make a big difference helping us rebuild," Tyler said.

"I'm a patriot, Captain, but I'm not suicidal," Clutch said. "Any notion at rebuilding is delusional until you put an end to the militia and fold them under your command. Do it before it's too late."

"Zeds!" Griz yelled behind me, and gunfire blasted from the Humvee.

The noise was deafening, and I gripped my rifle tighter. I snapped my eyes from one window to the next. Then I saw through the windshield several zeds collapse on the road.

"Are we clear?" Tyler called out after the shooting stopped.

"All clear," the gunner yelled, and the Humvee sped up.

I leaned back and caught my breath. I looked at my window, contemplated rolling it down so I could shoot if needed, but decided to leave it up—the glass would provide some protection against zeds. I glanced to my right at Clutch. He gave me a questioning look. I forced a half-smile, and he turned his gaze back outside.

Tyler made a couple calls on his radio. Every few minutes, the gunner fired, and a zed fell. When we crossed Fox River, zeds floated in the water. Some lay on the mud banks. All dead. In a muddy field not far from the river, sat a tractor riddled with bullet holes. Inside, a body lay slumped over the steering wheel. "You've cleared out this entire area?" I asked.

Tyler nodded. "As much as we can. But more show up every day. Most are coming down from Chow Town. There's simply too many there for us to clean out without risking lives and burning through too much ammo. So we wait and hit the ones that migrate in our direction."

"How about the survivors still in town?" I asked.

"We used to make drive-throughs every day. At first, we'd fill our trucks with survivors. But after a couple weeks, we were lucky to find one or two, if any. Then a mob of zeds took down one of our Humvees. So Lendt cancelled the drive-throughs. The risk wasn't worth the payout." He pointed outside. "We're almost there."

In the middle of a flat marshland stood an old farmers' cooperative. Three large grain silos reached for the sky, with smoke billowing from the top of one. Tall chain fences reinforced with plywood and two-by-fours buffered the buildings from the road. What hung outside those walls made me grimace. Surrounding the militia camp, every fifty feet or so, a dead zed hung from a pole like a scarecrow.

"Do you think the zeds get the hint?"

"Doubt it," Clutch muttered.

On an ancient-looking billboard was written faded letters. I had to squint to read the words:

Doyle's Iowa Surplus
& Paintball Supplies:

Open Seven Days a Week.

The paint had long since faded, leaving only the bold capital letters *D-I-S* on the first line easily legible from a distance. Still, I shivered when I read Doyle's name. This made what we were about to do feel all the more real.

"It seems odd to have a surplus warehouse in the middle of farm country," I said while Clutch rolled down his window.

"Camp Fox is only five miles straight east of here," Tyler said. "This place is owned by a retired farmer, Dale Doyle. He had a connection with some brass at Fox a while back, and he worked out a deal to buy surplus at a hefty discount. It was right about the time they built the new farmer's co-op on the other side of town, so he bought this place at a rock bottom price."

"And it looks like the deal has already been sweetened," Clutch muttered, nodding toward the two armored vehicles sitting at the gate. "How many M1117's did you guys hand over to Doyle?"

"They needed lead-in trucks for survivor runs," Tyler replied quietly.

"Christ, Captain," Clutch said. "You're handing Doyle everything he needs to take over the Camp."

"Watch your tone, sergeant. The militia has been instrumental in clearing zeds from the area and locating survivors. Doyle may have one hell of a temper and a superiority complex, but he's turned farmers and kids into a militia that gets results."

The Humvee slowed to a stop at the gate.

Guard towers stood behind the fence, one on each side of the gate. A man in each tower had his rifle aimed at us. Two more men—one of them Sean—with automatic rifles stepped through a small door next to the gate.

Sean saw Clutch and visibly tensed. After a moment's hesitation, he warily walked up to Tyler's window, while the other man stood back several feet with his rifle leveled on the Humvee.

Sean nodded toward us in the backseat. "What are they doing here, Captain?"

Tyler rested his arm on his door. "Open the gate, Sean. I'm here to see Doyle."

Sean pursed his lips, clutching an AR-15 that matched the rifles Tyler's team carried. "I'm afraid I can't, sir." He nodded in Clutch's direction. "I can't let in any unauthorized people. Not until I clear it with Doyle."

"It's not the reserve militia's place to turn back any citizen," Tyler gritted out.

"Doyle's orders," Sean replied.

"I have the authority here, Private," Tyler snapped. "Open the damn gate!"

The man behind Sean lifted his rifle. "You assholes from Camp Fox don't tell us what to do. That bastard killed our friends!" His wild-eyes homed in on Clutch at the same time he aimed his rifle.

I sucked in a breath. Pulled up my rifle. Clutch was in the way. I couldn't get a clear shot.

"Fuck this," Clutch muttered as he lifted his rifle and pulled the trigger.

PART SIX
ARROGANCE

THE SIXTH CIRCLE OF HELL

Nine

The Dog yelped, dropped his rifle, and cradled his hand to his chest.

"Cease fire! Cease fire!" Tyler yelled, jumping out from the front seat.

I waited for the Dogs to gun us down, but they never did. Clutch sat, unmoving, next to me, with his Blaser leveled on the whimpering Dog.

"Beware the man with only one gun, because he knows how to use it. Ain't that right, Clutch," an older man with a voice that sounded like he'd smoked a pack a day for forty years straight said as he emerged from the door at the gate.

"Doyle," Clutch muttered under his breath.

I frowned. *This* was Doyle?

This man could have been anyone's grandfather. He was tall and slim, with a casual swagger in his step. His cap and sunglasses hid many features, though weathered skin and tufts of white hair curling out from his cap hinted at an advanced age.

Nevertheless, I held my breath as he picked the rifle off the ground and handed it back to the whimpering man who now sported a bullet hole through his hand. Tyler stood between the Humvee and Doyle, as though protecting us.

"At ease, men," Doyle said. "We don't turn folks away. Especially one of our own."

"But, Doyle," Sean said with a frown, not lowering his rifle from Clutch and me. "You said—"

"But, nuthin'," Doyle interrupted. He motioned to one of the guard boxes above the fence. "Open up."

Metal clanged and two Dogs pushed open the creaky gate.

Wary, I kept an eye on Doyle as he stopped in front of Tyler. The older man looked harmless enough, though I knew to trust my gut. And my gut was screaming at me to shoot him already, grab Clutch, and get the hell out of there.

I'd seen enough. We needed to get as far from these guys as we could and fast.

"Sorry about the confusion, Captain," Doyle said. "My boys simply tend to get a bit energetic in protecting their families."

"Bullshit, Sergeant Doyle," Tyler snapped. "You need to get your minutemen in line."

Doyle smirked, and then shrugged. "Guess you're just going to have to eat that bullshit, Masden. I report to Lendt, not you. You can't touch me, not as long as my little militia is handling your zed problem. You know it, and I know it."

I watched Tyler tense as he seethed with anger. "Lendt's given you leniency, true, and I trust his judgment. But he also trusts my judgment. And after the stories I've been hearing from several survivors—including the ones with me today—I'm not convinced your militia should remain separate from Camp Fox, let alone continue to receive supplies."

Doyle narrowed his eyes at Tyler but said nothing before moving around Tyler to lean on Clutch's door.

Clutch was clearly tense but he pulled his rifle back inside the window and rested it on his lap. I readjusted mine so that I could take out Doyle in a split second if I had to.

The older man looked me over. His gaze narrowed and his lips turned downward. When Tyler slammed the front door shut, Doyle returned his focus to Clutch. I knew he'd already made his mind up about me: he didn't like me, plain and simple.

My lip curled in return. *Feeling's mutual, bud.*

"We need to talk," Clutch stated.

"We'll talk," Doyle said, giving Clutch a wide smile. "But first, let's get you folks inside where it's safe. Damn zeds are starting to come out of the woodwork." He swaggered back through the now-open gate.

An ominous feeling grew heavy in my gut as our Humvee passed through the high gate and several Dogs closed in around us. "Well, we're in," I said, my voice barely a whisper. "And I'm ready to leave."

Clutch watched me for a moment and then gave a nearly imperceptible nod.

I cradled my rifle as I kept an eye on the Dogs. The man Clutch had shot held his injured hand to his chest as he disappeared inside the first building. Except for one, the remaining men warily watched Clutch like he'd do the same to them. The only guard who didn't seem concerned was the one too busy leering at me.

I'd seen him once before, when he'd called dibs on me at the greenhouse. I had wanted to shoot him then, too.

When we made eye contact, the weasel wagged his tongue and blew me a kiss. I would've flipped him the bird if I wasn't holding my rifle so tightly. Instead, I turned away to find Clutch watching me, his jaw tight. "Don't leave my side," he said gruffly.

I swallowed a nervous chuckle. Like I'd even want to. "I just want to get back to the farm as fast as possible."

Tyler turned in his seat. "No matter what happens, there's not to be one more shot fired here, understood? This situation is a tinderbox that's been getting hotter for some time."

"Unless we're forced to protect ourselves, you mean," I corrected. "Where'd Doyle get these guys? Prison?"

Tyler's lips pursed. "Stick with me, and everything will be okay. Doyle knows better than to fuck with Camp Fox. Still, I'm surprised none of them got trigger-happy when Clutch shot one of their friends. We're damned lucky to be alive," Tyler replied.

"That shit-for-brains was less than a second away from opening fire on us," Clutch grated out.

"How do you know that for sure, Sarge?" Tyler asked.

Clutch inhaled and then narrowed his gaze on Tyler. "I've seen that look before, plenty of times. I know."

Clutch's words evidently sunk in because Tyler seemed to accept them and turned away.

Inside the fence wasn't any more pleasant than outside. I counted twenty armed men in the camp. No telling how many more were either hidden behind doors or out looting the countryside. I looked at Tyler. "How many Dogs did you say there were?"

"Eighteen," he replied quietly.

Which would've made sixteen after their latest garbage drop-off today. "Looks like Doyle's been adding to his ranks."

"Yeah," Tyler replied, sounding none too pleased.

Doyle stepped in front of the Humvee, and Nick brought us to a stop. The gate behind us closed with a loud clank, locking us inside the camp, which appropriately, felt like a prison.

"They've got quite the setup here," I noted, and Clutch nodded, not looking any happier than I felt.

Second-guessing Clutch's idea to gain intel on the militia, I stole a glance at him when he reached for the door. He had on his "hard" look, making it impossible to see any emotion except badassness. "Stay with me," he repeated his words from earlier as he opened the door, grabbed his pack, and climbed out.

Rather than opening the door next to me—and closest to the leering Weasel—I slid across the seat and followed Clutch.

"Seen enough yet?" I whispered.

"I don't know what Doyle's endgame is yet," he replied just as softly.

Nick remained with the vehicle, while Griz and Tack got out to stand next to Tyler.

"Leave your gear in the Humvee," Doyle said as he walked toward us. "You're safe within these walls. You won't need guns here."

"No," Clutch said simply, adamantly.

Doyle looked at me.

I gripped my rifle harder.

"As long as there are zeds, they can keep their weapons," Tyler said. "That's an order."

After a guffaw, Doyle relented with a brush of his hand. "Have it your way. Keep them, but you won't need them. You're under my protection here."

I didn't exactly feel safe under Doyle's "protection," and from the look on both Clutch and Tyler's faces, they felt the same.

"While we're here, you can also brief me," Tyler said. "I've told you this before: I've got concerns about how many rations you've been going through lately. And you have no authority to grow your numbers, not without Lendt's approval."

Doyle grunted and turned, leading our group through the militia camp. Three rundown grain silos towered into the sky. A line of smoke trailed out from the dome of one. A faded Iowa Hawkeye logo was painted across one silo. A large white cross was painted on the side of a long tin building with writing and graffiti all along its side. Overgrown grass and dandelions cropped up everywhere not covered by gravel. People milled about, including even a few children.

Woodsy smoke corrupted the fresh spring breeze. As we passed a small fire with a turkey fryer filled with boiling water, I asked, "What are all the camp fires for?"

"Cooking. Purifying water," Doyle replied. "Our generators aren't big enough to power the entire camp, so anything we can do the old fashioned way, we do. Besides, the smoke also helps keep the smell down."

"Not worried about smoke or the smell of smoke attracting zeds?" I countered, knowing that we only cooked at night to mask the visibility of smoke.

Doyle smiled. "I say, let 'em come."

As we moved into the shadows of the silos, I noticed two young women stirring a pot on a fire. The scraping of metal against metal overpowered the crackling wood. As we walked past, one of the women jerked up, revealing a black eye. Utter despair radiated through her swollen, red eyes. She quickly looked away, focusing all too intently on the pot.

My jaw tightened. "Tell me, Doyle. How many folks are here by their own free will?"

"Everyone is given a choice when they arrive," he replied without turning. "They can choose to abide by my rules and stay here or go it alone outside the walls."

"But only the minutemen and their families stay here," Tyler added, while watching the young woman. "The militia has strict orders to bring all other survivors to Camp Fox."

"Of course," Doyle replied. "And others have chosen to stay to support the militia."

Glancing back at the young woman, I doubted Doyle's words. If Clutch hadn't been with me that day at the greenhouse, I suspected I'd be in her situation now: trapped. I found both Tyler and Clutch stopped, still eying the woman, before glancing at one another. Whatever passed between them, I couldn't see, but they both started to follow Doyle again.

The gravel crunched under my feet as Doyle led us alongside a long warehouse. The words "Gone but not forgotten" were painted on the faded wood siding under the white cross, with dozens of names painted around it.

Many names were separated into smaller groupings, each under a different last name. *Lynn, Wahl, Hogan* ... the names went on and on, and I realized that while I didn't trust the Dogs, many of them had suffered as much, if not more, than I had.

At the end of the building, Doyle opened a door and gestured, "Welcome to my office and my home."

Tyler stepped inside, followed by his men. Clutch waited for me, his hard expression impossible to read. Just as I was about to step through the door, I heard a wretched cry. Pausing, I turned to the smallest of the silos. Then another cry, louder, almost forlorn, and I could make out a single syllable in its whimper. *Please.*

I shot a glance at Clutch before looking to Doyle. "I didn't realize zeds cried."

His lips curled upward. "Didn't you, now."

He turned and disappeared inside, and I stared at Clutch, frozen.

Because we both knew that zeds didn't cry.

TEN

Clutch stepped through the doorway. "What the fuck is going on inside that silo?"

"It's our smokehouse," Doyle replied calmly.

"Not that one," Tyler said. "I heard it, too. It sounded like a person in the middle silo."

Doyle lifted his hands. "It's not what you think, gentlemen. Any survivor who wants to join the militia must go through survival training. I need to know that every man on my team will obey me, no matter what the order. No man becomes a minuteman until every man on my team knows he can count on him with his life. What's going on within that silo is nothing more than a hazing ritual every man undergoes when he's ready to take on the title of 'minuteman'."

"Then show us," Clutch demanded.

Doyle smiled smugly. "I'd be happy to, but first, let's eat. I'm starving."

No one moved.

"You have my word," Doyle added. "Now, come and have a seat. I've asked for some leftovers to be brought in for us." Doyle motioned us to a table. The room, with one large bay window, offered a generous view of much of the camp. In the corner sat a large wood desk covered in stacks of papers and books.

We moved cautiously inside.

Doyle laughed silently, as though he found something funny. "You know, Clutch, most folks wouldn't have the balls to rob me like you did."

"I figured your store was fair game," Clutch replied. "How was I to know you survived the outbreak?"

Doyle held up a hand. "Fair enough. But you killed five of my men. You're lucky I didn't repay kind with kind."

"Seven. The two men you sent today are dead," Tyler said, and Doyle's face tightened. Tyler continued. "While their deaths are tragic, I'm not arresting anyone. Attacking civilians stops now, Doyle. If anything like this happens again, I'm putting you in the brig and having your militia reassigned to Camp Fox."

Doyle's lips tightened. "Most of my men are simple farmers. The stress of the outbreak may have proved too much for some to handle. But I don't have anyone with military training here to help. If Clutch joined my team, I could ensure there'd be no more...misunderstandings."

Clutch and Tyler chortled in stereo. I frowned. Where the hell had Doyle gotten the idea that Clutch would join the Dogs? Hell, he'd been attacking us for the past week, and now he thought Clutch would sign up with a smile. He should hate Clutch for killing his men. It was almost as if he'd wanted Clutch to come to him all along. But why?

"You don't have the authority," Tyler said. "This man is Army and has been reactivated. He goes to Camp Fox under Lendt's command."

I could feel the tension roiling off Clutch, yet he sat there, saying nothing.

"Bah!" Doyle waved a hand through the air. "It'd be a waste for Clutch to join Fox, and he doesn't want to, anyway."

Tyler narrowed his eyes. "How would you know?"

Doyle blew him off. "Besides, the National Guard has never been anything but wet nurses. The militia is the people's real protector. I've seen the future, and it ain't pretty. The only way to protect people is to be hard. That Clutch took out two of my men today proves it all the more. Clutch would be a good fit here."

"Excuse me? You don't have the authority." Tyler came to his feet, and the two soldiers with him stepped closer.

Doyle ignored him. "Really, Clutch, tell me. Do you think you can hold down your farm against the zeds that will be pouring out from every major city with only a kid and a wetback?"

My jaw dropped, and I stood. "Wetback?"

Clutch grabbed my arm, whether to protect me or keep me from going for Doyle's throat, I didn't know. He glared. "Watch it, Doyle."

I put a hand on my hip. "My mother was Puerto Rican, and my dad was Irish. I was born here, just like my parents, and my parents' parents before them. That makes me as American as anyone in this room, so fuck off."

Doyle smirked. "No wonder you're keeping this one for yourself. She's feisty. She'd make good bait."

I went to raise my rifle, but Clutch latched onto my forearm. I tried to rein back my temper, failing miserably.

"Fucking racist," Griz gritted out from behind me.

I nodded.

"Enough!" Tyler slammed a fist on the table. "This ends now, Doyle. You hear me? No more games. We're all in this shithole together and need to be working together."

A door off to our side opened, and I swung my rifle around.

The three women carrying platters entered the room and froze, eyes wide.

Doyle motioned to the women. "Come in, come in." He sat down as though everything was dandy. "Have a seat. Oh, and Captain, I've already sent a plate out to your driver."

"Thank you." Tyler eyed the room cautiously as he and the soldiers with him pulled out wood chairs. He waited until Clutch and I took our seats before taking his own chair. I propped my rifle against the table next to Clutch's, keeping it in easy reach.

As Doyle poured the wine, I realized that all we were missing was Jesus because it sure as hell felt like we'd been brought in for the Last Supper.

Even with the heavy atmosphere, my mouth watered and my stomach growled as the aroma of roasted ham wafted through the air. Clutch hadn't yet let us butcher a hog or cow, not until we worked the kinks out of the smokehouse. When the older woman set down the tray full of meat, I made a mental note to finish the smokehouse tomorrow.

"It looks delicious. Thank you, my dear," Doyle said, briefly holding the woman's hand.

She smiled and kissed his forehead before leaving the room.

On the second platter lay a round loaf of bread and spring greens. "Mm, I missed bread," I murmured and craved to dig in, but I didn't trust Doyle. I watched him, and he smirked like he enjoyed having that kind of power over me. He took his time tearing off a chunk of bread and popped it into his mouth. After he swallowed, I pulled off a piece. As I took my first bite, I found Clutch watching me with a hint of a smile.

I savored the first taste of bread in two months. It had a heavy, whole-grain taste, making it easy to eat without any butter. I tore off a piece for him. "I like carbs."

Before leaving, two of the women bowed to Doyle as though he was a god. There seemed to be a lot of that going on around here. I watched the two Dogs standing behind their leader, not eating. After swallowing, I turned to Doyle. "Why do you make your guys shave their heads?"

"It started as a matter of hygiene," Doyle said while carving the ham. "It took me less than a week to start up the militia, but within two weeks, three men already had lice. Now, it's become a badge of honor, and all new minutemen have their heads shaved before their training even begins."

"But you didn't shave your hair," I said.

"No, I didn't." He took another bite.

As I chewed, I suspected their shaved heads had little to do with hygiene and everything to do with Doyle's need for control. Not that I would ever say those words to his face, and I started to believe that Doyle had wanted Clutch to come to him all along.

Doyle handed plates to Tyler, who then passed them along to Griz and Tack.

"You keep this much extra food around?" Tyler asked.

"My men need to keep their strength up," Doyle replied.

"No wonder why you're going through rations at over twice the per capita rate at Camp Fox," Tyler said. "Last week I let it slide because of the survivors you brought in. But, your ration list is even longer this week. Yet, you've brought no more survivors to the Camp in four days."

"Just because we haven't found any more survivors, doesn't mean my men aren't working hard." Doyle handed a plate to Clutch, who then handed it to me.

I waited impatiently for Doyle to eat first. Could I trust the man enough to not poison us?

Hell, no.

"You need to start rationing better," Tyler said. "Camp Fox doesn't have enough supplies to keep this up. Our munitions are already under forty percent. With how many more zeds are projected to show up over the next few months, you need to conserve."

Doyle handed a final plate to Clutch before taking one for himself. "Without supplies, we can't clear out Fox Hills and make it habitable again."

Tyler didn't look happy. "I have three times as many men as you, yet you're going through more supplies. You're forcing my hand. I'm going to talk with Lendt about cutting your rations."

Doyle gritted his teeth. "You don't have the authority, Masden. Lendt runs the show, not you. And with Clutch joining up, we're going to need more supplies so we can hit the zeds even harder."

Clutch pounded a fist on the table "Godammit, Doyle. Get it through that thick skull of yours. I'm never hooking up with you and your crew of lowlifes."

"I bet with the right persuasion, you would," Doyle replied quietly.

Clutch looked at me. "Let's go." He came to his feet, grabbed his rifle, and headed straight for the door.

The scrape of silverware on plates turned to silence.

Still chewing, I jumped up, grabbed my rifle, and followed Clutch.

"Hold up." Doyle shoved to his feet.

Clutch paused, his hand on the handle.

Doyle approached, his two Dogs alongside him. "Let me show you something."

Tyler stood, throwing a worrisome glance in my direction. Griz and Tack didn't look any happier.

Clutch stepped to the side, and Doyle walked outside, and we all followed him toward the northern edge of the camp. I kept eying Clutch, and I suspected that he knew, as I did, that Doyle's attempt at pretenses had just vanished.

As we walked, the sickly sour reek of decay became more and more prevalent.

Clutch was scowling. "What is this about, Doyle?"

"Patience. You'll see soon enough."

A Dog wearing a surgical mask stood at a chain-link door built into the plywood-covered fence. Doyle wrapped a bandana around his face and motioned to the guard, who hastily unbolted the lock and held the door open. He tilted his head as his leader walked through.

Cautiously, I followed Clutch through the door, with Tyler, Griz, Tack, and Doyle's two guards at my back.

I nearly threw up the food I'd just eaten. The stench was horrific. No wonder they'd had so many fires burning within the fences. They weren't for preparing food and water. They were to cover the stench of death.

With my hand covering my nose and mouth, I edged toward the rim of the deep pit piled high with bodies. Hundreds of zeds were piled onto one another. None moved. All showed severe head trauma. Many had been burned, but the bodies on top were fresh, not yet burned. Half-rotted corpses sprawled upon one another, as though they'd been dumped there, dozens or more at a time.

The zeds on top looked like they'd been killed within the last couple days. What had been an older woman in a floral apron lay contorted, with one leg bent behind its back, staring lifelessly at me through gray glassy eyes.

Not far from her lay a toddler with a Tonka truck in a death-grip to its chest. She'd been young when she died, smaller than the ones I'd seen at the school.

The school.

I swayed, and Clutch leaned closer, his solid mass grounding me.

"Zeds rely on their sense of smell more. The stink seems to serve as a natural deterrent," Doyle said. "And it helps mask the scents that humans live within the fence."

I shook my head, unconvinced. The risk of disease seemed too high to have this much death near the camp.

"Why are you showing us this?" Clutch asked from my side.

"Zeds are an inconvenient bunch." Doyle said. "My men have taken out nearly five hundred deadheads since the outbreak. But we're seeing zeds passing through in greater numbers every week. My militia is the only thing standing between genocide and survival."

"*Your* militia?" Tyler asked. "Careful, Doyle. You're toeing the line."

Doyle brushed him off with a wave of his hand.

Tyler frowned. "I've given you leeway since your men have been doing a good job at taking down zeds. But that doesn't mean you're not replaceable."

Doyle's face reddened. "You have no concept of the type of leadership that's needed in times like these."

Tyler took a step closer. "I have a better idea than you think."

Clutch chortled. "I'm done with this bullshit. I'm taking Cash and we're heading back to my farm." He pointed at Doyle. "And from this moment on, your Dogs will leave us alone and stick with their job of killing zeds. Any act of aggression toward my people will result in more of your men being killed. Got it? I'm not fucking around, Doyle."

Doyle stiffened. "You need to remember one thing: You don't want to be my enemy."

ELEVEN

"Are you threatening me?" Clutch demanded, stepping between Doyle and me.

"If I was threatening you," Doyle said. "I'd have said how easy it would be to have you all shot and thrown into the pit to rot with these corpses and no one would be the wiser. I'm simply saying I'm someone you'd much rather have as a friend than as an enemy."

I glanced at Clutch who looked as tense as I felt. Without looking down, I checked my rifle to make sure the safety was off. I realized now it had been a mistake coming here today. Doyle was a power-monger. And he clearly wanted Clutch. That Doyle wanted Clutch alive or dead, I hadn't yet figured out.

"Watch it," Tyler said. "You're grossly overstepping your bounds."

Doyle pointed at the pit full of zeds. "My men are protecting the Fox River valley. If we hadn't destroyed these monsters, how many more lives would be lost by now? We are not asking for gratitude. All I ask for is a little support and regular supplies. You need to talk to Lendt and get him to grant my men full access to Camp Fox's resources. Enough of this rationing bullshit."

"No," Tyler said. "From what I've seen lately, I'm going to advise Lendt that the militia should be reassigned under my command."

Doyle pulled down his bandana. "And exactly what do you think you've seen, Masden?"

Tyler jutted out his chin. "I know you're feeding me bullshit every week. For starters, do you think I wouldn't notice that you have a hell of a lot more people on this camp than just the militia and their families?"

"It takes a lot of support resources to run a successful militia."

"If you haven't been killing so many zeds and bringing in survivors, I would've shut you down a month ago," Tyler snapped back.

Doyle watched Tyler carefully. "You should tread carefully, Captain. Times have changed. Nature will take its course, just as it always has. The weak will die, leaving only the strong. If we waste our efforts protecting the weak..." Doyle shot a gaze at me before turning back to Tyler, "then we will all fall to the zed horde. You are incorrect, Captain. As the leader of the militia, I have the right to do whatever it takes to ensure my men are the strong."

"You're fighting each other when we should all be fighting the zeds together," Clutch growled out. "You two can work out your own shit. I'm out of here."

With that he turned, shot me a look, and headed back to the door, with me at his side. The guard from earlier blocked the door.

"Out of my way, boy," Clutch ordered.

The man looked nervously past our shoulders and didn't move.

"Think it through, Clutch," Doyle called out, sounded exasperated. "You're trained to analyze every situation. You know joining with me is the only logical decision."

Clutch's back straightened and he turned around. "And if I don't?"

"Then you'll realize your mistake when you find you're unable to protect your own people."

"Now *that* sounds an awful lot like a threat," Clutch said.

"Enough, Doyle!" Tyler yelled out. "Sarge isn't militia. He's retired military and has been recalled to active duty as of thirty seconds ago," Tyler said, his voice deeper and louder than before. "How he serves is Lendt's decision. We'll continue this discussion later at Lendt's office."

I heard it then. The hearty growl of a big engine. I searched until I found a green garbage truck barreling toward us. This truck was undamaged and didn't have all the armor plating, but it was from the same garbage company. When it approached, I tensed.

It stopped, then turned and backed up toward the pit, the sound of *beep-beep-beep* echoing around us. The back lifted and dumped two more bodies onto the pile. I covered my nose and scanned the pile to make sure none were moving.

"You see, Captain," Doyle said. "How many lives did we save today?"

Tyler didn't reply.

Smugly smiling, Doyle turned to the man getting out of the truck. "I trust everything went well, Keith?"

The driver bowed to Doyle before speaking. "No problems."

I gasped. "You."

The man looked. His eyes widened, and he froze.

We'd found the fourth rapist. The one who got away.

Clutch and I raised our rifles at the same time. Doyle's guards and Tyler and his men raised their rifles in response.

"Whoa." Tyler held up one hand above his rifle. "What's going on here?"

"Stand back," Clutch nodded to the newcomer Keith, "That rat bastard is responsible for the rape, torture, and death of a young woman."

"Do you have proof?" Tyler countered, though Tack and Griz both moved their rifles onto the Dogs.

"We both saw it," I said. "She tried to escape and he was one of the four chasing her."

"I didn't do nothing!" Keith shrieked.

I looked at Clutch. His hard gaze told me everything I needed to know. I aimed my rifle and fired. Keith fell back, into the pit, a bullet hole through his forehead.

I expected to be riddled with bullets, but surprisingly, no one else fired even though everyone except Doyle held a rifle.

Doyle's lips thinned. "You'll be sorry for doing that, girl."

Tyler leveled his rifle on Doyle. "We have laws, Doyle. I'm arresting her, and she's coming with me to stand trial."

"If you'd seen what he and his friends had done, Captain," Clutch growled, "you'd have done the same thing."

"Everyone, stand down," Tyler commanded.

None of the Dogs lowered their weapons, and so no one else did.

"Doyle, your men are ordered to stand down," Tyler said, reaching out to me, but Clutch grabbed me first and pulled me against him.

"That Dog got what he deserved," Clutch said.

He took us a step back, and then froze.

"No!" I cried out when I saw Doyle's pistol aimed point blank at Clutch's temple. I turned to Tyler. "Clutch is innocent."

"The only way anyone leaves here is if I allow it," Doyle countered.

"You are disobeying a direct order, Doyle," Tyler stated. "This camp is under the jurisdiction of Camp Fox. If you do not have your men stand down now, you will be stripped of rank and deemed outlaws. This is your last warning."

Doyle snorted. "My camp, my rules. It's you who need to lower your weapons."

"If your men open fire," Tyler said, keeping his rifle aimed at Doyle. "You'll be the first one dead. Now, you are *ordered* to stand down!"

Clutch's eyes were completely focused on me. "Let them go, Doyle," he said, "and I'll join your crew."

I shook my head. *Don't do this.*

After a lengthy pause, Doyle pulled away his pistol and sneered. "You're lucky I'm in a good mood today, Masden. You have five minutes to clear out of my camp."

"Get her out of here, Captain," Clutch ground out.

"The militia is done, Doyle," Tyler said. "Effective immediately."

Doyle belted out a laugh. "Camp Fox needs me. I don't need you." He sobered. "And you're wasting your minutes."

Tyler reached for me. "You don't have to do this, Clutch," I begged.

Clutch's face hardened and he turned away, gritting his teeth while one of the Dogs disarmed him.

"Well, this worked out better than I expected," Doyle said to one of his men.

Tyler grabbed my wrist. He pulled me through the doorway and through the camp, flanked by Griz and Tack.

Knots tightened in my gut with every step. Doyle had wanted Clutch. Defeated and under his control. And we'd let him do it. He'd expected Clutch to kill the rapist so he could imprison him. When I killed the man, Clutch had volunteered to stay, making Doyle's job easy. Doyle had got exactly what he'd wanted. Clutch was no longer a threat, leaving those he cared about easy game for the Dogs.

With a surge, I twisted free and grabbed Tyler's arms. "Clutch is a good man. He doesn't belong here. Promise me you'll try to get him out of here."

Tyler watched me for a moment. Maybe he understood, maybe he saw something in my eyes. He gave a thin smile. "I'll do what I can."

When his words registered as truth in my mind, I nodded and inhaled. "Good." I headed to the waiting Humvee, a thousand rescue scenarios running through my mind.

The only problem was, without Clutch, I couldn't do anything, let alone pull off a rescue.

Before I climbed into the Humvee, I looked back one last time to find Clutch, but only saw Doyle watching us smugly, promising retribution. Clutch had sacrificed himself for our freedom. And it was a waste, because Doyle wouldn't stop until we were all dead.

PART SEVEN
VIOLENCE

THE SEVENTH CIRCLE OF HELL

TWELVE

I remembered the feeling of plastic restraints cutting into my wrists from my first night with Clutch. I understood why Tyler felt like he had to arrest me, and before the outbreak I would've agreed with him.

But the world had changed.

I felt even edgier without the weight of my gear and weapons. Being defenseless in the middle of zed country, with Clutch undergoing who knows what back at Doyle's camp, unnerved me.

I sighed. "You didn't need to tie me up. I'm not a danger to you."

Tyler turned from the window to me, looking none too pleased. "You killed an unarmed man today."

If he only knew the facts. "And I don't regret it."

Yes, I'd shot that criminal knowing that shit would hit the fan as a result. The man was dead, anyway. I'd simply fired before Clutch did. He was going to pull the trigger. I'd seen it in his eyes, just like he'd seen it in the eyes of the Dog he shot back at Doyle's gate. So, I killed the man to keep Clutch safe. I just hadn't figured that Clutch would be a victim in the ensuing cluster fuck. When I saw him again—and I promised myself I would—I was going to wring his freaking neck for playing hero.

Nick shot me a tender glance before returning his focus to driving, and I could feel eyes on my back from Griz and Tack behind me as well. None of them had seen what the Dogs had done to that poor girl. Still, being this close to the militia camp, they must've seen things or heard stories when it came to Doyle and his cronies.

"You know Doyle," I said. "He never would've let you take one of his Dogs into custody to stand trial. Face it, the only thing that kept that rapist from getting off free was my bullet."

Tyler narrowed his gaze. "How can you be so cavalier about taking a man's life?"

"You didn't see what they did," I replied quietly, remembering her broken body and hollow eyes.

He was quiet for a moment. "In case you haven't noticed, there aren't many of us left. We have to keep faith in justice. We'll never make it if we each take the law into our own hands."

I chortled. "We'll never make it if we *don't* take the law into our own hands." It was futile trying to convince Tyler that the world was no longer wrapped with a comforting blanket of rules and traditions. We could no longer afford the luxury of hiding accountability beneath layers of red tape. Doyle wouldn't follow the rules. Neither could we. In a matter of days, we'd toppled from thinking we were wolves to realizing that we were only rabbits.

I broke eye contact to look out the window. We were approaching tall chain-link fences, topped with razor wire, surrounding what looked to be at least ten acres of a National Guard base.

Camp Fox.

Too wide open for a solid defense. Too many areas for zeds to break through.

A white wind turbine rotated smoothly, towering above the base. My jaw dropped. "You have power?"

Tyler nodded. "Camp Fox has had its own wind energy for over five years now."

"Showers?"

His lips curved. "Yes, we even have hot water." I rested my head on the seat and fantasized about standing under a steamy shower as we approached the gate. Unfortunately, I couldn't allow myself the luxury of fantasies. Not with Clutch's—and my—current situation.

Several Humvees and armored vehicles rested on the other side of the tall fence. Camp Fox certainly wasn't lacking firepower, though Clutch and I had watched on television while cities like D.C. and L.A. fell, despite having massive military power on their streets.

Two soldiers stood while a third stepped inside a guard's box and opened the gate. They saluted Tyler as we passed through the gate, and he saluted in return. It was then I realized that I might never see the farm again.

"Will Smitty stay with Jase and Eddy tonight?" I asked, knowing that Jase had to be getting worried before long.

"I'm having the boys brought here tonight," Tyler replied. "I'll see that you connect with Jase tomorrow morning. I thought it would be safer than leaving him at the farm."

"I suppose so," I murmured, though I wasn't exactly confident in Camp Fox's strength, not after seeing the way Doyle had scoffed at Tyler.

Beyond the gate stood several small pens holding livestock. A lone bull with wide horns stood in a closed-off area across the road. No doubt this setup was to protect the animals from zeds, but to me, it was like setting out bait. Once zeds depleted the local population, they'd come in hordes to Camp Fox in search for food.

A single zed was easy to kill. They were dumb, slow things. Easy to outthink and outmaneuver. But a herd never tired. Tall fences and bullets couldn't protect these people. They were rounded up for an all you can-eat smorgasbord. I felt a hundred times safer at the farm, where we were ready to bug out at the first sign of herds.

As the Humvee curved around the Camp's winding roads, people milled around, some worked the gardens while others carried loads. Two young children played with a ball. Several looked up as we passed. Many smiled and waved as though these men were their saviors, which I supposed was true.

Seeing so many people in one place, I couldn't help but feel a pang of hope. Maybe Jase would be safer here than alone at the farm, for at least now. Maybe Tyler was right. Maybe Camp Fox could recreate civilization. Maybe, just maybe, they could withstand zeds.

We continued past several barracks, all of which had people in regular clothes walking nearby. After another few blocks, Nick pulled to a stop outside a square brick building with a sign that read Camp Fox HQ outside.

Griz and Tack climbed out back before Tyler opened his door. Each man grabbed my arms and pulled me across the seat. With my wrists tied, I nearly stumbled climbing down from the Humvee.

As soon as Tack shut the door, the Humvee drove off, leaving the four of us standing alone in the small parking lot. The sun had already begun to set, casting a warm orange glow onto the red bricks. Clutch was in the direction of the falling sun. What would he be doing now? Would he be tied up like I was, or was he playing along with Doyle?

Tyler tugged me along and I had to hurry to keep up with his longer strides. Griz and Tack followed us up the steps and through the double doors.

Inside, the building seemed innocuous. With the exception of military insignias, the main area could've passed for any town hall. Tyler stopped us at the front desk, where a man and woman sat. He was in uniform, while she wore jeans. "Is the Colonel available?" Tyler asked.

The woman spoke first. "He is. Shall I let him know you're coming?"

"Yes, thank you," Tyler nodded and then turned to me. A pained look flashed across his face before he turned to the two soldiers with us. "Escort the prisoner to interrogation room one." He gave me a final, almost-pained glance before turning on his heel and hurrying down a hallway.

Tension grew in my muscles.

"This way, sugar," Griz said.

With one man on either side, they walked me down a hallway, stopping when we came to an opened door.

Tack flipped a switch, and light flooded the room. The room sat empty except for a table and two chairs.

Griz nudged me inside, and I winced at the sudden brightness. With his rifle, he motioned to a chair. "Take a seat."

I swallowed and obeyed and was somewhat surprised that they didn't restrain me to the chair, not that I was an expert on interrogations. The sum of my experience came from what I'd seen on TV. They left me alone, closing the door behind them. I suspected at least one of them remained just outside the door, but I could neither see nor hear them.

The room was small, maybe eight-by-eight, without any windows. No one-way mirror covered the wall, though I supposed video cameras had long since replaced one-way mirrors.

I closed my eyes. Focused on my breathing. Silently repeated my mantra to soothe my nerves until I realized there was no way to get the upper hand in this situation.

I was at their mercy, plain and simple.

Long after my butt had gone numb in the cold metal chair, the door opened, and I started.

A man I didn't recognize walked in first, followed by Tyler. The newcomer was tall, his face craggy, and looked to be in his late forties. He took the other chair, while Tyler stood off to the side.

"I'm Lieutenant Colonel John Lendt." The man sitting across from me looked every bit the leader Tyler had made him out to be. A piercing, sharp gaze, hard jaw, and strong shoulders hinted that this man was confident in both his intelligence and strength. He was downright intimidating without even trying.

"I'm Cash. I'd shake your hand, but my hands are preoccupied."

"Just Cash?" He raised a brow.

I shrugged. "I'm no longer who I was before."

One corner of his mouth rose. "I disagree. Who we were shapes us into who we are, and who we are shapes us into who we'll become." He leaned back. "But we're not here to talk philosophy, are we. Captain Masden witnessed you shooting an unarmed man without provocation today. What do you have to say to that charge?"

A thousand different responses shot through my brain. I settled on simple honesty. "Yes, I shot him, but I had provocation."

His brows tightened. "You realize that under military law the punishment for murder is death."

I looked down at the table and swallowed.

Lendt came to his feet. "Sergeant Nicholas Lee has volunteered to lead your defense. I'll have a tribunal scheduled for the day after tomorrow. No need to delay this messy business, but you have my word that you'll be treated fairly."

Tyler followed Lendt out of the room.

I frowned. This was an interrogation? No questions about why I'd done it?

"This way."

Griz stood in the doorway, motioning to me, and I rose and followed him, feeling as though my doom was already sealed. Numbness coated my thoughts as they escorted me out the other side of the building and across a wide sidewalk to a low one-story building. Inside, the short hallway was lined with several cell doors and more hallways, though I could hear no one else nearby. They put me into the first tiny, windowless cell with a narrow bed and a steel latrine and sink.

"Hold still for a moment," Griz said just before I felt a tug and the plastic restraint snapped free. I rubbed my wrists and faced the two soldiers as one shut the steel door.

Tack faced me through the bars in the door's window. "The bastard got what he deserved," he said before disappearing, leaving me alone in my cell.

I collapsed onto the bed and stared at the gray ceiling. How had everything gone to shit so quickly?

Silence boomed off the walls in response.

I thought of Jase. He knew people here. They could look out for him. But Clutch...

For all I knew, he was lying dead in that zed pit right now.

The sound of boot steps echoing down the hallway brought me back, and I pulled myself up and walked toward the door in time to meet the driver from the Humvee.

He was looking to his left. "Open up."

"I can't, sir," an unfamiliar voice said. "Colonel's orders. He said the prisoner is a flight risk."

Nick rolled his eyes before turning to me. "Hi, Cash. I'm Sergeant Nick Lee."

"I remember," I replied. "Good to see you again."

"I'll represent you at your trial. Since you already admitted to the murder, I think our best defense is to prove that there was no premeditation, and, therefore, this wasn't first-degree murder. That way, you'll just get time in the brig, and the death sentence gets ruled out."

I watched him for a moment. "Why are you helping me, Nick?"

He shrugged, and then lowered his voice. "I've seen some shit. Bad things that have happened to women *and* men. We've all heard rumors. If you said both you and your friend saw this guy hurt a girl, I believe it. Now, if we can get your friend to testify, it will help your cause. The fact that he's a veteran is even better." He paused for a moment. "But, honestly, I don't think we'll be able to get him here for the trial."

Not that I was surprised. Still, having my thoughts spoken aloud burned. "Can't Lendt order him to come to the Camp?"

"Sure, but I don't think it will do any good. Colonel Lendt ordered Doyle to come to the Camp after Masden filled him in, and Doyle hasn't shown up yet." Nick grinned. "And, Colonel Lendt doesn't take kindly to being screwed with. I think he's finally going to make Doyle come to heel and break up the militia."

"Watch out for Doyle," I said, a rock forming in my gut.

"What's he going to do? Attack Camp Fox?" He smirked. "Don't worry. We have many times the resources and firepower that Doyle's got. We're safe enough here. Let's start prepping for your trial. Start at the beginning, and tell me everything."

———

Several hours later, I woke, sweating and heart racing. I dreamed that Clutch was in the room with me. Except that he was a zed.

A siren pierced the night's silence, and I lunged to the door. "What's going on?" I called out, hoping someone was nearby.

"Echo Four reporting in, requesting status. Over."

The soldier's voice was to my right, but I couldn't see him around the corner.

"All units report immediately to assigned defense points. Camp Fox is under attack. Zed Alert. Code Five. This is not a drill. Over."

The voice on the radio repeated the message two more times before my guard stepped in front of my door, his eyes wide.

"What's going on?" I asked.

He stared at me for a moment, and then took off running. A door opened and closed. Then silence.

"Damn it," I muttered, kicking at my door. Without any visible doorknob or hinges, all I could do was shove at the door, but it was solid steel. Still I tried. Trying was better than accepting that I'd die in this tomb, either from starvation or when the zeds would finally find me. I turned and walked over to the bed. Pulled at the frame but it was screwed into the concrete floor. I returned to the door. After long minutes of kicking, a door opened somewhere. Buried under the piercing siren, I heard gunfire and screams.

Nick's helmeted visage filled the window in my door, startling me. "It was Doyle," he said, panting. "His men cut through the fence and laid down flares. Set off the sirens. They must've gone out and drawn all the zeds in the area here."

He pulled off his helmet and wiped his forehead. "Doyle zed-bombed us."

Thirteen

"There are zeds everywhere," Nick said, putting his helmet back on. "I can't believe it. Doyle attacked us. He really did it."

I pressed my hand over my heart as his words sunk in. While I didn't doubt Doyle's ruthlessness, the reality that he'd attack hundreds of innocent people made no sense. I pressed against the door. "Let me out. I can help."

Nick noisily fidgeted with keys. "This is your only shot. Lendt will make you stand trial, and you'll end up either in the brig or worse. And that's just not right. I've seen shit the Dogs have done. You've got to run."

More rattles, I heard a click, and the door swung open. I jumped out of my cell to find Nick already jogging away, his boot steps echoing through the empty hallway. When he opened the door, the gunfire sounded way too close, but there was no way zeds should have managed to cross acres of the outer camp to get to the center.

Before I stepped outside, I paused. "I have no weapon."

He patted a couple pockets with his hand not holding an AR-15 and pulled out a folding knife with a camo paint scheme. "It's not much, but it's all I can spare."

I opened the blade. "Better than nothing."

Nick gave my shoulder a quick pat. "Head east. That's the quickest way out of here. I got to get to my squad. As soon as all the civvies are in their barracks, we're going to start unloading the heavies on the zeds." Nick sprinted toward the tanks and Humvees rolling in, likely to congregate around the barracks in the distance, and I hoped that Jase was safe.

Movement in the darkness off to Nick's left kicked me into action. "Your nine o'clock!" I shouted, running toward him.

He twisted to his left where at least a dozen zeds tumbled out of the shadows. He held down the trigger, firing into the onslaught and taking down several zeds, but most bullets embedded harmlessly into their torsos and limbs.

I sprinted to close the distance between Nick and me.

A zed wearing a business suit emerged from the darkness behind Nick. I spun around it and embedded the knife up to its hilt into the back of the zed's skull. I hadn't been sure the blade was long enough until the zed collapsed.

Nick's rifle clicked on empty. He dropped it and pulled out a pistol that looked like a Beretta 9mm.

"Conserve your ammo," I said as I picked up the empty rifle. "Remember to go for head shots!"

Wild-eyed, he fired into the thinning group, and I pocketed the knife. I jogged over to the zeds on the fringe, ones too shot up to walk, and swung down the rifle butt, making sure to crush each skull before moving onto the next.

After Nick quit shooting, I slammed the rifle into the last moving zed.

Walking back, I held out the AR-15, now dripping with brown sludge. He finished reloading his pistol, holstered it, and looked up. He grimaced at the rifle, but took it and reloaded.

"Hasn't anyone trained you guys on the art of killing zeds?" I held a finger to my temple. "Always go for headshots. One shot, one kill. Anywhere else is a waste of ammo unless you're overwhelmed and have to slow them down."

"Lay off me, I'm just ROTC," Nick said, reloading the rifle. "It's just different when they're right *there*. They should never have gotten this far into the Camp."

Screams erupted in the distance, and we both jerked around.

Nick's eyes widened. "They breached the barracks!"

No. Jase!

We took off running toward the barracks, where gunfire flashed like lightning bugs in the night.

Several zeds lumbered after us along the way, but we easily outran any Nick didn't take down with headshots.

By the time we reached the first barrack, cries seemed to be coming from everywhere. Zeds pounded at each of the doors and windows of the barrack. The people inside stood huddled together under the lights, making them look like fish in a fishbowl. Soldiers in full battle armor, unable to fire without risking casualties to friendly fire inside, used bayonet-knives, axes, and crowbars to take out the zeds and were making headway.

I came down on a knee by a soldier who'd lost his helmet and had been chewed to a pulpy mess. I relieved him of his rifle and knife before rummaging through his pockets to find two fresh magazines. His warm blood soaked my hands, making the mags slippery.

After reloading the rifle, I found a pale Nick nervously waiting for me instead of helping his comrades, his lack of experience all too obvious.

.30 cal machine guns belted out rounds into the darkness.

The first barrack had been nearly cleared by the troops. I tugged Nick's arm. "Let's check the other barracks."

We ran down the long building to the second barrack. Only a few zeds shuffled by its doors and windows. With no lights on inside, it was impossible to see if the barrack was inhabited, but I suspected these civilians had been smart enough to hide from the zeds.

The third barrack was a different story. Its doors were thrown wide open, and the soldiers were firing directly inside. The lights were on, and I couldn't make out who was zed and who wasn't.

I ran toward the building, searching for Jase. I wasn't used to the AR-15 so I got close to the crowd before I fired. My first shot went right through a zed's brainpan. The rifle had less recoil than I was used to, and I took down two more zeds before running to a more open spot and repeating the process.

The ground was covered with hundreds of zeds, some not moving, some dragging themselves toward prey. But, for every zed on the ground, there were four still on their feet. I didn't count my rounds, knew I couldn't have more than a dozen shots left if I was lucky.

When the rifle clicked on empty, I swung it at the zed nearest me. The rifle got tangled in the zed's clothing, so I let go and dodged to the side, narrowly missing a petite zed. I pulled out the longer bayonet knife I lifted off the dead soldier and planted it through the zed's eye, and it tumbled backward, collapsing to the ground.

I tried to get closer to the barrack, slashing at zeds, but it was impossible. More zeds were closing in every minute. I was forced to retreat and I ran toward the first Humvee. Manning the .30 cal was Tyler. A soldier leaned against Tyler's back, clutching a neck wound, but still managing to fire rifle shots at zeds coming at them from behind.

Something grabbed my foot, and I looked down to find a zed missing half its torso gnawing on my boot. I lifted my foot and brought it down on its head, breaking its nose. My next stomp was met with a pleasant-sounding crack of its skull fracturing.

I jumped onto the back of Tyler's Humvee. The other soldier had collapsed, either unconscious or dead. I relieved him of his rifle, checked him for ammo (found none), and shoved him off, knowing he could turn any moment.

I hadn't seen Jase yet, so I had to assume he was safely locked inside one of the other barracks. The alternative I couldn't deal with. As for Clutch, I hadn't seen any signs of militia yet, and I prayed that he hadn't been pulled into this cluster fuck.

Zeds, for all their viciousness, had a tough time climbing. Several relentlessly tried to get onto the Humvee but kept falling back. But, it wouldn't take long for enough zeds to surround us that they'd literally get pushed up onto the vehicle.

I searched around the bed of the Humvee for a mag, finding nothing for my rifle, but I did pull out a fresh belt of .30 cal rounds from under the pile of used shells and held it up for Tyler. He fed the belt into the gun, gave me a quick nod, and started firing again.

I noticed the Beretta in his holster and I tapped his arm as a heads up before freeing the pistol from his holster. At the back of the Humvee, I shot any zed that got too close. Then I stopped.

"Fuck," I muttered when I watched the others use the bodies of the fallen to get higher. I swallowed, backed up a step closer to Tyler. We were surrounded on a small island that was about to get a whole lot smaller. I switched from killing zeds to my original plan of kicking them back.

An artillery blast nearby blinded me momentarily, and I remembered Nick's comment about bringing out the heavies. Through the windows of the long barrack, zeds were tearing into the people, ripping them apart like ravenous harpies. Many people had been dismembered, bodies covering the floors like gnarled stumps, while zed continued to feed. Dark blood covered everything.

Even with all the chaos, the noise and smells around the third barrack drew all the zeds to it. Civilians began to emerge from the other barracks, carrying weapons and joining the fray.

My heart lurched. The familiar saunter was unmistakable. *Jase.* I watched as he fought alongside Eddy, each teenager firing his own AR-

15, and Mutt tucked into a pocket, seemingly fearless. "Be safe," I whispered before being forced to deal with my own issues.

I fired my last two bullets into a zed that made it onto the Humvee and resumed kicking the monsters back. My muscles burned and shook from exhaustion, but I kept pushing.

Finally, somehow, the tides began to shift. With the zeds centralized around the third barrack, Tyler shouted commands into his radio, and the troops formed a front against the mass. Soldiers with grenade launchers unleashed a fury of explosions onto the undead invaders.

Tyler's .30 cal clicked on empty. The sudden lack of vibration and noise washed despair over me. Tyler and I shared a knowing glance.

The soldier I'd shoved off the back had turned and now jumped at the truck. Freshly turned zeds were nearly as fast and agile as humans, and it worked its way through the lumbering rotted lot to climb onto the Humvee. It lunged at Tyler first, who was already pulling out his knife. I grabbed the zed's shirt to slow it down. It twisted around and lashed out at me. I jumped back, nearly tumbling off the edge and into the sea of waiting arms. As the zed came at me, Tyler shoved a blade through the skull of what used to be one of Camp Fox's loyal soldiers.

The zed collapsed, and Tyler fell to his knees, his shoulders slumped. "Jonesie was a good man."

I rested a hand on his back.

Tyler's head sagged. "He was the last of my original squad."

I stood there, staring out over the clawed hands reaching for us. Every now and then one fell. Confused, I scanned to find several troops shooting their way toward us. The heaviness from my chest lifted, and I was able to suck in a breath. "Look." I pulled Tyler up. "See? It's going to be okay."

By the time the soldiers reached us, no zeds were left standing. Single shots were fired sporadically as soldiers put down zeds still moving.

I jumped down, stumbling over bodies. The Camp was utter carnage. Blood mixed with brown goo. I searched for signs of Jase, and found him with Eddy, finishing off wounded zeds. I smiled. *You're going to be all right.*

My smile faded when I caught a glimpse of camouflage propped against the side of the barrack, and I burst toward him. But I wasn't fast enough. "Nick!" I cried out right as the badly injured soldier shoved his pistol in his own mouth and pulled the trigger.

I collapsed to my knees.

I never saw the zed until it fell upon me.

Fourteen

I rolled over, kicking away from the zed, and stabbed it through its eye before I realized that someone had already shot it from behind. Brown sludge seeped from the eye like half-set pudding, and I fell onto my butt, gagging at the stench.

"You okay?"

I looked up to see Griz standing before me.

"I am now," I said.

He held out a hand and pulled me up. "Hoorah," he grunted before heading after another zed that needed put down.

I stood near the third barrack—what remained of it, anyway—which was now a giant campfire, with flickers of embers and glints of soot showering us. Corpses covered the ground around me. Most lay unmoving. One zed had a blade through its mouth, pinning it to the ground. It chewed at the handle even while it convulsed and spasmed.

Someone had turned the sirens off, but the remaining sounds—cries of the dying—were heart-wrenching. A woman's weeping drew me to the shadows to my left. I edged closer, keeping the knife ready. She lay amid the corpses, her shoulder and leg badly chewed. She didn't have long before she turned, not with injuries that bad. She was clawing at the dirt with wretched, bloody hands, trying to pull herself toward something. "My baby," she cried over and over.

I frowned and looked to where she was trying to drag herself. A tiny body lay unmoving on the ground, its limbs twisted in unnatural ways.

I kept the knife ready in case the infant had turned, though I supposed it'd have no teeth to bite with. I rolled the baby over to find myself looking at the lifeless eyes of an infant, his fear frozen in his features at death. With such severe injuries, if he were going to turn, he would've by now. I'd seen a handful of people who'd died instead of turning. Maybe their bodies weren't strong enough to support the virus, maybe they had some kind of immunity, who knew. I figured those were the lucky ones.

I lifted the baby's broken body as gently as I could and carried him over to his mother. She reached out with her uninjured arm and pulled him to her. She buried her face in his hair and rocked him, murmuring loving words into his ears.

I left her alone while I went back to where Nick lay propped against the building and got what I needed.

I reloaded the Beretta as I walked toward the woman. Tears blurred my aim, but I was close enough it wouldn't matter. I fired twice at point blank.

Her suffering was over.

A hand touched my shoulder, and I snapped around to see Tyler.

He grabbed my free hand. "Come with me."

He led me down the block. He only let go to shoot a stray zed.

At the end of the block, he commandeered a Jeep. He drove in silence, taking me through the winding roads. As we approached the open square, I stared at the silhouette of the lone gallows under the moonlight.

"You were going to hang me?" I asked. "Is that part of your so-called justice system?"

"It wasn't for you," Tyler said quickly. "It was for a convict who killed one civilian and injured another when they caught him stealing food."

I rode numbly as Tyler drove us to an area of the camp where several large garages stood. In the fence was a gate that had been blasted open.

Tyler parked and looked me over. "Lendt's a stickler for rules, so even though you helped tonight, he'll still have you stand trial. I agree with him that you should stand trial, but the game's changed. But, I also think that, sometimes, the rules need to be broken. With all the chaos, it would've been easy for you to escape."

I cocked my head at Tyler's words.

"Though I wish it wasn't the case, we have to part ways. At least until I can get the charges against you reduced," Tyler said.

Before getting out, I paused. "Take care of Jase. He's a good kid."

Without waiting for a response, I jumped out and set a brisk pace into the darkness.

"Hold up," Tyler said, catching up.

I swallowed, then turned. He handed me another clip and then placed his hand behind my neck and kissed my forehead. "Be careful out there."

I gave a small smile and started walking again.

"Watch your six," Tyler called out behind me.

I paused for a moment, and then took off at a full run through the gate and into the night.

———

The east horizon was growing lighter than the west, meaning that dawn wasn't far behind. I jogged down the road to cover as much distance as possible before the sun would betray me to any Dogs and zeds in the area. I ran around a few zed stragglers on the roads, but didn't stop to kill them, instead, moving as quickly as I could before more showed.

My lungs burned. My body was drenched with sweat, and I'd run less than five miles because I could just make out the outline of Doyle's camp in my path.

I wanted to burst into the camp and save Clutch. Except stupid heroics would only get us both killed. Clutch had always told me to never go on an offensive without being prepared. He'd told me often, "Whatever you didn't plan for, that's what's going to happen." Worse, after the Camp attack (What the fuck was Doyle thinking, to go after Camp Fox like that?), the Dogs would be on high alert, waiting for repercussions, and ready to gun me down the moment I stepped near their camp.

"I'm coming back for you," I promised Clutch and kept jogging.

As the first rays of sunlight ebbed over the horizon, I detoured through a field that had been freshly plowed in the spring but already showed signs of being retaken by prairie grasses. The ground was rough, and I slowed to a walk to not twist an ankle. Within minutes, I entered the woods that lined the field, where the trees could hide me from both zeds and Dogs.

But trees could hide zeds just as well.

When the sun lit up the world, I moved slowly but steadily toward the farm. I figured I had around thirty miles to go, which would take me a full day at the rate I was moving.

Spending a night in the woods with zeds wasn't my idea of fun, but any nearby houses could have Dogs. So I kept moving through the woods like a predator but feeling more like prey.

When I came to a road, I didn't cross. Still too close to Doyle's camp. I walked alongside the highway, weaving through trees until I came to small creek running under the road through a round culvert. Keeping my larger knife firmly in my grip, I crept closer, stepping into the water. Cold water climbed up my legs and trickled down into my boots, and I grimaced. Soggy feet would be hell in a few hours.

I moved slowly to prevent splashing water. Finally, I reached the metal culvert, and thankfully it was empty except for a few inches of water rippling through it.

My throat was parched. I wanted to drink from the stream so badly, but between farm runoff and the potential for zeds or dead bodies to be lying in it upstream, there was too great a risk of dysentery.

The culvert was small. I had to wade through it on my hands and knees, and with every move forward, I prayed that nothing hungry waited on the other side. God, I wished there was another way, but I had to cross. The road curved around to the east, and I needed to go west.

When I came out the other side, it was blissfully peaceful, with nothing but the sounds of the water burbling into the creek below. Feet forward, I pushed myself out but slipped on the wet metal.

I hissed at the sharp pain. "*Shit!*" I watched the blood as it grew from the deep slice across my palm. Red tinted the water as the blood dripped from my hand and washed downstream. Having no gear meant having no first aid kit. I leaned back and held my hand up to slow the bleeding. The cut was deep and wide and would likely get infected if I didn't take care of it properly soon.

The sun was high overhead. My tongue felt like it had doubled in size from dehydration and sat like a giant cotton ball in my mouth. My stomach growled, but hunger was an easier thing to ignore.

With my hand still bleeding, I continued moving through the woods, surprised at the absence of zeds, especially with their seemingly excellent sense of smell. Doyle's Dogs did a hell of a job, either by keeping their area cleaned out or by leading every zed in the area into Camp Fox. Regardless, it made my trip back to the farm easier.

But it wasn't faster. I still had to pause at every tree to scan for movement.

I came across my first zed in the woods sometime during late afternoon. It'd been a man about my age, wearing a sporty T-shirt with a big logo. I couldn't see any injuries. In fact, as the dull infected features went, its were almost gentle behind gold-rimmed sunglasses. That was, until it sniffed the air and snarled.

Taking a breath, I stepped out and it lunged. I jumped around the tree and came up behind the zed, shoved the knife through the base of its skull, and pushed upward.

Its body shuddered, and then collapsed.

Zeds were vicious monsters, but they had their Achilles heels. One of those was that they couldn't corner worth a shit.

I bent down and lifted the zed's left wrist with a silver watch strapped around it. *Five-fifteen.*

Less than three hours until sunset. I was moving slower than I'd planned.

I couldn't make it much longer. I had to find clean water soon. Taking on the risk of creating noise, I moved faster through the woods, sloshing through two more creeks until I stopped at a mulberry bush laden with green and dark berries. Most weren't ripe, but I ate several handfuls, anyway.

With my energy somewhat renewed, I continued searching for a house to stay in for the night. When I finally saw the shape of a house in the distance, I sighed. "Thank God."

I set off into a jog toward the clearing. When I emerged from the woods, I slowed down, and then stopped. "Oh, fuck me."

Because standing before me wasn't just one house. It was Chow Town.

Fifteen

I'd traveled too far north.

Clutch's farm was southwest of town. Camp Fox was southeast of town.

I never should've gotten close to Chow Town.

Without a GPS or compass, I'd let the woods guide me right to the backyard of a large two-story house in a row of cookie-cutter two-story houses in a newer sub-development for as far I could see.

"Sonofabitch."

I walked past the play set and up to the patio door. Certainly, not *all* of these houses had zeds inside. I crossed my fingers. After looking inside and seeing no signs of zeds or violence, I rapped on the glass. A clamor erupted from somewhere deep inside the house.

I sprinted over a short chain-link fence and into the next yard. That was the good thing about zeds. They clung to the *out of sight, out of mind* philosophy and lost focus on their prey quickly if they couldn't see, hear, or smell it. But once they'd homed in on a target, they could be damn near relentless.

I didn't even knock at the next house. I could see overturned chairs, something dead and furry and on the floor, and a shape hovering at the kitchen window. I crept away from the patio door.

Finally, at the fifth house—one with a nice rock garden in its back-yard—I rapped on the glass and waited and rapped again.

Silence greeted me.

Even better, the patio door had been left unlocked, and it slid open silently and smoothly. I pulled out my larger knife and stepped inside, carefully closing and locking the door behind me.

The air was stale and hinted of rotten fruit but didn't contain the all-too-familiar stench of infection and decay.

I tiptoed across the open dining room and noticed drawers left ajar in the kitchen as though someone had left in a hurry. I bypassed the kitchen to the adjacent living room. No signs of struggle. Checked out the hallway, closets, a nicely finished basement, and upstairs. The master bed hadn't been made yet, and several shirts lay strewn across the mattress. "Thank God," I muttered and hustled downstairs. Whoever lived here must've left town as soon as the outbreak hit. If they got lucky, maybe they got to wherever it was they'd been headed.

Back in the kitchen, I turned on the faucet. Nothing, as expected. Before checking the refrigerator for liquids, I walked into the large walk-in pantry and smiled. Inside was bliss. It wasn't fully stocked by any means, but a dozen or so cans of food, several bottles of wine, and a case of flavored water waited on the shelves. I went straight for the water, tearing through the plastic, and grabbed two bottles. I chugged the first down without stopping.

I leaned back against a shelf, careful to avoid the fuzzy green bread. There was enough here to last me a week, maybe longer. Since this neighborhood hadn't been looted yet, the Dogs must've had the same idea as us when it came to Chow Town. The risk of drawing out a herd of zeds in this town was too high to take as long as we could still find food in solitary, secluded farmhouses with no more than a few zeds to deal with at one time.

It was a good reminder that I had to remain silent and unseen. I'd already stirred up zeds in at least three nearby houses. I could only hope they'd given up by now and gone back to lumbering around their homes. They could easily break out of the homes, especially through the all-glass patio doors. Clearly, they hadn't had a reason to...until possibly now.

No matter. I planned to be back to the farm by dark, which was only an hour or so away.

I closed the kitchen blinds and patio shades to hide my movements.

I grabbed a can of fruit cocktail and looked around for a can opener. "Of course," I muttered when I noticed the power opener on the counter. Rather than wasting time hunting around for tools, I opted instead for a jar of peanuts while sipping a second bottle of water.

Finished, I grabbed my knife off the countertop, and headed back up to the master bedroom and adjacent bathroom. I peeled off my clothes caked with sludge, blood, sweat, and dirt.

Without water pressure, a shower was impossible. Instead, I grabbed a half-empty bottle of shampoo and soap from the shower. I dipped a washcloth in the tank behind the toilet and thoroughly scrubbed myself. After I'd used nearly all the water in the tank and made a mess of the floor, I grabbed a tube of Neosporin and Band-Aids for my palm that still oozed blood.

Leaving the wrappers on the counter, I headed into the walk-in closet and sifted through clothes until I found a pair of jeans and a long-sleeved T-shirt that fit. I hurriedly dressed, fastened my belt and weapons, and ventured to the garage. I tapped lightly on the door and heard nothing in response. This time, rather than going slowly, I threw open the door and scanned the three stalls.

I sighed with a smile and leaned back against the wall. Not only was the garage clear, but a Ford sat in one stall. After a quick sweep under the sedan, I opened the car door and a beeping tone reverberated throughout the garage, energetically telling me that both the keys were still in the ignition and the battery wasn't dead. I turned the battery on and found that the car still had over a half tank of gas. I turned off the battery and patted the dash. "You'll do just fine," I said as I hopped back into the house.

It took me several trips to carry all the food to the car. After another search of the house, I found a baseball bat. By then, the sun had long since set. Without knowing the roads—and roadblocks—in this area, I did one final sweep of the house before settling in for the night in an upstairs bedroom facing the street.

Even though there was no way zeds knew where I was, I didn't sleep well. After an especially violent nightmare of Clutch being attacked by zeds, I shot awake as dawn was just beginning to light up the street.

I went down on a knee to look out the window, and fell back on my butt. Now, at least twenty zeds milled around the street below me, sniffing the air, as though sensing prey in the area. Their sheer numbers could crush the car with me in it.

I cupped my head in my hands. *How the fuck...*

After watching the herd for over an hour, I accepted the fact that they weren't going anywhere, and I changed my bandages and ate cereal out of the box.

And waited.

Their numbers never changed throughout the day. Some came, some went. Zeds shuffled in lazy circles as though waiting for food to come to them.

It wasn't until night returned that something snagged their attention and the street cleared except for a few stragglers. *Now.* I hustled to the garage. When I opened the car door, something thumped on the other side of the garage door.

I stood there, holding my breath.

Another thump.

I edged closer to the garage door and inched onto my toes to peer out the high windows. Under the moonlight, I could see a single zed on the other side, but as it banged at the door, it drew the attention of others. I came back down on my heels, my breath coming in short pants. Soon, a second pair of fists joined the first at the door.

"Shit!" I whispered.

If I waited any longer, the noise could draw out every zed in the area. It probably wouldn't take more than the weight of twenty or so to push in a garage door.

They had me exactly where they wanted me: in a gift box, ready to open.

I did a slow three-sixty, looking for anything to distract the zeds, trying to concentrate above the ruckus.

Then it hit me.

Get 'em where I want 'em.

I wanted them as far from the garage as possible.

I went back to the car, pulled out the bat and headed back into the house. I headed down the hallway and to the office near the front door. I took a swing and smashed the front windows. *Home run.*

I rushed back to the garage, looked out through the windows and found the thumping had stopped. I tossed the bat onto the front seat and grabbed the cord on the garage door.

One, two, three.

I yanked the cord, and the door opened with a clatter. I jumped into the car and slammed the door shut as I slid the key into the ignition. The car roared to life, and I had the tires squealing in reverse.

A zed slammed into the car before I was out of the garage. The car lurched over its body. More zeds shuffled from the darkness, filling the street with their relentless groans. As soon as I was on the street, I slammed on the brakes, shoved the car into drive, and rammed into zeds head-on.

The car snagged on bodies as I drove over them, and the right wheel ended up off the ground, leaving only the left front wheel with any traction, and it was burning rubber uselessly. I rocked the car between gears, using reverse and forward to try to nudge free like I was stuck in snow.

By now, the zeds that I'd drawn to the house had turned their attention to the car. The window behind me shattered. I pulled out my Beretta while keeping my foot on the gas. Zeds pushed against the car as they tried to get to me from all sides. The extra weight pushed the car forward, and the right tire caught traction. The car took off, pitching to a near stop when plowing through a wall of zeds trying to block me in.

Somehow, the car made it through and the strays slid off the hood. I took the first right, realizing too late that it was a cul-de-sac. "Fuck!" Spinning around, I got back on the main street.

When the number of zeds dissipated, I chanced a glance in the rearview mirror. One reached out to me under the moonlight. It looked young—too much like Jase—though months in the sun had baked its skin into a jaundiced husk.

I sped away. Since I was on the edge of town, it took only three turns, some lawn driving around a roadblock, and a couple curb-checks before Chow Town disappeared behind me.

I drove west until I came to a familiar stretch of road. The car made a clacking sound and the steering wheel shuddered if I went over twenty, not that I could drive any faster without headlights, which would give away my location. According to the car's clock, it took me over an hour to make it to the gravel road the farm was on.

As I turned onto the gravel road, I slammed on the brakes. Taillights in the distance signaled a vehicle leaving the farm. After the taillights disappeared and no other lights appeared, I crept forward and parked the car by the garage of Jase's old house, making sure it was hidden from the road. After a wistful glance at the beat-up sedan with an arm caught in the bumper, I stepped into the night.

I didn't like the idea of walking at night, but I couldn't risk driving into an ambush at the farm. The smell of smoke was strong in the air, and a bad feeling formed in my gut.

As I closed the distance between Jase's house and Clutch's farm, the smell of smoke grew stronger every minute. When I noticed the garbage truck had been shoved into the ditch, I avoided the lane and walked through a field that never got planted and into the trees enclosing the farm. I crept soundlessly through the woods, expecting a zed to pop out from behind every tree.

Not a single zed sniffed me out, likely thanks to the blanket of smoke over the area. Soon, I could see a glow through the trees and hear the crackle of a large campfire. I cautiously moved close enough to see the yard.

Or what was left of it. I gasped and covered my mouth. "*No.*"

The Dogs had burned everything to the ground.

Sixteen

I gripped the baseball bat as I fell to my knees. The house was nothing but a charred framework and a pile of burning ash and blackened debris with still-glowing embers.

This farm had become my home when the outbreak hit. It was a fortress. I was safe here. Months of hard work, the supplies, weapons, all the food we'd stored, *gone*.

It made no sense. Clutch had willingly joined the Dogs. Why would they destroy his farm? They wouldn't do something like this to one of their own. Which meant...

"No." I had to lean on the bat to keep from collapsing.

Clutch was dead.

I clenched my eyes closed. If only I'd gotten here earlier. If I'd returned to the farm last night, I could've prevented this somehow.

I chortled. Who was I kidding?

Like I could've single-handedly held back the Dogs.

Furious, I pulled myself back to my feet. In the distance, I saw two men with shaved heads leaning against their truck parked in the lane several hundred feet away. Too far away for me to overhear their conversation. I looked for more Dogs but found none.

I heard a rustle to my right and saw three zeds encircle me, groaning through jaws that no longer worked. They were badly burned, their arms and faces charred.

I grabbed the baseball bat and swung, crushing the first zed's skull like it was a T-ball. The second zed was on me too quickly and I kicked its ankles together, knocking its feet out from under it. I left it floundering on the ground, while I swung at the third, nailing it in the chest. The force knocked it back, and my second swing crumpled its head.

After smashing the zed on the ground, I turned back to the house.

All the food, weapons...*gone.*

Everything Clutch, Jase, and I had built was destroyed. The Dogs had burned the fuel tanks, and it looked like the explosions took down two of the three sheds. Only the smallest shed still stood, though its door was open, and I suspected any valuable contents gone. They'd even slashed the tires on the poor Prius.

After giving the house a final brokenhearted look, I headed past the burnt gardens, careful to keep the still-burning house between the Dogs and me, and cautiously around the backside of the largest shed, held up only by Clutch's combine. Feathers littered the ground, though I couldn't find any sign of the chickens.

Coming down on a knee, I pulled at the tin and debris as quietly as possible. Blood dripped from my hand. When I finally pulled away the last bit of plywood, I sighed in relief.

The Dogs hadn't discovered Clutch's TEOTWAWKI bunker.

I opened the round door and climbed down a few steps. With one final look around, I noticed the Dogs were still lounging by their truck, and I tugged the plywood up so it'd cover the bunker door.

"Damn Dogs," I muttered before shutting the door and descending into the darkness.

Knowing I was secure, I curled up on the floor and slept.

That was, until the door overhead opened.

SEVENTEEN

"Why the hell didn't you lock the door?" Clutch demanded in a gruff whisper, the moonlight casting him in an imposing silhouette.

"Clutch?" I asked, pointing the Beretta at him.

"Lower the gun, Cash. I'm coming down," he replied before closing —and locking—the door above him.

A lantern in Clutch's hand suddenly cast a gentle glow in the small space.

"I forgot the door locked," I said in a daze as I watched him climb down the ladder. Sweat glistened off his shaved head. Then I dropped the pistol and jumped him from behind. "You're alive!"

He was hot and sweaty and I didn't care. He turned around and pulled me into a full embrace.

"How?" I asked, holding on tight.

He rubbed my shoulder. "Doyle sent out most of his Dogs that first night. He left me in the silo with only one guard." He paused. "I got out. That's all that matters."

I pulled back to look at him. Emotion laced his words. "Let me guess. You pissed off Doyle in the process."

"Yeah." He ran a hand over his now-shaved head and grimaced, like he didn't enjoy the feel. "Were you here when they..."

"No," I replied quickly. "I got here after."

"Good." He paused. "Jase?"

"He's at Camp Fox. He's safe."

Clutch sighed, and then looked around. "We can't stay here. Dogs will be sniffing around my farm until I'm caught or dead. There were two waiting outside tonight."

Probably the same two that I'd seen. "I'm glad you're here," I said softly. I felt safe with Clutch in this bunker, but I'd already realized it could all too easily become our tomb. Only one way in or out. Only one air vent that could be too easily blocked from the outside.

He slid to the floor. "The captain let you go?" he asked gruffly.

"Yeah."

"Good. I couldn't tell if he was playing to get you away from Doyle or if he was actually thinking of arresting you."

"He let me go," I said instead, sitting back down. Clutch didn't need to be burdened with the details. Not with his home lying in ruins above our heads. I wrinkled my nose. "You smell."

He grunted, resting his head against the wall. "Thirty-six hours in the woods will do that."

I grabbed a bottle of water and tapped it on his arm. "Here."

He took the bottle, and then grabbed my wrist. "What's this?"

I tugged back my injured hand. "Just a cut I picked up yesterday."

"Why weren't you wearing your gloves?" He narrowed his eyes and frowned. "Whose clothes are those?"

I shrugged.

"Hell." His jaw clenched. "Masden didn't let you go, did he?"

"He let me go," I replied. "I just had to find my own way back home."

Clutch pounded the floor. "Sonofabitch. When I find him, I'm going—"

"You're going to do nothing," I interrupted. "We've got enough shit to deal with right now than take on Camp Fox, don't you think?"

"And your gear?" he asked, hoarsely.

"Somewhere at Camp Fox."

Clutch glared for a moment before taking a long draw of water and leaning his head back again, eyes closed. When his eyes opened, he leveled a hard gaze on me. "You all right now?"

I smiled and moved to sidle up next to him. "Yeah, I'm okay." I laid my uninjured hand on his knee. "You?"

He grunted again—his typical response of consent—and rolled up his sleeve. "I got lucky."

My eyes widened. "Holy shit."

There, on his forearm, was a dark bruise in the perfect semi-circle outline of human teeth.

"I was lucky I had long sleeves. But still, when they lock on, they bite hard. The bastards have got jaws like pit bulls."

I gingerly touched the marks and whistled. "I think you got *very* lucky."

"Your turn." He nodded to my hand.

"I cleaned it this morning," I said as I pulled back the first Band-Aid. Even in the dim light, the skin around the cut was red and swollen.

His brow furrowed. He grabbed a first aid kit off a shelf and motioned for my hand.

I held it out, and he gently peeled off each Band-Aid. He pulled out a small plastic bottle and poured it into my palm. I hissed as liquid fire shot through my arm. "Jesus, Clutch. Are you trying to kill me?"

"It's just alcohol. Don't be a baby."

I wasn't being a baby. It seriously *burned*. He dabbed a cotton swab at it until the sharp agonizing pain numbed into a constant throb. He covered my palm with a bandage and wrapped gauze around it.

"I'll clean your cut again in the morning," He said after putting the kit back.

Then he grabbed my uninjured hand and rested his forehead against it.

I rubbed his thumb. "It'll be okay." And I meant it. I knew that as long as Clutch was with me, everything would be fine.

He chuckled drily, the sound devoid of humor. "We've got no weapons, no food, no shelter. Doyle crippled us with one easy blow. Jase is at Camp Fox. And Masden made it clear that if we go after Doyle, we're attacking Camp Fox."

"Doyle's no longer with Camp Fox," I said. "He zed-bombed them a few hours after we were separated."

"Jesus." Clutch's muscles tensed under me. "So that's where the Dogs went."

"I guess Doyle saw a shot and took it."

"Were you there?" he asked quietly.

I nodded and laid my head on his shoulder. "They lost one of their barracks along with several troops in the attack." I thought of Nick. "They lost some good folks."

"The Camp will be better prepared against Doyle next time."

"You sure there will be a next time?"

"Yeah, I'm sure," he said, his voice low. "Doyle has a hard view on how to survive, and he assumes everyone will see that he's right." He chuckled. "He actually believed I'd willingly join his Dogs. Doesn't matter now. The only good thing is that Doyle will no longer get support from Camp Fox. I bet Lendt's guys are keeping the Dogs running as we speak. That should distract Doyle enough until we can secure a new location. We'll scout out places in the morning. How are we on weapons?"

"I've got a Beretta with nine rounds, a baseball bat, and two knives. And whatever else you have."

"It's not enough," he said.

"It'll be enough," I said, snuggling closer. I wasn't worried. I had Clutch back. I knew everything would be okay, and I found myself falling soundly asleep, safe in his arms.

———

I woke up with my entire body stiff from lying on hard, damp concrete. Being underground, I had no idea what time it was. I could've been asleep for only an hour or ten hours. I'd slept soundly, except for when Clutch's nightmares began, and I'd held onto him until he fell back into a more peaceful sleep.

Unfortunately, PTSD isn't curable. It's a way of life.

Clutch was already awake and heating something in a tin can. When he noticed I was awake, he tossed me a Gatorade. I caught it with my injured hand and winced. He then handed me a metal spork and a tin can wrapped with a towel.

I yawned. "What time is it?"

Clutch put another can on the tiny stove and glanced at his watch. "Five-forty. It should still be dark enough to take out the Dogs that are topside before they see us."

After we ate our refried beans, Clutch rummaged through the shelves and pulled out a shotgun that had been vacuum-sealed in plastic. He loaded several shells into it. "I go first. If there's more than two, we'll wait them out. You stay by the shed and take out any Dogs who try to get away."

I checked the Beretta and grabbed the baseball bat. "Ready."

Clutch slung the shotgun over his shoulder and climbed the ladder. At the top, he slowly unlocked and opened the door a couple inches. No light came in. After a long moment, he held up a single finger and pointed to my right.

Only one Dog? Could we get that lucky?

I followed up the ladder and outside. The cool, damp morning breeze swept away any lingering sleepiness as I crawled behind a pile of tin while Clutch moved toward a four-by-four truck sitting in the drive. The Dog was sitting in his truck, facing away from us and watching the driveway.

It was too easy. Clutch snuck up behind the truck and had the shotgun leveled point blank through the open window before the Dog even noticed.

"Hands on your head," Clutch ordered.

The Dog obeyed instantly. Clutch opened the truck door and stepped to the side. "Out of the truck and on your knees."

"Don't shoot!" the scrawny teen cried as he fell from the truck and onto his knees. An AR-15 tumbled harmlessly off his lap.

"How many are with you?" Clutch asked, kicking the rifle away.

"I'm alone. I swear it," the guy answered, keeping his hands on his head. "Please don't kill me."

"I won't if you keep telling the truth," Clutch said.

"You...you won't?" The young man sounded genuinely surprised.

I could've asked Clutch the same thing. I scanned the area and saw a shape shambling around the edge of the woods. I pulled out the bat and stalked toward it while keeping an eye on the Dog kneeling before Clutch.

"I'm going to ask you some questions," Clutch said. "Take my advice. Don't lie."

The Dog nodded furiously.

"What are your orders?"

"Wa-watch for you. Call in if I see you."

"That's all?"

"Yes!"

"Why are you alone?"

The Dog didn't answer.

"Don't make me repeat myself," Clutch said.

"Camp Fox invaded our camp," the kid quickly replied. "A lot of guys are busy relocating their families."

The zed had noticed the two men and was making its way toward them. At first, I thought it was bloated, but then I realized it was pregnant, probably near-term when it'd been bitten. Bile rose in my throat as I readied the bat. A purse hung across the zed's body, and it hobbled in one sandal. It hissed and turned to me when I approached. I swung. Its head broke open like a beanbag.

"When's the next shift arrive?" Clutch asked, turning back to the Dog after watching me kill the zed.

"Eight o'clock," he replied, his voice cracking.

When I approached the Dog from behind, Clutch nodded, and I disarmed him, startling him. The Dog was young, not much older than Jase, and obviously scared shitless.

"Cripes, kid," Clutch said. "You're too young to be caught up with the likes of Doyle."

The Dog jutted out his chin. "Doyle saved my life. We're going to make Fox Hills safe again."

"Keep telling yourself that, kid," Clutch said.

I lifted a two-way radio I'd found on the Dog's belt.

Clutch narrowed his eyes. "How often do you report in?"

The Dog swallowed. "The bottom of every hour."

Clutch glanced at his watch. "Looks like you got seven minutes. What's the code for all-clear?"

He didn't answer.

"The code for all-clear?" Clutch asked more firmly, lifting his shotgun.

"The eagle soars," he replied quickly.

Clutch held out the two-way radio. "Report in. This time, with the *right* code for all-clear, and I'll let your last fib pass."

The Dog's jaw dropped before he snapped it shut. He nodded tightly. He took the radio, took a deep breath, and clicked the side. "Hamster reporting in. Over."

"Base. Report. Over."

"The swallow has flown, repeat, the swallow has flown. Over."

A slight pause.

"Affirmative. The swallow has flown. Over."

The Dog handed the radio back to Clutch.

"You aren't a bad kid. It's too bad you got hooked up with Doyle."

"I owe my life to Doyle," he replied.

"And he's made sure he gets exactly that from you," Clutch said. "Dammit, kid. You shouldn't have lied on the radio."

"Wha—what?" The Dog's wide eyes shot up. "No!" he cried out the instant before Clutch blew his brains out.

My mouth fell open.

Clutch slung his shotgun back over his shoulder. "The Dogs need to work on their codes. The Swallow Has Flown is an acronym for the Shit's

Hit the Fan. Code 101." He kicked at the gravel. "Goddammit, kid, why'd you have to go and force my hand?"

"How much time do you think we have?" I asked, staring at the Dog's body.

"If he was telling the truth that Lendt hit Doyle's Camp, then it may take them awhile. Then again, they could have a unit close by already."

"We better hurry, then."

We ran back to the bunker. Clutch disappeared inside and came back seconds later with a stuffed backpack. He fastened the door closed and set a combination lock that I hadn't noticed on top of the door before. We covered the door with tin and debris.

Clutch eyed his big rig, which looked like the Dogs had fun taking a bulldozer to it. "She was a good rig," he growled.

"We'll take the Dog's truck," I offered, not seeing Clutch's pickup truck or Jeep anywhere. "I left a car at Jase's house along with enough supplies to get us by for a few days."

We sprinted back to the truck and tore down the lane. Clutch turned onto the gravel road, and fortunately, there was no dust in either direction indicating that Dogs were on their way. "We got lucky this morning," Clutch said.

"I'll take every bit of luck I can get," I said.

Clutch nodded. "We can't risk stopping and grabbing the car right now. We'll come back for everything else in the bunker and the car after we've secured a new location."

I leaned back, a weight on my chest. I'd already been thinking through how soon I had to transplant the seeds from the garden before it was too late. Not to mention having to start all over with looting runs. It was hard the first time, when we had so much to work with. Now? We were fucked. I swallowed. "Any thoughts on where we can hide that's safe from Dogs?"

Clutch shrugged. "They avoid Chow Town."

"Oh, hell, no," I said in a rush. When he eyed me suspiciously, I tacked on, "Trust me."

"Any farm we move to won't be any safer than mine was," he said. "That leaves our only option to head out of the area. Or...wait a second." He snapped his fingers. "I got it."

He cranked a hard left on the next road and stepped on the gas.

"Where are we headed?"

"Fox National Park. It's as far from any town as we can get without venturing into unknown territory."

Thirty minutes later, we drove through the park's winding narrow roads. Clutch took us deep and high into the hilly park, and we saw no zeds, though I knew the monsters lurked in these woods just like they had everywhere else. Clutch stopped at the DNR office that seemed to be near the park's highest point. Only a park ranger's truck sat outside.

"This might be the best location for our camp," Clutch said, reloading his shotgun. "We'll check the cabins, too. They should keep keys to all the cabins somewhere inside."

I looked around. The A-line cabin sat on a ledge, leaving only three sides vulnerable to zeds. The narrow park roads would be easy enough to block. The place gave me a good vibe. I picked up the rifle I'd lifted from the Dog. "Let's do this."

Birds chirped in the distance, and a warm breeze blew scents of evergreens over me. Side-by-side, we moved to the two-story cabin.

Clutch checked the door. It opened.

He glanced at me, and I nodded, clutching the rifle. He rapped on the window. Nothing. He rapped again. Still nothing.

After a moment of waiting, Clutch took the lead inside. A familiar stench polluted the air. *Dammit.*

Clutch grimaced.

I sighed before calling out, "Hey, stinkface. Where are you?"

Something shuffled from above. My gaze shot upward to see a lone zed move around the open loft. It was wearing a brown DNR uniform and had wild, shaggy hair. It groaned and tried to walk toward us, but the railing stopped it. It continued to batter the railing, reaching out, until finally it toppled over and crashed to the ground floor.

The zed landed head-first, the impact sounding like a shattered light bulb. Its brittle skull collapsed into itself.

"That was easy," I said. Then the stench hit me. I pinched my nose. "God, that's awful."

Clutch held his forearm over his nose. "Let's hurry up and get Smelly outside."

Each grabbing a foot, we dragged the corpse outside and sent it off the deep slope that went off each side of the cabin. It tumbled down, disappearing into the trees below.

The rest of the office was thankfully clear, and the zed had made surprisingly little mess upstairs.

"He was here alone," I said.

"He must've gotten infected before he came into work."

We stood on the second floor, looking out through the two-story window over the wide expanse of the park. Trees went on for as far as the eye could see. No signs of violence.

"I like it here," I said.

"Yeah. Me, too," Clutch replied.

It was even more peaceful than the farm. Here, it was as though we were alone, free, and safe. As long as everyone thought we were dead, we had a chance.

But, we weren't safe.

Because as long as Doyle and the zeds were still out there, we'd never be safe.

Part Eight
Malice

The Eighth Circle of Hell

Eighteen

Ten days later

The wet spring had turned into a humid summer. The park was lush and green, with only the sounds of nature as background music.

It was a pleasant mirage.

Clutch and I tried to make the best of the shitty situation. Despite having no fences, the park turned out to be a decent camp, its hills a natural deterrent to zeds. Another huge perk: the park's water supply was fed by a rural water tower, so water had suddenly become the least of our worries.

We were careful in our movements in case any Dogs passed through. After losing our stockpile, we had to start nearly from scratch. Fortunately, one of the rooms in the park's DNR office contained boxes of stuff either left at the park or confiscated by park rangers.

I used several hours of sunlight every day fishing and setting snares. But, living on protein alone was draining us, especially with the exercise regimen Clutch had us on. In just over a week, I noticed I had less stamina and energy. Even the cut on my hand was taking longer to heal.

I'd been sifting through the park's library to find out which plants and berries were edible in the area. The park no doubt had a wealth of food that could be eaten, but getting to it was the challenge. There was no telling what trees a zed could be lurking behind. And so I started to dig up soil around the edges of the office's parking lot for a new garden.

"Ready to hit the road?" Clutch said, coming down the stairs.

He looked set for battle in his camos while I'd been stuck in the same designer jeans for the past ten days, though we'd both been wearing T-shirts from the gift shop.

I grabbed the plastic water bottles I'd been refilling every day. "Ready."

Clutch gave a quick nod and headed for the door. Stubble covered his head now and would be as long as my thicker hair in no time.

"We need fuel," he said over his shoulder. "The truck has less than a half tank left."

"Seeds are critical, too," I added. "Ooh, and gardening tools. Maybe a net. Definitely food. Weapons would be nice."

Clutch raised a brow. "Anything else?"

I smirked. "I'll be sure to let you know." I followed him to the truck. "Do you know any farms in the area?"

He shook his head. "No, but there's a gas station not far from here. It was a hotspot for day-trippers loading up on ice and beer before heading into the park. They might also have some camping supplies."

I climbed in and rolled down the window. "Did you bring the hose?"

He held up a five-foot length of rubber water hose I'd found at the office and cut into sections. My life had become a state of improvising. Finding tools or weapons in everything.

He started the engine. "If we can get gas from the tanks, then we'll be able to head farther out for your wish list items. It's pretty rural around here and far enough away from where Doyle's camp was that it may still be good for looting without running into anyone."

As Clutch weaved through the maze he'd been making of the park roads, I kept an eye out for intruders. When I was working on food, he was busy blocking off the roads and marking safe routes on park maps. The roadblocks signaled that there were survivors in the park, but—more important—the roadblocks would slow down zeds and especially Dogs in getting to us.

Only three zeds had passed near the park office since we moved there, and they'd been on the roads. Since the roadblocks went up, no zeds had passed through. We figured the hills and trees caused too many problems for the decomposing shamblers, so they likely wouldn't show up at the office unless they were lost or had homed in on us. And we were far enough inside the camp, that zeds should have no way of hearing, seeing, or smelling us.

Still, without much for weapons, we'd been brainstorming ways to corral zed stragglers into traps. We had plenty of ideas, but so far no manpower or tools to make anything work.

We passed several of the park's cabins in the heart of the park. With over two dozen buildings, we could set up a small town of survivors here, though the park's rough and wooded landscape wasn't exactly ideal for growing food or scouting for zeds. When I mentioned the idea of bringing others onto the park, Clutch changed the subject. I suspected the loss of Jase to Camp Fox had hit him harder than he let on.

Ever since the run-in with Doyle, Clutch's PTSD had worsened. His nightmares lasted longer, and during the days, he often had a distant look. Whatever had happened had really hit Clutch hard. Since he refused to talk about it, all I could do was hope that time would help heal the wounds on his soul.

I pointed to a cabin nearly hidden by trees. "That's our bug out cabin, right?"

"Yeah. You're starting to get the park figured out."

I smiled and leaned back. Clutch had covered more of the park than I had so far. He'd found us the most secluded rendezvous cabin should we get separated and couldn't get back to the office. He'd shown it to me a couple times already, but it was easy to get lost in hundreds of wooded acres with no straight roads.

I noticed the time on the truck's clock. "Oh, it's almost nine."

"Got it." He clicked on the radio to AM 1340. Every day, for a mid-morning break, we'd sit in the truck to listen to Hawkeye's broadcasts.

Like clockwork, the usual static silenced in favor of a voice. The broadcaster was either a hundred miles away or had poor equipment. We could barely hear his broadcast unless we turned the radio all the way up.

"This is Hawkeye broadcasting on AM 1340.

I have more news about zed-free zones for you. It sounds like Montana has built a city with high walls. But, if you are thinking of making the trip to Montana City, think again. Right now, they are only allowing Montana citizens into the city. Anyone else will be turned away. But, what's important is that there are zed-free zones out there. There is hope from the plague monsters wandering our lands.

For news closer to home, Lt. Col. Lendt's announcement last week that requires any Iowa militia to be commanded by a military officer has stirred backlash across the state. I've heard rumors that some militias are banding together against Camp Fox rather than submitting to Lendt's power play.

The militias are made up of good people, folks who've stepped up and volunteered to fight against the zed scourge. And now the government is trying to control them.

Here's my question for today: if all militias are forced to report into Camp Fox, what's to stop Lendt from misusing his power and becoming a despot over us survivors? I leave you with a warning: absolute power corrupts absolutely, my friends.

This is Hawkeye broadcasting on AM 1340. Be safe, stay strong, and know that you're not alone."

Hawkeye rarely had good news and showed no love for Lendt, but the final words he spoke every day grounded me.

You're not alone.

Even though we hadn't seen another living soul for ten days.

A large sign displaying gas prices that would never change again peeked out from the trees. As we neared the station, the stink hit me, and I wrinkled my nose. "Oh, that's horrible."

"Jesus," Clutch said, holding his forearm over his nose. "Smells like the sewer backed up."

"Lovely," I muttered. Add one more annoying trait of the apocalypse to an every-growing list.

Today, we at least had the benefit of dealing with fewer zeds at the gas station than we would have if the outbreak had hit during tourist season. Even so, there were still a half-dozen cars in the lot. Four zeds wandering nearby bee-lined for our truck the moment we approached. One was covered in dried mud, one was naked and chewed up, and all four were shriveled by months under the sun.

"How the hell do some of these guys end up naked?" I asked. Seeing a zed was bad enough. Seeing *all* of a zed was enough to make a stomach roil.

Clutch shrugged. "Caught on the shitter, maybe."

They stumbled in our direction as though coming to greet us, and Clutch stepped on the gas, taking down two with his first hit. He put the truck into reverse and rammed into the third. The naked zed moved too slowly and was too far away to be a problem.

Clutch stopped near the underground gas tank cover.

I swung open the door and clobbered the female zed struggling to get up with two newly broken legs. Clutch was out of the truck with a tire iron and taking down the least rotted of the bunch, and I walked up to the crusty mud-covered zed and gagged.

Shit. Not mud. My eyes watered, and I swung extra hard to make sure I finished it off quickly and moved away.

When I turned to Clutch, he was just finishing off the naked zed that had finally reached us.

"Keep an eye out." He got down on his knees and pulled out his knife.

I stood at his back, gripping the bat covered in layers of dark stains, and analyzed the wide one-story building. The gas station was covered in slate and had three glass doors, one to each section: the gas station in the middle, the liquor side to the left, and a small café to the right. The glass was shattered on the large door to the gas station. Two zeds lay dead in the shadow of the overhang.

"Damn," I muttered. "Looks like we aren't the first here."

With some muscle, he pried the cover open and peered inside. "At least there's plenty of gas."

"How do you know it's not diesel?" I asked.

"Smells like gas," he replied, going for the hose. He dropped one end into the underground tank, and held out the other with a smirk. "Want to do the honors?"

I handed him the bat and grabbed the hose. "Sure." I opened the gas cap, and then sucked hard at the hose.

I'd never siphoned gas before, but it looked to be a relatively easy thing to do.

Nothing happened.

I looked up.

He smirked. "Keep sucking."

I scowled but did what he said. At first there was nothing, then came the fumes, then the liquid.

"Ack!" I coughed out in between spitting out gasoline and shoving the hose into the truck's gas tank. Tears ran down my face. "That shit burns." More coughing.

Clutch chuckled while he pulled out a five-gallon red gas can from the back of the truck. "That's why I didn't want to do it."

I flipped him the bird before spitting again. At least I couldn't smell the sewage anymore. "Next time, you siphon," I muttered when I could speak again.

After we finished fueling and resealed the underground tank, Clutch backed the truck up to the building. When he jumped out, he looked at me. "Ready to do this?"

I blew out a lungful of air. "Yup."

It was times like these when I especially missed the farm. We'd had enough weapons and ammunition to start a small war, over six months' supply of food stockpiled, and had it secure as any place could be without being a high-security prison. We'd reached the point where we didn't have to go into high-risk places like these to survive. I sighed. We had no choice now.

We either adapted or we'd die.

I held the baseball bat tight in my grip as Clutch rapped on the broken glass, sending several shards crashing onto the concrete. Every sound was razor blade to my nerves.

A distant thump greeted us. There was definitely something waiting inside. Clutch gave me one more look before stepping through the door. I quickly followed and pulled back the bat to swing, but no zeds attacked. Instead, a stack of pastel Easter bunnies smiled at us in front of long aisles shrouded in shadows.

The place gave me the creeps.

Whoever had come here before us couldn't have left with much. All of the shelves looked fully stocked. When I noticed the cash register open and a near-empty shelf of Marlboros, I rolled my eyes. Money and cigarettes. Whoever had that kind of shit for brains was likely shuffling around the countryside now.

Then again, their idiocy was a good sign. It meant more goodies for us.

"I look out, you fill?"

I turned to see that Clutch had grabbed all the plastic bags off the counter. I swiped a small item from a shelf behind the counter, pocketed it, gripped the bat, and did a three-sixty to scan for zeds. Hearing no signs of any predators—other than the constant thumping coming from the back of the store, I grabbed the bags.

"Let's do this."

With tension prickling my nerves, I started in the grocery aisle, filling up five bags with soup, canned meat, saltines, and anything else with a decent shelf life. The bags were flimsy and couldn't hold much weight, and I slid each bag onto my arm to start another. I skipped most of the candy bars, instead going for nuts and fruit chews. Then, out to the truck to drop off full bags and back inside for more.

While grabbing batteries, something thumped on the bathroom door behind us, startling me. Memories from a different bathroom on the day of the outbreak doused me with ice, and I dropped a bag.

"Don't worry. It can't get out," Clutch said, picking up the bag.

"I know." I hastily grabbed a few bottles of water, more for the reusable bottles than for the water and made another drop of supplies into the back of the truck.

After two more trips, one to the automotive aisle and one for soap and cleaning supplies, I leaned against the truck. "What else?"

"The best part." He headed left, and I followed him into the liquor section. Most of the top shelves were empty, and several bottles were broken on the floor. Clutch slid the bat under an arm and grabbed a couple bottles of whiskey and I pointed at the Everclear. He dumped the bottles into bags, and I grunted at the weight.

I glanced out the front window to find the parking lot still wide open. "Still looking good. Knock on wood."

Clutch shot me a glare. "Cash, don't jinx us," he warned.

I shook my head. For being a badass, he sure was superstitious. Smirking, I followed him back through the gas station and toward the front door. Before stepping through, I had a feeling of being watched and I paused. I looked to my left toward the café.

"Clutch," I whispered, and he stepped back in.

"What is it?"

I glanced at him before looking again.

A glass door separated it from the rest of the station. When we'd first entered, it was empty. Now, on the other side, two jaundiced pairs of eyes stared at us. Two zeds—one who'd been a boy no more than twelve and one who'd been a slightly younger girl—stood. They were likely siblings, with the same hair color and similar features, but it was always hard to tell after bodies started to decompose.

Neither moved nor pounded on the glass. They simply watched. That was eerie enough. But what spooked me more was that they were holding hands.

Clutch tugged me outside. "Let's get out of here."

Nineteen

It had been a surprisingly low-key day. Zeds were blissfully few and far between, and we'd yet to see a Dog.

After the gas station, we hit two farms. The first was a quaint white house with an old couple inside who'd taken fate into their own hands by blowing out their brains. They were ripe, had likely killed themselves not long after the outbreak. Annoying flies buzzed around my head while I said a silent prayer for them.

"...Amen." I tugged the shotgun from the old man's stiff grip and went about my looting.

We'd gained some spices, home-canned foods, and much-needed canning supplies (even though neither Clutch nor I had any idea how to can), taking a load off our biggest stressor of not having any way to store food for the winter. The old couple had also been avid gardeners, but all the sprouts in the garage had long since wilted from lack of water. I'd found a few packets of squash and several gardening tools. It was a start.

At the next farm, the only sign of the outbreak were two graves with blades of grass just starting to break through the dirt. Hope pinged at my heart for the survivor who'd dug these graves. We'd spent several minutes calling out and searching, but no one answered.

Inside, we found the cabinets empty and little else in the house. Though, I discovered that the clothes in a teenager's room were a near perfect fit, even though they were boy's clothes. When I stripped out of my jeans, I paused in front of the mirror on the back of the door.

I had a solid farmer's tan from spending nearly every day in the sun without sunscreen. Messy dark spikes did nothing to soften my blunt features. My curves had disappeared, leaving behind straight, hard lines. No wonder I could wear a boy's clothes. Sure, Clutch had become leaner, too, but he'd been in good shape before so the change didn't seem so severe. Me? Even my parents wouldn't recognize me.

Mia Ryan truly was gone.

In a daze, I emptied the pockets of my old jeans, grabbed an armful of new clothes, and headed outside.

Frowning, I scanned the open area. "Clutch?"

He poked around the corner of a tin building, and he was grinning like a schoolboy. "There's a fuel farm here. They've got an entire tank of gasoline. You won't have to suck gas for a while."

I couldn't help but return his smile. Another backup plan to our backup plans. "I'll mark it on the map. But *you're* sucking gas next time."

By the time we had everything unpacked at the park, it was time to cook my morning catch: two trout, one bass, and a small rabbit. It was a typical meal. Most days we burned more calories than we took in.

Every day, I'd wait until twilight to start a fire, when the darkness smothered the smoke, though I couldn't do anything about the smell of fire attracting notice downwind. After a couple dismal failures in the first days at the park, I had finally gotten the hang of cooking meats so that they'd last through the next evening.

It was the first night in a long time we had seasonings for our meat. I closed my eyes. "Mm, I never knew salt could be so decadent."

Clutch leaned back, rubbed his shoulder, and took a long swig of amber whiskey.

"Oh. I almost forgot..." I reached in my pocket and threw the can at Clutch. "Happy birthday."

He frowned. "My birthday's in December."

I shrugged. "I had no idea when it was, so I took a guess."

He looked at the can of chewing tobacco and smiled. "My brand, even."

I smiled. "I know."

He tucked it into his pocket.

"You're not going to open it?" I asked.

"Nope," he replied with a smile. "I'm saving it."

After a moment, he came to his feet and stared out the window. The park office had no generator. The two-story A-line window of the cabin faced the west, so we had plenty of light up until sunset. After the sun went down, we either had to use precious batteries (we had even fewer candles) or get by in the dark. Fortunately, the days were getting longer, so sunset meant bedtime, or as Clutch called it, rack time.

Clutch turned. "I'm going to lock up."

I wiped off the tin dishes we used, and arranged our weapons near the two twin-sized mattresses Clutch had taken from one of the cabins. I made sure the shotguns were loaded and looked over our bleak inventory. An AR-15 with three clips, the two shotguns along with an extra shotgun we'd found in a locked cabinet in the office, a box of shotgun shells, a baseball bat, a camping axe I'd found in one of the lost-and-found boxes, and a few knives. We'd also found a tranq gun in the same cabinet as the shotgun, but we figured we'd have to be pretty desperate to try that on a zed.

Darkness had taken over the world by the time Clutch came upstairs. With only the two of us and few zeds in the park, we no longer did patrols like we had at the farm. Since the office sat on a ridge, it was the safest lodging in the park, but it didn't yet have a fraction of the security features we'd built around Clutch's house. If someone managed to break through the door or windows we'd yet to board up, we were fucked.

He lay down without a word, and I watched the stars wink peacefully back at me until I drifted off.

I awoke to the sounds of Clutch's nightmares, just like I did every night. He mumbled and tossed and turned. Like every night, I crawled over to him and wrapped an arm around him. He rarely woke, but when he did, he'd roll over and pull me to him like I was his anchor.

His muscles tensed and he shot awake.

"Shh," I murmured. "It's just a bad dream." I pressed him back down and placed a gentle kiss on his forehead.

He looked up at me. In the moonlight, his gaze moved to my lips.

I ran a hand over his short hair and gave him a soft smile.

He cupped my neck and pulled me to where his lips met mine. It was just a brush, but then I deepened it, pressing my lips against his. For a long second, he didn't move. Then he grabbed me and rolled, pinning me beneath him. He took over. He came crashing down to me, kissing me hard and deep, with take-no-prisoners intensity, and a moan escaped from my lips and into his mouth.

My thighs spread to cradle him, and he shifted, lodging him tight against me. I'd been careful never to cross the line into intimacy, but now that we had, I'd rather give up breathing than his kiss. After seconds—or minutes—of kissing me senseless, he pulled back, leaving me gasping for air.

He, too, was breathing heavily. His calloused hand brushed against me, and I shuddered in pleasure as he tugged off my underwear and shoved out of his boxer briefs. He cupped my ass and pulled me tight against him. I could feel his cock, hot and throbbing, press against my core.

"Clutch," I begged and grabbed his head, pulling him into a brutal, raw kiss.

He replied with a growl. He slid his arms under my back, grabbed my shoulders, and plunged into me. I cried out as my body was forced to accept the sudden intrusion.

I raked at him, widening my thighs, pulling him to me with all my strength, but his weight held me in place. He clamped onto my hips to pull me even closer. He thrust hard and deep. Exactly what I wanted—what I *needed*.

He pounded into me over and over until I could do nothing but hold on. His low growls combined with my shameless cries. The next instant I cried out, freefalling into a climax. Clutch's back arched and he bellowed as he pulled out, shooting a burst of seed onto the blanket.

I lay there, boneless, while he rolled onto his side, panting and sweaty. He lowered his head to the mattress next to mine, and pulled me tight against him.

Time was lost while I floated, the mattress unfeeling below me.

"I killed her."

The words were soft, barely audible. "What?" I asked, confused.

"At the Dogs' camp..." Clutch rolled onto his back. "Doyle left me in the silo, with one guard outside. Only it wasn't a Dog. It was a woman."

I pulled myself up onto my elbows and watched Clutch.

"He'd threatened to go after you and Jase if I tried to escape. He assumed I wouldn't try it. He was wrong. He posted her outside my door. She had no training, no experience."

I laid a hand on his heart. His muscles tensed.

"I killed her. Broke her neck so I could get out. I had to make sure you were safe."

He jerked away, got up, and stood in front of the window.

I came to my feet. "It's not your fault. Doyle forced your hand."

"He didn't force me to kill her."

I walked over to him and watched him stare out over the dark valley below. "He did, in a way. He forced your hand. You did what you had to do. If you didn't, you wouldn't be alive today. *I* wouldn't be alive today."

He turned, looked into my eyes for a moment, then pulled away and grabbed his clothes and a bottle of whiskey. He paused at the top step. "She was Doyle's wife."

Twenty

Three days later

"There's one coming up your six," Clutch called out before diving behind a pew to reload. I twisted around and blasted buckshot into the head of an exceptionally overweight zed, pumped my shotgun, and then took out the aggressive one reaching for Clutch.

I continued shooting, taking out their legs if I couldn't get a good headshot. Clutch rejoined, and the church was like a Tarantino film, full of gunfire and gore. I used up my last two shells on a priest wearing a collar stained with dried blood.

"Reloading!" I yelled out and scrambled back several steps. I rushed to slide the shells into the shotgun while a zed in the form of a decrepit old woman stumbled toward me, its head askew with a broken neck. I'd only gotten five shells loaded when it closed in. I swung the gun up and shot it in the chest. The force sent it flying back, and my second shot was a direct hit to its face.

I looked around for what to shoot next but saw no zeds still standing. I frowned. "We're clear already?"

"All clear," Clutch said as he pulled out a knife.

I finished reloading my shotgun before slinging it over my shoulder and pulling out my knife. We went around to each zed, making sure it wouldn't come back. Shotguns packed a punch, but they didn't always get the job done.

Afterward, we stood at the baptismal fountain, washing up under the watchful gray gaze of a statue of the Virgin Mary. "Jesus," I said, and then glanced at the crucifix hanging at the front of the church. "Sorry," I mumbled. "Did everyone in a ten-mile radius come to church when the outbreak hit?"

"Plenty of folks get religious when things turn to shit."

My eyes fell on the priest. "Guess the priest would've had his hands full giving last rites."

"Too bad the dead didn't actually stay dead."

I dried my hands on my jeans and scanned the corpses and toppled pews. "We used up a lot of ammo."

"It'll all be worth it if this place hasn't been looted yet."

I grinned and clapped. "Let's check it out."

———

What we discovered quickly proved Clutch right. We'd struck gold at the Catholic church in the town nearest to the park, if you could call six houses and a church with an attached reception hall a town. According to the banner hanging outside, they'd been collecting donations for a local food pantry to help the needy at Easter.

And we definitely qualified as needy.

"See if you can't find a P-38," Clutch said as he rifled through cupboards in the kitchen.

"I have no idea what you're talking about," I called out in reply, stacking another box of canned food near the front door with the dozen other boxes. "You know, for a small town, these guys were really generous."

I headed back to the kitchen. "Everything's boxed up and ready to go."

"Aha, a P-38." Clutch held up a small metal can opener not much bigger than a razor blade. He pocketed it.

My brow furrowed. "It's a can opener?"

"It's a P-38."

With a sigh, I rolled my eyes. "Ready?"

"Ready."

We headed to the stack of boxes. "You carry, I watch," I said.

Clutch lifted two boxes and grunted. "Did you have to pack them so full?"

I patted his shoulder. "Just doing my part to help you stay in shape."

With the shotgun in one hand, I propped open the door with a brick. After a quick sweep of the area between us and the truck, I motioned Clutch forward. "Clear."

He carried the boxes outside, and I stayed close, constantly scanning a full three-sixty around us. Afternoon shadows of tall trees danced like taunting spirits across the tombstones in the quaint cemetery on the other side of the church.

I opened the back of the truck, Clutch slid the boxes onto the bed, and we headed back for more boxes. We were getting efficient at looting, but we both knew that there'd be nothing left to loot in another year. We'd deal with that problem a year from now.

On the third load, I came to a hard stop.

"Aw, hell." In one smooth move, Clutch set down the boxes and swung his shotgun around.

Parked next to our truck was a Humvee.

Don't let it be Dogs. Don't let it be Dogs. I treaded cautiously toward it, careful to keep the truck between us and them.

As I neared the vehicle, I let out a breath as Griz stepped out from the driver's seat and waved while still speaking into the handheld radio. Tack emerged from the other side of the Humvee. He casually gripped a rifle, looking none too bothered that we had two shotguns aimed at them.

When Griz put down the radio, I lowered my weapon. "What brings you boys all the way out here?"

"Standard recon," Griz replied. "Damn, I never expected to run across the pair of you. That teaches me for betting against Tack."

I lifted a brow.

Griz busted out a wide grin. "The odds were twenty to one that you two were zeds. Tack was the only one to bet on both of you."

Tack gave a nod.

"Thanks." I lifted a brow. "I think."

"So everyone thinks we're dead?" Clutch asked by my side.

"Everyone at Fox, anyway," Griz replied. "With the exception of Tack, me, and now Captain Masden."

Ah, so that was whom he'd been talking to on the radio.

Griz, joined by Tack, headed our way. Griz whistled at the church. "Gutsy move to clear out a church. We've learned to keep our distance from churches. They're right up there with grocery stores and police stations as being zed hubs."

"Beggars can't be choosy," I said.

Griz nodded to the boxes. "Here, we can help."

"We're good," Clutch said, grabbing the boxes.

Griz held out his hands. "We're not trying to take what you've rightfully stolen."

"Recon, you say? You guys still out looking for survivors?" I asked.

"Some, but our focus has shifted more to tracking down Doyle. His guys are still a pain in the ass."

My muscles tightened as I watched Clutch for any sign of emotion. I knew he'd never forgive himself for killing that woman. Not that Doyle would be any less forgiving if he found out Clutch was still alive.

"Lendt hasn't taken care of him yet?" Clutch asked.

Griz frowned and shook his head. "We busted into Doyle's camp and caught several of his men and freed some of his 'indentured servants'."

I cocked my head. "Indentured servants?"

"That's what Doyle told them," Griz said. "Doyle convinced them that Camp Fox wasn't safe. So, for food and shelter, they had to sign contracts to service the militia for seven years. Lendt figured his attack on Camp Fox was as much to convince people that with him was the only safe place."

My jaw dropped. "Holy. Shit."

"But he's surprisingly wily for his age," Griz added. "His guys have gone guerrilla on our patrols, but there have been no more attacks on the Camp, so we know we've got him on the run."

"I wouldn't be foolish enough to count on that assumption," Clutch said, pushing the box onto the truck bed and heading back for more.

"We're not," Griz said, keeping up. "But we'll get him one of these days. You can bet on it."

"It doesn't sound like you've made the smartest bets yet," I said with a smirk before stepping back to the reception hall. Tack and Griz followed.

Tack picked up a box, and Griz lifted the top. "Who would've guessed that cheap toilet paper would become a luxury item?"

"How's Camp Fox holding up? The civilians are all safe?" I asked, thinking of one in particular.

Griz sighed. "We're getting by, but Doyle's attack put a hurt on our supplies. Before long, we'll be out doing what you're doing."

Tack dropped the box into the back of the truck and faced me. "That friend of yours, Jasen Flannigan, he's all right. Fitting right in at the Camp."

I closed my eyes and breathed deeply. When I reopened my eyes, I smiled. "Thank you."

Griz and Clutch set down the last of the boxes.

"We'd better head back," Clutch said.

I checked the sun sitting just above the roof of a two-story house across the street. Zeds tended to disappear at night, especially on cloudy nights. I suspected it was some sort of instinctual need for self-preservation. They couldn't see any better than us, so they could walk right into a river or off a ledge in the dark. Not that they were bright enough to avoid doing that in the daylight.

Except last night was a full moon. Tonight wouldn't be much better, without a cloud in the sky. It would be a good night to be back at the park and locked in before the sun set.

"I saw what they did to your farm. That's a damn shame," Griz said. "Where you staying now?"

Clutch narrowed his eyes. "Why do you want to know?"

"I'm guessing it's out this way," Griz said, looking around. "We're tight on resources, but whenever we have a squad out this way, I can have them stop by to check in to see how things are going."

"Things are going fine," Clutch retorted.

"I read you loud and clear. But, the attack really cut into our numbers and decimated our ammo supply. We've started training civilians, but we could use all the help we can get."

"Help?" I asked with a hand on my hip. "Tell me something, do they still have the prison cell waiting for me?"

Griz's lips thinned and shook his head. "Lendt's wiped the slate clear on anyone charged with assaulting the militia. After the stunt Doyle pulled, Lendt realized that he had to revisit his approach to military law. Hell, you just might get a medal now."

I didn't share his confidence. "Clutch is right. We need to get going."

"Hold up." Griz jogged back to the Humvee and pulled out something. "This radio pack is fully charged, and it's got an adapter for a cig lighter. I already dialed in our frequency. Call if you need anything. Leave it on so we can reach you. If we see any herds or any of Doyle's guys sniffing around this area, we'll let you know."

Clutch nodded and took it.

"Thanks, Griz," I said and followed Clutch to the truck.

"Do you think they'll try to reach us?" I asked, closing the door.

"Yeah." Clutch paused. "The radio is Masden's way of saying I've been called back to duty."

TWENTY-ONE

"Why can't anyone just leave us the fuck alone?" Clutch growled as we drove back to the church two days later.

I reached out and intertwined my fingers with his. "That's because we're irresistible."

Neither of us laughed. I wasn't any more comfortable with the idea of tying ourselves to Camp Fox than Clutch. When Tyler had called in on the radio this morning and said he needed to meet with us, a rock had formed in my stomach and had been expanding ever since.

As we rolled up to the church, we found two Humvees waiting for us.

When Clutch turned off the ignition, the back door on the first Humvee flung open, a nearly full-grown coyote jumped down and a teenager with a wide grin stepped out.

My eyes widened. "Jase!"

He waved wildly and met me midway with a bear hug. Clutch came up from behind me and patted him on the shoulder. "Damn, it's good to see you, kid."

Jase took a step back. "Man, when Griz told me you guys were okay... well, it's just good to see you. Really, really good."

The golden coyote sat behind Jase, and I grinned. "I see Mutt's turned out all right."

He bent down and picked up the furry canine, and she licked his cheek. "Yeah, she's a regular zed hunter now. She comes with me scouting."

Clutch frowned. "You go on scouting missions?"

"Yeah." Jase nodded back at Tyler, Griz, and Tack, who were now walking our way. "They asked for folks to join up after the attack. Eddy and I are on Captain Masden's squad." He stepped to the side, making room for Tyler, while Griz and Tack stood back with their rifles ready, scanning the area.

Tyler smiled at me. "It's good to see you again." He held out his hand, and I shook it, having a hard time returning his smile.

Tyler didn't even try to shake Clutch's hand. Tyler never liked Clutch, and Clutch still held a grudge against Tyler for abandoning me in zed and Dog country. I wasn't angry. Not anymore. Tyler had simply been trying to do the right thing in a world where all the old rules had changed.

I still wanted to punch him.

"What do you want, Captain?" Clutch said.

Tyler gave a thin smile. "Always to the point, Sarge. I respect that. Griz said he filled you in on our current situation with Doyle and his minutemen."

"He said you guys were at war," Clutch said.

Tyler chortled. "It's been more like a hunt than a war. Though, Jase might have found a game changer."

"How's that?" I asked.

"Your boy here came across one of Doyle's outposts."

"When are you going in?" Clutch asked.

"Tonight."

Clutch narrowed his eyes. "But you're not here for a briefing."

"You're right, Sarge. To be honest, we're tight on resources. Before the outbreak, we didn't have many troops with real field experience. And Doyle's attack on the Camp put a hell of a hurtin' on us. You've served two tours, Sarge. I need you out there with my men tonight. It's not a request."

I watched Clutch turn and pace the sidewalk. When he returned, he ran a hand through his short hair. "What's the SITREP?"

"From what Jase and Southpaw reported, this isn't Doyle's primary camp, but we believe he's running out of multiple small camps instead of one larger camp now. Nevertheless, the camp Jase and Southpaw found would be a critical hit from a payback perspective. The payload is three fuel tankers, which we believe constitute all of Doyle's mobile fuel reserves. We could really use that fuel at Camp Fox, so we can't go in with guns blazing and risk blowing the trucks sky-high."

He motioned to Jase who handed Clutch his iPhone. After Clutch scrolled through the pictures, he handed the phone to me. Three fuel tankers sat side by side at a rest stop. Calling it an outpost was an exaggeration. There were no fences, hardly any people, and only the single building. If the trucks were lined up, I would've driven by without looking twice.

"As for tangos," Tyler continued. "We're looking at no more than five guys on duty at any time, but they're likely patched into Doyle through handheld radios we provided the militia awhile back. I think Doyle figured this place is far enough north that we wouldn't find it."

"Which rest stop is this?" Clutch asked.

"It's about twenty miles north of Chow Town, just south of the ethanol plant."

"I know the place," Clutch said.

"I'm leading the mission, and I'm taking my entire squad with me. That makes ten of us. With you, it'd be eleven."

Silence boomed, and I noticed Clutch watching Jase. "If I do this, both the kid and Cash are on my team."

Tyler nodded. "I was planning on that." He turned to me. "Since you're not ex-mil, I couldn't make you come along, but your assistance is appreciated."

I gave a tight nod.

Tyler faced Clutch and continued. "Griz has Alpha team. You'll take Bravo team. That brings our total to twelve troops for the mission. It should be an easy in-and-out."

Clutch shot me a strained glance before turning back to Tyler. "Hoorah."

Tyler smiled. "We head out at zero-three. I'll make sure you both have clearance into Camp Fox. We meet inside the front gate. Got it?"

"Cash and I need weapons and gear," Clutch added.

"Roger that," Tyler said. "Those are two things we still have in good supply. Ammunition is another story."

"How low are you?" Clutch asked.

"If we're careful, we might have just enough to take Doyle down. But we're going to have to get creative with the zeds."

Clutch nodded and headed back to the truck. I shot Jase a quick smile before following.

We drove away, and neither Clutch nor I spoke until after we passed by the farms we'd looted a few days earlier. "I guess it's official. We're with Camp Fox," I said.

Clutch took in a deep breath. "Yeah, guess so."

My eyes widened. "Wait. Turn around."

He hit the brakes and did a one-eighty. He frowned. "What'd you see?"

I hurriedly pointed to a house with a couple rustic tin buildings. "Turn in here."

He pulled into the drive. "Is that—?"

"Yeah."

He stopped the truck next to the old tree, with dozens of red apples dangling from it. I shot him a wide grin before we both rushed out to the tree. The apples were high, and I had to jump to reach one. When I bit into it, tart juices splattered, and I groaned. "*Mm, so good.*"

Clutch didn't reply. He was too busy chewing on his own apple.

It had been so long since we had fresh fruit. These tart apples were meant for pies, but they tasted like heaven. Clutch finished his before I finished mine and grabbed another apple. I tossed my core, and he held the apple out to me. I grinned, grabbed his wrist, and pulled him into a long, sugary kiss. *Bliss.*

I pulled away to find Clutch wearing one his rare smiles.

My smile fell at the same time the blood in my veins froze. "Watch out!"

He twisted around just as the zed tackled him.

I reached for my shotgun and realized I'd left it in the truck.

I pulled out my knife and ran at the zed snapping its teeth at Clutch, who was holding it back. I grabbed its legs and yanked it to the side, got to my knees and shoved the knife through its cheekbone. Clutch was next to me, stabbing it through its eye. Jumping to my feet I turned around to find at least a half dozen more heading our way, all looking less than friendly and more than hungry.

"We've got trouble," I murmured.

"Truck" was all Clutch said, and we both sprinted back to the still-running vehicle.

As Clutch tore out of there, I watched the zeds through the back window. They stood under the apple tree, watching us, as though daring us to come back.

I turned back around and sighed. For more apples, I just might.

Twenty-Two

"You'll stay at my side and do everything I say," Clutch said on our way to Camp Fox. "This situation could go FUBAR in a flash. I don't like you this close to the action, but I'd rather have you with me than alone at the park."

I yawned, then saluted. "Yes, Sergeant Bad Ass, *sir*."

He muttered something under his breath. I grinned and went back to scanning the dark landscape.

It took us two hours driving without headlights and around the ever-growing numbers of zeds to get to Camp Fox. By then, my nerves had amped up a million levels. I'd fought against zeds plenty. This was my first time playing the aggressor against other people, and I felt sorely unprepared.

At the Camp's front gate, we found a friendly reception and load of gear and weapons waiting for us. Clutch helped me gear up before fastening on his own armor. As I checked out my new sniper rifle, Tyler drove up with a Humvee full of troops with faces painted black.

They stepped outside and we all formed a circle around Tyler.

He looked over everyone, and then threw me a plastic container. I unscrewed the lid to find what I guessed was dark face paint. Clutch dipped two fingers in and started wiping it across his face, and I did the same.

"Sarge, you've got Tack, Southpaw, Cash, Eddy, and Jase," Tyler said. "Everyone else is with Griz and me. Here's the plan."

———

Two hours later, Bravo team lay flat on the grassy hill behind the rest stop, waiting for Tyler's signal. To my right, Mutt, an honorary member of Bravo, was sprawled out next to Jase, seemingly unconcerned that shit was about to hit the proverbial fan. Eddy was on Jase's other side, one of his legs shaking. To my left, with Clutch between us, was Southpaw, the other sniper in Bravo. Tack was silent and unmoving next to Southpaw, and I couldn't tell if he was even awake.

Clutch looked like he was analyzing the situation, and I turned my attention back to my target. There were two guards on the backside of the rest stop, one on each corner. Southpaw and I each had our assigned target in our sights for the past ten minutes. Just waiting for the signal.

We each had a role in the straight-forward mission: *Go at them from both sides. Take down the guards. Smoke out any hiding in the rest stop and neutralize. Grab the fuel trucks and reclaim any weapons and ammunition.*

Clutch tensed, and I suspected he was getting the call from Tyler. Camp Fox had been ill-equipped for war, leaving only the three mission leaders with headsets.

"Bravo. Received." Clutch turned to Southpaw and then to me. "Green light." He paused for a three-count while we each readied to fire. "Green light, *go.*"

I inhaled. As I exhaled, I pulled the trigger. My target fell to the ground, unmoving. My shot was echoed by Southpaw's rifle, and his target collapsed.

"Nice." Clutch held up two fingers and motioned back and forth.

Show time.

Clutch took the lead, with Tack, Jase, and Eddy lined up one by one in trail. Southpaw and I stayed behind to take out Dogs before they posed a risk to our guys, though I suspected Clutch's motive was to keep me out of danger, leaving Southpaw behind to cover me.

The rest stop, right off the interstate, was a smart location for moving large trucks. Instead of fences, every forty feet or so, there was a zed, buried up to its knees and chained to the ground. *Interesting defense.*

Lights erupted from an amped-up pickup truck and its horn blared.

"Shit!" I muttered.

"Guess the surprise is up," Southpaw said from my left, sounding none too happy.

Alpha team reached the rest stop as soon as the first Dog emerged. Clutch took him out with a clean chest shot.

Clutch slammed against the building, nearly dropping his gun. It was then I noticed the Dog he'd shot wasn't a man at all but a young woman. As Clutch leaned against the building, I wanted to shout, *she's a Dog, goddammit!* Instead, I fired off a shot at the next Dog coming through the door.

The shot snapped Clutch out of his stupor. He pulled up his rifle, shot a glance my way, and headed back into the fray. Jase fired off several shots, and I heard him yell. Mutt took off running and jumped onto an injured Dog trying to flee. The coyote tore at his throat and clawed at his skin until the Dog's screams found silence.

Clutch pressed his hand to his ear. He made a hand motion. Eddy and Jase ran toward one of the fuel trucks, with Mutt on their heels. Four of Alpha team met them at the trucks, and a pair climbed into each of the three trucks.

Heavy engines roared to life, and the lights on the fuel tankers came on one by one. As they started rolling, Southpaw and I continued to lay down fire whenever we saw a Dog.

Clutch held up a hand and shouted, "Pull back. Company's coming!"

When Clutch and Tack reached our position, Southpaw and I sprinted with them into the darkness. Bullets zinged past us and I wanted to dive for cover but kept running.

Southpaw stumbled, and I stopped to help him. He was trying to pull himself back up while holding his side.

"South's down!" I yelled, bending down to pull him up. Clutch moved me out of the way and he and Tack grabbed the fallen soldier.

I fired off cover fire as the guys ran past me.

"Haul ass, Cash!" Clutch yelled.

I fired off three more shots and reached the guys as they were loading Southpaw into the back of the Humvee. We climbed inside, and Clutch took the driver's seat. He was cussing at Tyler, but I couldn't make out the jargon.

But I did notice the onslaught of headlights in the distance, and they were coming right at us.

TWENTY-THREE

Clutch sped dangerously fast without headlights. I had no idea how he managed to keep the Humvee on the road. He pressed two fingers against his headset. "We have one man down."

A pause.

"Affirm. Bravo team is still a go. Repeat, Bravo is still a go."

A pause.

"Wilco. Bravo, over and out." Clutch grimaced and turned on the headlights.

My eyes widened. "What are you doing?"

Clutch clenched his jaw. "Alpha is rendezvousing with the tankers to provide firepower support to the Camp. We're to lead as many Dogs as we can away from the convoy."

I swallowed, found it hard to breathe, and immediately started reloading my rifle.

He glanced at me and then took a quick look in back where Tack was busy tending to Southpaw. "How's he doing?"

Tack didn't answer.

"Tack, report."

The soldier looked up slowly. "It was clean, through and through, no organs hit. But...I think he's gone."

Clutch hit the wheel. "Fuck!"

"I don't get it," Tack added on though in a daze. "It wasn't that bad of hit. He should be conscious and talking to us right now."

I looked around and noticed lights—a lot of them—closing in. "Do you know this area?" I asked.

"Not good enough." Clutch cranked a hard left, sending me against the door, and he barreled down the on-ramp and onto the interstate. "Let's hope for no roadblocks."

Something chinked the metal, sounding like a rock chip, except we were on pavement.

"Tack, take the .30," Clutch ordered. "Cash, feed him ammo."

I started crawling into the back.

"Fuck!" Tack yelled and jumped back.

"What's wrong?" I asked.

"It's Southpaw. He's turning!"

"How's that possible?" I fumbled with my rifle.

Southpaw plowed into the much smaller Tack, but I was close enough I barely had to aim. I fired an ear-ringing shot, and Southpaw collapsed on top of Tack.

Tack sat up and shoved off his comrade.

I kept my rifle leveled. "Are you bit?"

He kicked away Southpaw's body. "No."

"What the hell was that?" Clutch asked.

"No idea," I said, making my way to Tack. We hadn't been close to any of the zeds in the area. So how in the world had Southpaw gotten infected? More pings against the metal reminded me that I didn't have the luxury to think right now.

Tack fired rounds at the headlights behind us. The first vehicle swerved but then straightened out, but at least we now had more space between us and them. Another pair of lights came up alongside the first, and flashes of gunfire from both trucks winked back at us.

"Can't you go faster?" I yelled toward Clutch.

"Humvee," he replied as if that explained everything.

I fed more ammo to Tack.

Clutch jerked the Humvee onto an exit ramp, knocking me across the floor and onto Southpaw's body. As I pulled myself back up, I saw the sign that read *Fox Hills 3 miles*, and by the look on Tack's face, he'd seen it, too, though he went back to firing.

"You're taking us to Chow Town?" I asked.

"We can't outrun the Dogs, and they'd be crazy to follow us into town."

We'd be crazy to go into town, I wanted to say. Instead, I warned, "It's almost dawn."

Clutch kept on driving. "I plan on only making a quick drive-through."

As Clutch suspected, the Dogs backed off when we passed the sign that read *Welcome to Fox Hills, Midwest's hidden gem, pop. 5,613*. Clutch drove the Humvee off the shoulder and through the ditch, around the blocked road, and into the Wal-Mart's parking lot. Already, at least a dozen dark shadows lumbered toward us.

The truck behind us stopped but kept its machine gun leveled at us. The other trucks peeled out and headed in different directions. "Fuck!" Clutch stepped on the gas. "The shits are trying to block us in town."

Clutch turned left on the first street, running over a zed wearing a gaudy shirt, its sequins glittering in our headlights. "Come on, come on, come on," he muttered as he sped faster and faster.

When we reached the next road leading out of town, on the other side of the roadblock was one of the Dogs' trucks. They fired off several shots, and Clutch slammed on the brakes. He made a U-turn and headed for the next street. The gunfire had drawn zeds out from the darkness. Clutch dodged some and hit more on his way to one of the few roads leading out of town. Chow Town wasn't a large town. With a river running along two sides and all bridges blocked or destroyed during the outbreak, there weren't many roads leading out of town.

Clutch slowed, and I saw the Dogs on the other side of the roadblock.

The wheel creaked under Clutch's grip. "Shit."

"If we can't get out of town, we need to find a place to lie low until the Dogs clear out," I said, fear tightening my muscles as I remembered how well that worked the last time I was here. I looked from Tack to Clutch. "Any ideas?"

"My apartment is about three miles from here," Tack said.

I frowned. "Apartments sound too dangerous."

"When that sun comes up, anywhere is going to be too dangerous," Clutch said.

"How about the pharmacy we cleared out? It's not far," I said.

Clutch shook his head. "The glass windows will make it hard to hide."

"My girlfriend's house is across the street from First Baptist. She went to Des Moines with her parents shopping when...you know, so the house should be clear," Tack said.

Clutch sighed. "Let's give it a shot."

Tack gave directions, and Clutch weaved around cars and cut

through yards. A lump formed in my gut when I saw the zeds building behind us.

As soon as we hit a side street, Clutch stepped on the gas to put some distance between us and them. "We're going to have to move fast. Run to the back door. Don't be noticed. If you are, take care of any that home in on us. Tack, you make sure you get us inside fast. Then we're going into silence so no zeds get a bead on us. Got it?"

"Got it," I said.

"Tack, grab any extra ammo off Southpaw. I have a feeling we're going to need every round," Clutch said before relaying our next coordinates to Tyler.

A moment later, Tack pointed. "There. That two-story brick one. That's the place."

"Let's do this." Clutch cut the engine of the Humvee while it was still rolling into the driveway, and I jumped out.

It was dark enough that the herd of zeds about a block away was only an ominous fog of shapes. Sweeping trees cast ominous dark shadows over the yard, hiding God only knows what. Clutch scanned the backyard alongside me.

Tack checked the back door. When it didn't open, he lifted a flower pot and grabbed a key. He opened the door and disappeared inside.

I went to follow but stopped cold. I pulled out my knife, walked down the steps, and stood on the patio. A zed emerged from the shadows. It groaned, and I lunged forward and stabbed it through the top of its head. I looked around for more. Clutch tugged my arm and motioned to the door.

I followed him inside. He locked the door, and I found us in a kitchen. Aside from the earliest glimmer of dawn coming through the windows, it was pitch black inside. I moved slowly to not make any noise and closed the blinds on the kitchen window. I turned, leaned on the sink, and inhaled.

Death.

I smelled death.

I stepped cautiously into the living room, where Tack was closing the curtains. The smell was stronger here. He noticed me, held up a hand, and whispered, "It's Daisy."

"Daisy?" I mouthed back.

"Golden Retriever."

Relief replaced my tension. Now all we had to do was wait it out.

Something thumped against the window.

Tack and I both stiffened. Clutch walked silently into the room.
Thump.

I flattened against the wall and peered out of the crack at the end of the curtain. Several zeds grabbed at the Humvee. Even more zeds stood on the other side of the window, sniffing at the air.

Thump, thump.

I stepped back, mouth opened. Impossible. They couldn't possibly find us through brick and glass. Clutch exchanged places with me and he looked outside. Tack looked outside from the other edge of the curtain.

Both looked as surprised as I felt.

The pounding on the glass grew, and more zeds joined in.

"If I can get to the Humvee, I can unleash the .30 on them," Tack whispered.

"There's too many," Clutch said in a low voice. "When that glass breaks, we're going to have to make a run for it."

All three of us checked our weapons one last time.

The glass shattered.

Clutch yelled, "Run!"

And we did.

Twenty-Four

We bolted out the back door. Tack fired the first shots, clearing the patio. Clutch took the lead from there. I gripped my rifle as I sprinted behind him, with Tack at my side. It was still dark, but the coming dawn shed enough light to reveal outlines of zeds waiting in the shadows.

We ran in the opposite direction than we'd come. We ran through backyards, turning at fences and dodging zeds, shooting open escape routes. Once we broke from the herd near the house, Clutch set the pace at a quick jog, faster than any zed but slow enough that we could keep this pace for some time, if we had to.

And we had to. My clothes were soaked and my muscles burned by the time the sun reached into the sky. It was already easily eighty degrees and it was still morning. Body armor held the heat against my skin.

We could outrun any zed easily enough. But more just kept showing up. Around every corner, out of every alley. As soon as we got away from one herd, we'd find ourselves smack dab in the middle of another, and we'd have to zig and zag around houses and cars.

Tack ran out of ammo first. I was out eight rounds later. When Clutch's rifle clicked empty, I think we all sucked in a collective breath. With nothing but pistols and knives, we kept running. The sun baked my head under the helmet, and I had to drop my rifle and backpack to keep up with the guys' longer strides. My lungs couldn't suck enough air by the time the zeds' numbers dwindled and we reached an industrial park.

Clutch slowed to a stop, bent over with his hands braced on his legs, and panted. I fell back against a wall, sucking air. Tack walked slowly, his hands on his hips, while he caught his breath.

Tack huffed, pointed to the north, his finger shaky. "There's an old bridge that leads out of town just beyond these buildings."

Clutch reported our status to Tyler, and then faced us. "They got the trucks back to Camp Fox okay."

"Thank God," I panted out.

Clutch did a slow three-sixty. Sweat dripped from his brow. "We have to keep moving. Too much open space. We're easy targets out here."

As though on cue, two zeds stumbled around the corner. The first, a farmer in jeans and cowboy boots, lumbered forward. At its side came a heavily tattooed biker zed with an intricate dragon climbing its sunbaked arm.

Two shots and the zeds fell. I turned to find Tack with his pistol still leveled where the zeds had been standing a second earlier.

Clutch sucked in another breath. "Let's move out. It won't take long for these guys' pals to catch up."

It took all my strength to push off from the wall and propel myself forward. Every boot step pounded the pavement. Every building seemed a mile long. We wheezed air. I stumbled over a curb.

At the end of an old warehouse, a bridge waited, its iron trusses reaching upward like welcoming arms. Several cars were smashed on it, preventing any vehicles from crossing.

Bodies rotted on the ground, but surprisingly, there were no zeds walking around.

I came to a stop at the same time Clutch and Tack must've seen it. A truck was parked not far from the bridge. The machine gun mounted on back was pointed right at us.

The Dogs were waiting for us.

TWENTY-FIVE

"S hit!" I flattened myself against the wall, and Clutch and Tack did the same. "Think they saw us?" I asked.

"Maybe. Maybe not. But they had to hear Tack's shots," Clutch replied. "They're probably stationed there to hold us back until the herd gets here. They've got front row seats for watching us get shredded."

"There's no way we can cross that bridge without getting gunned down," Tack said.

"And there's bound to be zeds in the river," I added.

A zed came around the far corner of the building. It moaned and kept walking toward us, followed by at a least a hundred more, and more kept showing up. My heart lurched. "Looks like the party is about to start."

"Time's up," Clutch said. "We have to take our chances at the bridge."

"Wait," I said, and I examined the iron bridge. "What if we go under the bridge?"

Both men looked at me.

"The undersides of some of these bridges are just big I-beams. We might be able to shimmy across."

Clutch's brow furrowed. "It could work. If we stay low and behind the roadblock, the Dogs might not be able to hit us."

Moans and shuffling steps grew closer. The herd was halfway down the building now.

"Give it a shot?" Tack asked.

"Why not." Clutch took off in a hunched-over run.

I followed and Tack hung back to cover our flank. It was hard to run bent over, weighted down by what remained of my gear and exhausted from nearly four hours of running through half the alleys and backstreets of Chow Town. I stumbled and Tack helped me back to my feet. My legs were jelly, but from somewhere deep inside, fresh adrenaline numbed my body and senses, and I kept moving behind Clutch toward the bridge.

Two zeds emerged from the bridge and came at us, but they were easy enough to maneuver around. I dove to the edge of the embankment. Clutch already had a leg over the embankment. He held out a hand. "Grab on to me," he ordered. I reached out, and he snatched me against him and took a step down the embankment. He lost his footing and slid onto his back, pulling me against his chest. We slid several feet down before Clutch found traction again.

One of the zeds rolled past us and into the river below. The second followed a second later, grabbing Clutch's arm on its way down. We were dragged several feet before I was able to kick it loose, and it tumbled away.

Clutch held me tight. I lay against him, panting. I looked down, and swallowed. If we'd slid another fifteen feet, we would've landed right on top of a couple dozen hungry zeds hungrily trapped at the edge of the river. They couldn't climb the steep incline, and they couldn't enter the river without being swept away (which I suspected was what had happened to quite a few zeds already).

"Don't do that again," I muttered against Clutch's chest.

"Yeah," he replied breathlessly. Then he pressed a couple fingers to his headset. "Bravo needs pickup *now*. We've got half of Chow Town waiting for us on one side of the bridge, and Dogs set up to chase us down on the other."

Silence except for the growing hum of moans and shuffling feet.

Clutch scowled. "Copy that. Three hours. Over and out."

I pulled out a flask and took a quick drink. It was still half full, but no telling how long we'd be out here. There was no sound of engines, which meant the Dogs were still there but hopefully still oblivious to us. "Did you see how many Dogs were in that truck?"

Clutch shook his head.

I continued. "Once we get across we might be close enough to get clear shots."

"That's assuming they don't take us out while we're climbing across," Clutch replied.

"I guess we'll find out soon enough," I whispered and glanced back to find Tack climbing up onto an I-beam under the bridge.

I pulled away from Clutch but kept close by his side as I crawled toward Tack. The underside of the bridge was a zigzag of iron. After cracking my knuckles, I grabbed onto an I-beam. The beams were large, so there was plenty to grab on to, but I wasn't convinced I had the strength in my fingers and arms to get all the way across. I slid my legs around an I-beam and shimmied toward Tack.

He was already several feet ahead and putting more distance between us. I followed, with Clutch behind me. It wasn't a long bridge by bridge standards, but the arm strength it took for pulling myself across, it could've been the Golden Gate. Every time a gunshot rang out, I froze, waiting to feel horrible piercing pain. But none ever came. At only about a third of the way across, my arms shook, as much from my fear of heights as from my own body weight.

At the halfway point, two I-beams intersected and I was able to lean on one to catch my breath, though the humid air did nothing to help my breathing. Afraid if I stopped too long, I'd never get across, and so I continued. Minute by minute, putting one hand before the other, I made it to the three-quarters point, then only ten feet left. Eight, six, four.

By the time I reached the end, I had nothing left. I literally dropped off the bridge and collapsed onto the ground next to Tack. I rolled onto my back and grasped long grass with both hands.

Clutch dropped next to me, and we all lay there for several moments. When Tack moved, I stayed put, watching him Army crawl up the hill and scout the scene. This side wasn't quite as steep and—thankfully—zed-free. He backed himself down to us.

"SITREP?" Clutch asked.

"I see only two Dogs," Tack replied in a hoarse whisper. "One driver and one gunner. The driver looks like he's taking a lunch break. The gunner is busy watching the herd behind us. I think they've got him spooked. I count three zeds at the tree line. A few more dead on the ground."

Which explained the random gunshots.

"Can we get close enough to take them out without being seen?" Clutch asked.

"Maybe," Tack replied. "It looks like the gunner is still watching the other side of the bridge for us."

Clutch nodded and pulled out his pistol. "We head for the tree line. That way, if we're seen, we can still find cover. Cash, you take the driver. I'll take the gunny. Tack, make sure we're covered." He didn't wait for a response.

"There's no telling how many zeds are in those trees," Tack warned.

I shot him a quick glance, grabbed my pistol and crawled up the hill, and stopped next to Clutch while he scanned the area. The truck sat less than a hundred yards off. Easy shot with a rifle any day of the week, except I no longer had my rifle. The driver's side window was open, and he was taking a bite out of an MRE. The gunner in the back of the truck was leaning on the cab, still intently watching the bridge.

Clutch took off at a run toward the trees, and I dragged myself behind him. No shots fired from the truck. Clutch slid behind a wide tree, and I slammed into him, unable to stop my forward momentum. He caught me before I knocked us both down. Tack grabbed the tree next to us. A shadow moved several feet away, and Clutch took off, weaving around trees for the truck. A skinny zed emerged from a tree to our right, and Tack shoved a blade through its head.

When we reached the trees closest to the truck, we were no more than ten feet away from the zeds making their way to the truck.

"Ready?" Clutch asked.

"Ready," I whispered.

He motioned. "Now."

We ran out and started firing. Out of the corner of my eye, I could see the gunner spin the .30 cal toward us. Machine gun fire drowned out the pops of our pistols. My first shot planted harmlessly into the truck door, but as I closed the distance, my aim improved. The driver snapped back, and red splattered the passenger window. The .30 cal died soon after, leaving behind silence.

"Clear," I said.

"Clear," Clutch echoed before turning around. "How many zeds now?"

"Five," Tack replied, coming up from behind.

I sighed, and Clutch rubbed my shoulder. "Just a bit longer," he murmured.

The five zeds had broken from their way to the truck and reached out toward us. That zeds always seemed to prefer their prey living over the freshly deceased had never made any sense to me. I would've thought they'd go for the easy meal, but it seemed like they were predators at heart.

Tack took down the nearest zed. I fired a single shot at the zed on the left, and Clutch fired several shots to take out the cluster of three. No one bothered to make sure they were down for good. Seemed like we all had the same idea: get away from Chow Town as quickly as possible.

Tack jumped in the back of the four-by-four and threw the dead gunner off. I opened the door and found the driver still sputtering blood. Air hissed through the hole in his cheek. He wasn't moving, just in the final death throes. I grabbed his shirt and pulled him out the truck, let him collapse onto the ground at Clutch's feet.

Clutch rifled through the man's pockets. Movement caught the corner of my eye, and I noticed another zed emerging from the tree line. "There are more headed our way," I said.

Clutch climbed behind the wheel, and pressed his headset. "Bravo is Oscar Mike in a Dog truck. Repeat, Bravo is Oscar Mike. ETA is one hour, over and out."

I sat down on the leather seat and sighed. Every muscle in my body was exhausted. After two long breaths with my eyes closed, I grabbed bottles of water and protein bars off the floor and tossed them to the guys. Between bites, I sifted through the glove box, finding a box of condoms, a flashlight, and a six-shooter. I grabbed everything.

I checked out the handheld radio on the seat. "I wonder when these guys were supposed to check in."

"Fingers crossed, they just did," Clutch said. "We could use extra time to put some distance between their last location and us."

If Clutch had said anything else, I missed it. I fell asleep somewhere between ten and twenty seconds into the drive.

I awoke with Clutch nudging me, and I grumbled. "*Lemme sleep.*"

"We're at Camp Fox."

I may have snarled at him, but I opened the door, climbed out, and grunted at my quickly stiffening muscles. I wasn't going to be able to move tomorrow.

"Damn, you're a sight for sore eyes," Tyler said walking toward us with a wide smile.

Jase ran out from behind his captain and pulled me into a hug. Mutt hopped around us. Jase stepped back and wrinkled his nose. "Jesus. You guys need showers."

"Happy to see you, too," I mumbled, and I really was. Seeing the kid alive and well made me feel like everything we'd gone through had been worth it.

"How many were lost?" Clutch asked.

"Three brave souls," Tyler replied. "But we gained fuel trucks and cut into Doyle's numbers." Then his jaw tightened. "How'd Southpaw bite it?"

"It was the darndest thing," Tack said. "He was shot. Then he turned."

Tyler frowned. "Same thing happened to two of Alpha team. The only thing we can figure out is that the Dogs dipped their ammo in zed blood."

I raised my brows. "Wow, that's low."

"But smart," Clutch said. "They don't have to be accurate, only good enough to nick one of us with a shot, and we're no longer an issue." Then he frowned. "I'd think the guns would jam from sticky bullets."

Tyler grimaced. "It's messed up, true enough. Let's head to my office and debrief."

"Later," Clutch said. "Bravo team needs rest first."

Tyler moved his gaze slowly over the three of us before nodding. "Understood. But we need to debrief as soon as you're up. We have extra racks in the troops' barracks if you want to stay. Tack can show you around."

Clutch looked to me, and I shrugged. "Okay, for now at least."

Tyler smiled. "You'll find Camp Fox is more secure than ever. You're safe here."

"You haven't seen our camp yet," Clutch replied.

"No, I haven't," Tyler said. "Where are you at now?"

Clutch paused before speaking. "We're at Fox Park. Cash and I thought it could be made into a solid fallback location for the Camp. It needs a lot of work, but we should always prepare for the worst."

"Agreed. I'll mention the park to Colonel Lendt. A fallback location doesn't sound like a bad idea, though I doubt we'll need it. We've got Doyle on the run and the zeds will be gone come winter."

"What makes you so sure the zeds will die out when winter comes?" I asked.

"Their bodies are decaying, and they are running off the most basic of instincts," he replied. "They'll die from exposure because they're not smart enough to seek shelter. That is, if their bodies don't rot away by then."

After watching a zed continue to function completely under water for days, I had my doubts. "And if they don't die off or rot away?"

Tyler shrugged. "Then we keep killing them."

TWENTY-SIX

Ten days later

"One vehicle coming in at our two o'clock," Jase said while he adjusted his night-vision binoculars. "I can't make out how many are inside yet, but Mutt doesn't like this situation."

I threw a quick glance at the fidgeting coyote at Jase's ankles before returning focus to my rifle's scope. "Does she like any situation?"

"Sure," he replied. "Dinnertime, bedtime, walks, any time there's a chance to steal someone's food."

I chuckled as I lay on my stomach, the approaching vehicle in my sights. I was here in case things went to shit.

Hmph.

I'd figured things had gone to shit the moment two Dogs called Tyler on the radio, asking for amnesty, especially with one of those Dogs being Sean. How many zeds had he personally dumped over the gate at the farm? I didn't trust him. Not one bit.

Clutch had agreed. That's why he took a second squad to come at the Dogs from behind in case this was an ambush. I wanted to be on his team, but unlike Clutch and even Jase, I wasn't particularly strong in the field, making Clutch pleased since he preferred me to be as far from the action as possible. At least I was a good shot, and so I was made one of Camp Fox's designated snipers.

The truck came to a stop at the prearranged intersection one hundred yards from our current position. Tyler might be an idealist but even he knew better than to allow Dogs to enter the Camp unescorted.

I adjusted my scope on the driver. *Sean, what are you up to?*

I moved a millimeter to the left to make out the passenger. *Fucking Weasel.* This situation just kept getting better and better.

"I only see two Dogs," Jase said.

"Same here," I added.

"Okay. Give them the signal," Tyler said while lying on the ground several feet from me.

Eddy came to his feet and clicked his flashlight on and off three times.

A light flashed three times in response from the Dogs' truck.

"That's our cue." Tyler looked at the three of us. "These guys may be on the level, but play it safe. If anything smells funny, we cut and run."

"Yes, sir," the boys said, and I tacked on a "got it."

Jase and Eddy had become hardened soldiers seemingly overnight, though I guess that's what this world did to a person. They were young, and they clearly looked to Tyler as their hero, even though he couldn't have been more than ten years their elder. When not with Tyler, they were often with Eddy's mother, who had quickly adopted Jase as one of her own.

"Hold up. We've got incoming," Jase said.

"Dogs?" Tyler asked.

"No. Zeds. Ten o'clock."

"Cash, if you've got a shot, take it," Tyler ordered.

I adjusted my scope. It was dark, but the night scope lit up the zeds just fine. I focused first on the hunched-over zed. *Pop.* Then on the hunched over petite zed. *Pop.* Then on the large lumbering male. Fire engulfed it before I pulled the trigger.

I squinted at the sudden flames. "That wasn't me."

"It looks like someone from the truck threw a Molotov cocktail," Tyler said. "Jesus, just what we need. A flaming zed setting the country-side on fire" He pressed his headset. "Bravo, this is Alpha. Hold off. The Dogs are attacking the zeds only. Over."

"*This is Bravo. Copy that,*" Clutch replied in my headset.

Tyler turned back to me. "Finish this before Sarge gets trigger happy."

It was easy to find my target, since it was on fire and wobbling from side to side. "Swiggity swire, guess what's on fire," I murmured and pulled the trigger. Then smiled. "Swiggity swed, guess what's dead."

"All clear," Jase said.

"Then let's pick up our guests," Tyler said, coming to his feet. "Let's do this just like we planned. Jase, you're with me. Cash, you cover us and wait for pickup from Bravo. Eddy will have your six."

I gave Tyler a thumbs up.

"If these guys fuck with us, try to avoid kill shots. We need the information they have."

I gave him another thumbs up.

I heard the Humvee start up and pull away, but I never took my eyes off the Dogs, waiting for them to make a wrong move. But the two men stood in front of their truck with its lights on. They stood without rifles and arms held out.

A gunshot behind me startled me, and I yanked around to see Eddy standing, facing away from me "Eddy?" I asked.

"Just one zed," he replied. "All clear."

I refocused. The Humvee headed down the gravel hill and stopped in front of them. Tyler and Jase got out and walked toward the Dogs.

Clutch's voice came through my headset. "*This is Bravo. Get your asses out of there, Alpha. You've got a world of hungry trouble heading your way.*"

I looked up from my scope but couldn't make out anything in the dark fields. I narrowed my eyes and realized that the darkness itself was moving. My eyes widened. There went the assumption that zeds moved less at night. I looked through my scope to target the nearest risks.

"Be ready, Eddy," I said. "Because a shitload of zeds are headed this way."

Twenty-Seven

I took my time targeting the zeds nearest to Tyler's Humvee.

Get 'em where I want 'em.

Only when I knew I had kill shots, I fired. After four zeds fell, I clicked my headset. "This is Sweeper," I said, using the call sign Tyler had given me after seeing me take out a zed over a hundred meters out. "Clear out, and I'll lay cover as long as possible."

Eddy fired more shots behind me, and it took everything to not turn around.

"Talk to me, Eddy," I said.

"We need to get out of here soon. Very, very soon!"

I aimed and fired, accompanied by a symphony of gunfire to my right.

"This is Bravo. We'll pick up Sweeper as soon as you're clear."

I would've told Clutch to hurry the fuck up, but I didn't want to take my hand off my rifle for even a second. I fired three more shots before a Molotov cocktail flew through the air. I noticed Tyler yanking a Dog to the Humvee. As soon as the Dogs were loaded into the vehicle, I switched my sights back to the herd, with the fire spreading.

Eddy was sending off long bursts behind me.

"Alpha is Oscar Mike. Clear out!"

I continued to fire until I had to reload. The gunfire to my distant right became sporadic.

"This is Bravo. Sweeper, we're on our way, so be ready."

I clicked the mag into place, and turned around to help Eddy. A couple dozen dark shapes were tripping over their fallen comrades on their way after us. I lifted my rifle and started firing.

When they closed in too tight, I backed up and fired at their legs to slow them down. Headlights came up the hill from behind me, shining light on the zeds. It was a sight that I knew would give me nightmares for years. Jaundiced eyes reflected light almost like cats. Zeds opened and closed their stained mouths like they were imagining what it would be like to chew on us. They reached out to us with clawed, gnarled fingers—those who still had fingers, anyway.

The .30 cal on Clutch's Humvee cut down the first line of zeds.

I grabbed Eddy and we sprinted toward the Humvee. The back door swung open and we tumbled inside.

Griz sped off. Tack stayed at the .30 cal.

"You okay?" Clutch demanded from his position in the front passenger seat.

"We're good. We're not bit," I replied before rolling off Eddy and leaning back.

"Zeds take the whole 'you are what you eat' thing way too seriously," Eddy chuckled then dropped his head back. "Jesus, that was close."

"Yeah." I sighed and eyed Clutch. "The information those two Dogs have better be worth it."

———

"...The militias are struggling, but they're still fighting the good fight. Keep them in your prayers.

In further news, I've yet to verify the rumors circulating that a central-ized government is being organized and that new 'super' cities are being architected. I've asked Lt. Col. Lendt at Camp Fox for confirmation, but I've gotten no response. Same story, different day. But I'm going to keep asking. You hear me, Lendt? I'm going to keep asking until you give me an answer or send in your troops and shut me up.

Here's my thought for the day: The zeds are the enemy, so why is Lendt withholding information that could save lives? My advice? Trust no one, my friends, whether they have a pulse or not.

This is Hawkeye broadcasting on AM 1340. Be safe and know that you're not alone."

"That radio jockey is a splinter in my sphincter," Lendt said as he sat down at the table where Clutch, Jase, Eddy, and I were eating leftovers from dinner. Mutt was tearing into our scraps on the floor.

"Have you met with Hawkeye before?" I asked, twirling more spaghetti around my fork.

"He hasn't even tried to contact me," Lendt replied. "And I'm not exactly a hard person to find."

Hawkeye's transmission was a recorded broadcast, one that I'd heard earlier, but they replayed his daily transmissions every four hours at the request of the civilians on base. His voice had something familiar about it, yet I couldn't quite place him.

Not yet, anyway.

"Well, are you withholding information?" I asked.

"What goddamn information do I have to withhold?" Lendt countered, then cracked his neck. "Folks think that just because I'm a colonel that I have some super-secret handshake. I know as much as anyone else. NORAD hasn't made contact yet. Everything I hear is from other bases in the same boat as we are."

"Have you thought about tracking down Hawkeye to set the record straight? Maybe offer to have him interview you on the air?" I asked. "It sounds like he's trying to rile up the civvies against you." Then it hit me. Hawkeye disliked Lendt, just like Doyle had. Yet, Lendt had done all right by me so far.

Lendt chuckled. "He's definitely trying to rile folks up, but he's a conspiracy theorist, and that's what conspiracy theorists do. He's one of those people who's suspicious of anyone in authority. It doesn't matter what I say, he'd find a way to make me out to be the asshole."

Tyler set his tray on the table and saluted.

"At ease, Captain," Lendt said.

Tyler took a seat and started cutting his spaghetti. "The two men are being kept in the brig tonight for both their and our safety, per your orders, sir."

"They should be executed for treason," Clutch said.

"Agreed," I added quickly, especially when I discovered Weasel was the second Dog. I'd had the heebie-jeebies since.

"They will stand trial." Lendt smirked. "Then they'll be executed."

Tyler frowned and put down his fork. "They surrendered. They deserve a fair trial. Doyle put a militia together as quickly as Camp Fox moved into action at the outbreak. A lot of good men joined up to help, and a lot of the people here now owe their lives to the militia. Now, we're going to kill them for signing up to help and then going AWOL when they realized Doyle was no longer out for the greater good?"

"They'd had no problems obeying Doyle until now," I countered. "Why the sudden change?"

Tyler held up a hand. "I'm just playing devil's advocate, but maybe they did want out, but they couldn't get out until now. Have you thought of that?"

"Have you thought that they may be here under Doyle's direction?" Clutch asked, raising the same argument we'd been having ever since the Dogs contacted Lendt. "We should be thinking of what Doyle would want in this camp."

Twenty-Eight

Three days later

My aim was off. The machete slit the zed's windpipe wide open instead of cleaving its skull. The near-severed head swayed, and my next swing scalped it, sending half of its brain and what had been long blonde hair to the ground.

Clutch had brought Jase and me back out to the apple orchard to win back the apple tree and for some much-needed close-up fighting. I didn't realize how badly I'd needed the exercise. I had become so dependent on my rifle that I'd let myself get rusty in hand-to-hand combat.

I swung the machete I'd grabbed from Jase's stash and took off the arm of the zed reaching for me. It hissed and reached out with the other. I swung again. This time, the machete snagged on bone and didn't go all the way through. I kicked the zed back and yanked my weapon free. When it came at me again, I quit playing with it and finished it with a slanted blow down its face. Half of its head and face slid off, and I looked to see how many zeds remained.

Five.

Clutch demolished one.

Four.

I went for the ugliest zed next. Its nose had rotted off and only one ear remained. I made my way around it, careful to keep plenty of open space between me and everything else. It had been one of Clutch's first rules he'd taught me: *never back yourself into a corner.*

The zed followed my movements.

I let it come to me. *Get 'em where I want 'em.*

I raised the machete and brought it down in a straight line and shredded the zed from its chin down to its privates. "Oh, God." I stepped back, trying not to breathe, but the stench caused bile to rise in my throat.

The zed's organs tumbled out, jiggling with each step it took toward me. Clutch finished it off since I was too busy puking.

"Let's not do that again," Clutch advised, holding his arm over his nose.

"Yeah," I said, now dealing with the foul aftertaste in my mouth.

"Hey, guys. Check this one out," Jase said from behind us.

I wiped my mouth and turned to find Jase grinning. In front of him was the last standing zed missing its hands and the lower part of its jaw.

"Finish it," Clutch said. "This isn't a game."

Jase shot an adolescent glare before taking his axe and bringing it down on the zed's skull. We double checked every zed before I grabbed an apple off the tree and took a bite.

Jase turned to the shed. "C'mon, Mutt. It's all clear."

Mutt peeked from the shadows, and then trotted over to brush against her master. He handed her an apple.

"She's quite the fighter," I said.

Jase shrugged. "She's more of a lover than a fighter."

The coyote preferred to keep her distance from zeds. I remembered that feeling. While I still hated zeds, I no longer froze in terror when I saw one. Maybe I was numb to the violence, but I could kill without feeling a single pang of guilt. Sometimes, when I spent too much time thinking, I wondered if we hadn't reached the end of the world but that we'd reached the end of humanity.

Something hit my head, and I jerked around to find Jase pulling back to throw another apple at me.

"Nice. Real nice," I muttered and picked up the apple and stepped out of the way as Clutch backed the truck up to the tree. I hopped onto the bed and started plucking ripe apples from the tree.

Jase joined me and we plucked several bushels of fresh apples while Clutch stood watch. Jase said Mutt was on guard duty, too, though with the way the coyote was sprawled out in the sunshine, I found that hard to believe.

On our way to the park, our work at the Camp done for now, we stopped at the gas station to grab more supplies. Several more zeds had meandered onto the lot, but they were easily dispatched. I'd forgotten how much easier looting was with three of us, rather than just two.

When Jase went to open the glass doors to the restaurant, I stopped. "Not there."

The two kid zeds were nowhere in sight, but it still didn't feel right. I'd never seen zeds retain any semblance of humanity, but this pair had seemed different. Maybe I'd let them get to me and my mind played tricks on me. They haunted my dreams. But that day, when we'd seen them, they'd showed no aggression. It had seriously freaked me out.

I didn't tell Jase about them, and Clutch had simply nodded in agreement as he walked into the store and started clearing shelves.

I looked across the shelves, and hopelessness wrenched my heart. This gas station was an easy place to loot yet many of the shelves were still full, aside from what we'd taken the last time. Were there really so few people left?

Listless, I helped Clutch fill the large bags we'd brought. The only other sound was the zed still thumping against the bathroom door. We'd cleared out much of the store before I realized there were only two of us. "Where's Jase?" I asked.

Clutch nodded toward the liquor section.

I rolled my eyes, and we headed into the section to find Jase with a nearly full cart.

"Not that," Clutch said, grabbing the wine coolers from Jase's hands. "If you're going to drink, do it right." He handed the kid a bottle of whiskey. I grabbed the remaining bottles of Everclear and vodka, but didn't have any intention to drink it. Alcohol worked great for disinfecting wounds, starting fires, and especially cleaning zed goo off things.

I grabbed an armful of wine bottles. "We should get going," I said. "I want to get unloaded before dark."

Jase hurriedly grabbed a couple more bottles before heading out with us. Mutt waited in the back of the truck, chewing on an apple.

"Save some for us," I called out.

The coyote raised her ears and then bit into another apple.

Clutch took a draw of whiskey before climbing in behind the wheel. Jase watched, grabbed a bottle, and took a drink. He coughed and bent over.

I patted his shoulder. "You're in the big leagues now." I hopped into the truck and Jase climbed in the back several seconds later.

Clutch smirked. "You look a little green around the gills."

"I'm. Fine," he choked out.

"Give it time," Clutch said. "It'll get easier."

And it did.

By sunset, Jase was drunk for the first time in his life, and we discovered he was a happy drunk, finding pretty much anything and everything funny. We sat in the park office, and the booze helped the MREs from Camp Fox taste better. And I had long since noticed that apples and wine paired beautifully together for dessert. Clutch was quiet, though he'd already put a hurting on his bottle of whiskey.

Still, it had been a nice night. The three of us together again and not running for our lives.

A couple hours later, we'd all passed out, though I awoke to the sounds of Clutch's nightmares. They were even worse when he drank, and he drank often.

"He still has them," Jase said quietly.

I found Jase propped up on an elbow.

"Yeah."

"He should get help," he said. "There's someone at Camp Fox he can talk to."

"Get some sleep," I replied.

Jase collapsed with a thud, and I figured he was asleep by the time his head hit the pillow.

I wrapped myself tighter around Clutch, and he quieted somewhat, but I could never break through his pain. Sometimes I wondered if he thought he deserved the nightmares and depression because of the things he'd done. He'd never said anything to that effect, because if he had, I would've firmly reminded him that everything he'd done was to save lives and that he was a hero. But, those kinds of words would fall on deaf ears. Clutch was the hardest on himself.

In the months that I'd known him, Clutch had opened only a tiniest sliver of himself to me. He kept things bottled up inside, acting impervious all day. But a mind was a pressure cooker. It could only take so much before it must let off steam or else explode. Clutch's nightmares and killing zeds were his steam.

I was afraid of what would happen if he ever exploded.

Twenty-Nine

"Wake up! Wake up!"

I bolted awake and then grabbed my throbbing head. "Shh," I ordered Jase as I reached for a bottle of water.

Clutch pulled himself to his feet, and I grimaced at him before taking a long swig. How could he drink three times as much as me yet wake up ready to take on the world?

"What happened?" Clutch asked, stretching his shoulders.

"Captain Masden just called on the radio. Colonel Lendt was killed, and both Dogs have gone missing."

I got to my feet and stood, in stunned paralysis, as his words cut through my cotton-filled brain. While we'd been drinking and enjoying ourselves, the Dogs had escaped, killed Lendt, and did God only knew what else at the Camp.

We should've been there.

Clutch scrambled into his clothes, and I kicked it into gear and hurried as fast I could in a hangover haze. We were loaded into the truck in less than five minutes. Clutch drove while I finished dressing and we all took turns with the Tylenol, food, and water. Twenty-two miles later, I started to feel semi-human again.

When we reached Camp Fox, the gate opened and the guards motioned us through. Clutch sped down the winding roads until we stopped at a familiar brick building. I grabbed my rifle.

We jogged up the steps and through the doors of HQ, which had now become town hall, to find at least half of the Camp's population milling around. Some looked like they were in shock, others looked downright pissed.

"Tell us what's going on!" someone shouted.

"We have a traitor!" someone else shouted back.

"String them up!"

The shouting and finger pointing continued. I gave Clutch the look, the one that insinuated we were mice about to step into a mousetrap.

Tack motioned to us from across the crowd, and we weaved toward where he was blocking people from entering the hallway. He looked like he was about to be overrun. "Captain Masden needs every hand on deck. He's in the Colonel's office," he said, moving aside to let us through.

Clutch nodded, and Jase and I followed him down the hall. We stepped inside to find the walls riddled with bullets. Five body bags littered the floor, making dark heaps across the wood.

"Crap," Jase said breathlessly.

When Tyler saw us, he patted the injured man's shoulder and headed our way. "Glad you could make it. We've got a Charlie Foxtrot on our hands."

"The two Dogs," I said.

Tyler nodded tightly. "Likely, since they went missing late last night."

"How'd they escape?" Clutch asked, the tone inferring he knew they'd escaped all along.

"Someone killed the guard and let them out." Tyler rubbed his neck. "Damn it, I should've known better."

"Who carries the keys?" Clutch asked, ignoring Tyler's self-criticism.

"Doesn't matter," he replied, shaking his head. "The guard on duty always carries a set. They could've gotten the keys off the guard."

Clutch walked over to one of the five body bags and unzipped it, frowned, then rezipped it.

Tyler rubbed his temples. "Lendt had coffee every morning with the civilian leadership council. These guys knew exactly when and where to hit."

"What's the status on the Dogs, Captain?" Clutch asked, all business.

"Unaccounted for," Tyler replied. "I need every troop out there looking for who did this. I can't trust the civilians. They'd turn this hunt into a lynch mob."

"You can count on us," I said.

Tyler smiled weakly. "I know. Griz is on point. Go see him at the chow hall for your assigned sectors. You're relieved."

He turned and walked off, leaving the three of us standing alone.

"I guess Tyler's in charge now," I said quietly.

"C'mon," Clutch said and he led the way back down the hall and through the agitated crowd, several of whom threw us distrusting glares. When we reached the cafeteria, Griz was standing with Smitty. Both looked exhausted, though Smitty looked more tense than usual.

"Perfect timing," Griz said. "Jase, you're with Smitty. He'll fill you in."

"Yes, sir," Jase said and jogged to catch up with the slender, clean-cut soldier heading outside.

"Where do you need us?" Clutch asked before I could.

Griz turned and pointed at a spot on the map laid out across the table. "I've broken the Camp into sectors. We're too short-staffed, so every pair gets two sectors. You guys have sectors thirty-one and thirty-two, but stay together. Whatever you do, don't split up. Since everyone's been accounted for, the traitor is still walking around. If you find the Dogs, we need them alive to interrogate them."

"Understood," Clutch said. "That it?"

He handed Clutch a radio. "Let's find those fuckers."

Clutch and I headed out. Sectors thirty-one and thirty-two were on the far edge of the base so we drove there. We silently walked through buildings and examined every shadow, finding nothing. The Dogs should've been on their way back to Doyle by now. It made no sense for them to stick around after their job was done.

I smelled a familiar stench and stopped cold. I narrowed my eyes at the shadows near the outer fence. "What's that?"

Clutch took slow steps closer while I held my rifle at the ready.

I lingered until he got down on a knee and I came closer.

I kicked at the two zeds—one male, one female—tied together. They watched us, their mouths taped shut and their hands cut off. Each zed was cut wide open, with entrails oozing out. The stench was horrible, though they'd been open for long enough for some of the horrendous odor to dissipate. "What the hell is going on?" I asked.

"No fucking clue." Clutch stood, raised his rifle, and finished the two zeds.

These zeds were connected to Dogs, somehow. "Why would someone order a zed delivery here?" I thought aloud. "And why the hell would someone cut them open?"

Having zeds inside the Camp was dangerous enough, especially if they got free and leaked their infectious goo all over the place.

I took a step back. "Oh, shit."

"What is it?" he asked.

"The Dogs aren't done yet. They're going to spread the infection."

THIRTY

Clutch and I looked at each other.

We left the stinking corpses and took off running back to the truck.

A blast detonated in the distance, and smoke rose from the direction of HQ.

My heart pounded. "No!"

We raced back to find soot-covered people pouring out of the building. Many were injured and wet with blood. Clutch slammed on the brakes just as Griz and several troops ran toward the building. I jumped out and yanked Griz back. "Anyone who got hit with shrapnel is infected!"

Griz's brows furrowed in confusion. "What are you talking about?"

I pointed at the building. "They used zed-soaked grenades!"

His eyes widened. "Are you sure? You've got to be fucking sure about this."

Clutch came up. "Yeah, Griz. They're using dirty bombs."

The soldier muttered out a string of curses before raising his hand-held radio. "This is Griz. Anyone injured by the grenade blast is infected. You are ordered to eliminate anyone injured. Repeat. Kill anyone injured. Over."

Chatter erupted on the radio.

Repeat last.

Say again.

You're joking, right?

Griz sighed. "You heard me right! I'm not fucking with you! The Dogs used dirty bombs, goddammit. Kill the injured!"

"God help us all," Griz said and opened fire on survivors.

Screams erupted. People went berserk, running wildly away from us, seeking shelter.

I raised my rifle. My hands shook. My aim needed to be right. I took a deep breath and sought out the most injured. They would turn first.

I fired.

A woman holding her bloody stomach fell. From my side, Clutch fired into the crowd. The sounds of more gunfire from both sides filled the air.

I took down a man with a head wound. Then a kid getting trampled in the chaos that had overtaken the Camp.

As if spooked by something, people switched directions and starting running toward us.

A zed with a massive chest wound sunk its teeth into the neck of a screaming man. I fired off two shots back to back, taking both down.

Clutch grabbed me. "Run!"

We sprinted toward the truck. The stampede was nearly upon us. Clutch grabbed my waist and threw me onto the bed. I grabbed his shirt to pull him up, but he was yanked from my grasp.

"Clutch!" I screamed, but I couldn't find him anywhere in the mass of running people.

People reached for me but were smashed against the truck by the sheer force of numbers. The four-by-four wobbled from side to side. A woman shrieked like a yippy dog as she was squeezed between the truck and people until she drowned under the stampede.

"Godammit! Clutch!"

In a panic, I continued firing as I crept to the edge, searching for him on the ground. A familiar man shoved a kid down on his way past.

"Sean," I growled out. He looked up right when I shot him. Weasel was only a few feet behind Sean, and I killed him with my last round.

The truck was rocking so much that I dropped the clip while reloading.

The stampede thinned out as the people spread out. Bringing up the rear were mostly zeds. When they first turned, zeds were nearly as fast as humans, and they were taking down people left and right, like they were at a wine tasting party.

I went through three more clips before I pulled out the machete. I jumped off the back of the truck and stumbled over bodies on the ground. I hacked at zeds and slashed anyone still living who bore shrapnel wounds. I shoved bodies aside.

"Clutch!" I screamed until my voice gave out. I kept going, pushing over bodies, searching, until my gaze fell on camo fatigues.

I dropped to my knees and pulled the lifeless man onto my lap and started sobbing.

I'd found Clutch.

PART NINE
BETRAYAL

THE NINTH CIRCLE OF HELL

Thirty-One

Three days later

Forty-two.

That's how many Camp Fox survivors made it to the park. After surviving the zed outbreak, only one out of every seventeen civilians survived the Dogs' attack. Of that number, over half the survivors were troops, as they'd been spread across the base hunting the Dogs when the attack started.

Forty-two was barely enough to protect the park from zeds, let alone protect it against the risk of Dogs. Same story, different day.

I snuggled against Clutch and held his hand, just like I had every day since the attack. On the first day, his fingers had trembled, but the doctor said not to think anything of it, that the spasms were due to the swelling on his brain. Even though Clutch no longer showed any response, I still held hope.

Jase clung to hope, too. He slept alone in a beanbag chair on the other side of Clutch's bed every night. He no longer had his faithful sidekick. The timid coyote had sacrificed herself to save her master when a zed tackled Jase. It seemed like he'd lost enough that he no longer had much to say.

He blamed himself for her death. But no more than I blamed myself for Clutch's situation.

Griz, Tack, Smitty, Eddy, even Tyler had come through without injuries. A selfish, dark shadow deep inside me was angry that they were okay while Clutch lay lifeless on the bed. It had all seemed so unfair. But as soon as the guys stopped by to offer respect, I'd been ashamed of my thoughts. Those men were heroes as much as Clutch. They'd just gotten lucky this time.

Clutch had been crushed under the stampede. His back was broken, along with three ribs, both legs, and his left wrist. He also had a dislocated shoulder and a fractured skull. If—*when*— he woke, the doc said he could have permanent brain damage. And he'd be paralyzed from the waist down.

Still, I prayed for him to wake.

I *needed* him to wake.

On the nightstand next to his bed—against doctor's orders—sat a fully loaded Glock and the can of chewing tobacco I'd given him. The doctor—a general practitioner—figured that if Clutch woke up, he'd be suicidal, and would put a bullet through his brain. I disagreed.

The Clutch I knew would never pull the trigger.

I only hoped that when Clutch woke, he'd still be the man I knew.

In the background, Hawkeye's latest transmission droned on over the beeps of Clutch's life support system.

"*...The time is coming soon when we can all relocate to a zed-free zone. At the right time, I will give you all a date and time to meet, and we will head out together. A militia has volunteered to protect us on our journey. There is strength in numbers, my friends. Until tomorrow, this is Hawkeye broadcasting on AM 1340. Be safe and know that you're not alone.*"

Griz burst through the door and I nearly fell out of bed.

I got to my feet, gently, so as not to disturb Clutch's broken body. "What's wrong?"

"You better come quick."

I placed a kiss to Clutch's forehead and ran with Griz to his Jeep. "Where are we going?"

"Jase's cabin."

I sucked in a breath. *No!*

Fear stung my nerves. He'd been so quiet lately. He'd probably been planning on taking his own life since the attack, and I'd been so obsessed with Clutch that I ignored the signs.

I held on tightly as Griz squealed tires around winding roads through the dense morning fog. Three other vehicles were already parked at the cabin when we got there. I ran inside.

Expecting to find Jase's lifeless body, I was surprised to find Jase alive and well, and I let out a breath that I felt like I'd been holding since Griz grabbed me.

Then I noticed Jase had a rifle leveled at his best friend. Eddy kneeled on the floor, whimpering, with his wrists restrained behind his back. Tyler stood nearby, his arms folded over his chest.

I frowned. "What's going on?"

"Eddy couldn't take the guilt eating away at him anymore," Jase said with a cutting edge to his voice. "He'd figured his mom was exempt from getting chewed up by zeds. He figured wrong."

"None of that was supposed to happen. I swear it!" Eddy pleaded. "No one except Colonel Lendt was supposed to get hurt."

My jaw dropped. Eddy was the traitor? Of all people, a kid betrayed us?

Eddy sobbed. "I'm sorry, I'm sorry. I was trying to help everyone. I screwed up."

"What you did is *not* called screwing up. It's called treason," Tyler said coolly. "Your actions brought about the deaths of over three hundred innocent people, including your own mother."

Eddy lowered his head and sniffled, his body quivering.

"You can start making amends by giving us Doyle's location," Tyler said.

Eddy looked up, confused. He shook his head. "I had nothing to do with Doyle. Hawkeye arranged everything, even getting the two Dogs into Camp Fox."

Tyler frowned. "The AM jockey?"

The blood drained from my head as I finally placed Hawkeye's voice.

Eddy nodded. "Hawkeye had proof of zed-free zones that welcomed survivors. We could go there and be safe. But he'd said that Lendt didn't tell us about the zones because he didn't want to lose his power and control over everything and everyone at Camp Fox."

"And Hawkeye showed you this proof?"

"Hawkeye told me."

Tyler slowly shook his head. "Son, you were played for a fool. Hawkeye's the one interested in power and control. Not Lendt."

Eddy sniffled before looking across the faces in the room. His gaze stopped at one and morphed into a glare. "It's your fault. Mom would still be alive if it wasn't for you."

The room temp dropped twenty degrees when every pair of eyes turned to Smitty.

Smitty's gaze darted to Tyler. "I don't know what he's talking about."

Eddy's glare narrowed. "You said everything would be all right. That we were helping everyone."

Smitty fidgeted. "Stupid kid thinks to throw a scapegoat out to save his own ass. Don't try to pull me into this, Eddy. This is all on you."

Tyler took a step forward and shook his head. "You've always been a lousy poker player, Smitty." He nodded to Tack and Griz who I noticed both already had a pistol aimed at their fellow soldier. "Arrest him. Put him with Eddy."

Surprisingly, Smitty didn't rabbit. He stood, jaw clenched, while Tack disarmed and restrained him and Griz held the weapon level on him.

"I don't get it. Why, Corporal?" Tyler asked.

Smitty snorted. "When I joined up, I vowed to defend this country against all threats, domestic and foreign."

I rolled my eyes. How cliché. "And how does killing innocents fall under that?"

"None of that was supposed to happen. Hawkeye had said only the leadership had to go, so then everyone could relocate to the zed-free zone. The Dogs must've disobeyed orders. Maybe Doyle got wind of their plans and turned them."

"Hawkeye is Doyle, you idiot," I said and then walked out.

THIRTY-TWO

Two days later

Tyler led a public tribunal for Eddy and Smitty where shouts for death had erupted within seconds. Tyler passed judgment two minutes later and condemned both to die—not by hanging but by zeds. Not a single person cried for leniency.

It'd taken only three months for society to return to Old Testament ways of thinking.

Tyler delayed the execution one day to make arrangements and assemble volunteers. Jase had been the first to step up. I had been the second, quickly followed by Griz and Tack.

After I checked on Clutch, we headed out from the park in Camp Fox's heaviest duty truck—a HEMTT—that was nearly impenetrable against zeds. It made Doyle's garbage trucks look like Tonkas.

Tyler sat up front in the cab with Griz, who drove us to Camp Fox. Tyler rode along because he felt like it was his responsibility to see his decisions through. He'd become a recluse since the trial. I imagined the hard decisions he'd been forced to make were tearing him up inside. Me? I thought Smitty and Eddy had it coming after the pain they'd caused. They'd been idiots to believe there were safe zed-free zones out there, let alone that we could move hundreds of people across states to such zones. Before the outbreak, I never would've thought I could become so ruthless. Now, I realized it was the only way to survive.

The rest of us sat in the HEMTT's open back with the prisoners. The numbers of zeds in fields and on the roads grew as we neared the camp, though we'd already figured most would still be within Camp Fox. Zeds weren't exactly adventurous unless in a herd. They were lemmings like that. Now if we could only find a giant cliff and lead them to it.

As we passed Doyle's abandoned camp, I was surprised to find relatively few zeds in the area. I was even more surprised to find the gate closed. "I thought Lendt's guys had blown open the gate," I said.

Jase shrugged, not taking his gaze off Eddy sitting across from him. "Guess not."

The thought nagged at me until we reached Camp Fox. The gate stood wide open from when the base was evacuated, and several zeds wandered around near the guard box. Griz ran over three on his way through.

The HEMTT drove slowly down the road, swerving around bodies, and came to a stop a couple hundred meters inside. We couldn't risk going too deep into the Camp where the risk of being overtaken by zeds was too high. Even here, I could make out over twenty stragglers wandering around the open grass area.

I stood. "This is it."

Both Eddy and Smitty looked scared shitless, though Smitty also looked pissed off as though he thought he should be exempt from punishment.

Jase grabbed Eddy's arm and forced him to stand while Tack and I dragged Smitty to his feet.

Eddy looked across our faces with wide eyes as though one of us could pardon him. He watched me and paled. Then I realized he was looking past me. "Mom?"

Eddy tried to lunge forward, but Jase held him back. "Mom!"

About thirty meters away, a female zed with the same hair color as Eddy cocked its head and sniffed the air. Then it started to shuffle toward the truck.

"Mom." His lips trembled and tears fell down his face. "I'm so sorry."

The breath hardened in my lungs. Of all the shitty, rotten luck.

Tyler climbed up. "It's time. Eddy, you're up."

Eddy bit back a sob. "But my mom's out there."

Compassion flashed in Tyler's eyes. He opened his mouth to speak but clamped it shut. After a moment he nodded to Jase.

With a clenched jaw, Jase nudged Eddy to the edge and cut his wrist restraints. I half expected Jase to shove his friend off the truck as payback for Mutt's death, but instead he lowered Eddy gently to the ground.

Eddy stood there for a moment before looking up. "I'm sorry. I didn't mean for any of this to happen."

"I know," Tyler said quietly.

Eddy's feet looked like they'd been tied to sandbags with the way he trudged away from the truck and straight toward his mother. "I'm sorry. I'm sorry. I'm sorry."

The zed held its arms out and pulled Eddy into an embrace that almost seemed motherly. Until it lowered its mouth, jaws wide open, and clamped onto his throat. Eddy screamed and fell back, taking the zed with him.

Smitty jerked, and I tightened my grip. "You did this. Watch," I ordered, though it was taking all my strength to watch the execution play out. If I was here alone, I would've put a bullet through Eddy's skull to end his pain, but Tyler had been adamant about setting an example of what happened to traitors. There simply weren't enough of us left. We had to be able to depend on each other with our lives, or else we were all doomed.

Tyler had declared that Eddy's death would be first so that Smitty would have to watch what was about to happen to him. Everyone knew that Smitty had coerced the weaker boy to help. Eddy had simply been an unfortunate lackey, and I even found myself feeling sorry for the kid.

Smitty was the real traitor.

Eddy's screams turned into a gurgle before quieting. He spasmed as a nearby zed joined in on his shoulder.

On the HEMTT, Jase reached under the seat and pulled out one of the long wooden spears the survivors had been making from the park's trees. Camp Fox hadn't had much ammunition before the outbreak. Now, their ammo supply was dangerously low and would likely run out by fall. We were forced to find new weapons. Jase walked to the side and skewered a zed that had been trying to climb onto the truck.

Eddy had quit moving, and I let out a breath. His suffering was thankfully over.

The zeds stepped back. They didn't like the taste of their own.

It wouldn't take long now.

The smell of urine snagged me, and I looked down to find that Smitty had pissed himself. Not that I could blame him. Death by zeds wasn't an easy way to go, but it was easier than he deserved.

The two zeds drenched in Eddy's blood sniffed at the air and turned toward the HEMTT. At least a dozen zeds were already on the way from every direction. Jase killed another that had reached the truck.

Eddy's foot jerked.

Smitty tensed. "Don't do this. Please."

The two zeds reached the truck. Jase impaled the first, a male. He paused before killing what had been Eddy's mother. He inhaled. Then thrust.

What had been Eddy climbed to its feet. Blood was already congealing and browning around its throat and shoulder. It turned to the HEMTT and started jogging toward us.

Tyler turned. "Now."

We shoved Smitty off, and he collapsed, with his wrists still restrained, onto the ground ten feet below. He hopped up and started to run.

Tyler raised his pistol and shot the man in the leg.

Smitty grunted and fell onto his knee.

I reached down for a spear and killed an older zed bumping up against the back of the HEMTT.

Smitty tried to get back to his feet, but Eddy came up from behind and clamped onto his head. Smitty cried out and tried to shake Eddy off, but the zed held on, biting his scalp over and over. Smitty fell forward, screaming, twisting back and forth, but fresh zeds were strong, and Eddy hadn't been badly injured before he turned. The zed pinned the man and tore at his face. Smitty's high-pitched screams drew the attention of zeds that had been heading toward the truck.

Two more zeds joined in on Smitty's legs.

His screams abruptly stopped. A man could only take so much pain before the body shut down. Though his heart must've still kept beating since the zeds continued to chew for several minutes before backing away, leaving behind a mangled corpse.

Eddy was the first to reach the HEMTT. Jase thrust his spear through Eddy's eye, and the zed that had been Jase's friend fell.

Tack and I took out the next two zeds.

We waited. More zeds came, and we killed them.

Smitty's body quaked. It sat up. Its face and scalp were nearly gone, except for patches of skin and hair. For being a fresh zed, it took over a minute to climb to its feet with chewed up legs and restrained wrists. Once up, it hobbled right at the HEMTT.

Tack gave Smitty final rest.

"Let's go," Tyler said and thumped the roof of the cab. The HEMTT roared to life, and Griz drove, leaving nearly a hundred zeds slowly wandering toward us from the bowels of the camp.

Tyler sat next to me, leaned forward, and put his head in his hands. Jase stared off into the distance, and Tack pretended to sleep. When we approached Doyle's old camp, I stared at the gate. It didn't make sense that they'd lock up after they cleared the place. Light glinted off the silo with the faded Iowa Hawkeye logo, and I narrowed my eyes. The silos were old. Nothing should be *glinting* off rusted steel and dull aluminum. Then I saw another glint.

Binoculars.

I nudged Tyler. He looked up, his features worn by exhaustion.

"Doyle's camp isn't abandoned," I said.

He frowned. "I cleared it out myself. By the time I got there, the place was a graveyard. Doyle had already moved all his supplies out. Only three injured Dogs were left behind."

I shook my head. "So why is there someone up on the silo watching us?"

When the truth hit, he leaned back and air whooshed from his lungs. "Jesus. Doyle's been under our noses the whole time."

THIRTY-THREE

Three days later

"I believe we should take him off the respirator," the doctor said. "We simply don't have the resources to use equipment and medicine on terminal patients when it could be used on others."

I didn't let go of Clutch's hand. "You said he could still wake up."

"He *could*, and I've seen much worse cases wake up in the past. But given these primitive medical facilities—"

"As long as there's a chance, he stays on." I came to my feet, kissed Clutch, and walked past the doctor. I paused at the door. "And if you take him off, I swear to God, I will crucify you in the middle of Chow Town for the zeds to tear you apart."

Without waiting for a response, I stepped outside the park office AKA town hall AKA makeshift hospital. Wind cooled my cheeks, though anger still simmered just below the surface. It took several deep breaths before I could focus on what needed done.

My truck was parked just past the humming generators. I climbed in, gunned the engine, and put it into gear. With the window open, I rested an elbow on the door while I meandered through the park, savoring the fresh air, before finally heading into Tyler's cabin, where all troops not sleeping or on guard-duty sat.

It was the same as yesterday, and the day before that. Droning debates on how to attack Doyle with not nearly enough manpower and even less ammo. When it came down to it, there wasn't a single feasible plan that didn't run the risk of losing a life, and Tyler refused to sacrifice one more person for Doyle.

People rotated through as they rolled on and off shift. I listened, offering up a comment here and there, until it was my time to stand guard at one of the park's four entrances.

The hours at the gate alongside Jase bled by.

"I heard what the doctor said," Jase said a couple hours into our shift.

I leaned against a tree. "Yeah?"

"I would've punched him for even suggesting pulling the plug."

"Believe me, I considered it." I watched a bald eagle fly over.

"Don't give up on him," Jase said.

"Never."

———

The following morning, I kissed Clutch good-bye.

"Be safe," I whispered and left him.

Numb, I returned to my cabin, shaved my head, loaded everything I needed into the truck, and drove away from the park. I had a plan to take out Doyle that involved the loss of only one life, though I had "borrowed" some of Tyler's ammunition stash during the night to make it work.

The Fox Hills Municipal Airport was only a couple miles northeast of town, not far from the river. I parked next to the only row of hangars, where seven old tin buildings of various faded colors stood side by side. I geared up with every weapon I owned and grabbed the crowbar.

A decrepit, lone zed meandered down by the last hangar. I rapped gently on the first hangar. Nothing. I checked the door. Locked. I pried it open and looked inside. An old Cessna 172. It would work but the nose wheel would make it more difficult to land in a field. I checked the next three hangars. One was empty, one held a Beech Bonanza, and I stopped at the fourth. *Perfect.* Inside awaited a yellow taildragger. On its tail, the Piper Cub logo matched the tattoo on my forearm.

The old hangar door pushed opened easily without power, and I pulled out the small plane. I returned to the truck and grabbed the duffel bag, admiring the way the airplane shone in the sunlight as I headed back toward it. Its owner had taken good care of the classic.

The badly decomposed zed had finally made it within twenty feet of the Cub. I met it halfway, and finished it off with my crowbar. I opened the duffel, kneeled, pulled out my knife, but paused before I cut the zed open. After a moment, I stood, sheathed my knife, and lifted my chin. "No," I said simply.

I checked the Cub over, made sure the gas tanks were full, and loaded everything up. It took only two hand props to start, and I climbed inside, leaving the door and window open. I skipped the warm-up because engine noise would quickly draw attention, and a plane this small would never survive a collision with a zed. The wheels broke free from the runway at under fifty MPH before the first zeds emerged from the tree line.

The wind made the flight bumpy. They'd hear me coming, but I didn't care. If Doyle hadn't fled his camp already, he would never abandon his camp.

The silos of Doyle's camp came into view eight minutes later. I descended as I approached. I flew right over the camp, looking down to see shaved heads looking up at me. They looked filthy and half-starved. Then I saw the only man without a shaved head. He waved his arms at his Dogs, and someone fired. Then a symphony of gunfire sounded around me.

Where the hell had they gotten their hands on all that firepower? Camp Fox had cut them off, yet these guys were shooting like they had an unlimited supply of ammo. Nevertheless, I couldn't turn back now. I started my one-eighty.

Get 'em where I want 'em.

I grabbed the duffel from the seat in front of me. I set the bag on my lap and opened it. As I neared the camp with nearly all of its occupants outside firing at me, I searched out Doyle. When I found him, I pulled the pin on the first grenade and dropped it. But the wind and velocity grabbed at the grenade, and it blew at least fifty feet away.

"Dammit," I muttered and quickly pulled the pins on two more, dropping them.

Dogs were running in different directions while continuing to send fully automatic gunfire my way. I tightly circled overhead, dropping grenades onto the camp.

Sudden agony pierced my calf, sending searing pain every time I touched the rudder pedal, but I remained focused on my mission.

The propane tanks in the camp exploded, and the blast rocked the small Cub.

I righted the plane and continued to drop grenades until the bag was empty. Then I broke away and cut the engine to land silently in a hay field just on the other side of a band of trees, hiding me from the camp. I went to climb out of the plane and winced, grabbing my left calf. My hand came away bloody.

I'd been shot.

If they were using tainted bullets, the virus was now flowing in my veins.

Not much time now. I had to hurry.

I grimaced and tied a bandana around the wound and climbed out. I reached in for my rifle and started to limp my way into the trees and toward the camp.

I figured the Dogs would've assumed this was a hit-and-run attack. Since no trucks broke down their gates, they were now safe.

That's where they'd be wrong.

THIRTY-FOUR

hat came next had to be up close and personal.

I approached the camp from its backside. The zed pit was still there, full of rotting corpses. I held up my rifle, using the scope to scan the ground, then the silos. It still looked like an abandoned camp except for the smoke.

Even I hadn't given Doyle's camp a second thought when we'd evacuated Camp Fox. We'd all been fools to not double check.

As I limped closer, I could hear the voices. They sounded like an echo of the dying at Camp Fox. My heart clenched. I'd caused this. I knew not all these people were bad, some were simply misled. I inhaled deeply and moved forward. There was no other way.

Sometimes, only killing would stop further killing.

I'd planned to dip the grenades in zed goo and give them a taste of their own medicine. I'd believed they deserved the karma after the hundreds of innocents they'd slaughtered. But, at the last moment I realized I couldn't go through with that. I refused to sink to their level. These men were getting off easy.

Not all would be so lucky. The noise would attract zeds from Camp Fox, which was part of my plan. I was counting on them to take care of anyone I missed.

No guard stood at the gate by the pit, and I cracked the gate open and peered inside. Through the dusty, smoky haze, I could see contorted bodies littering the ground. Some moved, many didn't. I limped across the camp, quickly glancing from body to body. One man covered in blood reached out to me for help but I continued on.

With my shaved head, no one seemed to notice me through the haze. They were all preoccupied. After I ran out of bodies to check, I gritted my teeth and headed toward Doyle's office.

I'd really hoped to finish him off the easy way.

I didn't even pause before throwing the steel door open.

Inside, I found Doyle alone, sitting with one leg up on a desk, wrapping his bloodied forearm. When he looked up, his eyes widened, and he reached for his rifle propped behind his desk.

"Don't," I ordered, pulling shut and dead bolting the door behind me.

He leaned back and watched me. His faded yellow cap was stained and bloody cuts crisscrossed his soot-covered face. "Where's Clutch? I figured he'd come to finish the job himself."

"He's on his way," I lied.

Doyle seemed to relax. "So, you're here to keep me company until he gets here, is that it?"

"That's it." I kept my rifle leveled on Doyle. "I don't get you. You had a good thing going with Camp Fox. Then you had to go and fuck things up by going after them. Twice."

"Hmph." Doyle leaned back. "It never would've lasted. Both Lendt and I were spreading my resources thin protecting the weak. Everyone would've all died if I didn't change the game. It's really quite simple. The weak had to die so that the strong can thrive."

I stared at him for a moment. "That's insane."

He narrowed his eyes. "Think about it. We have limited food, limited supplies. Yet, too many people to do anything efficiently. Thinning our numbers for the strongest to survive has been the way of every species throughout history."

"But that's so...heartless," I said, finding it hard to breathe.

He chuckled. "There's no room for that sort of thing in this world."

"You're wrong," I said coldly. "There's no room for *you* in this world."

He and I looked at one another for a split second. A wide grin crossed his face. "Your rifle's empty."

I dropped my weapon and pulled out my machete. The rifle had served its purpose as a prop. It had gotten me in front of Doyle.

He lunged, and I was too slow. We crashed to the floor, and the machete slid across the floor. He was strong for his age, stronger and bigger than me. I wasn't able to buck him off, so I rolled, squeezing out from under him. He caught me from behind and put a chokehold on me.

I couldn't breathe and knew I only had seconds before the lack of blood to my brain would render me unconscious. I threw my head back in an attempt to break his nose, but I hit his collarbone instead.

He grunted and then chuckled. "I'm going to have fun killing you. Clutch took Missy from me. I wonder how he'll like it when I kill his whore."

I pulled out my knife and stabbed him in the fleshy softness on his side.

He cursed and his grip weakened.

I shoved back onto him and rolled myself off, jumping to my feet. The room was spinning but my tunnel vision was slowly widening.

Doyle pulled himself up, holding his side. It looked like a shallow wound, just enough to piss him off.

"I'm going to keep you alive even longer for that," he snarled out.

Someone knocked, and Doyle turned toward the door, "Get in here now!"

Whoever was on the other side yelled something and started kicking at the door.

I pulled out the last grenade from my pocket and pulled the pin. Doyle's eyes widened.

I smiled. "You had it backwards. I'm going to have fun killing you."

I tossed the grenade.

He rolled behind his desk. The grenade bounced off the wall behind him. He raised his rifle at me and sprayed bullets across the room.

I dove onto the table, knocking it on its side as I tumbled to the floor.

The room exploded.

I swam in a sea of vertigo and a high-pitched ringing. My body was numb and yet hurt everywhere at the same time. A faint pounding echoed somewhere in the distance. I dragged myself toward the over-turned desk and clawed at the body lying there. I saw six glassy eyes staring back at me with my triple-vision, and I collapsed on my back. The floor felt less solid here. I rolled over and felt around the wood. I pried at a floorboard, and it lifted easily, revealing darkness below.

I pushed myself in and crashed onto the rough-hewn floor. Rifles tumbled down, nearly suffocating me. The floorboard snapped shut, leaving scanty light filtering through the cracks above.

I clawed out from under the rifles to an open space. My fingers wrapped around an ammo clip. There were more weapons down here than Doyle had ever received from Camp Fox. Clearly, Doyle either had other connections or had been preparing for war for a long time.

A door slammed open and boot steps pounded the floor above me.

"Doyle! No!" A man's voice yelled, and the shuffling of boot steps increased.

They'd find me. Within a few seconds, I'd be dead. I no longer cared. I'd done what I had to do. Doyle would never hurt Clutch or Jase or anyone else ever again. I closed my eyes and the noise above me faded into oblivion.

———

I woke up.

It was pure dark in the hole. Not even a splinter of sunlight fought through the cracks.

I sat up, and every cell in my body hated me for it. Pushing through the pain, I felt around the wall until I found a light switch. With a click, fluorescent lights lit up a basement that went the length of the building above it. It was filled with racks and racks of rifles, surplus gear, food, and wooden crates. Not far from where I sat was a desk with what I guessed to be radio equipment.

All the time Tyler had searched for Doyle, he'd been quite literally under our noses.

Shaking my head, I pulled myself to my feet. My leg hurt worse.

I stood there for a moment.

I was still alive.

I wasn't a zed.

I'm alive!

Hope infused my muscles and I climbed the ladder behind me. I listened for long minutes for voices or movement of any kind. When silence greeted me, I pushed the floorboard up and pulled myself onto the floor.

The clear night sky blanketed the room with enough glow that I could see Doyle's mangled body still lying prone near the desk. I was surprised the Dogs hadn't moved him unless...

I crawled to the blown-out window and peered outside. Across the campground, zeds shambled, several with shaved heads. I ducked and glanced at the door standing wide open. It was only a matter of time before a zed discovered me.

The gates were too far away. I'd never reach them with a bum leg. I'd seen no vehicles. The silos were halfway across the camp.

A dark shape hovered near the door, and I pushed myself to my feet and pulled out my knife. As soon as the zed crossed the threshold, I shoved the blade through its temple. It collapsed, and I saw two more zeds turn toward me.

I stepped over the zed and outside into plain sight. Something moaned to my right, and I swung, hitting a zed's shaved head just as its arms reached for me. I twisted to my left, leapt onto the broken window ledge, and grabbed the edge of the roof. The knife tumbled from my grip and clinked as it bounced off the ground. With every ounce of strength, I pulled myself up. One of the fresher Dog zeds had nearly reached me by the time I pulled my feet up.

Panting, exhausted, I dragged myself onto the roof and rolled onto my back, staring into the night sky, the one place incorruptible by zeds.

I saw Clutch, wearing one of his rare smiles, reaching out to me for a dance. Standing not far from us were my parents, holding each other's hands and watching us with warm love in their eyes. Jase and Mutt were playing fetch. He looked up and laughed.

It was a good dream.

A soothing peace came over me, even while the zeds moaned and shuffled below.

I'd survived hell. Maybe there was such a thing as hope after all.

Taking a deep breath of fresh air, my body relaxed, and I smiled up at the night sky full of stars.

Deadland's Harvest

Part Two of the Deadland Saga

Part One
Purgatory

ONE

"Cash!"

I tried to open my eyes, but they were glued shut. I opened my mouth to respond, but my tongue was too parched and swollen. I couldn't even move through the shivers that racked my dew-drenched body.

"Cash! Damn it, where are you, girl? Cash!"

I willed strength into my arms to push myself up, but could barely lift my head.

I wanted to tell whoever was calling to me to be quiet, that the herd had disappeared only a few hours earlier. Instead, I could barely force out a rough, garbled syllable. "*Here.*" Trying to speak choked my sandpaper throat. Blood trickled from my cracked lips.

"Cash!"

The voice was closer and louder now, echoed by other voices, each one calling my name. I pried my eyes open, but the world remained a cloudy blur.

"Up here," I called out louder this time, though the words still came out as only a coarse whisper.

With the last of my strength, I rolled over the backpack that had been propping me up on the angled roof, and let myself roll down. As I picked up speed, I clawed at the shingles to slow my descent, but it did nothing but scrape the skin from my fingers. I fell off the edge and plummeted to the ground ten feet below. Agony shot through my abused body, and I collapsed, my head hitting the ground with a thud.

A pleasant numbness followed, and crystalline stars glittered through my vision. They were the first things in over a day that I could see sharply. As the stars faded, I could make out a man-like shape moving toward me.

A gunshot fired, and the shape collapsed. The acrid stench of plague and rot hit me.

Zed.

Another shape approached, and I tried to kick away, but my limbs weighed a ton, my movements sluggish. Arms wrapped around me, holding me in a relentless grip. I whimpered as I waited for dull, broken teeth to shred my skin.

"Cash, I've got you. You're safe now."

Once the words sunk in, the tension in my muscles gave way, and I inhaled the fresh soapy smell of a man who'd recently bathed. Through my blurry vision, I could barely make out the blond, clean-shaven soldier in full gear. "Tyler?"

"Yes, it's me. I've got you. Everything's going to be okay."

I felt myself lifted off the ground and I held onto his shirt. My leg that had a gunshot through it throbbed with each sway of Captain Tyler Masden's steps, but I welcomed the pain. It meant I was alive.

They found me!

It was hard to think, with black clouds drowning my happy thoughts as quickly as they came. I was jostled around and found myself laying on a cold hard surface. The rumble of a big engine starting reverberated through my body. My consciousness ebbed against the soothing engine vibration, but I didn't mind. I was safe now.

"Holy shit, she's alive." I heard Griz's familiar deep voice off to my left, sounding a million miles away.

"Here," Tyler said, lifting my head. "Drink this."

Something pressed against my lips. Cool liquid poured into my mouth and streamed over my tongue. I tried to gulp the water, but it burned, and I choked. I coughed out nearly everything I had drunk. When Tyler held the bottle to my mouth again, he only allowed a trickle of water to pass through. I took a tiny sip. Then another.

"You've been up on that roof for two days?" Tyler asked while I forced down the water my cramping stomach threatened to heave.

I tried to nod, but that sent more water dribbling down my chin and neck.

Tyler pulled the bottle away. "Whoa. That's enough for now. You have to take it slow, or else you'll get sick."

"More," I said, reaching for the water again.

Someone touched my calf, and I hissed. Pain from the gunshot wound burned up my leg, causing me to wince. Blackness tunneled my vision.

A whistle. "That's a nasty infection. You're damn lucky we found you when we did."

"Hurts," I muttered. I didn't feel lucky. I felt like hell.

"Everything's going to be okay," Tyler said, rubbing my shoulder. "You're safe now."

"*We're* safe. Doyle's dead," I said, finally able to get out more than one word just as I felt my body fade into a colorless place between day and night.

"I know. You did well," Tyler said. "We drove through the area yesterday, but the place was still crawling with zeds." A pause. "Damn. I'd just about given up on you, but Clutch was convinced you were still alive."

My jumbled mind tried to process words that made no sense. Clutch couldn't have said those words. It was impossible. That Clutch could've spoken *anything* was impossible. A vision of when I'd last seen Clutch cut through the clouds in my head. "But Clutch..."

Tyler gripped my shoulder. "Clutch is alive. And he's pissed—we're all pissed—you went after the militia on your own."

———

Thankfully, the next few weeks went by in a blur. When I remembered the flight over Doyle's camp and my attack on his Dogs—the militia— the memories were so fresh that they seemed like yesterday. I could still smell the smoke from the grenade blast, and I could still hear the neverending moans of the zeds surrounding me as I waited on the roof. Had I waited up there to die? To be saved? Hell, to be honest, it was a bit of both.

Fortunately, I didn't have to dwell on such things for long. After three days of being confined to bed and on IVs, Doc had cleared me to return to my cabin. It took me another ten days before I'd been able to walk without using crutches, but that didn't stop me from signing up for any tasks to keep busy.

Doc had said I'd gotten lucky that the bullet from the Dog's rifle had been a through-and-through and that it hadn't hit an artery or bone. I was even luckier that the bullet hadn't been dipped in infected blood as the Dogs had become notorious for doing.

Several times a day, I'd rub my leg to remind myself that it hadn't all been a just a bad dream. By some miracle, I'd gone into the pit of hell and came out alive.

Clutch hadn't been so lucky. It had taken another two and a half weeks before Doc had cleared him to leave the infirmary. With the injuries he'd sustained during the Camp Fox attack, he had a long battle ahead of him. No one said anything when Clutch went through painkillers and booze a bit too quickly. He was angry most of the time and a muted version of himself the rest of the time. His injuries had pulled him into a dark place that I hadn't yet been able to reach. But he was alive. That was what mattered most to me.

While we recuperated and worked on physical therapy, Fox scouts cleared out Doyle's basement that I'd discovered after killing him. The large underground space chock full of military surplus, weapons, ammo, and food was exactly what Camp Fox's morale needed. With those supplies and the militia no longer a threat, people finally felt like they had a shot at getting through the winter.

"You're wasting daylight, Cash. C'mon, rise and shine!" Jase yelled before jogging out of the cabin the three of us shared, the creaky screen door slamming behind him. Our cabin was the most hidden of all cabins at Fox National Park, which was why Clutch had chosen it when we'd first arrived here. We'd been alone at that time. Now, it was nearly impossible to find a place where we could be alone since the park had become the temporary Camp Fox until the zeds evacuated the real Camp Fox National Guard Base nearly thirty miles southeast of here.

"Off duty," I muttered as I stretched with a groan and rubbed my eyes. I sat up and swung my legs off the bed, and my still-healing calf protested by shooting a burning spike of pain up through my leg. Wincing, I reached for the bottle of water on the floor and took a long swig. God, I loved water. Couldn't get enough of it ever since Tyler rescued me from Doyle's militia camp. I'd been up on that roof for two days, and I wouldn't have made it a third day.

With a sigh, I strapped on my gun belt, and came to my feet. Pink scar tissue tightened over my calf, and it took a moment for the tension to release. The bullet wound always hurt most in the mornings, but I finally felt like I'd climbed out of hell. All the while, Clutch was stuck in hell's deepest tar pits. I glanced at his cot pushed up next to mine. Unmade and empty. The blankets were tangled and draping off the bed after another night of nightmares.

Each night, when I'd move onto his bed to console him, he'd turn the other way. For the past twenty-two days, he'd tell me to leave. The first night I gave him his space, and his nightmares returned worse than ever. The second night I stayed despite his words. He turned away from me, and I draped my arm over him, spooning him. Even though he grumbled, he fell back to sleep and the nightmares stayed away. Every night he tried to push me away, to emotionally isolate himself, but I made sure he knew he wasn't going through this alone. It wasn't easy, and I doubted myself sometimes, but I kept doing it anyway.

I had convinced myself that what Clutch asked for wasn't what he needed. He'd drawn so far into himself that he pushed others away. Jase and I watched as melancholy dulled his gaze. I loved Clutch's intensity, and it broke my heart every time I saw that strength missing from his spirit.

The third morning he'd left before we woke, Jase and I made a vow to see him through his recovery together, no matter how much of an ass he could be. Clutch had saved both of our lives. It was our turn to bring him back from the hell he was stuck in. We were his family now. Of course, cheering someone up in the middle of the zombie apocalypse was easier said than done.

Just like every morning since he'd returned to our cabin, he'd left before sunrise for physical therapy. He was relentless with his exercises; as if the harder he worked, the faster he would heal.

And, just like every morning, I loosely made all three beds, grabbed my rifle and the long spear that sometimes doubled as a walking stick, and headed out the cabin door.

Several minutes later, I found Clutch at our usual spot by the stream. After every morning PT session, I'd find him sitting there, watching the sun rise and scanning the trees, always ready to kill any zed or bandit who made the mistake of stumbling into our small part of Fox National Park.

I rubbed his shoulder as I walked by him. "Morning, sunshine. How'd PT go?"

He took in a long breath, and his grip on his rifle loosened, but he still stared ahead. "It went."

His short light hair with slivers of gray was still damp with sweat, and his scruffy face was pale. The veins on his arms stood out like they did every time after weightlifting.

I frowned. "You're pushing yourself too hard. It's only been a couple months. Doc says it's a miracle you're even alive."

Clutch chortled. "Doc was a family doctor before the outbreak. He had no idea how badly I was injured. Hell, he got half of his diagnoses wrong."

"Thank God he did," I said all too quickly and then forced a weak smile. "Doc's doing the best he can. He seemed to do a good job on your broken wrist and fractured leg. Yesterday, you even said yourself that your ribs weren't bothering you as much."

He shook his head. "The only thing Doc did was keep me on my back and drugged up so my body could heal itself with time. Just about any injury will heal in three months."

Just about, I thought to myself. *But not every injury.*

His lips turned upward into a smile that wasn't quite a smile. "The zeds aren't going to wait around for me to get back into shape. We've been too lucky lately, with only groups of two or three coming across the park each day. Our luck is going to run out sometime."

"That's why we have scouts spread out across the park to keep watch. With that and my recon flights over the area, we'll know if any herds are headed this direction."

"I know. It's just, when I'm not out there..." He rubbed his eyes with his forearm and clenched his fists. "Hell, I hate being useless."

"Whoa," I chuckled. "One thing you've never been is useless. You may be as stubborn as a mule but you're not useless."

He grunted, his tight features unchanged.

I sobered and knelt by him, placing my hands over his. "I'm serious. Do you think Tyler would have asked you to be his second-in-command if you were useless?"

Clutch didn't respond.

I wanted to knock some sense into him, if only a simple smack to the head would work. Exasperation came into every conversation with Clutch lately. It wasn't his fault. He was dealing with things the only way he knew how: by unhealthily shoving his feelings down, making his body a boiling volcano always close to exploding. I forced myself to breathe and not snap at him. "You could be tied down in bed and you'd still be far from useless. Tyler manages the day-to-day stuff around here, but you're the reason Camp Fox still exists. Even though Tyler would never say it, he knows it, too. Everyone knows it. Thanks to you, everyone's trained and prepared." I paused, then frowned. "You know that, right?"

His lips tightened before he finally spoke. "I just hate sitting on my ass all day when there's so much left to be done. Once winter hits, the same tasks are going to take twice as much work."

I sighed. "We'll get by. We always do. But you've got to give your body time to heal."

He gave an almost imperceptible nod, which I returned with a soft smile before turning in the sand. I pulled off my thermal shirt, leaving on my sports bra. I glanced down at the Piper Cub aviation logo tattooed on my forearm, which reminded me of how far we'd each come. A little over six months ago, I'd sat in a cubicle every workday in a big insurance building. I'd fly for fun every weekend and work on my little bungalow at night. Clutch had been a farmer and a truck driver. His skills had proven far more useful than mine, especially considering he was also a military vet. He'd saved my ass ten times over.

"At the rate you're healing, you'll be back to your old self in no time," I said before I dipped my finger into the cold water and shivered.

Clutch grunted. "Old is right. I've collected plenty of new aches and creaks in this old body."

I smirked at his grumbly response and noticed his eyes focused on my none-too-ample chest. I gave him an appraising look from head to toe and back up again. "Not too old, I hope," I said with a flirty smile.

A hint of lust twinkled in his gaze before his reality dampened his features again.

My heart skipped a beat. Even though it had been a fleeting glimpse, I considered it a success. *Any* improvement in Clutch's emotional state, even if for only a second, I took as a sign that there was still hope. In this world, any hope was worth treasuring.

I turned and splashed cold water onto my face. Goosebumps flitted across my skin as rivulets ran down my cheeks. In my wavy reflection, my cropped dark hair went out in every direction. I used the water to try to tamp it down, with little success. As I washed up in the cold stream, I dreaded what winter would be like. Even the outhouses being built by each cabin were already cold. Sitting in one when it was ten degrees outside would be absolute torture.

On this brisk morning, we shared the stream with three other bathers, but they were all a hundred or so feet away at their personal stations. Only those at a higher risk for infection, like Clutch, could use the park's showers. Until the water froze, the rest of us had to use the trout stream to conserve the half-full rural water tower that fed the cabins and campgrounds. With over fifty survivors—and new arriving each week—at the park, the trout stream was never without someone bathing or collecting water. We'd all quickly learned to shed our modesty, though some still clung to old values and had strung up shower curtains next to the stream for changing and bathing.

Each person had their quirks. Life had gotten hard fast, and every single one of us had found ways to survive without going crazy. Taking a cold bath was nothing compared to learning how to walk again with only a general practitioner for a neurosurgeon. I leaned back on my heels, turned, and saw Clutch watching the horizon. My gaze fell on his wheelchair, and I thought of the battle he still fought. Seeing his trampled body following the Camp Fox attack was the worst image of every image haunting my dreams every night. It was worse than the school full of zombie kids, worse than sitting on a hot roof surrounded by a hundred zeds, even worse than all the different ways I'd imagined how my parents must have died during the outbreak.

I hadn't seen how they died, so I tried to tell myself they went peacefully, that they hadn't suffered. Like anyone else, I hated seeing those I loved hurt. That's what terrified me about Clutch. He had been hurt so badly—and still hurt—that it nearly broke my heart every time I saw him wince from pain. And he winced far too often.

If he'd dislocated his back before the outbreak, modern medicine would have had him walking by now. Except there was no longer such a thing as modern medicine. His bones were healing, and the swelling on his spine was going down since he was regaining more sensation every week. Still, even though he had feeling in his legs and could sometimes move his toes, he might not ever walk again.

Since the attack, we hadn't had sex. While I craved a deeper connection, Clutch couldn't handle intimacy. He was struggling just trying to hold his personal demons at bay. I was afraid a simple kiss could topple his teeter-totter of control. So, I gave him his space, even though I felt so very alone.

The funny thing was that before the outbreak, I wouldn't have considered dating Clutch. My parents would never have approved of a blue-collar man fifteen years older than me. We were from two different worlds. It would've been a shame, too. Instead, it took a virus to destroy the world for me to find someone whose spirit meshed so perfectly with my spirit.

"What's wrong?" Clutch asked, and I started, looking up.

I shook my head. "Nothing."

After a moment, he gave a small frown and looked back toward the rising sun.

I splashed more water on my face. The rumble of a motorcycle drowned out the sound of the stream and my thoughts. I glanced over my shoulder to see Jase ride down the trail we walked to get to our section of the stream. The sixteen-year-old pulled to a stop, kicking up dirt and leaves, and revved the engine one final time before killing it. His sandy hair was in much need of a haircut, but it fit his personality. He had grown into his body over the past several months, but he was still clearly a teenager.

He gave his famously endearing grin before climbing off the bike, the grin I knew hid nightmares. It was a bad habit he was picking up from Clutch: burying his pain, pretending it didn't exist. Not that those two were alone in that bad habit. I found myself doing it enough, as well as most of Camp Fox. It was a survival mechanism. If we focused too much on the reality, it would swallow us whole. Every now and then, someone would break. Each person was different. Some would cry nonstop, some would eat a bullet, some would take on a blank stare, and some became hell-bent on destroying every zed in the world. I prayed that neither Clutch nor Jase would hit their breaking point.

Just like every morning, Jase pulled out a couple granola bars and tossed one to Clutch and me. For the first week or so after the Camp Fox attack, he'd rarely spoke. He'd lost too much in too short of time to be able to digest it all. Then, one morning, he'd awakened and started to speak. Acting like Teflon—like he hadn't lost Mutt or his parents—had become his coping mechanism.

He leaned on the handlebars. "Looks like another quiet day."

"Leaves are starting to turn," Clutch replied.

Jase ignored him. "I'm going on a run today. Doc is running low on towels."

"Count me in," I said.

"I'll go," Clutch added on.

Jase's brows rose. "But—"

"I'll be fine," Clutch interrupted. "I'll stay with the vehicle and scan for zeds. It's not like I'm going to jump up and run away."

I clenched my jaw shut to keep from saying anything. Doc would get pissed if Clutch left the park, but I also knew that being caged up was driving him crazy. The idea of him heading out before he was fully recovered bugged me, especially given the lack of any decent modern medicine. If something happened, his temporary paralysis could become permanent—assuming that it was temporary now. Clutch needed action to survive. Every day spent doing nothing but PT at the park, he lost a little bit more of his spirit.

Jase didn't look convinced but he also knew better than to tell Clutch no. "All right. I'll prep the truck. See you guys at—"

We all jerked around to see one of the Jeeps used for guard patrol barreling down the lane. The driver's white hair stood out. Wes came to a stop and stood up in the Jeep. He was one of the newer residents, having moved to the park less than a month ago. "We've got an all-hands call, guys. Captain Masden said I'm to grab every scout I can find and head to the church at Freeley."

I stood up and pulled on my shirt. I was one of the scouts, Camp Fox's protectors. Most were soldiers—National Guardsmen—but there were a few non-military scouts like Jase and me. Tyler had originally called us all soldiers, but then opted for a more neutral, "friendly" term. The label made sense. Scouting for supplies while watching for trouble was ninety percent of our jobs.

"What's up?" Clutch asked while I wiped my face with my sleeve.

"We've just found out about some survivors trapped in Freeley. Sounds like they've gotten themselves surrounded by zeds."

"On my way," Jase said as he revved up the bike and peeled out.

Jase was always energetic like that. Other folks had even started calling him Teflon, since the nastiness of the world around us seemed to roll right off him. But I knew better. Jase had seen a lot of shit and buried his memories, fears, and emotions under a thick coating of that Teflon. Back at the cabin, when he was exhausted after a hard day, I sometimes saw the real Jase. The Jase that was still a kid and was struggling to fake it through each day. He'd toss and turn all night, often waking up in a cold sweat. I'd sit with him until he fell back to sleep. By morning, he was back to being Teflon.

When two survivors showed up at the park with a dog, Jase had avoided them for over a week until the kid—and his dog—cornered Jase one day. I'd noticed Jase's eyes watered as he petted the dog that day, remembering things he tried so hard to forget. He wasn't afraid to pet the dog after that. In fact, he seemed to seek out Diesel. I'd thought about finding a dog for Jase's birthday but had decided it was still too soon. He had too many wounds in his heart that needed time to heal.

"Let's roll." Clutch headed toward the Jeep.

Wes looked confused. "Oh, I don't think you have to come, Clutch. You're—."

"I'm coming," Clutch interrupted. He then turned and pulled

himself out of his wheelchair and onto the passenger seat using the Jeep's roll bar and seat.

When I saw the intensity in Clutch's eyes, I said, "It's fine." I came up and grabbed the wheelchair, folded it, and set it in the back before climbing in next to it.

"Uh, okay. You guys need to stop for any gear before we head out?" Wes asked as he sat down and pulled the Jeep back around.

"We're good," I said, knowing that Clutch never left the cabin without being fully prepared for anything, a trait I'd quickly picked up after a run-in at an elementary school.

I checked my rifle. Loaded and ready. I just hoped I wouldn't have to use it.

Two

"How many zeds are we talking about?" I asked, my question muffled from trying to talk while chewing on the granola bar Jase had given me.

"A big herd," Wes replied as we drove through the opened front gate, which the two scouts on duty closed as soon as we went through. "Tack's report was twenty, maybe even thirty. Always hard to count when they look the same and keep shuffling around each other. Tack said that the zeds have surrounded a house full of survivors, somewhere in the middle of town."

"Shouldn't be hard to find, not with a town the size of Freeley," I thought aloud.

"These better not be bandits we're risking our lives for," Clutch said as he held onto the Jeep's windshield. "Or else they're going to quickly learn that they'd prefer the zeds' company to ours."

"Amen," I added.

Most survivors had already joined with settlements like Camp Fox. Since the outbreak, civilization had been regrouping, finding strength in numbers against the relentless zeds that kept spreading out from the cities. Camp Fox had become a new home for survivors in central Iowa. Even larger, more powerful city-states were being formed across the country.

Bandits were a different story, and they were becoming more common to see than survivors. While everyone looted empty houses and stores, bandits were greedy outlaws, taking anything they wanted from other survivors and leaving bodies and scarred victims in their wake. I hated bandits more than I hated zeds.

Zeds couldn't control their evil. Bandits could.

We drove past the gas station Clutch and I had cleared out before Camp Fox relocated to the park. We had avoided the station ever since, leaving it to other scouts to loot. No one else had come across the two zed kids that we'd seen there. They'd simply disappeared, even though all the doors to the restaurant were still closed. The pair we'd seen had watched us while holding hands, and it had freaked both of us out.

We'd run across a few non-violent zeds before, but what had really unnerved us was the intelligence in those kids' eyes. Zeds weren't supposed to have any kind of brainpower. If they did have the ability to think, we wouldn't stand a chance. We'd told others about what we'd seen, but no one believed us. Well, no one *wanted* to believe us.

They had racked it up as just seeing a bit too far into something, which was common. After all, when a zed could be hiding around every corner, survival required a bit of paranoia. But, if some zeds could think, it would tip the odds even more against us. Not to mention, I couldn't imagine the horror of zeds knowing who they were and the cannibals they'd become. I prayed those kids' intelligence was just a figment of our imagination.

Wes slowed down once we passed the sign that read *Freeley, pop. 498.* The sun had just crested, sending a warm glow over the trees. Clutch was right—the leaves were showing hints of changing color. Fall had always been my favorite season. But now, rather than enjoying fall, I dreaded the season that would come next. Even with the gold mine we'd found at Doyle's militia camp, we were nowhere near ready in terms of security and supplies. Plus, taking in more survivors meant that we'd have to pull together even more supplies and food before winter hit.

Wes drove the Jeep into the church parking lot near the edge of town. Aside from some corpses, I didn't see any of the zeds Wes was talking about. We pulled up next to the Humvee where two of Tyler's most trusted men stood on the hood. Tack was looking through binoculars while Griz kept watch.

Tack had joined the National Guard a few months before the outbreak. He'd finished basic training, but still looked like he belonged in high school. He was as scrawny as ever, but no one messed with him. He was too damn likable.

Griz, on the other hand, had over a year under his belt in the Army before the outbreak. He had plenty of muscle, and was a Golden Gloves boxing champ. A trader had dared to mess with him once. No one ever messed with Griz again.

Griz eyed Clutch. "You sure you should be out here today?"

"Fuck off" was Clutch's quick response.

Griz lifted his hands in surrender and smirked. "No harm, no foul, man."

Tack lowered his binoculars to look Clutch over. "Good to have you back, man."

I jumped out and walked over to stand at the front of the Humvee. Even from this distance several blocks away, it was easy to guess which house the survivors were in. Hanging from a second story window was a bed sheet with the word *HELP* written across it. And, it was the only house surrounded by zeds.

"Son of a bitch," I said. "There must be forty zeds." We couldn't take that many without burning through precious ammunition. "You sure there are even survivors left inside?" I asked, selfishly hoping we didn't have to go near a herd this size.

"I'm sure," Tack replied, not looking very happy about the fact. "They hung that sign after they saw us. And they've been antsy ever since."

The rumble of a big engine came up from behind. I turned to find Tyler and several more of Camp Fox's scouts arrive in a Humvee. Tyler jumped out. Sometimes, I thought he seemed too young to be leading Camp Fox, but then I remembered we were the same age. After the outbreak hit, being nearly thirty wasn't seen as young anymore. Especially since there was hardly anyone over the age of fifty remaining. Then again, there was hardly anyone of any age remaining anymore.

When Tyler saw Clutch, he raised a brow, clearly surprised. "Sarge."

"Captain," Clutch said as Tyler approached Tack and Griz's Humvee.

Over the past few months, Tyler and Clutch had *almost* become friends. Well, at least they put up with each other. Tyler respected Clutch's experience, but he'd never gotten over the fact that Clutch had refused to report to duty when the outbreak first hit. Clutch respected Tyler's leadership, but he'd never forgiven Tyler for abandoning me in the middle of a zed-infested wasteland. I knew the only reason Clutch stayed with Camp Fox was because of Jase and me.

Out of over thirty troops at Camp Fox, Clutch was the next-highest ranking officer after Tyler. Always one to follow the rules,

Tyler had gritted his teeth as he made Clutch second-in-command of Camp Fox.

"What are we looking at?" Tyler asked, all business.

Tack handed him the binoculars. "A large herd surrounding a house with six or more occupants, including at least one kid."

That a kid was with them was important. It meant that there was a good chance they weren't bandits. Bandits tended to ditch anyone that would slow them down—and they often ditched them by using them as zed bait.

"The front door is broken but barricaded. There are three vans parked outside, but there's no way for them to get through the herd and to their vehicles. I'm guessing they've been in there a while since the zeds aren't attacking, but there are some curious zeds sniffing around the porch. The folks holed up inside look to be in rough shape. I doubt they can hold out much longer."

"Well, they'll have to wait just a little longer," Tyler said, turning to face our group.

"Are we going with the Pied Piper plan?" I asked.

He nodded and then looked over all of us. "It saves our ammo and minimizes risk. The Jeep will lead as many zeds away as possible, and we'll take out the rest. My team will go in for the survivors. Griz's Humvee will take out any zeds that stay behind."

A chorus of *yes sirs* and *hooahs* erupted.

Tyler nodded in Clutch's direction. "Sarge's team is with the Jeep. We need to get the zeds at least three miles out of town before you break and head back to Camp Fox. Call in if you run into any problems."

Tyler had given us the easy job. Lure zeds away while keeping a safe distance. With each passing month, the zeds were moving slower and becoming less of a threat. I wasn't surprised he'd assigned us as the Pied Piper vehicle. It was by far the least risky role to play in this gambit. Wes was old yet often overconfident. Clutch...well, everyone knew Clutch's weakness. Heck, I was surprised Tyler was even letting Clutch participate today. He could've ordered him back to the park.

Then again, we all knew how well orders went over with Clutch aka Sarge.

As for my case, Tyler had always been protective of me, but assigning us as the Pied Piper vehicle was more than for my protection. It was a matter of practicality. For one thing, my injured leg was still slowing me down. Another reason Tyler intentionally kept me on the sidelines of trouble was my unique skill. I was Camp Fox's only pilot. My patrols were critical to helping us stay ahead of zeds in the area. I could easily cover a fifty-mile radius and report back any herds heading our way. We'd finally reached the point of being a step ahead of the zeds. It was our first break since the world had ended.

We were still waiting for a second break.

"Are the streets cleared?" I asked finally.

Tack shook his head. "The north and west has been mostly cleared, I think. But as far as I know, no one's started on the east or south yet."

"Avoid the east and south. Got it. We'll see you back at the park." I grabbed the extra bag of ammo Tack held out to me and headed back to the Jeep with Wes. We waited with Clutch while the attack-force with two Humvees checked their weapons. There were as many homemade machetes and spears as there were rifles. Next to food, ammo was the most valuable resource. We'd collected a couple hundred thousand rounds in Doyle's stash, but we knew that once it was gone, there would be nothing left. So, we were careful with every round.

Tyler turned to us. "You've got a green light. Be careful and keep a safe distance."

Wes started the engine and pulled out. Tyler waved as we headed past.

Two minutes later, we slowly approached the intersection closest to the white two-story house. It sat in the middle of a street surrounded by other houses. At the sound of the engine, the zeds turned in our direction. Some started heading our way. The disease that had taken everyone I'd known in my past life seemed to be slowly eating away at their bodies. Scouting patrols over the past month all reported the same: the zeds were definitely getting slower, smellier, and uglier. Now, if we could finally get a bit of luck, they'd all die out this winter. The poor souls deserved peace. Hell, *we* deserved peace. Until then…

"I'm ready," I said. "Lead the zeds either to the north or west. The south and east might not be safe."

"Let the games begin." Clutch turned on the CD player. Heavy bass blared as Avenged Sevenfold blasted through the speakers. The zeds around the house immediately turned and began to migrate in our direction en masse. A man came to the second-story window and held out his hand, waving wildly. A little girl with golden hair came to his side. She was clenching a stuffed doll against her chest, and she watched us with big eyes.

The zeds became more and more frenzied as they moved in our direction. It had been nearly seven months since the outbreak. The zeds that had managed to avoid the elements and keep well fed were still in relatively good shape. Luckily, most of these had managed neither.

They stumbled, crawled, and shambled toward us.

I let out the breath I'd been holding. "It's working."

Wes revved the engine.

"Not yet," Clutch said.

Wes gripped the steering wheel, his knuckles white.

I got up on a knee, supporting myself against the roll bar in case Wes hit the gas, and I readied my spear. The first zed was less than ten feet away.

"Now," Clutch said.

The Jeep lurched forward, then Wes slowed down somewhat.

Over the next block, I watched as the zeds behind us grew smaller. I yelled to Wes over the music, "Slow down! We're going to lose them. Three miles, remember?"

I kept my spear ready for any coming at us from the side, but it seemed like every zed in town had been at the house.

The Jeep came to an abrupt stop, and I was thrown against the back of Clutch's seat.

"The road is blocked!" Wes shouted.

I jerked up to see what looked like a nasty car accident blocking the entire street and debris littering the front yards. The wreckage was dusty, and the bodies inside the broken windows were little more than bones. The roads weren't anywhere near cleared enough. *Shit.*

"Then turn around and take the last intersection," Clutch said.

Wes did a hard U-turn, which put the zeds at our twelve o'clock. He stepped on the gas and sped toward the herd.

"Don't turn left," I said, noticing the dead end sign at the upcoming intersection.

Wes cranked the wheel hard left. Wheels squealed.

"I said *don't* turn left!" I yelled.

"You said turn left!" Wes yelled back.

I hollered out a string of profanity.

Clutch killed the music, and winced, grabbing his ribs. "Get us out of here, Wes. In one piece would be nice."

Wes whipped the Jeep around again. The zeds had come around the corner, blocking our escape route.

"Try that yard," I said, pointing to a yard without a fence that looked wide enough for a Jeep.

Wes jumped the curb, and Clutch yelped in pain.

"Careful!" I yelled.

Wes kept driving, maneuvering between a garage and a neighboring house. He knocked off a side mirror on a wood play set in the backyard. He narrowly missed the trampoline in the next yard, drove through two more yards, a chain link fence, and plastic deer. I clung onto the roll bars, unable to do anything except to keep myself from getting thrown out of the Jeep.

"Charlie to Alpha," Clutch said into the radio. "Charlie needs support."

No response.

"Charlie team to Alpha." After no response, he set the radio on his lap. "They must've moved in already. We're on our own."

I pointed to a large shed. "How about in there?"

"Let's try it," Clutch said quickly.

"Okay," Wes said under his breath while he gripped the wheel. He pulled up to the shed with a sign that read *Mac's Auto Shop*.

Panting from the wild ride, I jumped off the back, ran to the first garage door, and rapped on the metal. When no sound emerged, I yanked on the door. By some miracle it wasn't locked, and the door slid easily to the side with an unoiled squawk. Wes pulled the Jeep inside, bumped into a VW Beetle that was sitting in the bay, and pushed it forward. I scanned outside. Seeing no zeds in the vicinity, I tugged the door shut as quickly as I could.

Wes cut the engine. The three of us watched one another, all with eyes wide open and breathing heavily. I swallowed and forced each breath out slowly.

Zeds were dumb, but they were damn good at sniffing out prey.

THREE

Wes was already out of the Jeep, searching for zeds around the car and behind toolboxes. With nothing looking or smelling out of place, I'd already figured the place was clean. Zeds were a messy, stinky bunch with no talent for stealth.

I looked at Clutch to find him still gripping the windshield, his head lowered.

I went over and rubbed his shoulder. "Hey, you okay?"

"Yeah." He raised his head. Tension highlighted the wrinkles around his eyes. "Just got a bit bumpy back there."

I'd thrown my back out once, and it had hurt like hell. I couldn't imagine how dislocating it would feel. I gave him the gentlest of hugs. "Hang in there," I said softly.

He leaned back with a wince and closed his eyes.

When Doyle's Dogs attacked Camp Fox last summer, Clutch had been crushed in the stampede of fleeing survivors. Two vertebrae in his back had been dislocated, thankfully not broken as Doc had first guessed. Doc was doing the best he could do. It had to be tough to work in a world without x-rays and emergency rooms. A person couldn't just snap vertebrae back into place like a dislocated shoulder. Doc had been very, very careful to align Clutch's back. The backpack Clutch had been wearing was likely the only reason his back hadn't been broken; it had served as a buffer between his body and the trampling herds. Even then, the swelling on his spine prevented us from knowing yet if it had been permanently damaged or if it was simply the swelling that had paralyzed him from the hips down.

While his back had been his most serious injury, Clutch had also gotten three cracked—or at least badly bruised—ribs, two fractured—or badly bruised—legs, and a broken left wrist. He'd also had a dislocated shoulder and a nasty concussion. Any one of those injuries would have taken him out of action for a bit, but the combination of injuries had left him unconscious for three days.

It was a miracle he hadn't incurred any internal bleeding, deep cuts, or bites in the stampede. At the Camp Fox medical clinic, if someone couldn't heal on his or her own, there was little hope. After the attack, Doc warned me that if Clutch didn't wake in the first hours, he would likely never wake up due to the severity of his injuries. Doc didn't know Clutch. The Clutch I knew was too hardheaded *not* to wake up.

Aside from some minor memory lapses and random muscle spasms, he was well on the road to recovery. Despite Doc's pessimism, I knew Clutch would walk again because he could feel pain in his legs and wiggle his toes not long after he woke. He'd even been able to lift his legs a bit a couple days ago. It shouldn't be much longer until the pressure was off his nerve endings enough that he'd regain control over his legs and be able to stand on his own. I only hoped he could stand soon because being held prisoner by his own body was taking its toll.

My greatest fear was that if Clutch didn't have use of his legs, it would kill him. Well, he'd kill himself more likely. The idea of the strongest man I knew giving up terrified me. If he couldn't make it, how did Jase or I have a chance?

Wes stopped by the Jeep, his gaze darting to the garage door. "As long as they don't break down the door, I think we'll be safe in here."

I nodded before holding up my hand. "*Sh.* They're coming." It was the faintest sound of shuffling feet and low moans. It sounded almost like a flock of sheep passing through. Except sheep didn't tear apart anything that breathed.

This was the sound that caused me to wake up in a cold sweat every night. The herd that had followed us from the survivors had caught up. We stood frozen as the sounds outside grew louder. I exhaled as shallowly as I could and leaned on the Jeep, waiting for the zeds to sniff us out. *Please don't find us,* I prayed over and over.

If they found us, it wouldn't take them long to break through the old door. Clutch's eyes remained closed, and I couldn't even tell he was breathing, let alone conscious, though I knew he was listening as intently as I was. Wes kept his rifle aimed at the door. The sounds grew louder. My nerves felt like they were about to detonate. My tense muscles ached.

Something brushed against the shop, and the air in my lungs froze. With no windows on that side of the building, the zeds couldn't see inside. It also meant we couldn't see if they were stopping to sniff around the shop or merely passing through in their quest to find us.

————

Hours passed as the zeds checked out the shop, brushing against the walls on all four sides. They'd lingered for some reason, but whatever it was, it wasn't enough to work them into a frenzy. None pounded against the building. It seemed like they were more curious than anything.

And so we waited. My back ached from standing in one position. I sat on the ground as quietly as possible, knowing the smallest sound could draw attention. Wes had long since lowered his rifle and sat at a tool bench, but he still faced the door. I could tell by Clutch's pale, pained expression that he needed to be lying down, but he didn't dare move.

The sounds grew fainter until I could hear nothing but silence. Wes looked back and glanced from Clutch to me.

Wait, I mouthed. There'd be stragglers. There were *always* stragglers. Ones whose guttural wails would call the others back if they found us. And so we waited longer. I didn't take even one step toward the door in case there were any zeds still out there. That they hadn't sniffed us out meant that the various car and old oil smells in the shop had provided better cover than I'd anticipated. Or, the zeds' senses were deteriorating right along with their bodies.

After a forced count to one thousand, I glanced at Wes and then crept toward the sliding shop door. When I reached it, I put my ear to the crack and heard nothing. Taking a deep breath, I pushed the door open an inch. The rollers squeaked, and I cringed. I peeked through the crack.

At first, I saw nothing. Then, movement in the corner of my eye caused me to scan again. Sure enough, a pair of slow moving zeds was focused on the garage.

"Is it clear?" Wes whispered at my side.

I jumped at the unexpected question. "Clear enough. But I don't think we'll want to stick around here all night." I threw him a glance. "Let's go home."

"You don't need to twist my arm," he said before heading back to the Jeep.

Wes started the engine, and the two zeds continued their shamble toward the garage. I shoved open the door, grunting, finding it much harder to open this time. To my right, a zed that must've been pressing against the door spun around and was sent tumbling to the ground. I marched over, twirled my spear around, and skewered its head. The two zeds' moans grew louder.

When it no longer moved, I walked over to meet the pair of zeds. Their groans rose as they reached out for me. I speared the male through its forehead, yanking my weapon back to knock out the ankles of the female zed. It went down on its back, its head making a solid thump against the ground. I stood over it and brought my spear down, putting it out of its misery. I didn't know if zeds suffered, though they'd never winced whenever I cut off a limb or stabbed one. They just looked miserable.

I figured they just *were*. They existed—without feeling or thought—and with a single urge: to feed. At least that's what I told myself to make it easier to kill what had once been a person. The worst part about zeds wasn't their hunger or viciousness or stench. It was that each one resembled someone I knew before the outbreak. They were reminders of loved ones lost. Then again, maybe I was just trying to anthropomorphize something that was no longer human.

As Wes backed the Jeep alongside me, I turned away from the zeds, grabbed the roll bar, and swung myself onto the open back.

"Let's get the hell out of this town," Clutch muttered, his arm cradling his stomach.

Escaping a town where the herd of zeds potentially waited around any corner wasn't exactly easy. We had no idea if the herd had kept moving or if it had stopped around the next house. Wes drove slowly, creeping up to every intersection so as to not draw attention. We'd gotten lucky today. Once we were back on familiar streets, I think we all breathed easier. The herd was nowhere to be found. At the intersection not far from the roadblock, I finished off a lone zed that approached the Jeep. A block later, another zed lumbered toward us.

Wes sped up.

"Hold up," I said. "I'll get this one."

Wes slowed, and I waited until the zed was close enough that I could stab it from the safety of the Jeep. As we progressed through town, I took out every zed I could because every zed I killed was one fewer zed that would come across the park or join up with a herd later.

By the time we reached the church, the parking lot was empty. We drove by the house where the survivors had been. There were several corpses scattered around on the overgrown lawn outside, but fortunately no bodies wore Camp Fox fatigues.

Once we were safely out of town, Wes stepped on the gas. As we headed back to the park, I shivered in the October breeze. No one spoke. Without things like movies and sports, small talk had become an exercise of discussing what still needed done before winter hit. A person could only handle talking so much about the lack of skills and supplies.

As we approached the park's entrance, I cringed inwardly at the sight of the newcomers standing outside the gate. It was a larger group than I'd thought. At least ten, but it seemed like a hundred for the amount of food they'd eat. Wearing my actuarial hat, I figured we'd have to add an additional seventeen percent to our calculations of food needed to get us through the winter. The numbers became more and more dismal with more stragglers arriving every week. We'd have to start turning people away or else we'd starve. The question was, would today be that day?

Most of Camp Fox's scouts were on the other side of the gate, standing with their guns lowered but at the ready. Two scouts stood next to Doc while he attended to someone in one of the newcomers' three vans, the same vans that had been parked outside the house in Freeley. The rest of the newcomers were busily drinking from plastic water bottles.

Tyler was sitting in the passenger seat of a Humvee, also drinking water, with his window rolled down, and I had no doubt a rifle sat on his lap. His blond hair was matted from wearing a helmet, yet it did nothing to detract from his good looks. He had a killer smile and when he talked, he made you feel like he was talking directly to you, even if he was standing in front of a group of hundreds. There was something charismatic about him that made men want to be his pal and women swoon. He was a natural leader.

Wes slowed the Jeep down to a crawl as we drove past the newcomers and toward the gate. They were a dirty bunch and looked like they'd been on the road for some time. Some waited at the gate with desperate pleas for help. Four ATVs sat nearby to run down any zeds or chase fleeing bandits.

Tyler would have already informed the newcomers that Camp Fox had protocols. Any newcomer had to be fully vetted by Doc for bites, fleas, illness, and other infectious things before being allowed through the gate. Still, it tugged on the heartstrings to stand around when miserable, starving people needed help not even twenty feet away.

Seventeen percent, I reminded myself when sympathy rose in my chest.

Yes, they desperately needed our help. And, if I was on the run and came across a camp, I hoped they'd take me in. Still, I didn't know these people. What if they stole our supplies or hurt Jase? Keeping an image of Jase in my mind helped gird myself against my desire to help them.

Little Benji Hennessey held Styrofoam cups as his grandfather Robert, whom everyone called Frost, filled them with water. Frost's huge Great Dane, Diesel, lay sprawled out at his side. After each cup was filled, Benji handed it to a newcomer. Tyler always called upon the Hennesseys whenever newcomers showed up. It was a smart tactic that worked every time. A kindly grandfather and a young kid with Down Syndrome tended to put folks at ease. Little did any newcomer know that Frost would kill—and had killed without hesitation—anyone who threatened his grandson. Even more impressive, Benji had ridden a bicycle—with training wheels no less —miles and miles through zed-infested country to reach his grandfather. He hadn't killed a zed yet, but he was a survivor, through and through.

Wes pulled onto the shoulder to get around the vans. Clutch let out a pained groan when the Jeep's tires went off the edge of the pavement. I placed a hand on his shoulder. "We need to get you to the cabin and on your back."

"What I wouldn't do to get a woman to say that to me," Wes said.

I rolled my eyes.

That Clutch didn't argue was proof of the pain he was in. I was sure the jarring ride in the Jeep hadn't helped the swelling on his spine.

A small section of the gate opened, and we drove through, coming to a stop at Tyler's vehicle. He stepped out of the Humvee, setting his rifle on the seat. After giving us a once-over, he frowned. "What took you guys so long? You usually beat us back by at least a couple hours."

"Detour," I said. "We really need to clear all the main roads in these towns."

"I'll add it to the list of infinity."

He said it jokingly but it was true. Civilization had collapsed overnight, and it was going to take years to get it back, if it was even still possible.

"Any problems getting the survivors out of that house?" Clutch asked curtly.

"Nothing I couldn't handle," Tyler replied quickly, and then he whistled. "You look like shit, Sarge."

Clutch flipped him the bird.

I rolled my eyes. "In case you guys hadn't noticed, we've got nearly a dozen more mouths to feed standing at our gate."

Tyler's lips tightened before speaking again. "Doc's nearly finished with checking them out. I'm not too worried about these folks. They seem harmless enough. To play it safe, I want every scout on watch once I let them into the park."

"I'm no good to anyone right now," Clutch said, the words sounding forced.

After a moment, Tyler gave a single nod. "Understood. Get yourself to bed."

"I'll take Clutch back to the cabin and get right back," Wes said.

I squeezed Clutch's shoulder just before I climbed out. "I'll see you in a bit."

He touched my hand briefly. The Jeep pulled away.

Tyler watched the Jeep disappear around a curve. "It's too early. Clutch shouldn't have been out there today."

"Our detour today jarred him around too much," I said. "He needs more time in bed, but you know him."

He sighed. "Yeah, I do."

Doc waved toward Tyler and then gave him a thumbs up. The newcomers had been cleared. I walked with Tyler toward the ragtag group of newcomers. When we reached the gate, a middle-aged man with white hair and a scruffy beard stepped forward.

Tyler said, "Thanks for your patience. I apologize for the delay. I know you're tired and hungry, but we have protocols to follow."

"I understand. You've treated us fair," The man said and then held out a hand. "The name's Manny."

Tyler nodded rather than taking Manny's hand. "I'm Captain Tyler Masden, and this is the current base of operations for Camp Fox."

The man smiled. "Oh, I know who you are. We were on our way here to find you when the zeds found us."

Tyler frowned. "You were coming here?"

"I heard Camp Fox was a safe place."

"Word travels. We're the largest camp in the area for a reason. But you nearly didn't make it here. You're damn lucky one of my men saw your sign," Tyler continued. "We only scout Freeley once a month."

Manny smiled. "Luck? No. I'd call it a goddamn miracle you found us. We're mighty obliged you stopped to help. Most folks would have just kept on going. You saved our lives. To tell the truth, we were starting to lose hope."

"We're happy to be of service," Tyler replied. "Nowadays, we have to look out for one another. After all, there aren't enough of us left. So, where are you folks from?"

"Marshall," Manny replied.

"Marshall, Minnesota? You mean the group holed up at SMSU?" Tyler asked. "What are you doing this far south?"

My brows furrowed. Marshall, with all its radio and telecom equipment, had been one of the first to develop an entire network of communities, with Camp Fox being one of its weekly contacts.

Manny cocked his head. "You haven't heard? Marshall was overtaken. When the herds hit the university, we couldn't get back to the student center where everyone else was. We were out on a supply run, and the herds cut us off. Anyone else who couldn't get back to the student center scattered to the four winds. So we radioed the center and took off to scout somewhere safe from the zeds. We'll go back to pick up everyone as soon as we find somewhere safe in case the zeds pass through again. Before we lost contact with them, they'd said several herds were still there. They don't have much food in the student center, enough for a few weeks, maybe."

I gulped in shock. Marshall was a large settlement. With survivors from the Twin Cities, they'd had a couple thousand survivors and had set up walls around the small university. No herd should've gotten close.

"I don't get it," Tyler said. "What kind of herd could get past Marshall's troops?"

"Not just any herd. Many huge herds all moving together." Manny waved his hand. "One was at least a hundred thousand strong."

A hundred thousand zeds. I shivered. A herd of forty nearly got the best of us today. The last thing I could fathom was an endless herd heading straight toward us.

Manny continued. "They're slow, but they make a wide path, and they trample everything. The bastards are relentless. They only stop to feed. As soon as we'd get in front of one herd, we'd run into another. They got my Marcia when we first tried to leave the house we'd spent the night in. I tried to get to her, but...well, she's with them in hell now." He rubbed a hand through his greasy hair. "We'd finally put a couple hundred miles between us and them. We stopped at Freeley when the sun set. We were planning to come here first thing in the morning, but when we'd awoke, a herd had found us. We tried to get out, but we lost several good people. We'd been holed up in that house for damn near a week, losing time that we don't have."

"You think these herds are headed this way?" I asked the instant before I knew Tyler would voice the same question.

Manny nodded with a pained expression. "They're headed this way, that's guaranteed. We figure they're migrating. Near as I can tell, zeds from as far north as Canada are picking up small herds as they move south, until their numbers become like locusts."

Tyler pursed his lips before letting out a sigh. "Well, shit. I definitely want to learn more about this zed problem, but your folks need food and rest. We can talk more over dinner. Tonight, Vicki is making a rare treat, pumpkin for dessert. You and your people are welcome to stay as long as you need." He pointed down the road to the south. "I have a farmhouse set up about a mile from here for you to stay in tonight. As long as you play fair, you'll see no aggression from Camp Fox. If you want to make your stay more permanent and live within the park, we'll have to talk. There are conditions all residents must agree to." He motioned to Griz and Tack in the Humvee closest to the gate. "My men will take your people into the park for dinner and then to the farmhouse so you can clean up and rest. Sound good?"

The other man nodded. "I owe you my life and my thanks. Your offer is more than fair." Then he held out his hand.

This time, Tyler shook it.

A blond guy approached Manny. I could see the white tip of a thick scar peeking out from the V-neck of his shirt. He reached behind him and I readied my spear. Instead of pulling out a weapon, he held up a picture of a family. I assumed he was the man in the photo, though the beard and a hundred pounds less fat made it tough to tell. In the picture, a middle-aged man posed with a kindly looking woman and a teenaged girl. All three looked happy. Obviously, it had been taken before anyone had heard of zeds.

He shoved the picture in my face. "Please, you have to help me. My wife and daughter are still in Marshall. If you can give me some supplies, I can go back for them while the others go ahead and find somewhere safe."

"Bill, we've talked about this already," Manny said with a sigh.

"I know, but I can't leave them alone for much longer. I need to get back to them," Bill replied before looking again at me. "Please. It's my family."

My lips tightened. He was clearly trying to get me on his side, likely because I was a woman. He was playing to the wrong person. Of the pair in front of him, Tyler had the softer heart. He was generous, always ready to help someone in need. I was selfish. Everything I did was to protect Jase, Clutch, and me. With every stranger we helped, we put ourselves at risk. Our days were already full from sunrise to sunset with keeping Camp Fox clear of zeds and searching houses and gardens for food. The idea of giving up even one day to help someone I didn't know or trust brought on an instant tension headache.

"We'll consider your case later," Tyler said, pressing Bill's hand down. "You need food and a good night's rest."

The man frowned and fervently shook his head. "No. This can't wait. The herds will hit you here, just like they did in Marshall. Then there will be nothing left. I have to get my family and head south, find an island or somewhere the herds can't get to us. If we stay here, we'll die. Just like you're all going to die."

FOUR

Tyler let Bill ride back to the park square with us so no one else had to listen to his endless pleading. I couldn't imagine how he must've driven the other survivors crazy while they'd been cooped up in that house. Manny rode along, seemingly oblivious to his friend's chatter.

As we headed back to the park square in the Humvee, Bill detailed his plans about getting back to Marshall to find his family. Though, for pointing out all the obvious details, like stopping by farmhouses to look for food, his plan was really simple: drive back to Marshall while watching out for the herds.

Even though his constant talking grated on my nerves, I could relate to how he felt. If I'd been separated from Clutch or Jase, nothing short of death would've stopped me from finding them. However, as much as I understood Bill, I was also disgusted with him. He was too afraid to head after them on his own. It was bad enough he'd abandoned them in the first place.

"We're here," Tyler said a few exhausting minutes later, as he pulled the Humvee into the small parking lot for the park office, where all Camp Fox business took place, including three group meals per day. "Welcome to the Fox Park square. It serves as our command center, chow hall, and the place for just about any other group activity."

"The university's student center was our town square," Manny said, a hint of sadness in his voice.

Bill had quieted when we arrived, likely from the smells of dinner overtaking his senses. Starving, I headed straight for the door, and the three men were right there with me. A couple of the park's residents walked out the door as we approached. Tyler held the door open, and I politely followed the two newcomers inside. Even though Bill was a chatterbox, both he and Manny seemed like decent, albeit smelly, folk. Regardless, it would take longer before I trusted them enough to welcome them into the fold of Camp Fox.

Inside, I found Kurt already hitting on one of the women who'd arrived today. It was par for the course for the Guardsman who treated every day like a frat party rather than the end of the civilized world.

Tyler grabbed a tray, stepped into the cafeteria-style line, and nudged Kurt. "I need you to check on the north gates."

"I'm sure they're fine," he replied all too quickly before smiling again at the young woman basking in his attention.

Tyler's jaw tightened. "I wasn't asking."

Kurt's smile fell, and he stood straighter. "Yes, sir."

On his way out, he winked at the woman, and her flirtatious smile left no doubt as to whose bed she'd be sleeping in tonight. That was Kurt. He hit on every woman. Hell, he hit on me but mostly only when Jase was around, likely because it pissed Jase off. He obviously liked Jase even though he seemed to be constantly picking on him, so I figured it was some kind of friendship hazing ritual. Clutch, on the other hand, was a completely different story. Kurt didn't risk hitting on me when Clutch was around. Maybe because Kurt looked to him as Sarge. More likely it was because that any sense of humor Clutch had was lost in the stampede that crippled him.

The smell of beef stew made my mouth water and drew my attention to the small buffet line. Made with wild greens, berries, and some other local plants that I hadn't yet figured out, it was my favorite meal. As soon as Tyler got a bowl, Nate set a generously sized bowl of stew on my tray. Nate, like everyone else here, performed multiple duties. Like Kurt, he was also a Guardsman and a scout under Tyler, but he was also a damn good cook. Between Vicki and him, they planned all our meals.

It was easy to see that Nate thoroughly sampled each meal. He was one of the few scouts whose clothes fit tighter since the outbreak. After giving Nate a grin, I moved on and grabbed a handful of nuts and two crumbly chunks of cornbread, our daily staple. One thing the Midwest had plenty of was corn, but there was one big problem. Farmers planted *seed* corn, with only small pockets of sweet corn scattered across the area.

Seed corn was made for cattle feed or corn syrup. Hard and bland, it generally wasn't exactly consumable without being ground down into cornmeal. We'd grown accustomed to the simple taste. Hell, I even looked forward to Nate's corn hash every third morning.

That was the way things were around here. Everything had become a routine. Hard-boiled eggs or hash for breakfast, meat as dinner's main course every other day, and only vegetables and grains on the alternate days. Sugar and salt were restricted for medical use only. After a while, a person's palate became accustomed to a blander fare, finding new flavors in things like dandelion tea and root soup. But that wasn't always the case. Some things were just simply flavorless, or worse, tasted like weeds.

Tyler led us back outside to a picnic table. Manny and Bill followed us rather than sitting with their own people.

"Real beef?" Manny asked, swirling a spoon in his stew, while Bill slurped directly from his bowl, completely oblivious to us.

"It's nothing fancy," Tyler replied after taking a bite. "But it fills the stomach."

Manny chuckled. "No, you don't understand. I can't remember the last time I had meat that didn't come out of a can." He took another bite and frowned. "I can't make out the seasoning."

"It's marjoram," I said. "Deb found a whole bunch of it growing wild around the park. We ran out of spices a month ago and have been trying out what grows naturally. We're still getting used to the new flavors ourselves."

"We've also been collecting all the remaining livestock in the area," Tyler said. "Mostly hogs, but a few cattle and some chickens. There aren't many left, but enough to repopulate into something that can support us."

"Impressive," Manny said. "We've brought some livestock into Marshall, but nowhere near enough to support the numbers we need to support. You've got everything you need right here."

"Not yet, but being smaller helps," I said. "Right now, we're working on harvesting and canning fruit. There are quite a few apple trees, but other than berries, we don't have much variety. Not having enough vitamin C to last the winter is one of our greatest nutritional worries right now. Scurvy is a very real risk we will face unless we can get into town for food or vitamins."

Manny tilted his head. "Well, you're a step ahead of us. For winter, we planted some crops in the greenhouse, but we'd planned on living off anything we could find in houses. The pickings have grown pretty slim the past few weeks. We've gotten desperate enough to start picking around the edges of the Twin Cities. We've been saving seeds. Come spring, we're planting crops anywhere there's grass at the university. That is, if the herds haven't busted things up too bad."

"I'm sure you can rebuild," Tyler said with his famous, kind smile. "Were you in contact with any other survivors from Marshall?"

Manny frowned, and then shrugged. "We kept in touch for the first day before we lost contact. There were pockets heading in every direction. Some headed north, thinking the worst of the zeds were to the south. Some headed east or west, since the herds were moving south. I decided to take my folks south to get as far ahead of the herds while we still could, but as soon as we pulled away from one herd, we ran smack into another. All I know is that once we find a temporary place to hide until the herds migrate, we'll head back to Marshall for the rest of our people and rebuild at the school, if it's still possible."

"It's possible," Bill said, wiping his mouth with his sleeve. "The other zeds will join up with the herds, so they'll all be gone. We can focus on rebuilding, finally, instead of just watching and defending ourselves against the infected every day."

"You really think the herds are migrating for the winter?" I asked, sure that the doubt bled through my words.

"After seeing it with my own eyes, I'm convinced of it," Manny said before taking another bite.

"I think it's a good idea to check out those herds for ourselves. What do you think?" Tyler asked me. "Can you make the flight without a fuel stop?"

I shrugged. "It shouldn't be a problem."

"You're a pilot?" Manny asked.

I gave a quick nod. "If the herds are getting that big, they'd be easy enough to spot from a distance. I wouldn't even have to fly low. Plus, I could make a wide arc back to see if there are any other groups headed our way. It'll give us some idea where the herds are and where they're headed."

Bill's eyes widened. "You have to take me with you."

I held up my hands. "Whoa. I'm scouting the herds. That's all. I'm not touching down anywhere."

"If you could at least fly over Marshall, we can at least see if the herd did much damage," Bill pleaded.

I sighed before turning back to Tyler. "If the flight goes without any hiccups, I suppose I could check out Marshall the same way I did Mason City."

Tyler thought for a moment, and then nodded. "If the weather changes or you get any kind of bad feeling in your gut, turn back. This run should be as straightforward as they come. I also want Clutch with you to check out the herds. We'll wait until he's feeling better if we have to, but I need his experience on this one."

"So, you *aren't* going to check on Marshall?" Bill asked, each word climbing in pitch.

"I didn't say that," I said. "If everything goes as planned, I'll fly over it. If the heavens align, I'll *consider* landing. But if it is in any way unsafe to land, all I can do is drop a bag with any messages you and your friends want to leave."

Using bag drops had been Tyler's idea to improve morale. The first bag I'd dropped had worked like a charm at Mason City. It looked like no survivors had made it in the ravaged area, but that didn't matter. Even if no one came to claim the bag, Tyler was right. The action had brought hope to the families back at the park.

Manny smiled and patted Bill's shoulder. "That's a grand plan. If you have some paper and pens around here, I'll bring notes from my people in the morning. We'd done similar things over the Twin Cities when we still had a pilot with us. Though, I'm guessing Bill would be more than happy to ride along if you have room for an extra passenger."

Tyler looked to me to answer. I didn't like taking people I didn't know on a flight, especially one as desperate as Bill. Too many things could happen in the air that could turn everything to shit. I'd learned that lesson by watching my dad. He'd been a doctor and an avid volunteer in the Doctors Without Borders program. He had learned to fly to get into some of the world's most inhospitable places. He'd taken me with him one summer, where I became hooked on flying but also learned first-hand how easily a single passenger with a panic attack could nearly crash a plane. Now, I never flew anywhere without having someone I trusted on board to handle any passenger.

"Okay," I said and Bill's face lit up. "You can ride in back only if we have an extra seat. Jase is my co-pilot and rides shotgun. We'll try for tomorrow morning. If Clutch isn't up for it or the weather doesn't look perfect, we'll try again for the next day. If any other Fox scout wants to ride along, you lose your seat." I pointed a finger at him. "I'm in charge. You do everything I say. No questions asked. No arguing. I will not risk my plane or my life because you decide to do something stupid. Got it?"

Bill gave a fervent nod, smiling widely. "Yes, yes. I'll do whatever you ask." He cupped my hands. "This means so much. Thank you, I mean it."

I gave a weak smile. "Listen. There are no guarantees on this trip. Chances are, even if we make it to Marshall without having to turn around, there won't be any safe landing strips, so we'll only manage to make a bag drop. You're signing up for what will likely be a dull three- or four-hour flight."

"I understand," Bill replied, his eyebrows high. "We had a road cleared at the university for our pilot to land. You can land there."

"I'm not making any promises," I cautioned.

"Even if you can't land, I can at least get a note to my family," Bill quickly replied. "They'll know I'm safe and on my way back to them. They've got to be so worried right now." Bill reached into his pocket, grabbed a pen and notepad, and started drawing something.

"Much obliged, ma'am," Manny said. "Bill's been riding my back ever since we pulled out of Marshall."

"I'm not surprised," I said with a smirk. "And the name's Cash." I watched Manny for a moment. "What can you tell me about these herds? How are you so sure the zeds are moving south?"

"A scout told us he'd followed the herd for fifty miles before he figured out they were heading straight south. One of our radio contacts in North Dakota noticed zeds all started walking the same direction about the same time the birds started migrating. We put two and two together and figured they're migrating for the winter."

I shook my head. "The zeds around here aren't showing any signs of migrating."

"You're farther south. It's warmer here, so they might not have gotten the itch yet. Or, maybe they're just waiting to join up with other herds."

I thought for a moment. I dreaded seeing if this pair was telling the truth, but I also wasn't going to be an ostrich with my head in the sand. If there was danger headed our way, we needed as much advance warning as possible. Flying was the safest and most efficient way to do that. I sighed, came to my feet, and grabbed my tray. "Well, if I'm going to do this, I better start my flight planning." I turned to Bill. "Be at the park gate by sunrise. Don't bring more than five pounds of gear with you. I like to keep the plane as light as possible when we head out."

"Here." Bill handed me a piece of paper. "Here's a map of the university." He pointed to a long line. "Here's where our pilot used to land."

As I pocketed the paper, Tyler gave me a smile. "Get some rest. I'll try to catch you before you leave in the morning. *If* you leave in the morning, I mean."

"Good night." I gave Tyler a slight smile before stepping back and then paused, thinking of another problem of being cooped up in a small, enclosed space with a newcomer. "Oh, and Bill? Be sure to wash up. You guys really stink."

Tyler's smile widened into a big grin, and I couldn't help but return his smile. I turned and headed toward the food table. After dumping off my tray and grabbing a bag of nuts and an apple for Clutch, I walked back to the cabin. My leg needed the exercise, and I needed the fresh air. Aside from the random raider and zed herd, life had returned to something that vaguely resembled normalcy. I tried not to show fear, but if Manny was right about huge herds headed this way, I was downright terrified. We couldn't take out a single herd. How the hell could we defend the park against something ten thousand times the size of the herd we ran from today?

By the time I reached the cabin, the sun had set. Jase was doing push-ups on the floor while Clutch was sprawled out on the bed sound asleep, with a bottle of pills still in his grip. For a moment, my stress disappeared. These two guys were my family now. Like so many other "families" of survivors in this new world, we were just as close as any real family, and I loved them no less than if we were related.

Jase was a bit like the brother I'd never had, but he was more like a son I'd probably never have. He had a good heart. Even with all the shit he'd seen, there was still an unjaded piece left in his soul. I'd give my life for his in a heartbeat. He was a far better person than I was, and I was thankful that he came to Clutch's farm that day many months ago...the day our family was born.

The idea of a real-life son terrified me. I often thought back to the time Clutch and I had unprotected sex and was thankful that I hadn't ended up pregnant. I shivered at the thought of having a tiny, defenseless, *crying* baby surrounded by zeds.

Shaking the thought from my head, I walked over to the table, grabbed the stack of FAA sectional maps, and opened up the one for Minneapolis. I laid the map next to the hand-drawn map Bill had scrawled during dinner. On it, the buildings of the university were squares and rectangles, with a thick line drawn at the bottom indicating a road he was convinced would work as a landing strip. After lighting a candle, I scrutinized the sectional, circling every airport that had fuel along the route to Marshall and back. Taking off and landing wasn't much of an issue anymore. Any stretch of road without power lines worked, especially since the planes I flew weren't large by any means. I could feather the prop and land nearly silently. As long as no zeds were too close when I restarted for takeoff, I could be safely in the air before any got close.

"I didn't know you were doing a scouting run tomorrow," Jase said without stopping.

"*We* have a scouting run tomorrow. A long distance one," I replied. "If Clutch is up to it. Tyler wants him on this run."

Jase rolled over. His brows rose. "Really? Where are we heading?"

"The folks from Marshall said there might be some herds headed this way. I want to check that out. They seem to think zeds are migrating south for the winter. If that's true, the more time we have to prepare, the better."

Jase's guffawed. "Zeds migrating? Like geese?"

I shrugged. "I suppose so. I thought it sounded pretty farfetched, too."

He simply gave a disbelieving shake of his head. "How big of herds are we talking about?"

I thought about telling him what Manny had said, but decided Jase had enough bad things to dream about already. "I guess we'll find out tomorrow."

Jase's eyes narrowed. "They must be big for Tyler to want you to fly out that far."

I shrugged. "We head out at sunrise. This will be a top-off-the-fuel-tanks kind of mission. If we can, we'll also check out the folks still holed up at the university in Marshall. Otherwise, we'll at least try to do a bag drop."

"Cool." He then nodded to Clutch. "He was out cold when I got home. I'm surprised he's still asleep."

"Freeley was a bit rougher than we expected," I said. "I think it banged him up a bit."

He frowned for a moment before his features softened. "He'll feel better in no time."

I wished I had his confidence. While I knew Clutch would say he was feeling better, I also knew he would lie about his pain just to ride along. Clutch needed more time to heal, but he also needed to keep his spirit up. Being cooped up at the park was a constant numbing barrage against his spirit. I didn't know how to find the balance, and so I took the easy way out and let Clutch decide.

I circled another airport on the map. "Oh, and one of the newcomers will be riding along. He's got a wife and daughter still at Marshall."

Jase gave a crooked smile. "We could leave early, leave him behind."

"Believe me, I've already considered it, but this guy really needs this. That's another reason I need you along—to make sure he doesn't go stupid while we're up there."

"Won't be the first time."

I snorted. Yeah, the Cessna now had duct tape covering a bullet hole in the fuselage from the last time we gave a newcomer a lift. "Get some sleep. I have a feeling tomorrow is going to be a long day."

———

Bill was waiting—practically prancing—when Clutch, Jase, and I arrived at the gate the following morning. As we approached in the small red truck, he waved and jogged to the edge of the gate.

I gave him a full once-over. His hair was still damp, and he wore a fresh shirt. That he'd listened to me yesterday and cleaned himself up a bit gave me some confidence that he'd behave on this trip. "Morning," I called out. "Are you ready to go?"

He nodded with a smile, his eyebrows raised high. "You bet. Let's go." He lifted a small duffle. "I also brought some letters and things from the others."

"All right. Go ahead and climb in back." I gestured behind me, where Clutch sat in his wheelchair against the big white portable fuel tank, sipping coffee in a thermos while he eyed the newcomer. Before the outbreak, Clutch had never touched caffeine. Ever since his concussion, he guzzled the stuff whenever he had a chance.

As Jase drove us down the road, I craned my head out the window. Long wisps of white marred an otherwise clear sky. I leaned back in with a sigh of relief. "Fingers crossed, it should hopefully be a smooth flight today."

"Good," Jase drawled. "That last flight was not much fun. And by 'not much fun,' I mean it was pretty much the worst experience ever."

I chuckled, remembering Jase's face buried in a sick-sack thirty minutes into a two-hour scouting run. "Poor Jasen can't handle bumpy air," I cooed.

He gave me a droll stare for a moment and then flipped me off, and I grinned even harder.

Jase's stomach couldn't handle turbulence, but it was Clutch's back that couldn't risk any turbulence today. Over the past couple of months, Jase had filled in for Clutch on supply runs, and he'd become my co-pilot. He was no longer the kid who'd come to Clutch's farm—bloody and carrying his dying dog—six months ago. He'd only turned sixteen last week, but, aside from a youthful face, no one would ever mistake Jase for still being a boy.

In his eyes, anyone could see that he'd suffered more than most. Not many had to kill their own father like Jase had. Many would've been broken. Not Jase. He'd become the consummate survivor. He was the best of all of us. He did what it took to survive, yet he somehow managed to retain his humanity, something I felt like I had to fight to hold onto. Whether fighting zeds or on scouting runs, I easily trusted him as much as I trusted Clutch and Tyler.

I also hated bringing him into danger. I wanted to keep him safe behind the park's gates. Every time he left the park, some place deep within my heart panged with dread. A part of me craved to lock him in the cabin, but I knew that would be a disservice to him. He needed to learn how to survive on his own, and protecting him would only hurt him.

Still, it was hard.

Jase brought the truck around a curve in the road, bringing into sight the Cessna 172 and shot-up Piper Cub sitting in the small parking lot of a rest area, both ready to go at a moment's notice. For most of my scouting trips, I took the slower Cub. For today's long trip, I needed the speed and distance the Cessna offered, even though the 172 could in no way be called a fast airplane.

I kept the planes as close to the park as possible. It made sense given we kept the area around the park clear of zeds, and I felt safer knowing I could be in the air in less than five minutes in case shit hit the park. Jase parked on the edge of the road, and I stepped out. The air was cool and damp, and the early morning sun caused the dew to glisten on the Cessna's wings.

Bill jumped down and stared at the plane. "You take off on this road? Isn't that dangerous with all these trees?"

"Nah," I said. "It's a lot less dangerous than the airport." I headed to the back of the truck and dropped the lift gate. Clutch casually screwed the cap on his steaming thermos and slid it into the bag on his wheelchair. After twelve or so hours of rest, Clutch's pain had receded, and his mood had improved. His face seemed lighter this morning, and I knew he was eager for his first flight with me. I pulled two two-by-sixes out and made a ramp against the truck.

"The airport is close to Chow Town," Jase said, walking past us. "So the risk of zeds getting in our way on takeoff or landing is a lot higher. This road is straight and close to the park. Besides, it's not like we have to worry about traffic."

Clutch wheeled his chair down the primitive ramp, and we headed for the Cessna 172. "The weather looks good today," he said.

I looked out to the sky another time. "Yeah. It's great flying weather." I went down on a knee and began removing the tie-downs.

"Don't you have to land at an airport to get fuel?" Bill asked from behind me.

Once I tugged the first rope from the plane, I moved onto the next. "No. We truck the av-gas in." I pointed to the pickup truck we'd arrived in. "You see that white tank on the back of the truck?"

He looked and then frowned. "That's for the airplanes? I thought it was an extra tank for the truck."

I shook my head. "We have a full-sized gas truck for all of our cars and trucks. We use that tank just for the airplanes." We'd found the fuel tank on the back of some farmer's truck. We'd cleaned out the tank and filled it with aviation fuel at the airport. "It works pretty good," I tacked on before glancing over to see Jase helping Clutch get into the front seat. I looked back at Bill. "We'll be taking off soon. We'll be in the air for a few hours, so if you need to hit the bathroom, this is your last chance."

"It's okay. I'm ready to go." Bill wrung his hands and headed toward Jase.

"Jase can help get you strapped in," I said and walked my preflight checklist. After I made a final circle around the plane, I headed for the cockpit.

"We're all set. Clutch is up front since it would be too much of a hassle to put him in the backseat," Jase said as he held the door open.

"That makes sense," I said. "I guess it's time, then." While Jase stood off to the side of the plane, I climbed into the front left seat of the small four-seater.

In the seat next to mine, Clutch was busy stashing his backpack under his seat.

Bill was strapped in the seat behind Clutch and already had a headset on. I set my spear and rifle alongside Clutch's Blaser rifle between our seats, and buckled into the pilot's seat.

I smiled at Clutch strapped in next to me. "Our first flight together."

He nodded and for the first time in months, a genuine smile emerged. "I've been looking forward to it."

"Jase is my usual co-pilot. But since you're riding shotgun, you want to be my navigator on this run?"

"Sure." A sense of purpose spanned his features. "Do you have a map?"

A smile crept up my cheeks. "It's good to have you back," I said quietly as I pulled out the sectional maps I'd marked up last night and handed them to him.

He watched me for a moment, and the tiniest hint of a smile curled his lips. He opened his mouth to speak but then closed it, choosing instead to say nothing.

"All right," I said with a sigh. I pointed to black circle that marked the park and moved my finger an inch or so. "We're about here right now and our flight path is that penciled line there. We'll be on a heading of zero-one-zero. The map continues on this side." I flipped the large sheet over.

"I'm a Ranger," he replied with a smirk. "I've read a map once or twice."

"Oh, yeah," I said. "I guess you have." After a moment, I grabbed a pen from my pocket and handed it to him. "We need to mark down every large herd we fly over. Be careful to mark down their current locations. If you can see any kind of path they've trampled, try to note their trajectory, if you can. Hopefully, we'll be able to figure out if any herds will come near the park or if we're in the clear. If any are headed our way, I think Tyler's counting on you to help figure out some kind of response plan."

"I figured as much," he said, his smile fading.

"I'm still hoping Manny was exaggerating, and there aren't any big herds headed this direction."

"We'll find out soon enough," Clutch said quietly.

This morning, while we were at the stream, I'd brought Clutch and Jase up to speed on everything Manny had said. But, it wasn't until Jase had left to grab the truck that I'd told Clutch just how large the herds were reported to me. I swallowed and gave a tight nod before going through my pre-startup checks. Satisfied, I looked outside to Jase who was busy keeping an eye out for zeds. "Clear," I called out. I turned the prop on the engine and it came to life. The magnetos were starting to run rough. Unfortunately, I knew nothing about the mechanics of an airplane besides the most basic items, and neither did anyone at the park. There were two guys who maintained the Humvees, and they were doing their best to keep the plane in shape as much as their knowledge would allow. If the FAA still existed, they would've grounded this operation months ago. As it stood, it was just a matter of time before I'd have to find a new airplane for transporting cargo and going on longer scouting trips like today's.

Once the engine warmed up, I taxied the plane onto the road and ran through my pre-takeoff checks. It took a few minutes to tame the coughing engine by leaning the mixture and playing with the throttle. Once everything was in the green, I motioned to Jase who, after one final three-sixty, ran over and squeezed inside behind me. Takeoff was the most dangerous part of the flight. There was no way to mask engine noise and full throttle, and even though any zed that neared the park was quickly dispatched, more zeds showed up all the time.

As Jase buckled in, I put on my headset. While there was no use for headsets to communicate with control towers or traffic, they did make it easier to talk with the passengers and to report in to Tyler when we were returning from scouting trips so he could make sure the runway was cleared for landing. To not draw zeds to the area, I liked to fly straight in and with the throttle pulled back to keep my landing as quiet as possible.

"Everyone ready for takeoff?" I asked.

Clutch nodded. "Ready."

I looked to the backseat.

"I'm ready," Bill said, his voice coming through loud and clear through my headset.

Jase was still adjusting his boom. "Let's rock and roll," he said.

I smirked and then turned my focus onto the road in front of me. I pushed the throttle full forward, and the plane rolled ahead, slowly at first, and then passing each yellow divided highway line faster and faster. I tugged back on the yoke, and the plane lifted off the ground gently, the smoothness of the air instead of tires against rough concrete was the only sense of transition from the ground to the sky. As the plane climbed, I turned toward north on my compass heading.

I set the stopwatch taped on the panel, a backup to help remind me how much fuel I had remaining. I looked at Clutch. "While you look for herds, keep an eye out for landmarks and let me know if we start to veer off our flight path."

"Got it," he replied, all business.

"If I have to ride backseat, I call dibs on the music," Jase said, and I found an iPod dropped onto my lap.

With a chuckle, I plugged his MP3 into the audio input and kicked off the playlist he always listened to on our scouting runs. Flying was one of the few times we could listen to music without fear of zeds, and we always played rock-paper-scissors to see whose music would be played. Though, listening to *any* music was nice. Pop music filtered through our headsets, and I turned up the volume.

We flew for an hour, everyone given the same task: search for herds. I kept the plane three thousand feet off the ground so that any herds would be easier to spot. Bill nervously chattered, his voice cutting over the music. Once I threated to pull the plug on his headset, he was a better passenger.

The air was smooth and cool, and the sky was clear. It was an absolutely perfect flying day, and I found myself feeling lighter and breathing easier. There was something surreal about being in the sky, removed from the death and destruction below. It was the only time I could still feel completely at peace. After all, the sky was the only place left without man-eating predators.

"There's one! Down there, below!" Bill exclaimed.

"Down where?" I cranked my head around to see him pointing out the window to my right. I looked, searching for zeds. My gaze narrowed on a field of dirt that seemed to go on forever in the distance, and I turned the plane in that direction. As we approached, the dirt morphed into what looked like a giant, flat anthill. Chills covered my body because this was no anthill.

"Holy bejeezus," Jase said. "That's no herd. That's...that's..."

"Fuck," Clutch muttered.

"Yeah," I added, my jaws lax. As we drew closer, the movement began to split into individual humanoid shapes all moving together like fans at a music concert, only far bigger than any concert or sporting event could be. The herd was larger than I could've possibly imagined. Hell had opened up and spurted forth millions of demons from its gorge.

"I told you guys these herds were huge. And it looks like another one in the distance out there," Bill said from the backseat. "Now that you've seen it, can we check on my family?"

"Hold on," I said, as I continued to stare at the mass of zeds below us.

"I wasn't expecting a herd like that," Jase said. "What could we possibly do if it found the park?"

After a tense moment of silence, I pulled off to return to our flight path.

A heavy stone was already growing in my gut. I found it hard to breathe, and my chest pounded like I was about to have a heart attack. I could already guess their trajectory from seeing the relatively straight trodden path over a half-mile wide that went on for as far as I could see. Camp Fox didn't stand a chance.

As I flew north, parallel to the zed path, Clutch continually updated the map while muttering under his breath every few seconds. The herd had crushed all the grass and fields in its path. We lost the path a couple times when we flew over larger towns, but quickly found the path again on the other side.

"God," I sighed. "There's another one."

Clutch looked up and followed my finger. "Jesus."

Another herd, at least half the size of the first, looked like it was only thirty miles or so behind and headed the same direction.

"I'll mark it down," Clutch said as I tried to stay focused on my heading, but my eyes kept darting back to the herd. Worse, not ten miles later, another herd appeared in the distance.

"How can there be so many?" Jase asked from the backseat.

No one answered. In fact, no one spoke for many long minutes. I gripped the yoke and twisted my hands around it. Clutch scribbled on the map. I couldn't tell what Jase and Bill were doing behind me. My mind was too busy dealing with shock. I didn't need to be an actuary to do the math. There was nothing we could do to defend Camp Fox against such numbers.

We were absolutely, completely fucked.

My brows furrowed as I held back a sob. The unfairness of it all pissed me off. We worked so hard to survive. We'd finally gotten to the point where we felt a step ahead of the zeds.

And now this?

Like Manny's group, we could only run, but where could we go? The massive herds seemed to cover an entire line of latitude as they moved south.

Bill lunged forward and pointed straight ahead. "There," he said, wagging his finger. "See that? The university is coming up."

I jumped, startled. "Get buckled in!"

"It's SMSU. We're there," he said, not moving.

I squinted and made out the connected buildings. We were still at least five miles out and I throttled back to slow the plane and descend. "All right, guys. Keep an eye out for zeds."

"They would've all left with the herds," Bill said.

"Do you know that for sure?" I countered, adding in flaps to slow the plane to near stall speed.

He said nothing.

I sighed. "Where's that street I can land on, Bill?"

He leaned forward more. "Birch Street," he said as if I could read street signs from up here. "It's just to the south of the dorms. We kept it clear in case we had to pull out."

"It's east-west, right?" I asked, looking once more at his roughly drawn map.

"What?"

I made a motion with my hand. "Does the road go north and south or east and west?"

"Oh, east and west. You can't miss it. It's the main street for the university."

As we neared the small university, I slowed the plane and dropped in as much flaps as I could without stalling. Once I had the street in sight, I nodded. "I've got it."

I frowned as I took in the university. During a typical scouting run, zeds dotted streets of any town I flew over. Here, other than the random zed crawling across the ground or a rotting corpse, I saw nothing. The entire university seemed devoid of zeds. "You guys see anything?" I asked.

"Nothing yet. Just a few stragglers," Jase said.

"Same here," Clutch said. "From what I can tell, those stragglers look pretty decrepit."

"You're going past the street. Down there! Down there!"

I flipped off the intercom but could still hear Bill's yelling even through my headset. The street was narrow, only two lanes lined with trees and streetlamps. It had a ninety-degree curve on the eastern edge and a forty-five on the west. I could make it work, but there wasn't much room for error, and no room for a late-decision go-around.

Clutch squeezed my knee, and I turned. "You sure you want to try it?" he yelled since I'd turned off the intercom.

I looked back down at the street. I had to make the call. If I continued to circle, the engine noise would draw all remaining zeds into the area. I glanced at Bill. His eyes were wide and pleading. It would've been easy to fly over and drop a bag, letting the survivors make their way to their families and friends on their own. But, if I were in Bill's shoes, this close to my family…

"Damn it," I muttered and dropped in the rest of the flaps. There was no way I couldn't *not* land. I may have lost my parents, but if it was Clutch or Jase down there, I would have to see for myself. Bill deserved the same.

I lined up for a long final approach. I wanted to land as short as possible because neither the length nor the width of the street was forgiving for a botched landing. My grip was firm on the yoke. I had to get it right. The stall warning sounded, and the ground came up quickly. The wheels hit hard. The plane bounced before settling down. I stepped on the brakes to stop faster than I could with a taildragger.

I pulled off my headset and looked around to find no zeds running out to greet us. I bit my lip. "Well, that wasn't my finest landing."

"We didn't crash, so I consider it a success," Clutch said.

Jase tapped my shoulder. "I'll cover you while you get lined up for takeoff."

I nodded and opened the door. I brought my seat forward. He squeezed out from behind me and hopped outside. Bill leaned between Clutch and me as I started to taxi back the opposite direction I'd landed. Jase walked alongside the Cessna as I taxied, ready to take out any random zed that came at us.

"What are you doing?" Bill asked. "You're going past the dorms."

"We'll check them out on foot. First, I need the plane ready in case we need to make a quick takeoff."

He muttered something and leaned back. Suddenly, I found myself pressed forward against the yoke as he squeezed passed me. "Hey!"

Bill jumped out of the plane and ran back toward the dorms, carrying the bag of letters.

"Idiot," Clutch muttered.

I shook my head. "He's going to get himself killed." I taxied the plane all the way back to the eastern edge of the street and turned around, setting the plane up for an immediate takeoff. "I'm half tempted to just leave him and head back."

As I cut the engine, Jase walked around the front, still scanning the area.

Clutch grabbed his rifle.

I put my hand on his forearm and fought to say the words I needed to say. "You should stay with the plane, in case we need to make a quick takeoff." I inhaled before he had a chance to speak. "You know us. Jase and I won't do anything stupid. We're just going to check on the dorms, that's it."

"I know. I trust both of you. It's the other guy I don't trust."

"We'll be wheels up in ten minutes. You stay here and sweep for us in case zeds start trickling this way. Okay?"

He sat there, gripping his rifle. After a moment, he hit his legs, startling me.

"I hate this. I fucking hate this," he said before tilting his head back against the headrest.

My heart ached for him. "I know," I said softly and touched his cheek. "This is a temporary inconvenience, that's all. You'll be walking soon. I know it. We just have to take it one day at a time."

His lips tightened. "I'll see you in ten."

After a moment, I dropped my hand, unbuckled, grabbed my gear, and climbed out.

"Be careful," he said suddenly. "I've got a bad vibe about this place."

I gave a small nod and walked away, glancing back to see Clutch already focused on scanning the area.

Jase came up to my side. Looking around, he gave an exaggerated shiver. "This place gives me the creeps. Everything's been trampled. There's not even a shrub left."

To my right was a parking lot filled with cars. Most were parked askew, as though they'd been forcibly shoved out of their parking space and into the spot next to them. A couple had even been rolled over. I hadn't seen any mobile zeds, but no survivors came out to greet us, either. Both would've heard us fly over.

I slung my spear onto my shoulder and kept my rifle ready. "Let's make this quick."

We walked toward the dorms where Bill had headed. We took slow steps, constantly scanning our full three-sixty, though I knew Clutch had our six covered. While I wanted to get the hell out of there, I didn't rush. Just because Bill had run in half-cocked didn't mean that we had to put ourselves at risk.

A zed without legs reached out like a beggar. I stepped to the side, and it tried to drag itself to us. I didn't waste energy killing it; it was in such bad shape that the only way it could latch onto a victim was if someone fell on it.

The ominous feeling in my gut grew worse as we approached the first dorm. The doors were propped wide open by a mangled corpse. Bones, tufts of hair, and cloth shreds were about all that remained.

Jase and I eyed each other. With a deep inhalation, he stepped inside first. Glass crunched under my boots as I stepped around the corpse. We walked as carefully and quietly as we could, pausing to listen after every few steps.

Something fell on the floor in a nearby room. I swung my rifle around.

We moved as one toward the open door. I listened for any other sounds, but could only hear movement in the one room. When we reached the door, I twisted around and aimed. I lowered my weapon with a sigh. "Jesus, Bill. I nearly blew your head off."

He continued to rifle through papers on the table. "They're not here. I don't understand it. There's no note." He chewed on his bottom lip for a moment before he looked up and over his shoulder. "They must still be in the student center."

"Hold up," I said, reaching for him. That no one had cleaned up the body in the building they lived was a serious red flag. "They probably had to run and didn't get a chance to get back here to leave a note."

"Bill, hold on, man," Jase echoed.

He pushed open the door. "It's lunchtime. Everyone eats at the student center." He headed outside.

"He's a real pain in the ass," I muttered, not caring if Bill heard me or not.

"The idea of ditching him and heading back is getting pretty appealing," Jase added.

I glanced at my watch. Six minutes to go. I sucked in a breath. "Let's get this over with."

We followed Bill as he jogged down a sidewalk and up to a brick building with large glass windows.

"Hold up," I said and grabbed his arm before he opened the door.

He yanked out of my grip. "Everyone will be inside. It's okay."

"*Look*," Jase said and pointed.

"What?" Bill asked, and then he frowned. He cupped his hands against the glass and squinted. He let out a gasp. "*No.*"

Inside, the student center was a mess. Tables were overturned, chairs were scattered. There was nobody eating lunch. There was nobody, period.

"They must've run," I said hopefully.

Bill grabbed the door handle and yanked it open. As he ran inside, I lowered my head and shook it slowly. After taking a deep breath, I followed, staying protectively at Jase's side.

There were no zeds, not even any bodies littering the floors. The ominous feeling in my gut had morphed into fear.

Bill was doing a three-sixty, looking around. "Katie!" he called out. "Jan!"

"*Sh*," I hissed. "Keep it down."

A thump came from somewhere off to my left, confirming my suspicion. There were zeds still around here, all right.

A smile broke out on Bill's face, and the tension fell from his shoulders. "Oh, they're in the theater. Thank God."

"Don't," I warned.

Bill turned back to us. "It's all right. The theater is our emergency shelter. They've probably been staying in there until someone came to give them the all-clear."

"Then why is there a steel pipe through the door?" Jase asked, but Bill either didn't hear or didn't care because he rushed across the open space and to that exact door.

"I don't like this," I said, slowly walking toward Bill.

"I think we should get out of here," Jase said.

"Agreed."

"I'm coming!" Bill called out and glanced over his shoulder. "It's okay. You don't understand. This is part of our emergency procedures. Someone probably locked them in here for safety, so that zeds couldn't get to them. But now they can't get out unless we unlock it for them."

"Then why didn't they lock the door from the *other* side," Jase asked dubiously.

Bill slid the pipe out from the handles and pulled open the door. He stood there, staring into the darkness. "Katie? Jan?"

Moans echoed. Jase and I both lunged for the door the same time a zed tumbled from the darkness. Bill cried out and shoved it down. Jase slammed the door shut, and I slid the bar back into place. I spun on my heel to see Bill holding the zed back with his hands pressing against its shoulders.

Hundreds, if not thousands, of fists pounded against the metal door. It sounded like the entire theater was filled with zeds.

Jase swung his machete, taking off the top of the zed's skull, and it collapsed.

"Holy shit," Jase said, sucking in a breath.

"Yeah," I said breathlessly before turning around to find Bill frozen behind us. After wiping sweat from my face, I grabbed his arm. "We need to get out of here. Now."

Both Jase and I pulled at him, but he dug in his heels. "The theater was safe. No windows. How'd the zeds find them?"

"Someone was probably infected before going in there," I answered.

"That door isn't going to hold them for long," Jase tacked on. "We need to get out of here. Because those are going to be some fresh and fast zeds in there."

Bill collapsed onto the floor with his head between his knees, hugging himself. "I never should've left. I should've come earlier."

Jase and I looked at each other, hopeless. Neither of us spoke. I didn't voice the truth, that his family had probably never stood a chance.

The sounds of fists pounding against the doors echoed through the center. The bar through the door handles clanged as the door moved against it in a rhythmic wave. It would take minutes, at most, for them to break free.

I nudged Bill. "We have to go."

He shook his head. "What's the use in going on?" He looked up, tears running down his cheeks. "It's my fault. I should've come for them." His voice grew louder with every word, and I tried to shush him. Bill shook his fist at the theater. "You bastards! You're all bastards!"

I eyed Jase and he nodded. "We need to go *now*," he said, enunciating every word.

I nodded. We each grabbed one of Bill's arms and pulled him to his feet.

He tore away. "No!" He fell back onto his butt and sobbed.

I pursed my lips. "Bill, it's not your fault what happened."

"There's nothing you can do, Bill. Your family would want you to save yourself."

Bill didn't respond, instead he continued to sob.

We tried to pull him up again, but he shoved away and fell back down. The zeds' moaning and pounding were growing louder, echoing throughout the student center.

This time when I eyed Jase, his features hardened, and he shook his head slowly. I swallowed and glanced down at Bill one more time. The man had reached his breaking point. He'd chosen to give up rather than to keep on living. I wanted to yank him along with us, but I knew it would be pointless. If we took the time to drag him, we'd never get out of there alive.

My throat tightened and I stepped back. Then Jase and I ran back to the plane, leaving Bill behind with a theater full of zeds.

FIVE

"Where's Bill?" Clutch asked as Jase and I piled into the Cessna. I dumped my gear onto Jase's lap and pulled the door closed.

A distant scream broke through the silence.

"He's not coming," Jase said as I started up the plane without taking the time to go through any checklist, let alone buckle my seat belt.

Clutch didn't say anything else, but I could feel his eyes on me as I tried to smooth out the engine as quickly as I could. As soon as its rough grumble of fouling spark plugs cleared somewhat, I throttled full power and started my takeoff roll.

"A shitload of zeds coming in fast at our two o'clock," Clutch said loudly at my side.

"*C'mon, c'mon, c'mon,*" I muttered, pulling back on the yoke, trying to force the plane into the air. With the tanks only half full and one less passenger, the Cessna lifted off at the edge of the dorms. Zeds came running around the buildings and onto the street below. I leveled off my climb to build up speed just out of reach of the zeds below, because I didn't want to risk stalling and losing what little lift I had.

Once I could manage a decent rate of climb, I looked down at the crowded street below. If we'd been five seconds later, zeds would've collided with the Cessna, and we never would've gotten off the ground. I let out the breath I'd held on takeoff. "That was close."

Clutch craned his head to watch the scene below, and then turned to me.

I put my headset on, and he did the same.

"What the hell happened back there?" he asked.

"No one made it out of Marshall when the herds passed through," I said.

"They were still at the student center," Jase added.

His lips tightened and he looked over both of us. "You two okay?"

I nodded. "Yeah."

"That was too close," Jase said before sighing heavily into the headset.

After getting the plane set up on its heading back to Camp Fox, I turned on Jase's music. No one spoke the entire flight back to the park. We passed over the herds again, as they chewed their slow but relentless path toward our home. One herd had stopped at a farm and had all of its buildings surrounded. I hated to think what they were after.

Poor Marshall had never stood a chance, and it'd had a hundred times the population of Camp Fox. The herds could eat right through us and barely slow down. Seeing what had happened at the student center made me realize one thing. We couldn't defend the park against the herds like we'd done before. We had to run, and we had to do it soon. Because if we waited until the first herd was in sight, it'd be too late.

Clutch, Jase, and I could fly somewhere far enough north that we'd be safe easily enough, but I'd never be able to get the others out in time. Tyler, Tack, Griz...they'd all be doomed to certain death. *No*. I couldn't live with myself knowing I'd stranded fifty or sixty people for execution.

I spent the rest of the flight trying to think of viable escape plans that included everyone and our livestock at the park and the only solution that came to mind was a tall building. But I quickly dismissed it as too risky. No skyscrapers existed anymore after all major cities had been bombed. If any had survived, they wouldn't be structurally sound. As for tall buildings in smaller towns, most buildings wouldn't be more than five floors high. Sure, a herd could likely not reach us on the top floor, but if they knew we were inside, they could have us surrounded until we all starved to death. Or, worse, eventually they'd climb over one another to get to us.

We needed a better option.

When the park came into sight, Clutch radioed Tyler. Clutch simply said, "Come out and meet us."

I had no doubt it got the point across.

Sure enough, by the time we landed, Tyler was waiting for us. He watched from where he sat on the Humvee's hood as I taxied to my usual parking space.

Tyler jumped down and started tying down the plane as soon as I cut the engine.

I opened my door, and Jase squeezed out from behind me. "I'll get your chair, Clutch," he said from outside before opening the baggage compartment and pulling out the folded wheelchair.

After checking everything, I grabbed Clutch's and my gear and climbed out.

With Jase's support, Clutch lifted himself out of the plane by holding onto the spar and lowered himself onto the chair. I handed him his rifle and backpack.

Tyler came over and scrutinized each of our faces. "Well?"

I opened my mouth to speak but couldn't find the words. I searched for something to say, but nothing coherent formed. How could anyone describe what was headed our way? No one else spoke either, likely unable to find the words as well.

After a long pause, he clenched his fists and kicked at the ground. "Shit!" He took a deep breath and looked back up. "How bad is it?"

"Imagine your worst fucking nightmare times a million," Clutch said bluntly.

"I've never seen anything like it," Jase said. "Huge herds. Each one has thousands and thousands of those things."

Tyler was silent for a moment. "Do any pose a risk to the park?"

I swallowed. "We have a week, maybe two, until the first herd gets here. If we were a hundred miles east, we'd have longer. But the park is right in their path."

"God," Tyler muttered.

"Camp Fox is not equipped to hold off that many zeds," Clutch said. "The park's hills and waterways will slow them down, but they'll still plow right through the park. We'd burn through all of our ammo, and there'd still be more."

"We have to run," I added.

"Where will we run to?" Tyler asked quietly.

I shrugged. "I don't know. We can keep ahead of the herds for a while. Maybe Montana or Wyoming where they're building those super-cities we keep hearing about."

Tyler shook his head. "The herds could already be hitting through those areas now."

"Okay, then. We could go gypsy. Keep on the move until they pass through," I said, frustrated that I had no better answer. "As long as I have a plane I can scout out areas and make sure that we're not heading straight for another herd. Or, we can try the Pied Piper plan and lead them away from the park. That plan has never failed. If we're lucky, the herds will stick to the roads and steer clear of the park completely. After all, it's pretty secluded."

Even I didn't believe my words. Hungry zeds had a knack at sniffing out prey. A few dozen people in a small area would be a tasty snack for a herd.

"But if the plan failed, we'd be doomed," Clutch said.

"We can't sit on our asses and hope they bypass the park. I've already reached out to all my radio contacts. We have one potential option," Tyler said finally. "How'd Marshall fare? Did Bill find his family?"

I shook my head. "It's been completely wiped out."

Tyler sighed. "I was afraid of that. It's going to devastate Manny's people." He scratched his head. "And Bill?"

I gave him a slow shake of my head. He didn't need to know the ugly details.

"Damn it." He kicked a pebble on the concrete. "I need time to think. We'll talk more after dinner. I'll meet you all at the square," he said and took off.

As though we hadn't just seen the Grim Reaper headed our way, a grin grew across Jase's face and he hustled toward the truck. "Good. I'm starving."

Food, the best temporary medicine for a shitty day. It was the only time I knew Jase wasn't faking his happiness. Everyone loved food now, likely because we all knew how precious it was. Without the convenience of drive-throughs and grocery stores, food took on a whole new meaning. That, plus all the hard physical work we did each day, made mealtime an almost religious experience.

I glanced back at the plane. "I'll refuel in the morning. I didn't see any zeds worth worrying about in the area," I said when I saw Jase already loading Clutch onto the back of the truck. I hopped in, and Jase started the engine and stepped on the gas.

As we drove back into the park, many of the residents were outside working on their assigned tasks, such as gathering food, tending to gardens, and doing laundry. All were completely oblivious to the horde of death headed straight for them.

Jase headed straight for the park square and parked next to Tyler's Humvee. In front of the log building, three of the park's older residents were busy cracking walnuts, hazelnuts, and acorns that the kids had found. Everyone had a chore. No one got a free ride. Even the kids' games had a purpose. Flag football was a popular one, where we taught them how to escape zeds. There was no football involved. One kid started without flags, and they played the role of zed. Every kid whose flags the zed took had to join its herd and go after the others. It sounded a bit morbid, but we had to train them to protect themselves. For little kids, running and hiding were their only real options.

I forced a smile and waved at the trio cracking nuts on my way into the park square.

Tyler held the door open for us. "I should warn you. They've been waiting here since morning,"

Clutch rolled himself in first, and Jase and I followed.

The chow area was empty except for Manny and his people. The moment we stepped inside, all eyes turned to us. Manny stood with a wide smile and headed our way. "You're back!" He slowed down as he looked past my shoulder, then at me. "Where's Bill?"

I'd been expecting the question and didn't hesitate. "He decided to stay behind."

Faces lit up. Except for Manny, whose smile had been replaced by a dubious squint of his eyes. I tried not to make contact as I followed Clutch to the food line. Jase had somehow found his way to the front of the line. A woman hustled to me and held a picture in front of my face. "Did you see my husband?"

I shook my head. "I didn't see him." I picked up a tray and grabbed some leftover potatoes, nuts, and berries.

Manny's people quickly surrounded us.

"Are they okay?"

"Did you talk to Lyle?"

"What did you see?"

"Did you give them our letters?"

"Please tell us more!"

The woman who'd showed me the picture of her husband grabbed my arm. "Please take me north like you did Bill. We don't have to land, just look for Mike. I know he's out there. Please help me."

"I'm sorry, but I can't help you," I said, not wanting to be the one responsible for crushing their precious hope. "The chance of seeing anyone from the air is so miniscule that—"

"You took Bill there. I need to get back to my husband!"

Clutch wheeled between us, forcing the woman to loosen her grip. "Cash can't help you. None of us can," he said.

Even though he had to look up at her, he still radiated strength. The woman's lips pursed in anger. She spun on her heel and left us, mumbling, "Assholes."

"Will you go back tomorrow?" someone else asked.

"No," Clutch and I said at the same time.

"There's no place to go back to," Tyler said from behind us.

His words smothered the room. Even the sounds of silverware on plates silenced. In a rush, Clutch and I grabbed the rest of our food and headed to a picnic table in the corner.

The man who'd asked the last question followed. "What do you mean, 'there's no place to go back to'?"

I glanced down at Clutch, and then took a deep breath. "It's not safe there."

"What do you mean? Why won't you tell us? What happened? If it's not safe, why did you leave our people behind? Those are our families back there!"

I ignored him, eating with one hand while holding my Glock on my lap with the other.

"Because there was no one left to get out!" Tyler bellowed out as he sat down.

Manny clenched his eyes shut for a moment before opening them again and speaking. "We were too late."

I pursed my lips before I finally spoke. "Some had to make it out. If they made it to cars and stayed ahead of the herds, they could've made it." I wasn't lying; I believed my words. After all, someone had to have locked the infected in the theater from the outside. Whether they got away in time...chances were no one would ever know.

"I thought they'd be safe," one of the newcomers muttered without any inflection. "I thought the herds were following us."

"God," someone else said. "So many kids...lost."

"We should've gone back for them."

"My Ginny," a man said, pulling at his hair.

"Maybe they got out in time."

"We have to try to find any survivors," the woman who'd first showed me a picture said, though the picture was now crumpled in her grip. "Manny, we need to go back."

"We have to go back and find anyone we can."

The man who'd been pulling at his hair screamed, "Stop it! Stop it!

You all know they didn't get out. They're dead! We left them there to die! They're all dead or they're zeds!"

Manny held up his hands. "Whoa. Enough. We don't know that for sure. Some might have gotten out. Even if they did, there are all the herds between us and them. We can't search for them if we're dead. We have to look out for ourselves first. Once the herds pass through, then we can go back."

"How will we survive the herds? If Marshall couldn't survive, we have no chance here!" a woman cried out.

Tyler stood up. "I have an idea, but it's a long shot."

Six

The following morning's flight was a bumpy one, and I had to keep both hands on the yoke. The weather was unseasonably warm, and the heat caused thermals to pop up in the air. Tyler was strapped in next to me in the Cessna 172. Sitting behind us, Jase scanned the countryside for anything useful while Griz slept soundly, his snores coming over the intercom every once in a while.

Clutch, as Tyler's second-in-command, was in charge of the park whenever Tyler was offsite for longer than a few hours. When Camp Fox had relocated to the park, the pair had reached an agreement to never ride in the same vehicle because the park couldn't risk losing both of our seasoned military officers. Even though their knowledge and leadership had saved our collective ass many times over, I suspected the other reason they didn't ride together was because they pissed each other off as much as they needed each other.

Clutch couldn't come along today for three reasons. First, the air was too turbulent for his back. Second, Tyler was the only person who'd spoken with the guy we were meeting today. Third and most important, Clutch was shit as a diplomat. He was great at getting people in line—and was likely running all the residents through the training wringer right now—but when it came to begging for help, Tyler's smooth personality was needed.

Tyler currently had his head propped against the glass, looking outside, his hand tapping to the beat of the music piping through our headsets. He had his iPhone plugged into the plane's audio system, and the connector charged the device while it played. Right now, music from the Nadas filled my headset.

"The zeds around here aren't showing any signs of migrating yet. I wonder if they do leave, how far south they'll go," he said without looking up, the music volume auto-muting while he spoke.

"Who cares as long as it's a long ways from us," Jase replied from the backseat.

"I don't get it," Tyler said. "The zeds are rotting away. Why would they migrate when they're probably going to be dead within a year, anyway?"

The zeds still owned the area, but their bodies had slowed down as the plague ate away at their flesh and muscle. With how decayed many were, that they hadn't died off already made no sense. Then again, that anyone could have their throat ripped out and yet return as a zed made no sense either. The virus, in its cruel effectiveness, was terrifying.

Still, on this trip, our greater risk was survivors, not zeds. Most zeds remained near towns, with only herds roaming the countryside. If only I'd flown over these roads before and mapped out any roadblocks or signs of raiders, we could've driven today. This was the first time Tyler was meeting with this radio contact. I would've preferred to drive so that we could have taken more reinforcements.

Tyler's contact, a riverboat captain named Sorenson, had a community roughly the size of Camp Fox on a riverboat casino. He'd told Tyler he was confident his people would make it through the migration unscathed, and Tyler had believed him. The question was, would Sorenson take Camp Fox under his protection as well? That he had offered to meet with Tyler gave us all hope.

Right now, everyone at Camp Fox was busy packing up their belongings and pulling together all the food, livestock, supplies, and weapons for winter under the assumptions that Tyler's diplomacy would succeed and we could temporarily relocate to Sorenson's riverboat. If Tyler failed in gaining Sorenson's help today, our only option was to run. I hoped to God Tyler wouldn't fail.

On the ground, a few zeds dotted the landscape. Nothing like the herds Clutch, Jase, and I had seen north of us. Every hour I hoped the herds would stop their migration or at least pass through without coming near Camp Fox, but I knew better. I'd seen the herds and the paths they'd trampled. They moved like locusts intent on a mission. "Maybe the zeds in Chow Town will head out with them," I said, thinking of the only possible benefit of the migration.

"We can only hope," Tyler said. "It would be great to be able to get into town and clear out the stores before bandits get to them."

Right now, around three thousand zeds lurked in the streets of Fox Hills, now called Chow Town. I'd made the unfortunate mistake of getting myself stranded in town not once but twice, and I'd barely gotten out alive each time. No one was crazy enough to venture near Chow Town. Zeds had laid claim, and no one dared challenge them for it.

Every day, a few more would trickle out of Chow Town, and our scouts would put a quick end to them. Still, at that rate, it would take years to clear out the town that had once been Fox Hills.

We couldn't wait a decade for the zeds to clear out of Chow Town. We needed food and resources *now*. After Clutch's farm and Camp Fox were destroyed, it was too late to replant, leaving everyone to harvest wild crops and the few gardens that had been planted. It scared the beejeezus out of me knowing there were even more zeds on the way, eating everything in their path.

Swallowing, I glanced over my shoulder. "Hey, Jase. Did you bring the map that's marked up with the herds?"

"Got it right here."

"Good. If we get the chance to make a fuel stop, I'll fly us north. What do you think, Tyler?"

He nodded. "It's a good idea to see if they're still on track for what we calculated. I think we'll need to start scouting to the north every day."

"I'll use the Cub. It burns less fuel, and I don't want to use this plane except when we have to because it's in desperate need of an overhaul." I paused. "And we have another problem."

"Oh?" Tyler asked.

"The fuel tank at the Fox Hills airport is nearly empty," I replied. "I can get two, maybe three, more refills for the portable tank from it. Jase has marked every airport in the area that might have av-gas, but if I have to travel farther for refills, I need a bigger portable tank. A gas truck would be perfect."

Tyler chuckled. "Easier said than done. Every gas truck we've found is needed for ground support in case Camp Fox needs to become mobile. We can't sacrifice a single truck right now."

"I guess I'll start searching for a plane that runs off auto fuel."

His eyebrows rose. "There are planes that run off regular gas?"

I nodded. "Quite a few, actually. There weren't any at the Fox Hills airport, but I'm sure there's one at a nearby airport."

"Hey, it looks like a grass strip down there," Jase said.

I scanned from side to side and found a yellow crop duster sitting in tall grass. A single building and white tank sat near it.

"That's a good one. Be sure to mark it on the map."

"Already got it," he said. "There's no town for miles. The land is wide open. Might make a good fuel stop on the way back."

"The grass is awfully tall, but yeah, it could be perfect."

We flew in silence for the next several miles. I kept an eye on my flight path while Jase and Tyler scanned the countryside.

"That looks like a camp down there," Tyler said, his finger pressed against the glass.

"It could be a bandit camp," Jase said. "I don't see any kids down there."

"I'd rather warn bandits than not warn good people," Tyler countered.

I slowed the Cessna and descended a hundred feet. Finding survivors was rare, but they were easy to spot. All we had to look for was signs of fortifications, and nearly every camp we'd found was at a farm.

"Can you get any closer?" Tyler asked, ruffling through a duffle.

I smirked. "Afraid gravity won't catch the bag?"

"No, but it'd be nice to actually drop it within their fence."

I bit the inside of my cheek to keep from gritting my teeth. I'd grown an aversion to flying over camps. Every time I did, it brought back memories of Doyle's camp and getting shot at, even though I suspected most folks were out of ammo by now. With one hand wrapped too tightly around the yoke, I dropped in some flaps, slowed the 172 to near stall speed and brought it in to circle the settlement. A half-dozen or so people came to stand outside, looking up, and shading their eyes against the sun.

The engine began to rumble roughly, and my heart lurched. I added in power. "Damn engine is getting worse. We've really got to get it fixed," I muttered.

Tyler opened the window. Cool air blew into the cockpit, and he dropped out the hazard-orange painted bag filled with dirt and a single written warning about the herds heading south. He pulled the window shut and I turned back on course.

"Thanks," Tyler said. "Any time we can warn others about the herds is potentially another life saved."

Tyler had brought three more drop-bags, but we didn't use them.

We'd flown over what had definitely been a camp, but it looked like it had been abandoned or overrun some time ago. I often saw signs of abandoned camps, but I hadn't seen a new camp pop up in over a month. Maybe people were moving west where the government was supposedly pooling all resources into building new "city-states" defensible against zeds.

The rumored city-states gave us all hope, but they were too far away to be considered a possibility yet. The largest rumored city was in Montana, with three states of zeds between us and them. Until we had better vehicles, the trip was too risky. We had to survive on our own in zed country.

Mid-sized groups did the best out here. Too small of a group, resources were spread too thin between fending off zeds and finding food. Too large of a group and it became a magnet for every zed in the vicinity. Camp Fox, just crossing sixty residents if the newcomers stayed, was going to become quite tempting to zeds.

The wide blue landmark in the distance caused me to refocus. "We're coming up on the Mississippi. Start looking for our bridge," I said to no one in particular as I strained my eyes, searching the Mississippi River for its bridges.

If the GPS had still worked, it would've brought me straight to our destination since Sorenson had provided the bridge's coordinates. Now, I had to fly by sight, and I was often a mile or more off my destination. It was my fault. Like most, I'd become way too reliant on technology before the outbreak.

"Wait, I've got it. I'll check in," I said to no one in particular as I lined up to the giant yellow X that had been painted on a bridge. I pressed the radio's transmit button. "Cessna to Camp Fox. If you can still hear us, we're descending to land at the RP. Over."

Dead static came as the only response.

"Clutch might have heard us, but there's no way I could pick up his handheld from this distance. I'm not even sure he can pick us up," I said. "We both figured that'd be the case."

On the right day, the radio signal could cover the entire state, especially with the lack of other signals to hinder it. Today didn't seem to be one of those days.

As the river grew larger, I descended and slowed. No signs of zeds and —unfortunately—no sign of the riverboat yet. I flew over the bridge with two steel arches. "Everything looks clear, but I'm not seeing our guys. You guys see any zeds?"

"No. Nothing," came the response from my crew.

I lined up for the bridge again, this time running through my landing checklist. Touching down this close to the river set my nerves on edge, even though the highway was open for a quarter-mile before the bridge, and I had plenty of runway ahead of me. Still, it was discomfiting having all that iron and open water surrounding me. It wouldn't take too much to veer off and hit a wingtip, and then we'd be stranded over two hundred miles away from Camp Fox. And, once down, I'd have to taxi onto the bridge so we didn't have to walk to our destination.

The engine sputtered a couple times on final approach, and I throttled forward just enough to keep it from cutting out completely while still making the landing.

"That engine doesn't sound good," Tyler said.

"It's been acting up more and more lately. Joel says it needs some new sparkplugs," I said as I pulled the plane to a stop in the middle of the bridge so that I could take off in either direction at a moment's notice.

"He's been busy with Humvee Three, and that's his first priority right now. But I'll ask him to take a look," Tyler said.

"Yeah, I figured that." After double-checking to make sure everything was powered off, I set my headset on the dash and unbuckled.

"Rise and shine, Grizzly Bear," Jase said, and I heard Griz grumble something unintelligible.

Tyler smirked, grabbed his bag, and climbed out of the plane. I grabbed my backpack and rifle. Before I opened my door, I glanced back at the red five-gallon jugs filled with emergency av-gas to make sure they were still bungeed together in the baggage compartment, and then headed outside. Jase and Griz followed.

Griz stretched under the sun while I locked the Cessna's doors and turned to Tyler. "We're all set. Barring any big change in weather, we should easily make it back to the park without having to refuel." I thought for a moment. "I miss getting the weather forecasts. They sure did come in handy with flight planning."

"I kind of prefer the lack of news," he said as he pulled out his sword. "It was always sensationalizing the bad things."

"I'll check out the area to the east," Griz said. "I need to stretch my legs."

"I'll go with you," Jase offered, and the two sauntered off with their weapons drawn.

I started to head in the opposite direction.

"Weather reports were inaccurate as much as they were accurate," Tyler said. "I miss pizza delivery more."

I chuckled. "I miss pizza, too."

We both quickly sobered. It was no fun dwelling on things that we could never have again. We all had a trigger that brought everything we'd lost to mind. Shaking off memories of loved ones I'd never see again, I scanned the distance in silence, looking for any zeds that might have heard the airplane and come to investigate. The bridge and rural highway had no cars for as far as my eyes could see. This area was rural enough that it didn't have the telltale scars of wreckage and bodies that populated areas had.

The sun glistened off the blade a trader had given Tyler in exchange for penicillin. It was a nice weapon but it'd be far too heavy for me. I preferred my lighter weapons: the spear I'd made from an old broom handle, a machete from our first looting run in Chow Town, and a large tanto knife Clutch had given me right after the outbreak.

I checked my M24 rifle. We'd been through plenty together, and it bore as many scars as I did. Tiny scratches marred the black metal from a grenade blast that I'd never expected to survive.

"You look sad," Tyler said. "What's wrong?"

"My poor rifle has seen its share of abuse," I answered.

"We all have," he said softly.

I pointed to a gouge on the barrel that had shown up sometime between the time I was imprisoned at Camp Fox and when I got the rifle back. "This one wouldn't have happened if you hadn't thrown me behind bars."

He raised his brows. "Seriously? You're still beating me up over that?"

"Always," I replied. "After all, no one forced you to arrest me."

"I did it to save you from the Dogs," he said, referring to the Iowa militia. "Besides, you did break the law. No matter how you look at it, killing someone is still breaking the law."

"*Hmph*. You and I both know that scumbag Dog had it coming for what he'd done to that poor girl."

He nodded. "Maybe. But that wasn't for you to decide. You took away his right to a fair trial. I'm not saying he wasn't guilty and didn't deserve what he got. I'm just saying it wasn't the right way to go about it."

I could've brought up the young girl the accused had raped and beaten, but Tyler had heard it all before, and he still refused to budge from his stance on traditional justice. After the outbreak, I'd reverted to an "eye for an eye" brand of justice because mistakes and crimes committed now nearly always caused someone's death. We didn't have the time or resources for a full court system anymore.

"At least it was one fewer Dog to attack Camp Fox," I said instead. "But that's all water under the bridge now," I said, watching a sizable tree limb float down the river.

"I agree. I'm glad things worked out and that you decided to stay with Camp Fox." Tyler shaded his eyes as he looked down the river. "No sign of the riverboat yet."

Tyler had reached this guy Sorenson on the radio a month or so ago by sheer luck. He spent twenty minutes every day scanning all the AM, marine, and aeronautical frequencies. One day, they had both been scanning and reporting across the same marine frequencies at the same time. It was through Tyler's diligence that we'd connected with the folks in Marshall as well as several tiny groups scattered across the area. Sadly, for every settlement he reached, he seemed to lose contact with another.

Of all Tyler's contacts, Sorenson was best equipped to survive the herd migration. He was a riverboat captain and, since zeds couldn't swim, anyone who could navigate the rivers had done pretty well since the outbreak.

Tyler believed Camp Fox had found an ally in Sorenson.

I was doubtful. There was a big difference between talking on the radio and asking Sorenson if he'd take another sixty mouths to feed onto his boat. That's why we'd flown all the way here today—to beg Sorenson to add Camp Fox to his crew. Temporarily, of course.

After turning around and heading back toward the plane and across the painted X on the bridge, my stomach growled. I pulled out a plastic bag filled with jerky. Without freezers, all lean meat was made into jerky. Jerky and nuts comprised our protein staples on scouting runs. I chewed on a piece and held the bag out to Tyler, who grabbed one.

"Any thoughts on a backup plan to our backup plan?" I asked. "Just in case Sorenson doesn't come through."

"Besides running?" Tyler sighed and then shook his head. "No. We really need Sorenson to come through."

"Even if he does let everyone from Camp Fox hop a ride until the herds pass through, it's still a three-hour-plus drive over here, best-case scenario. Longer with the roadblocks we've marked on the maps." With the Cessna, I could only bring a couple people with supplies at a time. I'd never be able to transport everyone before the herds reached our latitude.

If today fell through, my assignment was to fly over potential routes and mark any roadblocks and herds on the maps. Even then, driving a convoy full of people and livestock in any direction was a dangerous plan. We'd surely draw out any zeds in the area.

Griz and Jase met up with us at the plane. "All clear to the east," Griz said, snatching a piece of jerky from my bag.

Jase grabbed the entire bag and dug in.

"Same to the west," Tyler said. "If the engine noise didn't draw any in, we shouldn't have anything beyond the random grazer to worry about today. Sorenson picked a good area. I can see for miles in every direction."

An engine noise in the distance snapped all of our attention to the river. Shading my eyes, I searched for the source of the sound.

"Over there." Jase pointed to the southeast.

I followed his finger and saw a white deck boat coming out from behind an island of trees and toward us.

As the boat approached, I could make out four men. They pulled to a stop where an aluminum extension ladder had been securely chained to the bridge.

A muscled man grabbed a hold of the ladder while a man with weathered skin motioned toward us. "Come on down. We're here to take you to meet Captain Sorenson."

Tyler didn't move. "I was under the impression that Sorenson was coming here to meet me."

The man shook his head. "You're meeting Captain Sorenson on the *Lady Amore* today. We've all seen the herds. He can't risk leaving the boat anymore. Now, we're burning gas. Are you coming or not?"

Tyler shot each of us a look before turning back to the men on the boat. "Yes, we're coming, though I don't appreciate the change in plans."

Griz took the lead down the insanely long ladder, and I followed, noticing that the ladder was actually three extension ladders fastened together with chains. It would be no fun for anyone scared of heights, like me. My muscles were tight, and I gripped too hard with each rung I descended.

One of the men helped me off the ladder at the bottom, and I looked up to see Tyler sliding his sword into its sheath. I stood off to the side, ready to pull out my machete in an instant if anyone tried to injure Tyler. After all, Captain Tyler Masden wasn't just the commanding officer of Camp Fox, he was its face. Clutch was a better strategist and a stronger leader, but he lacked Tyler's finesse in working with people. If something happened to Tyler, morale—which was thread-thin already—would snap.

Tyler climbed down, with Jase right behind him. One man motioned Griz and me to sit up front. As I walked past the boat pilot, I noticed the rifle propped next to him, and I swallowed. We'd have run out of ammunition months ago if I hadn't found Doyle's stash of old military surplus.

Once we all sat down, the driver throttled the boat forward gently, and we pulled away from the bridge and headed toward the small island. With every minute, I felt farther and farther away from Camp Fox.

Over a half hour later, the boat curved around the northern edge of a small island, and a riverboat casino came into view. It was still a good ways off, a mile or so at least, and our boat pilot seemed to be in no hurry, burning precious daylight.

As we neared the *Lady Amore*, my eyes widened. The riverboat casino was massive, yet perfectly hidden from anyone—or anything—on land and from air. Our boat rocked gently as it pulled up alongside the riverboat which was filled with people watching us from the deck above. At least six of those people had rifles pointed right at us.

Seven

"The password?" a white-haired man—who looked like the fellow on the cover of frozen-fish boxes—called out from the deck above.

"Mae West had nice tits," the man who'd spoken to us at the bridge yelled out.

"That password is correct, Otto. You all may come on board." Sorenson motioned to the armed people with him. "Lower your weapons. Everything's clear."

"His own guys have to use a password?" I muttered.

"Every time we have newcomers," the man named Otto replied. "It's a safety precaution in case we're being coerced into bringing bandits on board."

"It's smart," Tyler said as he came to his feet.

A ladder extended down the side of the tall riverboat. We climbed up in the same procession as we had at the bridge. At the top of the ladder, two men lifted me up and onto the deck.

Griz was already chatting with the white-haired man I assumed to be Sorenson. A small terrier sat by his feet. The man said something that brought out Griz's deep chuckle, and then the man narrowed his eyes at me. "You must be the pilot."

I nodded.

"It'd be handy having one of you around, especially nowadays. I'm

Captain Sorenson, and welcome to the *Lady Amore*." He held out his hand, and I accepted it.

"I'm Cash."

Tyler stepped onto deck, quickly followed by Jase. Sorenson smiled. "And I take it you're Captain Masden."

Tyler gave his irresistible Homecoming King smile. "It's great to finally meet you, Captain Sorenson. Under normal circumstances, I would've delayed our meeting until the spring, but some factors arose that forced the issue."

Sorenson nodded. "I've seen the herds with my own eyes, Captain Masden, so I'm not the least bit surprised at your visit." He gestured to his men. "You've already met four of my men. Otto, Hank, Chuck, and Pedro."

Tyler dipped his head at the men who'd just come up the ladder.

"You didn't come all this way to swap nicknames and exchange pleasantries," Sorenson said. "You've got a zed problem headed your way, and you need my help. Let's go somewhere where it's more comfortable to talk." He paused. "I'm a fair man, but I won't allow aggression on the *Lady*. All weapons must be holstered or sheathed at all times, or else they will be confiscated. Aggressors will be dealt with harshly. I'm assuming you find no issues with that?"

Tyler looked at all three of us first, then back at Sorenson. "I can assure you, no weapons will be drawn as long as there's no reason for them to be."

"Fair enough. I'd never ask for more than that," Sorenson—with his dog as his heels—led us to a side door and entered. We all followed into a well-lit hallway. I glanced back to see Otto and Pedro stepping in behind us, and Otto closing the door. Inside, the hallway was straight with doors every ten feet or so. It reminded me of an old-fashioned hotel, and I realized that was exactly what the *Lady Amore* was.

The end of the hallway opened into a winding double-staircase that led down to an enormous open area. Twenty or so poker tables dotted the colorful open space. Couches, beanbag chairs, and camp chairs looked out of place in the ornate room that reminded me of a scene from *Titanic*. The new furniture was likely replacements for the missing slot machines, and the area was now filled with people chatting and eating. At the far end of the casino was the restaurant area where a large buffet was set up against a wall. Twenty or so people stood in line.

Sorenson had a good setup here, a safe little paradise that no zed could get to…though I suspected it was a different story each time they had to go to land to refuel and restock.

He led us down the stairs and through the area, nodding, chatting, and smiling at folks as he walked. Beyond the buffet line, there was another winding stairwell. After climbing a flight of stairs and taking several hallways, we entered a bland corridor with beige walls and no artwork.

"This used to be the staff quarters. My quarters are right on the end up here," Sorenson said. "We're a bit cramped around here, so this is the best place to chat openly."

"I would've taken the biggest room if I was the boss," Jase said softly behind us.

"A family of eight lives in the Presidential Suite," Sorenson replied as he stopped at a door. "They need the space far more than I do. Besides, these quarters have been my home for nigh on thirty years. They're plenty enough for my needs and suit me just fine." He opened the door, and his dog bounded inside. Sorenson walked in and held the door open for the rest of us to enter.

Inside, the area seemed to be as large as any suite, which I supposed was probably common for captain's quarters. The room we stood in was a medium-sized living room area with a large wood conference table in the middle. A couch and TV sat in the far corner opposite a small kitchenette. Next to the refrigerator was an open door to a bedroom.

Sorenson gestured to the table. "Have a seat," he said before he opened the refrigerator and pulled out a bowl.

I took a seat next to Tyler, and Otto sat on my other side.

Sorenson set down the bowl. "Pickled bass. Help yourselves."

His dog yipped, and Sorenson picked out a large piece of fish and tossed it in the air. The dog jumped, caught the chunk, and swallowed it in a single bite.

Tyler reached in and grabbed a small piece of fish. "Bass? Haven't heard of that being pickled before."

"You can pickle just about anything that can be eaten. It keeps food from going bad and doesn't ruin the taste," Sorenson replied. "But we steer clear of the bottom feeders. In fact, I lost one of my people from bad catfish. Too many fish have ingested zed-infected bits to be safely eaten anymore. It makes fishing more challenging."

"I can imagine," Tyler said, after taking a bite. "We no longer hunt wolves since they've started going after zeds. We can't trust that they don't carry the virus."

"Speaking of zeds," Sorenson said. "Looks like a heap of trouble about to pass through."

Tyler gave a tight nod. "We have a theory that they're migrating south for the winter."

Sorenson cocked a brow. "Interesting idea, and what I've seen would support that. But I wouldn't put much weight on that theory. I've yet to see the herds do anything logical."

Tyler shrugged. "I doubt it's a planned event. I think it's nature. As they get cold, they just start heading to where it's not so cold."

Sorenson chuckled. "You're assuming they can feel *anything*. I've speared a zed right through a kidney and it didn't even wince."

"Call it a sense of preservation, then. Who knows what's driving them, but we've mapped their paths, and all signs point to the herds moving south and picking up numbers along the way."

"Which is exactly why the *Lady* is going to head further north to find safe ports and food," Sorenson said. "Once they pass through, the pickings should be easy."

What's left of them, anyway, I thought to myself.

"What's your plan when you come face to face with one of the herds?"

"Same plan as we have when we come across a herd of twenty. We're safe as long as we are careful under bridges and keep plenty of water between them and us."

"What will you do if one of these herds comes across the *Lady Amore*? What then? You think they'll ignore you just because they can't get to you?"

"No, they're persistent bastards. We'll head down river. If they're migrating, then they'll get the urge to keep moving. There are enough islands and turns in the river for us to break visual contact. You know zeds. 'Out of sight, out of mind' and all that."

Tyler looked dubious. "You're assuming the urge to migrate is stronger than their urge to eat. I'm guessing these zeds are hungrier than ever since they're moving."

Sorenson leaned back and cracked his knuckles. "I'd worry more about what you're going to do. You don't have a boat. What's to stop the zeds from walking right through the park? There ain't nobody out there with enough firepower to cut down one of those herds." A sly smile crossed his lips. "Then again, that's why you're here."

After a moment, Tyler nodded. "We need your help. If we can come aboard this riverboat, just until the herds pass through—"

Sorenson lifted a hand. "I'll stop you right now. The *Lady Amore* is at full capacity already. She can't handle any more people. We can barely purify water fast enough the way it is. As for food...well, that's all dependent on our next restock."

My heart plummeted. I wanted to jump in to talk about how they wouldn't have to feed us, but I didn't dare speak. Tyler was our leader, and we had to show we were one hundred percent behind him. We needed Sorenson to believe that Camp Fox would make good passengers on the *Lady Amore*, but after seeing the riverboat, I'd already suspected Sorenson wouldn't risk the good thing they had going by doubling his crew with strangers. We were desperate, and it pissed me off, but I couldn't blame him. I had the exact same mindset when survivors passed through the park. Still, knowing that we'd be on our own devastated me.

I looked across the table at Jase and Griz. Both looked the same way I felt. Filled with utter despair.

"It would only be for a week or two. Once the herds pass through, we'd head back to the park," Tyler said. "We'd bring enough food to cover all Fox personnel while on board. With more hands for boiling water—"

"You don't understand. It's not the manpower, it's the facilities," Sorenson interrupted. "We're boiling water twenty-four hours a day as it stands. We'd have to turn on another bank of stoves, which would burn more fuel, and that's our biggest concern. Fuel is our most precious commodity. It's not easy finding safe ports to refuel. Hell, siphoning from crippled boats is nearly as dangerous."

Tyler held up a hand. "I understand. I'm asking you for a favor I might never be able to repay. Believe me, if we had any other option I wouldn't be here. But the only way we'll all survive in this new world is by working together. If I put my people on the road, any direction we head except south, we'll run into more herds. If we run south, we'll just be staying one step ahead of the herds. Eventually, something would happen, and the herds would get us. We need your help, Captain."

"Please," I said softly, pulling my girl-card. But I wasn't acting. I desperately hoped he would help us, and I wasn't above begging.

He came to his feet. "I never said I wouldn't help you. Unfortunately, the *Lady* is full. I'm sorry, but I simply can't take on any more souls. Not without risking the lives of the ones on board now."

Tyler came to his feet as well. "Your riverboat is doing okay now, but just wait. What about the trade agreement we'd discussed? Your fish for my livestock. If Camp Fox has to go on the road, we won't be able to tend crops or share our livestock. Hell is coming our way, Sorenson. Don't be so naïve to think that it's going to bypass your boat."

Sorenson headed to the kitchen. He opened a cabinet and pulled out a bottle of whiskey.

The room sat in silence before Tyler finally sighed. "I get it. I know the strain taking on my people would add to an already full boat. I wouldn't ask if I knew of another way."

After taking a drink, Sorenson screwed the cap back on, turned around, and leaned against the counter. A moment later, he looked up at Tyler, then at his two men in the room. "As I told you before, I'll help you, but I can't take any more onto the *Lady*."

Tyler frowned. "Then what can you do?"

Sorenson paced the room. "Awhile back, I came across a decent-sized towboat that's run aground not too far from here. It'll work better than any building would for keeping zeds out. I'd been planning to use her for overflow survivors we find. I can mark it down on a map for you."

Hope sprang from deep within. There was a chance!

Tyler shook his head. "None of my people have any experience running a towboat, especially one big enough to support sixty-plus souls, our livestock, and food."

"There's no need for that. That towboat isn't going anywhere. It's dead in the water. It ran aground on a small island that goes underwater every spring. A few of her barges have broken off, but there's enough still connected that should hold you through until the island floods come spring. Even then, she should still hold together for a year or two."

I watched as Tyler thought for a long moment.

He finally nodded slowly. "It could work. We should only need it for a couple weeks. Until spring, that is, when the zeds might return."

Sorenson pulled out a stack of papers in the top drawer and headed back to the table. He dropped a paper on the table. A map.

Sorenson opened the map and pointed at an X marked on the water. "Here's the island you're looking for. It isn't far from the mainland, so you'll have a higher risk of zeds floating ashore, especially with how tiny the island is. But it's the best I can offer. We've already had to start turning away survivors. If we bring on any more, we risk the lives of the ones already on board. I can't allow that. These people are my responsibility."

Tyler sat down and examined the map before sliding it to me.

I looked at the small island toward the east side of the river, and not far south of a four-lane bridge. I much preferred the idea of being on the riverboat casino. From what I'd seen of the *Lady Amore*, they had plenty of space to take on more survivors. Hell, the boat was so large it was like a mountain on the water. The idea of being stranded on an island made me feel like a sitting duck. If any herd spotted us, there'd be no running. "So, zeds can still get to the island?" I asked after sliding the map across the table to Jase and Griz.

"Unfortunately, yes," Sorenson said. "They can't swim, but any that fall in the water could wash ashore easily enough. The towboat also likely had a crew of ten or twenty on her when the outbreak hit. That she ran aground isn't a good sign. She might have been evacuated because I didn't see any zeds on her deck. Even if she's not empty, with enough fire-power, it shouldn't take you long to clear her out.

Tyler sighed deeply and leaned back, closing his eyes. I placed my hand over his and he gripped it.

"It could work," I said quietly, as much to support Tyler as to convince myself.

"Oh, it can work all right. Trust me," Sorenson said. "Once you get the towboat cleared out, you'll only have to deal with zeds that get to the island from the water. I'm sure the barges are all clear. I don't see any reason why you couldn't start moving your people and supplies over right away. From what I've seen of the herds, you have about two weeks before they make it this far down the river. You've got a lot of work to do between now and then."

"Except there's a herd already coming straight through the center of the state," Tyler said. "We have to be over here within a couple days or else we risk getting cut off." He paused. "It can work. We'll make it work."

"You'll need to get moving then," Sorenson said.

Tyler nodded and motioned to us. "Agreed. Thank you for your help, Captain. I don't have any marine experience, but I'll take you at your word that this towboat and barges will make for a defensible position and that I'm not condemning sixty souls."

"Aye, she'll be safe as long as you're discreet and don't do anything to draw attention," Sorenson said. "I've kept an eye on her for just this sort of need. I'll make sure there's a pontoon or two for you to get to her by tomorrow. Be sure to bring enough folks to clear out the boat and possibly do some patching. The towboat is named the *Aurora II*. She's built for a small crew, so she won't hold sixty people. Maybe thirty if you push it. You'll have to use the barges to house the rest of your people and supplies."

"Fair enough." Tyler looked at his watch. "Sunlight is half gone. We'd better head back. We've got a lot of work to do."

"You're more than welcome to stay the night on board the *Lady Amore*," Sorenson said.

Tyler smiled and held out his hand. "Thank you, but we have to get started on preparations. We've got a lot of work to do."

Sorenson shook Tyler's hand before he headed over to the door and opened it. "Otto will see you back to the bridge. I'll see if a couple of my people will volunteer to help you patch up the barge once you clear it."

Suddenly feeling a hundred pounds lighter, I came to my feet and followed Tyler into the hallway. For the first time since seeing the massive herds, I felt like we stood a fighting chance to make it through the fall.

After Pedro, Otto, Griz, and Jase joined us, Sorenson shut the door, staying in his room. I wondered how much time he spent in his quarters to avoid having to deal with all the problems of having people living in a floating hotel.

Our trip back to the plane was uneventful. The sun had warmed the air, and I enjoyed the afternoon breeze blowing through my cropped hair as the boat cut through the water. When we reached the bridge, we said our good-byes and cautiously climbed the ladder, and Otto and Pedro pulled away.

Fortunately, no zeds had come across the plane or blocked our takeoff path. In fact, the countryside was still wide open. We piled into the Cessna, and I started the engine. It coughed and sputtered and growled. On the third attempt, it kept running but was rough. "Keep your eyes peeled for zeds. This could take a while," I yelled over the engine as I throttled up and checked the mags. The right mag had been running rough but now both sounded like metallic beasts about to explode. I leaned the mixture, trying to clean the spark plugs, to no avail. For several more minutes I tried to smooth the engine, all the while cursing and begging the plane.

After I knew it was hopeless, I pulled the mixture all the way out and the engine quit. I leaned forward, resting my head against the panel for a moment, knowing I was about to let everyone down. I hated times like this. My first urge was to cry, but I refused to be the weak one, the one the guys felt sorry for.

"What's the problem?" Tyler asked quietly at my side.

I leaned back and opened my eyes. "You heard the engine. This plane's not going anywhere. With both mags running rough, it's not going to be running for much longer. If the engine goes out while we're in the air, we have to land, and it doesn't matter if there's a town of zeds below us or not."

"Will it help if you let it sit for a while?" Jase asked.

"I don't think so." I scratched my head. "Fuck, I don't know. I'm a pilot, not a mechanic. I have no idea how to fix it. I just know it's not safe to fly it like this."

"Then we won't risk it," Tyler said. "We'll find another way back home."

We climbed out of the plane and stood on the bridge.

"Can I see the map?" I asked Jase.

He dug into his cargo pocket and pulled out the folded sectional.

"Thanks." I knelt and spread it out on the pavement.

Tyler came down on a knee next to me while I could feel Jase and Griz at my back.

I pointed to a spot on the map. "The closest small airport is here. It's not far, but it's on the edge of town. If we can't get to the airport, we should at least be able to find a car. Jase has been marking the routes on the map."

"Too bad Otto didn't stick around," Griz said, looking out over the river. "A lift could've saved us hours."

"That would make things easier," Tyler said. "But I'm not seeing any boats around here that we can use, so it looks like we'll be hoofing it. There should be a few farms between us and the next town. One of those farms is bound to have a vehicle we can use." He came to his feet. "Take five, and then we head out."

I was already dreading how much my leg would ache tonight. I headed back to the plane. I tried to reach Clutch on the radio but had no luck. Giving up, I rummaged through the baggage compartment. I pulled out a plastic bag and handed it to Griz to add to his rucksack. "There are a few protein bars, a couple bottles of water, and a first aid kit in there."

"It's time," Tyler said. "Let's get a move on. We've got less than four hours of sunlight left to get back to Camp Fox."

EIGHT

After an hour of jogging, we switched to walking once we realized there was no way in hell we'd make it back to the park before dark. My calf had ached for the first forty minutes until pleasant numbness finally settled in.

The rural road was rough but wide open, with trees to our right, where the river was, and fields to our left. A group of four zeds emerged from the trees and blocked our path. Luckily, only one of them was fresh enough to be halfway fast. Tyler took it down with a heavy swing of his sword. I pulled out my machete, and the rest of us each took down one without firing a shot. The zed I killed had been a man, wearing stained khakis and a golf shirt. My first swing knocked it to the ground. My second swing put it out of its misery.

Sounds came from the trees, but thankfully, no more zeds emerged. Still, we made haste to continue on. The first farmhouse we came to we didn't dare approach. Jase had counted at least three zeds inside, and we had no intention on riling them up. The truck in the driveway sat with the driver's side door open and no keys in the ignition. When Jase tried to hotwire it, nothing happened. The battery was dead.

We fared no better at the second farmhouse. A zed was enclosed in the SUV in the open garage. When it saw us, it pounded on the glass. Jase checked it out, but the SUV had been left running and had long since run out of gas. So, we moved on.

It took us another thirty minutes before we found a vehicle we could use. The white sedan we found sat in the attached garage of a newer looking farmhouse that showed no signs of zeds lurking within its walls. The four of us stood in front of the split-foyer house. Griz and Jase had already run around it, looking through each window. Luckily, the garage door was one of those with windows in it, making it easy to see the car as well as telltale signs of notoriously clumsy zeds.

"It looks clean inside," Jase said.

"Should we try the house or the garage first?" I asked.

Tyler stood quietly for a moment, his sword in one hand. "I'd say we waltz right up and try the front door." And he did exactly that. He cut through the lawn and onto the pebbled path leading to the doorsteps. Large bay windows were to the left, making it easy to see if any zeds came from that direction. To the right of the door was a wall, so we were going in half-blind.

Griz, Jase, and I followed. Tyler stood at the front door and knocked. A short pause later, he grabbed the door handle and turned but didn't open the door. He glanced back at us. "It's unlocked."

As I gripped my machete, I noticed both Griz and Jase tense as well. They stood a couple steps behind Tyler and me, in case we needed to jump out of the way. I stood off to the side, careful to avoid making myself a target through the windows. I peeked through the edge of the bay window. *All clear,* I signaled with my hand.

Tyler nodded. He threw the door open and then jumped back.

No zeds came at us. After taking a deep breath, I met Tyler at the door, and we stepped into a large living room. Griz and Jase came in behind us. I sniffed the stale air and picked up the telltale putrid sweetness of decay.

"It's not clear," I said softly.

Tyler motioned for him and me to take the left half of the ground floor, and for Griz and Jase to take the right. A couple minutes later, we met back up in the kitchen.

"All clear," Griz said.

"Same here," I said. "Other than the smell, there aren't any signs of zeds up here."

Tyler frowned as he looked at the basement door. "That means the smell is coming from down there."

We pulled out our headlamps and put them on. One by one, we headed down the stairs. As soon as I was off the last step, I saw the source of the odor curled up against a door. It was the corpse of a woman dressed in jeans and a sweater, and she still held a picture against her chest. A glass and empty bottle of pills lay next to her. With the rate of decay and her clothing, she'd likely killed herself not long after the outbreak.

Griz emerged from the single bedroom and covered the corpse with a sheet. "May God grant you peace," he said.

A thump against the door behind the body answered.

I jumped.

Tyler and Griz moved first. Griz grabbed the corpse's jeans and pulled the body to the side. Tyler stood at the door and knocked. The thumping became fevered. He gripped his sword in one hand and held the door-knob in the other. "Ready?" he asked Griz, who nodded in return, his machete held out in front of him.

Jase and I stood to each side, each holding our machetes ready. Tyler turned the knob and kicked the door open, sending the zed tumbling back. Stench wafted from the room. A zed, who'd been a teenaged boy, tried to pull itself up by grabbing on a black comforter. It looked to be about Jase's age. Its hair was even the same color, and a lump formed in my throat.

Griz rushed forward and slammed his machete through the zed's skull and it collapsed face-first on the floor, and I refused to look at it again. Tyler entered the room and looked in the closet and under the bed. "Clear," he called out.

Griz and Tyler hustled from the room, and I slammed the door shut behind them, as much to block the smell as to close us off from the zed that reminded me a bit too much of Jase. I breathed through my mouth, but the stench of putrid death always seemed to burn through my pores.

"All right. The house is clear. We'll camp here for the night," Tyler said. "Let's secure the perimeter. Griz and Jase, you guys check the doors and close all the curtains. Cash and I will check the garage. Once everything is secure, we can scout the house for supplies."

No one lingered in the foul-smelling basement. My leg was beginning to ache, but I forced myself not to limp as we walked through the small kitchen and toward the garage. On the wall near the door, a key rack hung on the wall, and I smiled. I shuffled through the sets of keys and pulled off a key chain that had a Chevy logo on it. I held it up and gave it a happy little shake.

Tyler returned my grin. "Let's hope the battery's not dead."

Undeterred, I followed him. Dead batteries had become a common occurrence, and I'd grown adept at jumping cars, but I'd always had a running car with me. We didn't have that tonight, and I suspected there weren't any new car batteries lying around.

Tyler opened the door slowly and carefully, just in case we'd missed a zed while checking the house earlier. Fortunately, silence and fresh air greeted us. A white four-door car sat in the shadowed garage.

I opened the car door and slid the key into the ignition and turned. The engine started without a hitch, and the gas gauge climbed halfway. I let out a whoop. "Looks like we've got ourselves a ride."

I turned off the car and stepped out. Tyler gave me a high-five. "It's about time we got a break."

He checked the garage door to see that it would open easily, and we headed back in the house. In the kitchen, Griz had several cabinets open and small stacks of canned food sitting on the counter.

Jase emerged from the bathroom with a bottle of rubbing alcohol. "I'll have a camp stove built and going in no time."

"The car runs," Tyler said. "We'll head out at dawn. If the airport isn't viable, we'll drive back to the park."

"Fingers crossed the airport is clear and has something I can fly. It will save us time."

Tyler wrapped an arm around my shoulder and gave me a hug, and I found myself leaning into his warm comfort. "It will," he assured. A moment later, he squeezed before letting go, and then led the way down the hall.

As Jase worked on making dinner, we searched every room for anything that could be of use. Over the next thirty minutes, we loaded the trunk with all the food, pills, and supplies we could find.

After we dragged two mattresses from the upstairs bedrooms into the living room, I plopped into a chair at the table and sighed as I rubbed my calf.

Tyler took the chair next to me, grabbed my leg, and massaged it. "How bad is it hurting?"

I shook my head. "Not bad. It just feels good to sit."

Even though Tyler touched me often, I knew he had no romantic feelings for me. Physical human connections helped ground him, and his touches didn't bother me once I realized that he was just seeking comfort and wasn't flirting. I was surprised that he hadn't taken any women to bed yet. It wasn't for lack of admirers. Tyler had plenty of those.

Tyler rarely touched me when Clutch was around, which was wise. Clutch wasn't in any way the jealous type, but it didn't take much for the two to get on each other's nerves. With their tense relationship, even something as simple as a harmless touch could set them off.

We watched the sun disappear beyond the horizon. With the smell of food cooking overpowering the ever-present scent of decay, the tension in my muscles slowly bled away.

"We'll rotate two-hour single shifts tonight," Tyler announced. "That will give everyone at least six hours of sleep."

"Dibs on first watch," I said.

Griz grumbled. "Just because you're a woman, I'll let you have it. I've got second shift, then." He put down a plate in front of me.

I leaned forward. "Spaghetti?"

"Yeah," he said, taking a seat across from me. "The pantry had a pretty good selection. Jase cooked the noodles in sauce and water, so it might be a bit gummy."

Jase guffawed. "You're lucky to have a hot meal." he handed Tyler a plate and then sat down with his own. "I'll take third watch, I guess."

Griz clasped his hands. "Lord, thanks for this food that we're about to eat. And thanks for another day where we get to eat food and not get eaten."

"Amen," we all murmured.

Silverware clinked against plates as we all dug in. Sitting around a table, eating spaghetti, felt like home. It almost felt like the apocalypse hadn't taken place around us.

Almost.

NINE

I could barely keep my eyes open after my watch, but unfamiliar surroundings and dreams of massive herds made sleep fitful, and I woke up every hour or so. I finally passed out sometime during Jase's shift.

"Cash."

I lunged awake, grappling for my machete.

"Whoa there," Tyler said and pressed me back. "There's no emergency. I just thought I'd wake you."

It took a moment for the night's fog to clear from my mind. I rubbed my eyes. "Time to head out?"

"Soon." His features softened. "You were having a nightmare."

"Yeah," I said breathlessly, my heart racing, remembering flying a shiny airplane with gold stripes. I sat up and wrapped my arms around my knees.

He kept a hand on my shoulder. "Want to talk about it?"

I thought back to the dream. Clutch, Jase, and I were flying somewhere. The engine stalled over endless fields filled with zeds. Tyler had woken me just before we crashed. "Just the usual stuff," I said after a bit.

He rubbed my shoulder and gave me a gentle look. "It was just a dream. We're all haunted by them. Don't let it get to you." He cupped my cheek before coming to his feet. He strolled over to Griz who was sprawled out on the mattress we'd dragged into the living room and nudged him with his foot.

Griz grumbled, and Tyler nudged him again.

I made out the words "go away" this time.

"Wake up," Tyler said. "There's some oatmeal on the table. We're heading out in ten."

I rolled off the king-sized mattress we'd taken turns sleeping on, stood, and stretched with a groan. With its cracks and pops, my body sounded—and felt—like it belonged to a fifty-year-old rather than one who wasn't even thirty yet. "I could've used another hour of sleep."

"I could've used another five hours," Griz said as he geared up.

I pulled all my things together, and we ate standing up at the table. A few minutes later, Jase lifted the garage door, and the four of us climbed into the car. Tyler backed the Chevy out of the garage and into the quiet darkness of early morning. We drove down the long winding road parallel to the river until the sun was halfway above the horizon.

Tyler turned at an intersection that had a green airport sign pointing to the left. "If you see anything that seems off, we'll abort and drive the two hundred miles. We'll find a fuel stop on the way."

"Let's not," Griz said, with his eyes still closed. "We need to get back to the park today if we're going to make a mass exodus to a shipwrecked boat before the herds arrive. We're on borrowed time already."

"We can't help our people if we're dead," Tyler replied a bit too quickly. He inhaled before continuing. "But, yes, I also agree with you. We don't have time for delays."

"There's the airport." Jase pointed. "Looks okay from here. No cars around. That's a good sign."

Tyler slowed as we approached the small municipal airport. Up ahead, the road became a roundabout, with turns in three directions. To the right were two large corporate hangars. To the left stood a row of T-hangars, each one large enough for a single airplane. Straight ahead was a single building surrounded by a wide tarmac that was unfortunately empty of aircraft. The pickings would not be so easy here.

Tyler stopped at the roundabout. "Which way do we go, Cash?"

I sighed. "Straight ahead. We need to hit the terminal building first. Lucky for us, it's a small enough airport that there probably weren't many people around when the outbreak hit, so there wouldn't be much reason for zeds to stick around here."

"Except for the ones still stuck in buildings," Jase tacked on.

I nodded. "I wouldn't be surprised if we find at least one in the FBO building."

"FBO?" Jase asked.

"Fixed Base Operator. Whoever ran the airport."

"Can we skip the FBO and go straight for the hangars?" Tyler asked.

"The keys to get into the hangars will be in there." I pointed at the building standing ominously alone just beyond the open airport gate. "We have to check it out."

"You sure?" Griz asked.

I shrugged. "I've never seen hangars left unlocked before."

"All right. We'll take it slow." Tyler stepped on the gas ever so slightly. The car crept through the open gate and he parked about forty feet from the FBO. It was an escape trick we all knew well. Zeds kept getting slower as they rotted away. If we had to leave in a hurry, putting a little distance between us and them made it easier.

I climbed out and breathed in the fresh morning air. No one moved far from the car. We took our time to scan for zeds. Jase was the first to head toward the building after taking several steps in a wide three-sixty. I followed him across the tarmac, crossing the white T-line marked for airplane parking and stepping over cracks in the old pavement. He stopped at the red door and looked through the glass pane.

"How's it look?" I whispered as Griz and Tyler joined us.

"Not sure yet. Give me a minute," Jase replied, taking a step back. "I'm going to check the other windows."

With that, he took off at a run around the building. Jase was Camp Fox's fastest runner. He was his high school football team's first-string tight end and a state track hurdler for a reason. Nothing could catch him.

I looked through the window and saw some papers scattered on the floor by the front desk. No blood or stains marred the walls or floor.

I heard a rustle and turned to find Jase returning from the opposite direction he'd left. He slowed down and then stopped. "I couldn't see any zeds through the other windows."

"We're burning daylight," Tyler said.

I grabbed the door handle. "You guys ready?"

"You open, I'll go in first," Tyler said from right behind me.

I twisted the handle and pulled. Fortunately, the door was unlocked, and Tyler went in, holding his sword before him. Griz went in next, followed by Jase. I stepped inside and closed the door with only the quietest *click* to signal someone had entered.

The air didn't stink of death, which was a good sign. Still, we moved through the building to make sure no zeds or bandits were lurking in shadows.

"This wouldn't be a bad place for a small group to hole up," I said after we cleared the building. "I mean, there's the fence on the side facing the road, which would deter looters, and on the other side gives a full view of the airport to see zeds coming from a mile away."

Glass shattered, and I jumped around to see Griz rummaging through a vending machine broken wide open.

"Not a bad place as long as you always had scouts on guard," Tyler said before joining Griz at the machine.

I walked around the front desk where papers had been scattered. Behind the desk, a small window was opened a few inches. "The wind must've blown the papers." On top of the desk was a clipboard with flight schedules. N-numbers and airplane makes and models were listed on each row, and I smiled. These were planes I could fly. Hanging below the counter of the desk hung several sets of keys. I set down my machete and leaned on the desk to rifle through the keys.

One keychain held a couple dozen nickel keys. It had a plastic fob with "hangars" written in black marker. The other key chains each held only a couple bronze keys, with Cessna or Beechcraft logos on the fobs. "We got lucky," I said. "All the keys are here. We have our pick."

I started plucking key chains off their hooks until a movement caught the corner of my eye. I looked down at the desk in time to see a rat—not a mouse but a huge fucking rat—run across my hand. "Ack!" I tumbled back, launching myself into the file cabinet. My head connected with the corner. Sharp pain blinded me, and I took a nosedive to the ground. Once the starred blackness in my vision began to recede, I let out the longest string of profanity I'd ever accomplished in my life.

Someone grabbed my arm. "You okay, Cash?"

I blinked until the two kneeling Jases became one. Warm liquid tickled my cheek. I touched it and then saw the blood on my finger. "Yeah. Damn rat. Surprised me, that's all."

Tyler stood behind Jase, frowning. "That's one hell of a cut." He turned away. "Griz, see if you can't find us a kit."

Tyler grabbed a box of tissue sitting on the desk and yanked out several. He handed them to Jase, who dabbed at my forehead and winced. "Dang, Cash. It was just a rat."

A moment later, Griz brought over a first aid kit from somewhere. Jase made room for him, and Griz came down on a knee. He grabbed the tissue from Jase and dabbed at my forehead and cheek. As the seconds passed, the numbness became a throbbing ache. Griz tore open a towlette and just before touching me, he paused. "This is going to sting."

"Just do it," I muttered, and he wiped my cut. I hissed and clenched my eyes shut. Burning needles shot through my skin everywhere he touched. Jase grabbed my hand, and I held on tightly. "Jesus. It feels like half my face is on fire."

"I can imagine," Griz said and he continued his torture.

I opened my eyes after a couple seconds of no new pain and found Griz sifting through small items in the first aid kit. He pulled out a suture kit and my eyes widened and my jaw dropped.

"I don't need stitches."

Griz chortled.

"Yeah, you do," Jase said at my side.

"Trust us," Tyler added. "Griz will do a good job. He's done this plenty of times."

I swallowed and positioned myself against the cabinet. "All right, but if that rat shows up again, you sure as hell better squash it."

The antiseptic wipe was nothing compared to getting stitches. The next ten minutes were raw agony. I begged for whiskey and morphine, but all Tyler gave me was a couple aspirin and a warm Coke. My hands were sweaty but I never let go of Jase.

Griz leaned back with a look of admiration. "That might be my finest work yet."

I chugged down more of the Coke before Jase helped me climb to my feet.

"Be careful to keep the wound clean. That cut could get infected easily enough," Tyler said, coming back over. He distributed the remaining candy bars from the vending machine, which we all dug into like kids opening Christmas presents. "Take as long as you need. If you're not up to flying, we'll drive."

I shook my head, and I instantly regretted the movement. My face throbbed, but I said in between chews, "It's just a cut. I'll be fine. We've already wasted enough time on me."

"All right. Let's head out, then," Tyler said.

I grabbed my machete off the desk and noticed a small mirror propped next to the PC. I looked at my reflection and nearly dropped the mirror. No wonder getting stitched up hurt like a bitch. A jagged enflamed line cut across my forehead and down my cheek, which looked almost like the number seven. I touched the skin around it. "Wow, that's *really* going to leave a mark."

No one said anything. I don't know if they were afraid I was going to cry or what, but the urge didn't even cross my mind. Times had changed. Before the outbreak, even though I'd always been a tomboy, I would have dreaded a big scar across my face. Now, the creek by our cabin was the closest thing to a mirror I had. Chances were this cut would leave a hell of a scar once it healed. Yet I'd probably not even notice it as long as it didn't hurt.

I swiped all the keys, all the while keeping a careful watch for the mutant-sized rat. We headed out of the building and back to the car. "Let's go for that row of hangars closest to the FBO first," I said, pointing. "The doors will be easier to open, and that's where the smaller planes will be."

"You need to learn how to fly a bigger plane," Griz said as Tyler drove us toward the row of hangars. "I hate small planes."

"How would you know?" Jase asked. "You sleep through every trip."

"Sleep is underrated," Griz said. "And I still think Cash needs to find a bigger plane."

"No, I don't," I said. "Bigger planes are more complicated to maintain. They require a longer runway. Besides, since I have no experience in them, the risks of me making a mistake go up exponentially. None of those constraints fits our current lifestyle," I said.

Griz cocked his head. "Good point. Small planes are good."

Tyler parked the car, and we went about checking the hangars, first for zeds, then for a plane that met our needs. When I unlocked the fourth hangar, I smiled. "This is the one."

While Jase walked around the hangar, I checked the plane over. Griz and Tyler pushed the large metal door open. Metal creaked against metal, making a horrendous screech. "Make it quick," Tyler said after dusting his hands off on his pants. "It looks like we've attracted the attention of a couple zeds in the field off the runway."

Unveiled by sunlight, a nearly new Cessna 172 sat in the hangar, the N-number on its tail matching a number on one of the key chains I carried. I stepped on the spar and looked at the sticker by one of the fuel tanks. "Hey, this one takes auto fuel! Let's get this outside." I grabbed the prop. Tyler and Jase each grabbed a strut. We pulled the plane straight outside. I unlocked the baggage compartment and Griz dumped an armful of food and supplies from the trunk of the car.

"I'm going to get this ready while you guys finish loading up whatever fits."

All three went to work at unloading the car into the plane. It didn't take long. The baggage compartment in the 172 was small, and with four of us, we were grossly overloaded. I started the engine, and it ran smoothly. "Thank God," I murmured as I ran through the checklist.

The guys climbed inside, and Tyler took the front seat next to me. "Better hurry because we're going to have a party in another couple minutes."

I taxied out without checking all the instruments. "Oh shit." My heart beat faster, and my eyes widened. "Zeds are on the runway already."

A few shapes peppered the middle of the runaway, but many more were headed straight for the pavement from the trees.

"There are too many for us," Tyler said, his brows furrowed. "Can you take off or do we need to drive?"

I looked at the airport for a long second, knowing this was one of those life-or-death decisions. "I'll take off on the taxiway." I did a quick pre-takeoff check and then throttled full forward on the taxiway. It was narrow, less than half the width of the runway, but I'd gotten used to landing on highways. At the halfway mark, the 172 was still grounded. At the two-thirds mark, I could almost get her wheels up.

"Uh, Cash?" Tyler asked, gripping the dash.

My heart raced, and my head pounded. Visions of last night's dream flashed through my mind. Maybe the plane was too overloaded. *Come on, come on.* After the three-quarter mark, I was able to force the wheels off the ground in time to miss the lights at the end of the taxiway as the plane struggled to climb. If there'd been trees, we would've flown straight into them. Slowly, the plane climbed out above the field and into the sky.

"Well, that was exciting," Jase called out from the backseat since we had no headsets.

Once we reached a safe altitude, I let my muscles relax and I leaned back in the seat. I handed Tyler the map. I didn't look back at the airport. I already knew a couple dozen zeds hungrily waited down there if we'd had a botched takeoff.

"Looks like you'll want a heading of one-nine-five, give or take," Tyler said, holding the map open.

I nodded and set us on course. I glanced back to find Jase looking out the window, jotting notes down for any roadblocks or zeds. Griz was already sound asleep, his head leaning against the window and his mouth open.

During the flight, Tyler, Jase, and I talked about how in the world we'd safely relocate Camp Fox across two hundred miles of zed-infested country. We'd need a crew to prep the shipwreck before the rest of Camp Fox arrived. All this before the herds passed through within a couple days.

For the plan to work, everything had to go absolutely perfectly. Nothing could go wrong.

I didn't think we'd have a chance in hell to make it work until after I landed and taxied over to where I used to park the old 172. Standing there, with no wheelchair in sight, was Clutch.

Hope blossomed. We just might have a chance after all.

Part Two
Pride

The First Deadly Sin

Ten

Thirty-one hours later

Wes and I pulled to a stop behind the first Humvee at the bridge crossing over the Mississippi and into Illinois. Even with having all the roadblocks mapped and only two small herds to detour around, it had taken over eight hours to make the journey. I would've preferred to have flown over, but our scouting party and supplies would have required a plane three times the size of the 172. So, we'd loaded up two Humvees and drove the route mapped for convoy to make sure it would work.

Tyler, Griz, Jase, and Nate climbed out of the Humvee in front of us while Tack stayed on the back of their Humvee to man the .30 cal machine gun. He scanned the area while Tyler and Griz talked between themselves by the river.

When Wes reached for the door, I stopped him. "We're not supposed to leave the truck unless Tyler gives us the all-clear."

Tyler's Humvee was the lead vehicle, while ours was jam-packed with tools, food, and weapons. It was our job to secure the boat, and we wanted to make sure we had all the gear we needed to get the job done.

Tyler had to lead this mission since he needed to be here to meet with Sorenson's people. Clutch had wanted to lead this mission, but his legs weren't strong enough to handle the stairs on the boat. He could stand now—thanks to the swelling finally going down enough and with the help of crutches. I loved seeing signs of the old Clutch return in his face. The glint had come back to his eyes, and his expressions were more alert now. It was like he'd been half-asleep and was coming back to wakefulness. Walking was still beyond his reach, but it wouldn't be much longer with how hard he was working at it. He had a renewed energy in everything now.

I think even Tyler wished we had Clutch's experience on this trip. Clutch had been in plenty of situations in the Army before the outbreak, while Tyler, Griz, Nate, and Tack were much younger. Aside from Griz, who had also been in the Army, none of the other soldiers at Camp Fox had seen action before the outbreak.

Even from a wheelchair, Clutch was Camp Fox's strongest leader. Tyler was trusted and loved, but Clutch was obeyed. No one argued with him, which made it all the more important he stayed behind to lead the convoy. If anyone could relocate sixty people and all our livestock across a zed-infested state smoothly, it was Clutch.

He wasn't thrilled that Tyler had asked Jase and me to come on the mission. Tyler had said he needed Jase's limber speed for scouting the barges, and my small size for squeezing through tight spaces, but I knew it was really Tyler's way of showing Clutch who was in charge...and to piss him off even more.

That Clutch had freaked out when we'd arrived home a day late with my face cut up was an understatement. He was downright livid at Tyler, even though it wasn't Tyler's fault. He'd blamed Tyler since he was in charge when my clumsy accident happened. Clutch had jumped from his wheelchair faster than anyone expected and tackled Tyler. Jase, Griz, and Tack had to tear them apart to prevent a fight.

Yeah, this mission had come at the right time. The pair needed space, and a couple hundred miles was just about perfect. Except that Clutch wanted Jase and me with him and not with Tyler right now. But even he knew that the safety of Camp Fox came first, and if Tyler said he needed us, then we had to trust his judgment. If something happened to either of us on this trip, I would dread being in Tyler's shoes.

This morning, even though he was still pissed about having to be separated again so soon, Clutch had acknowledged that he trusted Tack and Griz second only to himself when it came to looking out for Jase and me. It was the first time he openly admitted that someone besides the three of us had earned his faith.

Wes nudged me. "Tyler's heading this way."

I turned to see Tyler, Griz, Nate, and Jase walking toward our

Humvee. I rolled down my window. The breeze hurt my stitches, and I tried not to wince. As Tyler approached, Tack came jogging over.

"I see only one pontoon tied to the ramp right now," Tyler said. "It's enough for us, but we'll need to round up more transports to handle all the back-and-forths to the *Aurora* when the convoy arrives. I wish the towboat and barges were better camouflaged, but the towboat was clearly shipwrecked. No one should suspect anyone's there if we're careful, and since no zeds can walk there, it should be a great spot to hide out."

"We'll make it work," Jase said.

I looked out over the Mississippi at the small cropping of trees and a white towboat and eight long rectangular steel barges over twice the tiny island's size still attached to the boat, with two more barges that looked like they would break off at any moment. Four of the barges were plowed up on its bank, nearly out of the water. A couple more barges floated at an odd angle in the river, as though they were about to break away from the rest. "That's a lot of boat."

Griz frowned. "Yeah, we could really use more troops to clean it out. You think we should still go for it, Maz?" Griz watched Tyler for a moment, then Tack and Nate. He didn't look at Jase, Wes, or me. Something about the military guys. They always looked to each other for decisions, never to civvies. It didn't matter that I'd seen every bit as much action as most of those guys had. On the flip side, I could see where they were coming from. None of them meant any harm; they truly thought they were doing the right thing by protecting us.

Still, it pissed me off, but I was done grumbling about it because it did no good. They saw Jase as a kid—I was glad they saw it, too—and they saw me as a woman. Since men outnumbered women over four to one at the park, every woman was treated like delicate china. I was lucky that I had both Clutch and Jase on my side, or else I would've been relegated to only fly scouting runs a long time ago.

"Well, Sorenson seemed to think the barges *should* be clear since there was no reason for anyone to be on those. We should only have to clear out the towboat. We've got Camp Fox counting on us," Tyler said, then shrugged. "I don't see an option. We go in."

I squinted at the boat a couple thousand meters away. "Sorensen seemed to think there wouldn't be much of a crew on that small of boat. It should be an easy in-and-out."

"Except it's going to be dark in just a couple hours," Jase said.

"We'll park over there. On the slope under the bridge on the east bank looks like a good spot," Tyler said, pointing to an outcropping not far from the pontoon.

"That's got to be a thirty-degree incline," I said.

Griz chuckled. "It won't be a problem. Humvees can handle over forty degrees."

"Let's get them down there," Tyler said. "Time's a wasting."

The guys spent the next half hour hiding the Humvees and loading all the ammo, food and tools they could onto the pontoon. It sat low in the water, and there was still more in the Humvees. While they all worked as quickly as they could, I stood behind the .30 cal and scanned for danger, even though the area was rural and no zeds showed up. The only benefit of having less upper body strength was that I always got the easier job of keeping them covered while they hauled supplies. They could carry more and faster than I could.

Tyler wiped his hands on his cargos. "That's all that we can get on this trip." He waved to me, and I jumped down and met up with the men by the pontoon.

"I'll get the ropes," Jase said as he started to untie the yellow ropes that held the boat to the ramp.

Tyler looked back at the motor and climbed into the captain's seat. "It's been awhile since I've driven one of these things."

Having no experience with boats, I grabbed a seat across from Wes and near Griz, who held his rifle ready at the helm. Tack did the same at the back of the boat.

Tyler started the engine and looked up. "Okay, Jase."

Jase loosened the first rope and then the second. He jumped on board and climbed on top a crate full of tools.

Tyler revved the engine, and the pontoon slowly pulled away from the ramp. The boat swayed in the rough water. As we moved into deeper water, waves lapped at the sides, and I was forced to hold on so I wouldn't get knocked around.

"It's bumpy out here today," Wes said, stating the obvious.

I sat there and focused on the distance closing between us and the white towboat with *Aurora II* painted on the side. I wondered how many zeds were in the river, either buried in the murky bottom or floating just under the surface.

"Does anyone see a good place to tie up?" Tyler asked as he brought the boat around the backside of the *Aurora* so that no one could see our pontoon from the bridge, making us safer from bandits.

Jase stood on the crate, which was an impressive feat in the rough water. He pointed to the hull. "I might be able to get a hold right up here."

"It won't take long to get a basic dock built," Wes said. He'd been a handyman before the outbreak, so Tyler had considered him critical to have on this mission. The rest of us were Wes's manual labor. At least the guys were. My job was to squeeze into small spaces, to do tasks like looking for broken cables, if needed. I didn't enjoy my job, but someone had to do it, and I was the smallest of all the scouts.

Tyler throttled all the way back just before we bumped up alongside the hull of the *Aurora*. The deck of the towboat was nearly ten feet high in the water. Sorenson was right. As long as we were careful, it'd be a good place to hide during the zed migration.

We were all pitched forward as the front of the pontoon slid up against the sand. I looked over the side and saw something bloated with scraps of clothes floating just below the surface. "Possible eater here," I said. I poked at it with my machete. A chewed up hand rose to the surface, but the zed's most dangerous feature—its mouth remained underwater. I swapped my machete for my knife and slammed the blade through the zed's skull. I rinsed the blade in the water and reclaimed my seat. "Nothing to worry about."

We all scrambled to grab ahold of the towboat's hull to steady the pontoon. Jase hopped up and lassoed the towboat's railing. Tack, Nate, and Griz climbed off the pontoon and onto the beach. While Tack helped Jase secure the pontoon to a fallen tree, I jumped off and watched the woods. Wes joined me a few seconds later while Tyler stayed on board at the wheel.

"This island looks pretty empty," Wes said. "There's nothing here but trees and a shipwreck."

Of course, at that moment I saw movement in the trees. "Way to jinx us." I slung my rifle over my shoulder and pulled out my machete. I walked toward the tree, careful to make sure nothing else waited in the shadows. The zed that emerged was ugly—horrendously ugly—bloated with river water and weathered. Its balding head was the only thing that hinted at its gender when it'd been infected. It came toward me, arms outreached, as though it wanted to embrace me. It moved slowly and stiffly. I swung and took the top of its head off. It collapsed, and I immediately looked for more.

When no more zeds emerged, I headed back to the small beach to put space between the trees and me. By then, Jase had the pontoon securely tied to the towboat, and Tyler was checking his rifle. A pile of grain had poured out of one of the barges that had crashed onto the island. "I wonder if all the barges are full of grain," I thought aloud.

Tyler glanced up, and his brow lifted. "We can only hope."

"Yeah, hope that it's not rotten already. My uncle had a farm, and I helped him clean out a bin once. Man, rotten corn is nasty," Griz said as he walked around the towboat, with Tack at his side. He was searching the *Aurora*, though I wasn't sure what he was looking for. Nate stood, watching the water.

Tyler looked around. "I know it sucks, but we're down to an hour of sunlight left. Once we're aboard, we'll need to secure the towboat for tonight. In the morning, we'll clear out the barges so we can unload the supplies and get set up for Fox's arrival."

We'd left before sunrise this morning, while it was still dark, because we knew well the roads in the Fox River valley. We needed all the sunlight we could get for the long, slow drive over here. We'd known it would take several hours, but none of us had figured it would burn through nearly all of our sunlight hours coming here.

Griz went back to the pontoon and rummaged through a crate. He pulled out an armful of nylon cables and rappelling hardware. Tack helped while we watched him throw a hook over the first railing. He tugged on it and then turned to us. "See you on top." He climbed the short distance in under five seconds flat.

"I'll go next," Jase said, rubbing his hands together.

"Be careful," Tyler said. "No unnecessary injuries."

"I got it." He slung his rifle over his shoulder and grabbed the rope and made his way up to the deck.

I swallowed and glanced at Wes who looked like he was thinking the same thing. "Friggin' spider man," I muttered.

Tyler motioned to us. "Who's next?"

"I guess I'll go," I said, and I heard Wes let out a sigh. I dragged my feet over to the rope and snapped my sheath shut. I grabbed the rope.

Tyler pressed a warm hand against my back. "Use your legs and walk up. You'll find your rhythm soon enough."

If I hadn't had over twenty pounds of gear on me, it would've been easier. I definitely never found the "rhythm" Tyler had spoken of. Even though I was diligent with my workouts, I never had much upper body strength. Every vertical foot was a clumsy struggle, especially as I approached the railing and there was less slack in the rope. Two pair of hands reached down. I grabbed ahold of Jase and then Griz, and let them pull me the rest of the way. Below me, Wes was just getting started, and he was faring only slightly better than I had.

"Geez, Cash. I thought you were going to take a nap on the way up," Jase joked.

I flipped him the bird.

Griz helped me to my feet. "Don't listen to the kid. You did good, girl. It takes a while to get the hang of rope climbing."

I knew he was just being nice, but it still made me feel better. I unsheathed my machete. "Help the others. I'll stand watch."

A couple minutes later, we all stood on the deck of the *Aurora II*. It had three windowed levels above the deck, the second level half the size of the first, and a small high-sitting bridge on top. Anyone could see there were no zeds on the deck.

"The bridge will give us a three-sixty view of the area. It should be the most secure place to hole up for the night," Tyler said as he set down a huge duffle bag with a thud.

"The crew quarters should at least be comfortable when it gets cold er," Griz said.

"Where's that?" Tyler asked.

Griz pointed. "I'm guessing either the first level or below decks. I've been on bigger boats. Towboats are new to me."

"This boat wasn't empty when the outbreak hit," I pointed to the round, first-level window as a shadow lumbered by.

"We'll start on the top and work our way down," Tyler said. "I'm thinking we'll set up common housing in the barges. They'll be drafty, but open enough to have fires running for heat should we have to stay into the winter. Our first imperative is to get this boat cleared so we can get some power turned on."

"Then, let's do it," Griz said.

"Yeah, I'm getting hungry," Nate added.

"What are you making us tonight?" I asked.

Nate scowled. "MREs are all we have for tonight. The real food is still boxed up."

"C'mon, then," Griz said. The seven of us walked across the deck and climbed the first stairs.

"This room looks to be a good area for Doc's clinic hospital," Tyler said as he peered inside.

"It was probably the captain's quarters," Griz said.

The sun was beginning its descent, casting a softer glow on the wide river. Except for the road and bridge to the north, all I could see was water and trees for miles. "The view is really beautiful from here," I said, climbing the second stairs.

"Yeah, a regular vacation getaway," Jase said drily.

I grinned at his sarcasm but my smile faded as I kept focus on the task at hand. We slowed as we approached the bridge. It was a good sign that I saw no zeds in the windows. Since zeds rarely sat down, it meant that if there were any in there, they were either under three feet tall or in bad shape.

Tyler was the first to walk up to the window. He stood for a moment, and then turned to face us. "We don't want to stay in the bridge tonight."

"Why not?" Wes asked, and we all moved closer to look through the window.

Inside, three bodies lay sprawled on the floor, each one with a gunshot wound in the skull. A single revolver lay in the hand of one. They'd been dead for some time, with how their discolored skin clung to their emaciated forms.

Zeds were easier to deal with than corpses. I could convince myself that their humanity was gone, but corpses...they reminded me of what I was doomed to become someday.

"All right. Let's check the next level," Tyler said.

At the bottom of the stairs, we all went up to the glass to peer inside.

"Looks fine to me," Wes said, his nose pressed against the glass. "I wonder if the captain is one of the fellows we came across in the bridge."

Inside, the table and couch seemed undisturbed with no signs of violence and no place for zeds to hide.

"Good. At least one room that shouldn't stink like a shit storm," Griz said.

I glanced at the stairwell. "Ready for the galley?"

"We don't have much time until we lose our sunlight," Tyler said. "Let's go. Tack, you take point. Griz and I will cover. Everyone else, stand back until we clear this level."

Tack was Tyler's go-to guy for taking point, so he was used to it. He moved smoothly and rarely talked, but more important, he never freaked out. The slender man walked up to the door, held up his hand, and then motioned forward. Griz opened the door and Tack swung. A zed that had been on the other side of the door went down. Tack headed inside, followed closely by Tyler. Jase held the door when Griz followed.

I watched through the window as Tack and Tyler finished off the lone zed in the room.

"All clear," Griz called out, and we entered the large room. "Ready to check below decks."

"It'd be nice if there were only four in the crew," I said.

Tack was already at another door. Tyler and Griz joined up with him. He opened the door, and after a quick second, he touched his nose. A signal we'd come up with at Camp Fox for scouting runs.

The smell that caused Tack to signal us wafted through the air from below decks. The all-too-familiar rotten stench of zeds.

Damn it.

There were more than four in the crew.

ELEVEN

Tack held up four fingers. He turned to face us. "They're all at the bottom of the stairs."

Four zeds. Relief blanketed my nerves. Four more zeds we could handle.

Tyler looked across our faces. "Griz, since they can't get up the stairs, you want to clear out these one at a time?"

Griz nodded. "No problem, Maz."

"Okay then. Splitting up will save us time. Wes, you stay up above deck and start figuring out what needs done to get this boat ready for Camp Fox," Tyler said. "Tack and Nate are with me. Jase and Cash, you're with Griz. Griz, your team will clear this room. Move slow. It's going to be dark down there, so we have to be extra careful. We have sixty-plus souls counting on us, so there's no room for mistake. Tack, Nate, and I will start at the back and work our way toward you from below decks. Come to the deck if you hit 1900 and we haven't come across each other yet. Everyone clear?"

We all voiced agreement. Tyler, Tack, and Nate headed toward the back of the towboat.

I paused as I walked toward the door. Lying on the table was an open journal. On its cream pages was a beautiful drawing of a cloudy sky. I turned the page to find an ink sketch of a landscape. I flipped through pages of stunning art, and seeing it panged my heart. The outbreak had taken so much talent. It had murdered gifted people and criminals equally, children and the old. All that was left behind was remnants. I didn't have any special gifts. Before the outbreak, I was just one out of billions. Now, I was *necessary.*

The loss of a single life could bring us one step closer to the brink of extinction.

Ha. Who was I kidding?

We were already there.

I snapped the journal shut and looked up to find Jase watching me. His gaze questioned me, and I noticed that both he and Griz had their headlamps on; I clicked on mine. "I'm ready," I said quickly. The band rubbed uncomfortably against my stitches, but it was better than going in blind. Griz stopped outside the door, and I refocused on the mission.

As we stood behind Griz, I thought on Tyler's words. He didn't tell us anything we didn't already know. We all knew that this boat was Camp Fox's best hope. That's why I'd come along, even knowing it was a political play on Tyler's part. I sure as shit wasn't here because I enjoyed walking into the dank interior of a towboat with who-knew-how-many hungry zeds waiting around every corner and in every shadowy nook.

Griz glanced back at us. "We stick with the usual plan. I'll be on point. Jase, you're at my six. Cash, you'll be sweeper in case we need to break out the artillery."

"Yeah, got it," Jase said.

I nodded. "Just give me a minute to set up before you make contact."

Griz opened the door, his homemade machete ready. The stench wafted out. He stepped onto the top of the metal steps that led into the dark bowels of the towboat. Jase followed, and I brought up the rear. It didn't matter if it was Griz or Tyler. They both always put me in back. They kept Jase in back, too, if any of the other soldiers were involved. I figured it was because we didn't have military training, and they had some kind of idea that the military was the first line, that they were there to protect us civilians. I didn't waste the breath explaining that Clutch had been training Jase and me since the outbreak.

Griz paused at the top step, and I could hear a rustling below. Jase gave him plenty of space to retreat, but he didn't move back. Then, he descended a couple steps and waited. I stepped onto the first step in the darkness and looked down. My headlamp shone on the four zeds waiting at the bottom of the stairs, clawing out at us. Unable to climb the steps, they were almost comedic. Almost.

I lined up the sights on my M24. "Ready," I said.

Jase moved around me, and the two men descended down the steps.

Griz swung first, taking down the closest zed. Jase stayed behind. The second zed tripped over the first zed and tumbled toward Griz. Jase swung, and then kicked the lifeless thing away. Griz brought his sharp blade onto the head of the other zed the same time Jase finished the final one with a dramatic swing.

He held up a hand. "Stay here." He jumped over the bodies and paced around what looked to be the crew quarters. After he checked every shadowed corner and around every bed, he called up, "Clear."

I lifted my rifle and moved down the metal steps. With only our headlamps for light, shadows danced around the lockers and beds. We gathered around the next steel door.

"We can wait here, or do you guys want to keep going?" Griz asked.

"Keep going," Jase said quickly.

"I want to get this boat cleared," I added.

Griz smiled and then opened the door. A zed lunged at him. "Agh!"

Jase lunged forward and slashed the badly decayed zed across its face. Griz shoved the body off him and rolled to his feet, slamming his machete into the zed's head.

Moans erupted from the darkness. Jase jumped back and Griz slammed the door shut.

Ah, hell. We weren't even close to being done yet.

TWELVE

Once we had a chance to regroup, Jase opened the steel door, and Griz tossed a snap light into the room several steps below. A green glow lit up the open space. Several dark shapes clumsily and erratically ran into one another to pounce at the light.

Jase whistled. "There's got to be a dozen of them down there."

Griz let out a sigh. "It's too dangerous to take them out hand-to-hand. We could wait for Maz's team, but either way, sweeping the area is our safest option." He turned to me. Shadows danced across his face. "Cash, you're on. Jase, stand by the door. I'll yank Cash back if they get too close, and you shut the door."

"Yes, sir," Jase said, and he squeezed past me to the door.

I couldn't tell if he was being sarcastic or obedient, but I also didn't care. I had a job to do. Griz would never put me face to face with a zed where I could get hurt, but he had no problem with me taking them down from a distance. I didn't mind as long as I didn't feel useless. I was actually looking forward to some target practice. I still remember the first zed I killed. Hell, I remembered all of them, but when I killed them, I'd learned to compartmentalize. What I killed wasn't human or even *feeling*. It was a target, nothing else.

I ran a thumb over my M24. It showed some wear, but it shot true. After checking the stability of the handrail, I leaned onto the metal bar and aimed. "Don't worry. This won't take too long."

The zeds had begun to disperse from the snap light, having discovered that it brought no flesh that they craved. As soon as the first one sniffed us out, they all headed toward us. Still, I fired only when I was sure I had a kill shot.

My personal motto, *get 'em where I want 'em,* repeated over and over in my mind.

One. A zed fell. The shot resounded off the metal walls.

Two. Another fell. *Three. Four.* My ears rang.

I fired eleven shots in total and killed ten zeds. No one spoke while I fired. It was kind of like talking in someone's back swing. It just wasn't cool.

When I lifted my rifle, Jase smiled and gave me a thumbs up.

"Like fish in a barrel," Griz said with a pat on my back. "Good job, Cash."

He motioned forward, and then headed down the four steps and into the room holding what I assumed to be the mechanicals of the boat. I swapped my rifle for my machete; even though noise no longer mattered, ammo was a precious commodity. We checked the bodies to make sure they were good and fully dead. Not that I was worried. Each one was a solid head shot.

"God, it stinks down here," Jase said.

I nodded. "We need to find an air freshener warehouse."

"Boats need to be well-sealed or else they'd sink," Griz said, holding his forearm over his nose. "It's a good thing if we have to stay here through the winter. But damn, it's going to take a while to air it out. Jesus." He gagged and bent over. I thought he was going to throw up, but after a moment, he stood, pulled a scarf over his nose and stepped over a zed carcass.

Metal creaked.

"We're coming in!" Tyler yelled from the opposite side of the room.

"All clear!" Griz shouted back.

Beams from three headlamps emerged from the darkness.

"Everything covered from the back?" Griz asked.

"That's affirmative," Tyler replied.

He walked in and looked at the bodies.

"There were eighteen beds in the crew quarters," Griz said. "Add on one for the captain, we shouldn't come across more than nineteen zeds, and that's assuming they were running a full crew and not carrying passengers." He counted on his fingers. "Three on the bridge, one in the galley, and the pair in the crew quarters. We came across another ten in the equipment room, and they all looked like crew. No passengers. So, that makes sixteen."

"Make that nineteen," Tyler said. "We took out two hanging around the engines, and we found the final crew member dead on top of an engine, likely from dehydration. So there shouldn't be any more left."

"Sonofa—" Nate's cussing was cut off by a ruckus of metal crashing and shouts.

We all sprinted to Nate's position. My headlamp shone onto Jase's back as he slashed something on the ground. When he moved, I saw that it had been a zed. More noticeably, it had been female, wearing a skirt and sporting a badly broken leg. The likely scenario? The crew had brought her on board during the outbreak, not realizing she'd been infected. Their compassion led to their deaths.

"She bit me. She fucking bit me!"

I stepped around Jase to see Nate's wild eyes. Blood poured from his cheek and head. The zed had taken a couple good-sized chunks. He had less than an hour.

Jase knelt by the collapsed locker. "Aw, hell."

"Nate," Tyler said, falling to his knees. He shoved against the locker, trying to push it off the guardsman.

Jase breathed deeply and then joined in, and they pushed the locker off Nate.

Nate must've been in shock because he didn't seem to notice the locker. He only lay there and held his cheek. He stared at Tyler. "She bit me."

Tack leaned on his machete.

"Damn it," Griz said.

With a straight arm, Tyler pushed Jase back. He pulled out his sidearm and pressed a hand on Nate's heart. "You're a hero, Private Hawking. You've saved lives, and you've earned the peace that's coming to you."

Nate squeezed his eyes shut as Tyler lifted the sidearm. His hand shook, but he didn't waste any time. I jumped at the single gunshot. It still echoed through the room as Tyler stood and walked several feet away from us.

Griz came down on a knee, clasped the cross he wore around his neck, and prayed.

By the time he'd finished, I came to accept the fact that Nate was gone. It seemed like the more death I'd seen, the faster I moved on. I wasn't so sure I liked that change in me.

"The zed must've reached out and startled him," Jase said. "He must've banged into the locker and it fell over on him."

It'd been my job to clear this room. My fault. "I can't believe I missed one," I said breathlessly. My brows furrowed as I stared at Nate's body.

"It was hidden behind the cabinet," Jase said, grabbing my shoulder. "You couldn't have seen it."

I still couldn't help but think I *should* have seen it.

After a long minute, Tyler returned. "Let's wrap things up and get the engines running and lights on. We have less than forty-eight hours to get this towboat and barges ready for Camp Fox. We have to assume there could be more zeds wandering around here. Tack and Griz, you take the private above deck. Cash and Jase, you stay behind me."

We silently fell in line as he headed back toward the engine room.

"I hate these enclosed spaces," Jase said in a low voice, walking beside me. "If zeds got in here, there'd be no way out."

"We're safe now," I forced myself to say even though I didn't believe the words. Jase needed my support, not my doubts. "Zeds would have to climb the side of the boat to get in here, and that's not going to happen. This place will be a vault for Camp Fox, trust me. Once we get it cleared it, you'll be safe here. I know it."

"Easy for you to say," he replied. "You've been through more shit than just about anyone else out there. I still don't know how you made it through that elementary school."

"It wasn't fun, but it was nothing compared to Doyle's camp."

"The Dogs, then all the zeds...man, I can't imagine how much that must've sucked," Jase said after a moment.

"Yeah," I replied in a quiet voice. "But you know what? The Dogs and the zeds weren't the worst part."

He paused. "Then what was?"

I chuckled drily. "Everyone thinks I went after Doyle to save Camp Fox."

"You did."

I didn't answer.

"Didn't you?"

"Yeah, but I didn't need to go it alone. I also went after him because I was cocky enough to think I could pull it off all by myself without anyone else getting hurt."

Jase grabbed my arm, stopping me. "You *did* pull it off. You killed Doyle and took down the militia still loyal to him. You survived and no one got hurt."

"It was by sheer luck." I shook my head. "No. It was a miracle. I realized that when I was lying on the roof, waiting to die. Hell, if I had half a brain, I would've stayed in the cellar with all the weapons and food until help arrived. That just goes to show you how unprepared I was."

"You're being too hard on yourself."

"No, I'm not. I've made so many stupid mistakes that not only could've gotten myself killed, but also you or Clutch. It was at Doyle's camp when I finally came to realize that I needed to get my act together and quit thinking I had everything under control. I found out I didn't and I don't. Hell, if I were a cat, I'd be on my ninth life by now."

He smirked. "Well, then at least you still have one left."

I sucker punched him in the arm. "Funny, ha ha."

"Seriously, though," he said. "No one's perfect. We all make mistakes, and as long as you can walk away from them, it'll work out in time. Look, even your cut on your face is healing."

I lifted my hand to touch my stitches, but then dropped it. "Come on. Let's clean out our new home."

PART THREE
ENVY

THIRTEEN

The following morning

"Amen." Griz said after a lovely *hooah*-style prayer for Nate. Tyler and Griz rolled Nate's body off the edge of the deck, and he splashed into the river below. After him, we tossed over every member of the crew and the zed girl. Luckily, we hadn't come across any others during our search last night.

We still had no power. The towboat's fuel tanks were empty, and Wes couldn't get the engines started last night with only the five gallons he'd brought with him on the pontoon. Without heat, last night had been cold. The smell of death had managed to leak into the second level captain's quarters—in some part due to our clothes—so we'd left the door open to air out the room. The sweet, sickly stench had a way of seeping into everything and becoming a permanent part of a place. Zed stench didn't exactly smell like potpourri. In a way, it was like smoke. Once it got into a person's clothes, the smell lingered and nothing short of a heavy head-to-toe scrubbing could get rid of it. Our best defense for this night was the minty medicated ointment to help clear the lungs. We put a dollop of the stuff under each of our noses and took turns sleeping and standing watch.

Earlier, Tack and Griz had fastened a ladder onto the side of the boat to make it easier getting to and from the dock Tyler and the guys were building. Jase had lost at rock-paper-scissors, and he had to scrub away the old blood and bits of brain on the bridge floor. Thankfully, it wasn't carpeted, but it still stunk something awful.

I turned and went back to the pile of supplies we'd been carrying up one load at a time. While the ladder made climbing much easier, it was still a tiresome, slow progress carrying one load at a time up the side of the *Aurora*. Wes was busy building a pulley system so we could pull up larger loads, but there were some things that couldn't wait for Wes to finish.

I rummaged through the pile and found the cardboard box I was looking for. I untied the rope around it and pulled out two brand new cans of disinfectant. There was a gold star on each can that read, *Kills 99.9% of germs*, and I chuckled. If only killing zeds was that easy.

I headed to the bridge, took a deep breath, and entered. I didn't leave until I'd emptied half a can. In the galley, I finished the can. In the crew quarters, where there were fewer windows, I used an entire can. The other rooms would have to wait. With all the windows and doors propped wide open, I hoped for a good breeze today to freshen up the towboat. I was hoping we'd be able to sleep in the crew quarters tonight where we'd have real beds and it'd be warmer. Somehow, I suspected the crew quarters would take a couple more days to air out.

"All done in there?" Tyler asked as I stepped onto the deck, savoring the fresh air. He was wiping his sweaty brow. Tack and Griz were each drinking water.

"For now," I said.

"Good. Everyone, check your gear."

I headed for my weapons, and Jase took the empty Lysol cans from me.

He lobbed them over the water with an impressive throw.

"You've got a quarterback's arm," Griz said, walking over.

"Nah," Jase said. "I could never throw long straight."

"All right. Quit playing around and grab your gear," Tyler announced. "We have Camp Fox arriving tomorrow and barges to prep, so let's get to it," Tyler said.

———

One day later

Jase and I stood on the wood deck of the *Aurora*, watching the convoy approach down the highway from the west. We had hung the U.S. flag from the bridge, and it waved proudly in the fall breeze. The flag was our all-clear sign to the convoy. If the flag had been upside down or missing, our mission had failed and the *Aurora* wasn't safe. I could only imagine how nervous everyone in the convoy must've felt until they saw the flag.

I looked through the scope of my rifle. I counted fourteen vehicles in all. With the exception of a sports car for our scout vehicle, the other vehicles were all heavy duty: HEMTTs, Humvees, SUVs, trucks—one stacked with crates full of chickens—and a large semi pulling a trailer full of cattle, hogs, and goats. That the vehicles looked unscathed, coupled with the fact that they were slightly ahead of schedule, meant their journey was—hopefully—casualty-free. I continued to watch the vehicles, searching for signs of damage or injuries to their occupants.

Clutch sat in the passenger seat of the first Humvee. He was wearing sunglasses, and his arm rested on the doorframe, his window open. I slung my rifle onto my shoulder and gave Jase a wide grin. "Everything looks good. I see Clutch in front."

He returned my smile and let out a deep breath. "Good. I was hoping we hadn't stirred up any herds on our way over. I'll go tell the others." He jogged to the galley and toward the engine room where Wes and two of Sorenson's people were finishing repairs. The *Lady Amore* had stopped by yesterday, and Sorenson had left three of his people, including his daughter, to help us get up and running. Their help and expertise were invaluable. His daughter, Nikki, had been born with sea legs, and she had a salty demeanor that came from spending most of her life on the river. She had been the one to get the engines running. Over the last twenty-four hours, we'd completed far more than we could've done with everyone from Camp Fox combined.

Not that Sorenson had done all that out of the goodness of his heart. The new world was built on bartering, and he was one of the best at it. For three of his people to stay two days, Tyler gave him two pallets of MREs, which cut our MRE supply in half. Sorenson had delivered two more pontoons in exchange for the .30 cal on the back of Tyler's Humvee. I told Tyler he was being too generous, but he believed it was more important to get the towboat and barges set up to sustain Camp Fox.

If we had to stay the full winter on the *Aurora* or took on any more survivors, we didn't have a single ration to spare. Tyler counted on any remaining zeds in the area to clear out and migrate with the herds, leaving the Midwest free for us to get what we needed from the bigger stores in towns. I didn't have as much confidence. I knew for a fact that some buildings had quite a few zeds penned inside. I wasn't looking forward to finding out which buildings those were.

"Shit. Is the entire group soldiers?" Nikki Sorenson asked at my side.

I started, not realizing she'd come up behind me. I looked at the now-stopped convoy on the east bank, where people were getting out and stretching, including Manny. Until Manny and his people had arrived, Camp Fox only had about ten civilians, the rest being soldiers—mostly Guardsmen. It hadn't always been that way. After the outbreak, there had been well over a hundred non-military residents at Camp Fox. Doyle's attack on Camp Fox had changed all that. The head of the militia had attacked when nearly all the soldiers were fixing the camp's perimeter. No one had ever expected the attack to come from inside the base. The camp's population had been decimated, and I'd almost lost Clutch.

Only forty-two survivors had made it to the Fox National Park to rebuild Camp Fox. Even with stragglers coming in every week, soldiers outnumbered civvies three to one. I think that was part of the reason why Tyler and Griz were overly protective of Jase and me. They still saw us as civvies rather than soldiers.

"Most are, I guess," I said finally.

From this distance, even most civvies could pass as soldiers. Many of the Fox survivors, including myself, wore desert tan or olive drab from Camp Fox's supply rooms as it was our most abundant source of durable clothing.

"Must be nice to have that kind of protection," she said, her tone caustic.

I shrugged. "Yeah, I guess so, but it's not like we're not pulling our own weight. We all look after each other in some way."

Jase emerged from the galley and headed our way. "Wes says they're nearly done down there. We'll have power tonight, but there's not much diesel fuel left for the engines. We're going to have to go on a fuel run soon."

"Ha. Good luck with that," Nikki said. "There's no diesel fuel along this river for fifty miles in either direction. You'll have to go onto dry land to find any."

"We'll find some," I said.

"As long as you're not taking what the *Lady Amore* needs," she quickly added.

My brows rose. "We're not competing. We're all in this together."

With her droll look, I could tell Nikki wasn't convinced. "The *Lady*

Amore needs fuel or else we're dead in the water. The *Aurora* isn't going anywhere, so it's not like you need it."

I chuckled. "We don't need it for the boat. We need it for the generators. We're just shooting for a couple luxuries to keep morale up: lights in the barges, some hot water, some portable heaters, and a couple working toilets."

"Hmph." She pursed her lips. "I don't even understand why you couldn't just hop in a jet and fly all your people to safety."

My hands slid to my hips. I'd heard this all before, and it pissed me off every time. "Just because I have a pilot's license doesn't mean I can fly anything out there. You have a driver's license. Does that mean you can drive a big semi-truck or bulldozer?"

Jase cut between us. "It's all going to work out," he said. "Don't be so sensitive. Sheesh."

After a moment, I sighed. "We're all trying to just get by."

"Say that to the river towns," a man from the *Lady Amore* chimed in as he approached. I tried to remember his name.

"Hey, Bill," Jase said as he fidgeted with his binoculars.

Ah, Bill.

Bill nodded to Jase before continuing. "Those towns that aren't completely infested by zeds are having walls built around them. It's getting harder and harder to find an open dock that's big enough for the *Lady*."

"The towns are closing off their docks?" I asked.

"No, they charge docking fees. Not to mention the outrageous fees for fuel and food," he replied.

"It's a cutthroat world," I said, not knowing what else to say. Yeah, times were tough, but I'd seen the *Lady Amore* in action. They were managing just fine.

"Looks like they're getting ready to load the pontoons," Jase said at my side, looking through a pair of binoculars.

I lifted my rifle and looked through the scope. Everyone in the convoy, with scouts on the outliers standing guard, was busy unloading supplies around Tyler by the three pontoons. Two dead zeds floated face-down nearby.

"I wish we had a better place to secure all the vehicles," Jase said. "It sucks leaving them out in the open like that."

The vehicles, still laden with anything worth taking from the park, had been backed into a semi-circle around the dock to both protect the small boat ramp as well as enable efficient unloading. Soon, everything on the vehicles would be moved onto the *Aurora,* though I suspected loading the livestock on the pontoons would make for an entertaining afternoon show.

I pointed to the tree line near the dock. "Tyler thought we'd park them just off the road by the woods."

"We could try to camouflage them," Jase said. "Even so, I don't see how we can possibly hide an entire convoy. Is Tyler planning on keeping at least one scout on land to keep an eye on them?"

"I think so." I thought of long, cold nights outside ahead of us and shivered.

"Until the herds come," Nikki added. "Then you'd better hope there's no one still there."

Being reminded of the reason for this journey quickly sobered me. "Yeah. Until the herds come."

"Let me see, Jase," Nikki said.

I glanced away from my scope to see Nikki holding out her hand. Jase handed her his binoculars. After several long moments, her mouth slowly dropped open. "My God, it looks like the Army is moving in. How much stuff are you guys moving?"

"Stuff?" I shrugged. "Just the usual. Anything we can eat or use, we're bringing onto the barge to keep it safe."

Nikki watched me for a moment before looking through the binoculars again. "You should be careful. The more you have, the more you have to lose."

FOURTEEN

Nikki Sorenson's words pierced any hope I had at sleeping. It wasn't so much what she'd said. It was *how* she'd said it, like she was taunting us at how much we had to lose, like she knew something we didn't. Or it could've been just another one of her catty remarks. Unlikely the former, probably the latter.

I tossed and turned in my bunk, trying not to wake anyone else in the crew quarters below decks, which had become the new residence of Camp Fox's scouts. We filled up all eighteen beds, and eleven of the bunks were shared by scouts working alternating shifts. Using the crew quarters made it easier to rotate shifts than bunking with the civvies in the large, steel Number One barge, which would add at least five minutes onto any scout's response time.

The four barges closest to the towboat were in good shape, and two of Sorenson's people had been busy moving enough grain from the barges closest to the towboat to the barges further away so that we could use some of the areas for the general residence and livestock. Finding eight barges of grain, with most of it not rotten, was a goldmine. Of course, Sorenson's guy immediately claimed one hundred percent rights to the grain, but fortunately, Tyler talked him down to fifty percent more quickly than I'd expected.

Giving up on the idea of sleep, I shoved the blanket off me, sat up, and climbed out from the bottom bunk that had belonged to one of the towboat's previous crew. Probably one I'd shot.

From the top bunk, Jase rolled over. "What's up?" he asked, sounding wide awake.

"I'm going to check on the Number Three barge," I said softly so I wouldn't wake anyone in the crew quarters. "Something Nikki said earlier. I just need to make sure everything's secure. Then I'll be right back."

Jase sat up. "So it wasn't just me. Yeah, I got a bad vibe, too. How about I join you."

"Thanks." I reached up and grabbed my belt that hung off the corner of my bunk and latched it around my waist. By the time I'd finished fastening my holster and sheath, Jase was armed and ready to go. We headed up the stairs and into the galley, which made up the entire first level of the towboat. A lantern was lit on a table in the center, and Frost was reading a paperback that had seen better days. Diesel was missing and likely serving as a bed for Benji like the dog did every night.

"Where are you two going?"

I turned to see Clutch watching us from the couch that he'd turned into his bed. It was too much hassle for him to sleep downstairs in the crew quarters. He had regained minimal coordinating movement in his legs and still struggled with stairs. Every day, he made it a few more steps with crutches than the day before, but it was clearly exhausting for him.

I rolled my eyes. "Is everyone awake on this boat?"

"We're going to check out barge Three," Jase said.

He sat up. "Barge Three? Why?"

"We both had a feeling," I said simply.

"I'm coming, too," he said, tugging his legs over the edge of the bed.

"You don't have to," I said. "It's probably nothing. Just a suspicion that's been nagging me."

Clutch slid onto his wheelchair and grabbed his crutches. "And if it's not?" He took the lead, and wheeled out of the galley. Frost never even looked up from his book, though I'm sure he'd listened to every word.

As we crossed the deck of the towboat, I looked up at the bridge to see Tyler drinking coffee as he went through papers. He should've been sound asleep by now, but he was one of those folks that felt the need to always be in control. He bore all the weight of Camp Fox on his shoulders. Sometimes, I thought he was afraid the community would collapse without his leadership. Maybe he was our white knight. But maybe he just needed to have faith in the community we all had a hand in building.

I tripped over Clutch's chair and barely caught myself from tumbling over him. "Oomph. Sorry," I muttered.

"Graceful," Jase teased with a grin, his white teeth easily seen in the starlit night.

With a sigh, I saw the large, rectangular-shaped barges in the night sky. The general residence had been set up in Number One, the barge closest to the island and in the row of the four closest to the towboat, making it the safest barge from any bandits who might come across the highway bridge and notice us. Makeshift wood plank bridges had been built from the towboat to each barge. None of the barges were cozy by any stretch, but they would work.

Next to One, Number Two was our commons area. Numbers Two and Three were the easiest to get to from the towboat for a reason. As we crossed the manmade bridge of two-by-sixes to Number Three, Clutch's wheelchair made a nearly-silent rolling sound over the wood, while Jase's and my boot steps made thumps in the night.

Number Three held all our stockpile of canned and dried food, weapons, and other supplies. It was our own Fort Knox, making it critical that we could get to it easily from the towboat. To its right, the livestock was set up in Number Four, the barge facing the highway bridge. Cattle mooed softly in the night air. If the livestock were any closer, people would constantly complain about the smell.

The second row of barges wasn't used except for storing grain. Number Five, on just the other side of Number One, had hit the island at the wrong angle, and its hull had been compromised. Grain had dumped out onto the ground. The remaining three viable barges were full of precious grain. When we'd discovered it yesterday, we danced like maniacs and whooped like fools. For the first time, we knew with confidence that we'd get through the winter, let alone spring and summer, without starving. We'd get sick of grain and likely have some serious nutritional deficiencies, but we'd survive.

As we approached the wide opening to Three, our steps became softer and slower. I could hear nothing out of the ordinary. In the distance, Kurt waved before turning back to his guard duty. Wes had opened the bays to the first row of barges to air out the dangerous grain dust.

Jase looked down the narrow, metal stairway, pulled out his rifle, and clicked on his flashlight. "I'll take lead."

Clutch pulled up to the edge of the open bay. He set his crutches on the deck next to him and laid his rifle on his lap. "If either of you see anything suspicious, flash your lights in my direction."

I pulled out my sidearm and snapped the small flashlight onto it. The

Glock and all its accessories had been a surprise from Tyler for my birthday. I think it was his way to finally show that he wasn't angry with me
anymore for leaving him behind when I went after Doyle on my own. I
peered into the darkness, my nerves making my senses hypersensitive. "It
looks quiet down there. Knock on wood, everything will be just fine and
we'll be back in bed in no time."

Clutch narrowed his eyes at me. After a moment, I shrugged and
couldn't help but smirk at his superstitious nature. He was a firm believer
that if any of us said something would be easy, it was sure to have problems. Just because he was right *most* of the time only made the supersti-
tion a coincidence, not a fact.

Oh, and Clutch also didn't believe in coincidences.

Jase gave me a slow shake of his head before taking the first step into
the barge. I followed him down the steps, slowly scanning the floor and
pallets with my mounted flashlight. Nothing seemed out of place. No
tarps had been torn off. No supplies were scattered. The tension in my
muscles eased. My imagination had been working overtime. Everything
was fine. I'd been overreacting.

As I reached the last step, I could make out an almost imperceptible,
powered hum, and I frowned. "Do you hear that?" I whispered.

Jase paused and looked at me and then did a three-sixty. "Yeah," He
replied just as quietly. "Sounds like it's coming from that way." He
pointed with his flashlight and led us toward the long side of the barge.

Wes had gotten the engines running, but they weren't running right
now, and there were no generators running on this barge. Tyler had
mandated we needed to save power until we found more fuel and the
temperatures dipped below freezing. There were several small gas-
powered generators spread across the barges to help with lighting, cooking, and plumbing, but there should be none in a barge being used only
for storage. Yet, the noise grew as we drew closer.

"What the hell is a generator doing on down here?" Jase asked.

My eyes narrowed on a tarp against the wall. Unlike the other tarps
that sat squarely over pallets, this one seemed misshapen and tight against
the side of the hull. There, on the edges of the tarp, warm light bled
through the edges of the tarp.

"I don't like this." I raised my Glock and turned the light on and off
three times. A light from the deck above did the same back at us.

Jase turned off his light to have both hands on his rifle. Seconds later,
I heard the sounds of boots pounding down the steps.

The tarp moved, and a masculine shape crawled out from under it. "Lay off. I said I'll check it out."

As he stood, I leveled the light in his eyes. "Don't move!"

Philip from the *Lady Amore* held a hand over his eyes, and then spun around. "Run!"

The tarp was thrown open and two more shapes bolted out.

Jase stepped up to Philip and coldcocked him with the butt of his rifle. The man fell to the ground with a solid thud. The other two ran behind pallets, and we both took off after them.

Jase quickly took the lead and cut between the pallets while I ran straight ahead and took the next chance to get behind the pallets just in time to see Jase tackle a smaller shape.

As he yanked her to her feet, I noticed it was Nikki.

My mouth dropped. *Son of a bitch.*

"I've got her," Jase said. "Quit wiggling, dammit."

"Do you need help?" I asked, glaring at the woman.

"No, I've got it covered," he quickly replied.

"Right!" I took off running in the direction the two had been headed. When I reached the end of the barge, I made a hard right and climbed over a pallet of boxes. Pain shot through my scarred leg, reminding me that it wasn't fully healed. I needn't have hurried. Several feet away, Kurt had Bill from Sorenson's crew restrained, while another scout was dragging an unconscious Philip across the shadowed floor.

I headed back to Jase to make sure he had Nikki under control. She must not have behaved, because he now carried her lax form over his shoulder. "The other two guys are secure," I said. "I'll check the generator."

I jogged toward the tarp now hanging limply off to one side. Under it sat two work lights and the small, still-running generator they'd snagged from somewhere. Hooked up to it was the acetylene torch I'd seen Wes use many times. Confused, I went down on a knee and examined the wall of the barge. Chalk lines were drawn to make a large square on the wall, large enough to slide a crate through. "Son of a bitch," I muttered and jumped to my feet.

I zigged and zagged around pallets and up the steps to the deck, where a small crowd had gathered near the open bay to barge Three. Tyler stood next to Clutch in his wheelchair.

Bill and Philip stood before them, while Nikki—held tight by Jase and Tack—was just coming to.

"—too busy doing whatever it was they were doing, they didn't even see us coming," I heard Jase tell Tyler and Clutch as I approached.

"They were going to cut a hole through the hull!" I said breathlessly. In spring, when the water levels would rise, the barge would likely flood. Until then, where the barge was currently located, it made a perfect exit point for dropping supplies onto a small boat hidden between the barges below. "These bastards were going to rob us."

Frost shook his head slowly. "With all the grain dust around here, they would've set the whole barge on fire."

Tyler cocked his head at the three prisoners. "I made a generous deal with Sorenson for your time and assistance. Tonight, you've broken a trust between our communities. We have zero tolerance for theft."

"It's not like you don't have enough to share," Nikki spat out.

Clutch guffawed. "Does it look like we're any better off than you? We've had to completely uproot our home and are camping on a shipwreck."

"That barge is full of food and ammunition. I've never seen so much in my life," she retorted.

"Aside from sharing the location of this shelter, the *Lady Amore* crew hasn't offered my people a single thing without demanding heavy payment in return," Tyler said, his voice steady and calm but laced with anger.

"You don't understand. We are struggling to get by," Bill said. "Every day, we don't know if we're going to find more diesel or more food."

"Grow a pair," Clutch scolded. "We're all fighting to survive here. The world's a shithole. Deal with it."

Nikki grunted and twisted out of her captors' grasp and sprinted forward. Tack reached for her, but she jumped to the side. She must've twisted her ankle because she tumbled down and fell partway over the edge. Jase lunged after her, sliding on his belly to grab her, but she swung him away, loosening her hold, and she plummeted into the darkness below.

"Nikki!" Bill shouted.

Her scream was cut off by the sound of her body hitting the hard steel floor nearly twenty feet below. No one ran down to check on her. A drop from this height wasn't just deadly, it would've been *messy* deadly.

Everyone stood in stunned silence.

"What the hell just happened?" Tyler asked.

Jase climbed to his feet. "I don't know. She'd been standing so still. Then she just freaked out and tore away."

"You killed her!" Bill yelled, trying to lunge forward, but his scouts yanked him back.

"No," Tyler said harshly. "It was an accident. You saw for yourself."

"The captain's not going to see it that way," Philip said quietly. "That's his daughter down there."

Clutch grabbed his crutches and pulled himself to his feet. "He's going to see it that way because you're going to tell him the truth. You're going to tell him what you were doing here and exactly what happened. I'm going with you to make sure you do."

Tack stepped forward. "No, Clutch." He sighed. "I need to go. She was mine to watch."

"Bullshit," Jase said. "She was as much my responsibility. I'm going."

Tyler watched Tack and Jase for a moment before speaking. "Okay, by morning, the *Lady Amore* shouldn't be more than thirty miles or so south of here. You are both going, but under no conditions are you to board the *Lady Amore*. You drop Sorenson's daughter and his men in a raft and double-time it out of there. I'll write a note to make sure he knows the truth. It's our only shot at keeping our trade agreement. Whatever you do, don't let them get a bead on you. That's Sorenson's daughter lying on the bottom of Number Three. I don't trust him to be rational when he sees her. You drop the package and run. Got it?"

"Yes, sir," they both replied.

"You-you can't just dump us in the water," Philip said. "There are zeds in the water. If it's shallow at all—"

"You should've thought of that before you tried to steal from us," Tyler interrupted. "The only reason I'm allowing you to return to the *Lady Amore*—instead of staying on the *Aurora* for trial—is because of our trade agreement."

"Just let us go," Bill cried out. "We'll tell the Captain the truth. I mean it. You don't have to worry about anything. Please. Just let us go. Nothing will happen. I swear!"

Tyler ignored Bill's pleas and instead looked at the scouts holding the thieves. "Get these two out of my sight. Put them in the galley for tonight and keep at least four armed scouts on them at all times." He then looked to all of us. "I need volunteers to prep Sorenson's daughter for the trip in the morning."

Deb, one of the Fox survivors who volunteered for everything, unsurprisingly stepped forward. "I'll take care of it."

"I'll help," Tack said in a rush.

Deb gave him a sweet smile. "Okay. Thank you."

As the two headed into the barge, I couldn't help but grin. Deb may have been ten years his senior, but Tack didn't seem to care. The two had hit it off the moment she'd arrived at the park, and even though they thought they were hiding their relationship, everyone knew about it.

The crowd dissipated.

"I'm going to hit the sack," Jase said, sounding utterly exhausted. "I'm guessing Tyler is going to want us to get those guys off the *Aurora* at the crack of dawn.

"Listen, Jase," Clutch said. "If you want me to go, if you want an extra gun—"

"Relax. No worries. Tack and I've got it." Jase patted Clutch's shoulder. "Like Tyler said, we just toss them into a raft and bust out of there. Trust me, I don't plan on getting anywhere near Sorenson." With that, he turned and started walking away.

Jase spoke the words so nonchalantly, yet I had a hard time believing that an accidental death wasn't tearing him up inside. He'd seen so much death that he'd built quite the mask. So good that I couldn't even tell anymore if something was bothering him.

"Good night," I said, watching him. "I'll be in soon."

Clutch sat down in his chair and set his crutches across his lap.

The edge around the barge and deck had mostly cleared. Lanterns and flashlights blinked off one by one. I looked out over the river, the water peacefully reflecting the moonlight. In the far distance, wolves bayed. While people and domesticated animals had been devastated by the outbreak, some wild animals had flourished. Packs of wolves had become a new risk to scouting runs. I took in a deep breath of cool air. "Well, isn't this is a mess."

"I don't have Tyler's optimism," he said. "Any hope for a trade agreement is lying dead at the bottom of the barge."

"With the grain, we have enough food. We don't need a trade agreement," I said, pushing his chair. "So we're on our own. Then again, we've always been on our own."

"Yeah, but you're assuming Sorenson is going to let us be."

PART FOUR
WRATH

The Third Deadly Sin

FIFTEEN

Mid-afternoon, the following day

"You're getting a sunburn. It could slow your healing," Clutch said.

I touched my cheek where Doc had taken out the stitches a couple hours earlier. The bright sun warmed my skin. I looked down at Clutch. "What's taking them so long? They should've been back hours ago."

"Maybe the *Lady Amore* was farther out then Tyler thought."

"The herds could be showing up as early as today."

He shook his head. "The latest recon to the north shows them at least two days out, longer if they stop along the way. Jase will make it back okay."

Clutch didn't leave my side, so I knew he was as concerned about Jase as I was.

Just before the sun had crested this morning, we'd watched Jase and Tack disappear around the bend of the island. They'd been in the fastest deck boat we had, tugging behind it a large yellow tube containing the trio from the riverboat. Before the outbreak, the tube would have carried squealing kids as they bounced over the waves. Today's passengers were far more somber, especially considering one was dead.

Since Jase and Tack had left, Clutch and I had circled the deck countless times, taking breaks only for food and when Doc came for me. My anxious nerves were making it impossible to focus on anything. At noon, Griz begged Tyler to let him take a small crew out to find Tack and Jase. We all hoped that the reason they weren't back yet was because they'd had trouble finding Sorenson's boat. Any other alternative meant something had gone seriously wrong. I tried to focus on the positive, but as the day went on, horrible imaginings began to cycle through my mind.

I shaded my eyes against the sun and looked out over the river for any sign of either boat. Even with sunglasses, the glare off the water gave me a headache. An engine noise to my right pulled my gaze to find Kurt returning on a Jet Ski from his scouting run in the north. The Jet Ski, which we'd found at a dock a few miles upriver, had extra plastic fuel tanks strapped on both sides, and Kurt wore a large backpack. He'd had enough fuel and food for a three-day trip, but he'd been gone only two days. "I wonder how close the herds are now," I said.

Clutch wrapped his gloved hand around my mine. "Come on. Let's head back to the galley and grab a snack. There's nothing we can do out here except wear holes in the deck."

I looked to the south another time, still seeing nothing. "I guess you're right."

I moped as we headed back toward the galley. Clutch rolled slowly over the deck boards. After several feet, he came to an abrupt stop, peeled off his worn gloves, and picked at a blister on his hand, grumbling under his breath.

I picked his gloves off his lap and rubbed at the soft leather with holes and slashes. "Wow. These are worthless. You really need a new pair."

"That's not going to happen. I can't find any more. What I need is to get rid of this chair and back on my feet."

I wanted to snap back at his infuriating refusal to give his body time to heal. Instead, I dropped his gloves with a smack on his lap and gripped his shoulder. "A week ago you couldn't even stand. Just be patient."

"It's hard to be patient when we've got a shit storm of zeds heading this way."

Good point. I left my hand on his shoulder while I looked to the north. I forced a smile. "The zeds aren't here yet. So you can be patient a little longer."

"Hmph," he replied.

As I turned to look back down at Clutch, something in the distance caught my eye. I stepped back and lifted my rifle to look through the scope. Off the edge of the island, a deck boat with several people in it came jetting around the corner. I quickly made out Jase's sandy, shaggy hair.

I lowered my rifle and let out a whoop. "They're back! They must've had boat trouble since they're all loaded up in one."

Clutch narrowed his eyes and scrutinized the incoming boat for a long minute.

"Come on," I said. "Let's go meet them at the top of the ladder."

He didn't move. "I only count four on the boat."

"What?" I asked. "Are you sure?"

"Yes."

When I'd seen Jase, I hadn't bothered counting the crew. I squinted in the sunlight as I counted. Clutch was right. Griz had gone out with two other scouts today. There should have been five on that boat. "Maybe the fifth man is still bringing in the other boat," I offered hopefully.

"Maybe," Clutch said. "Let's get over there."

We hustled over to where the rope ladder and pulley-driven elevator platform hung. Deb was already there, watching each man climb up the ladder. Consternation filled her face.

Jase was the second man up the ladder. I grabbed onto his shivering, wet form and helped him climb over the railing. He collapsed on the deck, and I wrapped my arms around him to share my body heat. "What happened? Are you hurt?" I asked.

Clutch put a hand on Jase's back.

Deb kneeled by Jase. "Where's Tack?"

"Don't-know," Jase replied between chattering teeth and started to pull himself up.

I helped Jase to his feet. "Let's get you a hot shower."

By then, the others had reached the top. Griz's sleeves were wet, but everyone else was dry. He gave Clutch a hard look. "I think it's safe to say Sorenson is headed this way."

Clutch nodded. "I'll meet you on the bridge in five."

Griz and the other two scouts jogged across the deck, followed closely by Deb, who kept asking them about Tack.

Clutch looked up at Jase. "I need you to tell me exactly what happened."

Jase nodded, his whole body shaking against mine, as we took slow steps toward the galley. "We-we drove until we s-saw the riverboat." He sucked in a breath. "We c-cut the tube loose and took off. They must've seen Nikki or something 'c-cause they sent a speedboat with—swear to God—our own .30 c-cal after us."

"Shit," I muttered under my breath. "Thank God you didn't get shot."

"Tack?" Clutch asked.

Jase sniffled. "When they got close, they shot out our engine. W-we were dead in the water. They kept their distance until we ran out of ammo. They came up alongside, and Tack and I got ready to take them on, but then he shoved me into the water and took on all three guys by himself."

"Oh, God." That sounded exactly like something Tack would do. Even though he was only a few years older than Jase, Tack had taken him under his wing. I figured it had something to do with the fact that Tack had a younger brother about Jase's age. After the outbreak had hit, he searched but never found him.

Jase winced and then rubbed his hair. "I saw it all from the water. They tackled him. Then they tied him up and came after me. I had to ditch my life jacket and swim. I got lucky and hid under a tree trunk floating down the river. They got really close but I heard Sorenson on their radio and he called off the search. I think he assumed I was a goner."

He looked at each of us, his eyes pleading. "We've got to go back and get Tack."

"We will," Clutch said without hesitation. "We don't leave any of our own behind."

I hugged him. "We'll get him back. We have a hundred times the firepower that Sorenson has."

"What if they've already killed him?" Jase asked.

"If they wanted him dead, they would've gunned you both down in the water. I'm sure he's safe. Sorenson needs Tack as a bargaining chip," Clutch replied.

I tried not to frown, but whenever Clutch threw in extra words like "I'm sure" or "maybe", he didn't really mean it. A chill ran down my spine. Did he really think Sorenson would kill an innocent man? I swallowed and made a mental note to ask him as soon as we were alone.

When we reached the galley, Clutch stopped, lifted himself on his crutches, and turned to me. "You got this?"

I nodded. "Yeah, we'll be fine."

He started to climb the stairs to the bridge while Jase and I headed inside and down to the crew quarters. I propped my rifle against the wall, and helped Jase strip out of his gear and boots. His fingers were shaking too much to unbutton his shirt, so I took over, gently brushing his fingers away. Once he was down to just his pants and a t-shirt, I opened the utility closet near the shower and kicked on a generator hooked up to a small, tankless water heater Wes had brought on board. Within seconds, warm water came out of the shower. Jase stepped under the spray without bothering to take his pants off and stood, leaning against the stall.

I went to his bunk and sifted through his trunk for a change of clothes.

"You don't need to stick around for me."

"It's okay," I said, putting on a smile. "I've got nothing better to do."

He lowered his head under the spray. "To be honest, I could use some alone time," he said after a bit.

"You sure?"

"Yeah. I'll see you above deck."

I waited for a moment before taking a step back. "Okay, but I'll be here if you need me for anything. Anything at all."

"Thanks. I'll be fine," he said all too quickly with that deadpan tone.

I wasn't surprised that he was closing himself off, but I was still disappointed. I sighed. "I'll leave your clothes on the chair."

With that, I set his clothes down and headed back through the crew quarters. I heard shouting and I ran up the stairs, through the galley, and onto the deck.

One of the scouts was pointing to the river. "The *Lady Amore* is a couple clicks to the south, heading our way!"

Tyler was running down from the bridge, followed closely by several others. Clutch, being so much slower, brought up the rear. I caught up to him quickly. "Sorenson's here," I said, though I knew he'd already figured that out.

"We need to be ready for a fight," he said as he settled into his chair. "Do you have all your gear?"

I winced. "Shit. I left my rifle below decks with Jase's stuff."

"You might need your rifle for this one."

Griz's voice came over the loudspeaker from the bridge. "All scouts report to the deck. Everyone else, please go to barge Number One immediately. This is not a drill."

"I'll be right back," I told Clutch and headed back to the galley, only to have Jase nearly run into me.

"You left this." He handed me my rifle.

"Thanks." I checked my rifle and slung it over my shoulder.

"Is it the riverboat already?"

My body shook with anger. "Yeah," I replied, and I narrowed my eyes. "Let's go."

We ran to meet up with Clutch and Tyler. Griz was just coming down from the bridge. He held an extra rifle and looked around. "I guess none of you need one."

Clutch, who already had his Blaser on his lap, grabbed it. "I'll take a spare."

"Do you see Tack yet?"

I jerked around at the voice to see Deb right behind me.

"You should be in the barge right now," I said.

Deb's lips tightened.

"Or you can stay," I quickly added.

I turned my attention to the incoming riverboat. We were in a shallow part of the river, which meant a few zeds washed up on the island every day that we'd have to dispatch. It also meant that the *Lady Amore* couldn't get very close without hitting the river bottom, which was the first perk I'd seen about being on a boat that didn't go anywhere.

Deb's hand flung over her mouth. "Oh, God."

"What is it?" I asked.

Deb pointed to the riverboat. "*No.*"

Every pair of eyes followed.

There, on the bow of the riverboat, Tack was strung up like its figurehead. He hung limply, a dark clump of bloodied hair hinting that he couldn't be alive.

"No, no, no," Deb cried out and then collapsed.

I fell to a knee and wrapped my arms around her. Clutch, his brow furrowed, looked from Deb to Tack.

"Aw, shit. No," Jase said. The sound of his heart breaking couldn't be missed in those few short words.

"We've got incoming!" someone yelled.

I looked up to see flares being fired from the riverboat. Sorenson and his crew had dozens of flare guns, and they were shooting constantly into the air and directly at the towboat. All but one from the first round of flares missed the *Aurora*. The flare that didn't miss landed on the deck and lit up a tarp covering a raft. Kurt lunged for a fire extinguisher hanging near the stairs.

"To your posts!" Tyler yelled, waving his arm. "They're trying to burn us down! Teams Alpha and Bravo, prepare to launch a counterattack from the boats. Charlie, get those barge bay doors closed now! All other teams, get the civvies to barge Two *now!*"

Over a dozen scouts, including Griz and Tyler, ran toward the ladder to head to the boats. Jase and I were on Clutch's Charlie team, which meant we stayed behind to protect the towboat and its barges.

"You heard the captain," Clutch yelled as he grabbed his crutches. "We need to get the big generators running and those doors closed now."

A young man came up and stood there, looking in shock. He'd arrived with Manny and had just joined Delta team a day ago. His eyes were wide and looked like they were about to burst with tears. "I don't know what to do."

"Grab as many fire extinguishers as you can handle and distribute them," Clutch ordered. A commotion of cattle bellowing and pigs squealing came from barge Four. He turned to Jase. "Jase, take lead of Delta and Echo teams. Cash and I will get the bays closed. Save the barges."

Jase didn't say anything. Stress was instantly replaced by a smooth, hardened sense of purpose on his face. "Come with me!" He took off at a sprint, and the other scout followed.

Ever since Tyler had divided scouts into teams, we'd practiced, but we'd never needed more than three teams on a mission before. Delta and Echo teams were made up of only corporals and civvies. "You sure Jase can handle teams right now?"

"He's a natural," Clutch said. "Besides, he needs this. Let's go." He grabbed his crutches again, and we headed into the galley.

Starting the generators was an easy task...except that black smoke was bleeding through the doorframe leading below decks and exactly where the engines were.

Sixteen

Even with crutches, Clutch kept a good pace. After touching the steel door for heat, I opened it. Smoke dirtied the air and I coughed. Propping the door open with my foot, I tugged off the red bandana I kept tied around my wrist.

"Hold up," Clutch said and grabbed my bandana. He dumped water on it and handed the soaked fabric back to me. "Here. This will help."

"Thanks." I tied the wet bandana around my face while he did the same with a tactical scarf he'd retrieved from a backpack he always carried.

As soon as he had his face covered and his water bottle stashed in his pack again, I entered the short deck. The air wasn't pleasant, but there was no fire here. I looked up to see the heaviest of the smoke hovering around the vents. "The smoke must be coming in through the ventilation system," I said.

"We need to hurry," he said as he hustled around me. Each step of his was staggered as the rest of his body had to overcompensate for legs that didn't play along. He stopped at the door leading to the equipment room that would in turn bring us to the engine room. He touched the door. "It's cool. That's a good sign." He sifted through his backpack and pulled out a flashlight and a flat roll of duct tape. He clicked on the flashlight and taped it onto a crutch. He turned to me. He ran a hand through my hair, and his look softened. "Stay here. I don't know how bad it's going to be in there."

I guffawed and then smacked his hand away. "I should go, and you should stay. I can move faster."

He frowned. "You don't know how to work the generators."

I pulled out my handgun and pressed the flashlight. "Then we go together. If one of us falls, the other will get us out of there."

He turned back to the door. "I knew you were going to say that," he muttered as he opened the door. I shoved my bag against the door to prop it open. Before us was a filthy gray haze, hiding anything and anyone in the large room. Clutch took the lead, moving as quickly as he could, clearly pushing his body beyond what it was ready for.

My eyes burned. Every breath was bitter air. Clutch coughed. I tried to smother my coughs, but it was impossible. I supposed all these doors help protect the well-sealed towboat in case it flooded, but they were a pain in the ass because they retained bad air inside.

For all I knew, the barges were already on fire, in which case we'd be screwed. Even if it was too late to close the bay doors, we still needed water pressure to put out any small fires. We *had* to get the engines running.

When we reached the next door, I could barely see Clutch in front of me. My flashlight couldn't cut more than a foot through the haze. His coughs were about the only way I could stay with him. I grabbed onto his backpack so that we weren't separated. We didn't talk. When I tried, I only coughed more. Tears streamed down my cheeks. A coughing fit nearly had me bent over. Clutch wasn't doing any better, but his crutches seem to bolster our stability.

When he stopped, I bumped into him. Metal clanked, and I found myself yanked forward.

Clutch slammed the door shut behind us. The air was much better—though still not great. The beam from my flashlight cut through the haze to fall on the large engines and the short red generators covering much of the floor.

"Thank God," I said, which brought on a coughing fit.

Clutch headed straight for the engines. He tripped over a cable and fell down, so he pulled himself over to the control box. With my help, he got back to his feet. Using my weight to support him, he flipped a switch. Nothing happened. He frowned and then struggled to the next motor. Again, nothing happened. He stood there while I watched, feeling incredibly helpless. He was right. I knew nothing about engines and generators and mechanical things. After a long moment, he spoke. "Wes must've turned off the fuel line."

"I looked around the room. Where is it?"

"It's got to be in here somewhere. It should have a gas marking or warning on it."

I propped Clutch against an engine while I retrieved his crutches. Then I began my search. With only a flashlight, it was a tedious search. I tripped a couple times over the cables Wes has strewn across the floors.

"I see it," Clutch said.

I hurried over.

Clutch pointed. "It's too tight with my crutches."

I looked down the narrow walkway between two engines and saw a triangular "Warning: Extremely Flammable" sticker. "I'll get it." I had to walk sideways. It must've been a tight fit for Wes, but it was pretty easy for me. I knelt at the sticker. Below it was a round metal crank that looked like it rotated rather than a switch that flipped on and off. I tried to twist it counterclockwise, but it didn't budge. "Jesus, Wes," I muttered, and put all my strength into it.

Slowly, the crank moved an inch before it picked up speed and twisted a full rotation. I leaned back. "Try it now."

I heard an engine start up. "We're good!" Clutch yelled out.

Clutch had the engines running by the time I reached him, and had moved to a box of switches that Wes had built to run all the generators. While each of the generators had its own gas tank, Wes has talked about how he had everything set up to run directly off the towboat's gas tank to save someone having to constantly refill the generators.

As the generators started, the noise in the metal room became deafening, and I winced. Clutch rewet his scarf. He held the bottle to me, and I took a long drink before soaking my thin bandana.

"Ready?" He yelled. "We have to close the bay doors now!"

I could barely hear him but nodded. "Okay!"

He grabbed my hand and put it on his belt. "Don't let go!"

After taking a couple deep breaths, he opened the door, and we headed back into the smoky mechanical bowels of the towboat.

The smoke had faded some—probably due to my propping the door open rather than any fires being put out—making the return trip not quite as terrifying as our first time through. My throat was raw, worse than any sore throat I'd ever had before. The smoke was acid to my already stinging eyes. I closed them and held onto Clutch's belt loops as he clumsily took the steps as quickly as he could.

I had to steady him several times when he lost his footing or didn't get the crutches leveled right on a step. I grabbed my bag, and we burst through the crew quarters and shower room. Finally, when we climbed the stairs and reached the last door, Clutch threw it open, and we tumbled inside the galley. I kicked the door shut, and we both lay there, gasping slightly better air. Who knew how badly the boat or its barges had already burned. Worse, who knew how many zeds the smoke would draw to our location.

"Are you okay?"

I looked up to see Benji standing over us, Frost's Great Dane at his side. Diesel was as tall as the short boy and just as lovable.

"Benji." I propped myself up on an elbow. "What are you doing here? You should be in the barge." The words came out rough, like I was a life-long smoker.

"Grampa told me to stay in here. He heard the engines start and said he was going to close the big doors." He pointed up, referring to the bridge.

"Good," Clutch said and then coughed.

Outside I could hear shouting. I rubbed my eyes with my bandana and climbed to my feet. Through the windows I could see people running across the deck. Several were pulling a large water hose. "I guess I'd better get out there and help."

As I kneeled to help Clutch, the door leading to the deck opened. Three men entered, with their pistols raised. In the middle stood Sorenson.

I froze. Neither Clutch nor I could draw our weapon in time, and with Benji and Diesel in the way, I'd never get a clean shot, anyway. Benji didn't move. Instead, he just stood there between us and them. He was likely frozen with fear, but it didn't matter. He was going to get himself killed.

I reached out to pull the boy behind me.

"Don't move," Sorenson ordered. "And get down on the floor now."

I stopped mid-reach. I could hear Clutch's breaths next to me but was afraid to make eye contact with him. *Don't be a hero,* I mentally said to Clutch. I sat back on my heels, waiting for, hell, I had no idea what I was waiting for.

Benji cocked his head. "Are you here to help us?"

Sorenson frowned while he scrutinized Benji. He waved with his pistol. "Move to the side, kid. We need to get upstairs."

Benji didn't move. Diesel's shoulders bunched aggressively and his hackles rose as he stood next to his small master. A deep growl came from his throat and his teeth were bared.

Sorenson was trying to get upstairs? Why? To get to the bullhorn? To open the bay doors again? I glanced at Clutch, but he had on his poker face. I stayed silent, not willing to take the risk of pissing off Sorenson even more.

Benji patted the dog before looking up at Sorenson. "Are you going to use that gun? Because I don't like guns. They're loud. My mom shot a gun by my ear once. It hurt for a long time."

"Only if I have to, kid," Sorenson replied. "Now, get out of my way. I'm in a bit of a hurry and don't want to hurt you. I need to unhook those barges from this boat."

"Why?" Benji asked.

"Because some of those barges belong to me," he said.

"Why?" the boy asked again.

"Listen, kid. They just do. I need what's on them. Enough."

Benji crossed his arms over his chest. "No." he said sharply. "You look angry. People do bad things when they're angry."

Sorenson could've shoved the boy out of his way. Instead, he took a deep breath and his expression softened. "They hurt my daughter."

"My mom got hurt once."

"It's tough out there, kid. So you see, I have no choice. I need what's on those barges."

Benji shook his head. "Grampa says that people always have choices."

"Well, your gramps is wrong."

"Nuh uh." Benji shook his head even harder. "He's never wrong. He's really smart. He's been around a really long time. He's old. Like you."

Sorenson smirked and one eye narrowed. "Yes, I've been around and seen plenty. I've got to say, I liked the way things used to be a whole lot better than they are now."

"I did, too," Benji said. "I liked school. I had a lot of friends."

Sorenson's lips tightened. After a moment, he held up the hand not holding a pistol. "We're leaving."

"What?" the man at his side asked. "But the barges—"

"We've done enough for one day." Sorenson cut him off with a hard glare. "Everyone's had enough hurt for a lifetime. We're heading back to the *Lady*."

The man who had spoken seemed pissed, while the other looked relieved.

As they backed up to the door, Benji waved. "Bye. Be careful out there."

Sorenson gave Clutch and me one final glance before he turned to leave, like he'd just remembered we were still there.

"Game over, asshole," Jase said from the doorway, his rifle leveled dead-to-rights on Sorenson.

His men jerked around. "You move, I shoot," Frost said as he squeezed inside.

Clutch yanked up his rifle, and I went for my sidearm.

"We were just leaving," Sorenson said slowly.

"Not now, you aren't," Jase replied much more quickly. "Drop your guns."

Sorenson eyed Benji and then spun his pistol and handed it over to Jase. The other two men dropped theirs.

"Benji, are you okay?" Frost asked, cranking his head just enough to see his grandson while keeping his rifle aimed at Sorenson's pals.

"Grampa!" Benji said. He tapped his leg. "C'mon, Diesel!"

The Great Dane's growling dissipated and he trotted alongside the happy-go-lucky boy to the older man, both oblivious to the showdown of firepower under way. Sorenson watched as the pair bounded past him.

"Did they hurt you, son?" Frost asked, tugging Benji against him.

"I'm fine, Grampa," he giggled. "No one hurt me." He pointed to Sorenson. "He's just sad because his daughter was hurt, that's all. He wasn't going to hurt me."

I took a big breath and leaned into Clutch, who was breathing just as heavily. He knew as well as I did that the only reason we were still alive was because of a boy. A boy with Down Syndrome just proved that a little bit of kindness was sometimes more powerful than all the brute force and guns in the world.

PART FIVE
SLOTH

THE FOURTH DEADLY SIN

Seventeen

We held Tack's funeral the following morning.

Griz had used his Ranger skills and somehow managed to climb onto the riverboat and cut down Tack's body sometime during the attack without getting caught. Tack had been executed—shot in the head. That he hadn't been beaten was little consolation to any of us.

Deb refused to leave Tack after he was brought on board. When I stopped by to offer my condolences while she was preparing his body, she seemed oblivious, completely lost in her own world. By morning, she'd regained her composure and now stood strong, her blotchy cheeks and swollen red eyes the only outward signs of her mourning.

Even Manny and his people joined all of Camp Fox on the towboat's deck, just off the back, where the water was deepest. Frost and Wes had spent the night building a heavy casket out of wood leftover from pallets and various metal parts found on the barges so that Tack would find permanent peace at the bottom of the river.

Griz led the service. He and Tack had been best friends, and Griz had to stop several times during his speech to take a deep breath before continuing. After he recited a prayer, he asked everyone to share a story.

No one spoke. Then, after a long minute, Tyler stepped up and told everyone about Tack, the skinny new recruit on his team who wasn't expected to make it a week. He ended by finally sharing Tack's real name. Corporal Theodore Nugent. Yeah, the poor guy was seriously named after a rock star. No wonder he'd always gone by his nickname. We all laughed. Even Deb cracked a smile, though it was still a sad expression.

After Tyler, the stories came easily. Some were short like Frost's straightforward proclamation, "I'd have been proud to call him my son." Others, like Benji's, took fifteen minutes or more. For his story, the young boy went into detail about how Tack had shown up with a foam football for his birthday. Benji went so far as to run back to the barge, with Diesel at his heels, to reclaim the purple ball so we could all see the special present.

Jase talked of the time Tack had gotten him drunk for the first time in his life, and they'd tried to catch a possum with their bare hands. Jase showed us the scar on his hand that I'd always thought bore a striking resemblance to sharp teeth marks.

Clutch and I talked about the time the three of us ran through Chow Town and, by some miracle, managed not to become dinner for five thousand or so zeds.

The service lasted for hours, and we took snack breaks. Everyone was there except for the scouts on duty, but Tyler had instituted one-hour rotations to ensure everyone had a chance to say good-bye while remaining on full alert for herds and the *Lady Amore*.

We cried and we laughed as we celebrated Tack's life. When everyone had finished, Griz turned to Deb. She was the only one who had known Tack well and hadn't spoken yet. "Would you like to say anything?" he asked softly.

She looked across the faces and then touched Tack's casket. "I'm carrying his baby."

A lengthy pause followed. There was nothing that could be said after that. Finally, eight volunteers slid the weighted casket onto a makeshift ramp of two-by-fours. "Lord, grant Tack peace," Griz said before shoving the casket off.

We all watched from the edge of the deck as the casket splashed into the water. It floated for only a second before it descended into the darkness. Bubbles came to the surface, the final glimpse we had of Tack, aka Ted Nugent, a Corporal in the United States National Guard.

I looked up at the zeds surrounding the *Aurora*. There were only a few dozen, having been drawn in by the dark smoke. A few tried to walk through the water and were carried away by the current. Most had a basic sense of preservation and simply stood on the bridge over the river, swaying from side to side as they watched. The herds weren't here yet. Kurt's last scouting run put them out several days. The closest herd had stopped at a large river town, buying us time. If we didn't clear the zeds now watching the camp, they'd surely draw the attention of a herd.

But that wasn't our biggest problem.

The *Lady Amore* sat in the water about a mile south of us, an ominous reminder that we had her beloved captain locked up below decks. The riverboat hadn't shown any aggression since the attack. It simply waited, likely for its missing captain.

"All right," Tyler said. "We've got a lot of cleanup to do. Unless you've volunteered for a cleanup job, everyone stays in barge Number One until the zeds move on. Got it?"

People complained and dragged their feet as they headed back toward the barges.

"We're not doing this for fun," Tyler yelled out. "We're doing this to save lives."

His words cooled down the grumbling a bit, but people still weren't thrilled about being cooped up in a dusty, steel barge.

The *Aurora* was in rough shape. The deck of the boat, with its heavily shellacked wood, was charred in several places. Only one flare had burned through the deck and into the equipment room, which accounted for most of the smoke we'd come across yesterday.

The deck had been repaired, but barge Four, which had taken the brunt of the damage, was a different story. A flare had landed on hay bales, which had lit a fire. Our livestock had been decimated. No animals survived. Most of the animals had died from smoke inhalation, and the cooks were working non-stop to save what meat they could.

Still, we'd been counting on eggs for our breakfasts. Several cattle and hogs had been pregnant, and all of them died in the fire. Finding livestock after the outbreak was tough. It had taken us over six months to pull together the thirty head and several dozen chickens. To replenish our stock would take a miracle. It would take a bigger miracle to hunt and fish enough meat until we could rebuild our livestock.

At least no one had died from the black fumes, although Clutch and I had both suffered from killer headaches all night. We'd gone through a pot of coffee this morning, and it had only taken the edge off our throbbing headaches.

I pulled myself to my feet. "Want to go bug Jase with me before we join the cleanup crews?" I asked Clutch.

He gave a crooked grin. "Hell, yes."

I wheeled him toward the galley, giving him a twirl when we reached the door. He pulled himself up on his crutches, and we headed inside and went below decks. When we reached the equipment room, Clutch called out before he walked through the door. "Hey, Jase, coming in."

Jase waved at us, without taking his rifle off his prisoners. "Hey guys!" He was currently on guard watch over the three prisoners from the *Lady Amore*. The temporary brig was in the towboat's equipment room and was in no way set up to hold prisoners. It wasn't the ideal location, but we figured it would be more difficult to escape than from any barge near civvies. Rather than bars, the prisoners were all handcuffed to chains that had been wrapped around thick pipes. It had a medieval feel to it, but we had to make do with what we had.

Clutch stepped unsteadily down the few steps, using his crutches and upper body strength for support. Since his back injury, his upper body was stronger than it'd ever been to make up for the lack of strength in his legs. He'd also lost weight, making the contrast in muscles all the more obvious. I liked the look of his biceps. His tattoos wrapped around his arms in a sensual way. But his legs were too thin from lack of use, and I worried about how long it would take for him to rebuild muscle.

Jase stood and offered the box he'd been sitting on to Clutch. "How'd the rest of the funeral go?" he asked.

"It was nice," Clutch said as he took a seat.

"Griz did a really good job. The stories were great," I added. We'd worked alongside Tack for several months. When I'd heard the stories from the other residents, I'd realized just how many lives the man who'd rarely spoken had touched. He had truly been an example of actions speaking louder than words. I hated that one more good person had been unfairly stolen from the world.

I turned to Sorenson, who sat on the floor, his wrists cuffed in front of him. His two men sat next to him, one on each side. Their chains were long enough to allow some mobility so that they could reach the single bucket that served as their toilet.

They all watched us. Sorenson with a blank look, the man to his right glowered with disdain, and the man to his left simply looked exhausted. My jaw tightened, and I crossed my arms over my chest. "You killed a good man. A man who would never hurt an innocent."

Sorenson blinked a couple times, but his gaze didn't connect with mine. It was distant, dull. "I lost my daughter yesterday."

"There's no one left alive who hasn't lost someone they love," I said.

Sorenson's gaze sharpened as his brows furrowed. "When I left Nikki with the *Aurora*, she was alive and vibrant. When I watched those two men bring her back," he eyed Jase, "She-she was gone."

"It was an accident," Jase said. "I'm sure Tack would've told you that."

"I am sorry about your man. When I saw what had happened to Nikki, I couldn't bear it."

"And so you killed an innocent man," Clutch said, anger dripping from each word.

Sorenson gulped, frowned, lowered his head, and then shook his head. "It doesn't matter now. I can't bring him back any more than I can bring my little Nikki back."

"It does matter," I said. "Nikki slipped and fell. It was an accident."

"She's telling the truth," Clutch added.

"What happened to your daughter sucks, but it was an accident. What *you* did was murder," Jase said.

Sorenson scowled. "Is there even such a thing as murder anymore? We kill those who used to be family and friends every day, just because they get sick. Who are we to judge what constitutes murder and what doesn't?"

I shook my head. "Tack wasn't a zed. He was a young man who'd done nothing except help return your daughter's body to you."

Sorenson climbed to his feet and backed up several steps. "She was everything to me. Everything I'd done, taking passengers onto the riverboat, all of that was for her. She was the only reason I helped anyone." He picked up the now-lax chain and held it in his hands. He looked up. As long seconds passed, his distant gaze narrowed with intent. "I have nothing without her. Nothing!"

In a sudden rush, he wrapped the chain around his neck and sprinted forward.

I lunged to stop him, but wasn't fast enough. When the chain was pulled tight, Sorenson was yanked back, and he collapsed onto the floor.

"Captain! No!" His men each moved to kneel by him. One pulled the chain from around Sorenson's neck while the other watched as the man on the floor convulsed. I took a single step closer but didn't get within reaching distance of the prisoners. Sorenson's eyes were wide as he fought for breath that wouldn't come. His body shuddered on the floor. After a minute or two, his body became still and his hands fell.

"Is he—?" I asked, afraid to voice the word aloud.

"He's dead," one of his men said without looking up.

"His windpipe was crushed," Clutch said quietly at my side. "There was nothing anyone could do."

I stared at the now-slack chain and then at Jase and Clutch. By their wide eyes, they were as shocked as I was. I swallowed. "Shit."

We were going to have a war on our hands.

———

"Cash? You around here somewhere?" Clutch's voice cut through the fog.

"Over here," I answered.

"Where's here?"

"At the stern," I said.

I could hear footsteps, then a dark shape morphed into Clutch. He took a seat on the deck and set his weapon down next to him. He'd swapped his wheelchair and crutches for a cane yesterday. The swelling on his spine had finally subsided enough that he had decent control over his legs again. He couldn't jog, but at least he could put one foot in front of another. I'd been terrified that he'd never reach this point, which would've killed his spirit.

"There's not much I can do in this fog," I said. "I can't see five feet in front of me. I feel like I'm just sitting on my ass instead of being on duty."

"At least if we can't see them, then the zeds can't see us. Besides, we can hear better than they can." He handed me a thermos.

"Thanks." I took a sip of the steaming tea and burned my tongue. I winced and screwed the cap back on.

Since Clutch had dropped off his wheelchair with Doc, his mood had improved a hundred-fold. While I still believed he suffered from depression—and he clearly suffered from PTSD—it was nice to see him not staring off blankly into the unknown quite as often.

"This fog could save us," he said. "The zeds may move on since they can't see us."

Until the zeds left, there wasn't much we could do besides quietly get the *Aurora* back into shape. It was too foggy to go ashore or even down the river on any scouting runs. We'd used up a ton of fuel putting out fires and making repairs. The herds would be passing through any day now, so we couldn't go in search of any livestock. Thank God we still had the grain, though the lack of complete protein this winter would be hard.

"Hopefully we don't have to worry about the *Lady Amore* any time soon," I said. Immediately after Sorenson's death, Tyler had organized a truce with Sorenson's men. He'd offered them full pardons in exchange for no more attacks. He'd even offered another chance at the trade agreement, which they'd quickly accepted. However, many of us weren't nearly as confident as Tyler was that they wouldn't seek revenge or try to steal from us again. The riverboat had left minutes after we'd returned Sorenson's body back along with his two men, and the boat hadn't returned.

"I still think we should've gone in and hit them hard. They know they're outgunned and they wouldn't try something stupid again," Clutch said. "It all depends on Sorenson's replacement. They could be smart and know the value of working together, or they could be idiots. We'll have to stay on our toes until we know. It's too bad Sorenson killed himself. He was easy to figure out. He was a straight shooter, except that he let his heart get in the way. Whoever replaces him could be more of a challenge."

I nodded and then smiled. "At least we have his speedboat now. I'm looking forward to going for a ride." Tyler had given Sorenson's men one of our deck boats in a "trade" for their speedboat. He wasn't about to let them leave with our .30 cal again.

A light breeze blew through, and I shivered. My clothes were damp from the fog and offered little warmth. I held the thermos against me. "I need to start wearing a jacket."

"Here," Clutch said as he wrapped an arm around me.

I leaned into him, savoring his warmth and the closeness. We sat and watched as the sun burned through the fog. A low haze sat just above the water, but I could see the land over it.

"Look." I pointed to the riverbank. "The zeds have cleared out on the east side. You're right. They're leaving."

Clutch twisted his neck to take in the landscape. "Yeah, but they're still on the bridge and on the west side."

"Hopefully just one more day of us laying low and they'll leave like the others."

"Hey guys," Wes said through a yawn as he approached.

"Mornin'," I said, climbing to my feet.

Wes took a seat on the deck behind the rail where I'd been sitting. The boat was angled in the water in a way that allowed us to watch the bridge and see land from every direction without being seen by the zeds. "Man, I'd rather still be asleep."

"That's all everyone does anymore," Clutch grumbled. He used his cane to push himself to his feet and looked at me. "Feel up to some sparring?"

"You bet." I turned to Wes. "Don't have too much fun."

He scowled, and I headed off with Clutch.

Clutch had a point. Once the critical repairs had been made to the *Aurora*, there was little left that could be done quietly. It didn't take more than a couple days of relative safety for laziness to set in. Hell, if I didn't have Clutch's persistence at having me spar with him and Jase's contagious energy, I'd be heading back to bed right now out of boredom.

As we walked across the deck, I watched Clutch's legs as his stride nearly matched mine. "You're healing really fast now. I can already tell a huge difference from yesterday."

"Doc said that healing would happen in bursts. All I can tell you is that it can't happen soon enough. I'm sick and tired of being a cripple."

I rolled my eyes, because Clutch may be a lot of things, but he was no cripple. He proved it during our sparring session in the towboat's engine room. Even though his legs were weak, his upper body strength more than made up for it. I almost got in a high kick once, but he'd taken me down with him. I imagined it would always be that way: Clutch the master, me the student. He had too many more years of experience.

After a day of doing little, as the sun began to set, we headed to the commons area in Barge Two to meet Jase for dinner. The area was already filled with people. I stepped into the line while Clutch spoke with Tyler. I looked for Jase, but he wasn't at our usual spot on the floor yet.

I grabbed a tray, and Vicki, Fox's best cook, slid chunks of white meat onto my tray.

My eyes narrowed. "Fish?"

Vicki nodded. "They finished the nets this morning and fished off the south end of the island so the zeds wouldn't see. Fish for everyone tonight!"

I grinned. "Awesome."

Normally, the fishermen caught no more than a dozen fish using fishing poles. They figured the zeds rotting in the shallow waters scared them off. The livestock from the fire was being dehydrated for the winter, so we'd been living on canned meat, beans, and grain. As I worked my way through line, I noticed everyone was in a better mood. The fresh fish, the zeds starting to disappear, and the repairs to the *Aurora* relatively complete gave everyone hope.

I sat down on the floor and dug into the fish.

Jase sat down a minute later with his food. "What kind of fish is this?" he asked.

I shrugged.

"It's catfish," Frost said as he and Benji ate a few feet away from us. Diesel had his head buried in a bowl of dog kibble.

The fish suddenly went down like a rock. "Catfish?"

"Wait," Jase said. "Isn't catfish a bottom feeder?"

"Yes, why?" Frost said.

Jase's eyes widened as he looked at me. "Didn't anyone tell the cooks?"

"Tell them what?" Frost asked.

I dropped my fork. "Bottom feeders are tainted from feeding on zeds. Sorenson said they'd lost a crew member to bad catfish."

Frost grabbed Benji's hand that held a fork full of white meat, but the boy had already cleaned much of his plate.

"Maybe these fish are okay," Jase said to the pair before giving me an *oh-shit* look.

We jumped to our feet at the same time.

"Where are you going?" Clutch asked as Jase and I ran past.

"To warn Vicki," Jase said.

I took the stairs two at a time to reach the kitchen faster. Halfway up the second flight, a stomach cramp doubled me over.

I felt Jase's hand on my cheek. "Cash, are you okay?"

I clenched my teeth as I grabbed my stomach. "Bad fish."

Eighteen

The day was a horrifying blur of dry heaves, chills, high fever, and bizarre dreams. All around me, people moaned and cried. They lay in bed, the slightest move causing them to retch.

Jase and Clutch took turns at my bedside. They helped me and the others without rest. Since neither had eaten the catfish, they hadn't gotten sick. They were in the minority. Thirty-three residents had eaten the tainted meat. They kept all of us in barge Number One and had opened the bay door to let in fresh air.

By night, I finally regained some semblance of myself. I felt like I had one foot solidly in the grave, but I'd lived to see another day. Others weren't so fortunate. I'd seen Mrs. Corrington covered with a sheet and carried out. What a miserable way to die.

Clutch squeezed water from a rag into my mouth. The other healthy people, like Jase and him, constantly moved about, checking on the sick. Meanwhile, others filled in as scouts above deck to keep watch for the herds or any signs of trouble from the riverboat. Deb was the only person who hadn't eaten the fish that Tyler wouldn't allow to help. Her pregnancy had come to represent the hope of Camp Fox. Tyler didn't want her around anything that could pose a risk to her pregnancy. After Tyler's adamant orders, she'd reluctantly stayed in the crew quarters on the towboat.

I rolled my head to see Jase still with Benji, who was up to eating crackers already. That kid had a cast iron stomach. If only I'd remembered to tell the cooks what Sorenson had said about the fish, then none of this would've happened. I felt so stupid, but was too weak to stay angry at myself. No one had remembered to tell the cooks. Jase blamed himself, and I'd seen Tyler's face when he walked through. He blamed himself the hardest of all.

Twenty-four hours later, I could finally hold down small amounts of water, and Clutch was relentless at sponging drops into my mouth every couple minutes.

The poor man looked utterly exhausted, with dark circles and bags under his bloodshot eyes. I licked my chapped lips. Sometimes, a pessimistic devil sitting in my soul would make me wonder if all of this running and work was in vain, that all we were doing was delaying our inevitable doom.

I lifted my fingers, though they weighed a ton, and touched his hand that was holding the rag. "You should get some rest."

"I'm fine," he said rather tersely, making it clear he wasn't going anywhere.

"Can't believe I ate catfish," I said on an exhale.

He shook his head and dribbled more water into my mouth. "You couldn't have known."

I closed my eyes.

"You're going to get better," he said. "You don't give up. That's why I brought you with me to my farm at the outbreak. I knew you were a fighter."

When I reopened my eyes, I saw Clutch watching me, taking his eyes off me only to soak the rag again. Sitting there, his broad shoulders cast a shadow over me. His quiet strength showed through his gaze. When he looked at me, I always knew I'd be safe.

I grinned, weakly. "You're an oak."

His confused expression tightened into a look of consternation. He pressed a hand against my forehead, and I treasured his touch.

I needed him to know the truth. "I love you," I said, but my words slurred. My eyes grew heavy.

"What's wrong?" Jase asked, sounding distant.

"Get Doc. She's got a fever."

"Mary Corrington had a fever right before—"

"I know. Get Doc *now*."

PART SIX
GREED

THE FIFTH DEADLY SIN

NINETEEN

Lucky for me, I was both younger and healthier than Mrs. Corrington. My fever of one-hundred-four broke the following morning, but it took me an entire day before I could stand without getting a nosebleed, and another day after that before I could handle a flight of stairs without getting light-headed.

I woke up early in the morning, quietly climbed out of my bunk, and crept past Clutch. He'd been able to move down to the crew quarters once he had no longer needed his wheelchair. Being careful not to wake him, I grabbed my boots, clothes, and gear and headed up to the deck. I stopped in the shower room to finish dressing. Since the catfish incident, I'd lost a few pounds and had to buckle my belt a full notch tighter. Not that I'd had any fat on me before, which meant my body had burned through muscle, and, Christ, I was feeling it.

That was just one of the little things that had changed after the outbreak: there simply weren't overweight people anymore. Without proper food and medical care, things like food poisoning or dysentery were even more dangerous than ever. Everyone who'd gotten sick from the catfish had a gaunt look. At least everyone who'd survived. We'd lost four to bad catfish.

I took a seat on a bench and inhaled deeply the smell of fresh coffee as it finished brewing. Moments later, I poured myself a small cup and headed outside. I walked slowly so I wouldn't slip on the deck still slick with frost. The coffee steamed, and my breath made small puffs in the morning air.

I slurped the coffee, holding the warm cup in both hands, and tried not to shiver. The warm sun was rising, and its light glistened on the wet deck. I headed to my usual spot that overlooked the open river. A light morning fog blanketed the water. An eagle soared above the tree line. It was beautiful, serene. And the best part? No zeds. They'd finally moved off while I'd been sick.

I really thought I wasn't going to make it. I'd never felt so miserable in my life. Thankfully, I didn't remember much of the past couple days. Only Clutch's gentle touch and him never leaving my side.

I set down my coffee and started my yoga routine. Sometime during Downward Facing Dog, Clutch bent over and looked at me.

"Mornin'," I said with a smile.

He stood back up. "I called your name three times."

"You did? Oh. I guess I was in my zone."

"It's good to see you getting back into a routine," he said.

As I changed position, I saw him looking out over the river.

"I feel fine, other than the fact that my body thinks it was in bed for a month instead of days. I can promise you that I'd rather starve than eat catfish ever again."

"You had me worried there for a while," Clutch said.

I stopped and turned to find him watching me with a strange intensity, his eyes full of emotion. Then he quickly turned away. Disappointment panged in my heart. "Well, moving around in the fresh air and stretching has helped as much as anything. It's nice that the zeds left so I can do yoga outside rather than in the dark, stuffy boat."

"We still have to be careful. Yesterday, Jase saw a couple small groups still in the area. There." He pointed. "And there."

I squinted and couldn't find them, but my vision had never been as good as Jase's. "As long as they're not fixated on the *Aurora*, they shouldn't draw any interest of the herds." I stood up and grabbed my coffee.

He took in a deep breath. "Kurt returned from another Jet Ski trip to the north. He thinks the first herd will pass through this area by tomorrow. Tyler wants all boats and a couple Humvees out today to search the area for anything we can possibly grab before the herds arrive. Fuel, food, chickens, anything. We don't know how long we'll have to lay low once they arrive."

I clapped my hands. "I'm ready."

He smirked. "Feeling cooped up?"

"Feeling *very* cooped up."

"Sounds like exactly how I felt being stuck in that wheelchair."

"You were a bit grumpy," I teased.

"Speaking of grumpy, how about you go wake up Jase so we can head out."

I lowered my arms from my stretch. "Want to play rock-paper-scissors for the honor?" By honor, I meant who had to deal with getting a pillow —or worse—thrown at them by a teenager whose one last pleasure he'd held onto from pre-outbreak days was sleeping in late whenever he could. Today was supposed to be one of those days.

Clutch shook his head. "Hell, no. I had to wake him last time. It's your turn."

I scrunched my nose at him and then tossed him my empty cup. "Fine. Wish me luck."

As I trudged toward to the galley, I could hear Clutch chuckling.

When I reached Jase's bed, I grabbed the spear lying next to his cot and took a step back. With four feet of space between us, I gently poked at the pile of blankets with the flat end of the spear. A grumble emerged, and the blankets wiggled. "Go away."

"Wakey, wakey, eggs and bakey," I said softly in a singsong voice.

I grinned when he grumbled louder and rolled over, taking the blankets with him and leaving his back exposed. "Lemme sleep."

Too easy, I thought to myself. I ran the dull wood bottom of the spear up his spine, and the insanely ticklish teenager jerked up.

He whipped around and went to throw his pillow but held onto it, which was a good thing. It wouldn't have taken much to land me flat on my ass.

I laughed.

He scowled and hugged his pillow. "Not cool."

I laughed. "Rise and shine. We've got a run this morning."

I think he might have actually growled at me, but he did kick his blankets away and sat up. I handed him his spear and he plucked it back.

"I'll see you in the galley," I said, still chuckling, and left him rubbing his eyes.

An hour later, after Jase had time to ingest caffeine and some breakfast, he was back to his usual self. The boats had already left on their scouting runs. We were one of the two teams assigned to make a land run. Jase, Clutch, and I took one Humvee, while Griz and two other scouts took another.

Our Humvee was the easiest to spot out of all Camp Fox's Humvees. It had a coyote head painted on the hood and front doors, thanks to Jase. He'd dubbed our team the Charlie Coyotes and the name had stuck. Luckily, only one zed still lingered around our vehicles this morning. Jase easily dispatched it, and we headed out for a day of adventure.

The plan was that we'd drive east and Griz's team would drive west, since it was far too risky to drive north. We'd check out rural gas stations and farms and meet at the boat ramp in four hours. If any of us succeeded in finding fuel, the six of us would bring a fuel truck with a Humvee lead vehicle back to the places to fill up. Getting the diesel to the ramp was the easy part. Getting the diesel onto the *Aurora* would be a bit more complicated since we had to move it in fifty-five-gallon drums on pontoons.

Jase took his favorite position manning the .30 cal on the back of Charlie team's Humvee. He had a warm leather coat on to fight the late fall chill in the air. I drove. Clutch was by far a better driver, but since his legs were still healing, he rode shotgun.

I drove slowly, even though we had a lot of ground to cover. We had to be careful to avoid the river towns that dotted the river. The good thing with towns every ten miles or so was that zeds tended to group together and hover around populated areas rather than in the fields and around farms. The bad thing was that we couldn't find a single rural gas station clear of zeds. "I guess the fuel will have to wait until after the migration," I said.

"Let's see what else we can find," Clutch said. "Try that gravel road."

We searched farms for the next three hours, finding only a few dozen cans of food, which we tossed into duffle bags. As I turned off a gravel road and onto the winding river highway, I hit the brakes. "Shit. You see that?"

"They're not biters," Jase called out from above. "What's the plan?"

A group of ragged survivors were standing near a vehicle in the intersection. The van hadn't been there when we'd passed through the area a few hours earlier. Steam pouring out of the open hood gave hint at why it was there now.

It was a group of mostly women, and they looked in rough shape. A man stood by the hood. A hunched-back elderly woman stood in the middle of the road, staring off into the distance. A teenaged girl stood near a little girl playing hopscotch. A pale woman lay against the van. They had crowbars and spears, but no one seemed to be carrying rifles or pistols. Still, it could have been a setup.

Another man walked around from the other side of the van, saw us, and started waving wildly.

Jase kneeled to our eye level. "They've seen us."

"Hold on," Clutch said before he picked up the radio. "Charlie calling Alpha."

A couple seconds later, Griz's voice came on the radio. *"Alpha here. Report."*

"We have a sit rep. Charlie has come across at least six survivors ten clicks straight east of the RP."

"Are they raiders?"

"Negative. Just civvies. Looks like their vehicle broke down."

"Alpha is heading your way. Do you want to wait for backup?"

Clutch looked at me, Jase, and then back at the group. "Negative. We're going to check it out."

"Roger. We're on our way."

He hung up the radio. "Here's the plan. We'll pull up close. If anything throws off a red flag, we're out of there. We all stay with the Humvee. Only if we're absolutely sure they're safe, Cash and I will get out. Jase, you stay behind the .30 no matter what happens. You never, ever leave the .30, got it?"

"Yes," we both replied at the same time. We'd been together for enough months that we understood one another.

Clutch checked his rifle one more time. "Okay, Cash, take us in nice and slow."

As we approached, the man quit waving and stood between us and the woman propped against the van. The little girl stopped playing her game and jogged over to stand by the man. The other man, the one who'd been standing behind the hood, grabbed the teenaged girl and pulled her to him.

Clutch rolled his window down.

I pulled up alongside the van and stopped, but left the engine running.

The craggy old woman limped over to us first. Her hands were gnarled with arthritis that looked like it'd taken over much of her body. How she'd survived this long was beyond me.

"I need you all to stay at least four feet back," Clutch ordered.

Her gray eyebrows rose, but then she stopped and smiled warmly. "Oh, I'm not any danger to you, I promise. I knew God would answer my prayers. He's never let me down yet. He's really outdone himself this time, sending one of those big Army trucks and strapping, able-bodied young men," she said, her voice crackly. She noticed me and touched her chest. "Oh my. Young men and woman. Well, God bless you for coming. Your timing couldn't have been better. You see, we've gotten ourselves into a pickle." She motioned her people. "We've been on the road for days, only stopping for gas and rest breaks, and I'm afraid we overworked our poor van. Praise the lord for sending you to our rescue."

"Save your prayers, lady. God didn't send us," Clutch said with a grumble. "It was just luck we happened to be passing through."

She chuckled. "Well, you can call it what you like. It's all the same. You're here now. I can't tell you how relieved we are to see you. I'm Margaret Fielding, but you can call me Maggie."

Clutch nodded at her group. "Nice to meet you, Maggie. I'm Sergeant Seibert from Camp Fox. Where are you from and where are you headed?"

"Well, you get straight to business, don't you, young man? I can understand, with all those infected folks out there. We were staying at the Wisconsin Dells, but things went downhill. We were planning to keep driving until we found another group of God-fearing folks like your-selves. In fact, you're the first people we've seen since we've left. I must admit, when our van broke down, my faith was tested. But as soon as I saw your truck, I knew everything would turn out fine."

Clutch didn't speak for a long moment while he scowled at Maggie while she continued chattering away. When he finally spoke, he pointed to the pale woman sitting against the van, and interrupted. "What's wrong with her? Is she bit?"

Maggie turned. "Thank goodness, no. When we ran, Brenda cut herself on some old tin, and I'm afraid it's become infected and she's caught herself a bit of a fever. We've cleaned it as much as we could, but we don't have any bandages or medicine. I don't suppose you happen to have anything that can help her?"

After a moment, he took in a deep breath and grabbed our first aid kit. "I'll take a look."

"Oh, thank you," Maggie said, clasping her hands together.

I narrowed my eyes suspiciously at him, but he didn't make eye contact. He propped his rifle on his seat, unsnapped his holster, swung open the door, and stepped out with his cane in one hand and the kit in the other.

I put the Humvee in Park, grabbed my rifle and stepped out. I only took a few steps and propped my rifle on the hood so that I could get behind the wheel quickly while also keeping a clear view of Clutch and the refugees. I threw a quick glance at Jase to see he had the .30 cal leveled on the refugees.

As Maggie hobbled next to Clutch, she commented, "You don't get around much better than I do."

I smirked when Clutch grunted in response. He didn't like his faults being pointed out. I could only imagine how much it annoyed him to be compared to a little old lady.

As Clutch approached the injured woman on the ground, he nodded toward the man near her who had the young girl pressed tight against his leg. "I need you to take a step back."

The man didn't move. "She's my wife."

"It's all right, Don," Maggie said. "He's here to help Brenda. Let him help."

Keeping a watchful eye on Clutch, Don took a tentative step back, holding who I assumed to be his daughter against him. Clutch went down on his knees before the woman. "I need to take a look. I'm going to have to lift your shirt."

The woman—Brenda—was pale and sweaty. She was clearly in pain, every movement stiff. With a small nod, she let her hand fall to the side, giving Clutch access. Her husband stood tensely to the side, his eyes darting from Clutch to Maggie and back to Clutch.

Clutch gingerly lifted her stained shirt and then quickly dropped it, covering his nose. He winced at me before turning back to the woman.

He pulled out a small syringe from the first aid kit. "This will help with the pain," he said just before injecting it into her thigh. After a moment, her features relaxed and she lay there limply. She looked almost peaceful.

He closed up the kit and pushed himself to his feet, using his cane for support, and faced Don. "I gave her some morphine for the pain."

"Thank you," Don replied.

As Clutch stepped away from the woman, Don's eyes widened. He shoved his girl behind him and he grabbed Clutch's arm. "What are you doing? You have to help her! She needs antibiotics!"

Clutch looked down at the hand on his arm and then pulled away. "There's nothing I can do for your wife. And back the fuck off."

The man glared for a moment before lowering his head. "But Brenda...she needs help."

"I can't help her," Clutch said more softly this time. "It's too late. She has gangrene, and it's too far advanced for anything to help. The morphine will ease her pain for a bit, but there's nothing else I can do. Any supplies we use would be wasted."

"Wha-what?" Don asked, seemingly unable to process Clutch's words.

Clutch said it more bluntly than I would've, but he'd never been one for beating around the bush. He gave me a hooded, tight look as he set the first aid kit back in the Humvee.

The man's bottom lip quivered. The girl hugging him looked up and whimpered. "What's he saying, Daddy?"

"There must be something that you can do," Maggie said, wringing her hands. "It was only a cut."

"Wait!" The man called out. "Maggie's right. There's got to be something you can do. You can't leave her like this!"

His daughter started to cry. Big tears rolled down her cheeks as she clung to his leg.

Clutch grabbed his rifle and shook his head. "There isn't." He turned away. "I'm sorry."

The second Humvee pulled up from the other side, and Griz jumped out.

"They're with us," I told Maggie, though it should've been obvious.

"You can't leave us like this. You've got to help my wife, damn it!" Don cried out.

Clutch ignored Don's pleas and curses, instead focusing on Maggie. "Tell me about what happened at the Dells."

She frowned at the change in subject, watched Don and Brenda for another moment, and finally nodded and inhaled deeply. "I don't understand where they're coming from, but there's so many of them, and they seem to be coming from everywhere. We were so well hidden, we were so far from any town, but they still found us. We lost so many." Her gaze fell and she shook her head slowly from side to side. "Too many."

Griz came walking over, holding his rifle.

Maggie lifted her head, looked at Griz funny, and then broke out into a wide smile. "My, I haven't seen a black man in months, and such a fine-looking young man you are."

Griz raised a brow in amusement.

Clutch spoke first. "How far behind you are the herds, Maggie?"

"Oh," she stammered and fidgeted. "They're not far. Not far at all."

"Exactly how far is that?"

Maggie didn't answer.

Griz motioned to Clutch. They walked around to my side of the Humvee.

"We don't have time for this," Griz said. "Did you find any diesel?"

Clutch shook his head. "Nothing we could get to. You?"

Griz scowled. "It's going to get hard fast without any power on the boat."

"You heard the lady," Clutch said. "We can't keep looking. The herds are nearly here."

"I know," Griz said. "We need to be below decks and silent by the time they show up. It's getting risky staying out here."

Clutch frowned. "What do we do about these folks? We have the room, but we don't have the food. Not since the livestock was destroyed. We can't leave them here. They'd get slaughtered."

Griz pointed to the west. "There's a farm a few miles straight west of here. We found a black SUV in the driveway that runs. You can't miss it. I can take one of them to go get it. That'll help them get some distance between them and the herds."

"Until they run out of gas," Clutch said. "If we don't take them in, they're zed bait."

Griz gave him a knowing look. "They could distract the herds from us."

My heart pounded. Even though my brain was telling me the same thing, my gut was screaming at me at how wrong this felt.

Clutch gave me a look and his features softened. "We take them with us. It's only six—well, five—extra mouths to feed."

Griz looked relieved but then frowned as he looked at the injured woman. "She bit?"

Clutch gave a slow shake of his head. "Gangrene."

Griz grimaced. "We came across a vet clinic this morning. We have the supplies on board to give her peace. It's the only thing we can offer her."

"I'm not sure her husband and daughter would agree to that," I chimed in. Without modern medicine, people often died horrible, painful deaths from infections. Euthanasia was one of the few things we could offer the doomed, and vet clinics offered plenty of the drug guaranteed to bring painless death.

"Then we give them the choice. They can either stay here with her or come with us," Griz said. "Gangrene isn't contagious, but we can't risk bringing any new sources of infection onto the *Aurora* in case she's got more than a case of gangrene. Not with how many are just recovering now."

Clutch stiffened and snapped around as Don hurried toward the Humvee.

"Stand back," he ordered Don.

Don kept walking toward us. "I heard what you said. You can't leave Brenda behind. You don't know her. She's strong. She'll recover."

"She has gangrene," Clutch said simply, as though that answered everything.

"She may also have contracted a secondary infection that could potentially spread. We can't risk it," Griz added. "Now, please step back."

The man's features morphed from desperation to anger. "So you're going to leave her here to die all alone in the middle of the road? What kind of sick monsters are you?" His fists clenched and he rushed Griz and Clutch.

Griz hit him in the stomach with the butt of his rifle just as Don reached them. "Get on the ground! Face down and arms stretched out!"

His daughter screamed, and the teenager rushed over and grabbed her to keep her from running to Don.

"Keep her quiet," Clutch snapped.

"Don't hurt my little girl!" Don cried out.

"Please," Maggie limped forward. "Let's all take a moment and talk. Don's just worried about Brenda. He doesn't mean anything by it. We've all been through a lot lately."

"She's going to be dead soon," Clutch said. "It sucks, but wishing for something different isn't going to keep her alive."

"She's not coming along," Griz said. "If you want to stay with her, you can."

Maggie wagged a finger. "We're good people. We work hard and wouldn't wish harm on anything. Please don't leave us here."

"The choice is yours," Griz replied.

Don guffawed. "That's no choice. I won't abandon my wife."

"Uh, guys?" I said, motioning to the tree line. "We need to make a decision and fast."

Several deer ran out from the trees and across the road. Deer were skittish creatures, tending to hide unless spooked by a predator, and, there was one predator in abundance around here.

Zeds.

Twenty

I stepped around the Humvee. Don climbed to his feet. No one spoke while we waited to see how big a herd we had to deal with.

Finally, a single shape emerged. We all let out a collective sigh. Maggie's hand fluttered over her heart. "Oh, thank God."

The huge, mangy wolf—or large dog; it was too hard to tell from this distance—stepped out from the shadows, eyed us as though deciding which would be easier prey, and then slowly turned to follow the deer. The deer had made a large U-turn around us and stopped only a couple hundred meters from where we stood. Wolves had multiplied since the outbreak. Large dogs were now joining their ranks, and these new packs feared neither humans nor zeds. Both became their dinner.

Once the wolf was a safe distance away and no others appeared, I let out the breath I'd been holding.

"Anyone in the mood for some venison for dinner?" Jase said from atop the Humvee.

I glanced at Clutch, and his lips curved upward.

We each raised our rifles. "I'll take the big one on the left."

"I've got mine," Clutch said.

"Three," Jase said quietly. "Two."

We fired at the exact same instant.

Two deer fell, and I grinned, thinking of the first real meal I'd have since the catfish ordeal.

"Let's hurry up and grab them in case the noise draws attention," Griz said.

"They're all yours," I said, still smiling. While I enjoyed eating fresh meat, I hated seeing it when it was still literally doe-eyed and bushy-tailed.

Griz smirked. "I'll haul them back, but I think I've got the better end of the deal. You guys will have to haul this group if they're coming." He gestured toward the small band of stranded newcomers. Then, his features hardened. "I'm sorry, but we can't take in a casualty. It's against protocol. You know that, right?"

I swallowed, glancing back at the woman who was starting to groan again, holding her stomach. The morphine was wearing off too quickly. Don was already growing tense again as he watched us.

"Get us a kit," Clutch said tightly. "I'll handle it from here."

Griz gave the slightest nod before heading around the back of his Humvee.

"What kit are you talking about?" Don asked. "What are you doing?"

Clutch didn't say anything, and Don turned to me. "What are you talking about doing to my wife?"

My lips tightened and I gulped before forcing the words out. "We can't heal her, but we can take away her pain." I liked to think I could bring peace for someone I loved if they were doomed, but I wasn't so sure I had the strength for it. Seeing the agony on Don's face, I was thankful it wasn't my decision to make.

Griz walked back with a vial and syringe and held it out for Clutch. "We'll meet you at the RP in twenty."

Clutch took it. "See you there."

Griz gave the group a troubled look before heading toward the van.

"What is that?" Don asked, backing up step by step.

"It's an anesthetic," Clutch said and held up the vial. "It's called pentobarbital. Just one shot, and your wife will fall asleep. She won't hurt anymore."

"But she'll wake up, right?" Don asked, his voice rising in octaves. "Right?"

"She won't wake," Maggie said. "That's the same stuff they use to put down dogs for good. They want to kill Brenda." She hobbled over to stand between Brenda and Clutch. She crossed her arms over her chest. "I won't stand for it. I will not allow you to commit murder."

I stood near Clutch, my rifle ready, in case they tried to attack. A quick glance at Jase showed that he had us covered.

Clutch held the vial out to Don. "It's the humane way. Your wife won't feel any pain. She has no chance of recovery and can't come with us. I'm offering her a peaceful way out."

Maggie scowled. "Who are you to decide who lives and who dies? Only God can do that."

"Zeds do a pretty good job at it, too," I snapped.

"Don," Brenda said, her voice barely above a whisper.

He moved like she'd shouted. He dropped down and clasped her hand. His young daughter, being held by the teen, took a couple steps closer.

"You-you must keep Alana safe," Brenda said.

He brushed hair from her face. "I won't leave you. Not like this."

She winced and fisted her shirt. "You have to go."

His body shook as he held back sobs. "No." He turned back to us. "You have to let me take her. We've been married eight years. We've never been apart."

"You're only prolonging her suffering," Clutch said. "She has a day left at most. If you want to stay with her today, we can take one of you to get a vehicle. It's your call."

"You can't give us ultimatums," Maggie countered. "We've done nothing wrong. You're taking all of us with you."

"No," I said, exasperated.

"Take us!" the other man stepped forward, pulling the teenaged girl alongside.

"Hugh," Maggie chided. "We don't leave anyone behind. We stay together. Always."

"If that's how you feel," Clutch said with far more calm than I could manage. "There's a vehicle not far from here. We'll take one of you to go get it."

"You can't leave us!" Maggie cried out.

Clutch pointed to the man named Hugh. "You. I'll take you to get the vehicle." He turned and started walking back to the Humvee, and I stayed at his side. I glanced up to see Jase still standing at the .30, alert and ready.

Hugh ran forward, dragging his daughter with him.

"She stays. Just one of you can come along for the SUV," Clutch said.

The man looked none too pleased, not that I could blame him. He didn't know that Clutch was only protecting us by minimizing risk inside the Humvee.

The man glanced back at his group and then pulled his daughter with him. "I don't need the SUV. Just take us with you," he pleaded.

"Hugh!" Maggie shouted. "You can't be serious!"

"They don't get it," Hugh continued. "We can't stay out here. The herds are coming. I don't plan on staying out here." Then he thrust his daughter at Clutch. "She's all yours to do with as you please. Just take us with you!"

The girl's eyes grew wide and she shoved against her father. "Dad!"

Uncaring, he pushed her again at Clutch. "She's pure! Hali will do anything you want. That should cover our room and board. Don't leave us behind."

Clutch grimaced at the daughter and then glared at the father. "Christ. Do I look like a pedophile to you? You'd sell your own fucking daughter for safety?"

The man winced but then stood firm. "I just want us to be safe. Take us with you. If you leave us behind, the zeds will get us for sure. You don't understand. We barely made it this far."

"Stop it!" Brenda cried out, her pale face twisted in pain. "All of you stop it!"

Everyone turned toward the dying woman. She turned to Don. "You must save Alana."

Don shook his head. "I won't leave you. I can't."

"Save Alana," she said with more strength than I thought she'd be able to muster for how close to death she looked.

He sobbed and then buried his head in her neck. "I love you so much."

"I love you." She looked up to their daughter. "Come here, my little garden sprite."

The young girl ran over to her mother with tears in her eyes. "Mommy!" Though she couldn't have been older than five, she still clearly understood the severity of the situation.

Brenda released her husband and hugged her daughter. Don held both of them in his arms. They cried and kept repeating their love for one another. After several long minutes, Don held out his hand and motioned for the syringe.

Clutch handed it to him.

"Don't do this, Don," Maggie said. "It's murder. Don't let these devils lead you astray."

"Maggie, I need you to look after Alana right now," he said.

When she didn't move, Don yelled, "Do it, Maggie!"

The old woman glowered, but she pulled the crying girl against her.

"You should go through the vein," Clutch said. "It will go faster."

Don's hand shook like crazy. His wife watched him and tried to smile but it was all too quickly drowned by pain.

He'd nearly pierced the skin and then tore away. "I-I can't." He grasped his hair with one hand while the other hand holding the syringe fell limply at his side.

"Okay." Clutch stepped forward.

"No. I'll do it," I said, stepping around him. Clutch had enough nightmares already. He didn't need another one. To make it easier, I'd already figured I'd imagine her as a zed and that I wasn't taking a life. At least, I figured if I did it quickly enough I wouldn't think myself out of it.

He grabbed my wrist, gave me a sharp look, and then tugged me back. He cupped my cheek and shook his head. "I won't let you do this."

He turned, bent down, and took the syringe from Don. Clutch didn't waste any time. He grabbed the woman's arm and rubbed his thumb over the vein at her elbow.

As the needle pierced the skin, her eyes widened, and she tried to yank away. "No! I—"

Her eyes fell closed, and she never finished whatever it was she'd had to say.

"Brenda!" Don cried out and pulled her to him.

Clutch fell back on his heels, and I pulled him up and away from the pair. He stared at the syringe, gave it a look of disgust, and then threw it across the road.

We stood around, silently waiting as Don held his wife's body. I held onto Clutch, knowing it had nearly killed him to do what he'd just done.

Maggie glared at us. "You committed murder. You are a sinner and will burn in hell."

I glared right back. "We're *all* sinners, lady. And if you don't back off, we're leaving your ass on this road."

Did euthanasia feel wrong? Hell yeah, but the alternative was so much worse. That woman was going to die anyway. We simply took away a few hours of suffering. At least that's what I told myself. I didn't try to think of the few hours of life we also took.

A strange sound in the distance yanked my attention back. "What was that?"

Clutch, shook his head and looked around for the source. "Sounded almost like a jet."

I looked to the sky but saw no trails. The ground...I bent down and put my hand on the pavement. The slightest sensation of a vibration. The noise, while distant, was becoming audible. There was no breeze today, yet the leaves began to tremble on the trees.

"No! They're here!" Hali yelled.

Hugh twisted around and reached out to me. "We have to go!"

"I've got a bad feeling about this, guys. I think we'd better boogie," Jase called out.

"It's too late," Maggie said, standing stoic, looking toward the north. "They're already here."

My brain finally deciphered the sound of a gigantic swarm of mosquitoes into a hundred thousand moaning zeds. Cold filtered through my blood, and my breath came short. My legs nearly gave out.

The first herd had arrived.

Twenty-One

Clutch yanked open the back gate of the Humvee and motioned everyone in. "Move it!"

"But our things," Noah said.

"We're going to be packed like sardines the way it is," I said.

"No time!" Jase yelled. "Move it, people!"

Hali didn't even hesitate as she shook free from her father and bolted for the Humvee. Jase grabbed her arm and pulled her on board. No one else had yet moved.

I rolled my eyes. "We'll come back and get it later," I said. "Now, get inside or else you're getting left behind."

My words finally got through to Hugh, who then caught up with his daughter.

Maggie was still praying over Brenda's body, and Don stayed by his wife's side. "I can't leave her here like this."

I ran over and squeezed Don's shoulder. "We have to go."

He wiped his eyes and picked up his wife's body. He laid her inside the minivan and closed the door.

"Come on, Cash," Clutch said, climbing into the front seat of the Humvee.

I ran around the front of the vehicle and climbed behind the wheel. Don pushed Maggie in and then climbed in, holding his daughter in his arms.

"Daddy! Mommy's still back there!" the little girl cried.

Jase pounded on the roof. "Everyone's on board. Go!"

I stepped on the gas, and we lurched forward. Don's kid was crying for her mother, and everyone was talking over one another. Clutch pointed to a lone zed on the roadside, and I swerved around it. Shots from Jase's .30 cal echoed non-stop through the Humvee. Alana cried out and covered her ears.

I glanced in the side mirror and saw zeds pour out from the woods. I would've said, "Holy shit," except my jaw was clenched too tightly to speak. I sucked in air.

Clutch said something, but I couldn't hear.

"Would you guys please shut the hell up!" I yelled, rubbing a hand down my legs one at a time before gripping the wheel just as tightly again. "I'm trying to get us out of here."

They quit trying to talk above the .30 cal.

"Drive," Clutch said. "I'll keep an eye out for the herds."

I had the gas pedal floored and didn't let up until we reached the bridge. Every muscle was tight. I slowed down only to pull off the road, and then drove down the steep slope of the east bank and stopped hard just before the ramp. Griz and his team already had their payload loaded on the pontoon and were waiting for us.

Griz's smile faded when he saw us. "What happened?"

"The herds are here," Jase said as he jumped down.

"Shit."

Everyone tumbled out of the Humvee and toward the pontoon in a chaotic mess.

"Where are we going?" Maggie asked.

"Get us out of here," Clutch ordered Griz.

"You don't have to tell me twice." Griz jumped behind the wheel and started up the boat's engine, and we scrambled for seats on the pontoon. Little Alana clung to her father. Jase had managed to grab one of the duffels filled with canned food on his way out of the back of the truck. Maggie limped on last, nearly tripping over one of the deer carcasses as she found a seat.

I helped shove the pontoon away from the boat ramp, and Griz throttled the engine full forward to get us into the river. But we weren't safe yet. We still had to get to the *Aurora* without attracting the attention of any zeds. It only took one zed to home in on us, and others would notice. Griz ran the engine full out to close the short distance to the barge.

"Is *that* where you're going?" Hugh asked.

"Yes," I said, and then turned to Jase, who was busy searching the surrounding area. "Any sign of them yet?"

"Not yet," he said without looking at me.

"Hopefully we were able to get in enough distance between us and them that they won't find us," I said as we pulled up to the dock.

Fortunately, the small dock for the *Aurora* was on the south side of the towboat to better hide us from predators. "We should be safe now, as long as they don't smell or hear anything," Griz said.

"Not if they see anyone on the deck," Clutch countered and squeezed Jase's shoulder. "Hustle up and warn Tyler."

"You got it." Jase leapt off the boat and climbed up the rope ladder.

Wes waved from the deck above and lowered the platform.

Tyler's voice came over the loudspeaker. "Code Red. Code Red."

He didn't say anything else, and he didn't need to. Everyone had been prepped for this moment since we'd arrived at the *Aurora*.

Maggie, Don, and Alana were sent up on the platform since none of them were in any condition to climb the ladder. We slid the deer onto the platform with them, not wanting to let the meat go to waste. I scrambled up the ladder as quickly as possible, with Clutch coming up right behind me.

Griz was already moving the newcomers toward the barge.

Jase waited for us. "Everyone's headed below decks. I think we're set."

We crossed the deck as quickly as Clutch could walk and entered the galley. The room was packed, but no one said a word. Not even prayers were voiced aloud. People huddled together, many holding hands. I squeezed my way through to look out a window.

Time dragged by more slowly than my Corporate Finance class my junior year at college. I focused at not making eye contact with anyone except Clutch or Jase. We played cards, but even that grew dull. I eventually settled on daydreaming about flying the Cub over fields free of monsters.

As the sun set, dark shapes filled in the landscape, making the land look like an eerie ocean of ripples. By morning we'd know if they'd zeroed in on the *Aurora*. Until then, all we could do was wait.

And so we waited.

———

We were able to move above deck freely after the sun had set, though silence was critical. With over fifty people crammed on board the *Aurora*, whispers and the sounds of shuffling feet were the only breaks in silence. We'd all prepared for this moment, we'd practiced it over and over. But the five newcomers were foreign to us and our plans, adding a huge element of risk to our plans. Maggie and Don avoided us, glaring at me whenever our paths crossed. I wanted to glare right back. Instead, I tried to take the higher road and simply ignore their unthankful asses. Hali, still pissed at her father for offering her up, had isolated herself in a corner of barge One.

Even though Clutch thought it too risky, Tyler allowed Vicki to cook the deer for dinner since the wind was out of the north and the bay door was closed over the barge. Everyone ate in silence. The tension was higher than it had ever been.

Through the hull, the sound of the moaning herd made nails on a chalkboard almost melodic. As I lay in my bunk and stared at the springs and mattress of Jase's bunk above, I prayed that they would have moved on before morning. I tried to sleep but settled for staring at the ceiling.

I headed up to the galley sometime before dawn. I didn't bother checking my watch. Upstairs, Jase was kneeling on a bench, his hands clasped and his head down. Clutch sat at a table nearby, cleaning his rifle. I took a seat next to him and watched Jase. I hadn't seen him pray since we'd buried his dog, and it worried me to see his façade gone.

Clutch glanced up before turning back to his work. "He's been at it all night," he said softly, also looking worried.

Seeing Jase's ragged appearance, it was clear the stress was getting to him. His hair was mussed and dark circles underlined his eyes. I headed over to the countertop and poured a cup of coffee, and then set it down next to him.

He looked up, startled. "Oh. Thanks."

I sat and wrapped an arm around him. After a moment, his tension gave way and he leaned into my embrace. "It'll be okay," I murmured. "We're safe here."

He nodded slightly before reaching for the cup and taking a drink. Holding the cup, he watched me for a moment, and then placed his forehead against mine. "I hope we're safe." When he pulled away, he put the cup down and traced the fresh scar on my face and he winced. "That's still a doozy."

"Do you think it'll hurt my chances at getting a date?" I asked.

He gave me the smallest hint of a smile before he looked back out the window and wrapped his hand around the cross he wore.

I sat there, with my arm around Jase, while he prayed. Clutch eventually joined my side. We watched the night sky turn from black to dark gray with hints of gold in the east. As light gave definition to the shapes and trees, any hope I had plummeted.

I could make out the zeds filling the bridge and road to either side. Not a blade of grass remained. They'd filled in the entire area to the west, disappearing into the trees, and were still spreading out. Our Humvee at the boat ramp was being rocked as zeds fought to get whatever they smelled inside.

A leaf in the wind caught my eye, and I noticed it was blowing north, which meant the wind had switched direction sometime during the night. My eyes widened, and I grabbed Clutch's arm. "The wind."

He looked. After a moment, he nodded tightly and then pointed at the zeds. "I think we just entered hell."

"*No,*" Jase said.

Clutch wrapped an arm around him, then another around me. I clung to him but could find no comfort in the embrace. My stomach clenched with terror. A tear rolled down my scarred cheek as I held onto Jase and Clutch and stared outside. One hundred thousand pairs of eyes were focused on Camp Fox, and they looked ravenous.

Part Seven
Gluttony

The Sixth Deadly Sin

Twenty-Two

Two very long weeks later

"It seems like the ones in back and on the edges are moving on," Tyler said as he walked down the steps and into the crew quarters. "Only problem is that there's still at least fifty thousand or more out there sticking around."

"Figured that was the case," Clutch said while he did another lunge. "I have to hand it to them. Once they zero in on something, the bastards are persistent."

"It really sucks being at the bottom of the food chain," I said, matching Clutch's lunge.

Eight of us were going through daily exercises. We'd just finished several sets of push-ups and sit-ups. We tried to keep it interesting by having each scout come up with an exercise, but after a while, even that got old. There were only so many variations to a push-up.

But the herds outside just kept coming. Even though it seemed like tens, if not hundreds, of thousands continued on their journey, enough stayed behind, seemingly too hungry to continue for the slight chance for prey. Two herds currently surrounded the *Aurora* from the bridge and both sides of the river. They couldn't reach us, not through the water, but at least a hundred tried—or were pushed—each day, and at least a couple dozen of those made it onto the island. I'd quit looking out the window on the fourth day. It made it easier to pretend that we weren't caught in the middle of the world's worst shit storm.

"C'mon. Just one."

I turned to see Griz with his open hand stretched out.

Jase shook his head. "No way. Go find your own."

"Why? You have a whole case of them."

"I risked my life for them." He held up a half-eaten candy bar. "These Snickers are my one and only joy in life so you'll have to pry it from my cold, dead hands."

"Don't tempt me."

When I turned back to Tyler, he had moved closer to Clutch.

"We need to ration harder. Vicki says we need to move to a diet of at least ninety percent grain," Tyler said in a low voice. "Without fresh meat and vegetables, we're going through our food stores four times as fast as we calculated."

Clutch's lips thinned. "People aren't going to like to hear it."

I winced. They weren't going to like to hear that news at all, but we had no other option. Heading to the mainland was out of the question. Worse, enough zeds had fallen in the water and scared the fish away, not that I could yet take a bite of fish without gagging. More and more zeds were washing ashore and now lingered on our island.

As long as the zeds were out there, we were stuck in what could easily become our tomb. "We need to get the zeds away from the *Aurora*," I said my thoughts aloud.

Tyler chuckled. "Want me to get on the bullhorn and order the zeds to leave?"

Clutch was watching me all too closely.

"I'll do it," I said after a moment. "I'll lead the herds away from the river barge."

"Cash..." Clutch warned.

I gave him a pleading look. I knew the odds. I'd been an actuary before the outbreak, but I figured the odds out on the river couldn't be any worse than staying on the boat. Staying on the boat was only delaying the odds. "If we don't do something, who knows how long the herds will stay. If we wait until we are out of food, it'll be too late. You know how long it took to build up the reserves we're burning through. The winter may kill the zeds, but without our livestock, it's going to kill us, too. I'll take a boat and run the Pied Piper plan."

"We've only tried that with tiny herds, a few dozen zeds at most," Tyler said.

"The plan hasn't failed yet," I countered.

Clutch watched me for a moment—it was a calculating gaze—and then turned to Tyler. "I'll lead the mission. I want Cash and Jase to stay on the *Aurora*."

"Like hell," I said. "Camp Fox needs you more than it needs me."

Clutch grabbed my arms. "What happens when you come up against a lock or a dam?"

"I'll figure out something. What would you do?"

He shook his head. "Leading them away is one thing. How are you going to turn around and get past them and back to the boat?"

"I'll bring plenty of supplies and hide out until the coast is clear."

His brows rose and his lips tightened.

"The idea could work," Tyler mused. "But it's dangerous. It's awfully dangerous."

"What other option do we have?" I asked. "If I fail, you still have time to figure out other options."

"If *we* fail," Clutch added. "We're a team."

I tried not to look relieved, but the idea of not having Clutch along terrified me. I smiled and gave a single nod.

"I'm in," Jase said, and I looked around, realizing we'd drawn the attention of everyone in the room.

Clutch glared at Jase. "Now, hold on a minute."

"This is a Charlie team mission, right?" Jase asked. "I'm a Coyote. You're not going to make me sit this one out. We're in this together."

Part of me wanted to scream at Jase to stay behind where it was safer, and I suspected it was exactly how Clutch felt about both Jase and me. But Jase was right. We were in it together.

Clutch sighed. "We don't even know if the plan could work on this scale."

"What could work?" Manny asked as he entered the quarters.

"We're forming a small team to lead the zeds away," Tyler said.

"I'm in if the kid ponies up a candy bar from his stash," Griz said.

"Heck, no," Jase said, and the two poked jabs at each other.

"This is not something to take lightly," Tyler said harshly. "I won't order anyone on this mission. It will be volunteers only."

"Well, son of a bitch. You guys can't go without me," Wes said. "I'm the best mechanic around here. With a herd that big, you can't afford to break down."

Tyler held up his hands. "Whoa. That's enough. Five of you will fill a boat and have eyes in every direction. Clutch, you're senior officer so you have lead. Now, we all need to take time to think through this. If anyone backs out, I won't hold it against you. Everyone, take sixty. We'll meet in the galley in an hour to work out the mission details."

Clutch nodded. His features were still set hard, so I rubbed his back. He sighed and looked from Jase to me. "I know trying to talk you two out of this is a waste of breath, so either of you want to spar instead?"

I grinned. Whenever he was stressed, he needed action. Of course, I was the same way. "You bet."

"Yeah, why not," Jase said after stretching his neck from side to side.

I grabbed my thermos from my bunk. By the time I returned, Jase and Clutch were already chatting about setting up the boat.

"Mind if I join you guys?" Griz asked as he caught up.

I motioned him along. "Only if you're ready for an ass whooping."

Griz chuckled. "Oh, it's not me who's—"

Shouting erupted from above deck and I snapped around. "What's going on?"

We ran up the stairs and to the galley. Outside, Maggie was screaming at the herds. "Go back to hell, you devils! You'll never get to us! Never!"

"Shit," Griz muttered. "Our first cuckoo has flown."

No!

I reached for my pistol, but the others bolted outside, and I followed.

Griz reached her first. He yanked her back and covered her mouth. "I should've figured out you'd be the first to go nuts."

She mumbled something but he kept her mouth covered.

I scowled at Maggie, keeping my hand on my holster. "Fucking nut. You trying to get us all killed?"

Lucky for her, Griz still had his hand over her mouth because if I heard what she seemed to be saying, I might have changed my mind and shot her right then and there.

Clutch and Jase helped drag Maggie back inside.

Before I reentered the galley, I looked out at the herds to see every pair of eyes watching us. The wind whipped at my face.

"Well, that does it," Clutch muttered. "This mission just became critical."

"Yeah," Jase said. "The tough part is that it sounds more like Mission: Impossible."

I swallowed and turned away from the ocean of zeds.

No, it wasn't just an impossible mission.

It was a suicide mission.

Twenty-Three

All of Camp Fox squeezed into the galley the morning we left. It was standing room only in a room made to seat twenty comfortably. Weighted down with food and gear, I followed Jase as he weaved through the crowd. I noticed Hali squeezed his hand briefly as he walked by.

Maggie, who now had a scout assigned to her twenty-four/seven, eyed us with her usual glare of disdain and suspicion. Thanks to her, zeds had proof that we were still here, and their numbers were growing. Her little tirade guaranteed Camp Fox would remain under siege until we starved. I craved to put a bullet between her eyes.

Even so, she wasn't the hardest to deal with in the room this morning. Everyone else watched with hope. They put all of their faith in us to save them. If our gamble failed, everyone would starve to death because of us. Those were the ones I really avoided eye contact with, as their gazes followed us silently through the room.

On the island, we chose a deck boat instead of the speedboat since we could load a lot more extra fuel on it. The .30 cal was useless, and we only had to be faster than the herds. The speedboat also couldn't hold nearly the amount of supplies a larger boat could. And boy, did we fill that boat. After all, we had to be ready to live on the river for up to a couple weeks.

Tyler and several scouts had speared the zeds on the land by the *Aurora* so we could load and get out. Even then, hands reached up from below the surface at us. A vision that would no doubt haunt my dreams for the rest of my life.

While I strapped down our food and gear, Clutch and Jase tied the leftover deer organs to the sides of the boat. Vicki had saved the deer organs "for a rainy day." The sweet, iron smell of deer innards was strong and unpleasant but not as bad as I would have expected. Vicki had devised a cellar system on barge Four that helped preserve food, and surprisingly the deer had only the slightest smell of decay.

I pulled out one more item from my backpack, unfolded it, and strung it up on the flagpole at the back of the boat. The wind was just strong enough today that the American flag flapped proudly in the breeze. I sat back and admired it. "I think we're all set."

Griz tossed me a life vest.

I looked at it and scowled. "It's going to be harder to shoot with one on."

He shrugged his vest on like it was body armor. "We play it safe. No unnecessary risks."

"As soon as you know the herds are moving on, get back here as soon as you are safely able," Tyler said.

I gave him a salute. "Aye, aye, captain."

His eyes narrowed with the hint of a smile before he turned and climbed up to the deck.

Kurt had spent much of his childhood boating and water skiing, so he was our pilot. He was also the only one who hadn't volunteered. Tyler had assigned him to the Pied Piper team since we needed Kurt's experience with boats.

We had a perfect team for the mission. Jase had eagle eyes, so he sat at the bow along with Griz, who was a master at strategy. Clutch and I, both crack shots, sat across from each other behind Kurt to have our sides covered. Wes, our mechanic, sat near the motor to keep an eye on our six. I also suspected the engine vibration comforted him as he couldn't swim and really disliked water.

"Everyone ready?" Kurt asked.

A chorus of yeses replied.

He backed the boat from the shoddy dock that had been hastily constructed our first days on the towboat. Wes had a long stick to push away any zeds close to the motor. Kurt piloted the boat slowly and smoothly, and I appreciated that his nerves didn't relay through the controls.

Things started to feel *real* when we pulled around the side of the

Aurora and the herd came into sight. I felt like we were the stars of a sold-out concert. Kurt pulled the boat around, and we moved away from the river barge and toward the zeds.

The boat rocked gently in the river current as Kurt piloted it forward, into the U-shape of zeds on the surrounding land and bridge. The zeds looked like extras in an old-time horror film. Filthy, they were all the same shade of brown-gray. Most were emaciated. Many sported fresh boils and old injuries.

"Don't get too close," Clutch warned. "We don't want zeds to start dropping in on us."

It was like someone had wound up the zeds. What had been slow shuffling before became a frenzied dance as we approached. When we approached the center of the U-shape, their moans reached a crescendo.

"That's close enough," Griz said, sounding nervous.

I didn't blame him. I was practically frozen, and it wasn't just because of the cold air. My hands trembled, and I gripped my rifle to me like it was my lifeline.

Kurt cranked on the CD player, and the previous owner's choice in music—Motor Boat City's "Pontoon"—blasted through the speakers. If the smells of deer organs and visuals of uninfected humans weren't enough to snag their attention, they couldn't ignore the noise. We hadn't had time to rig up louder speakers, but the stock speakers seemed to be doing the trick. Dozens of zeds tumbled into the water, pushed in by zeds behind them.

"Think we got their attention?" Kurt asked.

"Yeah," Clutch said. "We don't want them to keep falling in the water."

Kurt brought the boat closer to the western bank and turned the boat toward the south and cut the engine, letting the current do the work. As we drifted past the *Aurora*, the deck was empty and I could see no signs of inhabitants, though I knew everyone was watching from the galley.

Back on the towboat, we had debated for less than two minutes whether to lead the herd south or north. Leading them north seemed counterproductive. Leading them south meant that we had to lead them past the *Aurora*, but it was the direction they seemed naturally inclined to head.

The plan was to lead the herds far enough away—at least twenty miles—from Camp Fox and then hide in a cove until they had all continued in their migration. We had no map of the river, so it would be all guesswork, and we were counting on Kurt's experience to help navigate the river. We'd loaded up enough fuel to run for at least three days straight, but the plan was that we wouldn't need much.

We used paddles to keep the boat close—but not too close—to the western bank, so that the zeds from the east would work their way across the bridge to the west. Without the engine, the music blared even louder. Wes had rigged up a second battery so we wouldn't drain the primary one.

Jase stood up and shaded his eyes. "It looks like they're all following. Even the ones way in back are moving. Cash, you were right. They're just like lemmings."

I leaned back on the white vinyl seat. *Thank God.* We'd been counting on the zeds sticking with their herd mentality. That once a critical mass moved, the rest would tag happily along. Zeds weren't very bright, to say the least, and it wasn't too hard to outthink them. Except what they lacked in brains, they made up for in numbers and ferocity.

Unfortunately, no matter how simple and foolproof the plan was, when you're surrounded by a hundred thousand zeds, it just might not matter. Predictability can fly out the window. Griz and Jase relied on prayer to make the difference. The rest of us were relying on luck.

The current carried us faster than the herd walked so Kurt started the engine every thirty minutes or so to bring us back to the herd. It was a slow process. Two hours later, we were barely a mile south of the *Aurora*. At this rate, it would take us an entire day to get the herd out of the sight of the towboat and its barges, and a few days to get the herd back on their migratory path.

When the sun reached high in the sky, Kurt lifted the boat's sunshade. The music dampened the constant moaning. Wes had long since fallen asleep, his snores filtering through the wide-brimmed straw hat covering his face. If I closed my eyes and ignored the smells, the boat ride was almost tranquil, and I could pretend it was just another day on the water, in a world where the outbreak had never happened. There was a sense of safety in the boat, knowing that the zeds couldn't swim out to us. When I opened my eyes to a landscape filled with zeds, with zeds reaching out to us as they stumbled along the riverbank, reality soured my daydream.

For lunch, we each had a can of tuna and some flatbread. We didn't carry water. Instead, we carried carbon-filter straws made for camping, and drank directly from the river. Every time I leaned over the side of the boat to drink, I had a near panic attack from imagining hands reaching up and grabbing me. Fortunately, the only thing out of the ordinary was a faded beer can floating by.

We chatted, but small talk was hard ever since the outbreak. Without sports, politics, and celebrities, there were only so many things a person could talk about that didn't dredge up the topic of death or zeds.

I stared off at the treetops that lined the Mississippi. "This river has a lot of levees and little islands," I mused.

"It shouldn't be too hard to find a good hiding place once they get back on their migration," Griz said.

"The landscape can change within just a few miles. Let's hope there will be cover available when we need it," Kurt cautioned.

"Hey guys. There's a lock and dam coming up. We'll be there in a few hours at this rate," Jase said as he pulled out his binoculars.

"How's the lock look?" Clutch said from behind Kurt.

"Nuh-uh," Jase said. "It looks like it's blocked by a big boat."

"Damn. I was hoping we'd get lucky and the lock would be clear," Kurt said.

"Can we get through another way?" Clutch asked.

"Doubt it," Kurt said.

Clutch muttered a string of profanity, his words echoed by complaints and curses by every single one of us. When she wasn't being a bitch, Nikki had told us how various crews had opened all the locks after the outbreak to travel the river easier. We'd been counting on having a wide open path. With a lock blocked, we quite literally had nowhere to go except back.

I looked at my watch and tried to mentally calculate our location. We'd been on the river for nine hours. I bit my lip to keep it from trembling. "We can't be more than four or five miles from the *Aurora*."

"That's not far enough," Griz said and turned to Clutch. "What's the plan, Sarge?"

Goosebumps flitted across my skin. Once we reached the lock, we'd be fucked. The zeds would close us in. We couldn't turn back without bringing the herds with us to the *Aurora*. There were no islands or outcroppings of trees to lose the zeds in.

Clutch's lips thinned as he looked at the herd and then ahead toward the lock. After a moment, he spoke. "We keep going."

Tension throbbed between my temples as I wracked my brain for ideas, but there were few options in a wide open river. We passed a couple outcroppings of dead trees, which would offer some cover, but we were still dangerously close to the river barge. An hour later, the game changed when we could see which boat was blocking the dock.

The *Lady Amore* was sitting sideways in the lock. It looked like it had tried to shove past the smaller boats and logs jamming up the lock but had gotten itself stuck. Without Sorenson to captain the riverboat, it looked like Sorenson's remaining crew lacked the skill to navigate through the open locks and around dams.

"Oh, hell," Jase said.

Clutch made his way toward the front of the boat where Jase was. "What is it?"

There are zeds all over the lock. It looks like they're dropping down onto the boat."

"What do we do?" Kurt asked.

"Our primary objective is to deter the herd," Clutch said bluntly. "Everything else has to come second." He turned to Kurt. "Will that small grouping of islands and trees over there work to hide us?"

Kurt bit his lip as he thought for a moment. "It should. It's nice and close to the lock, so as long as we get there without them seeing us, it may work. Why?"

"Because the riverboat is going to draw their attention from us," Clutch replied.

Kurt frowned. "There might be people still on board."

Clutch narrowed his eyes. "The *Aurora* is counting on us."

"He's right," Griz said quietly. "We're not far enough away. If we turn around, we could lead them right back to the *Aurora*. The *Lady Amore* will distract them enough that they'll forget about us and then keep going. It's the only way."

Clutch unsheathed his knife. "Turn off the music, Kurt. Griz, help me cut the meat loose."

As the pair started to cut the cords holding the deer organs onto the sides, Kurt shook his head as he started the engine and turned the boat around. "I don't like this. It's not right."

"And exactly how do you expect us to rescue anyone in that lock?" Clutch asked as a chunk of deer meat plopped into the water.

"It's not right, but tell me what in this godforsaken world is right," I added, frustration bleeding over my compassion.

"They wouldn't have saved us," Wes said from my right. "Besides, we'd all die if we tried to help them."

Kurt remained silent. He piloted the boat against the current, bringing it in between a small island and a group of tall dead trees with their trunks underwater. I peered into the trees on the tiny island. A zed's hollow gaze leveled on me, and I shivered. It walked to the edge of the bank and stopped at the water's edge. It didn't growl or try to come closer. It only watched me inquisitively.

Kurt dropped the anchor before spinning around to face Clutch. "What now?"

"We wait."

And that's exactly what we did.

We had nowhere to go. As long as the herd was still here, we couldn't go north without drawing their attention. The south was blocked by the lock and dam. We had to ride out the herd. An occasional scream blasted through the groans of the herd, and I winced each time. I focused on breathing in the smell of the river water and tried to imagine I was in a different world, one without zeds, but the relentless sounds were an iron maiden to any daydream. I curled up into a ball and covered myself up with a blanket as I watched the zed watching me while everyone on board the *Lady Amore* was eaten alive.

TWENTY-FOUR

I'd hid and waited zeds out plenty of times, but this time was the hardest. Kurt was right about one thing. It felt wrong to sit by while people were slaughtered. I racked my brain for solutions, but it came down to the fact that Clutch was also right. There was nothing we could do for the riverboat. We were too late by the time we'd first seen it. Anything we did now would put both our lives and potentially every Camp Fox life at risk. The mission had to come first. The *Lady Amore's* demise was our wild card. We needed it to distract the herds from both us and the *Aurora*.

We waited while the zeds that fell onto the riverboat gorged themselves on its occupants. No one spoke, not even when I could hear someone screaming for help. To better hide our scents, we covered ourselves with blankets, which also helped to ward off the cold. Only our heads peeked out so we could watch for any approaching zeds, but the blankets did little to muffle the sounds.

The zed on the riverbank just stood there and stared, strangely not in a frenzy to reach fresh food. Its gaze seemed more curious than vicious. Still, I would've preferred to kill it, but it would have been a waste of a good arrow since the zed couldn't reach us. Instead, I kept a close watch on it while the sun set.

When sunlight morphed into moonlight, the lone zed remained easy enough to spot. Its jaundiced eyes reflected light in the dark akin to a cat's. Fortunately, unlike cats, zeds' vision sucked at night, making their eyes a giveaway to us, as long as the moon was bright.

Clutch assigned shifts using hand signals, but I don't think anyone slept. The constant moans of the herd cut through any imagined sense of safety. It sounded like a madhouse orchestra, with every instrument out of tune, and every note a screech. For the first time, I could *almost* commiserate with Maggie. I wanted to scream at the zeds to stop. They were driving me mad, but I was sane enough to know it would do no good. Instead, I focused my hate on Maggie, blaming her for our situation—even though I knew she wasn't to blame. If she hadn't gone nuts, someone else would have broken eventually. Still, hating her helped ground me.

Sometime during the night, we huddled together for warmth, rotating as we went on and off night watch. Each of our breaths made a tiny white puff in the night. It had to be below freezing because frost built on the wispy edges of my hair.

By morning, we were all snuggled together in the center of the boat, except for Clutch who'd taken the final night watch. Kurt copped a quick feel under the blanket, but I pretended I didn't notice. Even though I wanted to kick him in the nuts, there were just some things a woman learned to deal with when outnumbered ten to one by men in the field.

I opened my eyes and found Clutch watching me. I smiled, and he returned one of his all-too-rare smiles before turning back to watch the river. Suddenly warmer, I closed my eyes, making sure his smile stayed imprinted in my memory. There were too many bad memories in my head already. I had to work hard to keep the good ones. I spent the next several minutes dreaming of our cabin and snuggling with Clutch. He gave me that smile before kissing me and pulling me to him.

Unfortunately, Kurt's groping ruined the fantasy. When his fingers crept to my inner thigh, I decided I'd rather be out in the cold than under a blanket with him, and I shimmied out with a grumble. His finger looped around my belt, but I gave a sharp heel to his stomach, and he let go with a grunt. Clutch cut Kurt a hard look before giving me a questioning look.

I replied by focusing my smile completely on him and sitting next to him on the frost-covered seat. Cold wetness seeped through my cargos and into my bones. I shivered, and Clutch wrapped his blanket and a cold arm around me. He was shivering too, and I snuggled into his embrace. I found my breathing found a pace with his, and I placed my hand over his steady heartbeat. He leaned toward me and pulled me possessively closer. Feeling a rare peacefulness, we watched the sun rise over the trees.

Behind us, the zed on the water's edge had disappeared at some point before morning. We'd gotten lucky that the herd had followed us along the western bank of the river. If they'd taken both sides, we were just close enough to the eastern bank that we could've been seen or sniffed out.

I figured we deserved the luck. All too many times, we'd been unlucky, and it had become expected. Statistically, things were bound to go our way once in a while. But when they did, like now, it felt unnatural and worrisome. Not that I was worried enough to not savor our temporary fortune.

Jase and Griz joined us next. Jase grabbed my arm. He had a huge grin on his face as he pointed toward the lock. I looked and my mouth opened. I grabbed Clutch's hand but he was already looking, too.

The herds were moving on!

My heart nearly leapt from my chest and I squeezed Clutch's hand. A line of zeds had begun to head south, and the ones left around the lock were following. It would take them a long time, but their trajectory was clearly the opposite direction of the *Aurora*. I hadn't looked earlier because I was afraid of what I'd see. I grinned like a little girl as I snuggled in between Jase and Clutch and we spent the next several hours watching the exodus in silence.

By lunchtime, I was starving. Clutch had finally given the okay to eat. Last night and this morning, we couldn't risk the smell of food getting out. While we waited out the herds, we crunched as quietly as possible on nuts and some kind of flatbread cracker that Vicki invented. Even after letting each cracker sit in my mouth to get soggy, they still crunched. With every bite, I grimaced, wishing Vicki sent something mushy along, but I was too hungry to go without food, and so I kept crunching away.

It wasn't until nearly six hours later that Griz and Clutch broke the silence.

"Don't hate me for saying this, guys, but I think we ought to check out the riverboat," Griz said with an almost pained expression, like the words hurt to say them.

"Too dangerous," Clutch replied. "I can still see the back of the herd. Too much noise could draw their attention back this way."

"There might be survivors," Kurt said.

"There will definitely be zeds," Clutch countered.

"Just think of how much food and supplies are on that boat," Wes chimed in.

"And how many zeds do you think are on that boat between us and any supplies?" Clutch asked.

"You're lead on this mission, but what's the harm in just going in near enough to scout it out?" Griz said. "As long as it's stuck in the lock, it could be an emergency food run if it's not too heavily damaged. Besides, we can't head back to the *Aurora* yet, not until the herds are further away."

We all watched Clutch hopefully. While I trusted his judgment—his gut was never wrong—a part of me imagined the *Lady Amore* as the *Titanic* and that we could rescue any survivors who remained. Since the outbreak, nearly everything we did revolved around simply surviving. The chance to save even one person from the zeds brought hope that we could eventually win this war. Even though the realistic part of my brain pointed out the hopeless odds of surviving a zed herd.

Clutch sighed. "All right, but we wait until we are sure the herd can't see, smell, or hear us. So, dig in. We have at least a couple more hours to wait."

And the waiting continued.

Three hours and forty-seven minutes later, Clutch broke the silence. "Okay. We'll go in slow and keep to the east bank. We can't do a thing to draw the herd's attention, got it?"

We all came to full attention. No one smiled because we all knew that going near anything where zeds had been a day earlier was dangerous.

"It's the right thing," Kurt said as he climbed into the pilot's seat.

"Before we go, take five," Clutch said. "We're not heading into that clusterfuck half-cocked."

After we checked and double-checked our weapons, Kurt started the motor, and then reached back and pulled up the anchor. He kept the motor at idle as he weaved through the trees that had camouflaged us all night. The wind was out of the northwest, so any noise from the boat was carried harmlessly to the southeast.

Once clear of the trees, Kurt cut the engine, and we rode the current toward the lock. We all searched for survivors as well as for zeds. No zeds remained on the ledges, but I could already make out at least a hundred on the top deck of the riverboat. Kurt kept the boat on the eastern edge, so the tall, concrete lock served as a wall between us and the migrating herds. Even though they were now several miles away, we'd all long since learned that one of the secrets to survival was to be overly, obsessively careful. The other secret? Having a shitload of luck.

"Careful not to get caught in the lock," Griz said.

"Trust me, Sarge. I know what I'm doing," Kurt replied.

I'd almost echoed Griz's words. The riverboat blocked the entire opening to the lock, with smaller boats and debris lodged around it. Kurt pulled the boat closer and slowed to a stop.

Any hope I had of finding survivors, or at least access to food and supplies, was quickly drowned. The riverboat was *filled* with zeds. Through the windows, we could see zeds standing shoulder-to-shoulder. "We're not going in there," I said quietly. "Any food or supplies is a lost cause."

Clutch grimaced. "The riverboat is a no-go. Let's head back to the levee."

Kurt started to turn the boat around. Something thumped against the hull.

Griz leaned over the edge and then staggered back. "The water is full of zeds! They're floating just below the surface. Get out of here!"

Kurt throttled forward, but the motor ground and then died.

"They're getting tangled in the props!" Wes cried out.

"Grab the oars," Clutch ordered. "No gunfire."

We all lunged for oars. I dipped mine in the water to paddle and hit something solid. I pulled back and tried again. This time, something heavy nearly pulled the oar right out of my hands. I gasped and put all my weight into yanking the oar out of the water, and a zed still holding the oar reached for the boat. Every nerve was on edge as I twirled the oar free. I swung and cracked the zed's skull, and it fell back below the surface.

My brow furrowed with confusion. Zeds couldn't swim, but these hadn't sunk yet. Then it hit me, and my heart thumped harder. These zeds were climbing on one another to get to us. "Jesus, how many fell off the lock?" Goosebumps covered my skin even as adrenaline sent a surge of heat through me.

Everyone was too busy dealing with zeds clawing at the boat to say anything except curse the zeds. We were making no headway, and more hands were grabbing onto the sides. We wouldn't live much longer if we didn't get out of there soon.

Frantic, I swapped the oar for a machete and hacked away any arms that managed to grab onto the boat as the guys continued to paddle. Every foot we made north was a battle against both the current and the relentless zeds. Even in the cold temperature, sweat ran down my face. My arms ached and I struggled to keep a firm grip on my machete.

After fifty feet or so, fewer zeds reached up the sides, and the boat moved more smoothly through the water. I swapped my machete for the oar and paddled upriver. With all of us rowing, it took only a few minutes to close the rest of the distance to the trees where we'd hidden last night. Once there, Kurt threw out the anchor and then collapsed on his seat.

"Jase," Clutch said. "Do you see any zeds heading this way?"

Jase pulled out his binoculars and looked to the south, and then to the other directions. "No. It looks like the coast is clear."

"Good," Griz said on a sigh. "Wes, get that engine fixed so we can get the hell out of here."

"You don't need to tell me twice," the older man said. He stepped out onto the deck and opened up the engine cover. Water splashed. "Agh! Help!"

I jumped over the seat and grabbed Wes by his belt. His arms were thrashing around while he reached out. A zed was trying to pull him into the water and had his head underwater already. Wes lost his balance, and it became a tug-o'-war as I tried to pull him back. His yells were garbled by the water. Others joined in, and we all tumbled onto our backs on the deck, yanking Wes back with us.

I jumped up to make sure we hadn't brought the zed with us. "Holy shit, that was close."

"Ah, hell," Clutch muttered.

I turned around and saw the blood. "No."

Wes lay on his back, looking up with utter terror in his eyes. He was holding his neck, where crimson covered much of his shirt. He coughed and blood leaked from his mouth. I fell on my knees. His lips moved, but no sound came out. With blood loss came lethargy. His features relaxed. He looked around to each of us, though his eyes couldn't seem to focus. He reached up and touched my face.

He went to say something, but coughed and wheezed as he bled out on the deck. I knelt by him, my hand on his chest, offering what little comfort I could. There was nothing we could do. We waited until he lost consciousness, and tears caused my vision to blur, and I could do nothing but watch. I didn't wipe the tears away. Griz and Jase recited a prayer. Even Clutch joined in, the first I'd ever heard him pray. I couldn't find my voice.

His breathing became shallow until I could no longer feel it under my palm. His heartbeat disappeared seconds later. "He's gone," I said bluntly and without emotion, even though inside I seethed at the unfairness of it all. Jase tugged me back toward the main area of the boat, and Clutch stepped in. He swung his machete and then rolled Wes off the back of the deck. In the water, the zed tore into him like a piranha. My tears stopped, blocked by numbness, and I sat there, watching my friend be eaten by something that used to be human.

PART EIGHT
LUST

THE SEVENTH DEADLY SIN

Twenty-Five

We made it back to the *Aurora* just before sunset. Once we'd killed and disentangled the zed in the prop blades, the motor had started. It had run rough—some things were probably bent up inside—but it'd gotten us back to Camp Fox.

We'd returned to receive five minutes of fanfare, but then it was right back to work. Our problems were nowhere over yet. We found ourselves in an endless debate about what to do next. The herds had moved on, but a couple hundred zeds had stayed behind, watching us from the bridge that crossed the river. That number wasn't even counting the hundred dead or nearly dead scattered on the ground that had been trampled by the herd. Those would be easier to clean up but still posed some risk to walking to the vehicles.

The next morning, Griz led another Pied Piper boat, but the zeds we'd dubbed the "bridge bastards" remained undeterred. Over the next few days, we tried scouting runs to the north using the river since we couldn't get to our vehicles. Traveling under the bridge was dangerous, and we had to speed under each time. With no land vehicles parked to the north, we were limited in our search radius, and the riverfront had been picked clean by other boats on the river like the *Lady Amore*.

We'd brought a pontoon full of scouts to the nearest river town to empty the grocery store, but bandits had beaten us to it. They must've been right behind the herds because every place we went showed signs of being recently picked clean. Every vehicle we came to that looked like it could run was missing its keys. Likely, the only reason bandits hadn't come across our vehicles yet was the bridge bastards.

Without access to vehicles, we were running on borrowed time. We couldn't get the fuel or food we needed without making land runs. Relocating from the *Aurora* was deemed not an option. Tyler had queried the residents, and no one had wanted to leave. They felt safe there and were tired of looking over their shoulders.

So another option presented itself, one the residents embraced and the scouts balked at. Of course, none of the residents planned to get their hands dirty. They planned on watching us from the safety of the barge.

"We'll have to burn them at sunset, so the smoke won't be seen," Griz said before leaning back in his chair.

"It's risky," Clutch added. "We could set the whole countryside on fire."

Tyler shook his head. "Not if we control it. We'll set up boundaries."

Clutch's eyes narrowed. "Tell me. Exactly how are we going to dig up ground and not get torn to shreds?"

"Fine," Tyler replied. "We'll skip the boundaries. So what if the fire spreads? It won't reach the *Aurora*."

My eyes widened. "It could spread over miles and miles. We could destroy everything around here. Any food, animals, everything."

"Why does it matter?" Kurt asked. "There's no one left out there but bandits, anyway. A fire would destroy a lot of the rotting corpses and clean up the countryside."

Clutch clenched his fist but stopped himself before he hit the table. "Sure, the fire will take out all the zeds in this area, but it could also destroy any plants and wildlife. We'd be dealing with the same issue we have now, and that's no food."

"We still have the grain," Tyler said. "Deer are faster than zeds and can run. We'll hunt them later."

"It sounds too dangerous," I said.

"It's safer than using up our ammo on them," Kurt said.

"I disagree. We can't waste our gasoline," I said. "I think it's safer to shoot them, but I'd prefer to find a third option."

"Gas will start going bad before we use it all up," Kurt replied.

Griz stood and poured himself a cup of tea. "The people need to be free from zeds. Being watched by zeds day in and day out wears on morale. They need the break. Even if it's only for a few months."

"And when spring comes?" Clutch countered.

"We have no idea if they'll even come back," Kurt said, rolling his eyes and sighing in exasperation. "Every month, they rot away more and more. They can't last much longer before their bodies completely fall apart."

"We've been saying that for months now," Clutch said.

Jase finally spoke up. "You're not thinking straight. You're all too desperate to live without zeds. Going after a couple hundred zeds is really dangerous. We've never done anything like this before. We'd have to burn them to the point that they can't physically move, or else they could still survive."

"Then we need to make sure they are thoroughly burned because not going after them is even more dangerous," Tyler said. "Every day we can't get to our vehicles and start land searches, the bandits clear out more of the surrounding area."

"Well, if this boat is the new permanent location for Camp Fox, we need to make sure it's not going to float away in the spring floods. The residents need to kick up their efforts at turning this from a temporary base to a home," Griz said. "We'll have to focus completely on building up our food reserves. Vicki thought we should build a greenhouse so we can grow vegetables this winter."

The banter was giving me a headache, and I rubbed my eyes. We could argue these points until the zeds died off, even if it was twenty years from now. None of these discussions would keep us from starving. "Even if we find enough food to last the winter, we'll need acres and acres of land in the spring to feed everyone. How can we do that if everyone stays on the *Aurora*? Who's going to farm it?"

"Staying on the *Aurora* long term is too risky," Clutch said. "Griz makes a good point about the spring floods. How the hell are we going to anchor the towboat and barges here so we don't get washed away or broken apart in the spring?"

Tyler came to his feet and leaned forward on the table. "We've been rehashing this for too long. This isn't a democracy, and the matter is no longer up for discussion. As commanding officer of Camp Fox, the *Aurora* is hereby renamed Camp Fox, so deal with it. Since it's no longer our temporary location, we need to strengthen the infrastructure to support us long term." He pointed at the window. "We're burning those bridge bastards outside tomorrow and converting this camp into a sustainable fortress. Anyone who isn't one hundred percent on board with me as CO—commanding officer—is free to leave right now."

There were no retorts, and I assumed everyone had been stunned into silence like I had been. I stared at Clutch, who was looking right back at me. I was sure I looked as frustrated as he did. In the corner, Jase sat with his head in his hands. I didn't know the answer, but this plan had too much complexity and too many risks to feel right.

"You heard the captain," Clutch said, the sergeant tone coming through his voice. "We've got a bonfire to plan and a base to protect."

———

At fifteen hundred hours, twelve scouts in full gear loaded onto two pontoons and headed around the southern edge of the island to stay hidden from the bridge bastards. Zeds lingered on the small island, and we skirted around them rather than kill them, to not draw the bridge bastards' attention. As we broke away from the island, I thought about the plan. It was a simple plan that seemed like a wasteful use of precious fuel and ammo while putting eight people at risk. The plan? Pen the zeds in on the bridge, and burn them. Shoot any outliers.

My pontoon, led by Clutch, was tasked with sneaking onto the eastern shore, where there were more trees to hide our approach. Trees could also hide zeds, but they tended to shuffle their feet, while we could move nearly silently. We were counting on the zeds' tendency to herd together and hoping that one of those herds weren't lingering in the woods. Our pontoon's job was to lay gasoline on the east end of the bridge while the west team distracted the zeds.

The other pontoon, led by Griz, was to distract the zeds' attention from our movements until we were in position. Then, they'd land on the western shore, so we could burn the bridge bastards from both sides.

Clutch, the eternal pessimist, wasn't so confident things would go that easily. He'd voiced concern about the fire weakening the bridge, which could mean we'd have to find another bridge to cross the river. He'd talked about how few explosives were needed in Afghanistan to bring down a bridge if they were placed right. He'd said that a hot enough fire at the wrong points of the bridge might do the same. Only problem was that we didn't have a single bridge expert or engineer among us. So, the general consensus was that a gasoline-fed fire wouldn't burn long enough to weaken the steel and concrete structure.

Tyler had made it clear that he was the boss, and if we didn't like it, we could leave. Honestly, we were tempted. Clutch, Jase, and I had even talked about it last night. But Jase was adamant that Camp Fox needed us far more than we needed them. It was our duty to help.

Everyone craved to be free from zeds. Hell, I wanted it, too, but they were letting hope overshadow their logic. If we took out these zeds, there'd be more. There were *always* more.

When Clutch and Griz each gave their *ready* signal, our pontoon went east while the other went west. The island sat on the eastern half of the river, so our trip to the shore was brief. The pontoon hit the river-bank, and we all lurched forward. After regaining my balance, I looked over the side to make sure no zeds had washed ashore with us. Jase was the first to jump out, and I followed. Landing at the dock would've been far easier, but the bridge bastards would've seen us. Instead, Clutch picked out a heavily wooded area on the eastern bank a quarter-mile south of the dock.

"Let's move out," Clutch said in a hoarse whisper as he joined my side. "We need to be ready to go the moment the West team engages."

Four men on my pontoon each carried a five-gallon gas jug. Both Jase and I had our hands free since we were on point to take out zeds in the woods. One on point was probably good enough, but Clutch always believed in being doubly prepared.

I had my rifle slung over my shoulder, and my machete held at the ready. Silence was crucial until we were in position. Jase and I led the four others through the woods, each of us with two men following behind.

The leaves had turned colors, and many had already fallen, allowing sunlight to reveal a zed lying next to a log. The zed couldn't walk and was in pretty rough shape. Jase finished it off with two swings so that it couldn't make noise and alert others to our presence.

We moved slowly, being extra careful to not slosh the gasoline. We came across a second zed, but it had been torn apart, likely by wolves or wild dogs. When the trees opened onto the road, we saw the devastation Camp Fox's vehicles had taken while parked on the eastern bank. All had smears of zed sludge. A couple had been rolled over. A HEMTT sat askew in the road. Trampled zeds dotted the road.

For our pontoon, Kurt was going to drive the fuel truck while Joe, another one of Tyler's trusted guardsmen, shot gasoline onto the zeds to make sure they'd burn to death. The five-gallon jugs were to set up a wall of fire at the end of each bridge to help hold the zeds in. As the fastest runner, Jase's job was to light the fire. I had my usual job as sweeper to shoot any zeds that got too close to the scouts managing the fire.

The bridge was big. It spanned the width of the Mississippi, which made penning the zeds easier. Except that herding zeds was a lot like herding cats—a whole lot easier said than done.

Careful to avoid the zeds on the ground with some life still left in them, we looked under the vehicles to make sure no other zeds were waiting to jump out at us. We squeezed between the Humvees and HEMTTs and made our way toward the bridge. We paused at the last fuel truck we came to. Kurt set down his gas can, and opened the door. A second later, he stood back and gave a thumbs-up.

We stood behind the vehicle closest to the bridge, a big HEMTT, which would be our RP (rendezvous point). Clutch signaled to me, and I climbed up the back of the HEMTT. Jase came up right behind me. Until Jase started the fire, Clutch wanted him with me to provide suppression fire, but I knew it was also to keep us both safe.

Once I had my rifle set up, I noticed the pontoon in the middle of the river. The West team was in play. I motioned to Clutch, and he nodded. He signaled to our team and the four men with gas cans—Clutch, Kurt, Bryce, and Joe—jogged toward the bridge, though Clutch's jog was more of a walk. The bridge bastards were completely entranced by the West team, who was slowly making its way to the western riverfront. The zeds followed, mimicking the direction of the pontoon and moving onto the western half of the bridge.

The East team poured gasoline in a thick line across the eastern opening of the bridge.

So far, so good.

Clutch signaled to Kurt and Joe, and they took off at a sprint for the gas tanker truck. Clutch stood there, in plain sight, at the end of the bridge in the middle of the road. Bryce stood off to the side, more skittish.

Once Kurt and Joe both gave a thumbs-up that they were in position, Clutch waved his arms toward Griz's team's pontoon. They waved back, and went under the bridge to where they'd go ashore on the western bank.

"Hey!" Clutch shouted.

Several zeds toward the back of the group turned.

"Yeah, you! Come and get me, you dumb fucks!"

It was irresistible bait, and I wanted to run to Clutch and yank him away from danger. The zeds moaned as they changed direction to head back down the bridge toward Clutch. The West team crept up around the edges of the bridges and started pouring gasoline across the bridge, just like the East team had.

Clutch waved at the zeds and gave them the bird. "Come on, you slow shits!"

I had to remind myself to scan the entire area, not just the bridge, with the noise Clutch was making.

Behind me, the gas truck's big engine started, and I turned to see Kurt pull the truck out and back it toward the bridge. Joe was on top of the tank holding the hose. When Kurt approached the bridge, Clutch stepped to the side with Bryce and held up his hand. Looking in the side mirror, Kurt stopped the truck.

Clutch and Bryce climbed up on the back of the HEMTT, and I could hear them take position around us.

"You're up, Speedy," Clutch said.

Jase held up a lighter. "I'm way ahead of you." He got to his feet, climbed down from the HEMTT, and sprinted toward the bridge.

Movement in the tree line caused me to adjust my aim. I fired.

"Nice shot," Bryce said after the lone zed fell.

While I continually scanned the landscape, out of the corner of my eye I saw Joe stand on top of the truck and started spraying gasoline over the incoming herd as the truck pulled slowly away from them. They continued until they reach the end of the bridge.

Joe waved frantically. "I can't get the hose to turn off!"

The zeds were nearly to the truck.

"Leave it! Get out of there!" Clutch yelled, motioning them to us.

Joe continued to work with the hose and then finally tossed it away. Gas continued to spray out. With the engine still running, Kurt jumped just as Joe was climbing down the back. A zed grabbed Joe's leg, but Kurt shot it several times until its gripped relaxed enough for Joe to tumble onto the ground. He regained his footing and took off at a sprint along with Kurt toward us.

As soon as Kurt and Joe passed Jase, he lit a small, weighted rag and tossed it onto the gasoline-soaked bridge. Fire erupted down the line, forming a wall of flames across the western end of the bridge. Jase ran back toward us and was back up on the HEMTT in a couple seconds flat.

Even though they weren't smart, zeds tended to step back from fire. That was, if they weren't preoccupied with trying to get to us. These zeds stepped right into the flame, like we were counting on. As each gas-soaked zed touched fire, it went up in a whoosh.

Garbled hisses came from deep within the flames. Human-like shapes writhed and moved in a macabre dance in the fire. The zeds that passed through the flames made it several feet, sometimes even more, before they finally collapsed into abstract, angled shapes as their bodies cooked and brains melted. Zeds smelled horrible, but barbequed zeds smelled even worse. Burning rot and flesh made my eyes water, and I swallowed back bile to keep from throwing up.

Clutch put a hand on my back. "Don't look."

I hadn't realized I'd been staring.

Clutch and the others climbed down to dig up the ground to prevent the fire from spreading. As they frantically worked, I forced myself to scan for zeds coming at us from other directions. But my gaze kept going back to the charred zeds burning at the edges of the flames. Another memory to haunt my sleep.

We couldn't see the flames spread from behind the wall of fire, but it didn't take them long to reach the gas truck. A massive explosion blasted us and rocked the HEMTT. I clenched my eyes closed, but the heat nearly cooked us. My eyes watered and my cheeks felt seared, and I leaned my face against the cooler metal of the HEMTT. Once my tears slowed, I looked back up to the fire. Heat still tingled against my skin though we were a couple hundred feet away. Even when we were confident the zeds were all dead, we still had to wait until the flames died down before we could return to the *Aurora*. Not that we had any way of putting out the fire. We could grab buckets of water from the river, but it wouldn't make a dent on the searing flames that hadn't yet died down.

An hour passed, and the flames still didn't die down, even though the bridge was made of steel and concrete. Dread filled my gut, and looking at each of the men up there with me, they were thinking the same thing. I didn't understand all the science behind fire, but my lack of knowledge didn't change the fact that the bridge was burning.

A screeching sound of bending metal made me jump to my feet. My mouth opened. I pointed, and yelled out, "Did you see that?"

Clutch's jaw clenched. "I see it. The bridge is going to collapse."

Twenty-Six

There was nothing we could do as fire-tortured steel made horrendous cries. The northern edge of the bridge gave way first. When the arch's cables snapped, the pavement curved before setting off a chain reaction of concrete and rebar porpoising down the bridge. An avalanche of fire, steel, and dusty concrete plummeted into the Mississippi with a sonic sizzle. Much of the bridge sunk, sending up waves down the river. Many huge chunks of debris still littered the surface and burned while the current grabbed at it.

"Oh, shit." I could no longer watch for zeds. I stood and helplessly stared as the burning debris floated directly toward the *Aurora*. My hand flew to my heart and I clutched my shirt. My stomach churned as people ran out on the deck, screaming and shouting. When the first debris slammed into the towboat, I gasped. Someone fell off the edge and screamed the ten short feet down to the water, where the sound was abruptly cut off. As debris piled up against the boat, both it and its barges rocked.

The two barges that had been barely hanging onto the rest of the group broke away with a drawn-out metallic screech. Embers on the grain in barge Number Eight erupted into dark clouds of smoke.

I jumped off the back of the HEMTT before remembering to take a cursory scan for zeds. I stopped, found none, and ran up to Clutch, whom everyone had been gathering around. "What do we do?"

"They need our pontoons to speed up evacuation. Bryce, Kurt, and Joe, you're with me on the pontoon to help with rescue at the *Aurora*."

"How about me?" Jase asked.

He pointed to where I'd spent the last couple hours. "You and Cash need to keep this area clear of zeds, so Camp Fox can safely land. Make sure none of these grounded zeds can endanger people as they get to the dock."

"Okay," I said.

Clutch and the three other men took off running toward the woods and back to the pontoon. "Be safe," I called out, but I had no idea if he'd heard me.

Griz's pontoon was already in the water and halfway back to the *Aurora*, but they were having trouble zigzagging through the debris and kept having to back up and go for a different route.

I swapped my rifle for my machete and made a winding path through zeds on the ground. I stopped at each one that still had life in it and swung. Jase and I carved a path to the boat ramp in ten minutes. We spread out to make a wider path.

"Hey," Jase called out. "Three tangoes at my eleven o'clock."

I jogged back up the eastern bank and followed his finger. I saw the shapes exit the trees across the road. "I'll start on the right."

I had my rifle out and had taken two shots by the time Jase took the last one. After making sure no more emerged, I turned around and headed back toward the ramp. I lifted my rifle and looked through my scope at the *Aurora*. Clutch and his team had made it onto the towboat. People were running at him like a flock of sparrows. Against the rail, Clutch was shoving people back who couldn't take the ladder. Many were weighted down with bags, and I could see Clutch was yelling and motioning at them to drop their things. No one seemed to be listening.

When the smoke blocked my view of Clutch, my heart clenched. "Be safe," I whispered, suddenly knowing in my heart that I didn't care if anyone made it to shore as long as Clutch made it back safely.

"What?" Jase asked.

Anger at the stupid fire hardened my features. "Nothing."

The flames had engulfed the outer four barges and were already spreading to the four closest to the towboat. All of our grain...gone. My heart pounded, and I found it hard to hold my rifle. At least the fire hadn't overtaken the closest barges or towboat yet, but smoke was shooting out from everywhere. I could still make out barges Four and Three through the haze, where Kurt was taking a crate of ammo from another scout who'd just emerged from our armory. Smoke bled through where the bay doors met in the middle. "Hurry," I whispered as they carried out our irreplaceable supplies.

A fire shot up, and Kurt disappeared. I squinted to see smoke and flames pour out from a hole where Kurt had been standing a second earlier. *Oh, God.*

"The fire—" Jase didn't finish.

The sound of automatic gunfire drowned out the sound of everything else, and we both ducked. I quickly realized it wasn't automatic gunfire but the sounds of ammo going off in the fire. My legs were suddenly wobbly and I leaned against our Humvee that still sat next to the boat ramp.

We were about to lose everything. Our food, ammo, everything. And there wasn't a single fucking thing we could do except watch Camp Fox quite literally go up in flames.

Twenty-Seven

Embers showered down like glitter around the *Aurora* while ammo continued to go off in barge Three by the box-load. Clutch's team was already on board the towboat and helping with the evacuation. Joe brought over the first pontoon packed shoulder-to-shoulder with coughing, crying people. Joe's face was covered with black ash as he pulled the pontoon up to the dock on the eastern bank by what was left of the bridge.

Jase and I looked at one another, and then we both ran toward the pontoon. Other than smoke inhalation and shock, no one looked seriously injured. Jase and I helped anyone who seemed to be struggling off the boat and onto the bank. Once it was clear, I jumped on the pontoon to where Joe was curled over the steering wheel. "What do you need help with?"

Joe's reply was smothered by a cough, although he eventually looked up with tearing, bloodshot eyes and gave me a thumb up.

I held my rifle out to him. "I can take the next trip. Can you cover the people here?"

He nodded, still holding his chest.

"I'll drive," Jase said as a matter-of-fact and set his rifle down next to him.

I sat down just as he throttled full forward, and the pontoon cut through the water. Midway, we met Griz's boat, also filled with people. All of the barges were covered in flames, and the towboat was covered in smoke. Someone plummeted into the water to our right as we headed around the boat to the boat dock. I couldn't make out who he was because as soon as he surfaced, something yanked him right back under. I searched but could find no one under the murky water.

I swallowed and sat back. As we approached the dock, a zed was chewing on Hugh, while his daughter Hali was trying to pull him free. He looked unconscious, which was small consolation. I grabbed Jase's rifle and fired two shots: one into the zed and one into the doomed victim. Hali stood back, stunned, her big blue eyes and mouth opened wide. Jase cut the engine and jumped out. `

He wrapped his arm around Hali and led her back to the pontoon. "I've got you. It's going to be okay now." She went with him like she was a robot, seemingly oblivious to his presence.

On the other side of the dock, the deck boats were being filled, with Deb leading the effort. I searched for Clutch but didn't see him anywhere. I handed Jase his rifle back. "I'm going to find Clutch. Can you keep it clear down here until we get back?"

He looked at me directly and gave a single firm nod, still holding Hali with his other arm. "Hurry."

I ran for the ladder and waited for two scouts to climb down. Both were laden down with olive drab duffles. As soon as they were on the ground, I grabbed onto the ladder. "Just about everyone is down, and this is the last of the supplies we could get to," one of them said with a hoarse voice. "The final team is wrapping up on deck now."

I didn't wait. The metal was warm under my palms, and I climbed as quickly as I could. As soon as I reached the rail, I pulled myself over and stood. There was fire shooting up through the deck everywhere. Smoke burned my lungs, and I coughed on the black air. The bow was engulfed in flames. Two charred bodies lay hunched over in the fire, and I prayed neither was Clutch.

Frantic, I searched for anyone alive on the chaotic deck. Then I saw them. My heart leapt and air shot from my lungs. Clutch was helping a man down the edge of the deck onto the lift. Right behind him, Tyler was carrying Maggie who was quacking on about something. Even in this hell, I couldn't help but smile in relief at seeing Clutch and Tyler. Keeping a hand on the rail, I hustled to meet them, careful to avoid burning or smoking deck boards. I reached out and grabbed his arm, just to feel him and know he was real. "Is that everyone?"

Clutch, his face blackened, frowned in shock. "What are—"

"Is this everyone?" I asked again. "Can we leave now?"

"I think so," Tyler said.

I noticed the unconscious man Clutch was dragging was Don. But his daughter wasn't with him.

My stomach dropped. "Where's Alana?"

Clutch and Tyler looked at each other.

"Shit," Clutch said. "I didn't see her."

"Where'd you find Don?" I asked.

"The bridge," Tyler said.

I patted Clutch's chest. "Get to the ground. I'll see you guys below!"

His eyes widened. "No! It's too dangerous!" Clutch yelled.

I pursed my lips. Every nerve in my body was shouting to stay with Clutch, but I couldn't leave a child behind to burn. My bottom lip trembled. "Get those two to safety," I said and then burst away before I changed my mind. Clutch yelled after me, but I kept going.

"Alana!" I shouted and coughed. To my right, flames licked at the varnished wood and I flew up the outside stairs, taking the steps two at a time. When I saw no one outside the bridge, I jumped inside. "Alana!"

I could barely hear her whimpering above the noise of the fire, but I heard her. Jesus. Why did kids always have to hide? I bent over and found her hugging herself under the navigator's station. "Come here. I'm bringing you to your daddy."

She didn't move, and I didn't plan on taking the time to encourage her to come out on her own accord. I grabbed her arm and yanked her out. She cried, but I didn't take time to console her. A crying kid was a hell of a lot better than a dead kid. I lifted her into my arms, and ran outside and down the steps. The heat was excruciating. Alana kicked and squirmed, and I nearly dropped her. Suddenly, Clutch was there, and he took the girl from me.

"You're supposed to be on the boat!" I yelled, angry that he was still in danger.

He ignored me, and I followed him down the steps. It was hard to move fast when trying not to breathe. Alana continued to wiggle in Clutch's arms, but he was able to keep a hold on her. By the time we'd reached the deck, fire lapped at the deck boards all around us.

"Catch!" Clutch called out to Tyler, and then tossed the girl.

She flew several feet through the air. Her scream stopped abruptly when Tyler caught her. She sobbed in between coughing fits. He put her down next to her father on the already full platform and she clung to him. Tyler looked up. "We'll see you on the ground."

Tyler worked the pulley system that Wes had built, and the platform lowered. I glanced over the edge to see the hull around the aluminum ladder smoking. I bent over and touched the ladder with a gloved hand. It hissed like a hot iron, and I yanked back. "It's too hot."

Clutch frowned and then squeezed the pulley's ropes used for the platform. "We'll rappel down the ropes once Tyler's down."

Heat seeped through the rubber soles of my boots. I nodded quickly. "Got it."

The wood cracked beneath my feet. I grabbed for the rail, but was too late. The floor gave away, and I found myself falling into a furnace. My hands scrambled to grab onto anything. Clutch gripped my wrists, and pulled me up. The heat sizzled straight through my clothes, and I clenched my teeth against the oven temperatures.

When he pulled me to my feet against him on the deck, my breath came out and I leaned my forehead against his hot neck. I looked up at his burned red face. "You caught me."

His frown was overcome by his intense gaze, and he squeezed me hard against him. "I'd never let you go."

A tear escaped my eyes and I squeezed him right back. "Good" was all I managed to get out.

Flames licked up from the hole. Clutch twisted us around and before I knew it we were sliding down the outside of the hull. I made myself as small as I could and clung to him like a koala bear. I fought to keep from coughing, trying to keep completely still so that he could more easily handle both of our weight. I didn't know how he managed to support both of us, but he did. As soon as I felt his legs hit the wood dock, I stood but refused to let go.

"Come on, guys!" Jase yelled out.

Clutch and I looked around at the same time to see Jase standing alone on the dock. When I didn't see the pontoon, I frowned. "Where's the pontoon?"

"Tyler's driving it back," he replied. "Come on."

Clutch grabbed my hand and we hurried behind him across the island. Zeds reached out to us, but we ran past them. The speedboat came into view behind a thick bush. The motor was already running. We tumbled onto the floor while Jase backed us away from the bank.

As Jase navigated through the debris- and zed-infested water, I looked down at Clutch. He brushed his thumb across my cheekbone as he looked into my eyes. I mean, he *really* looked into my eyes, as though I was the only thing in the world, and it was perfect. His warm breath tingled my lips. After a while, he smirked. "There's not a single thing I could say right now that wouldn't sound completely idiotic."

I smiled, closed my eyes, and rested my head on his chest. His heart, still pounding from our narrow escape, beat strong. My head rose and fell with each breath he took. "Try it."

He didn't.

"Hang in there, guys," Jase said. "We're coming up on the dock."

I grudgingly rolled off Clutch and sat up. Clutch pulled himself onto a seat. It took several long minutes while we waited for boats to be moved before we could get to the ramp. When we stepped onto the rocky soil, Tyler was waiting for us with a hard look. "Take ten to regroup and load into your Humvee. We're heading out to the first house we find and staying there tonight."

None of us replied or acknowledged. We simply trudged up the rocky bank. At the top, I turned around to see the *Aurora* lit up like its namesake.

After I reclaimed my rifle from Joe, I headed back to our Humvee with the Charlie Coyote on the hood. Jase already had the engine running.

Two hours later, after the sun had long since set, we lay on the living room floor of an old two-story farmhouse with nineteen seventies decor. My eyes burned from smoke, and my skin still felt hot, even in the cold house. Exhaustion forced me into a sleep that I don't think my mind would have otherwise allowed. Not with all the fresh images of flames, lost friends, and burnt corpses filling my head.

When I awoke some time later, I found Clutch and Jase awake, one sitting on either side of me and leaning against the wall. I pulled myself up, squeezed in between them, and wrapped an arm around each of them. With my "family," I felt safe. But the devil was in the details. Sure, I felt safe right now, but we had no home, no food, and no weapons. Nothing except for what we had on our backs, and outside it was snowing.

PART NINE
NEW EDEN

Twenty-Eight

Thirty-two Fox survivors remained after the fire, but more should have survived. Most of those who died were lost below decks when they went in to grab their possessions. It was a funny thing how, even at the end of the world, people were so attached to their possessions that they risked their lives for them.

The final casualty, Don, was found dead this morning when he didn't wake. Doc figured the man had succumbed to an internal injury since his lower back was bruised and distended. His daughter, Alana, refused to let go of him and had to be dragged away. She screamed until she fainted.

The snow covered everything in a light blanket of white, making the world look deceptively clean. The house smelled like pungent smoke since no one had washed up last night, and we only had the smoky, filthy clothes on our backs. It took nearly an hour to hook up the only surviving portable generator to the well pump, and another four hours for everyone to wash up with ice cold water.

We didn't get on the road until noon, and we had no breakfast or lunch served. Vicki, with some help from Joe, had collected wild leaves and made tea to curb everyone's hunger. About a dozen of us, who always wore "every day carry" packs, had protein bars and water filters. I'd given one of my bars to Benji but none to anyone else. It wasn't because I was selfish. It was because we needed to maintain our strength so we could find food for the others. It didn't stop people from eying me with disdain as I zipped up my backpack and slid it over my shoulders, though.

Clutch and Tyler had constantly told people to always carry emergency bags, but few actually did. I wanted to tell each and every one of them to fuck off, that I'd gladly give any one of them a bar if they were willing to go find food. Except they didn't want to earn the bar. They just wanted the handout.

"Let's load up," Tyler announced to the room full of people, without making eye contact with anyone.

I frowned. Always before, Tyler had an underlying warm tone to his words. Since yesterday, everything he said was hard and to the point. He kept his arms crossed over his chest, and he didn't even respond when Vicki hugged him. It was like he'd completely closed himself off from everyone.

"I'll take the lead vehicle," Tyler said. "Griz and Jase will take the scout vehicle. They will advance ahead of the convoy and recon any houses for food. Clutch and Cash will cover our flank. We'll head north until we can safely cross the river. We'll stop outside the first town we reach today to split up and search for food. Any questions?"

"Why don't we stay here?" someone asked. "Have the scouts go for food like they've always done."

"Since we know the area around the river has already been picked clean, we need to move on. There's nothing here for us."

"What's our destination?" Frost asked. Diesel sprawled around Benji, both napping next to the older man. Frost had never given the dog any food meant for people, but when the *Aurora* burned so had all of Diesel's kibble. The dog, just like everyone else, no longer had anything to eat. Already, the griping had started. Complaints that the dog would take precious food.

Complaining about a dog wasn't a serious issue, but it revealed the mood of Camp Fox. If relationships were collapsing the first day on the road, we wouldn't last three days before everyone was at one another's throats.

"We're heading back toward Fox Hills since we're familiar with the area and the herds should've passed through there at least a week ago. We'll stop along the way at any place that's safe and has food, including every military base and armory so we can replenish our gear."

"What if we don't find food," someone else asked, and several others chimed in agreement.

Tyler didn't even pause. "Then we go hungry."

After Tyler's uncharacteristically harsh response, no one else voiced any more questions.

Fifteen minutes later, everyone had split into four Humvees, one HEMTT, and the two gas trucks. With fewer people and no gear, all other vehicles were left behind simply because we didn't need them anymore.

Less than an inch of snow covered the ground, so we didn't have to deal with shitty road conditions on top of everything else. Griz and Jase pulled out first in Bravo team's Humvee—the one with a pinup girl painted on the hood—and disappeared out of sight. Clutch and I had time to wait since we would be the last vehicle to head out. I was glad I was with Clutch rather than Tyler since Tyler's mood had been so sour since the fire.

Not that anyone was in a cheerful mood.

I drove, and Clutch stood behind the .30 cal. We'd decided we would switch positions every hour so neither of us would get too cold. This morning, we'd counted our rounds that we kept in the Humvee. Just over two hundred for our rifles and fourteen hundred for the machine gun. Not bad, but I would've liked to have had ten times that for a cross-country trip.

Tyler led the convoy and he kept us slow, below thirty miles per hour. That speed allowed plenty of time to prepare for any zeds that discovered us, and made it easy for Clutch and me to alternate positions. The slow progress also allowed for a chance to admire the beautiful day outside. Snow dusted the trees lining both sides of the winding river road. A gentle breeze pressed against the branches, sending maple seeds spinning to the ground like tiny helicopters. The sense of peace was surreal, given all the chaos in our lives over the past several days.

Jase reported in on the radio every thirty minutes. He and Griz had found a dented can of creamed corn under a kitchen counter at one farm. Two other farms offered nothing, and all three farms had clearly been looted. Whether the looters were still alive or not, we couldn't know, so Tyler warned Griz and Jase to proceed with caution.

The road map showed that the closest bridge over the Mississippi was near Parkerstown. If the zeds had cleared out of town, Tyler announced we'd camp there for the night after searching every store and house. With a large sporting goods store, it offered the possibility to restock gear. That was, if it hadn't been looted yet.

The convoy came to a stop before us, and I craned my head out the window to see why. "Do you see anything?" I asked Clutch.

"Everything looks clear up ahead," he replied.

Tyler's voice came over the radio. *"Contact across the river in the trees. Looks like a single troop with eyes on us."*

I scanned the tree line across the river, but didn't see anyone. "Do you see him yet?"

A moment passed. "I have him," Clutch said. "Looks Army issue."

"Scout vehicle to proceed with extreme caution. Make contact only if you're confident he's Army. Report back in ten."

Griz's response came. *"Roger. Scout vehicle closing in now."* Then he tacked on, *"If he's military, he's a damn beautiful sight."*

I scowled at the idea of Jase and Griz heading blindly into a possible ambush. Tyler and Griz had far more faith in an altruistic military structure than I did. I'd figured that the world collapsing didn't exclude the military. Still, we needed food, shelter, and protection. If this guy was the real deal, then we couldn't *not* make contact.

After a few more minutes, the convoy moved forward again. The next hour was tense as I kept waiting to hear from Griz, but there still was no response by the time we reached Parkerstown. Rather than leading us into town, Tyler brought the convoy to the huge store not far from the river.

We parked in the open parking lot. Several snow-covered cars sat, but there were no fresh tire tracks or footprints in the snow. The glass entrance doors were shattered, leaving the building wide open. Joe and Bryce pulled their Humvee close to the entrance. They stepped out and after a minute of looking inside, they walked through the doors.

They emerged about fifteen minutes later. One pulled out his handheld radio, and Bryce's voice came through. *"All clear. Not a single zed on initial pass. The place looks to be cleared out of ammo and guns."* With the exception of Clutch's handheld radio he'd had with him when we'd burned the bridge bastards, all the other handhelds were all still on board the *Aurora*, making Clutch's a valuable commodity.

"Roger that," Tyler responded. *"All right everyone, we're camping in here for the night. All scouts report to the front to make a full clearing pass. Everyone else, stay in your vehicles until I give the all-clear."*

The two gas trucks couldn't get the same frequencies as the military vehicles, so Tyler stopped by each to relay his orders.

"That means we're up," Clutch said as he climbed down. We still had our rifles, but the scouts off duty when the fire broke out on the *Aurora* couldn't get to their rifles in time. Many still had their machetes and swords, but were at a definite disadvantage if shit hit the fan now.

I grabbed my rifle and stepped outside. My boots left sooty prints in the snow. When Clutch joined my side, we headed slowly toward Tyler.

Scouts now made up about half of Camp Fox. Before the fire, three out of every four Fox survivors were scouts, and nearly all were Guardsman. Manpower had been Fox's greatest strength. But when civilians ran out during the fire, many scouts ran in to save who and what they could. So many had been lost. Camp Fox wouldn't intimidate any enemy now.

As we approached the huge store, I noticed the pile of burnt bodies near the building. Still covered with snow, I could only assume—and hope—they were zeds. I stepped through the doors. Glass crunched under my boots.

Inside, we walked under a ceiling of antlers that led to a wide-open space of clothes and merchandise. Much of it had been knocked over and shoved into piles. "Spread out," Tyler said. "Stay in pairs and yell if you come across a tango." He pointed to each team and then in a direction for them to head. After he motioned for us to head toward the boat section, Clutch and I started walking.

As we searched our section, I couldn't help but admire the rows of new boats and jet skis. "This place is a goldmine."

"I agree. There's plenty of gear still here that we can use," he said. "But I'd bet any food is as far gone as the ammo. We'd better find something for everyone by tomorrow or else their moods are going to turn shitty."

"Shittier, you mean," I said with a smirk, and we continued our search.

After making sure the store was absolutely, positively clear of zeds, Camp Fox was reestablished for the night in the hunting area toward the back of the store. The entrance was blocked off with a Humvee.

As people settled in new clothes and sleeping bags, Tyler tried to reach Griz and Jase on the handheld, but the signal was weak in the building. He decided it wasn't worth the risk of going outside after dark, and set up his sleeping pad and bag next to the wall.

"Do you want Clutch and me to go check on them?" I asked hopefully. The idea of being safe and comfortable while Jase and Griz was who-knew-where and caught up in who-knew-what seemed like a betrayal, and the guilt was eating at me.

Tyler didn't look up. "No. Get some rest."

"They might be looking for us."

"We need to keep everyone as centrally located as possible. I can't risk sending out scouts at night. I'll try to reach them again in the morning."

I never moved and watched him for a moment. He had his hands in his pocket and he seemed to be staring off into nowhere, though his jaw was clenched tight. "You want to talk about it?"

"No."

I stood there for another long moment and finally sighed. "Okay. Sleep tight."

I started to walk away, but then Tyler said something I couldn't hear.

"What's that?" I asked.

He nearly collapsed as he sat down. He rubbed his temples before looking up. "I screwed up."

I frowned and took a seat next to him. I placed a hand on his shoulder. "How so?"

"The fire." He leaned back against the wall. "It's my fault."

Confused, I cocked my head. "How is it your fault? The plan was solid. No one knew the bridge wouldn't hold."

"I ordered the mission. It's my fault."

Clutch, who'd just walked up, handed Tyler and me each a plastic bottle with a price tag still on it. "Water," he said. "It may still have a bit of charcoal taste, but it's okay to drink."

"Thanks," I said and waited for Tyler to continue. When he didn't, I did. "Someone had to take charge on the *Aurora* or else we would've kept debating until it was too late. You may have ordered the mission, but I volunteered for it. If you're looking for blame, it falls on every single person in this room. We're all in this together. Wins, losses, they belong to all of us."

Tyler's lips pursed and he looked off to the side.

"You know something?" Clutch asked after taking a drink from his own bottle. "If you didn't feel the weight of making tough decisions, then I couldn't ever respect you. I've got to admit, I didn't like you at first. I wanted to kick your ass, to tell the truth, but you earned my respect. You're the right leader for Camp Fox. You're not afraid to lead but you've also held onto your compassion. That's rare nowadays. You're exactly what we need."

Tyler's brow rose and the tension seemed to bleed from his features. "You mean that?"

Clutch held up a hand. "Jesus. Don't expect a hug or anything."

Tyler chuckled, and it was the first time I'd seen his smile for some time. "You two had better get some rest. Who knows how long a trip we've got ahead of us."

Reluctantly, I set up a sleeping bag next to Clutch, and we waited for

Jase and Griz to show up. Vicki warmed up the camping area by lighting fires in small charcoal grills.

Near dawn, shouting snapped me awake. Blinding light from flashlights shone on us from every direction, and I shaded my eyes, searching to make out the source. Shots were fired, echoed by cries and more shouting.

"Faces down! Don't move! If you move, we will shoot you!"

Before Clutch and I made startled, terrified eye contact, I saw one of our assailants dressed in full camo hunting gear.

Bandits.

Twenty-Nine

"Jesus. Except for their vehicles, these guys don't have shit," one of the bandits said to the man in charge while we all knelt on the freezing ground outside the store. Well, we all knelt except for the two Fox guards who had been on duty when the bandits arrived. No one had seen them since, and I suspected we would never see them again.

One of the bandits had moved the Humvee that blocked the entrance and was now rummaging through all of our vehicles. "Where's your food?"

"We don't have any," someone said.

Every single one of the bandits had a mean look, like they were all pissed off at the world and thought they deserved special treatment now. The leader, missing three fingers on his left hand, had the cruelest look of all. One of his men had called him Hodge, and we all avoided meeting his gaze. He had a mean look, like he'd been this way even before the outbreak. His eyes—cunning like a fox—seemed devoid of any emotion as he looked over the Camp Fox survivors like we were nothing more than cattle.

Our backpacks sat, opened and empty of contents, in a pile behind him, along with our coats. All of our weapons had been confiscated and carried into the store. The bandits who had disarmed me had been overly thorough. I'd wanted to scream and bite as they'd groped, but I'd stood perfectly still with a clenched jaw, afraid of what they'd do to Clutch if I'd reacted. When one was busy checking under my bra with his cold hands, he commented, "Too bad. This one wouldn't be too bad looking if her face wasn't so messed up."

The other one chuckled. "Easy fix. Just turn her around."

Clutch managed to tackle that one before three others knocked him to the ground. He'd gotten a black eye and swollen cheek, but they moved on from me after that. I felt sorry for the other women, who received the same treatment.

When Mary was grabbed, her husband lunged forward and they kicked him in the stomach. As they dragged her back toward the store, she begged them to stop. Her husband, still holding his stomach, climbed to his feet and ran toward her. A bandit raised his rifle, and my eyes widened. Shots cut through the night air, and I jumped. He collapsed, and she screamed. The bandit holding her punched her and she went limp. Tension hung in the air as she disappeared inside.

"If any of you idiots try something stupid like that," Hodge said, pointing to the body. "You're going to end up the same way. Got it?"

No one moved.

Hodge weaved through us, looking at each person one at a time. As he stood behind us, he spoke. "Many of you are wearing uniforms. Are you associated with New Eden?"

No one spoke.

Something moved, and somebody cried out. I swallowed back my fear.

"I've never heard of New Eden," Tyler said from several feet to my left.

The leader came walking around and stood in front of Tyler. "If you're not with New Eden, what base are you with?"

Tyler didn't answer.

Hodge bent to stare him down, his smooth brown hair covering some of his face, but Tyler stared straight ahead. "Yeah, you're military, all right." He looked up and narrowed his eyes at Clutch. "I'd bet quite a few of you are." He walked over to Deb and held his pistol to her head. She whimpered and tightened her lips. "Since I'm not, I'll ask one more time. What base are you with."

"We're with the Camp Fox National Guard base," Tyler ground out.

Hodge lifted his pistol. "Never heard of it, but that doesn't matter. You military folks are all in bed together, so you are going to help me."

"Please," Vicki said through shivers. "We're hungry. At least feed the children."

The leader looked up. "Tell me boys. How does a beggar earn food around here?"

"Fuck for it or fight for it," several bandits replied in unison.

A cruel grin curved upward on Hodge's face as he bent down to get eye-level with Vicki. "So, which is it going to be?"

Her lips tightened, and she didn't answer.

He stood, nodded to his men, and they walked around and yanked the adult men forward and made them kneel in front of us. I bit back my cry when they pulled Clutch away and made him kneel with the others. I wanted to lunge forward, to grab him and run, but I didn't move, feeling like a failure.

Soon, every adult man was kneeling in a row before us in the snow. Clutch and I never broke eye contact. I'd never seen him look as pissed off as he did right now. I prayed he didn't do something stupid and heroic. Hodge walked behind each of them, holding his pistol in his hand. "So tell me, which one of you are in charge of this little group?"

No one spoke.

"I'm not going to ask again." He nodded to one of his men, who went to stand next to Vicki, holding his pistol against her temple. She closed her eyes, and tears fell down her cheeks. "In three seconds, I'm going to have my colleague here kill this woman."

He looked across our faces. "One."

Clutch opened his mouth to speak. My brows furrowed, and I shook my head once. *Don't you dare.*

"Two."

"I'm in charge," Bryce said hurriedly from next to Tyler.

The leader's brows rose as though he was genuinely surprised, and he sauntered over to Bryce. "You? Really?"

"You've got me. Release my people. They've done nothing wrong," Bryce added. Even though his voice cracked, he put on a good act. I almost believed it myself.

"No, I don't believe I will." He raised his sidearm, and clicked off the safety.

"Stop!" Tyler yelled. "I'm Captain Tyler Masden, commanding officer of Camp Fox."

Hodge smirked. He grabbed Bryce's hair and yanked his head back to look him in the face. "That was stupid of you. I already knew that asshole was in charge. Everybody knows that whoever speaks up first is a hero, an idiot, or in charge. Usually all three are the same."

He looked up to his men. "Get them to their feet."

Tyler, Clutch, and the other fifteen men were pulled to their feet by the eight bandits. I could see in Clutch's, Tyler's, and all of the Fox men's eyes that they wanted to turn and attack. We outnumbered them, but they outgunned us. It would be a massacre.

The leader stood in front of Tyler. "Now I know how far I can push you and how loyal your people are to you. Disappointing on both counts."

He walked down the line of Fox men and back to Tyler. "You are going to help us draw that New Eden squadron into an ambush."

"We won't help you," Tyler said harshly.

"I should clarify. I don't need your help. Your *uniforms* are going to help us draw the New Eden squadron into an ambush. Now, strip."

It took rifles shoved into their backs for them to take off their fatigues. As a scout, I wore fatigues, too, but I wasn't ordered to take off mine, probably because I was smaller and mine wouldn't fit any of the bandits. I knelt there and watched as Clutch and the others pulled off their boots and stripped down to their T-shirts, socks, and underwear.

They stood nearly naked in the freezing morning air, their breaths making cloud puffs, while two of the bandits carried their clothing away. Goosebumps covered Clutch's tattoos on his arms.

"Hey, Hodge. We'd better hustle," a bandit called out as he came running up. "The New Eden pricks are just about to cross the bridge."

I think everyone's gaze turned toward the bridge in the distance. Trees with golden and red leaves blocked much of the view, but it was impossible to miss the squadron of heavily armored vehicles approaching in the distance.

"Well, then." Hodge checked his pistol. "Thank you for your service."

He walked over to Tyler, held his pistol to Tyler's temple and fired. A thunderous shot broke the silence. A woman screamed. Tyler fell face-forward, and a pool of dark blood spread out from around his head.

Air flew from my lungs and I couldn't breathe. My heart felt like it'd stopped. Someone clung to me—Vicki, I think—and I embraced her numbly. Ice zapped the strength from my legs, yet I somehow managed to stay on my feet. My vision swirled. Not Tyler. He couldn't die. He was too good to die.

People cried out. Hodge held his pistol against Bryce's temple and looked across our faces. He fired, and Bryce collapsed. He moved to the next man, again looked across the group of survivors, and fired.

My mouth opened as I watched in shock as the bandit stopped next to Clutch. My world spun and my legs gave out. I reached for Clutch. "No!"

THIRTY

Instead of executing Clutch, Hodge nodded to one of his men who raised his rifle and slammed it down on Clutch's head from behind. He collapsed into a pile. Tears fell down my cheeks, and I realized the leader was watching me with keen interest.

"You're a bastard," I said simply, the ice in my body having given way to boiling hatred.

He smiled broadly. "You see," he said. "I keep the ones with something to lose. It's entertaining the things I can make them do to try to save each other. I think I'll have fun with both of you."

Never, I thought to myself.

"Boss," one of the men said. "They're coming up fast."

He looked toward the bridge, before turning to his men. "Get the rest inside. We'll finish later. We have to get changed before the squadron arrives."

"On your feet," one of the bandits ordered, waving his gun at us.

Clutch was just coming to with a groan, and I helped drag him up. The back of his head had a wet spot from an open gash. I slid his arm over my shoulder. His skin was freezing cold. Deb came up and grabbed his other arm. The bandits rushed everyone back into the store and back to our small campsite. The seven small grills still had glowing embers from last night's fires.

Deb and I helped Clutch onto his sleeping bag, and I wrapped my bag around his shoulders. I swallowed and my eyes blurred. The shock of everything was starting to give way, and adrenaline and the cold made me shake nearly uncontrollably. I held tightly onto Clutch, and he wrapped his arms around me, shaking just as much.

"I can't believe they shot Tyler," Deb said in a monotone voice.

All but two bandits disappeared into the back. The pair who remained kept their rifles leveled on us while the others changed. One of the bandits was busy admiring his new rifle: Clutch's Blaser.

Less than a minute later, Hodge came out in Guardsman fatigues, walked over to the pair standing guard over us, and said something I couldn't hear. When he turned to us, his eyes narrowed. "If any of you try to run, you will be shot. Got it?"

He didn't wait for a response. He left with the others dressed in clothes our guys had been wearing minutes earlier, and I wanted to see his blood stain the clothes he stole.

I clung to Clutch, partly to warm him and mostly because I needed to feel him—his breathing, his heartbeat, his *life*. His breathing steadied my own, and I felt my pounding heart return to a level where it didn't feel like I was having a panic attack. After a minute or two, his grogginess wore off and he no longer swayed or shook as badly. He gingerly touched the back of his head and winced. "*Fuck.*"

I looked up at him. I wanted to ask if he was okay, but when I opened my mouth, a sob threatened to get in the way.

He cupped my face with both hands. He didn't kiss me, only pressed our foreheads together as though he needed the physical connection as much as I did. Tears streamed down my cheeks. He brushed away a tear with his thumb. "Sh. Don't cry," he whispered softly.

The soft words were such a contrast to his rough palms, yet both were full of emotion and I leaned into him. "I almost lost you," I whispered back, my voice cracking.

He looked up and glared at the bandits, each on opposite sides of our indoor campground, before looking back at me. "You shouldn't have cried out," he whispered. "They'll use me to hurt you now."

If I hadn't cried out, he'd be dead right now. Rather than saying that, I simply shrugged.

Around us, the remaining Fox survivors all sat in shellshock. Many were crying in despair and loss, some stared blankly into nothingness, and others looked downright pissed, like they were about to go kamikaze on the guards. I don't know how I looked to them because I was feeling all of those emotions at the same time.

Tyler's rumpled blue sleeping bag sat empty, along with a few others, and I turned away, not having the strength to think about the permanence of what had happened. I could only hope that Jase and Griz were safe.

The two bandits didn't stop Benji as he walked around the clothing racks, picking out clothes and bringing piles to each of the men. Diesel barked from one of the back rooms. The dog had gotten lucky. When Diesel had growled when the bandits manhandled Frost, one of the men had raised his rifle to shoot the dog, but the bandit leader took a shine to the dog and claimed him as his. Though, I wasn't yet convinced the leader wanted Diesel as his pet or for dinner.

"How did everything go so wrong?" I finally asked against Clutch's tattooed chest. "What do we do now?"

He watched the guard, and didn't speak for at least a minute. His body tensed and his gaze hardened. "I'm getting my rifle back."

THIRTY-ONE

"Let me know if the guard on the rock looks this way," Clutch whispered.

I frowned, peering into his brown eyes. "Okay."

I could feel his arm move behind me. *Oh.* Careful to reveal nothing, I forced myself to stare blankly in the bandit's direction as Clutch signaled to the other scouts. The bandit was lounging on a manmade rock next to a stuffed bear.

The game continued for several minutes. Clutch signaled while I kept an eye on one guard and he watched the one nearest us. I squeezed Clutch's thigh any time the man I watched looked in our general direction.

"We're set. We just need a diversion now," Clutch whispered finally.

I tried to think of anything I could do to distract the bandits. Outside, I could hear the sounds of big engines, signaling the approach of New Eden. I hoped they saw through the bandits' charade, but I couldn't count on it. As I concentrated on thinking of a diversion, I noticed Vicki watching us intently. Her cheeks were splotchy from crying. With the slowest movement, she gave a nod like she knew Clutch was up to something. I supposed, since she was sitting in between Clutch and the other scouts, chances were she was quite aware of exactly what was about to happen.

Vicki stood abruptly.

The bandit nearest us swung Clutch's rifle around. "Whoa there, lady. What do you think you're doing?"

Vicki pointed to Deb, who was lying on her side. "She's pregnant. If she doesn't eat soon, she'll lose the baby."

"So? Why would I care?"

Vicki took a deep breath and then untucked her shirt. "I'm buying her a meal."

It took a moment for her offer to register, and then a huge grin spanned the bandit's face. He looked up to his partner. "What do you think?"

The other bandit shrugged. "As long as you do it in here, the boss won't care. Just keep your rifle on them."

The bandit turned back to Vicki. "You got yourself a deal. A meal for the broad. Come here."

She stood adamant, and her jaw jutted out. "Give her something to eat first."

He thought for a moment and then shrugged, reached into his vest pocket, and tossed a small bag to Deb. "Okay. Done. Now, get over here," he motioned to Vicki. "Grab onto that clothes rack. Face your friends."

I found myself holding my breath as Vicki took slow, tentative steps to the bandit. I slowly pulled away from Clutch so he could make his move, whatever it may be. My arms wrapped around my abdomen on their own, and I swallowed back fear and hate.

The bandit grabbed Vicki's belt and yanked her to him. He almost put his rifle down to go for her pants, and then seemed to realize he was still guarding us. "Pull your pants down."

She moved stiffly as she undid her belt and unbuttoned her jeans, one slow button at a time. He watched her, but every second, he glanced nervously up at us. As soon as she unbuttoned the last button, he turned her around and yanked her pants down. "Grab that rack. Don't let go or else."

She reached out and grabbed the silver bar. I felt Clutch move away from me, and I'd nearly forgotten why Vicki was up there. I heard the sound of big engines outside. The New Eden squadron had arrived.

Vicki stood there. Her determined gaze leveled above our group while the bandit struggled with unfastening his belt and pants with only one hand. The other bandit had leaned forward, captivated by the scene and oblivious to Joe and three other scouts inching closer to the rock. Clutch still sat next to me, but I noticed he now had his feet poised under him, like he was a sprinter at the gate.

The bandit finally had his pants undone, and he grabbed Vicki's hip. As he moved close to her, she shoved her head back and nailed him directly on the nose.

"Uh! Bitch!" he cried out, taking a step back, momentarily stunned.

She grabbed the barrel of his gun, and he tried to yank it from her. Clutch shoved off and closed the ten feet to them with more strength and agility than I thought he had regained. I jumped and ran after him. A couple shots fired from the direction of the other bandit, but I didn't look.

Clutch reached the bandit as soon as he yanked the rifle from Vicki and knocked her to the floor. Clutch tackled him, and I grabbed the bandit's rifle and kneeled on his wrist. He cried out, and I pulled the rifle free. Clutch chopped the guy in the throat and rolled off him. The guy got to his knees, struggling to breathe.

Vicki reached for the rifle. I handed it to her. She raised it and shot the bandit in the gut. He took a step back, tripped, and lay there, holding his bleeding stomach. She handed the rifle back to me, fastened her jeans, and then headed back to the group. I'm guessing she was aiming lower, but I didn't care as long as he was down.

Several had gathered around the other, clearly dead bandit, and I saw Joe on the floor, a stream of blood trailing from his neck. Deb looked over and sadly shook her head.

Outside, there was yelling, and then the sound of gunfire erupted. Several bandits sprinted into the store. Hodge, whose eyes were already wide, froze when he saw us, and anger tightened his visage.

"Incoming!" I yelled. I tumbled with Clutch behind a toppled display and handed him his rifle.

Clutch shouted, "Everyone, take cover! Head for the back rooms!"

He laid down cover fire while the women and children ran. The scouts took up position behind various forms of cover. The bandits fired wildly as though they were trying to decide which direction they wanted to go. White fuzz exploded from sleeping bags. Someone cried out in sharp pain.

"We need to get to a better position." Clutch looked around. "This way."

We ran and slid across a sales counter. No one seemed to be firing at us, but the entire store was filled with the sound of gunfire, and I suspected the bandits were now shooting at the New Eden soldiers and not us.

"I'm going to give you a push, and we'll take position there behind that big support beam." Clutch pointed.

I looked up at the rock ledge filled with various stuffed animals. Toward the middle, just above the giant aquariums, was what I figured had to be the support beam Clutch was talking about: a tree trunk going from floor to ceiling.

"Ready?"

I nodded. We both climbed onto the glass counter. I jumped up at the same time Clutch heaved me, and I flew onto the ledge above. He tossed me his rifle and then climbed up. I slung the rifle over my shoulder, grabbed his jeans, and helped pull him up the last bit. We ran around the animals and behind the disguised support beam. Clutch crouched, took aim, and fired. I was behind the beam and couldn't see, but knew that since Clutch hadn't fired a second shot, a bandit had just gone down.

A grenade exploded, and I peeked around the other side of the beam. Dust and flames flickered near the front sales counters. Then, a massive explosion shook the building. Something big and black crashed down onto me, and I tumbled off the ledge and into the stagnant fish tank below. The falling object landed on top of me, knocking the air from my lungs and pressing me against the bottom of the tank.

I tried to shove out from under it—a stuffed grizzly bear—but it weighed too much. Stale water filled my nose and crept down my throat. My lungs burned as I struggled harder against the bear. I grabbed at its fur and tried to twist away. Blackness and stars overtook my vision. A pounding sound reverberated through the water, and I felt a wave around me as the water flowed away. I coughed and breathed, but the bear was still crushing me. Arms yanked at me. My limbs were going numb, and I felt like I was falling.

"Cash. Godammit, look at me, girl."

The voice sounded like Clutch but it was so distant. Gradually, it drew closer and louder until I found myself coughing water and sucking air.

"Thank God," Clutch said as he held me in his arms. "Are you okay?"

After a final cough, I held up my thumb.

He gave me a hard kiss and then pulled me to my feet before I'd even realized what he'd done. A blend of shock and thrill brought me back to reality.

"They're bringing this place down with artillery fire. We need to get out of here."

Thirty-Two

Clutch practically dragged me through the store. I recognized a couple of the bodies lying motionless on the floor, but, thankfully, nearly all of the Fox survivors were nowhere in sight. I had to believe they'd made it out okay. No one was shooting at us. The fight seemed to have moved back outside, but rounds were still going off everywhere around us. When we reached the hallway under the Exit sign, Clutch took the lead.

We ran past a room where Mary's body lay crumpled next to a desk, her lifeless eyes staring at us. Not far from her, I saw our weapons in a big pile. The bandits must've dumped them there when they were in a hurry to prepare for the New Eden guys. I stopped and pulled Clutch back. "Wait. We'll need these."

He stopped but didn't let go until he noticed the weapons. We rushed into the room, and I picked through the pile to find my rifle and knife. I couldn't find my pistol, so I just started pulling out anything that looked like something I could use. The entire time I focused completely on the weapons and refused to look anywhere even close in the direction of Mary's broken body.

Clutch did the same. I noticed he kept his eyes focused on the weapons, looking at each one. We each took the best machetes, knives, spears, and sidearms. Clutch even grabbed an extra rifle, but I took only mine to keep the weight down. The last thing he picked up before he came to his feet was Tyler's sword, still in its sheath.

"He would've wanted you to have it," I said between slinging what I could over my shoulder and fastening everything else in my weapons belt.

His brows rose but he quickly regained his composure. "Let's go."

We hurried toward the exit. Clutch threw the steel doors open, and we found three soldiers aiming their rifles at us.

"Whoa!" Clutch yelled, holding his rifle up. "We're not bandits!"

They didn't lower their weapons, but one soldier nodded in my direction. "They don't look like bandits."

"Where are you from?" another soldier asked. "And you'd better answer quick."

"I'm with Camp Fox," Clutch replied. "Sergeant Joe Seibert with the 75th Ranger Regiment."

His answer seemed to suffice because the soldier motioned toward the parking lot. "There's a HEMTT by the road. You can join the rest of your group on it. You'd better hurry."

We ran around the corner of the building and the HEMTT came into view. It was surrounded protectively by Humvees. A soldier I didn't recognize was lifting five-year-old Alana into the back.

Our biggest challenge was getting to the HEMTT. The bandits had taken our keys and now had our vehicles, making the battle closely matched. Every few seconds, a bandit ran out from behind one of our Humvees and lobbed a grenade at the New Eden vehicles as another bandit drove slowly, using the Humvee as a shield.

Rounds went through the Humvee's window, blood splattered, and the Humvee sped forward until it ran straight into one of New Eden's Humvees. Red and violet flames burst from the ensuing explosion.

"Wait. Look!" I pointed to a bandit trying to reload the .30 cal on our Humvee.

"Son of a bitch." Clutch took off as quickly as he could run toward the Humvee. He lifted his rifle and shot the bandit in the back. Clutch handed me his rifle and we both climbed up onto the back of the Humvee. He manned the .30, turning it from the New Eden trucks to the bandits in the Camp Fox vehicles. Three bandits stood on the back of Camp Fox's HEMTT. One had a rocket launcher while the other two had rifles, laying down cover fire. Clutch and a soldier from New Eden zeroed in on the risk at the same moment. Two bandits fell with shots from different directions, but the bandit with the launcher fired before he fell.

I watched as the rocket shot through the air, leaving a smoke trail behind it. When I realized its trajectory, I cried out. "No!"

My shout did nothing to stop the rocket from hitting the HEMTT. The vehicle went up in an explosion. Fire engulfed the large vehicle. Debris flew twenty feet in every direction.

Every single person that was here from Camp Fox was on that HEMTT. Everyone we'd fought to protect over the past several months, everyone we'd saved from the fire, everyone we cared for, was gone in a single blast of heat. I don't know how long I stood there, numbly watching the HEMTT burn. All my senses seemed to shut down until the sounds of battle grew in volume.

The New Eden soldiers fired .30 cal rounds back at the bandits, but the sounds of gunfire were growing less and less frequent. Either they were running out of ammo or they were running out of people. Artillery and grenade blasts rang in my ears.

I looked at Clutch to find him staring at the burning wreckage. Slowly, his jaw clamped shut and his eyes and lips narrowed. He maneuvered the .30 cal and began firing relentlessly at the bandits. The sudden sense of loss was blanketed by adrenaline-infused anger. "Kill them all," I ordered, though my words were drowned out by machine gun fire.

Clutch turned to me. "I'm out."

I looked around. The store behind us had become a massive fire. The soldiers who had been around back came running around the store, and were gunned down as soon as they appeared. I twisted to find the source and then saw the bandit who'd given Clutch a black eye standing behind one of New Eden's .30 cals. The Humvee took off, and I saw Hodge in the driver's seat.

I jumped up onto the roof of the Humvee and took aim. I didn't account for their speed properly, and my first shot missed. My second clipped the bandit's neck, and he fell off the back. It'd been awhile since I'd killed a man, but the fact didn't faze me. In fact, I found pleasure watching the blood spray from his neck.

I aimed at Hodge, but he turned sharply, and I couldn't get a clear shot. He pulled out of the parking lot and sped onto the road. I fired off three shots, but I doubted any found their target. Even if we took off after him in our Humvee, we'd likely never catch up in time. So, Clutch and I watched helplessly as the bastard drove off.

When he disappeared behind the trees, I noticed that there were no more sounds of gunfire. Fires crackled everywhere, and I heard someone calling for help.

Unlike massive climatic scenes in movies where the bad guy got his due, this battle had simply...ended.

My ears were ringing, and my adrenaline numbed my nerves. I stared off at the burning HEMTT. Across the parking lot, no one was walking. There were bodies everywhere, but no one was standing. There was no one left except us.

"We're all that's left," I said emotionlessly, though I knew my emotions were still in there, too beaten down by hopelessness to dare rise. "There's no one left."

Clutch wrapped an arm around me and I found myself holding onto him like he was my lifeline. "We have each other."

THIRTY-THREE

Our first pass through the aftermath was search and rescue. Out of all the Camp Fox survivors, New Eden soldiers, and bandits, we found only one person who wasn't dead or near-death. Marco, a soldier from New Eden, had taken a shot to his helmet and had been knocked out cold. When he woke, it took him some time to come to grips with the loss of his entire squadron. For the first few minutes, he moved restlessly around, counting vehicles and searching for his squadron. When he finally realized they were all there and he was the only one left standing, he collapsed.

Once Marco came to terms with reality, Clutch asked him several questions while I sat and stared at the fires. The HEMTT continued to smoke, but no more flames licked out from the vehicle. I could only imagine the smell of so many dead inside. I tried not to think about any of the bodies belonging to someone I cared about. There'd be too much time for thinking later.

New Eden was a new super-city in Colorado formed by the military at Cheyenne Mountain. Dozens of squadrons just like Marco's had been sent out with the sole mission to save any survivors they could after the herds passed through. On their mission, they'd run across a feudalistic, ruthless group called the Black Sheep that was quickly spreading across the Midwest. The bandits who'd taken us hostage were from that group, and Marco showed us the mark on one of the bandit's body: a brand of a ram's head with curled horns.

"At least we got all these guys," Marco said. "If any got back to their captain, they'd likely come back at us with a vengeance."

I shook my head. "No. Their leader got away."

Marco's face fell before fear widened his eyes. "He'll bring back reinforcements."

Clutch climbed to his feet. "We'll be out of here long before then. But we should hurry and get wrapped up here, just in case."

I looked up to see Clutch holding a hand out to me. I took it and he pulled me up and into an embrace. Strangely, I never cried, even knowing that I'd never see Jase again, or anyone from Camp Fox, again. It broke my heart, but my brain refused to process anything. It felt like I was on autopilot, and the circuit breaker to my emotions had been turned off, and I was thankful for that small mercy.

Later, as I walked around and inventoried the wreckage, Clutch and Marco collected dog tags and carried the dead of those we knew as close to the burning store as we could in hopes the fire would take care of them before the zeds found them. When we came to Tyler's body, neither Clutch nor I could move. For the longest time, I simply stared at Tyler's limp form. I noticed Clutch did the same. His lips quivered, then he sobered and we carried Tyler away from the burning building and laid him under a tree. Clutch walked back to a Humvee and returned with a shovel. As he started digging a hole, I also grabbed a shovel and helped.

The ground was soft, but it still took a while to dig a shallow grave. Clutch grabbed Tyler's shoulders and I grabbed his legs and we lowered him as gently as possible. We stared down at Tyler's peaceful, though bloodied, features.

"Lord," Clutch said. "Bless this soldier who gave his life in the service of others. Watch over his grave so that he finds peace."

"Amen," I said with him. It was the first time I'd heard Clutch pray.

"Sorry for your loss," Marco said.

Startled, I turned around, not realizing he was standing there. I swallowed, unable to find any words. It wasn't that I was hollow inside. Anger, terror, despair, grief, misery, it was all there but isolated in a safe room. I could feel the emotions boiling like a volcano, but there was a heavy, cold stone covering the top of the volcano, letting nothing escape. It was like my body and spirit had split and were fighting to come back together.

My body went through the motions. We buried Tyler and went back to work pulling together anything salvageable. Every vehicle had taken hits, but some were still in decent shape, so it was just a matter of siphoning gas, and tossing weapons, ammo, and supplies in a pile to sort out what could still be used.

As I carried a gas can from our old HEMTT, a dog barked. The sound was deep, hair-raising, and familiar. I turned to see a Great Dane bound out from the woods, followed by someone I'd never expected to see again. I set the can down and stared. "Jase?"

At the sound of his name, he jerked and then saw me. His eyes widened. He took a step from Hali. He started to jog and then run. "Cash!"

He picked me off the ground and twirled me around.

When the realization hit me that it was really Jase, something snapped inside, and tears poured out. I hugged him so hard. I grabbed his jacket hard enough that I swore I should've been able to tear it. I kissed his cheek over and over. In between sobs, I was able to cry out, "You're alive! How?"

"When we met up with the New Eden guys, they wouldn't allow us to radio you in case we were connected with the bandits they were following. Once they figured out we were all right, we couldn't reach Tyler on the radio. So we joined up with them to find you. It was pretty easy to find the Camp Fox vehicles sitting out in the parking lot. When I saw Tyler..."

He sighed and shook his head. Hali came over and stood by us. Jase gave her a look before continuing. "I thought we were too late. Then, those guys came out wearing our fatigues, the New Eden CO figured out the ambush right away. He sent several of us around the back of the store to look for survivors, and that's when we saw Deb and Vicki run into the woods. Griz and I went after them while a few soldiers stayed behind to get anyone else. It took us a while to round up everyone hiding. I've been searching the woods forever for you."

I stared at him for a moment. Then I punched him in the arm before embracing him again, unwilling to let him go in case he was an illusion. "I thought you were dead."

He guffawed. "I was going to say the same thing. Don't scare me like that ever again."

Over his shoulder, I saw other familiar faces emerge from the woods and I smiled.

Diesel led the way for Benji and Frost. They walked up to us, and Jase patted the boy's shoulder while the dog circled us, seemingly unbothered by the recent violence. "It turns out Benji is pretty dang good at hide-and-seek."

Griz was walking with Deb and Vickie.

"Thank God," I said on a sigh. "I thought we'd lost all of you."

"We're Camp Fox," Jase said. "We're too tough to die." He looked around. "Where's everyone else?"

I frowned. "They're gone."

"Gone where?"

I tried to swallow the lump in my throat. "They're dead."

It was Jase's turn to frown. "Wh-what?"

The others had also heard me. Vickie and Deb clung to each other. Hali walked into Jase's arms. Griz gave us his back. Benji started asking his grandfather complicated questions.

Clutch came over, and Jase's face lifted.

Clutch stared at Jase, his mouth opened wide, as he looked him over in disbelief. After a pause, he stomped forward and pulled Jase into his arms. Each had their eyes clenched shut as they hugged each other.

"You're all right," Clutch said, his voice unsteady and muffled by Jase's coat.

Marco jogged up to us. "We have to hit the road. There are zeds heading this way from both the east and the west. All that artillery noise and smoke probably drew their attention."

I jogged out to look down the road and saw a few dozen zeds making slow but steady progress toward us. When I looked the other way, I saw several dozen more. "They must've been too decrepit to migrate," I wondered aloud.

"All right, Frost, how about you help Benji and the others load up." Clutch waved his arm toward the Humvee I'd been loading up. The one with the coyote head painted on the hood. "Scouts, let's double time it and grab any beans and bullets we can."

"Beans?" Benji asked. "Why beans?"

"Food," Clutch corrected. "Find any food you can."

I smiled. "We're going to need a second Humvee."

He slowly returned my smile when he realized the meaning of my words. "Yes, we have too many people for one Humvee."

Several hours later, we were back in Iowa on the first leg of our trip west to New Eden. When the sun crept low in the sky, we set up camp near the Des Moines River for the night.

Charred zeds swayed like totems on the other side of the river, the side closest to Des Moines. They had no eyes or ears or noses, but they remained. They were an ominous reminder of why we kept from crossing the river and nearing the city. I refused to watch them.

I also avoided looking at the skeletal ruins of Des Moines's tallest buildings. I hadn't seen my parents since the outbreak, and I'd accepted the fact that I'd never see them again, that they never got out, along with a million other doomed souls in and around the city. At least I knew they were at peace. The bombing had taken out most of the zeds in the city, with the exceptions of the charred zeds—burnt beyond recognition—standing like shadowy guards at the edges of town, always on the lookout for prey.

The military hadn't bombed a wide enough radius to take out all the zeds, but they had done their job on the central part of the city. Bombs weren't precise and would've taken out uninfected and infected alike. Bombs existed only to destroy and took out anything in their path. They were a bit like zeds in that: they were both destroyers.

After taking a cold-water bath, I sipped some pine needle tea and lay in the back of the Humvee with Clutch and Jase. Our legs tangled around the machine gun, but we'd all slept in more uncomfortable positions before. In fact, having both with me, safe and sound, was the best feeling I'd ever had.

Deb lay awkwardly around the back bench seats, and petite Hali fit comfortably up front. Griz, Marco, Vicki, Frost, and Benji were still working out the sleeping arrangement in the other Humvee, though I suspected Benji would tell them how it'd be. Diesel lay curled in a ball next to the vehicle, outwardly sound asleep, but I knew from experience he'd bolt awake at the smallest threatening sound.

Camp Fox had taken a heavy hit. It would never be the same, but enough of us had survived to continue the effort. Yet, I knew that as long as I had Clutch and Jase with me, things would turn out okay.

"There's one," Jase said, pointing to the sky.

"That makes twelve," Clutch said.

I closed my eyes and savored this moment, knowing that we'd be on the road again tomorrow, running from who knew what and heading toward something I wasn't sure I trusted. When I opened my eyes again, I relished the night's peace where there were no zeds and no bandits and no death.

"Another one," Jase said.

"Eagle eye, I swear," I said with a smile.

Clutch chuckled. "Thirteen."

It was probably a meteor shower, and we all enjoyed the distraction. It was by far the best entertainment we'd had in some time. Before the outbreak, I would've gotten bored. Not now. Tonight, we were together and safe.

"Oh, there's one." I pointed.

"That's a satellite, silly," Jase said.

Clutch chuckled, and we both joined in. Lying in the back of that Humvee, without any manmade lights to block the sky, we laughed as we continued to count the shooting stars.

DEADLAND RISING

PART THREE OF THE DEADLAND SAGA

PART ONE
UNCERTAINTY

ONE

The fresh blanket of snow created a pleasant illusion. With Des Moines covered in silent white, I could almost imagine that concealed underneath the disguise was not the charred, desolate remains of a city littered with hundreds of thousands of corpses.

Another round of shivers racked my body. I hugged myself to fight off the morning chill and slid off the hood of the Humvee. Pants, boots, a long-sleeve T-shirt, and a mid-weight jacket weren't nearly enough to ward off the looming Midwest winter. The cold wasn't the only reason why I was shivering, though. I shivered because I felt utterly empty and afraid.

We had nothing. No food, no supplies, and less than a day's worth of gas left.

A lot had changed in two days. I think we were all numb, still operating on autopilot. Ten of us were all that remained of Camp Fox. To call our ragtag group "survivors" was being generous.

Clutch leaned next to me against the Humvee. He watched me with those warm brown eyes. They were often his only betrayal of emotion. He tried so hard to remain stoic, always in control, but his eyes belied his hard-fought façade. He was exhausted...and worried. "How are you holding up, Cash?"

I forced a smile. "Hanging in there. You?"

He rubbed his neck. "Hanging in there." He handed me a bag of homemade granola he'd found while searching vehicles after the bandit attack alongside the Mississippi River.

As I chewed on a handful of crunchy seeds, nuts, and oats, I stared at the large store on the other side of the interstate in the far distance. Sitting on the outskirts of the city, the building had somehow survived the bombing of Des Moines. After the outbreak, the military had tried to stop the spread by bombing all large cities, but their attempts were too late to do much good. I pointed to the store. "That's a Bass Pro Shop. It could be worth checking out. If it hasn't been looted already, it would have winter coats."

Clutch let out a long, quiet whistle. "Awfully risky. I'd prefer not to get any closer to Des Moines than we are now."

"That's the same reason why most looters would have avoided it, too," I replied. "It's worth the risk. Now that most of the zeds have migrated south for the winter, this could be our best chance before these places turn into a free-for-all."

He pushed off the vehicle, opened the driver's side door, and pulled out a pair of binoculars. He scrutinized the area for long minutes before handing the binoculars to me. "It looks in good shape. There's going to be zeds still locked inside."

I adjusted the binoculars to see through the store's shattered windows but could make out nothing in the interior darkness. "We won't know until we check it out."

"Farmhouses would be safer."

"And looted already." I lowered the binoculars. "I don't want to go into a place that big and that close to the city, but we're going to freeze out here otherwise."

After a pause, he sighed. "I sure would like to get my hands on some decent fishing gear."

I chewed on my lip. "What do you say? It could be like Christmas for all of us. Just a couple months early."

Slowly, his lips curled upward. "Christmas, eh? Jase has been talking about wanting a new backpack. We still need to figure out a plan," he said.

"Plan for what?" Jase chimed in as he walked toward us, hefting a black garbage bag filled with river water ready to be filtered and boiled.

"We're going to check out that Bass Pro Shop over there." I pointed.

He cocked his head in that direction. "Cool. Count me in. After breakfast, though. I'm starving."

"You're always starving," Clutch retorted.

The insatiable teenager shrugged and headed straight for our small campfire, where Vicki was busy making some kind of wild herbal tea to go with a bucketful of walnuts and two small trout Frost had caught.

As we all gathered around the fire, Clutch and I shared our ideas regarding the store. While no one was excited about entering a sporting goods store so soon after the run-in with the bandits in a store far too similar to this one, everyone agreed that we would freeze to death without warmer clothes.

If only we had food and supplies, I would've preferred to skip the store and head straight for Fox National Park. Several of us knew the area blindfolded. Alas, we had neither food nor supplies, and there was snow on the ground. Overnight, we had changed from the survivors handing out the food to begging for food.

Marco, the only person in our group not from Camp Fox, was the only man left alive of a squad sent to search for survivors. Marco's home base was New Eden, a large sanctuary in Nebraska. He'd said New Eden had enough supplies to feed hundreds well into next year. Even better, the town had been built around a missile silo. They'd survived the herds by going underground, and could do it again. Marco was anxious to get back to New Eden, and his hope was contagious. The decision had been unanimous.

We'd accompany Marco to New Eden.

Little Benji finished breakfast first to hustle back to playing fetch with Diesel, a massive Great Dane that stood taller than the boy and would protect his short master with his life. Benji had Down syndrome, yet he'd managed to survive the outbreak on his own and ride a bicycle for miles through a zed-infested landscape to search for his grandfather.

I chuckled while I watched the two chase each other. Benji, oblivious to the ruined world around him, proved more resilient than the rest of us. He didn't seem to carry the emotional or physical scars we'd collected since the outbreak. Sometimes, I wondered if we needed Benji more than he needed us. Frost smiled at me before turning back to watch his grandson play. The older man rubbed his knuckles, a sure sign his arthritis was acting up again.

A cold wind blew through. "*Brr,*" Hali said as she snuggled closer to Jase. The teenagers tried to look casual about their friendship, but everyone knew the pair carried a flame for each other. Even the apocalypse couldn't stop young love.

"Here you go, dear. This will warm you up." Deb poured steaming tea into Hali's water bottle. Deb was moving slowly due to her daily bouts of morning sickness. She wasn't showing yet, but Vicki had said the first few months of pregnancy were always the hardest. That Tack, Deb's lover, had died only a couple weeks ago, didn't help. The woman was struggling to hang on—physically and emotionally—and there wasn't a goddamn thing any of us could do.

"I say we take a full day in the store, pull together what we can, and then spend the night inside," Griz said before quickly adding, "Assuming it's safe."

"I was thinking the same thing," Clutch said. "But, I don't like how many assumptions we're operating on right now." Clutch and Griz could've been twins with how they thought alike, despite their different personalities. I suspected much of that came about because both men were Army Rangers and every day was another mission.

"Then we'd better get packed up and check out the place," Jase said. "Maybe I'll find a new backpack. Did I mention that I'd like a new backpack?"

"Every day," Clutch groaned, giving Jase a small smile before his features tightened. "All right, everyone. We head out in fifteen. Cash, Jase, and Griz, you're with me to recon the store."

"Got it," I said, echoed by affirmations from Jase and Griz.

Clutch continued. "Marco, you'll lead the second Humvee with everyone else crammed in. I know it won't be comfortable. You'll park at the far edge of the parking lot to watch for zeds. At the first sign of trouble, you'll radio us, and we'll rendezvous back here. Otherwise, we'll bring you inside once we have a defensible position for the night. Any questions?"

Griz spit out a piece of walnut shell. "Dibs on the candy aisle."

"Each man for himself," Jase said with a sly grin.

"Okay, the two words of the day are 'quiet' and 'careful,' everyone," Clutch said as he climbed to his feet. "This place could be a goldmine, or we could be walking into a buffet line for zeds. Let's pack up and roll out."

"Or a trap set by bandits," Vicki said bitterly.

I clenched my jaw. No one needed reminded. I jumped abruptly to my feet and focused on brushing walnut shells off my pants rather than on the truth in Vicki's words.

Twelve minutes later, we were driving toward the store. Adrenaline made my knees knock. I rubbed my cold hands together. For the size of their engines, Humvees had shit for heaters, though I'd be rubbing my hands together even if it was the middle of summer.

We all had weapons. Clutch still had his Blaser rifle that he'd owned for far longer than he'd known me. I checked my pistol: a Glock on which I'd spent an hour cleaning off its previous owner's blood. I holstered it and then checked both my knife and machete.

I hoped that none of us would have to waste what precious little ammunition we had left. I had to get up close and personal to use my machete, but I figured—hoped—that the cold temperature would have slowed down any remaining zeds.

Since the zed migration a couple weeks ago, I assumed that most of the zed population would've joined the herds as they headed south. With how few zeds we'd seen since the herds passed through, my theory seemed proven. Otherwise, going this near to a city was suicide. Of course, I also knew that if the zeds couldn't have gotten out of the building to join the herds, they would still be inside, safe from the elements and starving for food.

At the edge of the parking lot stood a lone, charred zed. Snow dusted its head and shoulders. Its eyes, nose, and ears were all burnt or rotted off, which explained why it wouldn't have known to follow the herds. It wore fatigues, and I wondered how it ended up here. We drove close enough to the frozen zed that I could read the bloodied and blackened badge it wore: Pvt Jonathan Hart.

What happened to you, Private Jonathan Hart?

As soon as the thought crossed my mind, I scowled and looked away. I'd never forget his name now. I hated humanizing zeds, even though they weren't anywhere near human anymore. That much was clear. It was as though they'd transformed, or *transhumanized,* into something entirely different. Except, when they wore something that revealed the person they'd once been, it added one more vision to an already overflowing cornucopia of nightmares.

Fortunately for us, the only other zeds in the parking lot except for Private Jonathan Hart were collapsed lumps on the concrete. Even covered by snow, I knew those lumps belonged to someone's family at one time. Hell, they could've been *my* family, who I'd abandoned in Des Moines when I'd selfishly fled the city during the outbreak.

I tried not to think about the greatest regret of my life, instead focusing on the massive store before us. *Be here, now,* I ordered myself.

Other than the completely demolished glass doors, likely from the bomb blast, the building from the front was in one piece and looked to be in pretty good shape. Unfortunately, through those shattered doors, I could see sunlight. A large section of the roof must've caved in, which meant the store wasn't going to be winning any prizes for being structurally sound. Not only would we have to be careful to not set off any more seismic events within the store, we'd have to deal with concrete, roof, and rebar while searching for supplies. The bright side was any zeds that had been trapped inside *should've* been able to get out and leave with the herds.

Griz whistled. "She looked prettier from a distance," he said from the backseat, pointing at the building.

"It's what's on the inside that counts," I replied optimistically.

"Depends," he said. "Are we talking about girls or stores?"

Jase snorted.

I rotated in my seat to find Griz smirking and Jase grinning from ear to ear. "You guys are hopeless."

It was then I noticed a green sprig weaved around Griz's helmet, another one of his personal air fresheners. Without deodorant, we'd all found new ways to deal with not having baths anymore. Today, his sprig reminded me of a laurel wreath, as though he were the mighty Apollo ready for battle. "What. No wreath for me?" I asked.

"If I make one for you, I'll have to make one for everyone," Griz replied.

"You made one for Benji," I said.

"The little trickster conned me into making him one."

"Diesel even has one on his collar," Jase added.

Griz shrugged. "He conned me, too."

I dramatically acted put out. "You made one for the dog before making one for me?"

"Yup," he replied simply.

"Time for game faces," Clutch said. "We're coming up on kick-off."

I smiled and shook my head at Griz before turning my attention back to the store.

Clutch drove around the perimeter of the building, where we found part of the western wall had collapsed from a fire. That explained the sunlight we'd seen, but the blackened debris worried me. "I hope the fire didn't burn through the store," I said.

"If it did, it'll be a quick trip," Clutch said as he brought the Humvee to a stop twenty feet from the main doors. We stepped outside. Gripping my machete, I searched the area for any signs of life. The only thing I saw was my breath in the cold air. After we spent many long seconds walking alongside the front and sides of the building, we stood outside the doors.

Inside the store, snow covered a portion of the merchandise, making a playground of shapes that could be anything. We shared *the* look. The one where we both wanted to get the hell out of there, but knew we had to go in. It was the look of dread.

"It doesn't look looted," Jase said. "That's a good sign."

Clutch glanced upward, shading his eyes against the sun with his hand. "Well, we can't wait around. When the sun warms things up, the zeds will start moving around again. We need to either go in now or write it off."

"At least the snow will make it easier to spot footprints," Griz said, coming to a stop next to me.

I closed my eyes and turned my face toward the sun, feeling its warmth on my cold skin. After taking a deep breath, I turned back toward the team. "We're already here."

Clutch pulled out his handheld radio and clicked the mike. "This is Team Charlie. We'll check back in twenty minutes. Radio silence otherwise. Be ready to roll out if this run turns to shit. Do not come after us. Confirm."

"*Got it,*" Marco's voice came through the radio in response. "*Be careful in there.*"

Jase took the first step forward. "Let's do this."

The four of us moved toward the hollowed-out front doors. As one, we stepped through the frames, our boots crunching on broken glass.

A single zed lay in our path in the entryway. Its skin was ripped from its body, flayed by glass shards, several of which were still embedded in organs.

"The thing must've been pushed up against the glass doors when the bombs fell," Griz said quietly as he gripped his machete.

Sprawled under a ceiling where the elements couldn't get to it, I could see the zed's organs, even its lungs and heart, beneath its shattered ribs. Its mouth moved only slightly, as though it was trying to tell us something. I'd seen horrific things before, but this zed caused us all to pause. It didn't attack, though with how ravaged its body was, it probably couldn't. Instead, it did nothing but lay there and watch us. Its gaze seemed more curious than sinister.

I couldn't take my eyes off the zed. Not until Griz put it out of its misery with a single thrust of his blade. I took a deep breath and swallowed. The aggressive zeds were so much easier to deal with. They'd come at me with evil in their eyes, and I instinctively fought back. Then, there was the tiniest minority of ones like this one that stuck with me. I called them Zen zeds, the ones that simply stared and never attacked. They haunted my nightmares worse than the violent ones, because these seemed like they retained a shred of their humanity. The act of killing them felt more like euthanasia than self-defense. I assumed they preferred death. At least, that's what I told myself.

Clutch began to move forward again, and the rest of us fell in behind him. We stepped cautiously until we were out of the narrow entryway and stood at the edge of the huge store. Clutch took point, and we followed him as he headed to the right, toward the boat section. Earlier, he'd said that he wanted to clear this section first. With its open spaces and the collapsed outer wall, it would be our Plan B in case we had to leave in a hurry and couldn't get out through the store entrance.

Rows of fishing boats sat in mish mashed rows on the floor, tossed and blackened by a surge of heat that must've hit the entire west side of the building. The bomb blast had been enough to break out all the glass. The sprinkler system must've still been working at the time of the bombing, as only the edge of the store had burned.

Fingers crossed, the good stuff was still safe.

Interspersed around the boats stood unmoving snow-covered statues.

Zeds.

I held my machete in a defensive position, ready to swing out at any moment. Griz came to a stop in front of the nearest zed. We encircled it, and my grip tightened on my machete. The duct tape I'd wrapped around the handle to give it a better grip creaked under my grasp.

Like Private Jonathan Hart, this zed's skin was crisped, and it had no eyes, ears, or nose. Slowly, Griz waved his blade in front of its face. It made no movement.

"Do you think they're dead?" Jase asked quietly.

"Maybe they're just frozen," I whispered back.

"I figured more would've migrated," Griz said. "But, these must be in too rough of shape to drag themselves out of the store."

Clutch looked across the area. "We'll take them down one at a time. Don't get too close if you can help it."

Jase waved his arm in front of a zed. It didn't flinch or show any recognition. "Kinda hard, with them standing around like bowling pins all over the place."

"They must be deaf and blind," I said. "None of them seem to have sensed us."

"Let's keep it that way," Clutch said.

Griz swung and lodged his machete in the first zed's temple. He pulled out the blade and the zed collapsed. We all stood and watched as he wiped the blade on the zed's shirt.

Clutch spoke. "I don't like how many are still around. Let's stick together until we clear the building. It'll take more time, but if we get this place cleared, we can drive the Humvees right through those big doors tonight to hide them in the off chance anyone passes through this area. Plus, that'll give us more time to do our shopping. With this"—he gestured to the building surrounding us—"We'll need plenty of time."

A rat scurried under a boat, and I jumped back with a squeak.

Clutch's gaze snapped to mine. "What is it?"

Heat flushed my cheeks. "Nothing."

"Nothing?"

"It was a rat," I said sheepishly.

His brows rose.

I added, "It was a really big rat."

He eyed me suspiciously for a moment before returning his focus to the task at hand.

"Chicken," Jase whispered as he walked by.

"It was *really* big," I countered, but he'd already moved on to killing a zed.

We spent the next several minutes killing zeds, the entire time I kept on the lookout for rats. I hated rats nearly as much I hated zeds.

Once we finished clearing the boat section, Clutch checked in with Marco on the radio. "There are plenty of stinkers in here," Clutch reported. "It will take a little longer than planned."

"*Need help?*" came Marco's response.

"Negative. Nothing too challenging here. I'll check in every hour. If anything goes wrong, you bug out and don't look back. Protect the civilians."

Marco didn't respond fast enough for Clutch's humor.

"Tell me you'll bug out," Clutch demanded.

"*I've got it covered,*" Marco replied.

We worked our way closer to the center of the store, zigzagging through debris. We finished off any zed we came across, but as we worked our way inward, they were becoming fewer and fewer. Leaning on a table of folded shirts, a zed seemed to stare off into nothingness as though contemplating the mysteries of life. Oblivious to our presence, Griz and I approached. This one was dressed in suit. On its lapel, it had a pin with two laurel leaves crossed over a book and a shepherd's hook.

"What's that mean, I wonder," I said without thinking.

Griz's lips thinned. "It meant he was a chaplain."

I frowned. "Oh."

Griz lifted his blade and paused for a moment before finishing the deed. I turned away in haste, trying to pretend this zed never existed, and I bumped into the clothes rack. A petite zed wearing a store uniform lashed out, and I jumped back. "Shit!"

My reflexes kicked in and I swung my machete, crushing its head in a single shot. "Not frozen," I said breathlessly before yanking my machete out of the zed's skull.

"Guess there's some life left in them yet," Griz said. "Good to know."

"Be careful," Clutch cautioned.

"Yeah," I replied as I grabbed a folded shirt and cleaned the blade now coated in the thick brown sludge that had once been blood. Killing zeds had become easier over the months. Not just because I'd gained skill and became desensitized to them, but because the zeds were becoming weaker. Their bones had become brittle, to the point my machete rarely became lodged in their skulls or necks anymore.

I crept more carefully as we scoured the store for more zeds. It didn't take long for us to finish the wide-open area. With the offices in back completely burned or collapsed, we turned our attention to the restaurant on the eastern side of the store.

"Looks in pretty good shape," Jase said while the four of us stood outside the closed glass door. The area beyond the glass was draped in darkness, making it impossible to see what hid within. "Do we go for touchdown?"

Clutch and Griz stepped up to the glass pane and both looked through.

Griz spoke first. "If there's anything in there from before, it hasn't gotten out yet, which means it likely is never going to get out."

"Let's leave it for now," Clutch said. "We'll post a guard in this area to play it safe."

I looked back at all the merchandise in the store waiting to be plucked, and I grinned. Just as I was about to say *let's go shopping*, something clanged on the other side of the door.

"Ah, shit," I mumbled.

A zed's visage appeared through the glass. Then another face emerged from the darkness. More kept coming. These zeds, protected from the elements, looked nothing like the ones we'd just killed. These were *healthy* zeds, and there were at least thirty of them.

"You guys really think that door will hold?" Jase asked.

Griz and Clutch both shook their heads.

"Not a chance," Griz said.

"Son of a bitch. Let's get out of their line of sight and see if they settle down," Clutch said as we were already taking steps back.

Instead of calming, our retreat seemed to rev up the zeds even more. They pounded on the door, fighting to get past one another at us. One zed tripped as others shoved at it from behind. Its head slammed into the door, and the glass shattered. Pounding fists tore through the weakened glass. With only the metal handle bar across the middle of the door to hold back the zeds, they worked into a frenzy to get at us.

The zed that had broken the glass with its head was on the ground and crawled out from under the bar. More followed, some tumbling over the bar while the shorter ones crawled under it.

"Outside to the Humvee!" Griz shouted, and we ran.

We jumped over debris and around fallen racks. The linoleum floors had become slick with the melting snow, and we slid our way through the store. I fell hard on my knee, and stars shot through my vision. Clenching my jaw, I jumped up and forced weight on my injured leg.

"To the RP!" Clutch yelled into the radio. "The store is overrun. Get out of here!"

Two

Griz pointed to the collapsed wall beyond the boats. "Plan B! Keep going. We can't risk the front entrance. We need to put more distance between us and them."

As we ran passed the entrance, I risked a glance behind me to see three dozen voracious zeds tumbling after us. Rats scurried under racks of clothes and counters. Fortunately, the slick floors were proving difficult for the zeds, and we were getting well ahead of them. I followed Griz as he weaved through the fallen boats and toward the open space where a huge glass door had once been used for moving boats in and out of the store.

Part of the ceiling had collapsed above the door, leaving debris piled several feet high. I stumbled over the rubble and caught myself before falling onto dangerous glass shards. Outside, the sun shone brightly enough to blind me. It took me only a second to get my bearings, and I ran toward our Humvee.

Something had drawn some of the zeds away from us and back to the main entrance. There, the loud engine of the other Humvee slashed through the area. The fast-moving distraction, with six people piled inside, plowed through the herd. Frost stood in back with a rifle and took shots at the zeds that got back up.

With them working on the herd outside, I turned and focused on the dozen or so climbing over the rubble. I unslung my rifle, took aim, and fired. A zed dropped. A shot rang off to my left, and another zed fell. A third shot joined in. We finished off the small herd in less than four minutes.

After I checked out the bodies in the rubble to make sure none survived, I turned to see Marco walking around the dead in the parking lot. I couldn't see Clutch's face, but if his slow, heavy march toward the other man was any indication, he wasn't pleased.

I hustled toward the pair as Clutch threw his arms in the air. "I told you to bug out if things turned to shit. Tell me exactly how bringing everyone into a zed swarm is bugging out?"

"I wasn't going to let you have all the fun," Marco replied.

"What part about it being a direct order didn't you understand?"

Marco pointed to the east. "My boss is lying dead across the state line right now. I'm not like you or Griz. I wasn't some G. I. Joe Rambo before the outbreak. I was a volunteer, not a soldier, and I'm not good with following orders. Hell, before all this, I was a consultant who had just about reached Delta's Million Mile status."

Clutch wagged a finger at the younger soldier. "Someone could've died back there. That'd be on you."

After a pause, Marco spoke. "I know. If things got hairy, I would've made sure they were safe. You have my word. I'd never put them at risk."

"C'mon guys," I said as lightly as possible. "The store is just about cleared. I'd really love to do a little shopping. Okay?"

Grudgingly, they turned their attention from each other and back to the store.

It took five hours before we had the stragglers in the building dispatched and enough rubble cleared to back our vehicles inside and park them in between the boats. From outside, no one could see any sign of survivors.

We couldn't risk bandits finding us here like they had at the store on the Mississippi. We'd been exhausted and let our guard down then. It had proved to be a fatal mistake.

Never again.

The guys worked at clearing multiple exit routes, with one route to the vehicles and backup routes, one to each direction. With how prepared we were, everyone had agreed to spend as many days here as needed to sift through supplies, give the Humvees an oil change, and prepare for the long trip ahead.

I straddled an ATV, taking in the huge store surrounding me. My jaw slackened as I rested. Aside from the basic looting of cash, guns, and ammo—all of which probably happened during the first day of the outbreak—the store was relatively untouched.

I hugged myself in the shearling parka with golden cream fleece lining I'd found. I looked like an Eskimo in it. It was too warm to wear very long, but I still savored its softness and refused to take it off as I stuffed backpacks and duffels from the luggage section with my discoveries.

A smile crossed my face as I looked at the big pile of bags to my left. Everyone had a similar pile, and everyone's pile was full of similar things. Warm, *clean* clothes. Camping and hiking supplies, such as eating utensils, hydration packs, sleeping bags, blankets, and sleep pads. And even a little bit of one of the most important items: food.

Most of the snow had melted under the warmth of the sun, leaving everything damp, so I helped Hali string our new clothes on hangers to dry in the cold air.

We'd all had a good laugh at Benji's pile. He'd forgone bags and piled toys and games into a mountain. No one envied Frost as he "coached" Benji into trying on clothes and picking out the right color for a winter coat. After a lengthy debate, Frost succumbed to the boy's adamant choice on a fluorescent green coat since his grandfather had chosen a dark evergreen coat to blend into his surroundings. To Benji, green was green.

Marco and Vicki emptied the restaurant. I avoided going inside the restaurant, instead waiting at the door to haul their findings. Even with the inside door gone, the restaurant still reeked of zeds that had been cooped up inside stale air for the better part of a year.

The pair found several huge cans of tomato sauce and vegetables and several bottles of olive oil. The bags of flour and sugar had long been claimed by rodents. The little buggers had gotten to nearly everything not in a tin can. They'd even managed to chew through plastic tubs. Despite the lack of variety in food, I had no doubt that Vicki, who'd been Camp Fox's cook, would work magic with whatever ingredients she had available.

After loading what we could into our two vehicles, we quickly discovered we had a problem that was nice to have. We'd found so much stuff throughout the store that we would need to find a third vehicle.

Taking the risk for the store had proved to be well worth it. No one was injured, and we'd found enough supplies to get us to New Eden without stress of running out. We'd desperately needed this good fortune.

We took anything we could use, but we also left plenty of gear behind for any who came after. The food was another story. We took anything that could be eaten. With winter coming and no home, we couldn't afford to leave anything behind.

The surplus food we now had was crucial, since finding gas for vehicles was becoming harder and harder with each passing day, making supply runs more and more limited. Until this month, I'd had no idea how quickly gas started to go bad when it wasn't in well-sealed containers. The Humvees could handle dirtier fuel than most modern cars, but even now, the engines pinged after the last siphoning of gas from a car on the side of the road. We added fuel additive at each fill-up, but we only had seven bottles left.

Griz was the first to point out that vehicles would be obsolete within another couple years. Everyone would be walking, riding bicycles, and riding horses—assuming horses weren't extinct by then. I dreaded the day cars became nothing more than lawn ornaments and prayed we had a permanent home, free of zeds, before the gasoline became no longer usable.

In the twilight, I glanced over to where Deb was setting down a pot filled with something steaming onto an aluminum camp-style picnic table. As if on cue, my stomach growled. I jumped off the ATV and headed straight for the food line. Jase pulled Hali to her feet.

Earlier, with Jase standing watch behind her, she had set up a cozy camp for Benji, his cot surrounded by teddy bears. The boy, oblivious to their actions, was propped against a snoring Diesel and completely engrossed with his new toys.

Jase clapped once, and Diesel shot up. A startled Benji looked around. Jase pointed to the table where Frost stood, waiting for the kid. "Dinner time, Benny boy."

Benji's face broke into a wide grin. He jumped to his feet and took off running toward his grandfather. He wasn't a fast kid, but every time food was involved, he'd come close to breaking his personal speed records.

He slid into being the first in line, just like he did every meal. No one minded. Spoiling Benji was one of the few joys in this new world.

In the large soup pot was all the pasta that had survived the rats and mice. The noodles had no real sauce, only olive oil and spices found in the restaurant, but it all tasted pretty dang good to me.

Griz and Frost stood guard while the rest of us ate. Benji slurped the noodles while he fed Diesel one strand of spaghetti at a time. I twirled my noodles around my fork, savoring every bite. Jase finished first, as usual, and he always went back for seconds.

Marco tossed his Styrofoam bowl and plastic fork into a plastic bag.

He stood and motioned to Frost and Griz. "I'll take watch now for one of you guys."

It was standard operating procedure to have someone stand watch twenty-four/seven. We always had at least two people guard over our group. Even inside a building like this. *Especially* inside a building like this.

Griz grabbed his dinner and sat down next to Vicki. She didn't even acknowledge him. I remembered the exact moment her personality had changed from kind and optimistic to cold and hard. It was the moment when Tyler was killed. She hadn't smiled since.

Deb burped and covered her mouth. "Excuse me," she mumbled.

Vicki had mentioned first pregnancies were even harder once a woman was in her thirties. Deb was thirty-four, and couldn't keep much of anything down. She was losing weight too quickly, and I worried how much longer she could go without losing the baby.

"Another tummy ache?" Benji asked.

Deb gave a small smile and nodded.

"Mom gives me warm milk when my tummy hurts." His face fell. He said the same thing every time he noticed Deb wasn't feeling well. I knew what Benji was going to say next. We all knew. "I miss Mom."

Diesel always seemed to notice when Benji's mood faltered, and the dog nudged the boy with his big, shiny nose. Benji scowled and wiped the slobber from his arm. The boy's features soon eased, and he rubbed the dog's ears. When he went back to his eating-slash-feeding-the-dog routine, we ate and talked about our findings as well as tomorrow's plans.

"There's a truck rental company not far from here, so maybe it wasn't destroyed," I said. "I rented a truck once to move into my house."

As soon as I said the words, a weight fell on my chest. I'd been so caught up in keeping busy that my mind didn't have the time to dwell on the past. My house, an adorable little bungalow I'd been fixing up, was likely a pile of stones sitting fewer than ten miles from here. My parent's house, not far from downtown, would've faced the same fate.

I still hated myself for not coming back for them. Not only had I left them behind, but also I never came back for them. I had planned to. In the first days, all I thought about was how I could get back into the city to find them. My dad was a doctor, my mother a nurse and a diabetic. Even though they were both retired, I knew they would've been at the hospital, helping out where they could in the most dangerous place of all.

Still, I had tried to work out a plan to make it to them. Then the news had come that the military had bombed Des Moines and all other large cities. They never stood a chance. Still, not having the chance to say good-bye—not trying to save them—would be something I would have to live with for the rest of my life.

I sensed someone watching me, and I noticed Clutch sitting in a camp chair. He motioned to the empty chair next to him. I dumped off my bowl and fork and headed to the seat Clutch had saved. I sunk into the seat, and my muscles loosened.

Clutch pointed to the night sky through the open roof. "Looks like we're going to have quite a full moon tonight."

I looked upward. The moon seemed as though it was racing to claim the sky, even before the sun relinquished its fleeting hold. "The days are getting too short. Soon the days will be shorter than the nights."

We sat as darkness bled out from every corner in the building. Small lanterns were lit, and the light licked at the dark. Without any light to mar its beauty, the moon became a brilliant pearl.

With night, came the beasts. The animals that came out of hiding after the zeds migrated. With little to fear, they searched to fill their empty stomachs.

A howl in the distance was returned by another. These weren't the coyote howls from old westerns. These howls sounded like mad men, as though the demons of the night were cackling at what the world had become, taunting us that humans were no longer the most feared predators on the planet.

The howls had become familiar, but they still unnerved me. Especially when they were the only sound of the night. Trying to ignore the distant wails, I focused intently on the moon. The iridescent pearl was stained by moon spots, and I wondered how each of those scars came to be. I mused if someone on the moon could see similar scars on the earth from all the bombings and fires.

I spoke softly. "Do you think the earth will ever be a place where we can live without fear?"

"Don't know," Clutch said. "But if we don't believe things will get better, why do we keep trying?"

"Yeah," I whispered. "I guess you're right."

As Clutch dozed off, I pulled out a small mirror and reflected the moonlight in it. The way the light shimmered and reflected in the glass would've made a pretty picture, if only I had a working camera. Instead, I focused on remembering this moment. Of the peaceful moonlit night and Clutch at my side.

Moonlight reflected off the stand of mirrors hanging nearby, all containing mirrors identical to the little one I held. A reflection beyond the stand caught my eye. I leaned forward. As I turned the mirror to move the light around, I noticed even more reflections scattered around the dark building.

Griz, nearing the end of his shift, paused to take in the reflections.

One of the reflections blinked.

I clicked the safety off my rifle. "Griz? You see that?"

"Yeah," he replied as he took a step back and did a three-sixty. "The Humvees. We need to get to them *now*."

I nudged Clutch, and he came awake with a deep inhalation. He grunted and rubbed his neck.

I held a finger to my lips. "Sh."

I could see his frown in the moonlight as he took in the situation. He let out the breath he'd been holding in a rush.

Slowly, I stood and walked over to Jase. A howl from inside the building woke him up before I could get there. Diesel returned with a flurry of barking. Howls surrounded us and echoed off the walls. We'd all heard the howls before.

But never in this great a number.

And never all around us.

THREE

"Wolves!" I yelled and yanked Jase and Hali to their feet. "To the trucks!"

We had camped next to the Humvees for easy escape, so we had only a few feet between safety and the pack. However, three feet looked like a mile when countless reflective eyes were racing toward us.

Ever protective of his grandson, Frost already had Benji safely inside the Humvee with a coyote's head and the words *Charlie Coyote* painted on the hood and doors.

Deb and Vicki raced to the other Humvee—the one with *Betty Bravo,* the pinup girl Griz had painted on it—while Marco and Griz fired rounds into the dark, their gunshots echoed by yelps.

When I opened the door of Humvee Charlie, I paused to make sure Jase and Clutch were right behind me, but I found myself shoved onto the backseat, with Clutch landing on top of me and slamming the door closed.

"They're safe," he said as I crawled out from under him. I crawled across the backseat and pressed the massive Great Dane to the floor so I had a place to sit. I looked to the other Humvee to see Jase cramming Hali into the front passenger's seat.

Vicki stood at the door of the other vehicle and fired off shots while Deb climbed inside. When Marco reached Vicki, they quickly disappeared inside, and their doors shut. The last one standing, Griz laid down a burst of automatic fire while Frost pulled Benji onto his lap.

Not far from our vehicle, a wolf tore into one of Benji's teddy bears. The boy gasped and wagged a finger at the animal. "Bad dog," he scolded, his voice cracking.

Diesel cringed at the words, and I rubbed the dog's back. Benji bit back tears. Frost pulled his grandson closer, and Benji tucked his head into the older man's shoulder.

There had to be hundreds of animals in the store. They leapt over their fallen, trying to reach us. Griz stopped firing, jumped into the driver's seat, and slammed the door just as a wolf smashed against the metal and glass with a sharp cry. A wet mark of saliva remained on the glass where the wolf had slid off. Another jumped up against my window, startling me.

Diesel growled at the wolves and dogs outside our Humvees, and I rubbed the dog's fur. "It's okay. They can't us get in here."

Griz started the engine and shifted the truck into gear, which only seemed to drive the pack into more of a fury. The dogs pounded against the sides like hail on glass. Many were sickly and couldn't jump high. Some could, and their looks of determination scared the hell out of me. Some attacked the dogs nearest to them in their frenzy to get closer.

Griz pulled ahead slowly, keeping an eye on the Humvee next to us. One large but skinny dog managed to leap onto the hood, and it stood there, watching us with bloodshot eyes through the windshield. Its mouth frothed as it bared its teeth. I could hear its growl through the glass.

Griz stepped on the gas pedal, throwing the dog against the windshield, and then slammed the brakes. The dog slid off the hood, trying to claw and scratch to stay on but to no avail.

"Bad meat," I muttered.

"What?" Clutch asked.

I nodded toward the dog growling at us. "They remind me of the catfish. After eating infected meat, they're all getting sick and going crazy, like rabid animals."

Clutch watched the dog and then tilted his head. "Zeds were probably the only food they could find after the zeds killed everything else."

"Getting bit by one of these would be a bad deal," Griz added, pulling in behind the other Humvee.

"The zeds are easy prey, and they obviously have no trouble eating them. I wonder why they're trying to go for us," I said.

"I'd bet we taste better," Griz replied.

"Maybe they like the hunt," Jase said. "We'd be prime rib compared to rotten zed meat."

"They're starving," Frost said. "Most of the zed herds have moved south. And, the dogs can't get to the zeds stuck indoors. There's just not enough food left for the number of animals out there."

Once we were outside the store, the Humvee in front came to a stop, and Griz hit the brakes.

Deb's voice came over the radio. *"I know the plan was to head back to last night's camp, but we think that might be too close to be safe. Where do you think we should go?"*

"Hold on," Griz replied and threw a quick glance at us. "The only option I see is we drive until we lose our uninvited guests, but it'll burn through our gas."

Clutch nodded. "We'll get an early start on our day. Drive until we ditch the dogs. Then we come back and look for a truck to transport our remaining supplies. We'll head back here, load up during the daylight hours, and bug out before the mongrels realize what's going on."

Griz got back on the radio. "Coyote will take lead."

"Okay. We'll be right behind you."

Griz stepped on the gas, and the Humvee thumped over several bodies. I cringed. I loved animals, and even though these were after us, I knew they chased us only because they were starving. I hated what had become the way of things now: *kill or be killed.*

As we weaved around cars and down streets, animals broke off until eventually we were free of the packs. In the morning twilight, we roused zeds in our haste. Unable to get to us, they pounded against windows of the buildings and cars that trapped them, leaving brown streaks on the glass.

After four hours of sunlight, all the remaining snow had melted, leaving the world in its autumn colors once again. We still hadn't found a truck for the supplies we'd left behind. Every vehicle we checked had either no keys or was wrecked. We tried to jump-start a truck, with no luck. We'd even tried a moving truck that had had a zed inside the cab. The stench was unbelievable. Even if the truck had started, I doubted I could've driven it.

We finally gave up and returned to the store. The building left an entirely different impression today. Yesterday, it had represented hope. Today, it represented the fact that nowhere was safe, no matter how carefully we prepared. The world was full of bloodthirsty beasts that would never stop coming.

We rushed to hook up a trailer to one of the Humvees and cram as many supplies, bicycles, and warm gear as we could squeeze into it. Clutch and Griz didn't enjoy having a trailer hinder our mobility, but they liked the idea of leaving the supplies behind even less. The dogs began showing up again—at first one or two at a time, then a half dozen or more in groups appeared. Clutch latched the trailer door closed. We left the store to the mongrels, and continued our pilgrimage to New Eden.

———

Marco pointed to a dot on the map. "We should try to make it here for tonight. It's the first exit we can take to where the interstate opens up again. It's also one of the places New Eden teams stop to refuel and stay when they need a place to crash on overnight trips. There isn't much in the area, so we've never had much of a problem with zeds around there. It's a good place to stop."

Clutch examined the map. Griz spoke up first. "How big is that town right there?"

"Three buildings and a gas station," Marco replied. "They've all been cleared, and the building has been fortified. Like I said, it's a New Eden way station."

Using my forefinger and thumb, I measured the distance from our current location to the dot Marco had made to mark New Eden on the map. "That's a heck of a lot of side roads to cover with only a half-day's worth of sunlight left."

Marco nodded. "I know, but I've been on those roads several times. The route is clear of any roadblocks."

"And bandits?" I asked.

"The Black Sheep are the biggest threat around here, but we've never seen them on those roads. They avoid the Des Moines area. Too many zeds."

"Not anymore," I added. "Otherwise, we wouldn't be here, either."

"Cash is right," Clutch said. "Right now, they're probably as busy searching for food as New Eden is searching for survivors."

"We've been lucky we haven't run into them already," Griz said. "I don't want to stay out in the open."

"I know," Marco said. "I want to get back to New Eden as soon as possible."

"Coffee break's over. Let's hit the road," Clutch said. "If we stop only to look for gas, we shouldn't have any problem making it sixty klicks in five hours."

"When did you become Mr. Optimist?" I asked him with a smirk.

"Since I got myself a nice, cozy sleeping bag and pad," he said as he turned and got behind the wheel of the Humvee with the trailer hooked behind it.

We piled into our vehicles. Marco navigated and we followed, checking in on the radios every ten minutes. Every five minutes, Marco tried to reach New Eden on the radio, but either they'd changed their frequencies, or no one was in the area.

Even with the newfound rarity of zeds, it took us nearly six hours to reach our destination. Twilight had turned to darkness. Marco had us stop next door to the gas station at a restaurant with a sign that read *Marcie's Café: Home of Iowa's Best Hamburger.*

"Mm, a burger sounds good," Jase said as he clicked on his shiny new headlamp and stepped out of our Humvee.

I turned on my headlamp and followed. I pointed to the sign on the glass door. "I think I'll have the special."

Jase gave me a look of disgust. "Meatloaf? You've got to be kidding."

"You'd love my mother's meatloaf," Clutch said as he walked past us and stepped up to the door next to Marco, who had pulled out a key hidden in the doorframe.

I shrugged at Jase. A movement in the distance caught my eye, and I squinted. "Um, guys?"

They turned, their lights blinding me.

Clutch spoke first. "What is it?"

I fidgeted. "Well, I...I swear I just saw a nun crossing the road."

Clutch frowned, and Jase smirked. "Is that a start of one of your lame jokes?"

I shook my head. "And she didn't look infected."

Their gazes—and headlamps—moved to the paved road we'd driven a few minutes earlier. I pointed to where I'd seen the woman, but saw nothing. "My eyes must've been playing tricks on me," I muttered.

Then, our lights fell on her. Sure as shit, a nun wearing full habit was standing next to a tree watching us. She shielded her eyes. "No need to blind me," she grumbled.

"Are you alone?" Clutch asked quickly as we all raised our guns.

"You don't have to worry about me none," she said as she hustled toward us. "I was just on my way back to Connie's for the night. You should get yourselves inside. It's less safe after dark."

"Keep your hands where I can see them," Clutch commanded. "And walk slowly."

"Can you at least turn down those lights?" she replied. "I can't see a thing with them pointed at my eyes like that."

"We will once we know you don't mean to do us harm," Clutch retorted.

"Heavens, do I look like I can do you harm?"

"So you say," Clutch whispered softly. He didn't lower his weapon.

I scanned the area but saw no movement.

The nun stopped. "I figured you must be with New Eden since you knew where the key was."

Marco frowned. "We are, but I've never seen you around here before."

"Connie and I were staying at her house; it's about fifteen miles southwest of here. However, we couldn't stay there anymore. We were out looking for a new home when we ran into a few nice fellows from New Eden. They offered to give us a lift to New Eden, but we preferred to stay out here." She pointed. "They dropped us off at the house down the road, and so here we are."

Clutch edged closer to Marco and whispered, "What do you think? She telling the truth?"

Marco shrugged. "She could be. We've cleared several houses, including the one she's in, for survivors we find but don't come to New Eden. Either by their choice or by ours."

The woman motioned to the café behind us. "Are you staying there tonight?"

Clutch kept watching Marco.

"I think she's telling the truth," Marco replied.

Clutch turned to face the woman. "We are."

"It's cold out. Connie and I don't have much for food to offer, but we still have a bit from what the nice fellas from New Eden left us. We also have a fire to keep you warm tonight. The house is quite safe. All the windows are covered. Nothing can see the fire from outside."

Clutch glanced at me, and I gave a small nod. He, too, seemed to be considering her words. She looked trustworthy enough. She was a nun, for Christ's sake—or at least dressed like one. However, that didn't mean I was going to blindly follow her.

I spoke quietly to Clutch. "If there are only two of them like she says, we have them outnumbered."

Clutch nodded and replied quietly. "They know about us already. I'd like to find out more about them. If anything sets off our instincts, we'll be better equipped to deal with it."

Clutch looked across all our faces. When he looked at Deb, he nodded. "We'll take you up on the offer. But, we'll provide dinner for you two tonight."

That Clutch had offered dinner didn't surprise me. A small part of it was to make it a fair trade, but a much larger part was because Clutch didn't trust other people's food, not unless he watched them prepare it.

She smiled. "It's settled then. You can park in the driveway, and I'll let Connie know." Without waiting for a response, she hustled up the street toward the lone house to the north of the café.

Clutch motioned us together as if we were a football team in a huddle. "We play it safe," he said. "Keep your eyes open and your ears peeled. Just because we're taking her up on her offer of hospitality doesn't mean we should trust her. No risks."

When we reached the two-story brick house, the nun and another woman stood on the front porch. As we approached, they introduced themselves.

"I'm Sister Donaldson, but all my friends call me Picadilly. And this is Connie."

I stood, frozen. Memories flooded forward as I recalled a good friend talking about his sister, a nun who'd always gone by her nickname, Picadilly. "You...had a brother named Wes?" I asked, already knowing there could be no coincidence.

Picadilly's eyes widened. "Yes. Are you from this area? Have you seen him?"

"Yes," I said and then swallowed tightly while Wes's final moments flashed through my mind...of Wes leaning over the back of the boat, of a zed lunging up and tearing out Wes's throat, of Clutch giving Wes eternal peace. I took a deep breath. "He was a good man and a dear friend. I'm sorry."

She cast her gaze downward for a long moment before looking up. "Did he suffer?"

"No," I said too quickly, afraid she'd hear the truth in my voice if I'd waited.

"Thank God for small blessings," she said softly. After another pause, she stood straighter. "Let's get you inside. There are too many things that go bump in the night to stand around outside after dark for long."

Griz and Marco did a final check of the vehicles and gear, and we entered the house with our sleeping gear and weapons. The fire in the hearth warmed my face as I crossed the foyer. The fire provided the only light except for our headlamps, yet the place felt somewhat homey. Two mattresses leaned against the wall to the left off the fireplace, with a stack of bedding to the side. A cast iron Dutch oven was propped above the flames. Several small stacks of home-canned jars and tin cans of food were on the other side of the fireplace.

Suddenly, I felt selfish we had so much stocked away in our vehicles.

Vicki carried in a cardboard box. "I'll get started on dinner."

"I'd be happy to help," Picadilly said as she begun to roll her sleeves.

I dropped my sleeping bag next to the couch. "I guess that's my cue to secure the house."

"There's no need," Picadilly said quickly. "We're safe in here."

Connie watched us nervously and stepped closer to the stairs.

I frowned and looked upward. The light from my headlamp lit up an empty hallway and closed doors. I motioned to Jase, who was already pulling out his machete.

Clutch dropped his gear and pulled out his sword. "What's up there?"

"Nothing," Connie replied, but she didn't move.

I pressed past her and took the first steps.

Connie came up behind me. "You're guests here tonight. You don't need to raise a fuss."

At the top of the stairs, the woman moved around me and stood in front of a closed bedroom door.

"What's behind that door?" I asked, feeling confident with Jase and Clutch on either side of me.

"Nothing you need to worry about," Connie replied coldly.

Picadilly ran up the steps. "Connie's right. There is nothing here you need to worry about."

I ignored her and grabbed the door handle to find it unlocked. Before I turned, I glanced at Clutch and Jase to find both ready.

Connie grabbed my forearm. "Please don't."

I opened the door.

Inside, my light shone on a single zed sitting on the bed. His jaundiced eyes reflected the light like a cat's eyes at night. He came to his feet.

Jase lunged forward to strike at the same time Connie shoved her way into the room. "Don't hurt him!"

She managed to squeeze her way in between us and the zed, making it impossible to kill it without going through her.

She cupped the zed's cheeks. "There, there. It's all right, Henry."

The zed didn't attack. Instead, he simply stood there, watching the woman with a dull gaze. I already knew what he was.

A Zen zed.

I couldn't find the words. Clutch spoke first. "What the hell is going on here?"

"This is Henry, Connie's husband," Picadilly said. "And you don't have to worry about him."

"The hell I don't," Clutch replied. "He's a goddamn zed."

Picadilly wagged a finger at him. "You will not take the Lord's name in vain in this house."

Connie dabbed a tissue at something on Henry's cheek, and I cringed.

"Henry was never quite right after he was bit. The fever caused some brain damage and hurt his vision, but as long as you're patient with him, he's okay. He's a bit like a toddler, but he's never been violent, not once."

"How long has he been like this?" I asked.

"Since the first day of the outbreak," Connie said while still watching her husband. "He picked up Freddy from school after some fights broke out in the classrooms. Poor Freddy had gotten sick, and when the fever hit, he bit Henry without thinking."

"Fred is Connie's son," Picadilly said. "He's back at Connie's house. Unfortunately, the fever hit him harder, and he got quite the mean streak. Grace doesn't seem to rain equally from God. When he got too much to handle, we were forced to move."

"These are zeds you're talking about," Clutch said.

Connie snapped around. "Look at him. He's not a zed."

A gasp behind us, and I realized we'd drawn the attention of everyone.

"He's..." Hali started.

"He's a survivor," Picadilly said before shaking her head with a sad, slow movement. "With the right medical care, I think he could recover more fully. We're trying the best we can, but honestly, we don't know what to do."

Henry stood there, rocking from one foot to the next. While he didn't look or smell rotten like other zeds did, he bore the gray pallor of someone whose heart no longer beat within his chest. He made a small moan, and Connie wrapped an arm around him.

Clutch pursed his lips. "How do you know he won't go crazy one day and attack you both? You've got a time bomb ticking in this house."

"We have to have faith," Picadilly replied.

Connie nodded. "When there's nothing else to go on, we can still go on faith."

"Before Connie and I came to be together," Picadilly said. "I was forced to break my vows. I murdered a parishioner who was attacking people in the church. I'm not proud of my actions, but I also know I had to do it. With Henry, we don't have to kill anymore. He keeps the zeds away. He even kept Fred in line until the boy became violent."

"He protects you?" I asked.

"As much as he can," the nun replied. "He moves a bit slow, but he means well. He's a bit scared right now, but once he settles down, you'll see him open up after a bit."

"Henry won't bother you tonight. I'll stay up here with him to keep him warm," Connie said.

"No," Clutch said. "It's your house. Your fire. But, I can't risk having my people stay in the same house with a zed. After we eat, we'll stay at the café and head out in the morning."

Few words were spoken through dinner. No one said anything when Connie filled a bowl of soup and carried it upstairs. By the time she returned, we'd all finished and were ready to head out.

"As long as you promise not to hurt our Henry, you are still welcome to stay the night," Picadilly said, but Clutch hadn't backed down, and I was glad. I didn't think I could sleep with a zed—or whatever Henry was —upstairs, even if he was harmless.

As we drove the several hundred feet back toward the café, Picadilly and Connie's waving forms disappeared in the rearview mirror.

Once I settled into the cold, dank café, my mind raced. I looked around the café. Memories of the two zed kids at the gas station filled my mind. They had been like Henry, likely forgotten survivors in this new world. I remembered other times when zeds had watched me and not attacked. Some I'd left, others I'd killed. Now, I couldn't help but wonder how many harmless people I'd murdered simply because they'd been infected.

I'd convinced myself that zeds felt no pain, had no conscience. It was the only way I could kill without remorse. Holy hell, if not all zeds were mindless monsters, how was I going to fight without hesitating?

My God. How many innocents had I killed?

FOUR

Minutes before we headed out the following morning, I faced a recurring debate with Jase.

"Fox Park is hidden," Jase said, his eyes pleading with me. "All anyone can see from the road is miles and miles of wilderness. I know it'll be hard, but we can make it work."

I put a hand on Jase's shoulder. "We'll make it back there. I promise. Just be patient a little longer, okay?"

Jase muttered something under his breath and went back to cramming his sleeping bag into his stuff sack.

I wanted to go back to Fox Park, too. More than anything, I wanted to return to something I knew. I also craved to be enveloped in the easy safety of New Eden. A familiar home versus trusting a man I'd known for barely a week. It was a tough choice. And I worried that we weren't making the right one.

My mood became monotone after that. We drove for hours, stopping only to refuel from the gas cans we carried onboard. Every gas station we came to had been drained, with the exception of one that looked like it had gone up in a massive explosion.

As we covered miles on the westbound I-80, I stared out the window at the landscape. Leaves had long since turned color. What few crops were planted before the outbreak were now brown and well past ready for harvesting, and I wondered if we could use it for food or seed in the spring. Most of the fields remained unplanted and were already returning to their natural state of prairie grasses and weeds.

However, the biggest difference in the landscape from that of a month ago was the distinct lack of zeds. Before the massive migrations, zeds dotted the landscape, with herds grouping around towns. These days, I saw the rare corpse, recognizable as once human only by the tattered remnants of clothing draping it. The landscape was devoid of life, with most animals being taken down by zeds or wild wolves and dogs. Before the outbreak, I'd imagined hell as a desert-like environment, full of fire and brimstone. Now, I knew exactly what hell looked like. It looked like wherever I was.

Jase and Hali were sound asleep in the front seat next to Griz, who was behind the wheel. "Do you think we're over the hump?" I asked Clutch, who sat across from me in the backseat. "That maybe we don't have to worry about the zeds coming back?"

"I think that's wishful thinking," he replied before adding, "But it'd be nice."

"Yeah, I guess you're right." I continued to watch the landscape passing by outside. I looked back inside to find Clutch watching me with concern.

"It's only natural to worry," he said, as though reading my mind. "It means you're human. Just don't let it screw with your head out there."

My brow rose. "You're telling me that you worry?"

"Of course. I'm only human."

I watched him for a moment before giving him an almost-smile. We were the lucky ones. We were part of a small world of survivors, who were still capable of thought. That was, if my prior assumption about zeds still held any weight. "Henry really came out of left field," I said.

Clutch nodded slowly. "Yeah. I didn't see that one coming. But it doesn't change anything."

"Doesn't it?" I asked.

"Believe me, if I could change the past, there'd be plenty I'd do differently." He shrugged. "But, I can't, and you can't either. We have to accept things as we see them and keep on living."

"Yeah, but what if there are a lot more zeds like Henry who can think and feel. What kind of hell must they be going through? Or, even worse, what if all the other zeds can think and feel, but can't control their urges?"

He considered for a moment. "I think if zeds had control of their senses, they wouldn't give into violence. So, no, I don't think zeds know what they're doing. I don't even think there was anything going on in Henry's head. If there was, I'd think he'd want to be put out of his misery."

I cocked my head while I considered his words. "Who are you trying to convince: you or me?"

He shrugged. "Things aren't so bad. We're alive. We've got food, and we've got a place to go." Even though he was a pessimist, Clutch always seemed to have more faith than I could muster. He reached over and gave my hand a gentle squeeze.

Then he did something he'd never done before. He didn't let go.

I sighed, my stress dissipating as I held his hand, and realized he was right. Even in this shitty world, things weren't so bad.

"*We're less than twenty miles out,*" Marco's voice alerted us through the radio.

Clutch let go of my hand and leaned forward in between the two front seats to talk to Griz. "Do you see any good place to stop?"

After a pause, Griz pointed. "How about that machine shed on the farm over there?"

"It's worth a shot," Clutch replied.

I looked out the window and saw a small farmhouse with a couple small outbuildings, including a decently sized white tin shed.

Clutch picked up the radio. "Take the next road to your left. We'll stop at the first farmhouse."

"*Copy that, but I still don't think this is necessary,*" Marco replied as they led us to the farm.

Clutch didn't respond.

We parked and approached the shed. The doors were all still closed, and it took us less than ten minutes to verify that the building was devoid of any life, except for a cantankerous family of raccoons. A combine harvester, a couple tractors, and three wagons filled most of the interior, but there was still room for one Humvee with the trailer. We emptied everything from the remaining Humvee, leaving only enough food and supplies to keep us fed, warm, and protected for a couple days.

Humvees were taller than most residential garage doors, making it a bit more challenging than a car to hide. When Griz and Jase pulled the metal door closed, we all looked at each other. From everyone's faces, they were as uncomfortable as I was about leaving behind over eighty percent of our "stuff." But, the alternative was too risky. If New Eden reappropriated our food and supplies when we arrived, we could be in far worse shape than not having it at all.

Everyone except for Marco had agreed we needed to play it safe until we knew if we'd be staying at New Eden. If it became our permanent home, we'd share our food and supplies. Until then, we all felt safer with a cache.

As we piled ten of us into a single Humvee, Clutch stepped in front of Marco. "I need your word that you will not, under any circumstances, tell anyone about this."

Marco scowled. "I already gave you my word. I won't tell anyone. I get it. Hell, I'd probably do the same thing if I were in your shoes."

Clutch grunted, and Jase tacked on a "we'll see."

Griz didn't have anything to say because he was busy claiming the driver's seat. Marco took the passenger seat, and Benji sat on the floor between his legs.

Somehow, we squeezed five of us into the back bucket seats, with Clutch and me on one seat, Deb and Hali sharing the other seat, and Jase on the incredibly uncomfortable hump. Behind us, in the unheated part of the Humvee, Frost sat with Diesel, and Vicki leaned into the pair for warmth...or probably because there was no other space due to all our food, gear, and weapons stacked around them.

Marco continued to try to reach New Eden on the radio, but with no success. We were still a few miles out from New Eden when movement caught my eye before the engine noise registered in my ears.

Three SUVs approached us from the west.

Marco leaned forward. "That's the New Eden flag. They must've seen us coming," his excited voice echoed through the vehicle.

The incoming SUVs flew American flags with an eagle stitched over the center.

Griz squinted in the bright sunlight. "Can you confirm? It could be a setup."

"I recognize them. It's New Eden!"

"We need to wait until we get close enough for you to verify their faces," Griz said.

Equal parts of fear and excitement fluttered through me, and I leaned forward to watch the SUVs come to a stop and form a roadblock in front of us. People with rifles jumped out and stepped behind the SUVs, using the vehicles for cover while leveling their sights upon us.

"They could be playing it safe," Clutch mused. "But I'd still make sure we can make a hasty retreat if this turns to shit."

"Already thinking the same thing," Griz said as he stopped our

Humvee at least a hundred yards back in a diagonal position on the highway.

I sucked in a deep breath. "Here's hoping they recognize Marco."

Marco chuckled. "They'll recognize me. It's not *that* big a town."

Hali came awake with a stretch. "Are we there yet?" she asked.

"Almost. Assuming we don't get shot first," Griz replied bluntly.

"Not funny," the girl replied.

"I wasn't joking," he replied.

As soon as we stopped, Marco stepped out of the Humvee.

"Be careful," Clutch said as he climbed out and stood by the open door with his rifle.

"I will," Marco said. He waved his arms in the air as he approached the newcomers. A man emerged from a white SUV and met him halfway. When they embraced, I think we let out a collective sigh. Marco motioned for all of us to come out.

"Hot dog," Griz said. "Looks like they're friendlies."

Energy tightened my muscles. "We really made it, didn't we?" I said to no one in particular as I opened my door.

"It looks like it," Clutch replied, sounding just as surprised as I felt.

Our group of nine approached the SUVs. Jase looked at me and smiled. Hope flared and my lips widened into a broad smile. Likewise, I turned to Clutch, and he grinned. He embraced me and I nearly squealed. We were safe.

Marco was grinning from ear to ear when we approached. "We did it, guys. We're almost home."

"Welcome to New Eden." The man next to Marco said. "Now, surrender your weapons."

FIVE

"I thought these guys were supposed to be your friends," I snapped at Marco.

Marco held up his hands. "They were. They *are*." He turned to the man at his side. "What's going on? I tried to reach you on the radio but never got a response."

"We haven't had the resources to listen on the radios lately," The man replied. "There's been a lot going on."

Marco's lips thinned. "You'll have to fill me in later, after we get these folks to New Eden. Come on, we've been on the road a long time and are beat. I gave them my word we'd be safe at New Eden."

I had to shade my eyes against the sunlight to make out the man's features. He was short, fair-skinned, with curly brown hair that had likely been much shorter and groomed before the outbreak.

The man's lips thinned. "It's nothing personal, but we've had to take new precautions since all the squadrons followed the herds south. Ever since the migration, the Black Sheep have really put a hit on New Eden. They sent in two assassins last week alone. So, you can see why we can't let anyone armed enter New Eden without quarantine and interviews."

"That's bullshit," Jase said at my side. "We're obviously not bandits. Look at us. Half of our group is women. We even have a kid with us. Have you ever seen bandits like this before?"

The man scowled. "And one of the assassins was a teenaged girl. Listen, I get that you're not happy. That's fair. But, it doesn't change the rules. I won't negotiate on this. If you want to enter New Eden, you have to surrender your weapons until you're cleared."

Clutch took a step forward. "And how long will that take?"

"Since Marco led you here, probably two days at most," the man replied. "The choice is yours. I'll give you five minutes to make your decision."

The man tilted his head at Marco. "In the meantime, you can fill me in. Where is the rest of your squadron? Why did they send you ahead?"

Even though we'd all gathered around Clutch, no one spoke. We all watched Marco.

"I'm all that's left," Marco said after a long pause. "The Black Sheep had ambushed their community." He pointed our way. "We moved in to help, but things went bad. There's no one left. Everyone's gone."

The man placed a hand on Marco's shoulder. "I'm sorry for your loss. I hope your squadron was able to put just as much a hurtin' on the Black Sheep."

"We did, but one managed to get away." Marco took a deep breath. "And, these folks say he was missing three fingers on his left hand."

"*Hodge,*" the man said, the name dripping with hatred. "That son of a bitch just won't die. Well, I guess we couldn't expect to be that lucky. At least you got the rest. Not that it helps the pain. Good people were lost, and the news is going to hit New Eden hard. Especially since the capital had ordered all but one of our remaining squadrons to the south."

"South?" Marco asked. "Why?"

"A lot's happened this week. I'll fill you in once we reach town. You've been through enough and probably want to sleep in a safe place tonight."

"Do I ever," Marco said quickly. "Give us a moment."

The man nodded and took several steps back.

Marco joined us. "How about it? You guys ready to give New Eden a shot?"

After a moment of internal debate, I shrugged. "We didn't drive all this way for nothing. I'd say we give it a shot."

"Oh, what the hell," Griz said. "We didn't come all this way for a Sunday drive."

Others chimed in before Clutch spoke loudly. "We've come a long way. And, we all could use a place to kick up our heels for a bit. Marco's like us. He's a survivor, and I believe him. New Eden is worth a shot. All right. We've had this debate a hundred times. This is the last vote. New Eden or Fox Park. Each person has to make his or her own decision." He lifted a hand. "All in favor of New Eden, raise your hand."

One by one, the hands went up. Benji was watching Frost, and his small hand shot up as soon as his grandfather raised his hand, like always. Jase and then Hali grudgingly lifted his hand after all other hands rose. It was unanimous.

"Okay," I said, not really knowing what to say. "I guess it's settled. New Eden, it is."

Marco grinned at us before waving Justin back over. "You guys won't regret it," he said. "New Eden is good people."

The man stepped over, followed by several others. "So you've decided?"

Clutch made eye contact with each of us one last time before speaking. "We have. We'll follow you to New Eden under the condition that we can each retain a weapon for self-defense."

"That's not our policy," the man replied.

"Where we came from, we'd let folks keep knives," Jase said. "You can't leave folks completely defenseless, not in this world."

"No guns," the man said after a moment. "Not until you're cleared."

"No guns," Clutch echoed.

"Fair enough." He motioned to their SUVs. "I'll ride with Marco in your vehicle. You'll ride with my people and follow us to New Eden."

"What are you going to do with our Humvee?" Griz asked. "Because I've got a lot of hours with her and would hate to see her go."

"We'll park it—*her*—until you're done with quarantine, at which time she's all yours again."

"Including everything inside?" Griz countered.

"Including everything inside, as long as it doesn't pose a risk to New Eden citizens. Marco's been with us since the beginning, and I trust his judgment. If you don't mean to do harm to anyone in New Eden, you'll have nothing to fear from us."

He then called to his men to collect our weapons. "The name's Justin, and I serve as the mayor of New Eden, the safest place in the Midwest. You have my word. You'll be safe there."

He motioned to Marco. "Marco, you can fill me in on what's happened in the past month."

We'll see, I thought to myself as I gave up my rifle. Sunlight glistened off the barrel as I handed it over in exchange for the promise of safety. I was relieved we stashed most of our supplies, but I had a tough time believing Marco would keep his word. After all, New Eden was his home. Why wouldn't he tell them?

I didn't have long to dwell on the situation, because the short drive felt like it took only seconds before we came to a fenced-in small town flying a huge American flag with an eagle stitched over it.

New Eden.

We had arrived.

Part Two
Ambition

Six

New Eden was the exact opposite of Camp Fox in one manner. Whereas we had protected ourselves through seclusion, New Eden broadcasted their location to anyone for miles. Like most of Nebraska, the small town was surrounded by flatlands for as far as the eye could see.

The New Eden flag proudly flew at the front gate. The size of the flag reminded me of ones I'd seen while eating breakfast at Perkins restaurants, and I realized that was probably where they'd found it.

A mishmash of fencing at least ten feet high—layers of wire, wood, and poles—closed off New Eden from the rest of the world. When we pulled up to the gate, we were all asked to step out of our vehicle. I took a deep breath, feeling better that Clutch, Jase, Griz, and I were still together.

As Justin's men led us through the gate, I could now see the town, which looked like it had been an old, broken-down, small town before the outbreak. There were wood guard towers erected inside the fence. Every tower was manned, and every guard kept a wary eye and semi-raised weapon pointed in our direction. Everything was exactly as Marco described it except for one thing: there were none of the military vehicles and soldiers Marco had spoken about. If we wanted, I had a feeling we could've rammed through the gates in our Humvee, and they could've done little to stop us.

People emerged from around buildings. None looked too thin, and most looked relatively clean. Only a couple people could've passed as beggars. A medium-sized dog galloped forward to sniff Diesel. Diesel sniffed back, and they did a friendly "nice to meet you" doggie dance around each other.

"Buddy's harmless," a man who looked about my age said as he approached. "Unless you're a zed, then he turns into the Terror of the Plains. The rest of the time, he just trots wherever he feels like around town and startles the feral cats. But, they're the bosses around town. They keep the mice away." He walked alongside us. "The name's Charlie. I'd offer my hand, but we have a twenty-four hour quarantine period for travelers on the off chance you're infected and turn. I'll be one of your hosts tonight."

Justin stepped out of our Humvee, and we all watched as Marco pulled the vehicle into a garage to be locked away during our quarantine. As Justin approached us, Charlie spoke. "You'll want time to get settled in. I'll stop by later."

Justin motioned to town. "Here's New Eden. Well, sort of. This is the edge of town. The real town starts another block in. You'll get the tour after your quarantine is up. For your first night, you'll be staying in the building right over there." He pointed at a small brick building with a U.S. Postal Service emblem etched into the glass door.

He motioned for us to follow, and he started walking. Several guards kept their distance but made it clear they were herding us toward the building. I swallowed and took the lead, checking to make sure the rest of our group was right behind me. People stood around, watching us.

Justin held open the glass door, and I cautiously stepped in. Inside, six beds filled nearly the entire space. When Clutch entered, I saw him take in the whole place—no doubt searching for weaknesses, surveillance, and whatever it was he always looked for. As for me, I looked for places that would be safe from zeds, bad guys, and animals. Beyond that, I didn't know much else to look for.

"We don't have enough beds for everyone. We'll see if we can't scrounge up some mats, but at least it's only for one night," Justin said. "Truth is, we haven't come across any groups larger than four in months."

"Believe me, we've slept in worse conditions," I said.

Justin motioned around. "You have free run of this building, but you can't leave. There are guards stationed outside every wall. There's a single toilet and sink right down the hall. It's not much. What you see is what you get."

My eyes widened. "You have running water?"

"Yes. We also have electricity, and somehow natural gas is still pumping through the lines, but blackouts are common. We're still working on a better long-term solution."

"Impressive," Clutch said at my side.

"Supper will be brought in just before sunset. I have a couple errands to take care of, so Charlie and I will be back to talk with you later."

Justin waited until everyone was inside before he stepped out, meeting Marco on the way. Justin gave him a smile before leaving.

Benji started to jump on a mattress, burning more of that never-ending supply of energy eight-year-olds possessed. Frost sat down on the floor next to the boy's bed.

Clutch and I stood off to the side as people claimed beds for the night.

Some things never changed. All the men waited for the women to choose beds before claiming theirs. Jase quickly claimed the one next to Hali, though he tried to look all cool about it. I was planning to unroll my sleeping bag on the floor, but I sensed eyes on me and noticed both Griz and Clutch were motioning me to take the last bed. I shrugged with a smile and then jumped onto the mattress. "If you insist."

Marco sat on the floor next to Deb, and I frowned. "Why are you in here with us, Marco? Guilty by association?"

He looked up. "Standard operating procedures. Anyone who's been outside for more than a day has to stay in quarantine overnight."

"We just can't get rid of him, can we?" Jase muttered, and everyone chuckled.

Truth was, I was happy to have Marco with us. Someone with a foot in our world and a foot in New Eden's. Especially since as long as he was with us, the less chance he had to tell others about our secret cache. Although, I supposed he could've told Justin about it already.

Whether Justin knew about our other Humvee and supplies, he gave no hint when Charlie and he returned a couple hours later with bowls and a stockpot filled with something steamy that smelled of carrots.

"Potato and carrot soup," Charlie said as he set the pot down. "We don't have anything fancy around here, but it gets the job done."

Justin started handing out plastic bowls, cups, and spoons. "Marco had said you've done a pretty good job in regards to eating balanced meals, and I can tell. You can't understand how much hope it gives me to see that you're not only healthy but thrived out there."

"*Thrived* is a strong word," I said.

"You have a pregnant woman, a child, and none of you are sick. That alone is a miracle. Many people here will be excited to hear about you. Most folks who arrive at New Eden's gates look half-starved and a day away from getting turned into zeds. Nevertheless, we're always happy to see any survivors make it here. In fact, the capital has announced that's our primary directive: to save and rebuild."

"Hm," I said as I thought through it. "Shouldn't the primary directive be holding off zeds?"

"We don't have to worry about zeds anymore."

I frowned. "The herds will be back in the spring. We have to be ready for them."

Justin shook his head. "No, they won't."

"What makes you so sure?" Clutch asked as he handed me a bowl of soup and sat down with a second bowl for himself.

"They won't be back because we nuked the South."

I jerked back. The spoonful of soup I was about to eat splashed off the spoon. I barely registered the gasps around me. "You—"

"—bombed the South?" Clutch completed the question for me.

"As in nuclear warheads?" Jase added.

Justin replied. "Yes, the government dropped nuclear bombs on the south to wipe out the herds. Any remaining zeds will be dead soon enough, because the capital ordered all available resources to head south to finish off zeds that escaped the kill zone. Marco's squadron would've been sent south as soon as they returned. So, you can see why zeds aren't our primary issue now. They're nearing extinction."

"No more zeds," Hali said softly.

"But we released nuclear warheads on our own soil," Griz said.

Justin stammered. "Well, yes. More accurately, what's left of the United States, Canadian, and Mexican governments released warheads on U.S. and Mexican soil."

"But, there would've been survivors down there," Vicki said with a frown. "How many innocent survivors were killed?"

Justin answered. "When the herds started to cross into Missouri, the capital sent every plane and bus south to save survivors before the herds reached them. From what I hear, they pulled out over ten thousand total, which is a lot better than the alternative. With the numbers in the herds, it's safe to say the herds would've found anyone alive down there."

Marco had mentioned some part of the government had survived, but I hadn't realized they had control over that much firepower—let alone that many resources—that they could support taking on that many survivors. I hadn't even imagined there could be ten thousand total survivors left in the world. Hearing the number sent a strange sensation through my body. That number, coupled with the idea of the zeds going up in flames...It almost felt like...*hope.*

Justin continued. "We'll clean up the zeds in this area as we come across them, but we have to first focus on pulling in survivors before winter hits. Every province has been charged with rebuilding the country. New Eden may be one of the smaller provinces, but we have to pull our weight, just like everyone else. Unfortunately, all we have left is the New Eden security force and part of one squadron. So, every able-bodied man will be a huge benefit to us."

"How'd the government contact you?" Clutch asked. "Camp Fox was on the radio every day trying to reach someone, and this is the first I've heard of it. We were never contacted by anyone in government—no military, no politicians, nothing."

Justin shook his head. "They didn't find us by radio. They use drones to fly over the country and take pictures. They map out all survivors sites and reach out to any settlements of significant size. They said that for the longest time, they were losing more sites than they were finding. There were too many zeds spread everywhere for them to provide rescue support. It wasn't until the migration started in Canada that they started planning Operation Redemption: eradicating the zed threat and building our new country."

"It's crucial we find survivors quickly," Charlie said. "There are so many more deadly risks besides zeds out there."

"Like dogs," I said.

"And bandits," Vicki muttered coldly.

Charlie nodded. "Yes, but there are even far worse threats out there, which we have no control over."

"Like what?" Jase asked.

"Winter, for one," Justin replied. "Most folks in the freeze-zones don't know how to survive without electricity. Outside of New Eden, I expect we'll lose many survivors this first winter to cold and starvation. Then, there's dysentery and all the diseases that come with that. It was a miracle you made it here. Marco told me the route you took here, from the Mississippi River to Highway 20, onto I-380, and then across I-80."

"Yeah, so?" I asked, confused.

"There's a nuclear plant down between Highway 20 and I-380. Its reactor melted down last week, probably within a day after you drove through."

"Holy shit," I muttered, but no one else spoke.

"That's probably going to happen to every nuclear power plant in the world. Without maintenance—and most of these have had no maintenance for nearly a year—it's only a matter of time."

"You made it, but most won't make it on their own. They need our help."

"And you have enough food to take on more?"

Justin grimaced. "It's not easy, but we'll make it work. The capital has distributed rations and has promised to send more. But, we have to be able to rely only on ourselves."

"That's smart," Clutch said. "It's never a good idea to put all your eggs in one basket, especially when that basket involves politicians."

Justin smiled. "Marco told me a couple of you were in the military, so you may have a bit more experience with politicians than I have. I sold insurance before this. I could get you the best rates for your auto, house, or boat. I loved what I did. I went home each day knowing I was doing my best to ensure people were protected so when disaster struck, they'd be back on their feet in no time. In a way, I still have the same job, except it's more important than ever. If we don't get people back on their feet after this disaster, they'll die, and we'll never get the chance at building a new country. It's going to take every single one of us working hard day in and day out to rebuild this world so our children can thrive. It won't be the same world as before, and maybe that's a good thing. But, if New Eden is a sign of things to come, it's going to be worth it."

Justin was about to say more, but an armed guard stepped inside, and looked straight at him. "Thea's looking for you."

Justin stood. "Duty calls. Charlie will answer any more questions you have. Please remember, you are not to attempt to leave this building under any circumstances. We don't mess around inside the fence. Security's orders are to shoot-to-kill anyone and anything that may pose a risk to us. With that said, I hope you make the best of the situation. You are safe within these walls, so sleep well."

Not waiting around to take questions, Justin left with the guard.

Charlie chuckled. "Funny when Justin talks about sleeping, since he never sleeps. He'd have to stop working for five minutes first."

"And, Charlie sleeps enough for both of them," Marco joked. "From what I hear, your wife complains you're out like a light the moment your head hits the pillow. That's no way to please a woman."

"I can assure you, Sarah has never been disappointed in my husbandly duties," Charlie replied quickly.

"That's because she's never been with a real man," Marco added.

Charlie raised a brow. "Just because you're popular with the local sheep, doesn't make you a man."

"Ha, ha," Marco replied drily before flipping the other man the bird.

"I think a few more of my brain cells killed themselves," Jase said.

"Not to interrupt this fascinating conversation," Hali said, "but, what happens next? Once we're done with quarantine?"

"Finally," Griz said, "someone says something intelligent."

"Your quarantine will end at three p.m. tomorrow, once you each have a physical exam. Marco vouched for you, so Justin is bypassing your interviews. He said it's clear you're not bandits. I'll give you a tour, and if you decide to stay, you will be assigned homes, and you'll sign up for jobs. You may not get your first pick, but I can guarantee there's something for everyone."

"Sounds fair enough," I said. After all, the system mirrored what we'd had at Camp Fox.

Charlie stirred the stockpot. "It's almost curfew, and I need to get home to Sarah before she starts to worry. Whatever leftover soup you have will be your breakfast, and you can get drinking water from the sink. Any last thing before I head out?"

No one needed anything, so Charlie left, and I heard the lock click in place. Griz went around and turned off all the lights except a small lamp. He turned and eyed Clutch. "What do you think?"

"I think we're safe here for the night. Tomorrow, we'll see."

I could see Griz shrug in the faint light before he turned off the lamp, leaving us in darkness, with only moonlight from the window.

Clutch went to lie on the floor. I tugged his arm, and he crawled into the small twin-sized bed next to me. I lay in his arms as I tried to clear my mind of nuclear bombs, zeds, and winter.

"What about the zeds like Henry? What if they can recover?" Deb asked softly, to whom, I had no idea. "If they went with the herds to the south, they would've been killed too, along with other survivors, like us. What if we lived a couple states farther south?"

When no one answered, I spent the next couple of hours pondering her questions until at some point my mind mercifully drifted off.

———

Charlie Martel and his wife, Sarah, made excellent tour guides. After cold soup for breakfast and a light lunch of applesauce and flatbread, the couple proudly granted our freedom from quarantine and led us outside.

Charlie spoke. "If you decide to stay—"

"And we hope you do," Sarah interjected before handing out business cards to each of us. On the front read, *Charles Martel, Chief Operating Officer, S&C Technologies.* Scrawled across the back of each business card were handwritten numbers one through fourteen, but several numbers were already punched out.

"These are your ration cards," Charlie said. "Every Sunday, everyone gets ration cards. Each card has fourteen punches, which comes out to two meals per day. How you use those punches is completely up to you, but once they're used up, you're waiting until Sunday for your next card. Since this is Tuesday, we already took off what would've been the last two days' worth of rations."

"How do we get new cards?" I asked.

"You'll take a job," Charlie replied. "Everyone who takes a job gets a weekly card. Any exceptions must be approved by Justin."

"Rations are available in the general store. Over there." Sarah pointed. "It's about two blocks from your house."

Charlie added, "Justin has house number Twenty-Six set aside for you. Most survivors are assigned rooms in other houses. We try to fill up each house before starting with an empty one. But, Marco said you'd all prefer to stay in the same house if possible. Twenty-Six is a three-bedroom bungalow. But, it should fit ten of you fine."

"Ten?" Deb turned to Marco. "You're staying with us?"

"Yeah," he replied. "I used to stay in the squadron house number Three." He sighed, "It doesn't feel right now—"

"I'm glad," she said.

"You're one of us," I added.

He smiled. "Thanks."

"How about house keys?" Clutch asked.

Sarah shrugged. "Sorry. We don't have any keys. We only found keys in a couple houses. And, we don't have the ability to make keys. So, pretty much all the houses remain unlocked, but I suppose you could put a chair against the door or something if it makes you feel safer."

"Hm," Clutch replied.

As we walked through the neighborhood, I observed how busy

everyone seemed. Two men were pushing wheelbarrows full of food into the general store, where a short line had already formed. I was surprised at how normal everything seemed. One woman was pruning a rose bush. Two kids were on swings that creaked with every back-and-forth movement. Many of the houses reminded me of my small bungalow in Des Moines. Old, nothing fancy, and needing some TLC. Even before the outbreak, this town looked like it'd been struggling.

"You can't even tell any herds passed through this area," I said.

"Oh, they came through here, all right," Charlie said. "It was the first time we had to use the missile silo. We stayed down there for a full week before we risked coming out."

"We quickly learned that the silo wasn't ready for long-term occupation," Sarah added. "Justin has doubled efforts to improve the structure and better equip the silo. Our goal is to have it ready by winter in case our power goes out or it's as bad a winter as folks up north are saying it could be. Below ground would be much warmer and safer if we need to hibernate."

Charlie motioned to a woman covering a garden with leaves and mulch. "We're expecting an early winter. Justin's contact in the capital says they already have a foot of snow on the ground."

My eyes widened. "Where's that?"

"Saskatchewan. Canada, the northernmost parts of Mexico, and the U.S. have merged into one nation. They're still working on names, laws, and all that, but we needed each other to survive."

"We're Canadian now?" Jase asked.

Charlie shrugged with a smile. "Yeah, I guess so."

"I'm not so sure about that," Hali added with a grin as she enunciated "about" as "aboot."

"I guess hockey is the new national pastime," Griz added.

"Well, the healthcare program can't get any worse," Clutch mumbled.

We laughed, and Charlie ushered us along the tour.

When we turned onto a street of small houses—most reminded me of the pillbox-style houses from the 1940s—Hali frowned. "Why do you cram everyone inside these small houses?"

Charlie's brows rose. "What do you mean?"

"We drove by a new housing development a few miles back. Why don't any of you stay there?"

"Two reasons," Charlie replied. "One, we only have enough resources to defend this two-square-mile area. We won't leave any residents unprotected. And two, the missile silo is within the fence. It's our fail-safe. In case of any emergency, all residents immediately evacuate to the silo."

"We practice twice per week," Sarah added. "Every Tuesday and Thursday. We've gotten the entire population of four hundred and sixty four souls into the silo and sealed in nine minutes and twenty-eight seconds. Justin thinks we need to get it down to five minutes."

"Agreed," Clutch said. "If the fences were breached, you could easily be overrun in under ten minutes. What are your backup plans?"

Charlie frowned, and then shook his head. "The silo is it. We've been working non-stop at getting it back into shape. It hadn't been used in forty years. A good part of it was full of water, and some of the floorboards had rusted through. We've got it dried out, and we store our food in there for winter. The government flew over and dropped seven pallets of food about three weeks ago, so we're sitting pretty decent for the winter now."

"Let me guess," Griz said. "That's about the same time the bandits upped their game."

Sarah nodded. "Most of the bandits are hungry and scared, like us."

Charlie continued. "The difference is we got Justin and they got Hodge. Two leaders with very different approaches. Under Hodge, they first tried to offer "protection" in exchange for access to the silo, but Justin saw right through their bully tactics and refused unless they became New Eden residents. A few joined right up, but it didn't take Hodge long to make an example of anyone who tried to leave his group. Soon after, the assassination attempts on Justin started. According to the last assassin we questioned, they think if they kill Justin, the rest of us will fall in line."

They're probably right, I thought to myself. Without Tyler and Clutch, Camp Fox would've crumpled against attacks. Though, in the end, their leadership hadn't mattered. The Black Sheep had still managed to take nearly everything and everyone from us.

Charlie led us to a small brick house. "This is Justin's home and where most of New Eden business is handled. Come on in. Justin wanted to talk with you."

I was surprised that Justin lived in one of the smaller houses. There was nothing special about it. And, other than the New Eden flag hanging near the door, nothing indicated the house was different from any other down the street.

"Why did you change the American flag?" I asked.

"Justin figured it would be good to give New Eden a symbol. Since there's no longer a United States, we were all born here and wanted to keep the stars and stripes. We voted on the eagle as a symbol of our strength, and we ended up with the New Eden flag. Who knows, maybe it'll become the new state flag once all the dust settles."

As we filed through the door, I found Justin sitting at a large oak dining table. Two men sat next to him, both completely focused on the stacks of paper in front of them. A cat lay on a chair, seemingly oblivious to us.

As soon as Justin caught sight of us, he stood. "How's the tour going? I hope Charlie and Sarah are answering your questions."

"They did," I said. "Thank you for the hospitality."

Justin smiled. "Oh, it's not only to be nice. I'm hoping you all decide to become New Eden residents. We need all the people we can get. From renovating the silo, to managing the food and supplies, to securing the town and surrounding area, we're extremely short-staffed." He looked at Clutch and Griz before continuing. "Your experience would be invaluable here. Anyone with military experience served on our squadrons, and between the one we lost and the two the capital has taken control of, we have essentially no forces to scout, forage, and bring in survivors. We have a state trooper who runs our security forces behind the gates, and his teams have been running double-duty lately. So, you see how much I hope you decide to stay here with us."

"New Eden is a good place," Marco added. "I'm proud to call it home. We work hard here, but that's because we're building from scratch."

"Thank you, Marco," Justin said. "He's right. I know New Eden can become a sanctuary for all as long as we work together to make that happen."

Pride seeped through his words, and I wondered if he hadn't bitten off more than he could chew. "That's a bit ambitious, don't you think? How can you possibly support such large numbers of people?" I asked.

He shrugged. "I believe the only way we can rebuild is to move beyond surviving day-by-day. I believe we need a vision so we don't get lost. Perhaps it's a bit lofty, but I know we can get there. So, are you in to help rebuild the world?"

Clutch spoke first. "We need some time to mull it over."

"Fair enough," Justin replied. "You have probationary residency for two weeks. That should give you enough time to recuperate from your journey and get to know the folks and culture of New Eden. Then, you'll either have to leave or pledge residency to New Eden." He smiled. "And, I have no doubt you'll all fit right in. Now, if you'll excuse me, it seems that status meetings don't stop for the apocalypse."

We were shuffled back outside in a small flock, where we stood in a circle in the front yard. "Why's a pledge so important? We never had people do that to stay with Camp Fox," Jase said. "It's not like we're applying for citizenship or something."

"You very well could be," a man's voice said from behind.

I turned around to see a haggard old man approach. Unlike everyone else I'd seen, he looked like a beggar. As he approached, I wrinkled my nose. He also smelled like a beggar.

"Come on, Romeo. Don't scare them," Marco said.

The man muttered something and wandered off.

"Romeo?" Hali asked.

"A nickname," Marco replied. "He's harmless enough. Believe it or not, he was a successful businessman before the outbreak, but the stress screwed up his head. Sure, what he said could be true. The country we knew is gone. Who knows what will form out of the ashes. But, more important, Justin believes in the ceremony. He thinks the pledge helps people feel like they're joining something special, like they made the A-Team."

"If we're the A-Team, I'm B.A. Baracus then," Jase said.

"You don't have nearly enough bling," I said, pointing at the small gold cross he wore around his neck.

Marco rolled his eyes. "I was talking about sports. You know, the A-Team, B-Team, and so on."

Jase waved him away. "I'm still B.A. If a beggar gets a nickname, I think I deserve one, too."

"That's not how nicknames work," I said. "You can't pick your own. Take mine. Clutch came up with it the first day we met."

"How mushy," Jase said drily before he held up his ration card. "I don't know about you guys, but B.A. is hungry and going to get some food."

"Me, too," Hali said, and several others then chimed in.

"I'll bring you through the line the first time," Marco said. "It's pretty easy, but there's a process you follow."

Clutch held his ration card to Marco. "Grab me some chow. I want to walk around some more."

"I'll go with you," I said.

"Count me in," Griz added.

Clutch nodded and turned to the others. "Be at the house before dark. That gives you about one hour to grab grub, give or take."

Both Jase and Hali gave matching salutes. Griz and I held out our ration cards, and I held onto mine before Jase took it. "No stealing rations, hungry man," I said.

He smirked before tugging it away. "B.A.'s no thief."

As the rest of our group headed off to the ration line, I called out, "Calling yourself B.A. isn't going to make the name stick."

Whether Jase heard me or not, he didn't acknowledge.

I smiled. What an odd family we made. Even though I worried about each of them, I couldn't imagine not having them around. "We've got it pretty good," I said softly.

"Yeah," Clutch replied. "Now, let's secure the house."

Griz nodded. "I was thinking the same thing."

One hour later, we had gone through our new house from top to bottom. Someone had brought in enough mattresses for all of us, and I worked on setting up the bedrooms while Clutch and Griz talked through house security and escape plans. The house had only one bathroom for ten people. Rather than seeing that as a detriment, I squealed at the luxury. We'd gone months without electricity. Maybe Justin was right. To survive, we had to focus on something bigger than living day-by-day.

As twilight settled in, Clutch and I sat on the front porch, sipping tea, and watched people return to their houses for the night. Other than lights in many windows and a pair of security guards who walked the streets, the town seemed empty.

That was, until the howling started. This pack sounded bigger than the one that had surrounded us in Des Moines. I worriedly eyed Clutch.

"The fences must keep them out," he said and pointed to the security guards. "They don't look worried."

We were a block in from the fences, but every now and then, I could see a dark shape move outside the fence. After several minutes, there was an electrical *zap,* followed by a yelp. After a couple more repetitions of the same sounds at different parts around the town, Clutch frowned.

"They're searching for a weakness in the fence."

I shivered.

Of all moments, Romeo came jogging down the street, yelling something that sounded like verses from the Bible. As he passed our house, he pointed toward the darkness outside the fence. "It's a sign of the apocalypse. 666. The mark of the beast is now here. First we had wars, then we had the plague, and now the beast has arrived."

One of the security guards blocked Romeo's path. "C'mon, Romeo. You know the rules. Get on home now. We need to keep things quiet at night." The guard glanced our way. "No need to worry. Everything's safe."

Romeo giggled and bolted around, and the two guards followed in what almost looked like a game of tag.

After they disappeared around a corner, I turned back to Clutch. "Well, that was interesting."

"Yeah," he replied softly.

A cold wind blew through my coat, and I leaned into Clutch. He wrapped an arm around me, but after a moment, he bristled and pulled away.

"You know, with the zeds gone, we might be safe here. We can start fresh. *You* can start fresh. You don't need me anymore."

I looked at him and cocked my head. "What do you mean?"

"This thing. Us." He motioned from me to him. "It can't work."

My brows rose. "Really?" My eyes narrowed, and I crossed my arms over my chest. "Why the hell not?"

Clutch took in a deep breath and seemed to struggle to find words. Finally, in a rush, he spoke. "We both know you can do better than me. I'm no good for anyone. There's something inside me that's...broken. I was broke before all this happened. I'm not going to get better. This is who I am. I don't want to bring you down with me."

"Do you have feelings for me?"

"That's not the point. It's about what's best for you. There's something hollow inside, something I lost in Afghanistan. And, I never found it."

"So what? You have issues. Hell, we've all got issues. There's not a single person left in this world who isn't dealing with some fucked up shit in their heads. Sure, you were in the minority and had PTSD before the outbreak. But, by now, everyone has been pushed beyond their breaking points. None of us can be who we were before."

"But there are others who aren't as fucked up," he said, sounding utterly helpless.

I came to my feet, cupped his cheeks, and looked down into his eyes. "I accept you exactly the way you are. We'll deal with your nightmares and shit together. But, you have to meet me halfway. You have to accept yourself first."

His brows tightened when I bent down and kissed him. He didn't kiss back, but at least he didn't pull away.

I straightened. "You don't have to be with me if you don't want to be. Don't run away because you don't think you're worth it. I know you're worth it."

I didn't wait for a response. I headed inside and up to bed.

Clutch never came upstairs.

SEVEN

For the first time in weeks, I awoke feeling fully rested. I would've slept later except for the forgotten sound of a toilet flushing snapped me from dark dreams.

I stood and stretched. The small scar—the one shaped like a bullet hole on my calf—burned just like it did every morning until the muscle loosened. Once my old wound quit sending tiny spears of fire through my leg, I headed out into the hall and ran into Deb exiting the bathroom with a hand over her mouth.

I frowned. "Morning sickness?"

She nodded, swallowed, and then turned right back around and disappeared into the bathroom again.

I shook my head slowly and went down to the kitchen to make her some tea, one of the few foods not counted against our weekly rations. It took another ten minutes before she reappeared. Back when Deb announced she was pregnant, Doc had estimated she was about four months along since she had started to show. That was a month ago. Deb was losing weight with every passing week since there were fewer and fewer things she could stomach. Vicki had said it was normal for certain women to be sick throughout their entire pregnancy, but I had seen the worry even in her eyes.

I watched Deb as she slowly took a seat at the table and rested her head on her crossed arms.

When she didn't move, I spoke softly. "How are you doing?"

She raised her head ever so slowly and took a deep breath. "As well as can be expected for being knocked up after the end of the world."

I winced. "When you put it that way..."

She slowly leaned back. "Sorry. I'm not trying to be a Debbie Downer—"

A sharp burst of laughter escaped before I could muffle it.

"The name fits," she said with a shrug. "After everything we've been through, I should be thankful to be in a real house with real electricity and an honest-to-god working toilet. I'm tired of being tired and sick and cranky. I blame it on the hormones. Those prenatal vitamins are awful for nausea. The smell of oatmeal makes me sick, yet I would kill for a breakfast burrito with jalapeños right now. Go figure."

I handed her a cup. "I'm running low on jalapeños at the moment, but how about some tea? It's the real thing."

She grimaced before reaching out for it. "Not quite the same, but it seems to be one of the few things I can keep down."

While Deb and I sat in silence, sipping our tea, I heard the rustle of others getting ready for the day. Vicki was the first to make an appearance. She poured herself a cup and then waved as she headed to the door. "I'll see you after work."

Deb pushed herself to her feet. "I should be going, too."

I put my hand on her shoulder. "Rest. They'll understand."

"Late for my first day? I don't think so."

"Trust me," I said. "They know you're pregnant. They'll understand."

She watched me for a moment and then sunk back into her seat. "Thank you."

Clutch walked stiffly in. He eyed us both before heading to the teapot and pouring himself a cup. Whereas my calf ached, Clutch had to deal with an entire body that had taken more abuse than most bodies were made to handle. Dislocated joints and vertebrae, broken bones, and too many years of treating his body like an ATV were taking their toll. Headaches, stiffness, pinched nerves, and aches plagued him. Especially in the mornings.

After several long sips of tea, he turned around to make eye contact. "Ready to head?"

It was just like Clutch to pretend last night never happened. I pursed my lips. "I just need to grab my coat," I replied before turning back to Deb. "Need me to pick you up anything?"

She glanced at me hopefully.

"Anything except a breakfast burrito?" I added.

She sighed. "If that's the case, then, no."

"Is it morning already?" Jase said as he dragged himself down the hall with his eyes still closed, impressively not walking into anything.

"The sun's been up for ten minutes," Clutch said.

We both smiled, and Jase scowled. Even with an unpleasant expression, Jase looked more refreshed than he had in a long time. For being the opposite of a morning person, he woke up without his usual grumpiness. He hadn't even snapped at Clutch or me yet.

It made me realize just how exhausted we'd been. A single day at New Eden, and the difference was palpable. There was optimism in the air that I hadn't felt since we'd first arrived at the river barge. I hated to be too hopeful, especially when I didn't yet trust Justin or the people of New Eden, but I couldn't help but think New Eden could become *home.*

A place where Clutch, Jase, and I would be safe. Together.

"Are you all right?" Clutch asked.

I snapped back to reality. "Yeah. Let's get to work."

———

The next nine days were a blur of working, eating, and sleeping. We each worked ten-hour shifts doing menial jobs around New Eden. The first three days, I helped clean all the public facilities. The men were tasked to help transform an old drugstore into a community center.

The only adult member of our group who didn't work was Deb. Marco paid a visit to Justin on the first morning. That evening, Justin had made it clear, in no uncertain terms, that Deb was on bed rest until she had written permission from Dr. Edmund, New Eden's one and only physician.

Surprisingly, Benji was required to attend school. Diesel was even allowed to accompany the boy as long as the dog didn't distract the other six students. Since Benji had loved school before the outbreak, he had awakened before everyone else for his first day of school.

When all ten of us were together, the topic always returned to whether we'd stay at New Eden. Winter was lurking around the corner. We still had enough time to make it back to Fox Park, but we had no idea what we'd find there. New Eden seemed safe, but we were the outsiders here.

We all knew Marco was staying. He'd made it clear, just like he'd made it clear he wanted us—especially Deb—to stay.

On the second night, Frost said he was staying. He had Benji to think of, and he was convinced New Eden was the best place for the boy.

Deb's announcement came the following night. She was terrified of having a baby on the road and wanted to stay at New Eden at least until the baby was born. Here, she had a roof over her head, a semblance of medical care, and a perception of safety. Marco was ecstatic—he had a knack of always showing up whenever Deb needed something. Justin was especially happy that Deb would pledge allegiance to New Eden. Hers would be the first birth at New Eden, and everyone treated her as though she was the Virgin Mary.

On that same night, Vicki said she'd stay with Deb.

Jase announced he wanted to return to Fox Park at the first sign of spring, but he said he'd go wherever we went. He firmly believed the park was where we belonged, and Hali agreed. The teenagers had formed a fast friendship during her early days at Camp Fox—notably, right after her father tried to sell her for their safety.

As for the rest of us, we were still undecided. I had no doubt Clutch would go wherever I went, and vice versa. Despite our issues, Clutch wouldn't give up on me. I knew it.

Griz was tight-lipped, which was rare for him. He'd formed a fast friendship with Marco, but as a Ranger, he was a kindred spirit with Clutch. I suspected he'd go wherever he believed he could do the most good.

Tension around our indecision grew with each passing day. We craved to return to Fox Park...but we needed the safety of New Eden for the winter. Unfortunately, Justin gave us ten days, not a season, to pledge fealty. Then again, it wasn't like they could keep us here if we wanted to leave in the spring. Or, could they?

On the tenth day, while I was delivering lunches to the seven patrol officers on duty, Justin found me. I'd been trying to avoid him after Clutch told me Justin had cornered him the day earlier. I was one of those people who, before the outbreak, had always said 'yes' to everyone. It didn't matter if it was a party at someone's house, a request from a charity, or asking for a helping hand, I had always been the sucker.

As Justin and Charlie approached, I looked for a way out. I'd finished my last delivery and had a lunch break. I couldn't pretend I hadn't seen them. We'd already made eye contact. I looked to the left and to the right but saw no chance for escape, only a cat watching me from its perch on a window.

Charlie smiled and nodded toward the animal. "The cats keep the mice away. Luckily, they don't get sick like the dogs do. They've never gone after the zeds. There must be enough mice to keep them content."

Justin handed me a steaming mug. "I thought you might like some hot cocoa."

"Thanks," I said when he handed it to me.

"I ran into Clutch yesterday," Justin began.

I nodded. "He mentioned it."

He continued. "Today's your tenth day at Camp Fox. Have you reached a decision yet?"

I frowned. "Don't we have until tomorrow morning to give you our answer?"

"You do. I was wondering if you were on the fence. If so, I was going to see if we could answer any questions to help you make your decision."

"You've been more than fair to us," I said after a moment. "If we choose not to stay, it's not because of how we've been treated here. New Eden is a good community. You're good people."

Pride beamed through Justin's smile. "We try to do our best with what we have. We may not have much choice in what's thrown at us, but we do have a choice in how we cope. Free will may be the one thing that saves us."

"We have incoming!" someone shouted, and I twisted around to the front gate.

Justin ran toward the guard who'd yelled, and I jogged behind him. Already, two more guards were racing toward our position.

The first guard pointed to at least four vehicles in the distance. "It's still too far away to make out if I've seen any of those vehicles before. I can't tell if it's Black Sheep or friendlies right now."

"Call in all reinforcements," Justin said. "If they're launching a frontal assault, they won't find us to be easy prey."

"I've got it," one of the men said and took off.

"Give me a gun," I said. "I can help."

Justin watched me for a moment and then nodded. "Charlie, send all nonessential personnel to the silo. Arm anyone, including the Fox Group, who wants to be out here with us."

Charlie nodded and then took off running.

The newcomers slowed as they approached, and I counted five—not four vehicles as I'd originally thought. An old blue truck in lead had a long stick with a white sheet tied to it.

"They're here in peace," Justin said, though he didn't sound exactly confident.

A dozen armed guards lined up behind the fence's concrete pillars, showing a clear display of force. By the time the vehicles came to a stop, another fifty men were running toward us with weapons.

Clutch handed me my rifle. My hands instantly remembered the weight and feel of the weapon. It took me only a couple seconds to check to see that it was still fully loaded. I saw he had his Blaser rifle, and I smiled. "Just like old times, huh?"

He smirked. "Just like it." Then he noticed Justin, and his face hardened. "What's your protocol for dealing with threats?"

Justin nodded to the vehicles. "They're flying a white flag. We give them a chance to state their case. If they show us no hostility and don't pose a threat to New Eden, we'll allow them to come in under quarantine conditions."

"And if they pose a threat?" Clutch asked.

"Then we refuse them entry."

"That's all?" I asked.

Justin frowned. "No. We used to have one of our squadrons follow them to ensure they left. Showing we outman and outgun them has always been enough to scare off bandits. Let's hope that's enough today if these guys mean us harm, because we're running desperately low on firepower."

Clutch muttered something under his breath. "We'll have to ramp up New Eden's forces."

"We're a town, not a military installation."

"There's no difference, not anymore," Clutch said.

Jase and Griz came running toward us. They were covered in sawdust and still wearing their work gloves. Before reaching us, they paused and grabbed rifles off a stack of guns on an ATV parked nearby.

"Sit rep?" Griz asked when they met us.

"The situation is five vehicles flying a white flag," I responded quickly. "We don't know if they're friendly yet."

"So they haven't shown any signs of aggression?" Griz countered.

"They haven't shown their hand yet," Clutch said, and then he nodded toward the newcomers. "But it looks like we'll find out soon enough."

Two men stepped from the blue truck. They held their open hands in the air as they approached, one with a limp. Both men were terribly ragged, with soiled clothes and matted hair. One man lowered his arms to hold his ribs, but the other nudged, and he raised his hands again. No other people stepped out of the remaining vehicles.

"Jesus," I said. "These guys are in rough shape."

Justin moved toward the gate, and we each took a position behind vehicles, barrels, and poles, aiming our weapons at the newcomers. He glanced back at us as though making sure we were ready. Then, he turned back to the pair of newcomers. "Stop right there. That's close enough."

The men did as they were told and stood ten feet from Justin, with only the wire gate between them.

Justin spoke first. "Welcome to New Eden. Put any weapons you might be carrying on the ground."

"We don't have any on us," the taller of the two men said. "We left them in the truck."

Justin nodded to one of the sentries. Charlie opened the gate for the sentry to squeeze through and walk up to the two men, careful to stay out of our line of fire should the pair be violent.

The sentry checked the one who'd spoken, then the other, shorter man. He stepped back and held up a small revolver he'd taken from the second man. He tucked the revolver into his belt and backed off to the side, keeping his own firearm leveled on the newcomers.

Justin shook his head. "Lying isn't a way to earn trust."

"I need to protect myself. I wasn't planning on using it," he said.

"We need your help," the taller of the two men said.

"We got no place to stay. We were run out," the second man added.

Justin held up a hand. "I'll hear your case, but only when I know you don't intend to cause trouble. So, here's how it's going to work. I ask the questions. You answer them. Do you understand?"

They nodded. The shorter man spoke again. "Will you let us in then?"

Justin wagged his finger. "Tut, tut. Didn't you listen? *I'm* the one asking the questions. And, if I happen to not believe you or don't like your answers, you will not be allowed entrance."

The taller man punched his compatriot in the arm. "Shut up, you idiot. You trying to get us killed?" The smaller one glared and clenched his fists but didn't speak. I kept my rifle leveled on him.

"Let's start over," Justin said. "How many are in your party?"

"Nineteen. No, twenty-one counting Jim and me," the taller man said.

"Where are you coming from?" Justin asked.

"North of here," the man replied after a pause.

Justin narrowed his gaze. "Exactly how far north? That's Black Sheep territory."

The pair fidgeted, and I inhaled. "They're bandits," I said.

Justin glanced at me, and he gave a tight nod before turning back to the newcomers. "Black Sheep aren't welcome here. You can turn around and leave now."

The taller man tamped the air. "I ain't going to lie and try to deny it. Yeah, we were Sheep. But, we ain't Sheep no more. Once Hodge disappeared, we started to break apart. Then, we were attacked by some group of crazy survivors. After that, the mutts started to pick us off one by one. We got nothing. We're starving and about out of gas. If we stay out here, we're gonna die. Please, let us in. I never did anything wrong against New Eden, I swear it on my momma's grave."

Marco walked up to stand by Justin. "When did Hodge disappear?" he asked the Black Sheep.

"A month ago, maybe," he replied. "I don't know for sure. He took some guys out east to clear the river but never came back."

I smiled and glanced at Clutch. He caught my gaze with the same look. *Hope.*

I had shot at Hodge a few weeks ago but was sure I'd missed.

His gang had attacked us in the middle of the night. We'd set up camp in the middle of a massive sporting goods store on the banks of the Mississippi River. Our security had been lax that night. Hours earlier on that same day, we'd survived having our last home burn to the ground and were exhausted. We paid dearly for our mistake. Nearly all of Camp Fox was murdered; leaving only nine of us to remember.

Hodge had been the only bandit to escape, and I carried the shame of letting him get away. Now, the possibility that he hadn't survived lifted a metric ton off my chest.

"Let me get this straight," Justin said. "You guys fell apart and now need help from the same people you've stolen from and tried to kill. Did I get that right?"

Neither answered for a long time, until finally, the taller man spoke. "We're hungry."

"You should've been making friends rather than enemies," Justin said. "Let me guess. Those 'crazy survivors' that attacked you fought back because you attacked first."

"It wasn't like that," the shorter man named Jim said. "It was self-defense."

"I find that hard to believe," Justin said. "Since twice in as many months you people tried to kill me and take over New Eden. I imagine you got what you had coming. Now, if you don't leave, you will be arrested or shot."

Jim's face darkened into red, and he burst toward the sentry standing outside the gate. I fired a shot, but the taller man jumped in the way, and the bullet meant for Jim hit his compatriot in the chest. He went down. More shots fired from around me. Before I lined up a second shot, Jim had somehow managed to get behind the sentry, who he now held at knifepoint.

The bandits' vehicles, except for the empty lead vehicle, raced toward us. Shotgun barrels poked out from their open windows. I homed in my sights onto Jim's left eye, the only clear shot I had. Even then, if my aim was even the slightest off, I would be killing one of Justin's men.

"We have nowhere else to go. You gotta take us in!" Jim yelled.

I fired.

Jim collapsed, and the sentry ran toward the gate. Charlie grunted as he pulled it open.

The four vehicles were nearly upon us, but their driving was erratic, causing their shots to fly everywhere. As soon as the sentry was through the gate, Charlie pushed it closed. Instead of running away, once he latched the gate, he slid down. As he turned around, I noticed the red stain widening on his shirt.

"No," I gasped before yelling out, "Charlie's down!"

A sentry ran for the injured man, but gunfire forced him back. As the vehicles approached, we all focused our efforts on the occupants within. Windshields shattered. One SUV drove off the road and crashed into a tree. Of the three remaining vehicles, the first one slammed into the gate. Metal wire screeched and buckled under the impact, but the gate held. Charlie had managed to pull himself a few feet away; inches closer, and he would've been killed in the crash.

The other two vehicles stopped to the side and laid down fire while the first SUV backed up. With a loud clank of shifting gears, it launched forward. Blood splattered its broken windshield the second before impact. The driver's foot remained on the gas pedal. Metal cried as the SUV tried to force itself through the layers of wire fencing and wood boards.

Clutch ran past me, and my eyes widened. Crouched, he weaved through gunfire and stopped at the bumper of the SUV, on our side of the gate. He raised his rifle and shot through the fence at the vehicle's occupants. The engine immediately slowed but the SUV still pressed against the gate.

Metal clanged, and the top part of the gate fell inward. Clutch grabbed Charlie and pulled him clear, and two other people carried the injured man away. I focused on laying down cover fire, and I saw at least one of my shots find its target when one of the passengers dropped his shotgun and collapsed over his open door. Gunfire slowed, and then stopped from the two vehicles.

"Cease fire!" Justin yelled, waving his arms. He motioned to the sentries who'd been on duty.

I continued to scan the area as three men moved to the gate and pushed their way through the bent door. One pulled the dead driver from the SUV that had rammed into the gate and cut the engine. He held up his thumb.

Justin turned to the other two vehicles peppered with bullets. "Lay down your weapons and step out slowly. Any sudden moves, and you will be shot."

No one emerged, and I took advantage of the silence to swap magazines. After an endless minute, Justin nodded to the trio on the other side of the gate, and they moved slowly to the closest vehicle. With two holding their rifles, the third man checked the entire vehicle. He stepped back and shook his head in Justin's direction, and they moved to the last remaining vehicle.

I was careful to scan the area, to make sure there was no one else sneaking around, but everything seemed quiet. It was the eerie kind of silence that followed a gunfight, where my ears were ringing like after a music concert, yet everything felt muted.

At the last vehicle, the sentries dragged out a man who showed no resistance. His eyes were closed, and I couldn't even tell if he was conscious. Two of the sentries dragged him back to the gate and through the small door.

Justin met them inside, and I moved closer.

Justin came down on a knee. "Why did you attack?"

The man's head rolled weakly. "No—where else—to go."

I swallowed, knowing the feeling all too well. *Desperation.*

"If you hadn't shot at us, we wouldn't have shot at you," Justin said.

The man struggled and lifted his hand, only to drop it, and his last breath puffed from his lungs.

Everyone stood around, and then someone cheered. The sentries chanted out, "New Eden!"

Justin joined in. "It's over. New Eden is safe. Anyone who attacks New Eden will suffer the same fate."

I didn't join in. I'd never found anyone's death a time for celebration. Not Hodge's. Hell, not even Doyle's. There were too few of us left. With every death, I knew humanity was taking one step closer to the brink.

Clutch stepped up to me, and I looked into his eyes. "How's Charlie?"

His lips tightened. "We'll see."

I sighed. "Is there no safe place left in this world?"

Clutch didn't answer. Jase and Griz walked over.

Jase slung his rifle over his back. "It feels good to have my rifle back."

"Yup," Griz said without looking up from reloading one of his mags.

I spotted Justin watching us. He didn't come closer, but I knew what he was thinking. I chewed my lip before speaking. "We've got a decision to make. Stay or go?"

Griz clicked the mag into his rifle. "These guys sure could use our help. Even today, it was sheer luck they didn't have more casualties."

"They need our help. But, do they deserve it?" Clutch asked.

I thought for a moment. "Of all the roads we could've taken, and all the places we could've ended up, somehow—a full state over—our paths still managed to cross. I don't believe in coincidence. I think we're meant to be here, at this time."

Clutch breathed heavily and then nodded. "We should stay."

I turned to Jase and Griz.

"You know where I stand. I'm in," Griz said quickly.

Jase shrugged. "It's cold out there. We have electricity and food in here. I'm in. What have we got to lose?"

PART THREE
TEMPTATION

EIGHT

All of New Eden gathered around us, and I found myself fidgeting. My breath circled in tiny wisps of fog in the freezing morning air, and I hugged myself to keep from shivering.

Justin held up his right hand, and the conversations hushed. "Repeat after me."

The nine sole Fox survivors raised our hands.

"As a citizen of the New Eden province ..."

"As a citizen of the New Eden province," we answered in chorus.

"I pledge to defend and support our province, with all that I am..."

"I pledge to defend and support our province, with all that I am..."

"With the highest level of integrity and honor, I give this oath of fealty."

"With the highest level of integrity and honor, I give this oath of fealty."

Justin smiled. "Welcome to New Eden."

Cheers erupted. Someone patted me on the back, and we found ourselves swarmed by people welcoming us into the community. I glanced to Clutch at my side, and he wore a genuine smile. He wasn't exactly a people person, yet there was no mistaking his demeanor. He looked at me, and I returned his smile. He shrugged, and I knew why he was happy. I sensed the same happiness.

We belonged somewhere.

It wasn't Camp Fox, but it still felt good. *Safe.*

Even Jase looked happy, though he was a consummate extrovert and handled attention like a fish in water. He still wanted to return to Fox Park, but like everywhere we'd been, he'd quickly acclimated to New Eden. It seemed the younger the person, the more easily they adapted to change, and it made me wonder what we lost as we aged.

Justin made his way down the celebratory line and stopped in front of me. His smile was wide as he held out his hand. "New Eden is lucky to have you."

I accepted his hand. "We're lucky to have New Eden."

He shook Clutch's hand next. "We have the start of something good here. I know it. We'll talk more later. I need to get back and send your names to the capital. We keep track of all citizens. Seeing the lists grow gives everyone hope."

"What's the number up to?" I asked.

"Four hundred and seventy-three at New Eden, counting you. We're one of the smaller provinces. Colorado has the largest with nearly ten thousand. Over eighty-seven thousand across the new, combined country. We're hoping to have found and tracked at least a hundred thousand by the first of July."

"You think that many made it?" Clutch asked.

Justin nodded. "I'm sure of it. The problem is we're all scattered right now. We need to pull together to build a foundation."

"How's the rest of the world looking?" Clutch asked.

Justin shrugged. "Australia was the least hit. They're still at twenty-plus percent, and they're the ones who reached out to us and are connecting the rest of the world. They're still trying to get data on Europe, Asia, and Africa. Now, if you'll excuse me..."

He bowed out and headed down the street.

"A hundred thousand," Clutch said softly.

"Yeah," I added, just as softly. "The human race might have a chance after all."

"Why the long faces? Today's a big day."

I looked over to see Sarah pushing Charlie in a wheelchair.

I frowned. "Shouldn't you still be in bed? It's been less than a week."

"That's what I told him," Sarah said. "But, Charlie will never miss a party."

Charlie waved a hand. "Oh, I'm fine. Just a little tender."

"You were *shot*," I said.

"And, the bullet missed everything that needs to keep working," he countered.

"Still," Sarah added. "You have to be careful. There's only so much medicine lying around."

"I know, I know," Charlie said in a rush. "Enough about me. Have you picked your new roles? Today's your last as free agents."

Clutch chuckled next to me. "By picking new roles, you mean signing up for jobs?"

Charlie shrugged. "Roles, jobs, whatever you want to call them. But, seriously. Have you picked your role yet? It's important to select the one that's the best fit for you. It won't feel as much like a job if you enjoy it."

"So you say," I said with a smirk.

"Well, whatever you picked, I hope you enjoy it," Sarah said before placing a hand on Charlie's shoulder. "We need to grab on to any joy we can find nowadays."

Charlie held her hand, and they gazed into each other's eyes. She then backed up the wheelchair, and the pair departed without another word.

The crowd had thinned. People had returned to work or home.

"I suppose it's time for us to head to work," I said.

"See you after dinner," Vicki said, and I waved to her and Deb as they walked away.

Last night, we'd each settled on our roles, which we'd start today. We were all assigned the first shift since we were newcomers, though I suspected we'd each be assigned different shifts as we earned their trust.

Once a school dietary aide, Vicki volunteered to help with rations. Deb volunteered to serve as a medical aide after she went for a prenatal checkup with New Eden's only doctor and saw he had no help, but a waiting room full of patients with jammed fingers, splinters, and minor cuts. Dr. Edmund likely had agreed so he could keep a close eye on her health.

"Be careful," Hali said, eying Jase.

"I always am," Jase replied with a grin.

She jogged to catch up with Vicki and Deb, since their workplaces were all in a close vicinity to one another. Hali signed up as soon as she found out New Eden had no one to manage the distribution of clothing and non-perishable supplies.

Frost and Benji had long since disappeared. Frost, with his general contractor experience, had signed up for silo renovations, while Benji had full school days.

The rest of us had signed up for security. When we arrived at the security building, Justin, along with another man, was already waiting for us.

"Already report us to the capital?" Clutch asked, and I noticed a hint of something hard in his question.

"All done," Justin said, sounding pleased. Then he looked to each of us: Clutch, Griz, Jase, and me. "I was hoping a couple of you would choose the squadron. With you, we have a full team again."

He pointed to a SUV parked near the gate, where Marco leaned against the side of the vehicle and waved in our direction. "The squadron is meeting in about ten minutes from now. Clutch and Griz, they're expecting you. Clutch, since you're the senior-ranking military vet here, Marco proposed that you command the squadron."

Clutch pursed his lips. "A sergeant isn't exactly senior ranking. There's a reason sergeants aren't commanders."

Griz chuckled. "Yeah, they're too cranky to be one."

Clutch flipped him the bird. "It's yours. You're the only other soldier in this place."

"Oh, hell no," Griz said. "I might have more of a personality, but the last thing I want to do is babysit amateurs. That's up your alley."

I scowled. "What's that supposed to mean?"

Griz smirked.

"This is important," Justin said, not giving Griz time for a witty comeback. "After losing Marco's squadron to the Black Sheep and the capital claiming our other squadrons to locate survivors in the south, it's crucial we keep our only squadron running in tip-top shape. This is our only crew equipped to travel out of New Eden."

"You can count on me," Clutch said, any humor gone from his voice.

"Well, that covers the squadron then," Justin said.

My brows rose. "What, you're not letting Jase or me serve as scouts?"

Justin watched me for a moment before turning to Jase. "Jase, I'd like you to meet Zach. Zach runs the New Eden security forces, and you'll be on his team."

Zach held out his hand. "Welcome to the force."

Jase didn't shake it. Instead, confused, Jase looked from Clutch to me and then to Justin. "But, I'm with these guys. We work together."

Justin spoke first. "I know you're more than capable to have survived out there for so long, but it's New Eden policy to not allow anyone under the age of eighteen to serve on the squadron. It's safer within the fence," Justin said.

"That's bullshit," Jase said. "I'm as good as anyone else out there."

"I'm not doing this to be difficult," Justin said. "I can't break policy for you. You—the youth—are our future. If we don't work toward our future, we won't have a future."

"The force isn't some place for lackeys," Zach said. "Our job is as important—if not more so—than the squadron's. We're the last line of defense for New Eden. These people are trusting their lives to our ability to keep them safe. We take out any danger that comes up to our fences as well as handle any problems within the fences. We also serve as backup support to the squadron. So, you see, it's not going to be a walk in the park. You'll see plenty of action, I can guarantee it."

Jase frowned.

"Give the force a shot," Clutch said. "Maybe they'll reconsider later."

"We have more guns and more ammo than the squadron," Zach added. "Marco mentioned you were pretty good with a motorcycle. We have ATVs on the force, but I happen to have a Honda 250 bike sitting in the garage that's yours as a sign-on bonus if you want it. I won't ever lie to you, we're in desperate need of personnel. You won't be treated like a kid here, I swear it."

Jase's frown disappeared as he tried not to look excited. "Well, I suppose I could give it a shot."

Zach smiled and held out his hand again.

This time, Jase shook it.

"What about me?" I asked with narrow eyes.

Justin's lips pursed. "Just like we have a rule in place to protect our youth, we have a rule in place to protect our women. Have you considered an administrative job? Marco said you're good with numbers. I could use help with the supplies tracking."

"That's bullshit. You don't need me behind a desk." I pointed. "You need me out there. I can fly over the area and identify problems before they get close."

Justin shrugged. "We don't have an airplane anywhere near here."

"I can find one. Then, all I'll need is a fuel tank and a decent mechanic."

"Two things we have in very short supply," he countered.

I pursed my lips. "Okay, then. If I stay on the ground, I can still help. I can take down a zed from over a hundred meters away."

Clutch spoke first. "She's right. Cash is the best sniper around. You'd be doing New Eden a disservice by not leveraging her talent."

"Unfortunately, we're running desperately low on ammunition," Justin said. "We're down to our last boxes, and we've cleared every known armory and supply store in the area. None of us will have any ammo before long."

Exasperated, I nearly rolled my eyes. "Fine, Then use me to scout for supplies, survivors, and trouble. Just because I'm a woman, I'm just as capable in my own right."

It was the first time I'd seen Justin uncomfortable. "Look at it this way. Men survivors outnumber women over three to one here. Any loss of a woman or child kills morale. It makes sense for women to choose the safer jobs, and we have plenty of openings—"

"No," I said, and took a deep breath. "Listen. I'm not trying to be difficult. I'm only trying to be where I can provide the most value."

"Cash..." Justin said.

Zach cut in. "C'mon, Justin. You know how short-staffed the force is. And, Cash has been out there, with these guys, for months. I'd be glad to have her on the force. It's safer than the squadron, but she can still make a difference."

I bit my lip. While I wanted to be outside the walls—with Clutch—I also didn't want to burn my shot with Zach's force. It would be better than shuffling paperwork. I didn't enjoy our team being split up, but I knew we'd have to make concessions at New Eden. After all, we were the newcomers here and had to abide by their rules. Not that it made things sit any easier in my gut.

Justin finally relented. "Fine, fine. Cash and Jase will serve on the security force." Then, he wagged a finger at me. "But, you will both be careful and do exactly what Zach says. I will not have you risk your lives unnecessarily."

"I got it," I said, trying not to frown, holding back the sting of disappointment of being judged just because I had tits.

Justin looked over each of us and then clapped his hands together. "We're all set. Let's get to work."

———

When Zach had said we'd see plenty of action, what he'd meant was that our days would be filled with hotheaded disputes and fiery tempers. My first day on the job, Mary stole from Jim's garden, the meal rations weren't enough for Ron's 260-pound frame, and Diesel caught a rabbit that Saul intended to eat. The second day, I learned most people used up their ration cards a day early, and they all believed they deserved extra rations for working.

My partner was Zach. Even though he chose me because I was the only woman on the force and he was being protective, he wasn't a bad partner. He had far more patience than I did, but he didn't take bullshit from anyone. Not even Bryn, the pretty woman who'd been caught at least five times before stealing from people's houses. We caught her pilfering canned pumpkin from house twelve. I would've kicked her out of New Eden after the second time. But, Justin was too protective of any women in New Eden. And everyone knew it.

"It's the ones like her who will make it so no one can trust anyone," I grumbled after Zach locked Bryn up for the night.

He shrugged. "She's a hard worker. Justin says as long as she's adding more value to New Eden than taking away, she stays."

"Locking her up overnight and giving her a free meal doesn't do any good. She gets the same punishment after each offense, and she keeps on stealing. You need to up the ante each time. Make the punishment worse until she decides to be a team player or leaves New Eden."

"What would you do?"

I thought for a moment. "I'd start by pulling her rations the next time she steals. Then, I'd try humiliation, such as those public stocks they used in the Middle Ages. After that, I'd send her outside the gates."

"Remind me not to get on your bad side."

I chuckled. "If you think that's bad, you're lucky you can't read my mind as to what I'd really do." A cold wind blew, and I shivered. "It's hard enough the way it is to survive out here. We don't need interminably selfish people to make it worse."

I envied Clutch, Griz, and Marco. The squadron of twelve men hit the road each day and was home in time for dinner. While the only excitement we got was taking out every zed or sick animal that reached the fence. The zeds were easy. Most had rotted enough they moved slowly in the cold. When the temperatures dropped about ten degrees below freezing, they couldn't move at all. Easy to take out with a quick stab.

The animals were another story. Between them and the zeds, the landscape was depleted of meat, making us walking around in New Eden look like a feast in their starved gazes. I could've sworn the damn things were taunting us. Running up to the fence, barking to get our attention, and then running back off into the surrounding woods. By day, they'd come out one or two at a time. By night, they numbered in the dozens, as they searched for weak spots at our fences. Our job was to scare them off. Kill them whenever we could. I hated that part of my job more than anything else. Not only because I was killing something that had once been a domesticated animal, but also because those dogs scared me a lot more than I was scaring them.

Zach pointed to the two men headed our way. "Our shift is done, and not a moment too soon."

I rubbed my gloved hands together. "Good. It's downright freezing out here."

"It looks like a storm could be finally rolling in," he added as we walked to the force's headquarters, which was next door to the quarantine-slash-jail.

I glanced at the overcast sky blanketing everything in gray. "It's looked like that for three days now."

"Yeah, but the wind's picked up. I bet something's headed our way." He stepped inside and held the door open for me.

I paused. "What month is this? Are we still in November?"

"Yeah," he replied. "Thanksgiving is next week already."

I sighed and entered. "Well, I guess we're lucky to have gone this long before Mother Nature reared her ugly head again. When we got hit last month with snow already, I was expecting a hell of a winter ahead of us."

He nodded. "I was, too. Luckily, she's been focusing on Canada so far."

"Let's keep it that way."

When the next shift stepped inside, we quickly chatted and made notes in the daily log before heading our separate ways. The wind picked up, and I found myself jogging home. A block from my house, I found Jase walking home from his shift on the other side of town. Poor Jase was stuck with the deadbeat on the force, leaving Jase to do all the heavy lifting. A couple days ago, I'd found Jase walking his shift alone, his partner no doubt taking another "break."

We met in front of the house. "You don't look so hot. Are you feeling okay?" I asked.

He wiped his red nose. "Just tired. I didn't sleep great last night. And, this cold weather doesn't help."

I put a hand on his shoulder. "I'll make you some tea. Hopefully you'll sleep better tonight."

He sniffled. "Yeah."

"So, how'd Dick ditch you today?"

His partner's name was actually Richard, and he went by Rich, but we quickly decided that "Dick" fit him better.

Jase rolled his eyes. "Dick was a no-show. Caught the flu."

My brows rose. "And exactly how could Dick catch the flu in a fenced-in town?"

He shrugged.

I shook my head. "Gotta give the guy credit. He comes up with a new excuse every day. I bet he's faking it. I haven't heard any rumors about a flu going around. Geez, I hope he's faking it. The flu would be miserable to catch. It's not like we get sick days or time off around here."

"You're telling me," he said and took the porch steps one at a time.

I frowned. Usually Jase leapt up the steps to get inside and eat. That he was practically dragging his feet today worried me.

Someone coughed daintily, and I froze. In slow motion, I stepped inside. Hali was lying on the couch. Several wadded tissues peppered the floor. Jase had sat down next to her and was rubbing her arm.

Vicki came in from the kitchen, carrying two steamy mugs. She gave me a knowing look before handing Jase and Hali a mug. I followed her into the kitchen.

"The flu's here," she said as she rinsed dishes in the sink. "Hali's got it. Benji's been in bed all day. You know how kids are. He probably picked it up at school and brought it home."

I let out a deep breath. "How's everyone else?"

"Okay for now." She turned around and leaned against the sink. "But, I can tell I'm more tired than normal. I'm going to bed after a bit to try to fend it off. How are you doing?"

"I feel fine."

"Good," she said. "Deb is staying at the clinic. Marco's with her. They're quarantining her to make sure she doesn't catch it. It's probably your run-of-the-mill flu bug. Deb accused Justin of being overly careful. I have to admit, I'm siding with Justin this time."

The sound of familiar, heavy boot steps on the porch pulled our attention to the foyer.

"I'll put more tea on," Vicki said.

"I can do it," I said. "Get some rest."

After a moment's hesitation, she nodded. "Thank you," she said and headed up the stairs.

I put on the water to boil, and heard Clutch enter the kitchen. He came up behind me, and I leaned back and into his warmth. "I was beginning to wonder where you were."

"We were at Justin's," he said and reached around me and grabbed a handful of walnuts and pumpkin seeds from a bowl under the cabinet. "He had us scout the Omaha suburbs today."

I turned around. "Why?"

He popped some nuts in his mouth and chewed. "Justin wants New Eden to have a Thanksgiving feast. He thinks it's important for morale. Lincoln's closer, but it was more heavily bombed. And, we did find a store in Omaha that hadn't been destroyed."

I frowned. "But, the cities are too dangerous. We learned that when we tried to camp in the store by Des Moines. There are way too many things that want to eat us in cities."

He shook his head. "The zeds won't be a problem. The temperature's dropped enough that all the ones we've come across lately were popsicles. As for the dogs, except for the sick ones, the packs seem to come out only at night. They're still too skittish to come out during the day."

"Still..." I cautioned. "There could be a lot more of them around the larger city."

He flashed one of his rare smiles and ran a thumb over my cheek. "It'll be fine. The superstore we found isn't too far into town. It should be an easy in-and-out. But, we have to move fast. If we don't hurry and grab what we can, other survivors will get to these stores first. And, once we run out of gas, getting supplies out of the cities will be infinitely harder."

"I know," I said, frowning. "But, I still don't like it. Besides, how are you going to make it into Omaha, raid a store, and make it back here in one day? The squadron is too small to unload a store. You need more help."

"We'll be fine. The squadron is heading out first thing in the morning. We're taking all three haulers. We'll be gone for two nights."

"You need more hands," I said. "Jase and I—"

"Have to stay here," he interrupted. "Without the squadron, New Eden only has the police force to protect it. And, Justin mentioned there's a flu bug going around. You and Jase need to be careful."

"You're the one who needs to be careful."

His smile widened. "I always am."

NINE

The temperature hovered at ten degrees Fahrenheit the morning the squadron headed out. An inch of fresh snow covered the ground. I went with Clutch and Griz to see them off. Marco had stayed the night with Deb, and I could see he was reluctant to leave her when he dragged his feet to the gate at dawn.

As the squadron loaded up, I grabbed Clutch's jacket, pulled him down, and kissed him solidly on the lips. He wrapped his arms around me. Someone whistled, and I ignored it. When I let go, Clutch looked rather pleased with himself. Typical guy expression. I held up three fingers. "Three days. You better be home in three days, or else I'm coming to get you."

He chuckled. "We'll be back with time to spare. I don't plan to get on your bad side."

I stuck out my chin and tried not to smile. "Damn straight."

"Where's my kiss?" Griz asked, holding out his arms.

I grinned and walked into his embrace. I kissed his cheek as he squeezed me half to death. When he let me go, I scolded, "Be careful out there." Without waiting for an answer, I spun on my heel and walked away, though once I was around the building, I stopped and then watched them drive through the open gate from my relatively hidden place.

After the gate closed behind the loud trucks, my heart pounded. While I'd grown accustomed to Clutch heading outside the fence every day, worry chewed at my nerves when he wasn't home at night. Since the outbreak, I could count on two hands the number of nights we'd spent apart.

The first few times, I'd worried about how I could possibly get by without him. Then, my fear had switched gears. Somewhere along the line, my feelings for Clutch had morphed into something deep and tangible, and I constantly worried about what could happen to him out there. I wanted to be there to protect him, even though he was more than capable of taking care of himself.

After the gate closed behind the trucks, I hustled into the force's HQ, a small brick building that had once been Justin's insurance office.

It was freezing inside. It was New Eden policy to not use precious energy to heat any building no one lived in. Even then, the force checked out every house every week to make sure energy wasn't being wasted. With the exception of the medical clinic, thermostats couldn't be set higher than sixty degrees, which felt balmy to me after being outside most of every day.

"Just the two of us so far?"

I jumped and turned to see Zach. "Jase caught the flu."

He frowned. "Rich, Steve, and Jack all called in sick. I haven't heard from anyone else yet. That flu is spreading fast."

"It makes sense. We're all working long hours in cold weather and not getting enough nutrients. And, we're all in a relatively enclosed environment. Any virus that passes through is going to hit us hard."

"You're starting to sound like a doctor."

I shrugged. "My dad was one. My mom was a nurse. I guess it's in my genes."

"Why didn't you go into medicine?"

"I didn't like dealing with people, and I used to get queasy at the sight of blood. So, I went the actuary route, though it wasn't exactly the best career to prepare me for all this. Justin said you were a state trooper before the outbreak"

He chuckled. "I was a volunteer reserve officer. For my day job, I worked in a factory. I assembled modular components for wind turbines."

"That'll come in handy if we can put up a wind turbine in New Eden."

He shook his head. "Afraid not. I'm in the same boat as you. My skills are pretty much worthless nowadays. I worked on the RF module housing. The other ninety-nine percent of a wind turbine's components is beyond my expertise."

"Well, aren't we the pair?"

He grinned. "Yeah. The fate of New Eden is in the hands of a number jockey and a windmill monkey." He motioned toward the door. "Shall we?"

I glanced at the icy window and cringed. "Let's go defend the hapless citizens of New Eden against...well, the hapless citizens of New Eden."

———

Two days later

Justin, Zach, myself, and five other people stood around Charlie's bed. Sarah sat in a chair next to him, biting back tears while she held his hand and crooned her love for him.

I fidgeted. I'd never been any good around the dying. Probably because most of the time, the dying had been bitten, and I needed to be there to bring them permanent death after they'd died the first time. Today was different. Charlie had caught the flu, and it wasn't even a bad flu as flus went. Only the run-of-the-mill flu that made its victims achy, sniffly, and coughy. Jase, Vicki, and Hali had all returned to work already. But, to the weak and infirm, the flu was always dangerous.

Charlie had been still healing from his gunshot when the flu struck. It had knocked him down hard, and he'd quickly become bedridden. Earlier this morning, the doctor announced Charlie had pneumonia, and there was nothing that could be done. After that, Sarah had demanded the doctor return to the clinic to help those who could be saved.

Charlie's breaths rasped in lungs filling with fluid.

Zach and I stopped during each of our daily rounds. A line of people cycled through the house, giving their regards to Sarah and their final good-byes to Charlie, though both seemed oblivious to anyone in their home.

As a coughing fit wracked Charlie and Sarah let out a sob, I swallowed the lump in my throat. Charlie was a good man. My lip quivered. "It's not fair," I said softly, turned on my heel, and walked from the room.

Inside the hall, I took a deep breath. The cool air helped, but still a weight pressed upon my chest. Everyone died—that was a part of life— but the world had become nothing but death. Picking us off one by one. What hope was there if we were going to die, anyway?

I leaned against the painted wall, and stared blankly at the picture at the end of the hall. It was a print of a famous painting—The Birth of Venus. It fit in with the tapestries and clay pots, all that remained of the house's original occupants.

A wail erupted from within the bedroom, and I clenched my eyes shut.

Footsteps entered the hallway, and I heard the door quietly close. "It's over," Zach said softly.

I opened my eyes and rested my head against the wall. Everyone who knew Charlie loved him. I couldn't fathom him ever having an enemy. "Losing Charlie will be hard on New Eden."

The corner of his lip curled almost into a smile before dropping again. "It will be hardest on Sarah."

I remembered her swollen, red eyes, brimming with loss. "Yeah."

We stood there for a long minute before I pushed off from the wall. "We should continue our rounds."

Zach thought for a moment and then nodded. "I could use some fresh air, anyway. We'll check on Sarah later. She's got plenty of company right now."

We headed outside and continued our long, cold walk around the western half of New Eden. Even wearing my arctic coat, ski mask, stocking hat, and gloves, the cold bit at our fingers and noses, and we took indoor breaks every thirty minutes to prevent frostbite. As we did every day, we took a full hour to walk through the first floors of the silo. Our job was to make sure everything was secure, but truthfully, there was an inherent security to the silo, and the more stairs I descended, the safer I felt. Especially when Clutch was still away. He'd be home soon, probably even before I was off duty.

Knowing Clutch would be safe within the New Eden fences tonight, the heavy weight on my chest began to lift. Justin was right—a Thanksgiving feast would be a perfect event for New Eden—symbolic of making new friends and a new life together. Everyone was excited to see what Clutch's squadron would bring back from Omaha. Even though half of the town was still recovering from the flu, the impatient excitement in the air was palpable.

By sunset, my muscles trembled with adrenaline. I had to force myself to slow down to keep with Zach's casual pace.

Zach fought back a smile. "The squadron will be back before too long. Why don't you head home?"

I glanced at my watch. "We still have twenty minutes left on our shift."

He shrugged. "I can handle the daily log. Go on, I'm sure Clutch, Griz, and Marco will be starving by the time they get back."

I eyed him for a moment before pulling him into a big hug. "Thanks. I owe you one."

"I'll see you in the morning."

Zach headed toward the HQ, while I turned and headed the opposite direction. The nightly howls had begun, and I could see many pairs of eyes reflecting moonlight from the other side of the fence.

My pace picked up with every block, pausing only when I passed Charlie and Sarah's house. I stood there for a long moment before deciding to check in on Sarah to see if she needed anything. I bounded up the steps and didn't bother knocking. Inside, the house was nearly empty. On the table sat a variety of food and gifts dropped off by various friends and neighbors throughout the day. I continued down the hallway and into the bedroom. The bed now lay empty, and I suspected Charlie's body was now at the clinic, which also served as the town morgue.

A lone woman sat in a chair reading a leather-bound book. She looked up when I entered. "Hello, Cash."

I couldn't remember her name. I knew she worked with Vicki, but I'd never talked with her before. "Where's Sarah?"

She motioned to the bathroom. "Taking a bath. She wanted some alone time."

"Oh," I said. "I guess I can stop back later."

"She should be out any time. She's been in there ever since they took Charlie away."

"Okay," I said. I stood there, twiddling my thumbs, and waited for Sarah. After a minute or two, I sensed a gaze on me, and I looked at the woman. "What?"

"Is Marco your brother?" she asked.

"What?"

"Someone said he was your brother. I was wondering. I think it's pretty cool he found you out there. What are the odds?"

I rolled my eyes. "He's not my brother. He's Mexican. I've never even been to Mexico. Just because we're both of Hispanic descent doesn't mean we're related."

She shrugged. "Sorry."

I glanced at my watch. "How long can Sarah stay in there?"

She laid the open book down on her lap. "I don't know, but she's been in there for ages already. Two, maybe three hours? Everyone else left a long time ago. It seemed wrong to leave her alone, so I stayed."

"I'm glad you did." As minutes passed, a sense of foreboding formed in my gut. "Any sounds?"

She thought for a moment. "She ran a bath when she first went in, but after that...no, I can't say I've heard anything."

I walked over to the bathroom door and knocked. "Sarah? It's me, Cash." No response. I knocked louder. "Sarah, open up."

When I heard nothing, I tried the handle, but it was locked. My heart pounded at the silence on the other side. I ran my fingers along the woodwork above the door and found a long, hexagonal-shaped key. I slid it into the keyhole, and the lock clicked. "Sarah, I'm coming in."

Still nothing.

I glanced back at the other woman who was now standing, her eyes wide.

I took a deep breath and opened the door. Sarah lay in the bathtub, staring at nothing. The water was murky with red. One arm was in the water, the other strewn over the side of the tub, a still river of blood puddled on the floor below it. It took several seconds for the scene to register in my brain, and my lips quivered. "Oh, Sarah, *no.*"

A gasp behind me. "Sarah!"

I turned in time to barely catch the woman as she collapsed.

She pressed her face against my chest and cried. "I should've known," she whimpered. "I sat out there while she...she..."

"You couldn't have known. No one could've known," I said, stroking her hair while staring at Sarah's lifeless body. I didn't bother checking for a pulse. The amount of blood and her pallor told the entire story. Sarah had chosen not to live without her Charlie and taken matters into her own hands.

"I don't understand," she said. "Sarah couldn't hurt a fly. Why would she do that to herself?"

I didn't answer.

"It's not right," she mumbled and continued crying.

When her sobs slowed to a simmer, I helped her up, walked her down the hallway, and sat her on the couch.

She shook her head. "I've lost two husbands. One to cancer, the other to those creatures outside the fence. It tore my heart out each time, but I survived. If only Sarah could've seen that things would get better."

The front door opened, and I turned to see Zach step inside. He grinned. "I figured you were heading home." His smile dropped abruptly. "What happened?"

"It's Sarah," I said. "She—she's in the bathroom."

Zach headed down the hallway with intent and returned a minute later. Somber, he looked across our faces. "Cash, can you go get Justin and Doc Edmund? I'll stay here with Izzie."

I nodded and turned as though in a haze. "Yeah, sure. I'll be right back."

I barely remembered running to Justin's house or to the clinic. But, I ended up back at Charlie and Sarah's house with both men a few minutes later. They quickly took control. Justin made calls on the portable radio he always carried, and the doctor went immediately to check on Sarah.

I didn't stick around. I numbly walked to my house. I could no longer find the quick walking pace I had before. All the excitement I'd been harboring had been muted.

I shut the front door, and the shrill howls were muffled by the walls. I was glad to find the living room empty, with everyone else in bed still recuperating. I sat down in a recliner and leaned back.

And waited for Clutch to come home.

The following morning

"Still no word from the squadron?" I asked for the third time in an hour as I drummed my fingers on Justin's desk.

Justin didn't look up from the papers he was working on. "Not yet."

Jase stepped from behind me and leaned on Justin's desk. He had a tissue in one hand, and his nose was still red from being sick. He'd quickly recuperated, but the flu had left him in a rather cranky, groggy mood. "Don't tell me there was no Plan B? You know, in case they got stuck somewhere?"

Justin's lips tightened before leaning back. "I'm sure they had some alternative plans worked up while they were on the road. But, we didn't work on any additional plans in case they didn't return. It seemed to be a straightforward plan. Low risk."

The front door opened, and cold wind hit my cheeks. Justin lunged forward to keep his papers from blowing away. A man walked in. He removed his scarf before I recognized him as one of New Eden's handymen. He crossed his arms over his chest. "They're not back, are they?"

Justin sighed and dropped his pen. "Not yet."

The man stomped a couple steps closer. "I told you that they never should've left. We've lost our last remaining squadron, and it's your fault. You were greedy to demand a Thanksgiving feast, and now look what's happened."

"Calm down, Folsom," Justin said. "The squadron is probably running late."

"Late? You mean like Smith's squadron? Or Martin's squadron? How many more men have to die before you learn that we shouldn't send our squadrons out there?"

I winced at the man's biting words and flashed a glance at Jase, who seemed as uncomfortable as I was to be in the same room as this pair.

Justin seemed oblivious to the remark and gave the man a calm gaze. "Those were extenuating circumstances. The zeds are no longer a serious issue, and the Black Sheep have been broken and disbanded. It's safer now."

"Safer?" the man balked. "How about the wild dogs? How about all the bandits we don't know about? You keep sending men out to die, when we already have everything we need to survive within these fences."

"You're only thinking of the status quo. We don't have enough if we grow our numbers," Justin replied quickly.

The man waved him off and headed back to the door. He opened it, letting the cold wind blow in. He faced Justin one more time. "I'm raising a vote of no confidence at the next council meeting. Your dictatorship has killed enough men."

With that, he left and slammed the door shut behind him.

I watched the man walk outside the window and disappear down the sidewalk. Outside, the day was a dark gray, with the sun hidden by layers upon layers of clouds. It was almost as though something were casting a giant shadow over us. It was exactly as I felt.

Justin sighed. "Sorry about the interruption."

"He's not exactly one of your cheerleaders," I said.

Justin chuckled drily. "Folsom voted for the other guy."

"Ah," I said. "And, I'm guessing the other guy is campaigning again."

Justin shook his head. "My opponent was Randy Smith."

Jase elbowed me, and I shrugged and gave him my I-didn't-know look.

"Smith's squadron was overtaken by zeds near Lincoln last summer," Justin continued.

"Sorry," I muttered.

"It's okay." Justin smiled weakly. "I'm sure there are at least a dozen folks out there right now who want to be running this place. But enough about politics. Now, if you don't mind, I have more papers to read and sign."

I took a step back but didn't leave. I eyed Jase, and he returned a hard look. I nodded and then turned back to Justin. "Clutch always keeps his word. The squadron missed their deadline, which means something is up."

"We don't leave our people out there," Jase added.

Justin closed his eyes for a moment. "And what exactly do you propose?"

I began. "I—"

"We," Jase interrupted.

I smiled. "*We*—Jase and I—will look for them."

Justin stood. "No way. Absolutely not. There's no way I'll let a teenager and a—"

"Woman?" I finished for him, my brow raised. "Really, Justin, the times have changed. Jase and I are scouts. We know how to get around out there."

"Besides," Jase said. "We're new to New Eden. If something happened to us, it wouldn't be as bad as if something happened to Zach or you."

Justin shot a hard look. "You're wrong. You would be sorely missed." He grabbed his radio and barked a command. "Send Tom to my house." He set the radio down without waiting for the response. He eyed us. "If you go, I'm sending Tom with you."

I shook my head. "Jase and I can move quickly on our own. We're used to being out there. And, we don't want to put anyone at risk who doesn't need to be."

"Tom is with the squadron. He had the flu the morning they headed out, but he's doing much better now. If anyone went, I'd prefer it would be only Tom. The squadron may already be lost," Justin said. "It doesn't make sense to lose more people searching for them."

"Bullshit," I snapped. "It makes a hell of a lot more sense than sitting on your ass and signing your name a hundred times."

"This is important—"

"Oh, buy a rubber stamp already," Jase added drily.

"We're going, and we don't need your approval," I said. "The last time I checked, all citizens had the right to pass through the gates at any time."

"You're not prisoners here, but if you're gone for more than a day, you'll have to sit through quarantine again."

"Fine," I said.

"Fine," Jase said.

Tom strolled in at that moment, and the redhead with a full beard paused to take in the full scene before walking for Justin's desk. He reminded me of an easygoing lumberjack, and I suspected he even wore a plaid flannel underneath his brown coat and coveralls. Hell, he could've been mistaken for a model on the front of a maple syrup bottle. "What's up, boss?"

"Thanks for coming, Tom. Are you up for a little trip?"

He smiled like he already knew what Justin was thinking. "Sure. I could be ready to head out in thirty minutes."

"Cash and Jase have their minds made up to go and look for the rest of your squadron. You were involved in the planning. I want you with them."

Tom nodded. "I'm fine with that. We'll just be driving, so it should be safe enough. To be honest, I was planning on heading out to look for them today, anyway." He thought for a moment, then eyed Jase and me. "Are you sure you're up for heading outside the fence? We could be gone until dark."

"We're good," we replied simultaneously.

Tom shrugged. "If you're good, I'm good."

Justin's eyelids became heavy, as though he were physically drained. "What's the plan?"

"Easy," I said before anyone else spoke. "We'll take a single vehicle with enough fuel to get to Omaha and back. We'll follow the same route the squadron took."

"We'll need the map Clutch left with you," Tom said to Justin.

Justin ruffled through his papers.

Clutch had talked me through his mission the night before he left. Whenever we planned a mission of some kind, we talked through it together. It helped us think of risks or gaps we hadn't covered.

Last night, when Clutch didn't return home, I couldn't sleep. I tossed and turned in bed and checked the front door every ten minutes. The night's silence was broken only by the howling of the wild packs. I had tried to draw Clutch's route from memory, but the truth was, I always had lousy navigation skills. Jase, on the other hand, had a gift for navigating. There was a reason I always took him when I flew over the Fox Park area. But, unfortunately, Jase had been down with the flu when

Clutch went through the squadron's plan and route. If Jase hadn't gotten sick, we would've had a map drawn from scratch and been on the road already.

When the night had given way to a cloudy morning and Clutch hadn't yet returned, my heart had felt like someone had dropped a hundred-pound weight on it. I'd already made up my mind and was packed to go by the time Jase made an appearance in the kitchen. Though, he'd evidently had the same idea, since he met me in the kitchen fully geared up. "I'm ready," was all he said, and it was all he needed to say.

"Ah, here it is," Justin said before flattening a map on the table. He pointed to a line drawn with blue marker. "This is the route they were taking both ways, and these dots are the general area of the big-box stores they were going to check out." He tapped on two X's on the map. "The interstate is blocked here and here." He continued to speak as he drew lines along smaller highways. "If you run into trouble, I recommend you take these roads. We know they're clear."

Jase took the map, folded it, and stuck it inside his coat.

Justin looked at Tom. "Is your radio fully charged?"

"I had it on the charger all night," he replied.

Justin nodded. "Okay, then. Report in every hour until you're out of range, which is roughly twenty miles. And, as soon as you're back in range, you better report in."

"I know the routine," Tom added.

"I know," Justin said, sighing. "And, take the F-150. It'll be the best for the trip."

Tom turned to Jase and me. "How soon can you be ready? You'll need food and warm gear to get through a couple days. I'd like to get on the road as early as possible."

"We're ready now," Jase said.

Tom smiled. "All right then. I left my bag at my house. We'll head out in thirty minutes."

We turned to leave, and Jase paused, glancing back at Justin. "Don't worry. We'll bring the squadron back with us."

I kept silent, praying that when we brought back the squadron, we'd be bringing back our friends and family and not a truckload of corpses.

Part Four
Prudence

TEN

The day was cold, but the sun shone brightly. Cold enough and bright enough that two rainbow sundogs appeared on either side of the sun, haloing the brilliant star like celestial gems. I shaded my eyes and slid on my pair of aviator sunglasses.

There was a strange nostalgia about being back on the road. While being on the constant lookout for trouble was exhausting, I found it easier to breathe in the open space. Especially now that any zeds we came across stood frozen in place like statues in a Tim Burton film.

With most zeds having made what I hoped was their final pilgrimage south, I wondered if the worst was over. The fence kept out animals easily enough, but it never could've kept out the herds of zeds. If the capital hadn't nuked the south, it would be a matter of time before the herds had killed us all.

Had it only been nine months since the outbreak? It seemed like ages ago. Yet, it had taken only a sliver of the years I'd lived to see the world decimated.

Jase coughed and popped a cough drop into his mouth. Even though he'd recuperated, it seemed the junk in his chest would linger longer. It was the same with everyone who'd caught the bug, and I worried how many of those cases would turn into bronchitis or life-threatening pneumonia.

Spring couldn't come soon enough. I remembered the feasts my mother would prepare for each seasonal equinox. It was a tradition that had been passed down through her family for generations. I remembered the dates of the equinoxes as much as the dates of any holiday. After all, they were a holiday in my family. I frowned. "What's today's date?"

Jase shrugged. "I don't know. Why?"

Tom concentrated. "Is it November 24? No, maybe it's the 25th" His lips tightened. "I can't remember. Thanksgiving is in two days. That's all I remember."

"I'll find a calendar," I said. "It's important to keep track of dates."

Jase rolled his eyes. "You're such a nerd."

I poked my tongue out at him. He grinned and turned away. Tom drove us in silence for the next hour while I stared hazily out the window. Hints of snow bunched in the shallow crevices of the plowed fields. Dozens upon dozens of unmoving, white wind turbines stood watch, silent scarecrows in the endless fields. No sign of the squadron, let alone any remnants of humanity.

Movement ahead caught my eye, and I squinted to make out the shapes. Ahead of us in the ditch were several furred shapes. They were tearing into something. When I saw a piece of blue clothing, I sighed. "Just a zed," I muttered to no one in particular, hoping that was true.

"I can't imagine they taste good," Jase said.

I nodded. "Eating diseased meat can't be good for them."

"They're starving," Tom said. "It's hard to imagine. In a single day, there were so many dogs and other pets abandoned by their caregivers. They were suddenly forced to hide from something that looked like their masters and search for their own food. I'm amazed as many survived as they did."

The dogs looked up as we passed by and cocked their heads, as though they were trying to remember the sound of engines. They didn't look healthy. Their fur was matted, and their eyes glassy.

"What will happen when they run out of zeds to eat?"

I swallowed. "I'm guessing they'll either turn on each other or starve to death. Either way, it won't be pretty. Poor things."

"Sometimes I'm glad Betsy didn't make it," Jase said softly, fingering the small gold cross he wore around his neck. "If something happened to me, I wouldn't want her out here, living like this."

I remembered the day he showed up at Clutch's farm, cradling his injured dog, which had been attacked by Jase's zed father. The small collie had sacrificed herself to protect Jase from his own father and had paid the price.

"It's hard to believe," Jase continued. "All these dogs were someone's pet at one time."

"Yeah," I said, hoping he'd move on to another topic.

"I never see any small dogs. They must've been killed by zeds or the packs in the early days."

I thought of my parents' adorable Shih Tzu, Peaches. How the little fur ball would curl up in my lap within five minutes of my being in the house. She was the sweetest thing, always happy to see me. And, boy was she smart. That little dog somehow knew my mom needed her insulin even before my mom did.

"I'll try to reach Clutch again," I said abruptly and ran through all the channels we used on the radio. After a few minutes of hearing nothing but static, I rummaged through my backpack and pulled out a can of Spam and some crackers. We'd taken all our rations for the remainder of the week to play it safe.

When we'd left this morning, we'd said no good-byes. Instead, Jase and I had dropped a note on the counter before we'd made our way for Justin's house. By then, we'd already known that we were either leaving to search for Clutch, Griz, and the rest of the squadron or getting arrested.

I grabbed a spoon and popped open the can of salty meat. "I'll eat an early lunch, and then we can switch seats, Tom," I said before scooping out a sliver of the meat and squeezing it in between two stale crackers.

Tom didn't take his eyes off the road. "I can eat and drive."

"Tut, tut," Jase scolded from the backseat. "Clutch hasn't ground that rule into you yet?"

"Which rule is that?" Tom asked.

"Everyone needs to focus on his one job. The driver focuses on driving. The passengers focus on looking out."

"Cash is eating while looking out," Tom countered.

I nodded. "But all I have to do is sit here and look. You have to be ready to slam on the brakes or crank the wheel in case something happens."

Tom smiled. "And what do you think is going to happen out here? Any remaining zeds are too slow. The Black Sheep are gone, and the roads are clear."

I shrugged. "You never know. You have to be ready for anything. Or, like Clutch says, you always have to keep a step ahead." I found myself thinking back to everything Clutch had taught us. I knew I wouldn't have lasted the first day of the outbreak if he hadn't taken me with him to his farm. He'd saved my life, Jase's life, and that of so many others.

Still, he didn't think he was worth anything. Idiot.

"One time," Jase began, "Cash and I were flying over this one small town, looking for survivors, when we came across this flat-roofed building. Some folks had run out onto the roof. We turned to drop the official Camp Fox goody bag—some food and directions to Fox Park—when they started to throw bricks at us. For real. They even had a big slingshot set up and everything. If Cash hadn't banked hard right then, we would've been clobbered."

I chuckled drily. "Yeah, we didn't always get the welcome mat rolled out."

"But, you tried to help. That's what counts." He slowed down. "I'm getting hungry. Here's a good spot to refuel and switch. At this speed, we'll be to Omaha within a few hours."

"We'd be there already if Tom could drive faster than thirty," Jase said. "I think I just got my first gray hair."

I smirked but didn't say anything. Tom wasn't comfortable driving fast. Safety was more important than speed. Even though every fiber of my being wanted to rush into Omaha to find the squadron.

I dumped the empty Spam tin into a plastic bag, glugged a long drink of water, grabbed my rifle, and looked outside at the flat Nebraska fields, with only the interstate dividing the land.

Tom shifted the truck into Park and cut the engine.

When he went to open the door, I grabbed his arm. "Hold on."

He glanced back at me. "What?"

After a moment of scanning the wide-open space around us, I relaxed. "I'm used to zeds running out from every direction to eat me. I guess I'm not used to the quiet yet."

"It's okay," Jase said. "I had the same gut reaction, too. It's weird, not expecting zeds anymore."

"There are still plenty out there," I cautioned. "We still have to be careful."

"But they're frozen stiff by now," Tom said as he opened the door and stepped outside.

I couldn't open the door without scanning the area one final time. This particular section of the interstate had no cars on it. The roadblocks of crashed cars seemed to be centered at the cities and towns. Weeds grew tall in the shallow ditches and as bold tufts in the unplanted fields. Something could hide in there.

"Cash, it's all clear," Tom said.

"I know," I said and pushed open the door. Frigid air blasted my face.

Jase followed. He stayed near me, and it grated on my nerves to know that he felt the need to protect me, when it was supposed to be the other way around.

Tom was already up on the truck bed and unraveling the fuel hose and portable pump. He connected it to one of the three, 55-gallon drums of gas we brought along with us. He handed me the clear plastic hose. I slid my rifle over my shoulder and grabbed the end of the hose. Jase stood watch while I opened the gas cap and slid the hose in. "Ready," I said.

Tom started pumping. At first, a slow trickle of gas ran through the hose, and then more and more came. Tom continued to manually pump for a tedious ten minutes, and I listened to the gas going into the tank. Jase walked casually around the truck, doing a full circle every couple of minutes or so.

When the sound of the gas gurgling in the tank changed, I held up my hand. "It's full."

Tom stopped pumping and wiped his brow. Even in the freezing air, he was sweating from pumping gas. Once I shook out the last drips from the hose, I pulled it from the tank and handed it back to Tom, who unhooked the pump and rolled everything back up.

He jumped off the back of the truck and rubbed his hands. "We're all set."

I nodded and headed back to the truck.

"Shotgun," Jase said as he butted in front of Tom at the passenger door.

"After you," Tom said rather sarcastically before stepping back, opening the back door, and climbing in.

I strapped myself into the driver's seat and started up the truck. Immediately, warm air belted out from the heater, and I savored the heat on my skin. Jase picked up the map from the dash and studied it. A quick glance to the backseat showed Tom biting into some kind of tortilla wrap. I shifted the truck into gear and slowly picked up speed.

Before the outbreak, I'd had a lead foot. Two speeding tickets a year was my average. Now, I never drove above fifty-five for two reasons. One, the faster I was going, the less time I'd have to react; and two, driving any faster would hurt the gas mileage. Even though I was anxious to find Clutch, I would've been stupid to rush. For all we knew, they hadn't even made it to Omaha.

Tom spoke in between bites. "It's kind of peaceful out here with nothing to remind us of the outbreak."

"Yeah," Jase said before taking a bite of his own lunch. "If you don't count the complete lack of anybody on an interstate except for us."

"I don't miss the chaos of what life was like before," I said. "But, I sure miss a lot of the conveniences we had."

"It's like Mother Nature forced a reboot," Tom said. "When people knocked the world out of balance, she sent in a disease to knock things back into line."

I considered his words for a moment. "You're assuming the outbreak wasn't man-made."

"You're assuming it was?" Tom asked.

I shrugged. "No. Maybe. I don't know. I remember there was a lot of speculation in the first days, but no one came out and said, 'this is the cause.'"

"I think the worse assumption," Jase started, "is to assume the outbreak is going to reset the balance. This isn't Star Wars, and there's no 'force' out there to help keep a balance," he air-quoted. "You've seen what the virus is doing to animals that feed on the zeds. The virus has only one goal, and that goal is to destroy. It's the Grim Reaper of viruses."

"Wow," I said. "When did you become the philosopher?"

A red light came on the instrument panel, and I frowned. *Check engine.* "Uh oh," I said. "Tom, you don't happen to be car mechanic by any chance?"

"I didn't own a car until I was out of college," Tom replied. "Why?"

"What's wrong?" Jase asked.

I tapped on the instrument panel, even though I knew that did no good. "I think that last batch of gas was bad or had water in it. Either way, the engine isn't happy about something."

"It still sounds okay. Maybe it's a fluke," Jase said.

"Fingers crossed," I added.

Tom leaned forward to look over Jase's shoulder at the map. He pointed. "Take the next exit. If we need to swap vehicles, we should take a county road. There would be more houses, so hopefully, a better chance for finding a vehicle. If the battery is dead, we should be able to swap in the truck's battery. Then, we'll be good to go."

My muscles tightened as I gripped the wheel. It took only three miles before the engine started to make a clacking sound, metal pinging on metal in a regular rhythm.

Jase pointed. "There's the exit. Now, if only we can keep this beater going until we find new wheels."

Evidently, the truck didn't relish being called "beater," because the very next second the engine sputtered and died. Several lights blinked on the instrument panel. "Shit," I said. The truck's momentum slowed without power. My heart pounded with every foot of ground it covered. I found myself leaning forward, to edge the truck farther down the road, but it crept to a stop on the inclined exit ramp.

"Da da da dun," Jase chanted ominously.

I scanned the area around us for a house, danger, anything.

Tom spoke. "Robert Frost once said in a poem something like, 'I have taken the path less traveled by, and that has made all the difference.'"

"Yeah, but Frost never said if that difference was good or bad." I grabbed my rifle and my binoculars and stepped outside. I walked around to the back of the truck and climbed onto the bed and then onto the roof. Cold wind blew through my jeans. Shading my eyes against the sun, I made a count of the buildings in the area.

Jase climbed up next to me, and the roof dented in. "At least we have some options." He pointed. "I'm thinking we go for those two houses across the road from each other."

"I was thinking the same thing," I said, looking through the binoculars. "Both have all their garage and building doors closed. We could get lucky."

"But the house to the north is closer," Tom said from the ground.

"True," I said and hopped down. "But, there's not enough sunlight left to hit all three houses today. With two houses, we have twice the chance of finding a vehicle we could use."

"And twice the risk for trouble," Jase added.

"I thought you said you wanted to check out that pair of houses first."

Jase gave a weak smile. "I thought we *should* check them out first. I didn't say I *wanted* to check them out first. I *want* to stay in the truck and call AAA, but their service has really gone downhill this year."

"Well, I say let's grab our gear and hit the road. I don't like standing out in the middle of nowhere," I said and walked around the truck and grabbed my backpack. I rummaged through it and grabbed a ski mask, stocking hat, and gloves.

In less than fifteen minutes, we had the truck pushed back onto the interstate and parked under the overpass, the best camouflage we could think of to minimize its appearance in the unlikely event someone passed through this area.

Jase, Tom, and I walked up the exit ramp and turned left on the small highway. The pair of houses stood about a mile away. Close enough to see their garages were closed, but too far to see any signs of violence or danger.

We kept Tom at a quicker pace than he was clearly used to, but he didn't complain. I hated being out in the open, especially in an area I wasn't familiar with. We had no idea what could be hiding within any of those buildings or behind the small cropping of trees. I felt like a sitting duck.

At our quick pace, we reached the pair of houses in ten minutes. We slowed as we examined each one. "Which one do you want to try first?" I asked, looking from the white-and-brick ranch on the right to the blue two-story on the left.

Jase held up a finger. "Eenie meanie miney moe, catch a tiger by its toe. If it hollers, let it go, eenie meanie miney *moe*." He pointed to the house on the left. "The Smurf house, it is."

"All right," I said, rubbing my cold fingers. "Using a startlingly brilliant display of deductive reasoning, Jase has made the call. The garage is detached, so I'd say that's a great place to start."

Jase and Tom nodded, and we walked slowly up the driveway, expecting something to jump out from behind the building at any second. I watched the house as we walked by it to the garage, which was set farther back from the road.

"Cover me," I said and tiptoed onto the porch. The big oak door stood open, a screen door the only barrier between us and anything inside. I could already smell the rank odor of one or more zeds inside. A blend of putrid disease and decomposition. I stayed to the left of the screen door and threw a quick glance inside. Chairs were knocked over. I backed quietly off the porch.

"I'm pretty sure the house still has its occupants, so we should keep it quiet."

Jase was already slinging his rifle and pulling out his machete.

"They should be frozen," Tom said.

"You want to bet the farm on that?" I asked as I swapped my rifle for the machete I had strapped to the front of my backpack. "No need to draw any unwanted attention if we don't have to."

Jase put a hand on Tom's shoulder. "I don't know about you, but between Cash and me, we have thirty-five rounds of ammo left. I'd prefer to save those until I really need them if I can."

Pride swelled in my chest. In a matter of months, Jase had transitioned from a high schooler to a man. To see him morph into a leader gave me hope for his future. If anyone could make it in this world, Jase could. With everything he'd lost, what would've broken most seemed to have honed him. Out of us all, Jase still had the strongest connection to his humanity. Clutch had always been jaded, and I was certainly jaded. But, Jase...he was the best of us.

We spread out as we approached the garage. It was an older building with no windows, not even small ones in the doors.

Jase reached the door first. He put his ear up to it. After a moment, he looked to us and shook his head. I took off my sunglasses and nodded to Tom. "Get your flashlight ready," I whispered. I stood to Jase's right and held up three fingers. Two. One.

Jase pulled the door open and jumped back. I stepped forward, ready to swing the machete at anything that moved. Nothing came forward from the dark. The air was cold but fresh. A beam of light shone from over my shoulder, and I could see a single compact car sitting under a layer of dust.

"It's clear," I said and stepped inside.

Tom followed, and he shone his light around the small garage. The undisturbed dust showed no signs of recent activity, so I relaxed my grip on my machete.

Paint cans and boxes sat on open shelves. I walked past them and opened the car door. The keys were in the ignition, and I sat on the seat. Holding my breath, I turned the key but nothing happened. No lights came on, not even a growl of an engine trying to start.

I looked at Jase and Tom, frowned, and shook my head.

"This car won't work," I heard Tom say from behind the car. "Two flat tires."

He kicked the side of the car, and I cringed at the noise.

Jase popped his head in the door. "Geez. Can you make a little more noise next time?"

"Oh, sorry," Tom said sheepishly.

"Let's check the other garage," I said, not bothering to shut the driver's door.

Jase was still standing watch outside.

I slid my sunglasses back on. "See anything?"

"Not yet," he replied. "Maybe we're far enough out of any towns that there isn't anything out here."

"We can hope," I said.

As we walked down the driveway, Tom slowed near the house. "I wonder how all the people who were at home during the outbreak became infected."

I shrugged. "Maybe a loved one brought the virus home. Maybe a neighbor. Maybe they also ate the infected food. Given enough time, it seemed as though the infection found a way into every house."

We crossed the highway and approached the ranch. This one had an attached garage, with two grain bins and a white tin building in the yard to the left. The building reminded me of the stocked Humvee we'd hidden before we entered New Eden. We really could've used that vehicle today.

A doghouse stood next to the garage. A corpse that was nothing more than fur and bones lay inside the kennel. A chain attached to the doghouse was still connected to the dog collar. I swallowed and looked away. I always hated seeing reminders of how the virus killed things even outside its reach.

"Poor thing," Jase said softly.

I continued forward to the garage. This one had windows in the garage door, making it easy to peer inside. "Shit."

"What is it?" Tom asked from behind me.

"The garage is empty." I turned around and frowned. "I guess we have to check the bigger buildings."

None of us delayed in walking past the kennel. As we passed the grain bins, I made a mental note to check it for grain that we could use. Staring at the metal, vivid memories of the first innocent I killed filled my mind. She had been a young girl who'd been hurt worse than any doctor could fix. Her tears still haunted my dreams. When I put the barrel to her temple and pulled the trigger, I killed more than her. I killed something inside me that day.

My innocence.

When we reached the big building, I clenched my eyes shut briefly to squeeze away the vision. When I opened them, she was gone, and I sucked in a deep, cold breath to ground me.

Like the garage, this building also had windows in it, and had shrubs planted around it. I imagined it had been a meticulously maintained place by its proud owners, but weeds and grass had overgrown and given everything an unkempt appearance.

Jase jogged up to a window. He spun around, his eyes wide. "Hot dog. You guys have got to see this."

Tom and I cramped in around him and looked through the window. Sitting under a stream of sunlight sat a pristine, 1950s Chevrolet truck.

Tom whistled. "Now, that's style."

"If we can keep anything running, it'd be that," Jase said.

Tom's brows rose in disbelief. "An old truck? Why?"

"The old stuff isn't as finicky with gas. Fewer computers, I guess," Jase replied. Not staying around to converse, he hustled to the door and peered through the window. "Everything looks clear. You guys ready?"

I couldn't help but smile. He sounded like a kid at Christmas. I walked over to him. "I'll take the door. You can be first in."

His grin widened. He threw a glance back at Tom and lifted three fingers. He quickly counted down to one, and I threw the door open. Jase jumped inside, and Tom followed.

The windows let in enough light that we didn't need flashlights. I stood watch at the door, looking from outside to inside and back outside again. After a few minutes, Jase jogged over to the yellow truck and waved me inside. "All clear."

After one final look outside, I stepped inside and shut the door. The air smelled lightly of a car shop. Oil, rubber, and gas. On the walls hung various hubcaps and Chevy signs. A large chevron was painted across the center of the floor. Clearly, the truck's owner was an aficionado and loved this truck dearly.

Tom continued to walk around the shop, inspecting various items, and I watched Jase. He opened the door and sat gingerly onto the leather seats. He ran his hands across the dash. "This baby is a work of art."

"Yeah, but can this work of art start?"

He held up a hand. "You can't rush perfection."

After long moments of cooing words to the truck, Jase turned the key. The engine moaned but didn't catch. After a couple attempts, the engine moaned less and less as what little juice the battery had left was now gone. Jase patted the dash before stepping out. "The good news is she's full of gas and ready to start. We don't need to change batteries. She just needs a jump."

"But we don't have any electricity," I said.

Jase shook his head. "Don't need it. The battery from the other truck should be enough to get us going."

"There are some garden supplies in back," Tom said. "We could use the wheelbarrow to transport the battery. It will be easier than carrying it a mile."

"We have about two hours until sunset," I said as I checked to make sure the door locked. "We need a secure place for the night."

"Why can't we keep going? Omaha can't be more than an hour or two away."

"Which puts us getting into a town full of who knows what after dark," I said. "We can't risk moving at night. And, I think this is as good a place as any for tonight."

"I'd rather be out there searching for the squadron," Tom said.

"If you drove faster, we could be in Omaha by now," Jase countered.

"We're here for the night," I said. "Bundle up. It's going to get pretty dang cold in here, colder than it is already."

"Never fear," Jase said. "I saw one of those propane heaters on a shelf. That'll keep us toasty."

"That solves one problem," I said. "But the bigger problem is all these windows. If we use any light whatsoever once the sun sets, we'll be in a fishbowl. Anyone or anything in the area couldn't help but notice. Maybe the house will be easier to hide in."

Jase shrugged. "But, we've already cleared this shop. We can do what we used to do. We get settled in early so when the sun sets, we go dark. And, we rotate shifts through the night."

I smirked. "You really want to stay in here, don't you."

He grinned. "Heck, yeah. I don't want to leave this girl all alone."

I sighed. "Okay. Let's get this building secure for the night. When the sun sets, we go dark. Tom, you take first watch. I'll take the midnight shift, and Jase, you get early morning. As soon as the sun rises, we'll grab the battery and get Jase's new baby up and running."

It took the full two hours to prepare for the night. We had to clear things from the floor so we wouldn't trip in the dark. We set up a tin wire with tools tied onto it at the door to serve as a noisemaker in case someone managed to open the door without us noticing. We had to set up the propane heater—which was full of propane, thank God—and our bedding for the night. Jase, of course, quickly claimed the front seat of the truck. I unrolled my sleeping bag on the bed, while Tom set his bag on a camp chair he'd found somewhere.

We ate together as the sun turned from bright yellow to deep gold to finally a reddish glaze before disappearing. I tried to reach Clutch on the radio again, but we were still too far away, their batteries were dead, or they couldn't answer. I prayed for either of the first two options.

As I lay down to squeeze in a few hours of sleep before my shift, I felt the silence. There were no dog or wolf howls. It was a sound I'd grown accustomed to at New Eden. A constant reminder that danger trolled outside the fence. But here, even within sixty miles or so of Omaha, there was nothing but silence.

I fell asleep fast and hard.

I woke to the sunlight peeking through the windows, and I jerked up. I looked around to get my bearings. Tom sat in his chair, snoring softly. Jase was a tangle of limbs on the front seat. I jumped onto the concrete, ran to the door, and winced when my calf reminded me it didn't savor quick movements in the morning. Luckily, outside, nothing had changed. I double-checked to make sure the door was locked before going to each window and looking outside.

Once I was comfortable we were alone, I walked over to Tom's chair and kicked him in the leg.

His eyes blinked open. "Wha—what it is?"

"Why didn't you wake me? No one was on watch this morning."

He rubbed his eyes. "Oh. I must've dozed off. Sorry."

"You're sorry?" I opened my mouth and then closed it, glaring at him. "What if something happened last night? What if someone or something attacked?"

"Nothing did."

"If something did, we would've been sitting ducks."

"But, there's no one around here. We're safe in here."

"There's no such thing as *safe* anymore." I spun on my heel and stuffed my bedding into my backpack.

Jase had wakened, and he looked around, frowning. "Why'd you let me sleep through my watch?"

"I didn't," I said. "Tom fell asleep, and I slept straight through the night."

Jase scowled in Tom's direction. "Dumbass."

Tom held up his hands. "I said I was sorry."

I slung on my backpack. "Let's go get that battery so we can get back on the road."

Tom had the common sense to stay quiet during our walk back to the truck. He pushed the wheelbarrow. It squeaked relentlessly, adding a headache to my already frustrating morning. The good news was that the truck was exactly as we'd left it. The bad news was the battery took us longer than we'd planned to charge the old Chevy. Once Jase got the truck running, he found an oil leak, and the two men spent the next ten hours improvising a solution. By then, it was dark, and we stayed a second night. Tom fell asleep again, but I hadn't let myself sleep, so I was ready.

When Tom woke the next morning, neither Jase nor I had any interest in talking with him. I opened the shop door, Jase started up the Chevy, and we piled into the front seat. We drove back to our stranded truck and loaded one of the drums of gasoline onto the back of the Chevy. When we pulled away from the truck, I squinted at the house to the north. "Stop," I said and rolled down the window.

Jase hit the brakes.

"What is it?" Tom asked.

"Give me a minute." I rummaged through my bag and pulled out the small pair of binoculars. I zoomed in on the house the opposite direction of the two houses we'd checked out. "There are horses with saddles in the yard."

"You sure?" Jase asked.

I nodded and handed my binoculars across Tom to Jase. "See for yourself."

"We should stop and talk to them," Tom said.

Jase and I both stared blankly at him.

"What?" he asked. "It's the right thing to do."

"Yeah, if you want to get us killed," Jase said.

"It's not the smart thing to do," I said. "We have no idea how they would greet strangers. From personal experience, you've got about a ten percent chance they're going to welcome you with open arms."

"Cash was an actuary in a past life. She knows," Jase added.

"We have a mission already," I said. "We have to find the squadron and bring them home. No detours. It would be nice to be back to New Eden before Thanksgiving is over."

"So far, this Thanksgiving sucks," Jase said and hit the gas. He didn't stop until we reached the outskirts of Omaha. The dead city showed its gashes from being bombed. Splintered buildings stood in the distant city center. Only the suburbs remained somewhat intact, and many of those buildings had burned or collapsed.

With every mile, more and more stranded and crashed vehicles filled the interstate. But, unlike Des Moines, I saw no zeds standing outside. Only remnants of bodies. Lots and lots of bodies. I examined the map in between glances out the window. "We should see the store any time now."

Tom pointed. "There it is, a Costco."

Jase took the exit ramp. Vehicles had been pushed out of the way far enough for us to weave through a narrow path. The first zed I found was sitting in the driver's seat of one of the cars. The zed's hand gripped the steering wheel as it stared at us with lifeless eyes, but it made no movement.

"See? Frozen solid," Tom said.

I grabbed my binoculars. Frost-covered minivans, SUVs, cars, and trucks were parked outside the store. "No sign of the squadron's vehicles," I mumbled.

"They must've continued on to find another store," Tom said.

My eyes narrowed. "Someone blocked the main doors." In front of where the main doors should be, a semi-truck and trailer sat, obscuring any sign of entrance.

"There." Jase pointed up.

I followed his direction, and saw a man waving down at us from the roof of the building. I could see his wide grin, and my heart leapt. "It's Clutch."

I rolled down my window and waved back, squealing in delight. Clutch motioned to the back of the store, and I nodded. "He wants us to go to the back entrance."

"They must be parked behind there," Tom said.

Jase gunned the engine and sped around the corner. "Now, *this* is Thanksgiving."

Something wasn't adding up. "Why are they still here?"

When we turned the next corner, it started to make sense. "Where are the trucks?" Tom asked.

Jase put the truck into park. When he went to open his door, I yanked his arm. "Wait."

He turned to me, confused.

I pointed to the row of shrubs outlining the parking lot. "Look."

Hundreds of glistening eyes peered out at us.

Eleven

T he steel door to the back entrance opened a crack, and Griz's face appeared. "Pull up as close as you can to this door," he said. "That way, you can get inside without getting pounced."

Jase reversed and pulled the truck up to the entrance, leaving only a few feet in between the driver's side of the truck and the steel door. He cut the engine and grabbed the keys. I grabbed my bag.

Griz threw open the door, and it dinged into the truck. "Careful," Jase said as he opened his door and jumped inside. Tom slid across the seat, followed last by me. I heard movement behind me, and I shoved forward, falling into Tom and onto the floor of the store as the door slammed shut.

I looked up to see a hand reaching out. I grabbed it, and Griz tugged me to my feet and into a hard embrace. "It's good to see some friendly faces around here," he said.

"Now, we can get out of here and back home," Marco said.

"Hey, Marco." I gave him a hug.

Jase waved. "Polo!" Marco waved back.

"What happened here?" I asked. "Where are your trucks?"

"That's the question of the day," Griz replied. "We just about had them loaded, and then some asshats blocked the door and took off with our trucks, like we were a drive-through window."

"We tried to reach you by radio," Jase said. "You guys had us worried."

"Batteries are dead," Griz said. "Hard to believe, but there's nothing to recharge them in here. You'd think a giant store like this would have generators, but not a single one left on the shelves, and the store's backup generators were bone-dry."

Solar stake lights were lying down all the aisles, bringing light to the shadows. Three men came around a corner, and I ran toward them. Clutch barely had time to stop before I jumped into his arms. He lifted me, and I hugged him. When I pulled away, I gave him a halfhearted glare. "You see? I told you I'd come after you."

He smiled. "I figured as much." Then, his smile faded. "But, you shouldn't have come. It's dangerous out there."

I shot him a hard look, and he lowered me to my feet. "Which is exactly why we came for you. You don't think we'd leave you guys out here to die, do you?"

Jase came up and slapped Clutch's shoulder. "It's good to see you, man. What do you think of my new truck?"

Clutch's brow rose. "A 1957 Chevy? She's a beaut. How'd you come across her?"

"Long story," I said. "Jase can fill you in on the drive back. Speaking of which, what needs done so we can hit the road?"

"We've been waiting out the hungry mouths outside," Clutch replied. "Once we knew the bandits weren't coming back, we switched gears to finding new vehicles. Unfortunately, that turned out to be much easier said than done."

"That's an understatement," Griz said. "We didn't get more than five feet out the back door before a pack of mangy dogs came at us. Within an hour, there were probably two hundred of the buggers out there. Although, a city the size of this, there's bound to be thousands of dogs that managed to get free and survive. Anyway, we moved to the front of the store and cut through the back of the big rig. The bandits left it running when they used it to block the doors. But, by the time we cut through the box to get to the cab, its fuel tanks were dry. We'd already burned our ammo to clear the store, so we've been waiting for the dogs to find something more interesting. But, they're persistent and ornery little bastards."

"Why'd you have to kill the zeds inside?" Tom asked. "They should've been frozen through and through."

Clutch chuckled drily. "The ones outside may be frozen, but the ones inside still had plenty of life left in them. The building's insulation must buffer enough of the cold, and they must still generate enough body heat that the temps need to drop more to stiffen them up."

I grimaced, though I'd feared as much. "So, we still have all the zeds trapped inside buildings to deal with."

"At some point, yeah," Clutch said. "But, if we wait until the temps drop more, we can take them one building at a time, like we did this one."

"Except we won't have any ammo to do this to all the buildings," I countered. "We'll have to get creative."

"And, we will. Later. Right now, we need to send out recon to secure us some transportation home," Clutch said.

"I'm guessing you already have a plan," I said.

Clutch nodded. "An easy grab-and-go. Bring our transportation to us and load up. We've collected over twenty sets of keys from the shoppers still in the store. At least a couple vehicles in the parking lot should still have juice. But, the damn mutts are between us and our wheels."

"We figured they'd get hungry and leave," Griz said. "The numbers are already down quite a bit. Within a week or so, they would've been gone." He grinned. "But now we don't have to wait for the flea-bitten mongrels to leave or eat each other."

"We'll head out in ten," Clutch said. "Griz, Marco, and I will take the truck—"

"I'll drive," Jase inserted.

Clutch watched the teenager for a moment, before giving a tight nod. "Okay. Jase will drive. The rest of us will ride in the back."

"Isn't that too dangerous?" I asked. "Can't the dogs jump up and reach you back there?"

"They could," Clutch said. "Except all of them are half-starved and many of them are sick. We should be able to block the few that can get up that high." He pointed at me. "Do you have ammo?"

"Not much. A little."

"How much is 'a little?'"

"Thirty-five rounds."

He frowned. "That's enough. I want you covering us from the roof in case this heads south." He looked around. "Everyone else, be ready to defend a perimeter at the back door and load up. We're not going to stick around this shithole once we have transportation."

A guy named Jack led me to the roof, while everyone else stayed below and prepared for what Jase called Operation: Carjack.

On the flat, empty rooftop, frostbite posed the only danger. I walked the edge of the roof until I found the right spot overlooking the parking lot. I settled onto my stomach and set up my rifle. Below, I didn't see any dogs, though some of the ones waiting out back were bound to follow the truck.

The sound of the Chevy's engine cut through the frozen air, and I focused on waiting for the truck to enter my line of sight. Once it did, I watched Jase drive the truck, with three men standing on back. Clutch stood with his sword drawn. Griz and Marco each had machetes, and Griz had added an axe to his collection.

Behind the truck followed a dozen mangy dogs. Most were large, but there were a couple mid-sized ones, though I couldn't make out any particular breeds. The procession reminded me of the Pied Piper plan we'd used several times against the zeds. Only this time, we *didn't* want to be followed.

The truck drove slowly, and I watched Marco dump a bag full of keys onto the roof of the truck. He picked them up, one by one, holding them out toward the parked cars. When the lights flashed on a red minivan, Marco thumped the roof, and the truck pulled to a stop, making a tight 'T' with the van.

The dogs circled the truck. I could hear their snarls from my position. None had jumped yet, but I had no idea how they were going to get from the truck to the van. Then, Marco jumped off the truck and onto the hood of the van. A dog lunged at him, and I fired. The dog fell back with a yelp. This incensed the other dogs, and their growls grew in volume.

"Nice shot," Jack said, and I ignored him.

Marco wiped the windshield and looked inside. He gave the truck a thumbs up. Jase pulled away slowly, and Clutch and Griz yelled out at the dogs. Nearly all snapped around and followed them, leaving only two who seemed to be concentrating on Marco. He looked up at me, and I fired twice. Each shot took out a dog. Marco jumped down and was inside the van in no time.

The van's engine turned over and engaged, and I breathed a sigh of relief. I wanted this to be over. I hated killing animals, especially what had once been pets. There was something horribly wrong about it. The poor things were only trying to survive. We had done this to them. We had raised them as pets and then abandoned them. It only made sense for them to return to their wolf roots to survive. It made me think of Diesel. He'd be one of these dogs if he didn't have Frost or Benji to look after him. He could've been one of the dogs I'd just shot.

I squeezed my eyes shut and opened them. The truck stopped at a green SUV. This time, Griz jumped onto the hood. Fewer dogs followed Clutch's voice this time. They were learning. After I killed five dogs, at least one of which I could've sworn was a gray wolf, Griz climbed inside the SUV, and started it up.

All three vehicles—the Chevy, the SUV, and the minivan—headed back around the building.

The remaining dogs attacked their fallen comrades. It was a kill-or-be-killed world now. My shooting wasn't perfect today; they weren't all kill shots, and the injured dogs screamed in agony as the others tore into them. I couldn't get any clear shots on the poor animals. The bile rose in my throat, and I jumped to my feet. Without looking back, I crossed the roof in time to see the three vehicles form a tight semicircle around the back door.

For the second time, I got down and aimed my rifle. Now, nearly all the dogs cautiously stepped toward the vehicles. Their bristled fur and growls made it clear they weren't coming out to play.

The doors popped open, and the men ran inside. Thankfully, none of the dogs managed to get around the cars before the back door closed, so I didn't have to shoot anything else. I yanked open the access door and jogged down the stairs to find men stuffing items into shopping carts. It seemed about half of the carts were filled with beer.

Clutch shook his head. "This mission is a scrub. We don't have space for the supplies. We'll come back next week with a plan and better equipment."

"We should get the semi-truck going then," Tom said. "Take what we can now."

Clutch pursed his lips. "Good luck finding diesel. Besides, we don't know when those guys who left the truck will be back. We have no ammo and no plan to hold them off. We need to get back to New Eden and regroup. Our lives are more important than this stuff." He motioned around him. "We have three vehicles and fourteen people. Do the math. Take what you can, but what doesn't fit will get left behind."

There was some grumbling, but no one outright argued against Clutch's plan.

He continued. "When it comes time to move, you'd better move. I don't like the look of those dogs. Be careful out there. If you get rabies, game over."

"The dogs will eat anything," Jack said from behind me. "To buy us time to load, we should shoot a few. Give the rest something to keep busy with."

Shock sent me jerking around. "You can't be serious."

"It's a good idea," Clutch said. "We can use the distraction."

I hemmed for a moment. Finally, I spoke. "Why don't we throw them some food from here? There has to be something in here that we can feed them. They're starving."

"They're also sick. Their aggression could trump their hunger," Clutch said.

I narrowed my eyes.

"But, we can give it a shot," he added, and turned to the squadron. "Hey, Tom. Where was the dog food you came across earlier?"

"It's over by the shop area," one of the guys said.

Clutch held out a hand. "Then go get it."

He jumped, grabbed an empty cart, and headed in the direction he'd pointed. Two other men rushed to follow.

I took a seat and shook my head. "Why didn't you guys try feeding the dogs before? Maybe once they had food, they would've moved on."

Griz chuckled. "A city girl like you never had strays before, huh."

I frowned. "No. Why?"

"The food would attract anything hungry in the area," Griz said. "And once they got hungry again, they'd be back for more."

"This diversion will work one time," Clutch said. "It'll keep the ones here busy for a few minutes, but at the same time, it's going to draw in a shitload more."

"Oh." I stared off for a moment. "We can try something else instead."

Clutch shook his head. "No. It's a good plan."

Ten minutes later, we had hauled ten fifty-pound bags of dog food up to the roof. I didn't carry a bag, but followed them up the stairs. Outside, we all stood along the roof edge, looking down.

"Here goes nothing," Griz said, and dropped his bag. It fell the thirty-foot drop and exploded when it hit the ground.

A dog crept forward, and then three more followed. They sniffed the food before scooping up mouthfuls of the kibble.

I couldn't help but smile. "It's working."

"Bombs away," Jase said, and dropped his bag. The remaining bags dropped, and soon, all the dogs in the area came to enjoy the feast.

"That should buy us a couple minutes," Clutch said. "Let's get out of here."

We all jogged toward the stairs. "Thanks," I said when Clutch had me go before him. "It means a lot."

He didn't say anything, but I could see in his gaze that he understood. There was enough death out there already. Anything we could do to leave one fewer scar on our souls was worth it.

"Move it, move it," Clutch ordered, and we all rushed toward the back entrance. "Head to your DV!"

Several men had full carts, and I had no idea where they were going to find room for everything. Three vehicles for fourteen people? They must've figured we had clown cars sitting out there with bottomless trunks. Not wanting to get blocked behind their carts, I squeezed between them, and Clutch did the same. Jase managed to climb over the carts, and Griz and Marco shoved their way through.

All I took from the store was a bag full of mini first-aid kits, two paperback novels, and the insert I broke free from a religious photo frame. It had the Prayer of St. Francis of Assisi. When I was a little girl, my mother used to sing that prayer when she washed dishes. Clutch carried a single bottle of whiskey. I didn't see what Griz had stuffed into his backpack.

Clutch had his sword drawn, and I situated everything so I could hold out my machete. He peeked out the door, turned back to us, and nodded. "It looks good. Time to bug out. Watch yourselves out there." He yanked open the door and we rushed forward. Several dogs eating outside the semicircle froze and ducked, as though expecting us to attack.

We didn't. Clutch opened the Chevy's door and shoved me in, coming in behind me. Griz and Marco jumped onto the bed. Jase, who'd refused to give up the keys, quickly hopped in and shut the door. As he started the engine, I twisted around to see men climb into the other vehicles. We'd planned who would ride in which vehicle earlier so everything would move smoothly.

But, rather than climbing in, the others were busy unloading five shopping carts. Cases of beer were thrown on the roof of the mini-van. I saw movement come from under the SUV.

"Watch out!" I yelled through the glass, but no one looked up.

"God damn it," Clutch muttered. "Move, move!"

Jack didn't notice the dog creeping out from under the green vehicle until it was too late. The dog—it reminded me of a black Lab—lunged and knocked Jack onto his back. He screamed out. Someone swung a bat, and the dog was knocked away with a yelp. It limped but came at Jack again. He was pulled inside, and the door slammed shut the instant the dog made its second attack into the door.

"Lead us out of here," Clutch said, and Jase popped the truck into gear.

The vehicles were tight together, and it took Jase several turns before he was able to drive away. He winced every time the bumper hit the concrete wall or the minivan behind us. He gunned the engine but slowed down quickly to weave around the rapidly increasing number of dogs around us.

I kept watch behind us, to make sure both vehicles were following, and—more important—to make sure both Griz and Marco were safe. They had to be freezing out there, but they were both adamant about climbing on the truck rather than squeezing in the other vehicles to make the getaway faster. If only the others were as fast, Jack wouldn't have been attacked.

I wondered how Jack was doing. If he was seriously injured. I was hoping the dog hadn't bit through his clothes. If he caught rabies, there would be little anyone could do. Clutch thumbed the radio a couple times, but no one responded from the other two vehicles.

"They must not have their radios plugged in," I said. "It won't be too long before we can pull over and talk to them."

He plugged the radio back into the lighter, and dropped the radio on the dash.

Jase picked up speed once we made it onto the interstate, but he kept it slow enough that Griz and Marco didn't get knocked around too badly. Any dogs that followed drifted off, and soon we were leaving the skyline of a destroyed Omaha behind.

Griz and Marco were tucked low into the bed of the truck and snuggled together. I almost laughed until I realized how cold it must've been for them back there. I turned back to Clutch and Jase. "How much longer before we can stop? The guys will freeze back there."

"Go ten more klicks before we slow down," Clutch said. "That should be enough distance between us and the packs in the city."

Jase cocked his head.

"Drive seven more miles," Clutch added.

"Why didn't you say so?" Jase said.

"I did," Clutch answered.

They bantered for the full seven miles before Clutch pointed to an exit and overpass. "Take us up there."

"Yes, sir," Jase said with a hint of sarcasm.

He took the exit and came to a stop in the middle of the overpass. Clutch zipped his coat up, and I opened the door and slid out. From this vantage point, we could see for miles in every direction.

Griz and Marco climbed stiffly out of the back, and I could hear their teeth chatter from where I stood. I rubbed Griz's arm. "Why don't you guys sit in the truck for now? Warm up until we figure out who's riding with whom."

"Now, that is the best thing I've heard all day," Griz said through chattering teeth.

Clutch walked around the overpass, his eyes shaded against the sun, and scanned the area around us. I watched the approaching vehicles. When the SUV stopped, I walked over and opened Jack's door. He sat inside, grimacing, with boxes and bags piled on him and the others.

"How are you doing?" I asked.

"Dog got its teeth into my arm," he said.

"Do you need stitches?" I asked.

"It's not bad," he said. "It barely broke the skin. Hurts worse than it looks."

I sighed. "Well, let's hope it didn't have rabies." I held out one of the first aid kits I'd picked up at the store."

"I don't need it," he said. "I already cleaned it up."

I shrugged. "Suit yourself."

I turned away and saw Clutch pulling things out of the minivan. "C'mon, we need to be able to fit two more in here. And who the hell grabbed a baby seat?"

Clutch went to throw the big box, but Marco sprang from the truck. "That's mine." He grabbed the box from Clutch. "It's for Deb."

Clutch's lips thinned. "Strap it to the roof or something. It takes up too damn much room."

"Hey guys," Griz said, and we turned around. He stepped from the truck and pointed down the road to the north. "Recognize anything?"

I searched the road but only saw a few derelict vehicles that were covered in ash and grime.

"Son of a bitch," Clutch muttered. He jogged over to the truck and stood behind the hood, staring at something in that direction.

I pulled out my binoculars and ran toward him. I looked through them, moving across the landscape. "What do you see?"

"Let me see those," he said and took my binoculars. He looked through them for a minute.

I stared in the same direction and then finally spotted it. "Holy shit. Are those our trucks?"

"Yeah," he replied and handed me my binoculars.

In the distance, I could make out a church—St. Dominic's according to the stone sign up front. Tucked nearly behind the church were, sure enough, our trucks. Their beds were still filled with supplies. We never would've seen them from the interstate; someone had hid them carefully. But, they hadn't planned on us coming up on this overpass.

Clutch turned around to face the rest of our traveling companions. "Load up and regroup below this overpass. Let's see about getting our trucks back."

"But, it's too dangerous," Tom said.

I patted Tom's shoulder. "Look at the bright side. You said you were disappointed not getting to go to church on Thanksgiving. Here's your chance."

TWELVE

We moved in without waiting for the sun to set, figuring that if the thieves were halfway decent at surviving, they would've seen us long before we ever saw them.

Clutch was as hardheaded as they came, but he was also practical. We weren't going after the thieves, only our four missing trucks. The thieves had carried no guns when they'd stolen our trucks, so Clutch figured they had no ammo. Still, the plan wasn't without risk.

The plan was as simple and safe as we could make it: drive cautiously up to the trucks, check each truck for its keys, and drive off, all the while keeping an eye out for trouble. If the thieves tried anything, we were going to hightail it out of there.

Jase drove the Chevy. We'd emptied out the bed, leaving the drum of gas and extra supplies with the other vehicles under the overpass. Now, four men—Clutch, Griz, Marco, and Tom—rode in back, with each one going for a specific truck. I rode in back with them to look for any signs of trouble and to lay down cover fire if things turned messy.

I searched for movement as we approached the parking lot. Other than seeing some candles lit inside the church, I saw nothing. The parking lot was open, with few trees or shrubs to hide danger.

We didn't *need* the trucks and supplies. We could find more of both, but finding supplies wasn't easy or risk-free. The squadron had loaded all the canned food from the Costco into the trucks before they'd been stolen. To find as much food, we'd have to find another large store.

Finding stores that hadn't been destroyed, looted, or infested was like finding needles in haystacks. Simply put, going after these trucks was safer than the alternative.

More important, it was a matter of honor.

Jase pulled in slowly, the engine a notch above idle. That I saw no one worried me. They had to have seen us or at least heard the truck. Noise carried more now without the constant hum of traffic, jets, television, and phones. My ears had become more sensitive to sound in the past several months.

Still, the only sound I could hear was Jase's truck. The only movement I could see was us. As soon as I started to wonder if the thieves weren't around, I noticed a figure move within the church. I homed in my scope to count six people inside the glass doors, watching us.

"We have at least a half dozen people inside the church," I announced. "They're standing inside the entrance."

"I have them," Clutch said, soon echoed by Griz and Marco.

"None have rifles. I see only spears and blunt weapons," Griz said. "These don't look like high-risk bandits. But, keep your eyes peeled for any of their friends."

It was hard not to stare at the people staring right back at us, but I forced myself to scan the bushes and under the trucks for snipers.

Jase slammed on the brakes, and I nearly went flying over the roof.

"There are nails all over the ground," Jase yelled. "They could pop my tires."

I looked forward to see the concrete glistening with metal. They were trying to cripple us, to either send us limping off, scared, or to chase us down and finish us off on the road. Worse, I didn't know how we could possibly make it far with the trucks since there was a field of nails between them and the road.

Clutch tapped the roof of the truck. "Stay here, Jase, but be ready to hit reverse and haul ass out of here if I give the call."

He set down his sword, stood in the truck, and faced the church. "We've come for our trucks. You stole items that didn't belong to you, and we're taking it back. No one has to get hurt. Don't show any aggression, and we'll take our trucks and be on our way. You can have everything else in the store. I'll give you ten seconds to respond."

On the other side of the glass door, the figures moved, and I could hear a murmur of voices talking over one another. After a moment, the door opened, and an older man stepped outside, though he was quickly flanked by a young man wearing a gray SMSU sweatshirt and gripping a bat. Since he had the weapon, I narrowed my scope onto his chest. In small letters, above and below the acronym, his shirt read *Southwest Minnesota State University*, and I frowned.

It couldn't be possible. I'd been there. After the herds passed through.

The older man spoke. "We meant no ill will, but what you took from the store belongs to no one and everyone. You claimed it because it sat on shelves. We claimed it because it sat on the beds of trucks. There's no difference."

"Like hell there's no difference," Clutch said. "We laid claim the moment we sweat on that cargo. We'd earned it, fair and square."

"Clutch," I said to his back, and he cocked his head slightly to show he was listening. "These guys might be from Marshall."

Clutch stiffened. "How do you know?"

"Look. The kid's sweatshirt," I replied. "SMSU."

The older man began to say something, but Clutch cut him off. "Where are you from?"

The man frowned. "Why does that matter? Regardless of where we're each from, we all have rights to what's in that store."

"Where'd the kid get that sweatshirt?" Clutch countered. "Are you bandits? Did he take it off another survivor?"

The younger man visibly bristled. "It's my shirt. I'm a freshman at SMSU. We ain't bandits, you son of—"

"'Aren't,' Nathan," the older man said, placing a hand on the student's shoulder. "We *aren't* bandits." Then, he turned back to us. "I'm Professor Dominic Caler. I served on the faculty at SMSU. Nathan here was one of my students. Southwest Minnesota State University is a small university in Marshall, Minnesota."

"I know exactly where it is," Clutch said. "I was there after the herds passed through."

The man stood straighter. "*After* the herds, you say? Did you find survivors?"

Clutch shook his head. "No. We went there to look for survivors, but the herds hit it pretty hard."

The professor's eyes narrowed. "Now it's my turn to ask if you're bandits. Why else would you travel so far north unless you'd heard of a group of survivors to raid?"

"We're not bandits. A few of us are from Fox Park," Clutch said as though it would mean anything to the professor. "You happen to know a guy named Manny? About this tall?" He leveled his hand at his shoulder.

"Yes, I'm familiar with him."

"Manny had a small group with him. They had gone out looking for supplies when the herds hit and couldn't get back to their families at Marshall. They went south to stay ahead of the herds and joined up with our camp."

"I spoke with Manny's people during the first few hours. Many of them had family stuck in Marshall. They would've gone back for them."

"We had a pilot at the camp," Clutch said, referring to me. "She flew a few of us, including one of Manny's guys, to Marshall. But, when we got there, all we found was infected."

The professor's lips pursed. "We were last there about a month ago. It took us awhile to move around the herds and make it back, but we made it. When we saw the community center had been opened up, I'd hoped everyone had come out and connected with other survivors, but we haven't been able to track any of them down yet. We're still looking. We'd only planned to stop here to recuperate and restock for a week before heading back out again."

"Where's Manny now?" the professor asked.

I swallowed.

Clutch shook his head slowly. "I'm sorry to give you the bad news, Professor. We had a bad run in with some bandits. They took down nearly our entire group, including Manny and all of his people."

"That is bad news, indeed," the professor said. "And that sort of news seems to be all we hear nowadays."

"I tell you what," Clutch said. "Since you're from Marshall, we'll leave you two trucks and take two trucks with us. But you have to help us clear these nails."

"That is an acceptable deal. However, you must secure your weapons. I give you my word my people will do the same. My people will not raise a hand against you unless you threaten one of ours."

"You've got yourself a deal," Clutch said. "But, you try to hurt one of mine, and you won't like what happens."

The professor smiled. "Trust is earned in small steps."

Clutch had Jase cut the engine, and we left our larger weapons in the back of the truck. We still wore our side arms, knives, and whatnot. Clutch also hadn't mentioned that we each carried a radio and would call for backup the second shit went south.

The SMSU kid—his name was Nathan—found a couple brooms inside the church. This Marshall group was smaller than I'd expected. Where Manny had a dozen with him, I'd only seen four so far with this group. Aside from Professor Caler, the other three were college students. Peter had no interest in meeting any of us. He was thoroughly closed off from the rest of the world and had his nose buried in a book the entire time we worked at brushing nails away. Joachim, on the other hand, didn't trust us. He kept a safe distance and watched us from the corner of his eye. With his skepticism, he was probably the best equipped of his group to survive in this world.

The professor talked the most of any of them, though when I got closer to him, I noticed how frail he was.

"Cancer," he said when he caught my expression. "I gave cigarettes too many years of my life, and now they're demanding more."

After we cleared a path for the trucks, Nathan took the brooms back.

I caught Clutch and Griz looking out at the sky. I strolled over to them. "It's getting late," I said.

"We're going to have to hunker down soon or else we'll get caught in the dark," Griz said.

Clutch glanced over at the church, his lips tight.

"You're welcome to stay the night," the professor said, walking over. "You need a shelter for the night, don't you?"

"We should hit the road," Clutch said. "We'll find a place."

"The church offers plenty of room. We've already set up our camp in the undercroft. You can have the nave."

"The what?" I asked.

"We're in the basement," he replied, not sounding like I was an idiot for asking what was probably obvious to Catholics far more devout than I ever was. "You can stay where mass would've taken place, if you so choose. The pews should make adequate beds. I saw two other vehicles earlier. I imagine they would also stay."

"Give us a minute, and I'll check with them," Clutch said and turned away.

"Certainly," he said and headed into the church.

Clutch looked at me. "Where's that place you three stayed at on your way to find us?"

I thought for a moment. "A little over an hour from here, I think."

"That would put us there after sunset," Griz said.

"There was another group less than two miles up the road," I said. "I suspect they knew we were in the area, but we didn't stop to chat."

Clutch frowned. "I don't like going into a situation with an unknown quantity. Even though we don't know this group much better, my gut says we can trust this guy. What do you think?"

"I'm with you," Griz said. "If they were bandits, one of them would've given off a suspicious vibe by now."

"I agree," I said. "I get why they took our trucks. It's what most would do. I think they're just trying to get by."

Clutch nodded. "We'll stay the night. Let the others know. We'll run a double security detail to play it safe."

One hour later, we had camp set up within the church and had Jack slouched in a pew. He'd lost his color and was sweating profusely, and we all worried the infection he'd picked up from the dog bite was rabies. When the professor found out, he frowned. "I wish we could help, but we have no antibiotics here. There's a veterinary clinic a couple miles to the north, but we've already been through it. There's nothing but empty shelves and dead animals inside."

"Hang in there," Clutch said after checking Jack's bandage. "We'll get you back to the clinic tomorrow, and they'll get you fixed up."

Jack winced and leaned back. As he rested, we moved the rest of our weapons inside, despite the professor's complaints. He could complain all he wanted. It was one item which Clutch—or any of us—refused to negotiate.

Our trucks, including the two we'd reclaimed, were backed up to the church in case we needed to make a hasty exit. The only thing that stood between the doors and the trucks were two large concrete statues of lions, and they weren't going anywhere.

The Marshall survivors totaled seven—eight if you counted their small dog named Boy—but we'd only met six of them so far. Bonnie and Hugh had come upstairs only because Professor Caler had asked them to introduce themselves before they quickly returned to the basement. They were skittish and tended to stay to themselves. I was glad they didn't stick around. The only member of their group we hadn't met yet was "taking some much-needed rest after a long night."

We'd carried in two boxes of food to have a bona fide Thanksgiving dinner, if canned meat and gravy, instant potatoes, and canned cranberry sauce counted. We set out the food across the altar. I'm sure the professor saw some kind of symbolism in it, but it was really the easiest place to put everything.

Boy, the black-and-white dog that had been adopted by the Marshall survivors, anxiously sat as the lone guard of the feast. I think if he could've reached the altar, he would've pulled everything down. But he was a small mutt, and despite trying over and over again, he couldn't jump high enough.

While the food heated on small makeshift stoves, Tom walked around the pews, collecting bibles.

"What are you doing?" I asked. "We don't have room for all those books."

"They're not books, they're bibles," he replied. "And we don't have enough at New Eden."

I didn't bother arguing with him. I figured he'd find a way to fit boxes of bibles onto the trucks regardless of what I said. So I returned to the altar.

My stomach growled at the smell of warm food, and I inhaled the aroma. When I bent down to steal a spoonful of gravy, Jase slapped my hand. "You have to wait, just like everyone else."

I scowled at him before turning away. "I saw you sneaking a bite," I mumbled.

"I was tasting it for flavor. A chef's prerogative."

Professor Caler was examining the spread on the altar. "We're missing wine. I'll see what I can find in the priest's quarters."

"I'll help out," I offered.

The professor snapped around faster than I'd ever seen him move. "No, no, that's quite all right. I can manage."

I frowned at his sudden stubbornness and glanced to Jase.

He frowned before watching Caler disappear around the corner. "He must be hiding the good stuff back there."

"Or something," I murmured.

He stood and lifted the steaming pot with both hands. "The feast is ready."

"Woot!" I cheered and cleared a spot for the stew of meat, gravy, and vegetables Jase had mixed together from a couple dozen cans. That stuff alone was better than we had, but the coup de grace was the *spice*. They'd found boxes of salt, pepper, and seasonings at the store. I couldn't remember the last time my food had been seasoned with anything except some fresh-ground herb we'd found. I was more excited for this Thanksgiving feast than any other Thanksgiving in my life.

The professor carried food to the three members of his team staying in the basement. Everyone else sat around the altar, on the steps, or on pews, and ate. It felt like a real Thanksgiving, with old friends and new acquaintances sitting together around a feast.

All the church's candles were lit. We didn't bother covering the windows, since it was cold enough the zeds were frozen, and the church was far enough off the main roads that no one would see the light unless they were going directly by the church.

The seasoning was strong, nearly overpowering the stew, but I still went back for seconds—and thirds. The church wine the professor brought out was the worst I'd ever had, but I still had another glass.

Clutch took tiny sips from his bottle of whiskey, and I knew the only reason he was showing moderation was to stay sober. Once we were back within the safety of New Eden's fences, I knew that bottle would empty fast.

"Time for a toast," the professor said, and we all raised our glasses. "Here's to new friends and new starts."

"Cheers," we all said.

As everyone ate, drank, and conversed, the professor looked at Clutch. "I have a doctorate in human psychology. I consider myself a respectable judge of character. And, I believe you and your group are decent people."

Clutch nodded while he chewed.

The professor continued. "Our group used to be four times this size. We ran into trouble a little over two weeks ago. Some men who called themselves the Black Sheep demanded a toll for traveling through their territory. What they demanded, we couldn't pay. They attacked, and we defended ourselves. We fended them off, but our losses were terrible. You've met Bonnie and Hugh. They both lost their spouses, and struggle to get by. We wandered for two days until we reached Omaha. The sun caught off the stained glass windows of this church just right to catch my eye. It was a rainbow drawing us in. And, we've been here ever since."

"You were lucky," Clutch said. "We avoid churches. Just about every single one we found was full of zeds."

The professor chuckled. "Everywhere is full. Even hell is full."

Clutch raised a brow. "Hell is full?"

"A young girl told me that once." He motioned around him. "She said, 'Hell has to be full. That's why all the dead are now walking the earth.'"

Clutch shrugged. "It's as good an explanation as anything out there."

"So where are you going after this?" I asked.

The professor thought for a moment. "I'd like to say we'll continue our search for Marshall survivors, but I've seen the hopelessness in my friends' eyes. I'm afraid if we continue our search, it'll kill them. All they've seen is death. It's all they know now. Until we met your group today, I must admit, I was beginning to feel the same despair."

Clutch chuckled. "Was that before or after you ran off with our supplies?"

The professor smiled. "Would you have shared if we'd stopped and introduced ourselves?"

Clutch shrugged and then bore a smirk. "Maybe. If you'd asked nicely."

"Well, forgive me for my false assumption. I had mistakenly believed you would kill my people rather than share."

"That's generally a safe assumption nowadays," Clutch said.

"However, we did leave a full-sized tractor-trailer there for you. We already had your trucks. You couldn't give pursuit. We could've taken our truck, but we chose to leave it so you wouldn't be stranded."

"That didn't work out as planned. Since you blocked the doors with the trailer, I'm not sure how you expected us to get to the cab in time. And, with how quickly it ran out of gas, it had under a quarter tank of diesel in it when you left it running."

"We were perhaps a touch overly cautious in that we didn't want you to chase us," he said. "We only wanted to delay you until we could make it to the church. We had no intention of stranding you at the store. After all, you make an intimidating lot in your brown and green clothes and carrying swords and machetes."

The professor watched me for a moment. "You don't have the look of a soldier, yet you dress like one."

I shrugged and looked down at the hunting clothes I'd found at the sporting goods store in Des Moines. "They have lots of pockets and they hold up."

"I, on the other hand, am having a harder time each day 'holding up.'" He came to his feet. "On that note, I'll excuse myself for the night. We've had no problems since we've been here, so you can rest soundly."

"Thanks," I said.

Clutch waved as he walked away. The remaining Marshall survivors followed soon after.

"So..." Jase drawled out. "Are we taking them back to New Eden with us?"

Clutch spoke. "We haven't mentioned it to them, but so far I don't see why not."

"I'm cool with it," I said. "But, I want to find out why the prof is so protective of the priest's quarters."

"What do you mean?" Clutch asked quickly.

"He made it clear he didn't want anybody in the priest's crib," Jase said. "I figured he's keeping the good booze back there."

Clutch motioned to Griz, who nodded and came right over.

"You have your weapon ready?" Clutch asked.

Griz patted his back, where his machete was strapped. "Always. We got a date?"

"We need to find out why Caler doesn't want us anywhere outside this area."

Clutch and Griz quickly filled in the rest of the squadron, leaving them behind but ready to jump into action in an instant. I grabbed a candle. The four of us crossed the altar and walked past the confessional booths and down the narrow hallway lined with robes. As the hallway continued, we passed doors, each with a sign conveying what lay behind. When we reached the sign that read *Private Residence*, we stopped.

Clutch eyed each of us with his "you ready" look. I nodded.

He opened the door. The room to the left was dark, but a candle glow filtered out from the room on the right. Clutch and Griz took lead, and Jase and I followed. I held the candle in my left hand and my machete in my right.

Clutch stopped cold inside the doorway. He glanced to me and back to the room, his sword frozen in the air. I entered and became a statue.

In the bed lay two kids—their faces all too familiar to Clutch and me. We'd seen them once before. Many months ago. I'd never forget their faces, and neither would Clutch.

"What the hell?" Griz whispered.

"It's impossible," I said breathlessly, and I felt Jase hold me up.

The kids opened their jaundiced eyes and sat up, removing any doubt that these were the kids...the two zed kids from the convenience store.

THIRTEEN

"Stop," A man jumped from the darkened corner and stood between Clutch and the two zeds. "They won't harm you."

I frowned, my gaze flitting between the man and the pair sitting on the bed.

"They're not violent," The man continued before turning back to the two and stroking their hair. "But, they are special. Very, very special."

The zeds watched us with droll stares. The younger girl cocked her head, but no sign of emotion flickered on her face. They weren't like us, but they also weren't like the other zeds. They were something different.

"They're like Henry," I said softly. "Zen zeds."

The man frowned and eyed me. "You've found another survivor of the infection?"

I watched him for a moment. A sense of familiarity niggled the back of my mind. I raised the candle to illuminate his features. "Dr. Gidar?"

He blinked. "You know me?"

I nodded. "You were in Doctors Without Borders with my father, Dr. Ryan. I met you in Nigeria."

His mouth slowly parted before a smile crossed his face. "Mia? My girl, you're all grown up now. I didn't even recognize you."

"I was twelve during that trip," I replied drily. It had been the best summer vacation I'd ever had.

"Your name is Mia? Seriously?" Griz asked with a smirk. "Like Mama Mia?"

I smacked his arm. "No, like Mia Farrow. My mom loved scary movies."

"We can swap stories later," Clutch growled. "Right now, I want to know why this guy has two zeds in a building with the rest of us with no security to keep them from us."

"I told you," Dr. Gidar said. "These children aren't zeds. The virus didn't take over completely. I'd thought it was something miraculous about their genes since they are siblings, but you said you found another. Tell me about him."

"Later." Clutch pointed to the kids. "Once you secure those two, you're going to come out and tell us what you've been hiding in here."

Without waiting for an answer, Clutch motioned for us to leave, and I found my feet hustling from the room. Too many months of being chased by zeds made me skittish around them. And those two zed kids had haunted too many of my dreams already.

They were the first zeds we'd come across that had a spark of intelligence in their eyes. They were also the first that hadn't tried to eat us when they'd seen us. Instead, they'd stood there, holding hands, and watched us.

That happened before summer hit. Later, Clutch and I had racked our brains trying to figure them out, until we finally gave up. I'd done a decent job at not thinking about them again since we hadn't come across any other zeds like them. Until we'd come across Henry.

Once we reached the hallway, Jase blew out a breath. "Man, Cash. Those kids threw me. They remind me of the pair you and Clutch talked about."

"That's because they *are* the same kids," I said.

Jase frowned. "But you said you saw those two back near Fox Park. How'd they get all the way out here?"

"I have no idea."

When we emerged from the hallway, the rest of the squadron was waiting for us, armed and spread out across the open area.

"What'd you find?" Marco asked, nodding toward the hallway.

"They've got two Henrys back there," Griz said.

Marco frowned briefly before his eyes grew wide. "No shit?"

"What's a Henry?" Tom asked.

"They're zeds but they're different," Griz replied. "Not openly aggressive, but I still don't trust 'em."

"They have them in the open, with no restraints," Clutch said. "I don't know if they're dangerous, but it would only take one bite to ruin a perfectly good day."

"They won't bite you," The professor said as he entered with Dr. Gidar and Nathan at his side. Nathan carried his baseball bat, and I believed he would defend Caler to the death if he had to.

"They are the key to a vaccine," Dr. Gidar said before taking a seat near the altar. "They are the first subjects we've found who were infected but didn't fully succumb to the zonbistis virus or die, which means they carry the antigen in their blood. They suffered some level of neurological damage, but that their hearts still beat is a miracle in itself."

My jaw dropped. "A vaccine is possible?"

"Yes, I'm sure of it," the doctor replied. "I'm making progress on isolating the antigen, but it's been slow. At the university, I had the resources available, but we didn't have the children. I had hypothesized there would be survivors of the virus, but I had no proof until we found these children while we ran from the herds. The hospitals we've come across have either been bombed, are full of the infected, or have no generators to power the equipment I need to isolate the antigen from the virus and strengthen it to be replicable as a vaccine."

"We have power at New Eden," Tom offered. "And we have a medical staff. If you gave us a list of instruments you needed, we could search for them."

Dr. Gidar lightened up. "You must take us with you. This can change everything."

I glared at Tom for sharing information that no one outside New Eden needed to know.

"Tom," Clutch cautioned.

Tom looked at Clutch and frowned. "Well, it's not like we'd leave these folks behind. New Eden takes in all survivors who don't pose a threat."

"And, we haven't determined these guys don't pose a threat," Clutch said.

"I can assure you that we pose no threat. Additionally, you don't have to take all of us. At least take Richard and the two children," Professor Caler said. "But, Richard's work is far too important. Until we have a vaccine, we'll always be a step behind this virus."

"But, the government nuked the south," Jase said. "The herds are gone. All that's left are the stragglers."

"There's still a government?" the professor asked.

"They dropped warheads on the infected?" Dr. Gidar asked quickly. "That would've killed innocent infected as much as the violent infected."

"Like Caler said," Clutch chimed in. "We were always a step behind. We had to lower their numbers."

"But, that's not...well, I can't condone what they've done," Gidar said. "The south would now be a highly contagious zone."

"What do you mean?" I asked.

"Consider the case of the fungi found in the tropical forests. You see, there are several species of fungus lumped together and called the zombie fungus in layman's terms. They control the behavior of their host body —ants in this case—until the host body can no longer continue. The fungus then creates spores so that it can spread."

"But this is a virus, not a fungus," I said. "I remember seeing the news."

"Correct," he said. "But this particular virus is operating in a consistently similar fashion, but it is far more potent. *Zonbistis* controls the behaviors of its host body until the host body can no longer continue, but the virus can be contracted long after its host body's final death. You see, at the university, I tested the *zonbistis* life cycle in great detail. Not only did the virus survive in the host body nearly four days following death, it became tremendously more virulent until it finally burned itself out."

I frowned. "I don't understand. The virus spreads through bites and cuts. It needs contact with our blood."

The doctor shook his head. "Bites from the infected are contagious, but *zonbistis* is far more devious than that. When the virus loses its host, it puts all of its energy into spreading itself. I call this component the 'eleventh hour virulence,' and this is the reason why the virus spread so quickly at the outset."

"That's why the blood-coated bullets took down our guys so fast," Clutch mused.

"Bullets were coated with infected blood?" the doctor asked.

Clutch nodded.

"Well, that would certainly pose a high risk," Gidar said. "It wouldn't take someone long to succumb to the virus if it was outside its host body and within the four-day window."

"Holy shit," I said as the pieces began to click. We'd always been careful to avoid coming into contact with zed blood, but we'd all gotten it on us before. Plenty of times. I blew out a breath. "They said the virus started in a bad batch of lettuce and vegetables from the same processing plant. Something must've happened at the plant, and the virus tainted all the lettuce."

"Yes," Dr. Gidar said. "Produce was shipped across the country in under a day. The virus would've been at its highest potency at that point. It explains why people succumbed so quickly."

I swallowed. "We've been lucky."

"Very lucky," Clutch added.

Dr. Gidar continued. "The 'eleventh hour virulence' of *zonbistis* is precisely why the virus will never be defeated until we become immune to it. Think of measles. We've eradicated it from the U.S. before, but outbreaks continue to occur as long as the virus exists somewhere in the world. We will never completely destroy the virus—that's impossible, but we can better defend against it. There will continue to be outbreaks until we build immunity to the virus. Viruses can lay dormant for weeks, months, even years, and then erupt. We can't be myopic and focus only on the risk of infection today. We have to make the world safe for tomorrow."

I narrowed my gaze upon the doctor. "So, Dr. Gidar, you're saying you can produce a vaccine, which will keep any of us from getting infected?"

"I believe so, yes. But, I need resources, including this Henry fellow you mentioned. He, too, would carry the antigen."

"Give us tonight to talk about it," Clutch said. "If what you're saying is true, it can help end the zed threat. But, you're also talking about bringing zeds into a town filled with innocent people."

"I assure you, they pose little risk," the doctor said. "And, I'm sure we can work out an arrangement where they are secured from the general population."

"We'll be back up here in the morning," Professor Caler said. "To give you time to make your decision. I hope you understand that what you decide can change the entire world."

They came to their feet and headed toward the hallway.

"Wait." Tom jumped up. "You're a doctor, right?"

Dr. Gidar nodded. "I am."

"You need to help Jack. He was bit."

His lips tightened. "I'm sorry. I can't do anything for your friend."

"You don't understand. He was bit by a dog, not by a zed."

"Did the dog look ill?"

"Yeah. It might have had rabies."

He held out his hands, palms facing us. "I can't help him. There's no vaccine."

"He's got zabies," Nathan said. "We lost two of ours to dog bites."

"What Nathan calls zabies is a mutated form of the zonbistis virus," Dr. Gidar said. "It's a less severe strain, where the virus functions much like rabies."

"Are you saying the virus mutated?" I asked.

"Viruses constantly mutate," the doctor replied. "It's their nature. At least this strain only makes the infected sick and doesn't turn them into what we call zeds. In the case of animal bites, the virus runs its course in roughly forty-eight hours for humans. I don't have a lab with the security and equipment to determine a timeline for infected animals."

I swallowed. "What happens after forty-eight hours?"

He watched me for a moment before he understood the repercussion of my question. "At least your friend will not become a zed. Like rabies, this virus has a high mortality rate. He will succumb to the virus and die."

By the tone of his words, it was clear he believed death wasn't a bad alternative. By the raised voices in the room, everyone believed differently.

"There has to be something you can do," Tom demanded.

"I can offer some painkillers. It will ease the pain."

"That's not good enough," someone else said.

"You can't just let him die," another said.

"I am sorry, but I don't have anything to combat the virus," Dr. Gidar said. "Without equipment, power, and support staff, there's nothing I can do."

"Are you saying if we can get you those things, you can help?" I asked.

"No, I'm afraid even with unlimited resources, it could take weeks, or even months, before I make any kind of breakthrough in terms of a vaccine, and that's assuming a breakthrough is even possible. However, a vaccine is a prevention, not a treatment. As I said already, as is the case for rabies, there is no cure."

"What you will do is check on Jack every three hours and make sure he's doing okay," Clutch said after a long silence. "My guys and I are heading out at sunrise. We'll let you know if you're coming thirty minutes before we leave."

"We'll be ready," the professor said before adding with a smile, "In case you say we can accompany you."

Once they left, Clutch walked over to the pew he'd claimed earlier and shrugged off his backpack.

"Dr. Gidar is brilliant," I started. "My father admired him, which says a lot. If anyone can find a vaccine, I bet he could. I don't see how we can leave them behind."

"We'll take them to New Eden and hold them in quarantine until we talk with Justin," Clutch said. "That way, we can ensure they're safe without putting the town at risk. Now, if you're not on watch, get some rest. We head home tomorrow." He laid down on the bench seat and closed his eyes.

I glanced at Jase and smirked. He nodded. Clutch had never been one for long discussions. That I hadn't disagreed with him tonight was a relief. I was too tired to argue with him. Clutch was a lousy debater—he never gave up, no matter how lost his cause was.

Jase and I laid down near Clutch, and my world slipped away within seconds of closing my eyes. Somehow, I managed to sleep until my early morning shift, when Marco woke Jase and me. I was glad to be awake. I had been deep into a vivid dream where the two zed kids were chasing me, and I was trying to run through a deep stream. No matter how hard I pushed myself, I wasn't getting anywhere, while the kids kept walking toward me, holding hands.

I was still breathing heavily when I sat up, grabbed my gear and walked softly around Clutch to not wake him. Jase caught up to me, and we started to walk our first round, stopping to look out every window. He looked grumbly, like he did anytime he woke up, but he never complained when he was on duty.

At the third window, I looked out onto a world bathed in moonlight. As I tried to figure out the constellations, Jase fogged up the glass with his breath and used his fist and fingers to make little footprints on the glass.

"Cute," I said softly and started walking. "I should pick you up some finger paints."

"Watch out. I'd be the Michelangelo of the new world. All the girls would be chasing me," he whispered.

"And Hali will kick their collective ass."

He chuckled and then faked a straight face. "I have no idea what you're talking about."

I rolled my eyes. "Whatever you say, King of Denial."

We continued making our rounds for the next hour until it was time to wake everyone up. Professor Caler and the rest of his group came upstairs soon after. Dr. Gidar stood with the two kids before him, a hand on their shoulders. Everyone had bags, and several carried plastic totes.

"Have you reached a decision?" the professor asked when Clutch had his gear and strolled over to meet them.

"You can come to New Eden. You'll need to go straight into quarantine until you're deemed safe. That's non-negotiable. Can you live with that?"

Professor Caler scanned his people's faces before beaming a wide grin back at Clutch. "Your terms are acceptable. Thank you."

Clutch nodded. "We'll head out when the sun comes up."

"We're ready to go whenever you are ready," the professor said.

As moonlight gave way to twilight, we realized leaving the church would be more challenging than we'd planned.

"Aw, hell," Clutch said at my side.

I closed my eyes and rested my forehead against the glass door. When I opened my eyes, nothing had changed. Dogs—hundreds of them—weaved around the trucks, watching us.

"How'd they find us?" Tom asked.

"Dogs have an incredible sense of smell," Jase said. "And, the food supply is slim around here. They've probably been following us since yesterday and finally caught up."

"We'll have to sacrifice some of our food to distract them," I said.

Clutch scowled and motioned everyone to the center of the church. "We'll send a team at a time. One team per vehicle, except we'll leave the car behind in case we need it later. That's six teams. Carry only what you can run with. Leave everything else behind. We may be able to come back for it."

"The children can't run," Dr. Gidar said.

"Then carry them," Clutch retorted. "Team leads are Griz, Marco, Tom, Nick, Randy, and me. Leads, you have five minutes to pick your vehicle and teams. Let's move fast before those packs out there multiply. Trust me, they will get bigger."

"Why don't we wait them out?" someone asked. "You know, like we did at the store?"

"Because once the dogs knew we were in the store, they stuck around. The packs didn't start to thin until we'd stayed hidden for a couple days, and even then, there were too many. It could take a week or longer, and we can't wait."

"Why not?" the professor asked.

"Two reasons." Clutch held up a finger. "One, Jack doesn't have that long. And two," he held up a second finger. "I don't want to get snowed into this church for the winter."

"Snow? What are you talking—"

Clutch cut off the professor's words by pointing outside.

I moaned. "You've got to be kidding me." Sure enough, large snowflakes were beginning to dot the dogs' darker fur and the trucks' windshields. Without a weather forecast, we had no idea if we'd get a dusting or two feet. We hadn't found anyone with a knack at reading weather patterns yet, so we always had to play it conservatively. Without snowplows, it wouldn't take much to leave us stranded.

"But, we cannot leave my equipment behind," Dr. Gidar said. "I can't continue my research without it."

"We'll come back for it later," Clutch said, before adding, "We're heading out. Any more questions?"

No one spoke, and Clutch joined Jase and me in organizing everything we needed to evacuate. I wasn't the least bit surprised that Clutch hadn't named Jase or me as a lead. I didn't take it personally. I would've done the same thing. After all, we were family. We stayed together. Griz should've been with us, too, but Clutch and Griz had a different kind of relationship. I figured it was because they were both Army Rangers and that shared history meant something to them. They were brothers, and both treated Jase and me as though we were theirs to protect.

They had it wrong. We were each other's to protect.

Clutch took Jack onto his team. Since we had Jase's truck, four was plenty. Even at four, Clutch was going to take the back of the truck, which would make for a freezing ride back to New Eden. But, when I pointed that out, he didn't seem to mind one bit.

Each team had a crate of food they would toss out before they ran to their truck. They'd then use their truck to help create a blockade between the next team and the dogs. Griz volunteered his team to go first. Clutch's team would go last. We were the only ones with any ammo, and it was our job to take out dogs that got too close to any of the teams.

Griz's team waited at the door. Clutch and Jase stood at each door, ready to fling them open for the team and yank them closed the moment the team was through. Griz's team consisted of four able-bodied men. Clutch and Griz wanted a team outside to help fight off dogs if things went downhill.

"Ready?" Clutch asked.

"Let's rock and roll," Griz answered.

Clutch and Jase threw the doors open, and Griz's team lobbed out open cans of chicken. Dogs skidded around and dove after the food. Griz led his team as they sprinted out the door, which was closed as soon as they were outside. One dog turned and snapped at Griz, and he hacked at it with his machete. It cried out and fell, but other dogs that couldn't reach the food switched direction to go after the team. Griz had already made it to his truck—one of New Eden's supply trucks. He had the door open, and his men jumped in one at a time while Griz and they hacked at dogs.

Animals yelped and growled but kept coming.

I didn't let out the breath I'd been holding until Griz was in the truck and his door slammed shut. "Thank God," I said breathlessly. "One down, five to go."

Randy's team went next. Then, Nick's. Each time, the food worked, but more and more dogs showed up. Nick's squad spent as much time hacking as they did running. Clutch cracked the door open, and I took shots at the dogs coming up behind the team. One of their team may have been bitten, but at least they all made it into their truck.

Marco's team had the little girl and Tom's team had the boy since everyone thought having both kids on one team could slow down that team too much. Nathan carried the girl, but he moved clumsily with her. Before Clutch and Jase opened the doors, Marco cussed. "Jesus Christ, give her to me." He grabbed the girl, slung her over his shoulder as if she were a rag doll.

"Be careful with her," Dr. Gidar called out, but Marco was already outside.

The other two members of Marco's team were behind him. They threw food, but the dogs didn't go for it. Instead, they lunged at Marco's team. I opened fire at the mobs forming around Marco and his team. I prayed no shots ricocheted off the pavement and hit one of our people. They had nearly reached the truck when my rifle clicked.

"I'm empty!"

Clutch shut the door, but I noticed him gripping his sword. He moved from one foot to the other. A large dog leapt at one of Marco's men, and the man went down.

Marco tossed the girl inside the truck and shoved Nathan inside. Marco then turned for his other man, his features strained when he saw the dogs tearing into the man who had not once screamed during the attack. Though, that likely just meant a dog had torn out his throat.

Marco climbed inside the truck and started it up. Like the others, he pulled around to create a path for us to reach our truck and Tom's team to reach the minivan. Dogs ran under and around the trucks to come at us. The sickest of the animals didn't seem to remember what glass was and ran headfirst into it. Snow flew from their fur with each collision.

"We can't go," Tom said in a rush. "The dogs have learned. They prefer us to the canned food. We'll never make it."

"It must be something about the virus that even this strain makes them crave blood over food," Professor Caler said.

"I believe these dogs suffer from an iron deficiency in the same way those infected with zonbistis suffer," Dr. Gidar replied.

"Write your thesis later," Clutch said. "We've got forty feet between point A and point B with a shit-ton of rabid, pissed off mutts covering every inch. I could use some ideas right about now."

"I say we wait," Tom said.

"Then Jack dies," Clutch said.

"But, he—" Dr. Gidar started, but Clutch's hard glare stopped him.

"And we could get stuck here," Clutch added.

"What if we hide and the squadron heads out slowly and draws the packs away?" Jase offered.

Clutch turned. "Now *that* is an idea." He picked up his radio and relayed Jase's plan. After locking the door, we followed Tom down the hallway. Dr. Gidar led the boy. Jase had stuck Boy, their small dog, into his backpack. Clutch and Jase carried an unconscious Jack. Behind us, dogs howled. Trying to ignore the sounds, we headed down to the basement because Gidar thought it would provide us the best chance to not be heard or scented by the dogs outside.

Clutch spoke into his radio. "Church is secure. Bug out."

"*Affirm*," Griz's voice came through the radio. "*Squadron is bugging out. Will report in sixty.*"

The boy tried to walk back upstairs, but Gidar directed him back toward us. The boy then let out a howl, the first sound I'd ever heard him make. And it gave me the shivers.

The sounds of dogs outside grew louder.

Clutch scowled. "Christ, Doc. Shut that kid up or else the dogs will never follow the squadron."

Dr. Gidar bore an agitated expression. "There's nothing I can do. He gets uncomfortable without his sister. She will be even worse. They are quite dependent on each other."

"Can you give him something to settle him down?" Professor Caler asked.

Dr. Gidar shook his head. "He has a compromised system. He hasn't responded well to drugs in the past. I'm afraid it could make things worse."

"We need to give the squadron sixty minutes to draw the packs away," Clutch said.

Jack moaned and moved restlessly. I pulled out a tissue and wiped his sweaty brow. "Sh," I murmured. "Everything will be fine."

Dr. Gidar held the boy, who slowly returned to his vegetative state.

As we sat and waited, I watched the boy. "What's his name?" I asked quietly.

Dr. Gidar looked up. "I don't know. Neither child speaks."

I frowned. "What do you call him then?"

"I call them 'child,'" he replied.

"We decided it was impersonal to give them names that weren't theirs," Professor Caler said.

My brow rose. "More impersonal than calling them 'child?'" I thought for a moment. "I think I'd want a name, even if it wasn't my real one."

"Forty minutes to go," Jase whispered.

"I still hear the dogs out there. It doesn't sound like they've left," Tom said.

"Give the squadron a chance," Clutch said the instant before the sound of an engine and horn broke through the sounds of animals. "See? My guys know how to make a sales pitch."

For the next forty minutes, we sat there, the only sounds coming randomly from Jack and the boy. The boy grew more and more agitated, his jaundiced eyes flitting around the room, as though he was searching for something. The time passed interminably slow. I could hear fewer and fewer dogs. The engines disappeared.

When Griz finally called in, the radio startled me.

"We've led away what we could," Griz said. *"But, some refused to follow. There are some hardheaded ones out there. I hate to say it, but the snow is really coming down. These trucks don't have tires for snow."*

Clutch spoke into the radio. "We'll take it from here. Head to New Eden before you get stranded."

A pause. *"We'll come back for you."*

"Don't worry about us. Now, head on home." Clutch lowered the radio and came to his feet. "We have two options. We wait out these animals and run the risk of being stranded here, potentially for a month or longer. Or, we head out of here before the snow gets deeper and face the dogs that are still out there."

"I say we wait," Tom said.

Dr. Gidar shook his head. "No, I need to work on the vaccine. We can't afford to wait."

Professor Caler stood and walked toward the stairs. "There is another way. You're heading home today. The vaccine must be made and distributed."

"What's your plan?" Clutch asked, but the professor had already disappeared up the stairs.

Clutch and Jase hurriedly grabbed Jack and we followed the professor. I glanced back to see Tom waiting for Dr. Gidar who was coaxing the boy into his arms.

Professor Caler stood at the front door. When I reached him, I counted over three dozen dogs on the other side of the glass, watching us with glazed eyes. Caler seemed to stare off into nowhere. "Are you ready?"

"What are you planning to do?" I asked.

He kept staring out through the door. "I'll draw their attention and buy you the time you need."

"You can't do this, John," Dr. Gidar said. "You can't sacrifice yourself."

The professor sighed. "The day of the outbreak, I was receiving my first chemo treatment. My doctor had said that even with the treatments, my chances were only twenty percent I'd make it a year." He turned and faced us. His gaze was tired, showing the type of exhaustion that sleep couldn't fix. "I've had enough of this world. If there's one thing I can do that helps others one last time, then by God, let me do it."

I couldn't speak. Instead, I could only stare at the hard conviction in his eyes.

"We'll find another way," Tom said.

"Every minute you spend trying to find an alternative," the professor started. "More snow and more dogs arrive. Now, I'm stepping out this door in ten seconds. It's up to you if you let my last moments be in vain."

"Thank you, sir," Clutch said.

Professor Caler gave a slight nod and then unzipped his coat.

I pulled out my pistol. It had only one round left in it. I'd always refused to give up that single round in case I needed it for myself, but it felt selfish to hold onto it. I handed it to Clutch. He checked the mag, frowned, and then shoved it into his belt.

Professor Caler pushed open the door and ran with more energy than I'd thought possible. The dogs went after him. I couldn't watch. I burst out the door and swung my machete like a pendulum as I ran toward the truck. Already at least a couple inches of snow covered the ground, slowing my pace. I knew the others were behind me, and I kept running.

The professor screamed in agony as I opened the truck door. I found myself shoved inside with Jack thrown on me. Jase crawled in behind the wheel, and Clutch jumped into the back. Jase revved the engine and threw the truck into gear. The van moved, and I knew Caler's sacrifice had saved all our lives.

After I situated Jack in between Jase and me, I looked out the window to see the professor tangled in a rose bush. He writhed and screamed. A shot rang out in the frozen air. The man's head fell back, and he moved no more.

I looked back to make sure Clutch was safe. He held up a thumb. I leaned back and closed my eyes as Jase slipped and slid out of the parking lot. Jase drove, with the minivan behind us, for about thirty minutes before he stopped, and Clutch squeezed up front with us. It was tight, but he was in no mood to sit in the minivan. I pulled Jack onto Clutch and my laps and checked his temperature every few minutes. "I think his fever may be breaking," I said after the third or fourth check.

The snow kept coming down, and the winds picked up. We drove at a snail's pace. Jase recommended we stay at the place where he'd found his truck, but when I mentioned the people we'd seen on horseback, Clutch decided to brave the roads.

I don't know how many hours passed before Jase pointed. "Home sweet home."

I smiled at seeing the other trucks parked inside the gates. "We made it," I said and patted Jack's chest, only to find it wasn't moving.

Jack had already died.

PART FIVE
FORTITUDE

FOURTEEN

Twenty-four hours later

"It's perfect," Deb said as she looked over the baby seat Marco had brought back from the store. Marco beamed with pride as he knelt near her, helping her figure out the new baby seat. "Thank you," she added as she bent down and gave him a tender kiss. "Did you tell them?"

"No," Marco replied. "I thought you'd want to be the one to tell them the news."

Deb looked up at us, her face beaming, and grabbed his hand. "We're getting married!"

Surprise was quickly washed over with joy. Everyone in the living room cheered.

"'Bout time you manned up the nerve to ask her," Griz said, grinning.

I hustled over to the couple, and hugged them both. "Congratulations!"

"Way to go. Will you have white cake? It's my favorite," Benji said, evidently knowing what weddings were all about. He broke out into the chicken dance, while Diesel and Boy danced around him in mutual excitement.

"We'll have cake, Benji," Vicki said, wearing a rare smile.

Deb motioned for the older woman. "Vicki is going to be my maid of honor," Deb said.

Vicki laughed. "I'm long past being a maid. But I'll gladly be your matron of honor."

"Griz is standing in as my best man," Marco said.

"As long as I don't have to wear a tux," Griz said. "Although I would be the finest looking man around here."

"Justin is going to make it a town event next week. We hope you all can be there," Deb said.

"We wouldn't miss it for the world," I said.

After the celebration simmered down, I headed out to tell Clutch the good news. He'd been with Justin, debriefing him on the last several days' events while the rest of us had returned to the house as soon as our night in quarantine was over. The Marshall survivors were still in "quarantine," but really, Justin was keeping them in a separate building until he figured out how to handle them—and the two kids. He hadn't mentioned the kids to the rest of New Eden yet, and we weren't talking, though I had no doubt the rumors would quickly spread.

Marco had said the girl yelled until she passed out on the drive back to New Eden. I could only imagine how the two kids must've latched onto each other when they were brought back together. I suspected no one would be able to separate them as easily again.

I tromped through the six inches of snow that covered everything in a pristine white. My smile stayed glued on my face, despite the cold and despite having seen two men die only a day ago. Marco and Deb proved that good things could still happen in this new world.

Even though the baby wasn't Marco's, for all intents and purposes, he acted as though he was the father. Whenever Deb needed to go to the clinic or was too sick to pick up her rations, Marco was there, as though they'd been married for years. That was only one example of how things had changed since the outbreak. There were no longer things such as dating or drawn-out engagements. Life had no guarantees, especially now, and everyone knew it.

Their wedding would remind us that happiness wasn't extinct, a reminder each one of us desperately needed. Benji, with his innocent child resilience, had always been our poster child for a future that was worth protecting. Marco and Deb also belonged on that poster.

By the time I reached Justin's house, the cold had seeped through my skin, and I shivered. I jogged up the steps and walked inside. Justin was in his dining room—where he always was—with his two assistants, Clutch, Zach, Dr. Edmund, and Dr. Gidar. It was a full room.

Clutch glanced up while the others were deeply engaged by the papers on the table. "That should work nicely," Dr. Gidar said as he ran his finger down a list of handwritten items.

"We're working out a setup for Dr. Gidar to do his research," Clutch said. "I think we can make it happen without putting New Eden at any risk."

"That's nice," I replied before my smile grew.

"What is it?" he asked.

"Deb and Marco are getting married."

His brows rose before he nodded and grinned. "Good for them."

"So, it's official then," Justin said. "That's a relief. I wasn't going to be able to keep it a secret much longer. This will be the biggest event New Eden's ever had." He sobered. "We could use the good news. Folks can cope with not having a Thanksgiving feast. Losing Jack will be harder. He's been with us since the beginning. Hopefully, Dr. Gidar here can make it so we don't lose anyone else to this godforsaken virus."

"Well, there are no guarantees," Dr. Gidar started, but he didn't continue, because the door burst open and about a dozen residents hurried inside and fanned around the room.

"There are zeds inside New Eden?" a woman asked in a shrill voice.

"You're going to get us all killed," a man from the back called out.

"Calm down so we can discuss this," Justin said.

"Not until you get the zeds out of New Eden."

Yelling erupted.

Clutch came to his feet, pulled out his sword and slammed it against the table. The sound of metal on wood reverberated through the house. "Enough!"

The newcomers silenced.

Clutch continued. "I would never allow anyone through those gates who I felt was a risk to New Eden. Those two kids may be different, but whatever they are, they sure as hell aren't zeds. At least not zeds like we know them to be. Dr. Gidar here believes they are the key to creating a vaccine for the zed virus. I don't know about you, but I for one would like to see that happen. These guys have been working all morning on a plan, which I'm sure they'd be happy to share with you."

He sheathed his sword and pushed through the crowd. I followed. Once we were outside, I kept pace with him. "Wow, I didn't realize you were a diplomat."

"Irrational people drive me crazy," he said. "I've never gotten why some fly off the handle without thinking."

"Because they're being *irrational*," I joked. "It's a curse of being human. We're all doomed to act irrationally every now and then."

He smirked. "Speak for yourself."

I bent down, grabbed a handful of snow, and threw it at him.

"Hey!"

I jumped back, laughing. Clutch started making a snowball, and I did the same. We threw about the same time; mine hit his chest, while his hit me right in the head. "Oh! That's mean."

He laughed.

The ground rumbled, and I girded myself as though an earthquake was coming. But, this was Nebraska. Earthquakes didn't happen.

Clutch looked around. "What was—"

A house at the edge of town exploded into a ball of fire.

I gasped and brought my hand over my mouth.

"Fire!" Clutch shouted. He looked back at me, his eyes wide.

I knew mine were just as wide, because I was thinking the exact same thing.

We had no working fire truck.

We burst into action at the same instant, and we took off toward the fire. I had no idea what caused it. Had someone bombed us? What else could cause an explosion like that?

Justin came running up by us. "It's the gas lines! I heard about this happening at another town. We have to shut all the lines off. This fire will keep going wherever the gas goes."

"How do we turn off the gas?" I asked as we ran.

"There are shut-off valves outside every house," he replied. "Wrenches should work. Spread the word, starting with the houses near the fire."

"Do the gas lines go to the silo?" Clutch asked.

"No, the silo is on its own grid. Generators and propane tanks only," Justin said.

"Good," Clutch said. "I'm familiar with gas shutoff valves. I'll start turning them off. Cash, you tell everyone you can to get their valves shut off and fast. And then tell them to head to the silo. They'll be safe there."

"Okay!" I yelled and slowed down. I looked from side to side and had no fucking idea where to go first. When I saw Zach headed our way, I ran up to him and passed along the info. He headed west, and I headed east. I ran to each house. Most people were already standing on their porches, making my job easier. But, many were like me and had no idea where their shutoff valves were located. "Just find it already!" I yelled and moved on.

I kept running, even though the snow slowed me down, and I had no real plan of who to tell first, so I set up a path that would bring me to house Twenty-Six. When I reached it, everyone was already standing outside. "Turn off the gas shutoff valve!" I yelled, my voice coarse from the smoke tainting the air.

Frost nodded. "I was suspecting that was the case, so I already turned off our valve and told our neighbors to do the same."

"What do we do now?" Vicki asked.

A second explosion rocked the town. This one was in the center of town, nowhere near the first explosion, and I prayed Clutch was far from the deadly blast. The fires were spreading from both explosions, and smoke had blocked out the sun.

I looked back to Frost and the others. "Get to the silo!"

I jogged down to warn the next houses, but a third house exploded less than a block away, and I found myself trying to run faster, only to stumble and fall onto my knees. I climbed to my feet and stared at people running in the street. Clutch came running at me, a wall of smoke and fire behind him, and I blinked to make sure it was really him.

He didn't stop until he reached me. Even then, he pretty much plowed into me and pulled me to him. "Are you hurt?"

I shook my head. "I'm fine."

"We need to get to the silo," he said and grabbed my hand. "There's no stopping this."

We quickly caught up to the others. Jase and Hali were in lead, both of them like gazelles in the snow. Frost held Benji's hand, and Vicki hustled alongside them. Marco and Griz were helping Deb walk as quickly as she could, which wasn't nearly fast enough. The silo was on the other side of town, with fire and likely more explosions between us and it.

We made it about two blocks before Marco stopped and turned around. He pointed and said something, but Deb shook her head. "I can keep going."

Marco sprinted toward a wheelbarrow on the front porch of the house. "Hold on a second. I'm grabbing this for Deb!"

Everyone slowed and then stopped.

Marco grabbed the wheelbarrow, looked up and grinned while he stood on the front porch. "Got it!"

The house exploded outward, engulfing Marco in its flames. Glass shards shot from the windows. Heat blasted my face and burned my eyes. Debris pebbled my skin.

"Marco!" Deb screamed. She lunged toward the fire, but Griz held her back.

"God," Clutch muttered, and he tried to take steps toward the house, his arm covering his face, but the heat forced him back.

The flames licked out from the house. Still, I faced the house and tried to find Marco. I swear my mind still saw him standing on the porch, holding the wheelbarrow, but I knew it was an illusion. There was no sign of Marco. The explosion hadn't thrown him from the house. He had to be still up there, enveloped within flames that I could feel the heat of from sixty feet away.

Clutch returned and grabbed onto me as though I was his lifeline, and I sobbed, still watching the house.

"We have to go," Griz said softly to Deb.

"No, no, no," she said over and over again before she collapsed and Griz caught her.

The others had gathered around her, also searching for Marco. Jase had gotten closer to the house than Clutch had, but even he had to back off from the growing flames.

Griz carried Deb, his features clenched as though it was taking everything to hold back his pain. Like automatons, we left Marco behind. We weaved around streets and walked toward the silo. As we walked by the church, its cross burned radiantly, and its organ played an unholy tune of misshapen, dying notes.

We passed some people moving more slowly than us, while others hurried around us.

Clutch held onto me as we walked, and I held onto him. With every explosion, I cringed. When we finally reached the silo, before walking through the doorway, I turned around to see New Eden burning behind us. Numb, I blankly walked into the dark cavern where we would be safe. Most of us, anyway.

Fifteen

The next two days went by interminably slowly. At first, a team went up every hour to check the status of the fires and to look for any of the twenty-six missing residents—though at least three were confirmed dead. Stragglers arrived within the first few hours, including Dr. Gidar and the two kids. A riot ensued to keep the kids out of the silo, but Justin allowed them inside, assuring everyone that they would be secured in a locked room along with the doctor.

The fires continued to burn but had not come closer to the silo. From the higher floors, I could hear explosions and crashes as more and more houses succumbed to the fires. Once it was clear we were safe in here from the fires, Justin had teams go up only every four hours.

The lower levels still had standing water in them, giving the silo's air a cold dampness. Our clothes were saturated with smoke. Coupled with the heavy air, the smell of smoke hung everywhere. People coughed in the dimly lit corridors. Deb—and others—cried softly. It was dark enough that no one saw me cry.

Even after working every day, crews had only managed to repair the silo's flooring, lights, and vents. No rooms were ready in the silo yet, so everyone had to camp out on the metal grid floors, with only blankets for cushioning. Buckets were lined up in cordoned-off room, which served as toilets. Diesel, Boy, and the other dogs in the town had nowhere to go. Thankfully, most of New Eden's supplies were stored in the silo. Plastic bags quickly became the most useful resource.

At mealtime, each person was given an open can of beans. No one complained. We'd all been through tougher times and were thankful to be safely tucked inside a building when we could be out in the middle of a Nebraska winter with no shelter. Few spoke. After all, what could be said that didn't make matters even worse?

Unlike Clutch, Griz, Jase, Hali, and me who wore our backpacks everywhere, most had nothing with them—anything they'd owned was burning to ash outside. We still had our weapons, a change of clothes, and some basic survival supplies. I spent a lot of time curled into Clutch, and it wasn't just to stay warm. He grounded me. Griz sat with us, but he spent as much time doing sit-ups and push-ups as he did sleeping. Hali and Jase were inseparable, and our small group stayed within ten feet of one another. I guess we all felt the same. We'd been through homes before. When we had nothing else, we still had each other.

Frost had found a nice corner for Benji and his dogs. The boy was resilient, but he needed routines, and he exhausted easily. Deb hadn't fared as well. Contractions started during the first night, and Dr. Edmund was at her side every moment he wasn't helping the injured. Vicki stayed with her constantly. I made the mistake and mentioned that Dr. Gidar could help, but with the backlash I received from the New Eden residents, it was clear they weren't ready for "that man" to be out among them yet.

I didn't offer any ideas after that and rode out the time. I tried not to make eye contact with anyone while we took our hourly walks through the silo for exercise. When I failed, I'd see the exhaustion and despair in their soot-covered gazes. Hell, I probably had the same look.

I watched Clutch. We could carry on an entire conversation without speaking, and I know I gave him strength like he gave me.

New Eden's citizens stayed days in the silo before Zach returned to say the fires were just smoldering embers now. After Justin saw for himself, he gave the green light for everyone to venture out.

"Watch out for dogs and zeds," he'd said. "Everyone, analyze what needs done today to secure New Eden. But, be back to the silo before sunset."

Some rushed outside. Others dragged their feet. I was somewhere in between. Shit, I was beyond stir-crazy, but I dreaded seeing what awaited us outside.

And, I had good reason to dread.

Armageddon had come to New Eden. I could see all the way across town. No buildings obstructed my view. Sure, the skeletal remains of houses stood like splinters, but the fire had been thorough. Not a single house came through unscathed, but at least five houses were still usable. Surprisingly, much of the fence still stood. It had been built far enough out the fire hadn't consumed it. Sections were charred, and boards pressed against the wire, but it was better than standing out here naked to the world. There were clearly still some holes in the fences, because animal tracks dotted the snow.

When Clutch and I came across Romeo's body—New Eden's vagrant—all that was left was his coat and boots. Wild animals had eaten everything else. Most of the bodies of the missing residents were never found, like that of Jase's partner, Dick. Or the woman who always smiled when I met her on the streets.

Or Marco.

It was like he'd vanished, leaving no trace behind. Maybe it was better that way; then we could all pretend that he hadn't suffered.

The fires had raged in the area for days, and they weren't completely gone. Smoke rose in the distance, and an explosion was heard that had to come from fifty miles away. Evidently, the gas line was still seeking out new victims.

We walked the fence line and made notes of needed repairs, though Clutch and Griz thought it would be better to focus on reinforcing the fence that encircled the silo to make a smaller area more defensible. Besides, there wasn't much out here left to protect.

Everyone congregated around the few buildings that still stood. Justin had a table set up, and his assistants were taking down notes as people spoke of what they needed. Dr. Gidar, sans kids, had his hand raised. "I need assistants. I need to continue my work. That is more important than anything."

Someone punched him—I couldn't remember the resident's name—and people cheered.

Dr. Gidar held his bloody nose. "Fool," he said, his voice muffled as though he had a cold. "If I can't find a vaccine, we're all only one bite away from death."

People quieted down, but their gazes were murderous. Dr. Gidar needed to learn that empathy was still a valued trait. People weren't being naïve. They simply couldn't fathom looking ahead to tomorrow when they were struggling to get through today.

We didn't stick around. We headed back to our house to find it about halfway burned. Some of the windows were, amazingly, intact. Still, Frost wouldn't let us sift through the debris for fear the floor would collapse. So, we stood there and stared through the broken living room window. Still sitting on the coffee table was a melted and charred baby seat.

Sixteen

For the next several days after the gas lines blew, new fires popped up from old embers. After we buried the dead—those we could find—in the frozen ground, we worked frantically to repair fences and turn the silo into New Eden. With over three hundred people working in the silo, we had indoor plumbing in three days, and had the water drained from the lower levels in ten days.

Within two weeks, we had the fences repaired so the wild dogs couldn't get through. But, they didn't give up. Once the smoke dissipated, the numbers of wild animals trolling outside the fences grew. One of the best parts about the silo was that we didn't have to hear the animals' howls at night.

The silo was huge, but much of the space was open air and not set up in any kind of livable configuration, at least not yet. There were nowhere near enough rooms for any semblance of personal space. At least the dormitory rooms had been completed, and we had enough beds to require only two sleeping shifts. Three weeks after the gas line explosions, we fell into a comfortable routine of living in the silo.

Everyone stayed in the silo with the exception of Dr. Gidar, his assistants, and the two zed kids. They were set up in one of the few remaining buildings—a tiny, old house—using a generator to power their medical equipment and lights. The only heat in the house was from a wood fireplace. No one liked taking fuel from the silo generators for Dr. Gidar's house, but New Eden's residents liked the idea of the zed kids in the silo even less.

The busyness of working in and around the silo helped take our minds off what we'd lost, but it wasn't nearly enough to make us forget. If Clutch wasn't barking out orders, he didn't speak. Losing Marco threw Clutch back into that dark place where he'd close himself off from everyone. He developed a knack at not coming to bed until after I'd fallen asleep and getting up before I woke.

Deb acted much the same as when she lost Tack, the father of her unborn child: she buried her emotions and went on. She had contractions nearly every day, and Dr. Edmund told her she needed to lower her stress levels. I imagined that was tough for Deb to do when she watched her fiancé burn alive a few weeks ago. Her gaze revealed the losses she'd suffered, and I prayed she'd be able to keep it together long enough to carry the baby full-term.

"Here." Zach handed me a box of toilet paper before grabbing one for himself.

We were on duty, but things had changed because New Eden had shrunk from a town sitting on three square miles to a town of two city blocks, with each block—the silo and the buildings—sitting nearly a quarter mile from each other. The squadron and security forces had been merged, and our shifts were as much working on the silo as keeping the peace.

Zach and I carried our loads up a flight of stairs, I dropped off a half dozen rolls of toilet paper at the first bathroom, and we continued up the next two floors.

"We're lucky Justin thought to store everything in the silo," I said while Zach placed rolls by the next bathroom.

He chuckled. "Yeah. Good thing he didn't listen to me. I told him he should've stored everything in a building. I kept telling him that, with our luck, this silo would probably flood in the spring and ruin everything."

"Unfortunately, we didn't keep enough in the silo," Justin said as he walked up the stairs and overheard us. "We had only one radio with the range to reach the capital, and it's a melted mess of wires and metal. Being separated from everyone else is a bit unsettling." He sighed. "I know, I have to be patient. I'm sure they'll send someone down here to check on us and get us hooked back up." He looked at the boxes we carried and then looked back up at us. "Are you heading topside?"

"Yeah," I replied.

He smiled. "Can you bring this to the lab? Dr. Gidar said he needed more Q-tips."

I took the blue and white package of cotton swabs, and Justin tipped his hat before heading up the next flight of steel stairs and disappearing. We continued restocking our toilet paper until only a few rolls remained. I stuffed them into my backpack, zipped my coat, and pulled on my stocking hat and gloves. "Hopefully, it's warmed up a bit," I said. "It was frigid out there this morning."

"I haven't been out yet today," Zach said. "Fresh air sounds nice right now. Even if it is freezing."

I pushed open the door, and a cold wind blasted my face. I pulled my neck gaiter up over my mouth and nose.

"Good afternoon."

I looked to my left to see Frost leaning against the downwind side of the silo's concrete entryway. His arms were crossed tightly over his chest. "Dog duty?" I asked.

"Yep," he replied before glancing at three dogs hopping around the snow. A smaller black and white dog bounded under the bigger dog's legs.

"So you've adopted Boy and Buddy now, too?"

Frost grunted. "Buddy comes and goes. But, poor Boy was forgotten after the fires. Benji found him hiding under a burnt porch and decided we needed another dog."

I could only imagine the evil looks Frost would get now. First, one dog eating precious food. Now, two? Though, I suspected all the animosity of New Eden was far easier for Frost to stomach compared to the displeasure of his grandson letting a dog go without a home. Not that he was the only dog without a home. But, those still alive outside the fence were either sick, feral, or both.

I looked at the fences surrounding the silo. Only a few feral animals hung around today; evidently the weather was too cold for even them to stalk us.

I turned back to Frost. "See you later."

Zach and I headed to the small wood enclosure, which served as the guard station at the gate. The fence, connected to the gate, encircled the silo with a narrow, fenced path wide enough for a truck drive through. At the end of the path was a second gate that opened to the old New Eden. There, the fences had been somewhat repaired, enough to close gaps against animals but not strong enough to hold off a vehicle ramming it or a sudden crush of zeds.

Jase and Hali were at the guard station, cuddling in the cold. When they saw us walking toward them, they awkwardly separated. Hali waved, and Jase opened the gate. "Have a nice walk," he said as Zach and I passed through. "Bring me back something from Burger King."

"I'll get right on that," I said sarcastically, and started to jog down the path.

When Hali found out Jase and I left to go after the squadron, she'd made up her mind then and there that she wouldn't be left behind again. She was still learning how to use a machete and had never fired a gun before, but she had spunk. And she'd been relentless in asking Justin for the transfer to the security team, so he'd finally relented.

Now that the squadron and security forces were merged, Zach had stepped down to have Clutch be leader of the new, combined force. Zach and Griz were Clutch's seconds. Everyone had partners except for Clutch, who worked much of both shifts to drive things. He was working too hard and not sleeping enough, and it showed in his face. But, I knew it was his way of coping—of avoiding having to think of those he'd lost and blamed himself for. There was nothing Clutch could've done to prevent Marco's death, but I knew Clutch. That fact wouldn't have stopped Clutch from blaming himself, anyway.

I did the only thing I knew that seemed to work with Clutch. I gave him space and made it clear I was there when he was ready to come back.

I counted the fence posts in the quarter mile connector between the silo and the burnt-out city as Zach and I jogged. We jogged for exercise and for warmth. We didn't stop until we reached the next gate. Here, one guard watched while the other opened the gate for us, and we hustled through.

The gate closed behind us. I pulled out my machete. Before us stood the ruins of New Eden. Even though the fences remained, the town now had a forbidding presence. It could've been the lives lost here, or the hopes crushed. Either way, I no longer enjoyed walking these streets. Zach felt the same. Both of us were on edge, and neither of us spoke while we patrolled the "old" New Eden.

Justin believed we could rebuild the town in the spring. I offered up the idea of relocating the town to Fox Park, but many New Eden residents clung to the silo's safety. The majority of the town wanted to convert the silo into a permanent home, but some contemplated relocating to Moose Jaw to be a part of the new capital. I suspected that, come spring, some groups would leave the silo. I was planning to be in one of those groups.

Hiding underground was no way to survive.

The walk to Dr. Gidar's lab was short. The small cluster of surviving houses sat on the western end of the town, near the silo. The snow had been trampled down and was now as hard as the street below it. We didn't jog, because there were too many icy patches, but we still walked briskly.

I hurried up the two steps to the front door and stepped inside. The kitchen had been turned into the lab, while the zed kids had been set up in a baby pen in the living room.

Like Zach did every time we came here, he walked over and watched the boy sitting in the pen. The kid was watching a cartoon on a tablet computer they'd evidently charged off the generator. Zach seemed as captivated with the boy as the boy was with the show.

Currently, the little girl was in the kitchen, and Dr. Gidar had his stethoscope on her chest. The girl kept reaching for the instrument, and the doctor kept brushing her hand away. Hugh stood by and watched, slowly shaking his head. Bonnie was sitting at the kitchen countertop, placing droplets of a clear liquid on slides.

"Child B's heart rhythm is normal," Dr. Gidar said while Hugh jotted down notes. The doctor handed the stethoscope to the girl, who took it and examined it, making the metal reflect the light.

I set the box of cotton swabs and a few rolls of toilet paper on a table. "You still haven't named them?"

"They have names already," Dr. Gidar replied. "If they can learn to speak again, they'll tell us those names."

I shrugged. "Whatever you say. I still think they'd like to be called something else besides 'child.'"

"Do they look like they care?" Hugh said. "They're infected. They're a few fries short of a Happy Meal."

"Now, Hugh," the doctor said, "we don't know the extent of their brain damage yet. That they understand language and don't require diapers signifies some level of advanced cognitive function. Even more so, the boy had opened tin cans of food and kept both him and his sister alive for six months. That is not a sign of severely limited brain function. I suspect the virus targets the prefrontal cortex, but I don't have the equipment to run the tests I need."

"What do you need?" I asked.

"An MRI scanner, to start with," the doctor replied.

I smirked. "Good luck getting one of those."

"I know, I know. We're trying to continue modern medicine in a Dark Ages world. I'll make do. It will take longer, but I'll make do."

I watched while he prepared a syringe. "What's that?" I asked.

He looked up. "Prednisone. It's the only drug we have that helps her asthma."

As he injected the young girl, she snarled and snapped at him, and he jumped back. I lunged forward with my machete raised, but Dr. Gidar jumped in between us. "Don't harm her."

I slowly raised my weapon. "You do realize that if she bites you, you'd very likely become infected?"

"Possibly, not likely," he said. "My tests have shown these two children have fought the virus into remission. If she bit me, yes, she would transmit the virus, but she also may transmit the antigen her body has created to fight the virus."

"Then, you'd be like her?" I asked.

He scowled. "That is undetermined." He turned back to the girl and took her new toy. "Well, aren't you peckish today." He shook his finger at her. "No biting."

Once she settled back down, Dr. Gidar motioned to Hugh. "We're finished for now."

Hugh gingerly picked up the small girl as though she were a baby with soiled diapers. He carried her over to the pen and warily set her down. She moved to her brother and became instantly entranced by the show. Hugh took a step back with haste. Distaste wrinkled his features as he looked at his hands, and he disappeared around the corner. I heard the splashing of water seconds later.

I watched the children. Except for their jaundiced eyes and skin, they looked like any other kids slouching in front of a television, watching their favorite show. What went on in their heads? Did they feel fear or hunger or sadness and couldn't convey their needs? Or, were they vegetables, going through the motions of a child but truly a zombie inside?

"Are the kids showing any improvement?" I asked. "Do you think they can recover?"

"It's too early to tell," Dr. Gidar said. "Their health has improved, but for their ages, I'm amazed the children survived for six months out there alone. They were fortunate to have been left inside a restaurant stocked with plenty of food and safely out of harm's way. In fact, I suspect the children locked themselves inside there during the outbreak. They clearly show signs of intelligence."

"I'll take your word for it," I said. "I've never seen a zed with a fraction of those kinds of smarts before." I looked down at my watch. "Well, Zach and I need to get back on patrol. If you need anything else from the silo, make a list for someone to pick up tomorrow."

"I do have one thing I need," Dr. Gidar said as Zach and I walked toward the door.

I paused and slowly turned. I already knew what he'd ask for. He asked for the same thing for every day. "Listen. We can't go pick up Henry until the snow melts off the roads a bit."

"But, I saw the snowmobiles in the garage," he countered.

"No one wants a zed—or whatever Henry is—riding along behind them. The risk is too high."

"I've isolated the antigen," he said. "Only if I have different blood to test—blood that is unrelated to these children—will I know that the antigen is universal."

"I give you my word," I said. "As soon as the snow gets below three inches, I'll take a truck out to find Henry."

"Trucks can handle deeper snow than that," the doctor grumbled and then stepped over to Bonnie.

He said something I couldn't hear, and she looked up, aghast. "No, doctor. You can't."

"This is not up for discussion," he scolded.

She took a syringe, dipped the tip into the liquid she was working with, and pulled back the plunger. Dr. Gidar rolled up his sleeve.

A foreboding feeling built in my gut. "What are you doing, Doctor?"

When Bonnie held up the syringe, he snatched it from her hands and held it in the air. "You know me. I am not a foolish or impetuous man. But, developing a vaccine is more important than anything else we do. Yet, my team has been ostracized, and my work has been shoved into a freezing corner of a dead town. I do not want to do this, but I must. I will not put my team at risk, so there is no other choice."

"You always have a choice," I said.

"This," he held up the syringe, "is the antigen I've created off these children's blood. I have 94.5% confidence that this antigen will equip our bodies with the antibodies we need to fight off the zonbistis virus without loss of cognitive function. I could raise the level of confidence by at least one percentage point with a third test subject. But, I know when I'm being stonewalled."

"You're not being stonewalled," Zach said emphatically.

"We have to play things safe," I added. "When the roads are covered in snow, we could drive over a chunk of metal and shred our tires. Be patient a little longer."

"Patience I have, but not when it comes to delay tactics, one after the other. My work will never be taken seriously until after it's too late. People need vaccinated against this virus *before* they are bitten."

He took a deep breath. "I had a good life. I was giving a speech at Marshall on the day of the outbreak, and it was by a series of miracles that we survived. We did survive, and we had all the facilities we needed to work on a vaccine. We made leaps and bounds during the months we spent at Marshall, but were never able to isolate an antigen. Then, the herds came, and we were forced to leave everything behind except for my journals. For weeks we ran, until we stopped at a gas station for the night and found these two children—clearly infected yet non-violent—hiding in a small café. Within a week after studying their blood, I had reached a major breakthrough. These children gave me more than their blood. They gave us all hope there could be a world where the virus didn't dominate. Entire families have been wiped off the face of this planet for eternity, but the world will continue."

He smiled. It was a sad smile, devoid of anything. "Hope demands sacrifice. And, every vaccine needs its first live trial."

"Don't do this," I said.

"No, doctor!" Bonnie yelled, and the kids started to grunt in response.

Features tight, he injected the syringe into his arm. He pulled the plunger slightly and a tiny burst of red entered the syringe like a red lily in a clear field. Swallowing, he pressed the plunger down, and the liquid disappeared into his vein.

I stared as he pulled out the needle. "What have you done?"

He looked at the syringe before looking up. "I did what had to be done. Now, we'll see if my research is correct or if I'll become a test subject."

Seventeen

It took only twelve hours for Dr. Gidar to develop a fever. He said it was normal, but as his fever worsened, he couldn't hide the doubt in his eyes.

Justin and Clutch had both agreed Dr. Gidar needed to be quarantined until we could prove he was safe. Zach and I were assigned to watch him twenty-four/seven. We rotated shifts, and our days became alternating six-hour shifts. Hugh and Bonnie were allowed to return to the silo, but both had chosen to stay in the lab with Gidar and the kids.

The only people allowed to enter or leave the lab were Justin and Clutch. Even then, Justin had stopped in only once, on the first day. Griz had taken on much of Clutch's duties, so Clutch could be at the lab for much of each day. I could tell he hated that I was caught up in this mess, but he never voiced it. Instead, he hung out and kept a close eye on both Dr. Gidar and the kids.

Jase and Hali stopped by our porch at the beginning and end of their shifts, staying to chat through the window as long as they could. The others stayed in the silo, and I couldn't blame them. It wasn't exactly fun hanging out in an 800-square-foot house in the middle of a town graveyard and listening to the howls every night.

"Water," Dr. Gidar said weakly, and Bonnie rushed over with a glass.

Dr. Gidar worked until the third day, when he was too sick to continue. He still directed Bonnie and Hugh to run tests, this time on his blood, but neither had any kind of background or expertise.

The doctor now lay on the couch, while the kids watched the same cartoon they had one hundred times before. When Bonnie took the glass away, he struggled to sit up, and I rushed over to help. Clutch came to his feet and stepped closer.

"You must promise me something," he said.

"I know, I know. I need to bring Henry here," I replied.

He shook his head. "It's too late for that now. You need to bring my research to someone who can continue it."

I frowned. "Um. I would if I could, Doctor, but I don't know any hematologists around here."

"I know, but the government would have teams working on a vaccine."

I nodded, but we hadn't heard from the capital since the fires. "I'll try."

"No." He shook his head harder and pulled out a slip of paper. He held it out, and I grabbed it. He continued. "You must promise me that you'll deliver these items to the capital. You must do it soon, before the samples start to break down. Bonnie can direct you on the temperatures they need to be maintained at."

I read the list. His journals, blood samples from the kids, him, and Henry, and the antigen samples. I handed the note to Clutch and watched him as he read it.

"I'm dying," Dr. Gidar said. "But my research will save countless lives. That's why I need you to bring it to the capital. I know you'll have to leave the safety of New Eden. It's dangerous out there, but I remember your father telling me you had become a pilot." He smiled. "He was so proud of you. He spoke of how you succeeded at anything you set your mind to. You'll make it through."

He coughed and winced. Blood speckled his lips. "Your father was a man of his word, so I'm counting on the same from you. I need your word that you'll deliver these items to the capital as soon as you can."

I looked at Clutch, pleading for I don't know what in my gaze. He watched me, his jaw hard but his gaze soft. "If you do this, I'm going with you."

I gave a tight nod and inhaled deeply. "You have my word, Dr. Gidar. I'll deliver your research and samples to the capital."

"Good," he said, and he sank down into the couch.

He died several minutes later. Clutch and I stood there, Clutch with his sword, and I with my machete, ready for Dr. Gidar to awaken.

Thank God he never did.

We waited an hour before we let Bonnie check his pulse and take several blood samples. We carried him out the back and placed him in the wood coffin Hugh had built. The two of us stood outside, and I went to close the coffin, when Clutch put a hand on my arm. He pulled out his knife. "We need to play it safe."

I nodded and took a step back as Clutch stood by Gidar's head. I watched Clutch lift the blade and bring it down. No blood splattered, but I knew Clutch hadn't missed. He shut the coffin and we headed back inside.

Bonnie came running out. "Wait! Bring him back inside."

"But he's dead," I said.

"His heart rate had slowed too much for me to get a pulse. But, his cells were still alive when I checked them. He'll be like the kids, but he'll live."

I swallowed the bile rising in my throat. Bonnie must've seen something in our gazes because she shoved past us and to the coffin. She raised the cover and gasped. "What have you done?"

"We thought he was dead," I said weakly.

"I take full responsibility," Clutch added.

"You killed him." Her words dripped with venom.

"We couldn't risk him turning," Clutch said.

She watched us, her jaw lax, for a long moment. Finally, her eyes narrowed and her jaw clenched. "Don't let his death be in vain. Make sure you do what you promised him."

I lifted my chin. "We will."

I spun around and cut through the house and out the front door. Clutch caught up and kept pace alongside me. I reached out my hand, and he took it. He didn't let go, not even after we reached the silo.

Inside, we went straight to Justin's room. "Dr. Gidar is dead," I said. Not waiting for a response, we left and headed to the dorm where the remaining Fox survivors were eating. Clutch and I took turns in telling the events that had transpired and our mission.

"I'm in," Griz said.

"You're not going anywhere without me," Jase added.

"Without *us*," Hali said, giving Jase a look. "We're a team."

"You know I'll go," Vicki said.

"I would go, too," Deb started. "But..."

"I know," I said. "And, I understand."

"Are we going to fly?" Benji asked, his eyes wide. "I've never flown before."

I smiled. "You'll go on the next trip. We don't have much room this time. Actually," I said sheepishly. "I've never flown anything bigger than a four-seater."

"We can't all go," Clutch said. "We'll scout airports tomorrow. There are two within twenty miles of here."

Jase raised his hand. "Uh, we know the capital is in Saskatchewan, but that's a pretty big area. Any idea exactly where we're going?"

"A place called Moose Jaw."

PART SIX
JUSTICE

Eighteen

Christmas lights draped from the guardrails of the walkways, giving the silo a festive ambience. Except for the Marshall survivors, no one seemed to notice that a brilliant man had died yesterday. Justin had given everyone the day off. The excitement was palpable as residents prepared for tonight's Christmas Eve celebration. Nearly everyone—even the non-Christians—was helping decorate and plan skits. People were smiling. Benji was in a wild group of seven kids running down the walkways.

Clutch, Griz, and I were included in the few exceptions. We were fully geared up and on our way topside when we ran into Justin. "Good morning," he said with more enthusiasm than usual. "You'll be back before dark, won't you? Everyone's been looking forward to the banquet for some time."

"That's the plan," Clutch said.

"One, maybe two airports, and then invite Sister Donaldson and Connie to tonight's banquet," I said, neglecting to mention Henry's name. "It's a full day."

Justin nodded. "If they happen to bring Connie's husband, we'll have him stay in the lab with the others."

"Understood," Clutch said. "We'd better head out."

Justin stood off to the side. "It looks to be another sunny day. Be careful out there."

"We always are," Griz said as we walked past Justin and outside.

New Eden's vehicles were all parked outside the silo by a new gate installed after the fires.

Dozens, if not hundreds, of starlings flew over the ruins of New Eden. Birds were one of the few species that multiplied after the outbreak. Like mice and cats, they were everywhere now, and I had nightmares where the birds became sick like the dogs and wolves and would dive-bomb us. It wasn't as bad a nightmare as some.

Luckily, these starlings seemed to have no interest in us, to dive-bomb or otherwise, as we headed toward our vehicle. Clutch and Griz chose our Humvee since a few inches of snow still blanketed everything. It was full of gas, along with six five-gallon containers full—we always kept everything ready in case we had to make a sudden evacuation.

As we approached the vehicle, I glanced at Griz. "Shotgun, sucker."

Griz held up the key, a shit-ass grin on his face.

My eyes widened, and I made eye contact with Clutch. He took off running, and I leapt forward. He had a head start and reached the passenger side first. When he reached for the door, I tackled him from behind. He went down on a knee before catching himself and somehow managing to grab me and flip me over him. I landed on my back with a thud, and the air was knocked from my lungs.

I looked up to see Clutch standing over me. He tried to give me his mean look but failed, and he held out a hand. I grabbed it, and he pulled me to my feet. I pouted. "Bully."

"It was self-defense," he countered before he brushed snow from my hat. When he looked at me, I could see warm love in his brown eyes, and it melted me. I smiled and leaned into him, and he wrapped his arms around me.

The Humvee's engine roared to life, and we broke apart. Clutch opened the front passenger door, but instead of climbing in, he held the door open for me. I grinned and jumped in. "Thank you."

He climbed in the backseat, "Remember, paybacks are hell."

Griz drove through the gate, which the guards closed as soon as we'd left the safety of New Eden. The roads weren't as bad as I'd expected. Other than a few high drifts, which Griz seemed to take pleasure in plowing through, we made pretty decent time to the first airport, where we were able to fill up over fifty gallons of avgas into plastic containers and stack them in the Humvee. It was a small airport with fourteen hangars and without a zed in the vicinity. After we scared off the lone dog, we checked out each hangar. Unfortunately, not a single plane would start. We could jump start a couple, but I was hoping to find a plane that started without any issues the first time. Call me superstitious, but I felt more comfortable in a plane that didn't need encouragement to run.

After burning two hours there, we moved on to the second airport, which was only twelve miles away. The drive was peaceful, and I found it odd how not a single zed shambled around. No animals roamed the fields —the packs of dogs seemed to stay near towns. Every field we passed could've come straight out of a Bob Ross painting.

The second airport was larger than the first, with both a paved and a grass runway. I didn't like the row of trees off the end of the paved runway. Too many things—both two-legged and four-legged—could be hiding in there. The airport had twice as many hangars, with a large corporate hangar close to the airport office. Three zeds watched us from inside the office, and we quickly dispatched them.

This time, we only had to go through three hangars to find a plane that started. A big Cessna 210. It was more complex than anything I'd flown before, but it had four seats and could be loaded down with anything we could stuff into it. Like enough fuel to get us to the capital and back home again.

I gave one final look at the plane and put my hands on my hips. "Project Moose Jaw is a go."

"You're so adorable when you try to talk Army," Griz said as he and Clutch pulled the hangar door closed.

An eagle soared overhead, and I watched it ride a thermal. My soul lifted. Soon, I'd be up there again, like that eagle.

Our last stop of the day was Picadilly and Connie's house. The only other time we'd been there before, we'd left in a hurry. Since that visit two months ago, the squadron dropped off a box of food every other week... up until the snowstorm, when all travel had been halted.

We drove past the small store that served as a New Eden outpost and pulled up outside the two-story house. We cautiously stepped through undisturbed snow and up porch steps. I looked through the window. A wilted peace lily sat in the center of the kitchen table. "Looks like nobody's been here for a while."

After throwing a quick glance at Griz and me, Clutch knocked on the front door. "Sister Picadilly? Connie? We're from New Eden. Anyone home?" He waited for a minute before knocking again. "We're coming in."

He turned the handle and then shoved his shoulder into the door. It burst open, and we stepped inside. No fire burned in the fireplace, and I could see my breath. The boxes the squadron delivered sat in the kitchen, filled with empty cans and garbage.

"Hello?" Clutch called out.

I looked around. "Maybe they're out."

"Yeah, maybe they went to the mall," Griz said.

I flipped him off and followed Clutch up the stairs.

As soon as the smell hit me, I reached for my machete. *Death.*

Zeds smelled like death.

Two doors were open. The only closed door was to the same room Henry had been in when we were here last time. Griz moved from behind me and checked the first of the open bedrooms while Clutch checked the other. I stood in the hallway and watched the closed door, while glancing down the stairs every few seconds.

When Clutch and Griz returned, they moved to the closed door. I stayed behind them. Clutch rapped his knuckles on the door. Nothing. He looked back to Griz who nodded, and Clutch opened the door.

No zed jumped out, and Clutch stepped inside. Griz followed.

"What the hell?" Griz said.

"What is it?" I asked, still keeping an eye on the hallway.

Neither answered, and both emerged from the room and closed the door.

I looked at both of them. "What's in there?"

"They're dead," Clutch said. "All three of them."

I frowned while I tried to make sense of his words. "They'd survived so long. Why would they give up now?"

"Oh, they didn't give up," Griz said and brushed past me.

"What? What do you mean?"

"They were killed," Clutch replied.

"Are you sure?" I asked. "There weren't any signs of violence downstairs."

"Trust me," he said. "They didn't die by their own hands. Whoever killed them was thorough."

"Oh." Thankful I wouldn't have the images of the corpses of Picadilly, Connie, and Henry seared into my brain, I followed Clutch downstairs. "They were good people. Who would do such a thing?"

Downstairs, Griz stood by the back door and held up a hand. He made a gesture to Clutch, who nodded and moved closer to him. Clutch looked at me, held up his hand, and then pointed at the ground. *Stay here.* I frowned but nodded, not moving. What had Griz seen or heard?

Griz opened the door, and the two took silent steps outside. I moved to the door but didn't go outside. Clutch and Griz were at the small detached garage. They slammed open the door and rushed inside. A racket ensued as though an entire shelf of paint cans fell at once. Someone shouted and then there was eerie silence.

After an interminably long minute, Clutch and Griz emerged, dragging an unconscious man with greasy brown hair between them. I ran outside and stopped cold when I recognized who they'd found. He had three fingers missing from his left hand.

I felt myself grow faint.

Hodge.

NINETEEN

Christmas day

Hodge wasn't dead. The leader of the Black Sheep—Camp Fox's captor—was alive. He bore a scar from where my bullet had skimmed his neck. If my shot had been one inch more accurate, the murderer would've been dead.

I stood outside the silo, my shirt doing nothing to block the cold air. "They'd be alive if I'd killed him when I'd had the chance."

"It's not your fault, so get that thought out of your head," Jase said while he rolled snow into a ball. "There aren't any guarantees in this life. Picadilly and the others could've just as easily been killed by zeds or animals than by Hodge. That you clipped him while he was speeding away with his tail between his legs is amazing enough."

I sighed and rested my head against the concrete wall. "I can't believe that he's been near New Eden for months. We've been feeding him. For all we know, we led him to the house, and he killed them."

"You can spend all day wondering what happened, but unless he talks, we'll never know. So, quit beating yourself up over it."

"But, Camp Fox is gone because of him. He killed so many people...Tyler—"

"I know," Jase said softly before scowling and tossing the snowball at a tree. "But, he's not going to hurt anyone else ever again."

I sighed. "Yeah, I guess you're right."

He stuck out his chest. "Of course I'm right. Now, let's get inside before we freeze to death out here."

We entered the silo to find a flurry of activity. I stopped the first person we came to. "What's going on? I didn't think the Christmas stuff was starting for a couple hours yet."

"Justin decided to get Hodge's trial out of the way. They're bringing him up now."

Jase and I glanced at each other, and we both hustled toward the control room, which served as town hall. Justin stood there, with Dr. Edmund at his side. Clutch and Griz, surrounded by a dozen other guards, led a bound Hodge up the steps and before Justin.

Hodge was clean now, a stark difference from how he'd been a few hours earlier. My brain would be forever scarred with seeing his naked body after we brought him to New Eden. I'd stood guard while Clutch and Griz had stripped him out of his flea- and lice-infested clothes before bringing him into the silo. The man hadn't bathed in months and reeked of sweat and shit. He'd even had the gall to wag his tongue at me when he stood naked in the snow.

"Like what you see, don't ya," he'd said.

"Not impressed," I'd said drily.

Clutch had also replied for me with a punch to Hodge's stomach. I'd smiled when the man was bent over, dry heaving his guts out. It was then I'd seen the scar across the side of his throat—the one I gave him.

He should've been dead.

Instead, he stood in New Eden, healthy and fed.

"Hodge, you have been judged and found guilty by a jury of New Eden citizens. You are here today to receive sentencing for your crimes in leading a group of bandits into ruthlessly attacking, without provocation, the peaceful citizens of New Eden, Camp Fox, and other groups of survivors. Your Black Sheep are responsible for over one hundred murders of innocent people, including children. You have been a festering sore on the communities working hard to rebuild after the outbreak. What do you have to say for yourself?"

Hodge spat on the floor. "Fuck you."

"So be it," Justin said. "Whether you live or die will be in the hands of fate."

Hodge laughed. "You think you can live like you could before? That you can have laws and jails? That's bullshit. The zeds have already won the war. To survive, you have to be like the zeds. You have to take what you need, or else you'll die. Hell, you're dead already. You just don't know it yet."

"It's ironic you say you must be like the zeds," Justin said. "Because, in a way, that's your punishment."

Hodge cocked his head.

Justin continued. "Our people are working on a vaccine against the virus. We lost our lead researcher two days ago, but our research team, with the guidance of Dr. Edmund, has isolated an antigen. You will serve as its test subject. If you survive, you will serve out the rest of your life, however long it may be, in a tiny prison cell."

"Ha," Hodge called out. "Give me what you got. I'll outlive you all."

"We shall see." Justin motioned to Dr. Edmund.

The doctor stepped forward with a syringe. We all watched in silence as Dr. Edmund injected Hodge with the antigen.

"It's done," the doctor said and took a step back.

I prayed Hodge survived, because I wanted to be the one who killed him.

TWENTY

Six days later

The fucker survived. He hadn't even caught a serious fever.

I was one of the four guards on duty at the lab, and tried not to look at him while he ate New Eden food. Hodge was still imprisoned in the small house's dank cellar. One of his ankles was handcuffed to a chain that looped around the stairs. Each wrist was handcuffed to a chain looped through a cinderblock. No one was taking any chances at him escaping, though he seemed quite content to be in captivity.

No surprise there. He was safe, well fed, and didn't have to do shit for any of it.

He scooped up rice with his fingers (we refused to give him a spoon) and examined it. "This could use some salt," he said and popped it into his mouth.

We ignored him. Zach and I were stuck in the basement with him, while Jase and Hali were upstairs. We rotated with them every hour during our shift to keep Hodge from grinding too deeply on our nerves. Though, he tended to grind on my nerves within five minutes of every hour I spent in that basement.

"You know, your timing at picking me up was perfect. I just finished the last can of food you guys so generously dropped off."

I started a mental count to ten, trying my best to ignore him. Zach walked slowly over to Hodge, lifted his foot, and shoved the prisoner onto his back. Then, he snatched the bowl of rice, dumped it in the pail that served as Hodge's latrine, and returned to his position.

I gave Zach a grin.

Hodge pulled himself back up. "That wasn't nice. I wasn't finished yet."

"Oh, sorry," I said, my words laced with sarcasm. "With the way you kept yammering on and on, we assumed you must've been full."

He watched me for a moment and cocked his head. "Have we met?"

When I didn't answer, he continued. "You seem awfully familiar. Every day, I try to remember where I've seen you before. Have we fucked?"

I shot him a quick glare and turned back away.

"Don't worry. I'll remember, eventually."

I turned to face him then. "I'm surprised you don't remember me. You could say I left a lasting impression." I said as I ran my finger along the side of my throat.

When the meaning of my words hit him, his face tightened in an expression of pure rage. "You. You were a part of the group that put a hurtin' on my Sheep. I got stranded after that little adventure and didn't make it back to my Sheep until they'd all been wiped out, no thanks to the dickless wonders at New Eden." He chuckled drily. "And, you guys say you're peaceful. How many people have you killed?"

"We kill only those who've attacked innocents," Zach said.

"Innocents? Bah. There are no innocents anymore. All the innocents are rotting away while they eat their own families."

"Too bad the vaccine worked on you," Zach said. "I was looking forward to seeing you turn into one of those things."

Hodge sneered. "Instead, I have free room and board, and my own personal security detail. I'd say things worked out pretty good."

Zach's brow rose. "Pretty good, huh? You think Justin is going to keep you here and feed you? You really think that? You don't know Justin very well then."

Hodge's lips thinned.

Zach continued. "I can guarantee that whatever Justin is planning for you involves pain. Lots and lots of pain."

"We'll see about that," Hodge said. "I heard the lab rat talking upstairs. My blood carries the cure now. I'm carrying precious cargo."

Zach spoke. "Didn't you hear? Bonnie's done with you. That last liter of blood she took was all they needed to finish their research. Now, you're baggage." With that, Zach sat on his chair and stared at Hodge.

The prisoner turned his attention back onto me. His features relaxed, and his lips curled upward. "I remember you. You're the whore of one of those men my Sheep caught. You begged so pretty. I was looking forward to seeing what else you'd beg for."

I'd cried out when Hodge held a gun to Clutch's held, and I didn't regret it. My plea had saved his life. "You never would've gotten me to beg for anything else," I said.

"Oh, you would've begged. They *always* begged."

I heard boots hitting each step. Jase, then Hali, came into view. Their shoulders slumped; they looked as excited to be in this basement as I felt. "Thank God," I muttered, and turned from Hodge without another glance.

"Oh, goody," Hodge said from behind. "My favorite girl is back."

"Fuck you," Jase and Hali said at the same time.

"Soon enough, that's a promise," Hodge replied.

Jase sighed and shook his head.

Hali glanced at me. "I'm so glad this is our last hour for the day."

I gave her a knowing glance. "I promise."

With that, I took the stairs two at a time. Hodge was still talking when I reached the first floor, and Zach soon followed.

"Some folks grow on you over time," Zach said. "But, he's not one of them."

I dramatically shook my head. "No, he's not."

In the living room, the two kids were watching their same cartoon, while Bonnie was putting labels on vials. She glanced up. "I'll have everything packed and ready to go by tonight. Dr. Edmund said to keep everything below forty degrees and above freezing if you can. The samples can save the capital thousands of hours of work so they don't have to start from scratch from only Dr. Gidar's research notes."

"That shouldn't be a problem," I said. "As long as the weather holds, we'll head out first thing in the morning."

"What a way to kick off the New Year," Zach said before taking a seat by the kids. The boy looked at him, and Zach raised his hand. The boy mimicked, and Zach slowly moved his hand around. Zach looked up, surprised. "Hey, he's improving."

"They have good days and bad days," Bonnie said. "Without Dr. Gidar, we can't do anything for them except keep them comfortable and hope for the best. He planned to focus on the children once he worked out a vaccine. He truly was a brilliant man."

"Yeah," I agreed. Not only did his research lead to a possible vaccine, his blood had been the breakthrough he'd been looking for. His calculations and tests had gotten him as far as he could go. When he introduced the antigen to his own system, the antigen became stronger, but too much of the live virus had been included. It had taken Dr. Edmund—a general practitioner—only a few hours of testing Dr. Gidar's blood to verify the results and find Dr. Gidar's mistake. The doctor hadn't purified the antigen before injecting himself.

Fortunately, the hour passed quickly. Griz and three other guards arrived, and I pulled on my coat with gusto. "Have fun with him," I said. "He's a talker today."

A smile crept up Griz's face. "He can talk. But, he won't like what I do to him every time he opens that pie hole."

I grinned as Griz and his partner headed down to the basement. When Jase and Hali came upstairs, they joined Zach and me on the long walk back to the silo. On our walk, we met Vicki, who had her eyes narrowed in an intense stare focused on the lab in front of her.

"Hi Vicki," I said. "Heading to the lab?"

Startled, she looked at us. She lifted the bag slightly. "I thought I'd bring some treats to Bonnie and the kids."

"They'll like that," Jase said.

She nodded and then continued on her way.

"Wow, she was in the zone," Hali said. "I don't think she would've even noticed us if you hadn't said something."

"She's had a lot on her mind. Seeing Hodge again really upset her,"

"I'm surprised she'd go anywhere near the lab with him in it," Jase said.

"Yeah," I said.

Vicki had been Camp Fox's cook, and she had developed more than a little crush on Tyler. She'd been resilient. No matter what happened, she'd always been rational and strong. Then, she'd watched Hodge kill Tyler in front of her. After that, she was still strong, but she was quieter, more distant. When we brought Hodge into the silo, I saw the pain in her eyes. At that moment, it was as though she was watching Tyler die all over again.

The only other people we met on our walk were the guards at each gate. The dogs were building in numbers again. Once the weather warmed somewhat, they showed back up, with their numbers doubling every day. They were starving. The sunlight cast shadows under rib bones and hipbones. I wanted to feed them, but I knew that would only draw more to us. And they were sick. While Bonnie said Dr. Gidar had told her the vaccine might also have some effect on dog bites, he hadn't done any analysis to validate the possibility.

"Poor things," Hali said.

"Those poor things want to eat you," Zach said.

Hali didn't reply.

"It does suck, though," Jase said. "To think most of those dogs were people's pets at one time, and now they're sick and breeding out here. I wonder if there's hope for any of them."

"Some will survive," I said optimistically. "I would think they're like us. Some of us are surviving the outbreak. Some of them will, too."

"I hope so." After that, Jase said nothing else until we reached the silo and headed to our bunks.

I spent the next few hours with Clutch, planning our trip to the capital. It would be the longest flight I'd taken without GPS, so I wanted to be accurate on my flight plan, with any possible landing sites marked along the way.

Justin didn't have any radio frequency, let alone address, so I decided to fly into the Canadian Air Force base at Moose Jaw. I figured if any airport in the area were operational, it'd be that one.

At some point, Justin stopped by. "You two have a minute?"

"Sure," I said, stretching my stiff neck.

Justin looked at each of us. "Hodge is dead."

"He was alive and annoyingly well earlier today," I said.

"I'm sure he was. But, a couple dozen stab wounds didn't help."

"Wow," was all I said.

"Either of you have anything to do with it?"

My eyes widened. I looked at Clutch, who looked just as surprised, and back at Justin. "No. Not at all."

"This is the first I've heard of it," Clutch said.

Justin nodded and looked around. "Well, I figured as much. Griz and Joachim said they'd stepped away for only a few minutes. They said Hodge must've gotten a hold of a knife and stabbed himself. I think death by dozens of stab wounds is an interesting way to commit suicide."

"I'll talk to my people," Clutch said. "We had him under twenty-four hour surveillance. And none of my people had the authority to harm him unless he attempted escape. Griz would never disobey an order."

Justin shrugged. "It's okay. Hodge's death isn't a loss to New Eden, especially now that we have the antigen Dr. Gidar was seeking. If anything, it saves us time and resources. There will be an investigation, but I suspect we won't find anything. You know how these things go."

Clutch tilted his head into an almost nod.

"Well," Justin continued. "No need to keep you. You have to fly out early tomorrow. Get some rest. Just think, once the capital can create and distribute the vaccine to everyone, there will never be another zed again. Imagine that."

Once he left, I looked at Clutch. "Did you order Hodge's death?"

"I had nothing to do with his death."

"Do you think Griz did?"

"Griz wouldn't have killed him, not without talking it over with me first."

"You think Justin ordered it?"

"If he did, why ask us about it?"

I sighed. "Well, then we have a vigilante around here."

Part Seven

Temperance

Twenty-One

Clutch, Griz, Zach, and I had doused ourselves with no-scent spray made for hunters. We figured it couldn't hurt in case we came across any dogs at the airport. I'd never thought of using the stuff until we found some in the store at Des Moines. I mused if it would also work to mask our scent from zeds.

Jase was pissed that we were taking Zach instead of him, but Clutch had been obstinate. He refused to take Jase, because that meant Hali would come, and if things went to shit, Jase would be distracted if Hali got hurt. Jase denied there was anything between him and Hali, but Clutch refused nonetheless.

"Weren't you being a tad hypocritical back there?" I asked as we walked toward the Humvee, carrying a small cooler. "You're as bad as Jase."

Clutch shot a look at me. "What do you mean?"

"What if something happened to me? You'd be distracted, too."

"Nothing will happen," he said gruffly. "I'll make sure of it."

I shook my head and chuckled drily. "You're such a he-man."

"It's not that you can't take care of yourself," he said. "I know you're more than capable. It's that," he paused, "I want to take care of you."

I let his words linger for a minute before speaking. "I think that's the most romantic thing you've ever said to me."

He didn't smile. Instead, he reached out and pulled me to him. "I mean it," he said quietly.

"No one's getting lucky on this trip," Griz said as he walked around us. "Not unless I'm the one getting lucky."

"You think you'll find some sheep on this trip?" Clutch asked.

Griz flipped him off and didn't look back again as he headed to the Humvee.

I laughed. Griz was a hot catch for any woman. Even with men outnumbering women seven to one in New Eden, women flocked to him. It was likely because he was young, able-bodied, and easy to get along with. Jase and I, though, gave him crap about it. We picked on him that the ladies were intent on finding out if the "once you go black" urban legend was actually true. Griz denied it and said it was his sparkling personality.

Griz dropped his gear into the back of the vehicle before climbing into the driver's seat. Everyone else's gear was loaded into the remaining cargo space. We'd loaded the avgas for the plane yesterday. We had more gear than usual since we had no idea how long the thousand-mile trip could take. Before the outbreak, I could've flown to Moose Jaw in less than six hours flight time, not counting a fuel stop and immigration check.

In the middle of winter, we had about eight hours of sunlight each day. We were planning to make Moose Jaw tomorrow, stopping this afternoon to refuel and camp down for the night. Doing anything after dark was dangerous and a risk none of us were willing to take.

The sun hadn't yet peeked over the horizon; we had a good head start on the day. When we reached the airport, everything was still and silent. No new zeds appeared in the office window. No dogs sniffed around the hangar when Zach pushed the door open. The white Cessna with a yellow and orange stripe sat patiently inside. I smiled and tapped the engine cowl. "Soon, baby. You'll be dancing on the clouds soon."

We pulled the plane out of the hangar. Clutch and I topped off the fuel while Griz and Zach loaded as much fuel as they could fit into the baggage. The rest of our gear would have to sit on our laps. The plane was going to be weighted down. It'd need much of the runway, but I'd done my calculations. We'd get off the ground. On a hot, humid day, we might not be so lucky. But the cold air was a pilot's friend. Cold air was more dense, which meant it provided more lift. An airplane could lift off the ground easier and faster, and that was exactly what I needed for today.

"It's full." I handed Clutch the half-full fuel jug. Before sliding down, I sat on the top wing another minute and watched the tip of the sun break the horizon. It was going to be a beautiful sunrise, one of those fiery orange ones. Movement in the direction of the airport office caught the corner of my eye, and I squinted to make out the dark shapes emerging from the tree line in the distance.

I sucked in a breath.

Clutch held out a hand to help me down. "Ready?"

I glanced down at him, my eyes wide.

"What's wrong?"

"We're being stalked." I pointed in the direction of the animals.

Clutch moved away to see for himself. "Griz, Zach. We need to get a move on. We've got company coming for breakfast."

Griz and Zach were holding the last of our bags, and Griz closed the back of the Humvee. He looked in the direction of the dogs. "Sneaky little bastards."

"They couldn't have smelled us," Zach said.

"They could've heard us," I said as I slid down the windshield to stand on the engine cowl. "The Humvee isn't exactly a stealth vehicle."

"Shit." I glanced over to see Zach drop everything and kick at something. "Get away!"

Clutch grabbed his sword and ran over the same time Griz slammed his machete down on something. Clutch swung and a yelp echoed through the morning air. They each kept swinging until I saw three furred shapes lay lifeless on the ground.

Zach lifted his pant leg and looked up at the other two men. "Did you see them? Were they sick?"

"Yeah," Clutch said.

"Yeah, you saw them, or yeah, they were sick?" Zach asked.

A pause, then, "Both."

Zach swung his fist through the air. "Shit."

"Come on," Clutch said. "We've got to go."

Zach didn't move. "I think I'll sit this one out."

"They'll have a hospital at the capital. They can help."

"The earliest we'll reach them is tomorrow. By then, I'll be dead weight. No, I think I'll stick around here, watch the sun rise, and then head back to New Eden."

After a long moment, Clutch nodded tightly.

Griz patted Zach on the shoulder. "Take care of yourself." He grabbed his bags and put them into the plane.

Zach picked up the bags and handed them to Clutch. "I'll try to get their attention, draw them away from the plane and runway."

Zach looked my way and faked a grin. "Be careful with these two losers."

I forced a smile as well, while tears blurred my vision. "See you when we get back," I lied.

Unable to look at Zach without losing it, I slid off the Cessna and climbed into the pilot's seat. I pulled out the airplane's checklist, which I had spent hours studying last night, and laid it on my lap.

Clutch and Griz climbed in while I quickly went through each of the steps. I engaged the starter, and the Cessna's engine roared to life. The noise spurred the animals into action. No longer stalking, they ran toward the plane, slowing as they approached.

Suddenly, the Humvee sped in front of us, scattering the dogs and wolves in all directions. I taxied forward, using the distance to warm up the engine enough for takeoff. Zach drove the Humvee like a mad man, zigzagging around the airport and throwing the animals off their game.

When we reached the runway, I did a fast run-up on the engine before throttling back. I looked at both Clutch and Griz. "You guys buckled in?"

Clutch held up his thumb, and Griz said, "Let's rock and roll."

I checked the prop and mixture one last time, pressed the throttle in, and the engine roared. The plane moved forward, slowly at first, then quickly picking up speed. Even without Zach, the plane was weighted down, and the wheels didn't pop off until we were two-thirds of the way down the paved runway.

Careful to keep our climb shallow, I looked down to see the Humvee come to a stop, and animals gathered around it, as though waiting for treats. I shivered and fought to stay focused on flying. If I dwelled on the fact we'd lost a man before the mission even started, then I'd be tempted to return to the safety of New Eden.

But I'd made a promise. A promise worth keeping, even if it killed me.

PART EIGHT
HOPE

Twenty-Two

"Things sure look different from up here," Griz said. "I could get used to traveling first-class."

"I was beginning to think you were going to sleep the entire trip," I said.

"I wasn't sleeping," he countered.

"You were snoring," I said.

"You snore like a rhino with a head cold," Clutch added.

"You guys make this shit up," Griz said. "I'm too pretty to snore."

Smiling, I looked out at the endless earth beneath us. At this altitude, we couldn't see anything moving, which gave the world a serenity I hadn't felt in a long time. Unplowed roads hid under a blanket of pure white, with no tire tracks or road salt to taint the snow. Trees and quiet houses were all that broke the rolling landscape.

Clutch looked up from the map. "Adjust ten degrees west."

I did as he instructed and savored the feeling of flying. I knew my days of stick and rudders were limited. At some point, all fuel would break down enough that no plane would run.

Clutch pointed in the distance where the horizon loomed higher. "We'll fly right over the Black Hills. Should be quite the view."

Boy, was it ever. Tree-covered hills went on farther than we could see. It was nature's splendor, untouched by the virus. I sighed. "I want to find a cabin and retire here." I looked to Clutch. "How about it? Want to retire here?"

He smiled. "I'm all for that."

The Black Hills soon gave way to North Dakota's flatlands, whose simple landscape had its own flavor of surreal peace. Once we flew over the bombed ruins of Bismarck, we approached the point of our journey to refuel and stay overnight. I began our descent and watched the trees for signs of the wind's direction and strength. "We're lucky," I said. "Hardly a breeze today."

The airport came into view from nearly ten miles away. That was an advantage of flatter land. About twenty other buildings dotted the airport on a circular drive. I read through my checklist several times before handing it over to Clutch. "I'll fly over to make sure the runway is clear," I said. "Then we'll come back around and land."

Except for a snowdrift at one end of the runway, the rest of the pavement was relatively clear. "We got lucky," I said. "I was afraid we'd have to deal with snow, but they must've gotten some strong winds here."

Clutch read each step on the checklist to me as I flew the pattern and lined up on final. Adrenaline pumped through my veins and I clenched the yoke. "Guys, you better make sure you're buckled in tight. I've never landed anything as big as this plane before."

I was a few hundred feet off the ground when the stall alert sounded. "Shit," I muttered, realizing I was trying to land the 210 like my Cub instead of like the much-heavier airplane it was. I added in power to pick up speed and lowered the rest of the flaps.

The runway came up way too fast, and I clenched my teeth as I brought the plane down. I made the mistake and let it drop, and the plane jumped right off the ground. After porpoising through another bounce, the plane settled on the ground. But, the snowdrift at the end of the runway was quickly approaching, and I slammed on the brakes. Clutch grabbed the dash to keep from crashing into the instruments. Gear banged around, and something slammed against the back of my seat.

The plane came to a stop less than ten feet from the snowdrift. After a moment of stillness, I breathed. "Wow, that wasn't pretty."

Griz laughed. "Pretty? More like it was the damn near scariest thing I've ever seen."

"I guess I should've done a go-around."

"We're alive," Clutch said. "And the plane will fly again. I hope."

"I'm a bit rusty," I said as I turned the plane around and taxied toward the buildings. "And, in my defense, this plane is three times the size of my Cub."

"You did fine," Clutch said. "You're the best pilot I know."

"I'm the *only* pilot you know."

He shrugged and looked outside.

"How about I park by the airport office?" I asked.

"Which one is that?" Griz asked.

I pointed at the first building we'd reach. "I think that's the one."

"Looks as good as any," Clutch said.

"It's closest to the runway in case we need to make a fast exit," Griz said.

I taxied toward the small building, which bore the sign, *Welcome to Garrison Municipal Airport.* Three planes were tied down on the ramp, with small patches of snow accumulated around their tires. I pulled up to the small building and looked at its windows and glass door. "How's it look?" I asked. "We have a little over a quarter tank if we need to find another place."

"And have to go through another one of those landings?" Griz said. "Nah, this is good."

"You can fly next time," I offered.

"That landing was great," Griz said. "No complaints here."

I parked the plane and cut the engine, and Clutch climbed out first, following by Griz. With weapons drawn, they approached the small building. I stayed in the plane in case we had to make a hasty retreat. They checked the door, the windows, and walked around the building.

The nearest town had less than two thousand people, which was why I selected this airport. It was big enough to have a runway I could use, but small enough that there shouldn't be a great risk of zeds or wild animals. Bandits were another story. There never seemed to be any rhyme or reason as to where those assholes showed up.

A moment later, Clutch reappeared and gave the all-clear, and I climbed out. I reached into the backseat and grabbed my backpack, which was what had flown loose during landing. The cooler still sat, safe, on the floorboard. I opened the baggage and began unloading fuel containers while Clutch and Griz argued over how best to break into the locked office. Ignoring them, I found a ladder near the airport's fuel tanks and began to refuel the Cessna.

I sighed when I saw the pay-at-pump machine and missed the days of easy convenience. Now, however many hundreds of gallons were waiting in the airport's fuel tank would wait in there forever. Six plastic containers later, the Cessna was refueled and ready to go. I checked the oil and frowned.

"What's wrong?"

"Jesus." I dropped the dipstick. After I picked it up, I turned and scowled at Clutch. "Don't sneak up on me like that. Trying to give me a heart attack?"

"I didn't sneak up on you."

"You didn't mean to, but you did," I said. "It's that Ranger thing. Griz does it, too. You guys are just like sneaky little kittens right before they pounce."

Clutch straightened. "I am *not* a kitten."

"Kitten or not," I said. "Can you find me some oil? We're running a couple quarts low already."

"Only if you promise to never call me 'kitten' again."

I thought about it for an exaggerated moment. "Okay, I promise."

Clutch smiled. "I'll find you some oil. What kind do you need?"

I shrugged.

"Okay," he said. "I'll find you something."

"Luckily, tomorrow will be a shorter flight, so we shouldn't burn quite as much oil. Plus, we'll have plenty of fuel left."

"Let's hope we won't need it."

"I give up," Griz said from several feet away. He threw down the screwdriver.

"You were trying to pick a lock with a screwdriver?" I asked.

He rolled his eyes. "Aw, shucks. Why didn't I think of that? I left my lock picking kit at home."

He picked up the brick doorstop sitting by the door.

Clutch spoke. "Don't break—"

Griz smashed the brick into the door. Glass shattered and shards fell.

"What are we going to use for a door now?" Clutch asked.

Griz shrugged. "You're smart. Figure something out." He reached through, unlocked the door, and peered inside. "Hello? Anybody home?"

After a long moment, Griz turned back to us. "Smells fresh enough." He held the door open. "After you, my lady."

"Why, thank you," I said with a curtsy and stepped inside.

Griz must've been confident there were no dangers inside, or else he never would've let me go in first. Both Clutch and he were a lot alike. They always were the first ones to walk into danger.

Glass crunched under my boots as I crossed the tiled floor and grabbed several sectional maps for areas I didn't yet have. "This place is brand new," I said. "Most small airport offices are falling apart."

"There's your oil," Clutch said, pointing at a box by a display case.

"Well, that was easy," I said. "I should've held back from making that promise."

"Promise or no promise, it's the right thing to do."

I shrugged before testing the couch. "Ooh. Dibs on the couch."

"Go ahead," Griz said from the hallway. "I'm taking a recliner."

I followed him into the pilot's lounge where two leather recliners sat in addition to a workstation. After we checked the restrooms, we broke into the vending machines and stocked up on candy bars. I left the chips for someone else, as most chips tasted too stale anymore.

Ten minutes later, we'd each downed a soda and candy bars. No one had spoken for a while, and I had something to get off my chest. "Hey, Griz?"

"Yep?" he mumbled after tossing a handful of Reese's Pieces into his mouth.

"What really happened to Hodge?"

His chewing paused for a moment before continuing. "He died."

Clutch was carefully watching Griz.

"Did you kill him?" I asked.

"Nope."

"But, you did have something to do with it," Clutch said.

Griz shrugged. "There was someone who wanted him dead more than I did."

I leaned back when the pieces fell into place. The last time I saw her, she'd seemed like a weight had been lifted from her shoulders. It had been so obvious, yet I hadn't even thought of her. "Vicki."

Griz didn't respond, which was as much an affirmation as agreement.

After a while, Griz spoke. "We all wanted to do it. The bastard deserved it. She shouldn't be punished for delivering justice."

"She won't," Clutch said. "Hodge killed himself. End of story."

"End of story," I echoed.

"He begged," Griz said. "When we let her at him, he begged like the pansy he was."

"Good," Clutch said.

I inhaled deeply. I wanted to find pleasure in Hodge's death, but I only found retribution. It was good enough, and I took another bite.

Once we were full of food, we lounged around the office. It was cold in there and would be uncomfortable tonight, even with the small camp stove Clutch had brought along. But, it was better than flying at night and arriving at Moose Jaw in the dark.

I sat at the desk and perused the drawers for anything useful. In the drawer with pens and rubber bands, I found a key chain with a single car key on it. "Hey guys?"

"What's up?" Griz replied.

"Either of you see a Dodge parked around here somewhere?"

"Yep. A nice Dodge Challenger was parked in back."

I tossed him the key chain. "That must be their loaner car."

Griz smiled. "Nice." And he headed out the door.

A moment later, I heard a car start. My eyes widened. "I'm surprised it started."

Clutch, who had been lying on my couch, sat up and rubbed his stiff shoulder.

Griz hurried back in. "Anyone in the mood to check out the area?"

Clutch pushed himself up with a grunt. "Not a bad idea. Any locals would've heard us fly in. It would be good to know what kinds of risks we might have to deal with tonight."

I pulled my gloves on. "Let me lock the plane."

Once I locked the plane doors, we all stood in front of the airport office, staring at the broken glass door.

"I told you not to break it," Clutch said.

Griz held up a finger. "Hold on."

He disappeared back inside, the sound of pounding and banging ensued, and Griz returned with a wood door with a *Ladies* sign on it.

I sighed. "What am I going to use now for privacy?"

"You can use the guys' bathroom."

I scrunched my face. "You know how disgusting guys' bathrooms are?"

He didn't answer. Instead, he propped the door behind the other and pulled out some paracord. Once he had it tied onto the metal bar in the door, he took a step back and put his hands on his hips. Pride gleaned in his smile. "Problem fixed."

Clutch narrowed his eyes. "I could sneeze and knock that door down."

"I'd like to see you do better," Griz said.

"Well, it's enough that if any animals or zeds tried to get through, we'd know," I said. "But, it sure wouldn't stop a person with an IQ above forty."

Griz blew us off and headed toward the car. I climbed into the backseat, and enjoyed being chauffeured.

Griz played it safe, carefully plowing through snowdrifts. He stopped after we made a full circle of the airport.

"I could get used to this," I said, enjoying the quiet. We saw only a few animal tracks and no zed tracks. No tire tracks besides ours. Out here, it felt as though we were the only ones left in the world.

"Let's check out how many tracks there are at the edge of town," Clutch said. "It's close enough to the airport that it could be a problem."

Griz agreed. "My thoughts, too."

I enjoyed the view and heated air as Griz weaved down roads toward the town.

"Stop," Clutch commanded.

Griz hit the brakes. "What do you see?"

Clutch pointed to the right. "See those soccer fields over there?"

I slid across the seat to look out. The fields were still a half mile away, but something wasn't right about them. Instead of open fields, tall fences enclosed rows of white trailers lined up like they would be in a RV park. Griz drove toward the soccer fields, and I watched as we approached the fields. Zeds—at least a couple hundred—stood around. Reinforced fences surrounded the fields.

As we approached, no zeds moved, but I sensed their gazes upon us. "There are so many of them."

"They're frozen," Clutch said.

Griz brought the car to a stop not far from the fields. "This must've been a FEMA camp set up during the outbreak. It did a good job at containing them. The fences are still standing."

"Not quite," I said, and pointed to a place in the fence where a tunnel had been dug under. Dirt sat upon snow. Inside the fence, streaks of brown zed sludge stains led to the tunnel. Two large dogs were yanking at a frozen zed in a morbid game of tug o' war. The zed had no face—it had already been torn off by the dogs. When the zed fell, the dogs continued to pull. One fell back with its prize: an arm. The second dog soon followed with the other arm.

They carried their "food" back to the fence and crawled under. When they crossed the road, they paused to look at us. Deeming us no threat, they continued away from town, one of the dogs dragging the leash still connected to its collar.

"Wow," was all I managed to say after the dogs disappeared.

"It's like a deep freezer full of beef for them," Clutch said.

Griz chuckled drily as he turned the car around and started back toward the airport. "Now, that's the definition of irony."

"How so?" I asked.

"Zeds hunted the dogs. Now, the dogs hunt zeds."

Nothing about this felt ironic. It felt sad. Beloved pets had been abandoned and forced to do awful things to survive. They weren't much different from us, I suppose. We'd done some pretty awful things in the name of survival, too.

I noticed Clutch was eying me, and I tried to give him my "I'm okay" look.

But, it was hard to fake it when I knew we were nowhere close to being out of the woods yet.

TWENTY-THREE

After a cold night, we were anxious to sit in a warm airplane as soon as the sun rose the following morning. The Cessna lifted off the runway easier today, with less weight than when we'd taken off in Nebraska yesterday morning.

Clutch checked the airplane's clock. "We have under three hundred miles left, so we'll be there in roughly two hours, give or take."

"We'll have to be careful when we get close to Moose Jaw," I said. "We know they have an operational air force, and I'm not sure how they are at welcoming other folks flying into their airspace."

"We'll find out soon enough," Griz said.

Clutch dialed in numbers on the radio. "The radio's set to the frequencies listed on the map. If they've changed them, we won't have any way to know unless they're transmitting them."

When we were one hundred miles out, Clutch began to transmit our intention and location on the radio. When we were fifty miles out, someone responded.

"806 Romeo Bravo, this is Wing 15. Squawk 1219."

Clutch read back the instructions and set our transponder to 1219 so they could track us. When we were only ten miles out, the tower fed us landing instructions, which we followed to a T. When I was on final, I could hear Griz praying in the backseat, and I shot him the bird quickly before focusing on my landing.

Fortunately, for my ego and our well-being, this landing was spot on. When I pulled off the runway, the tower directed me where to go next.

"806 Romeo Bravo, take taxiway Alpha to the FBO."

I taxied toward a large hangar bearing an Air Force sign. A man jogged onto the ramp and flagged me to park at a location not far from the hangar.

"806 Romeo Bravo, cut your engines and stay in the plane until you are authorized."

I smirked. "We're the only plane with its engine running. It's not like they need to keep using our N-number."

"Guess they want to stay in practice," Clutch said.

Once we stopped and I cut the engine, I turned to Clutch. "We made it."

He smiled. "Thanks to you."

I couldn't help myself, and I leaned over and kissed him. "And thanks to my navigator."

"Don't forget me," Griz said. "It was my praying and good luck that got us here safely."

I laughed. "Thank you, Griz, for getting us here."

The flagger approached, and I opened my door to talk with him.

He had a wide smile. "Welcome to Wing 15. We don't see many planes that aren't based here. You can step out and stretch if you need, but please wait by your plane for another minute or two. Our official welcome wagon is on its way."

After a quick glance to each other, we climbed out with our gear, weapons sheathed, and I grabbed the cooler. We stood together. Clutch and Griz stood tall, tense, and still. I fidgeted, waiting to see what came next.

A black SUV came speeding toward us. I found myself shiver, not from cold, but from nerves, as the vehicle came to a stop only ten feet away. The front passenger door and two back doors opened, and three men stepped out, two of them holding machine guns. The third man, a younger one of perhaps twenty or so, walked over to us and smiled. "I'm Peter. Welcome to Moose Jaw, the capital of the Provinces of North America."

Twenty-Four

Peter escorted us into the large hangar where several military jets sat. His armed guards followed ten feet behind us. They had allowed us to keep our weapons, though a machete against a rifle wouldn't exactly be a fair fight.

I knew Clutch and Griz were as on edge as much as I was. We were in a new place, surrounded by unknown people. *Armed* people. And, these people were currently in control.

Despite Clutch and Griz's cool demeanors, I'd bet they were ready to jump into action the instant these people turned hostile. I knew that if they thought anything was off, they'd let me know. They always seemed to know how to handle these situations. I felt much safer that they both came along on this mission.

Peter talked as he led us through the hangar. "Most newcomers are found by our recon teams and brought here. It's pretty rare to have folks fly in here themselves."

"We're from New Eden, in Nebraska," Clutch said.

Griz added, "New Eden's radios were knocked out. Otherwise, we would've called ahead."

"I'm glad you came," Peter said. "We've been worried that something happened to New Eden. We had planned a trip down there, but mechanical issues have been grounding our drones, and fuel for manned flights has been restricted to training and high-priority missions only."

"We have time-sensitive material to get to an expert ASAP," Clutch said.

Peter held up his hand. "Aline already knows you're here, and I'll get you to her as soon as I can. I'm not trying to be a bottleneck, but we have protocols to follow. Before I can bring you into the capital, you need checked for bites or any signs of infection. Don't worry, we'll get you to the people you need to see."

Behind the jets stood a makeshift room built with plastic and tarps. Peter motioned to a person wearing blue rubber gloves. "Mason has done this a thousand times before. It doesn't take long if you do as he says. I'll take you into the capital after you pass inspection. Now if you'll excuse me, I'll need to get time slated on Aline's schedule so you can meet with her today."

"Who's Aline?" I asked.

Peter smiled. "Oh, Aline Palvery is the President of P.N.A., the Provinces of North America."

"I've never met a president before." I looked at Clutch and Griz. "It sounds like we're getting the red carpet treatment today."

"She's a good, strong leader. She does everything she can to get this new country up and running," Mason said. "Now, if you'll come with me, there are two rooms, one for the gentlemen and one for the lady. Set your gear and clothes on the table and step into the shower stall for a medical inspection and chem-bath."

I scowled. "Chem-bath?"

"To kill lice, fleas, and anything else immigrants tend to bring in. It doesn't hurt, I assure you. I've been through it myself." He must've caught my expression because he added, "Not that you guys have lice. It's standard operating procedures, that's all."

We entered the small room, and Mason directed us to our stalls. I eyed Clutch. He gave me a tight nod. I took a deep breath and stepped off to the right and undressed.

Thirty minutes later, after a thorough examination, chem-bath, and a detailed inspection of my backpack, weapons, and cooler, I was dressed and reunited with Clutch and Griz. Guards gave us water and flatbread while we waited in one of the hangar's offices.

Peter arrived soon after, smiling. "You all passed inspection with flying colors." He pulled out white stickers and markers. "If you don't mind, put your name on these, so folks know to introduce themselves."

My brows rose, and I looked at Clutch and Griz, who looked just as humored.

We put on our stickers, and Peter hemmed. "Uh, Cash, Griz, and Clutch? Those are your names?"

"They're the ones we go by," Clutch replied.

"Oh. Okay. Well, if that's the case, it's nice to meet you." He shook each of our hands. "I have an appointment set for you to talk with Aline." He glanced at his watch and motioned to the door. "It's in less than an hour, so we'd better be on our way. You can keep your weapons. Everyone carries in the capital, but the laws are strict. Anyone caught fighting or instigating violence is imprisoned until proven innocent."

He escorted us to the black SUV he had arrived in earlier. This time, he had no guards with him, and the tension eased. He drove us up to a fenced gate and waited for it to open.

"So, what do you do around here?" Griz said. "Besides being the welcome wagon?"

"I'm Aline's assistant," he said. "Basically, whatever she needs, I see that it gets done."

We drove down a mile or so before he reached another gate, this one manned by several armed soldiers. The gate was connected to a tall fence with razor wire that went on seemingly forever.

"Does that fence surround the entire city?"

"It surrounds about half of Moose Jaw," Peter said. "We lost the northern parts of the city before we were able to erect the fence through the center of town to save the southern half. We were one of the first cities that focused on defending our town rather than going after the zeds. That made all the difference between why we're alive today and not zeds."

"I heard you guys opened a can of whoop-ass on the zeds that migrated south," Clutch said.

"We did," Peter said. "And, there's a lot more coming. I'm sure Aline will fill you in."

Inside the fence, Peter drove slower because people were everywhere. Dressed in heavy coats, they moved around, working on construction, pushing carts, and carrying bags. It was a blur of activity.

"Holy crap," I said. "How many people live here?"

"Four thousand three hundred and eight. Eleven if you're staying."

"We're not staying," Clutch said quickly.

"We have family in New Eden," I added.

Peter smiled. "I understand." He motioned toward the city. "We're nowhere near the size of some of the bigger provinces, but we have the most resources. We were the best equipped to reach out to everyone, so it only made sense to establish us as the capital of the P.N.A., which is comprised of what used to be Canada, the U.S., and the northern states of Mexico. Moose Jaw is a good, safe place, though I'm not a big fan of their winters."

"Where are you from?"

"New Mexico. Our weather was a lot better, but unfortunately, the state had developed a problem with none-too-friendly 'illegal aliens.'"

He pulled up to a stop outside a brick building that looked as though it had been the city hall at one time. Different flags lined the sidewalk, and I recognized New Eden's about two-thirds of the way down.

Peter motioned to the flags. "As of today, we oversee twenty-four provinces. This winter has been rough, and we had to take down three flags this month. We were worried we'd have to take down another flag until you showed up today. Even though we're keeping a step ahead of the zeds, the cards are still stacked against us. When we're not fighting with each other, there are still plenty of zeds out there, wildlife is taking back the land with a vengeance, and even Mother Nature seems to be against us."

As we walked to the building, Peter pointed to the cooler I carried. "So, what's in there?"

"This," I lifted the cooler, "will prevent another outbreak from ever happening again."

Twenty-Five

We waited in the hallway while the president wrapped up whatever meeting she had before ours. Clutch looked at the cooler and then at me. "We're almost done. Then we can get back to New Eden."

The door opened, and Peter appeared and ushered us forward. Inside, a woman stood chatting with two middle-aged men. A large table was set with seven place settings and platters filled with pot roast, mashed potatoes, gravy, green beans, and fruit cocktail. The smell of food—*real* food and not some bland stew of some kind—made my mouth water.

Everyone turned when we entered, and the woman approached us and held out her hand. "I'm Aline, and this is James, the vice president, and Mike, our chief of staff."

Once introductions were made, Aline continued. "It's wonderful to see representatives from New Eden. When we lost radio contact, we were afraid that province was lost to us. I trust your journey wasn't too eventful?"

"It was fine, Madam President," I said.

"Please call me Aline. You'll find we're quite informal around here. Now, please, have a seat. We'll talk over dinner."

I set down the cooler, shrugged off my backpack, and took a seat in between Clutch and Griz.

"You'll have to forgive the lack of fresh fruit and vegetables. Our gardens are just beginning to produce. In the meantime, we're getting by on canned foods."

Griz chuckled. "This looks better than we've had in...hell, let's just say it's been a real long time."

"It's the least we can provide you after your long journey. Peter says you have much to tell me."

I began. "A hematologist came to New Eden. He'd been working on the zonbistis virus since the outbreak, and he had a breakthrough."

Aline's eyes widened. "You've found a cure?"

"Not a cure, but a prevention. A vaccine, to be clear." I reached back and hefted the cooler. "Dr. Gidar was able to isolate the antigen that allows a person to fight off the virus. With the antigen, you can create a vaccine. All of Dr. Gidar's research as well as blood samples are in here. All you have to do is reproduce and distribute the vaccine to everyone."

"That's...amazing." She rang a bell, and a young man entered. She motioned him toward me. "Take the cooler to Dr. Franzen as quickly as you can, and tell him I'll talk with him tonight."

"Wait," I said. "Don't you want us to talk with this Dr. Franzen, to tell him what we know?"

Aline smiled. "I'll make sure he can talk to you should he have questions."

I reluctantly gave up the cooler to the man, who hustled from the room. I eyed Clutch who sat there with a tight jaw.

Aline watched me. "Thank you for bringing this research to us. I can assure you that Dr. Franzen will look into it right away." She then looked across all our faces. "The promise of a vaccine will improve the morale of every citizen. After Operation Redemption is completed, the vaccine—if it's still needed at that time—will have a role in building the new nation."

I frowned. "Whoa. You're putting the vaccine on a back burner?"

"Tell us about Operation Redemption, and why you don't think we'll need a vaccine," Clutch stated pointedly.

"Yes, of course," Aline said. "Redemption is a multi-phased plan to eliminate the infected. Mike, if you'd please."

"It's a straightforward operation," Mike said. "The first phase was to reestablish government and build a network of survivors. New Eden is a link in that network. We continue to search for new groups of survivors every day. However, we've acquired enough resources to deem Phase One a success. Phase Two is now underway and nearly complete."

"Saturation bombing the south," Griz said.

Mike nodded. "Yes. Bombing was our initial offensive, followed by a cleanup effort. Our losses have been higher than originally forecasted, but we're still making headway."

"What happened down there?" I asked.

"Zeds proved more resilient to radiation than we'd planned. Those that didn't burn didn't die, despite receiving deadly radiation levels. Our fighting force is down over ninety percent since the offensive began."

"Jesus, that's not an operation. That's a slaughter," Clutch said. "How many troops are left?"

"At last report, eight hundred and sixty. But, don't worry. The zeds have suffered great losses as well. We estimate that there are fewer than one million left that pose any kind of threat."

My eyes widened. "Those are impossible odds. Every soldier down there would have to kill over a thousand zeds. Why haven't you pulled them back?"

"We need them to hold the line until we can implement Phase Three, which is our largest offensive yet."

"And, what would that be?" Griz asked, his words dripping with distrust.

"The Orange toxin," Mike replied. "One of the provinces led us to a warehouse supply of a highly improved version of the dioxin TCDD. You see, TCDD was first used in Agent Orange, and it still bears the same color. Orange has killed all the zeds in our tests." He took a breath. "Unfortunately, Orange also kills everything else. Even with carefully mapped drop zones, we expect significant losses when we deploy it. But, it's the only way to eliminate the zed threat."

"You'll kill everything," I said breathlessly, in shock at his words.

"Sounds like you're taking the 'throw the baby out with the bathwater' approach," Griz said.

"We're doing what's necessary to survive," Mike said.

"We didn't even know about the government or provinces until we ran into someone from New Eden," Clutch said. "There must be thousands of others like us. What are you doing about them?"

No one answered.

"Ah," Griz said. "You've already written them off. That's some plan you've got there."

I shook my head. "The Orange won't work. Dr. Gidar said the virus was resilient. He discovered that the virus becomes even more contagious outside the body. That's why the virus spread so quickly during the first hours of the outbreak. If you kill all the zeds, the virus will become even more of a super-virus for some time. You need to vaccinate everyone first.

Otherwise, your only other alternative is to kill every living human being on this planet."

Aline gave me a condescending smile, as though she were entertaining a child. "Well, let's hope it doesn't come to that. But, to your point, yes, we will employ the vaccine. However, a vaccine doesn't address the immediate threat of those already infected. You've said it yourself, the vaccine is a prevention, not a cure. We are at constant risk until we eliminate the current zed population. Therefore, spraying Orange must be our highest priority.

"Phase Three has long been approved for delivery," she continued. "The drones can't handle the weight, so we'll spray Orange via fire bombers. We will deliver it over areas outside the vicinity of each province under our protection. Then, each province will be responsible for eliminating any remaining threats outside the kill zones."

"How long will the toxin be viable?" Clutch asked.

"In tests, it has broken down in only seven days," Mike replied.

"As you can see, Phase Three will work," Aline said. "And, the matter isn't up for discussion. We are moving ahead with Operation Redemption."

I was less optimistic. "Orange kills everything. What will be left afterward? What about long-term effects to our food and water supply?"

Mike spoke. "Testing to determine any long-term risk isn't possible. But, we know Orange will work."

I shook my head. "Orange will work. Despite your good intentions, you're going to be responsible for genocide."

"I thought nuking several states was bad enough," Griz said. "That's nothing compared to willingly poisoning your own country."

Aline frowned. "We cannot afford to take moderate measures. People need to feel like we're doing something drastic. The troops in the south are down there to improve morale here as much as to hold back the herds. The idea of them down there, protecting us from the herds, is keeping hope alive here. The Orange is the same. Deploying it is as much for the citizens' hope as it is to kill zeds. The capital is in its infancy. Every step we take now must be to benefit the capital. I hate to be blunt, but no matter what, the capital must survive. If the capital falls, the entire country falls."

My mouth had dropped more and more with each sentence. I thought of Jase and how easily he could be killed by a threat he couldn't see. "You only care about the capital. That's—that's—"

"That's bullshit," Clutch completed for me.

"I was wrong, about what I said earlier," I said. "Your intentions aren't good, they're selfish. Provinces like New Eden and the squadrons in the south are nothing but pawns to you, aren't they?"

"We're not criminals. We value the provinces, and we're not intentionally killing anyone," Aline said. "In fact, we take the provinces into consideration with every plan we discuss. But, the end result must lead to the capital's survival. As long as the capital thrives, we can reform this entire continent. You can't say that for each province."

I came to my feet. "Where's this Dr. Franzen guy?"

Aline frowned. "Why?"

"Because you have no plans to deliver a vaccine to the provinces. And, I plan to make sure a vaccine is available to everyone that's left in this world."

Her lips thinned. "Once Phase Three is complete, if there is still a need for vaccinations, and if it can be safely distributed, we will distribute it outside the capital. I give you my word."

"Those are two suspiciously big sounding 'ifs,'" Griz said.

Clutch shook his head. "Just let us use your radio network. We can find someone else who can produce the vaccine in mass quantities so *everyone* can be vaccinated. That way, you don't need to pull resources, and the vaccine can be made. We'll stay out of the way of your operation here."

Aline sighed. "Believe me, I don't want anyone else to die. I'm not the Grim Reaper. Nothing would make me happier than to see the virus erased from the world. There has been far too much death already. However, the survival of this country is riding on my shoulders, and it's a responsibility I can't take lightly. The preparations for Phase Three are underway. At this time, a vaccine will only confuse people. They'll ask why they need a vaccine if we're destroying all the infected."

"Then tell them about the virus," I said. "Because any person with half a brain knows that killing every zed and every trace of virus on this planet is impossible."

James finally spoke up. "We'll kill every last zed in this country. I guarantee it."

"You sound like a politician," Griz said with a snarl.

After a moment of silence, Aline nodded to Peter who brought over a carafe of red wine from the bar. He poured some in each crystal goblet. She held up her goblet. "I'm disappointed that we aren't seeing eye to eye, but I believe we'll work out our differences. That you've brought us news of New Eden's survival is enough to celebrate. Here's to the future."

We reluctantly held our glasses up, and I took a sip of the sweet wine.

Aline smiled and took another long drink. "This isn't the best vintage, but wine has become such a rarity, I savor it whenever I can."

After I had another drink, I frowned and set the goblet down. A sudden case of vertigo overtook me, and I squeezed my eyes shut. When I opened them, everyone was blurry. I grabbed the table for support. "Clutch."

He kicked back his chair and pulled out his sword, but I heard the weapon fall, and he grabbed onto my chair. I tried to reach out to steady him, but my hands no longer obeyed me. Clutch fell, and I found myself falling.

"Fucking politicians," Griz slurred as everything went black.

Twenty-Six

I woke up with a searing headache in pitch darkness. Even blinking my eyes hurt. I groaned and sat up.

"I apologize for the headache. The tranquilizer is a bit strong, but its effects will wear off soon enough."

I recognized Mike's voice, but could only make out a male silhouette in the darkness. Surprisingly, my hands weren't tied.

"Where are my friends?" I asked.

"We thought it best to talk with each of you separately."

"You drugged us?"

"It minimized the risk of an altercation. You must understand. We preferred not to go this route, but when you and your friends showed animosity, you forced our hand. We need you each to be reasonable. Every survivor has a role in the new country."

I guffawed. "What makes you think I want to be a part of this new country?"

"We're not perfect, but we're trying to make things work. We're trying to save as many as we can."

"Killing survivors is not a good place to start," I said.

"Aline isn't afraid to make the hard choices. She must go certain lengths to ensure the new country succeeds."

"She's not a leader," I said. "She's a bully."

Mike sighed. "The human race is on a precipice of survival. We can't afford provinces to operate separately from us. If we don't work together, we'll all die."

He walked closer and flipped a switch. Light flooded the small room, and I shaded my eyes. The room looked to be a small apartment of some kind.

"We need everyone's help to eliminate the zed threat. We need capable pilots more than anything. Our air force has taken a beating, and we need to replenish. Pilots, no matter how little experience, are needed."

"So I'm being conscripted, is that it?"

"Everyone has a choice."

"And what's mine?"

"You can choose to fly missions, or you can choose to return to New Eden."

"What's the catch?"

"Nothing for you."

I let the words sink in. "And my friends?"

"If you choose to stay and fly missions, they'll stay here, safe. If you choose to return to New Eden, they'll be sent to join the squadrons in the south."

"So you'll send them to their deaths if I refuse."

"They could survive." He paced back and forth.

"Why are you doing this? You can train more pilots. You can find more loyal survivors. Why go to all this effort?"

"Because every survivor is crucial," Mike said before taking a long pause. "And the government is still in its infancy. We can't afford the toxicity of negative opinion to taint it. You would bring toxicity back with you to New Eden, and it would spread, just like the zed virus."

Ah, the truth finally comes out. I nodded as he spoke. "The jobs are to keep us busy. But, you wouldn't let us go home regardless of what my decision is."

"You have a decision," Mike said. "Be a crucial part of our new country."

"This 'new country' has already dropped nukes in the U.S. Now, you're talking about poisoning the rest of the country. What's going to be left for the survivors, if there even are any?"

"Idealism must be a nice trait to have. I haven't had that luxury for some time." He walked to the doorway and dropped a hotel keycard on the table. "You have until morning to make your decision."

He left.

I jumped off the bed, my throbbing head nearly sending me back on my butt. I pushed through it, found my backpack on the floor, and paused at the door. I remembered the plastic keycard, grabbed it, and headed out the door. The hallway was lined with more numbered doors. A hotel of some kind.

I started heading one direction, then changed my mind, did a one-eighty, and headed in the opposite direction.

I opened the door to the stairwell to find a stern-looking Griz and Clutch coming up the stairs with another man. My eyes widened. "You're okay."

Clutch's features lessened in an instant. He hurried forward and lifted me into an embrace. He held me tight. "You're all right."

"I love you," I said under my breath.

Clutch lowered me but didn't let go. He looked me in the eyes. He opened his mouth to speak, but the other man spoke first. "Your friend can show you your room for tonight. I'll stop back in the morning with breakfast. If you need anything before then, dial 0 and ask for Adam." He paused before heading back down the stairs. "Oh, and be sure to walk around town. Take in the scenes. It's really pretty here in the winter."

As soon as the man had gone, we looked at one another. "Where were you going?" Clutch asked.

"To find you," I replied.

We stood in the hallway for a long moment. "What do we do now?" I asked.

"It sounds like they've 'invited' us to stay the night," Clutch said, his voice full of venom. "That's what we'll do."

I pulled the keycard out of my back pocket. "I guess that's what this is for." Mopey, I led them back to the hotel room I'd been in moments earlier. Once inside, they locked the deadbolt on the door and spent the next several minutes looking for cameras or microphones while carrying on a casual conversation about the weather.

Finished, they shrugged at each other, and then Clutch motioned for us all to go into the bathroom. Griz turned on the shower as a sound dampener, and I stood there, watching both.

"I didn't find any bugs," Clutch said.

"Neither did I," Griz said. "But that doesn't mean we're not on someone's very own reality show." He then leaned against the counter. "I've never met a bureaucrat I liked," He rubbed his temples. "Damn, my head hurts."

"What'd they talk to you about?" Clutch asked me.

"They gave me a decision to make. Fly for them or else."

His lips thinned.

"What'd they say to you?" I asked quickly.

"They brought in a 'general' who clearly never served a day of his life. He told us that the military wasn't finished with us yet," Griz said. "The dumbshit droned on and on about the necessity of forming a stable government and how they can't afford to split their troops among the provinces, which was his way of saying we weren't heading home. That we'd find out our orders tomorrow."

"How can they do that?" I asked. "Just because you were in the military before doesn't mean you have to do what any officer wants for the rest of your lives."

"He said the zeds are terrorists. They've declared war on the zeds," Griz said. "So, yeah, they can basically make any citizen do what they want."

Clutch scowled at me. "And, I'd bet they have some kind of job for you, too."

I swallowed and looked away.

He cupped my cheek. "What did they do?"

I watched an invisible dust bunny on the floor for a while before I spoke. "They need pilots to drop the Orange toxin. If I don't fly for them, they said both of you would be sent to join up with the squadrons to die in the south."

"They can force us down there, but they won't be able to keep an eye on us all the time. We could go AWOL," Griz offered.

"They also hinted New Eden would be bombed with the Orange toxin," I said.

Clutch shrugged. "We didn't tell them that everyone's living in the silo. They should be safe inside from the Orange."

I shook my head. "They'll be safe as long as they're inside when the area is sprayed. But, if we can't warn them, anyone who went outside during or after the spray could die."

"These guys have got their heads up their asses," Griz added. "They're convinced they can kill off the zeds and then start fresh. It didn't work in Vietnam when we had less ground to cover and more resources. It's sure as hell not going to work now."

"The way I see it, we have three choices," Clutch said. "We can try to escape, but they have a dozen guards posted downstairs. We can tell them to fuck off and get shot or conscripted anyway. Or we can play along with their asinine plan, bide our time, until we find a way out."

"But the antigen will be lost," I said.

Griz smiled. "Not if we find a way to get it back."

I chortled. "That's an awfully big 'if.'"

"The capital has radios here that can reach most of the world. If we can get the word out that we have an antigen for a vaccine, then all we have to do is get the research and samples to the right folks."

"So," I drawled out. "All we have to do is find a way to prevent the entire North American continent from being poisoned, get access to the capital's radio network and broadcast news of the antigen, and not get killed in the process. In a nutshell, we're going to save the world."

Clutch thought for a moment, shrugged, and nodded.

Griz's brows rose. "Save the world? Yeah, that about sums it up."

I smiled. "I'm in."

PART NINE
COURAGE

Twenty-Seven

February

The fire bomber's wheels squeaked as they met the concrete, and the heavy plane settled onto the runway. My best landing yet. All fourteen pilots were required to make a test flight once per day until Aline approved the release of the third phase of Operation Redemption.

When we weren't flying, we were in the briefing room working on flight plans. The lead pilot walked to the front of the room and addressed us. "A warm front is coming through. The forecast is thirteen degrees Celsius tomorrow, which means it's finally going to be warm enough to load the Orange onto our birds and start missions. Expect the green light tomorrow afternoon," he said. "Get plenty of sleep tonight. You won't see much of it for the next couple months."

The tension was palpable in the room. Including me, nine of the fourteen pilots had been conscripted into service. At least five pilots were adamantly against spraying the Orange toxin and vocally raised their concerns daily. I was more careful. While I never voiced opposition, I never championed the operation. I tried to blend in so I wasn't noticed, though I suspected Aline kept a close eye on all of us.

She was a relentless wolf wearing the guise of a compassionate leader. Preoccupied with building a centralized government, she refused to see the blood she'd spill to make it happen. She never visited any of the provinces, preferring instead to stay within the safe confines of the capital. She'd convinced herself that as long as the capital survived, there was hope. But, she'd neglected to take one thing into consideration.

Loyalty.

She'd augmented her pilots and troops with people from the provinces. And, we didn't easily forget life outside the capital. The so-called Provinces of North America had forgotten about its provinces, but I hadn't.

The fourteen of us, along with other airport personnel, crammed into a bus and rode back to town.

"It sounds like tomorrow is going to be the big day," Akio, a fellow pilot, said.

"Yeah," I said. "It sounds like it."

He looked off into the distance and got closer to speak quietly. "Well, they can send me out, but they can't force me back."

"Your flight crew may have a different opinion," I said, reminding him that Aline had assigned at least one staunch loyalist on each crew.

He shrugged and leaned back. "They can't fly."

"No, but they can shoot you."

"There are worse things."

"Like what?"

He ignored the question and instead nodded to the sidewalk. "The riders are back in town."

I smiled. As soon as the truck stopped, I hurried to catch up with Griz and Clutch and gave them both hugs.

"How was the supply run?" I asked.

"The usual," Griz said. "A whole lot of nothing."

Clutch and Griz were riders, troops who went out on supply runs and scouted the area. It was the most dangerous of duties, and we weren't surprised when both Clutch and Griz were "randomly" selected to be riders after they were assigned to the capital's military division.

We headed up the steps of the Hotel, where everyone in the capital's forces lived. It actually was a hotel, and the three of us still lived in the same room we stayed in our first night in the city. If we had tried to escape, we wouldn't have made it fifty feet without being trampled by the entire force.

Our room was on the sixth floor, but we climbed all eight flights to the roof. We went up there to watch the sunset on every evening the guys were in town. It was the only place we were confident wasn't bugged.

The three of us stood at the edge, looking across the city. I could see the entire capital from this roof. It looked peaceful enough, but we knew it housed people who didn't care about other survivors, only about building a country in their own fashion.

"My flights start tomorrow," I said.

"Tomorrow," Clutch echoed.

The sun set, leaving only twilight.

Griz clapped his hands. "If tomorrow's the big day, I need a drink."

———

The following morning

"Good morning."

I scowled at the man standing in our room. "What are you doing here, Peter?"

Clutch and Griz spread out on either side of me so we formed a semicircle around our intruder. After breakfast, Clutch, Griz, and I had returned to our room to find Peter sifting casually through our drawers.

He smiled and held out an envelope. "Phase Three has been given a green light. We begin spraying Orange. I'm stopping by every pilot's room to drop off the flight schedule for today."

I took the envelope. "You could've slid it under the door."

"Yes, but I know how stressful these missions will be for the pilots. I wanted to be available to address any concerns you have."

"Consider knocking next time."

He frowned. "I wish I could change things. After all, we both want the same thing."

My brow rose. "What's that?"

"A world without zeds, of course," he answered.

I shook my head. "I want more than that. I want a world that we can live in after the zeds are gone, too. You've nuked the south. How long before people can live off that land? Now, you want to poison the rest."

"Orange is temporary. The rains will wash it away."

"Orange is a hundred times deadlier than its predecessor used in Vietnam. You said it yourself. It kills *everything*. How long do you think it will take for nature to recover enough to sustain life?"

Peter clenched his fists. "It will recover."

"Why has Aline set a one-hundred mile radius around the capital with no Orange drops?"

His face reddened. "She's playing it safe."

"For the capital but not for the provinces?"

He didn't reply.

Not caring if our room was still bugged, I continued. "She's not the president of the Provinces of North America, or whatever bullshit name you want to give it. She's president of Moose Jaw, and that's it."

By now, Peter's face had reddened enough that I thought he was about to have a coronary. "Go ahead and think whatever you want. But come this afternoon, you and the other pilots will start delivering Orange. You think you can disobey those orders?" He tossed an obvious glance at Clutch and Griz. "Go ahead and try it."

"I never said I would disobey orders," I said. "I'll be at the airport in an hour, ready to go. I hadn't realized freedom of speech was outlawed along with our freedom of choice."

"Freedom of speech isn't illegal," Peter said. "As long as you aren't talking about treason or hurting the country."

I laughed out loud. "You, Aline, and her henchmen are hurting the country enough on your own."

"Hey, Peter," Griz said.

Peter turned in time for Griz's punch. Peter went instantly down, knocked out cold. Griz rubbed his knuckles. "I've wanted to do that for a long time."

"Now, that was freedom of speech at its finest," Clutch said as he grabbed Peter's lax form. He bound his wrists and ankles with duct tape and slapped a long strip over his mouth. He took Peter's radio, checked the unconscious man's pockets, and pulled out a keychain with at least thirty keys on it.

Griz smiled. "Bingo."

Clutch and Griz dragged Peter into the bathroom and closed the door, leaving Peter inside.

They each checked their gear, and I went through my bag one more time to make sure everything was secure.

My nerves jittered like water droplets on a hot skillet. "I think I'm ready."

Griz hugged me. "Be careful. I'll see you when it's done."

He stepped away and left the room. Clutch pulled me to him, and his lips crashed down on mine. He held me, hard, while we kissed a lifetime of kisses in that moment. His lips softened as he held me, and he struggled to pull himself away. He rubbed a thumb on my cheek and then walked out of the room.

I took a deep breath and followed, though I went in the other direction. It didn't matter if anyone had been listening in on us. The coup had begun.

TWENTY-EIGHT

I took the ten o'clock bus to the airport. The bus was nearly empty, and I suspected that most personnel were still in their rooms. The first flight wasn't scheduled to depart for another three hours. I was one of the later flights, giving me roughly two hours before they would begin to load the orange-colored chemical onto the fire bombers and about four hours before the rest of my flight crew would show up.

The bus stopped outside the main hangar. I stepped off and let the sun warm my face. The air was still cold, but the early winter was already giving way to an early spring. I forced myself to act normal, though everyone had a nervous hustle in their actions this morning. Just like I did every day, I strolled into the pilot briefing room and looked at the weather reports before drafting a flight plan. Though, this flight plan wasn't tied to spraying Orange. This one was for our escape from the capital.

The pilots' missions were posted on a map covering a wall. Phase Three was being rolled out in a circular pattern moving outward from the capital. I'd been assigned to northern Minnesota today. Each load of concentrated pesticide would cover roughly 40,000 acres, which meant a shitload of flight missions. Iowa and Nebraska would be hit in less than four weeks.

Tucking the flight plan into a pocket, I headed out to the fleet of fourteen Convair fire bombers parked on the ramp. The airplanes had been modified from carrying water to carrying the highly corrosive

Orange. My plane was third from the end, and I walked around it, doing a pre-flight walk-around. Akio was under the wing of his plane, leaning against a tire. I gave him a casual wave before continuing my inspection.

I did one more walk-around, this time looking under the plane toward nine long, white tanks sitting in rows off the end of the ramp. No one stood around them, not yet, anyway. Thankfully, the airport's security force was small. Aline simply didn't have enough troops to spread across the capital and the airport. Aline had guards posted at every gate, but once inside the airport, everyone went about their business.

I walked toward the tanks filled with Orange. The tanks sat out in the open. There was no way in the daylight to approach them without being seen, so I made no attempt to hide. When I reached the tanks, still no one approached. I casually pulled a gas mask from my backpack and slipped it over my head. At the first tank, I flipped on the power switch, grabbed the handle, and squeezed. Orange sprayed out onto the ground, and I quickly tied a wire around the handle to keep it spraying. I dropped it, continued to the next tank, and did the same.

I continued until I reached the final tank. By then, someone must've seen me or heard the pumps, and a man came running out. "Hey! What are you doing?"

I ignored him and hurriedly tied a wire around the last handle.

I fell to my knees and pulled off my backpack.

When I turned to look at the man, he stopped and his eyes grew wide.

I pulled out the pipe bombs Griz had made. Designed to burn more than explode, I remembered his response when I'd asked him if they would do the job against double-lined steel tanks. He'd smiled and warned me to not stick around after igniting them to find out.

The man's jaw dropped, and he raced back the way he came. Then, he veered to the left and headed toward the emergency power shut-off valve for the tanks. The valve, kept at a small distance from the tanks for safety, was used to cut all power in case of a fire. He was too close before I realized his intentions. *No!*

The man stopped and swung out to hit the big red button, but someone jumped out from around the corner of the building. The pair toppled to the ground. Only one came to his feet, and he held a bloody knife.

Akio.

He watched me, and I pulled my gaze away to light the first pipe bomb. I set it down mere inches from the stream of Orange and ran. As I ran, I clutched the second pipe bomb and my lighter, ready to light it up if the first one failed.

But, whoa boy, the first one most definitely did not fail. I felt the wall of heat before I heard the *whoomp* of ignition. It pressed me forward, and I found more speed. Akio's eyes widened, and he motioned me toward him. He yelled something but all I could hear was the sounds of flames growing behind me.

Like Akio, I wore a Nomex flight suit like all the fire bomber pilots wore. Made of fire resistant material, it served its purpose well today. Exposed skin in between my suit and stocking hat burned against the oven heat at my back, and I hurried as quickly as I could to reach Akio.

He ran around the corner of the building, and I followed, finding a golf cart waiting for us. He climbed behind the wheel, and I more or less fell onto the seat. He floored the pedal, but being an electric vehicle, it didn't go nearly as fast as we needed it to go.

"That was the most ballsy thing I've ever seen," he yelled out with a laugh. "I can't believe you walked right up to 'em and lit 'em up."

"Let's hope it works," I said, cranking my neck to look behind us while hanging on for dear life. Bright flames shot high, with dark smoke climbing. The air around the first tank morphed a split second before the tank exploded.

I yanked Akio down as I flattened on the seat. The blast hit us, and the golf cart lurched. As soon as I could breathe again, I sat up and Akio kept driving. He slowed as we reached someone who was getting back to his feet. "Climb on."

The man, wearing the orange vest of a flagger, climbed on back, and Akio sped toward the gate. The gate stood open, and the guards were nowhere to be found, likely in search of emergency crews. Akio never even slowed as he drove us through the gate and toward the city.

I glanced back at the man. He looked a bit singed but otherwise all right.

"They have cameras at the airport," Akio said. "Once the fire's under control, it won't take them long to figure things out. They aren't going to be happy."

"They'll have other things to worry about."

"You did that?" the man behind me asked.

I grabbed out my knife handle, ready to unsheathe it, and turned around. "We'll drop you off at the Hotel."

"Take me with you. If there's something I can do to help, I'm in," he said with a heavy southern drawl.

Suspicious, I eyed him. "Why would you help?"

His jaw tightened. "I'm from Louisiana. Listen, I know I made a mistake coming up here when they put out the invitation. I've been looking for payback for some time."

I thought for a second and then held out my hand. "I'm Cash. This is Akio."

"I'm Greg."

Another blast sounded, and I knew the second tank had blown.

"Both of you, act injured," Akio said as he approached the city gate.

I leaned back in my seat, and I heard Greg collapse on the backseat's pleather.

Akio came to a stop at the city gate. "I'm on my way to the hospital," he called out.

I winced through half-closed eyes. Greg moaned.

"Go on." The guard motioned Akio to drive. "Hurry. And tell them to send help."

Akio floored the pedal again, and drove down the main road. "Where to now?" he asked without looking at me.

"Can you get me to the archives?" I asked.

Akio replied, "I can get *us* to the archives."

Greg leaned forward. "My wife works there. If you need a way in, I can get her to let us in the side entrance."

"That'd be easier than what I had planned," I said.

Another explosion, soon followed by two more. The entire airport looked like it was on fire.

"I think our birds are toast," I said.

"Aline's going to be pissed," Akio said.

I watched us approach the city. Fire engines roared past us. "The party's just getting started."

Twenty-Nine

"Hi, honey." Greg kissed his wife on the cheek after we squeezed through the door. "These are my friends."

"Thank God you're all right," she replied, oblivious to our presence. "I saw the smoke. Everyone's talking about a fire at the airport. What happened?"

"There was an accident with the Orange. The tanks ignited," he said. "How about you go home and take a long lunch?"

Her eyes narrowed. "Greg, dear. What's going on?"

He grabbed her hands. "Please, Jenny. No questions; not today. Do what I ask."

It took her a moment to process his request. "Okay, I guess..."

He smiled and kissed her again. "I'll see you at home. Now, go." Greg left her standing confused as he led us down the hallway. "The radio room is in the basement."

I stopped. "How'd you know I was headed to the radio room?"

"Besides books, that's the only thing in the archives."

"Oh. I guess that makes sense."

"The basement is open to the public, but the area that leads to the radio room is off limits. They assigned guards when too many people tried to access the radio room to locate their families." He motioned us down another hallway. "Jenny showed the radio room to me before. The back stairs lead to a hall where all the offices are. There are never guards in that area. That'll get you closer."

We followed him as he weaved through bookshelves and down a flight of stairs. Exactly as Greg said, we found ourselves at a hallway lit with bright fluorescent bulbs and lined with doors.

He slowed as we reached the end of the hallway, where we had to turn either left or right. "It's just right down here." He turned and stopped. "Strange. There's usually a guard standing at the door."

I moved around him and walked forward. "That means they're already inside."

Outside the door that read *Suite 3A*, I found a "V" drawn in white chalk scrawled on the wall. *Victory.*

I smiled and gave the secret knock.

Seconds later, the door clicked and opened, and I found Clutch pulling me inside and into his arms as though I were an oasis in the desert. When he released me, he eyed my compatriots, and I spoke. "They're okay. They helped me. This is Akio and Greg."

Clutch's gaze remained narrowed on the two men with me. He made no qualms about showing his distrust of them, but after a moment, he motioned them inside and locked the door behind us. Griz stood behind a man working at the radio bank. A restrained, gagged guard sat in the corner. Clutch turned his attention back to me. "How did it go?"

"It's done," I said. "All the Orange is burning."

"That's an understatement," Akio said. "The tanks are blowing like it's World War Three out there. The entire airport is going up in flames."

"How'd things go for you?" I asked.

"Easy," Clutch said. "All of Aline's people seem to be so focused on the fires that they didn't even go into lockdown mode. Aline's clearly a politician, not a military strategist."

"We're getting the radio set up for a mass broadcast now," Griz said, standing behind a man sitting in front of the radio. "Thanks to my new friend here." He slapped the man's shoulder who jumped at the contact.

I suspected "friend" wasn't quite the word the radioman would use to describe Griz.

"We should be able to broadcast before anyone gets their head out of their ass," Griz continued.

Someone pounded on the door. "Martin? Are you in there? Martin? Let us in!"

The man spun in his chair. He opened his mouth, but Griz pressed a knife against his throat, and he clamped his mouth shut again.

"Get those radios ready," Clutch warned.

Griz spun the man's chair back around and whispered something in his ear. The man shook and went back to work.

The handheld radio on Clutch's belt went off.

"Officer team twenty-two reporting in."

"Control station, twenty-two. Report."

"Yusef's not at his post at the radio room. The door's locked, and Martin's not responding."

"Hold your position. We'll send backup."

A brief pause.

"All available teams. Report immediately to the archives. The radio room is believed to have been taken by terrorists."

"Shit," Clutch muttered. "Someone just got their head out of their ass. Come on, Griz."

"It's ready," the man at the radio said softly.

Griz motioned for Clutch. "You're on."

Clutch walked over to the radio and lifted the microphone. He looked back at me once before closing his eyes. He was silent for a moment. When he opened his eyes, he brought the microphone closer to his lips. "This is the New Eden province reporting from the capital. We are hailing all provinces and all survivors. The capital bombed the south, and today we disrupted their plan to drop poison on the entire country. What this means is that if you live in U.S., Mexico, or Canada, you would've been poisoned. Only the capital city in Saskatchewan was exempt. In their attempt to kill zeds, they would've killed everything outside the capital. We found that plan unacceptable."

He took a long breath. "We destroyed the current supply of poison, but they can create more. If you agree with New Eden, do not send resources to the capital. Do not support their plans, which will cause the death of more innocents. There is a better way. We have found an antigen. A vaccine for the virus is possible. We brought the antigen here, but they have taken it and refuse to create a vaccine for anyone outside the capital. Who among you has the resources to create a vaccine so that we can prevent this virus from winning ever again?"

Something slammed into the door, and the wood cracked.

"The zeds out there can be defeated," Clutch continued. "And, if everyone can be vaccinated, we will be safe from future outbreaks. But we need your help."

The door slammed open, and officers rushed in with rifles. Behind them, two men threw down their battering ram. Shouts erupted as they flocked around us. "Down on the ground! Down on the ground!"

Someone shoved me to my knees, and I found myself on my stomach, my backpack yanked off, my hands pulled behind me. As I fought to breathe, I felt someone go through my pockets.

"This is Helena, Montana," a voice came through the radio's wall speakers. *"We have heard your broadcast. We have a fully functional CDC facility that is equipped to create the vaccine. Bring us the antigen, and we can produce enough vaccine for every single person in the world."*

"Shut down the broadcast!" someone yelled.

"This is Cheyenne Mountain in Colorado," another voice came through. *"We have air support and can—"*

The radio squealed and then silenced.

I was yanked to my knees and dragged to where Clutch was already kneeling.

When they dragged Griz over, he sported a bloody nose. Akio and Greg were soon added to our lineup.

I knew the odds of our mission succeeding were nil. We'd already accomplished far more than I'd ever anticipated. We'd prevented delivery of the Orange toxin, and we'd told the provinces about the capital's plans and the antigen. They would have to take it from there. The only part of our plan that had failed was for us to get out of the capital alive.

"We have subdued the targets," an officer spoke into his radio. "The room is secure."

A moment later, Aline walked in, with Mike and James on either side. She looked downright pissed, which cheered my mood...somewhat.

She walked in front of us. "Exactly what did you hope to accomplish today with these antics?"

None of us spoke.

She paused in front of Akio. "Why do you even care about what happens? This isn't even your country."

He slowly looked up at her. "Easy. I wouldn't want this done to my home. I couldn't stand by to watch it done to another's home."

"You're a fool." She looked at each of us. "You're all fools to think you've done any good here today. Four people died in the fire at the airport. They were innocent. Come spring, many more will die from the zeds that will unfreeze and start to walk again. Causing dissension among the provinces is treason. They need a strong capital to look up to, and you took that from them today."

"Lady," Griz said. "You overestimate your value. We got along just fine without a capital before. Hell, we didn't even know you guys existed until a few months ago. You can go ahead and keep on thinking you and your two sheep there are guardian angels, but you got it backwards. You're getting in the way by bullying defenders out in the provinces to do your bidding. From what I've seen, you're leeches, sucking resources and supplies from the folks who need them most."

She wagged a finger at him. "You're wrong. We've helped the provinces. We've distributed supplies to them. You have no idea what it takes to start up a government from ashes and to bring together groups of survivors into a network."

"You should've stopped there. You would've been remembered as a heroine," I said. "But, you didn't know when to stop. You screwed up when you switched from connecting folks to directing their destinies."

An officer hurried into the room. James held him back from getting too close. "Madame President?"

"What is it?"

"It's the squadrons from the south. They've returned."

Aline frowned. "What do you mean, 'they've returned?'"

"They're here, in the city. And they're demanding your immediate removal."

"That's impossible," Mike said. "What are they doing here?"

"Perhaps," Akio began. "They saw my note in the supplies I dropped last month. A note that may have mentioned the Orange toxin and how they were deemed to be acceptable casualties."

Aline walked over and slapped Akio across the face. "You fool. They'll lead zeds right to our doorstep." She faced the officer standing nearby, and pointed at Akio. "Shoot that man."

The officer's eyebrows rose before he shook his head. "But—"

A herd of heavy boot steps echoed outside the room, yanking everyone's attention toward the door.

The officers nervously held their rifles, the barrels pointing in all sorts of dangerous directions.

"Lower your weapons, and you will not be fired upon," a man yelled into the room. "We've had a lot of target practice, so I recommend you lower your weapons *now*."

The officers looked at one another. None, ironically, looked to Aline for direction. A moment later, they put their rifles on the floor and held up their hands.

Troops poured into the radio room and herded everyone—except for those of us on our knees—into the corner.

Aline refused to raise her hands, and the man who appeared to be the leader of the new troops walked in and straight for her.

"Hello, Paul," she said to the man with a bronze maple leaf on his collar. "Welcome home."

He smirked. "I bet you weren't expecting to see me around here anytime soon...or, ever."

He removed his helmet to reveal a scarred scalp. "You may remember, I had hair when I left. Radiation is an interesting thing. I've watched thousands of my men die, bleeding out of every orifice and coughing up their own lungs. When you denied my request to retreat, I knew you didn't give a damn what was happening."

"I did care," she said. "You were freeing the world from the infected."

He shook his head. "That's only a half-truth. You also wanted us gone. Us scarred-up soldiers bring back too many memories of what it's like out there. We get in the way of the fantasy world you're trying to create here." He smiled. "Don't worry. You're going to find out what it's like out there firsthand soon enough. I've got a nice spot picked out for you near Texarkana. We call it the devil's dance floor. We lost two thousand men there, and you'll get to meet them for yourself."

"Paul," she pleaded, "it was a hard decision to send you. But, we all have to work at containing the zed threat, in whatever way we can."

He nodded to two of his men, who restrained Aline.

"Paul!" she yelled, but the men took her away.

Paul then looked over each of us.

"You've got some flair for timing, Major," Clutch said. "And, we're mighty thankful to have you come save the day."

The major gave a slight nod. "That your voice on the radio?"

"Yes, sir," Clutch replied.

He smiled. "Your timing was perfect. We were pulling up to the gate when we heard your broadcast. I know Aline, and with a broadcast like that, I knew she wouldn't be anywhere else but here."

"Release them," the major ordered, and we found ourselves free of our restraints.

I grabbed my bag, climbed to my feet, and stayed closed to Clutch and Griz.

"The capital looks like it's fallen on hard times," he said. "Fifty miles out, we saw enough smoke that we assumed the whole capital was burning. While there are a few rats I'd like to smoke out of here, the capital is still a good place for survivors. More important, we could use some real beds to sleep in for a change. But, first, you're going to get me up to speed and show me where the antigen is."

"It's a long story," Clutch said.

"Then, find me a cold beer and a comfortable chair first."

Clutch smiled. "I know just the place."

PART TEN
REDEMPTION

THIRTY

After Major Paul Mallary and his officers laid claim to the President's home, we briefed him on everything that had happened since we had arrived. Akio was able to fill in the gaps of the time between when the squadrons were sent to the south and our arrival. I learned that Aline had started as a good facilitator with a knack at building relationships. As time passed, the relentless loss of survivors had a profound effect on her, and she'd developed an obsession to sculpt a new country, beginning with the capital.

The major kept his word. He imprisoned Aline, James, Mike, and Peter. Moose Jaw had two airports. The military airport had been destroyed, no thanks to me. But, the city's commercial airport remained functional. With an armed crew, Akio loaded the prisoners into a King Air and flew them south, where they were shoved out of the airplane with nothing but the parachutes on their backs. If the zeds didn't get them, the irradiated environment would. It was brutal, and I winced at the thought of how they met their end.

Akio, a commercial airlines pilot with tens of thousands more flight hours than I had, flew the antigen and research to Helena's CDC facility. I signed on to help deliver the vaccine as each batch was created. The CDC estimated that it would take three years to produce enough vaccine for the world's survivors—and even longer to distribute it—but we'd do it, assuming we could keep the planes running and full of fuel. Akio, I, and three other pilots would be the Pony Express of the twenty-first century. Clutch, of course, had volunteered to be my navigator and co-pilot before I had a chance to ask him.

The major retained control of Moose Jaw, but no longer called it the capital. Before the outbreak, he'd been a history professor in addition to being an Army Reserve officer. He believed the provinces were too spread out with not nearly enough survivors in between to support a centralized government. He called democracy an idealistic notion at this point in the game. Instead, he proposed a cooperative feudalistic system, believing the only way to survive until everyone "got back onto their feet" was to have each province control its own area, with trading and agreements with nearby provinces.

His opinion had its share of dissidents, with people accusing him of trying to bring us back to the Dark Ages. Personally, I agreed with him. The world was already worse off than what people faced in medieval times. We were homeless and struggling to survive day by day. I figured a feudal system had to be easier to achieve than Aline's idea of a centralized government.

Clutch stepped back from loading our supplies, which included new radios to talk with Moose Jaw and other provinces. He wore a T-shirt, which showcased his full-sleeve tattoos. "Ready to head home?" he asked.

I smiled and nudged into him. "You bet. Let's go home."

Griz had already climbed in the back along with Joe, the only remaining survivor of the New Eden squadrons sent to the south. My Cessna had been destroyed in the fire, and so I opted for a comfortable twin-engine, which could make it back to New Eden without a fuel stop and haul a lot more supplies.

I climbed in, and Clutch took his seat and organized the maps. As I taxied to the runway, Akio smiled and waved broadly from the edge of the ramp. I waved back and smiled, knowing I'd see him in a couple days when he'd come to pick up the zed kids and bring them to the CDC center in Helena.

I'd miss Moose Jaw. It was more than the sense of safety and the electricity and people like Akio. It was the city's potential. Moose Jaw was proof that we could live relatively normal lives, even in all this.

But we weren't ready for that. Not yet.

I throttled forward, and the airplane picked up speed and took to the air as though it couldn't wait to get off the ground. We climbed high, seeing only major landmarks such as rivers, forests, and cities. The sun glistened on a flooded river, and I hoped its floodwaters would wash away the zeds, leaving only pure water behind.

We touched down at the airport outside New Eden by mid-afternoon. Fortunately, there were no signs of wild animals today. The Humvee sat by the hangar, but there was no sign of Zach.

After we tied down the plane and moved the supplies from the plane to the Humvee, we leaned against the Humvee's bumper. Clutch handed me a bottle of water, and I drank greedily. The three of us stared off at the woods, watching the tree line. When nothing emerged, we all climbed into the Humvee and headed back to New Eden.

On our drive, we saw more creatures moving around than when we'd left. Not many animals—only the sick dogs and wolves seemed to venture out during the day. It was the two-legged ones.

Spring was here.

The zeds were thawing out.

Thirty-One

Later that night

Back in the silo was a bittersweet welcome party for Joe. While everyone had known the risks of sending the squadrons after the zeds, everyone had also hoped more would return home. I didn't stick around when people started grilling Joe about what happened out there. I had no doubt the man had been through a far worse hell than any of us.

Clutch had already disappeared to his tiny office in the lowest floor of the silo to catch up on the daily logs since we'd been gone. I hit the shower and stood under the hot spray for my entire five-minute ration. With my skin still steaming, I headed up to my dorm. I rifled through my backpack and pulled out the special items I had bartered for at the capital and hid from Clutch.

I set the bottle of wine and corkscrew down on the mattress. I pulled off my T-shirt and pants and slipped on the dress. Before the outbreak, I never would've worn anything like it. It was a slim-fitting, tiny white thing with spaghetti straps and dainty roses printed on the sheer fabric. It was as much a nightgown as a dress, but it fit perfectly. My shoe wardrobe consisted of two pairs of hiking boots, so I decided to go barefoot.

I stood in front of a small mirror. I tried to look past the jagged scar on my forehead and circular scar on my calf where I'd been shot. Hell, I had so many scars now, they crisscrossed my skin like spider webs Then again, Clutch bore far more scars than I did.

I didn't have model looks before the outbreak; I certainly didn't have them now. Curves had toned into lean muscle. My face had lost its softness. Taking a deep breath, I tried to focus instead on the dress and how it fit my body. *Get 'em where I want 'em.* I grinned, thinking of the one rule I had set for myself during the early days of the outbreak. It had meant that whatever happened, I needed to take control to get things to work out so I could survive. I'd never thought it applied to anything except fighting zeds. Until now.

I grabbed the wine and searched around until I found two red plastic cups.

"Holy shit, why are you wearing that?" Jase asked, startling me.

I nearly dropped the bottle. "Jesus. You about gave me a heart attack."

"She can wear what she wants, Silly," Hali scolded, giving me a knowing smile.

I scowled at Jase and walked past the pair. "Like Hali said, I can wear what I want."

"Have fun," Hali said.

"Where's she going?" I heard Jase ask as I entered the hallway.

I hurried down the steps, not wanting to run into anyone else. If Griz saw me, he'd never let me live it down. Fortunately, most folks were already in bed. My feet flew down the stairs until I reached the right floor.

Clutch's office door was open, and I peeked in to see his nose buried in a stack of paper. I knocked and stepped in the doorway. "Got a minute?"

"Yeah," he grumbled, dropped his pen, and looked up. His features changed from exhaustion to shock in an instant. I had no idea how I didn't laugh at the expression on his face. I'd never seen his mouth drop so quickly. He shuffled his papers to the side in a rush. "Yeah, um, yeah, come in."

He came to his feet rather clumsily, like a schoolboy, and I grinned. He seemed to struggle finding words. "You look nice tonight. I mean, you look better than nice." He finally settled with, "You look really good."

I held up the bottle of wine. "Happy Birthday."

His lips slowly curved upward. "I didn't think anyone knew."

I shrugged. "You told me once, a long time back. We never seem to get the chance to celebrate things like birthdays anymore, so I thought tonight would be as good as any to sneak in a little celebration."

He smiled. "I like that idea."

I shut and locked the door and gave him a mischievous grin. "I don't plan on sharing this wine. I had to trade my machete for it."

He frowned. "Your machete? You shouldn't—"

"I have another one under my bed." I set the bottle, corkscrew, and cups on the table. "Now, do you want a birthday party or not?"

He came to his feet. "Hell yeah. I can't remember the last time I did something on my birthday." He went to work at opening the bottle. He glanced up every couple of seconds while I watched. He filled each cup with the red wine, nearly draining the bottle, and he handed me my cup. "You do look really good."

"Thank you." I took a sip, watching him.

He took a drink, eyed me, and then took a longer drink. After a deep breath, he set his cup down, took mine, and set it down next to his.

He kissed me softly on the lips. "You asked me to say the words once. I couldn't do it. Not then. I was afraid that if I said them, something would happen, and you'd be gone." He swallowed. "But, I can say them now. I love you. With every fiber of my being, I love you." His shoulders relaxed as though a weight had been lifted.

"I know," I whispered. "But, I like hearing you say it."

He then gave me a kind smile. He deepened the kiss, our tongues meeting for a slow, passionate dance. Our bodies pressed tighter together, moving in a rhythm only we could feel.

He broke the kiss, and his smile widened then, enough to show the wrinkles at his eyes. He lowered himself, kissing first my neck, then moving a strap aside to kiss my collarbone. His kisses were innocent, yet they sent tingles across my skin. Already, my breaths were coming faster. His hands ran down my shoulders, my hips, my thighs, and then came back up under my dress. He chuckled when he realized I wasn't wearing underwear.

I held on to him; his heart pounded under my palm. He pressed tighter against me, and I wrapped a leg around him. I felt a shudder surge through him, rippling down his body into mine. He stared at me, the wildness on his face making my heart pound harder. Unable to stand it anymore, I tugged off his shirt as he unbuttoned his pants and shoved them down. He lifted me off the floor and took me right then and there. In perfect rhythm, he kissed me, devouring, violently satisfying kisses as he drove into me.

We made love, and it was sublime.

For the next hour, he went about showing me exactly how he felt about me, until someone pounded on the door.

"Hey, I know you guys are in there," Griz's voice yelled out. "These walls are thin, you know."

Clutch threw a stapler at the door. "Go away," he yelled back before grinning down at me.

"Come on," Griz yelled. "Wrap things up in there. Deb's water broke. She's having the baby!"

Thirty-Two

The following morning

Groggily, I woke when the chest under my head moved. "Hm?"

Clutch stroked my black hair, which I'd let grow out during the cold winter. "Vicki has an update."

I pulled myself up and rubbed my eyes. Everyone from Fox had been here all night. Benji lay sleeping on Diesel at Frost's feet. Other residents had come and gone, checking in to see how New Eden's first birth was coming along. The excitement was palpable. Nerves were on edge as everyone waited.

Vicki, one of the two people assisting the doctor with Deb's birth this morning, stood in her scrubs, smiling. "Dr. Edmund says she's fully dilated. It should be any time now." With that, she turned and hustled back into the room.

I stood and stretched. Jase and Hali stopped their card game to stand and watch the door. Clutch and Griz also came to their feet. Only Frost remained sitting, but his gaze never left the door.

Five minutes passed. We waited. I paced the floor. Jase and Hali joined me. Ten minutes passed. I wanted to be in there, with Deb, but the doctor had been adamant about keeping the room as germ-free as possible.

Deb cried out, and I froze.

"It's time," Frost said. "She's having the baby."

I could hear Dr. Edmund's muffled voice and Deb's cries through the door. The doctor was giving orders, and I heard a flurry of movement behind the door.

"She's seizing!" the doctor yelled. "Hold her down."

I moved toward the door, but Clutch held me back. With my back to his chest, I clasped onto his forearms that wrapped around me. My heart pounded as we waited.

As quickly as the ruckus began, everything silenced. Then, the sound started softly but grew in volume. A baby's cry.

I let out the breath I'd been holding, and turned in Clutch's arms. We smiled and kissed. "It's going to be okay," I whispered.

I tapped my foot, waiting for them to bring out the baby.

"I wonder if it's a boy or girl," Hali said.

Then, a second cry broke free, adding to the first. My eyes widened. I squealed and covered my mouth. "Twins!"

"Two?" Griz asked. "Wow, Tack had some strong swimmers."

A moment later, Vicki and Izzie emerged, each carrying a baby, and neither looking up from her precious cargo. We rushed the two women to see the babies. They were wrinkled and purple and adorable.

"Are they healthy?" Frost asked first.

"Yes, they are a perfectly healthy boy and girl," Vicki said softly.

"Can we see Deb now?" I asked, excited to congratulate the new mother.

Izzie sniffled and started to cry.

I swallowed and looked at Vicki. "Deb?"

Her lips trembled, and then she slowly shook her head.

"Oh, no," Hali gasped. "Not Deb."

"She hemorrhaged," Vicki said after a long silence. "She lost too much blood, and we couldn't stop it. We tried."

No one spoke. I found I could only stare at the babies, the weight on my chest making it hard to feel anything.

"I promised her I would look after his babies," Vicki said quietly.

I swallowed, then placed a hand on her shoulder. "You don't have to do it alone. We'll all take care of them. Together. Because that's what families do."

THIRTY-THREE

Easter Sunday, one year after the outbreak

"How about Jack and Jill?" I asked.

Clutch guffawed. "That's as bad as Griz's idea for Dick and Jane."

I shrugged. "Jase wanted Fluffy and Wuffy."

His eyes widened, and I held up a hand. "Don't worry, I shot those down."

"Their names are Ted and Debra Nugent," Vicki said, settling the debate.

Her words silenced the Humvee.

It took me a moment to place the male name before I remembered. Tack's real name was Ted. Theodore Nugent, to be precise. Vicki had named the twins after their parents.

My smile was bittersweet. "Those are good names."

The other Humvee pulled around us to take lead. Griz waved from the driver's seat. It was the vehicle we'd hidden in the shed before going to New Eden. It was still packed with all the gear and supplies we'd crammed into it. We'd told Justin about it and offered to share the supplies, but he'd been adamant that we needed everything we had if we were going out on our own.

I turned to make sure Jase and Hali were following us, flanking our tiny convoy. The old Chevy truck was dirty, but Jase didn't seem to mind

—if his wide smile was any sign. Of course, that could've also been because Hali was sidled up next to him.

Boxes piled high to Hali's right nearly hid her. All three of our vehicles were weighted down with food and supplies we'd bartered for in New Eden. Even our Humvee, with only room for the three of us, was chock full of supplies, including a radio so we could stay in touch with the other provinces and for me to plan flights with Akio.

Clutch drove. I sat in the front seat with one of the twins and a rifle propped against my hip while Vicki sat in the backseat with the other twin.

Frost had decided to remain at New Eden with Benji, which had come as no surprise. He'd made it clear he preferred to return to Fox Park, but he decided Benji fit in with the kids at New Eden and needed stability. We promised we'd stop by for a visit every chance we got.

When it came to Vicki and the twins, we left the decision up to her. We made it clear that we would stay in New Eden if she chose to stay. Not that she'd need help raising the twins, because she'd have an entire village to help with them, but because we'd given our word. Those babies were part of our Fox family. We'd do everything in our power to ensure their safety.

Vicki hadn't given her decision for a full month after the twins were born. During that time, Justin had tried his damnedest to convince Vicki into staying with the twins. But, on the thirty-first day, she stood before us and stated that Tack and Deb would've wanted their children raised in Fox Park and not a silo.

I was relieved Vicki chose Fox Park. The truth was, Vicki and the rest of us weren't cut out for city living. We'd all been on the run for so long that being confined in New Eden's silo suffocated us. We needed freedom and fresh air.

As Clutch drove, I stared out at the fields of massive white turbines, all still. I enjoyed the scenery as it became more and more familiar.

"We should be there in about an hour," Clutch said as he avoided a zed lying on the road.

With spring, the zeds reemerged, but they'd changed. Most had freezer burn. Bugs ate at their flesh, and they seemed to be putrefying in the warm air. Most could barely walk. They would rot away, and we'd burn the corpses.

When I saw the first zeds walking after the flight back to New Eden, I was terrified of having to face the herds again. It hadn't taken long to realize that the zeds were decaying. These were only the remnants of the vicious monsters that had erupted from the depths of hell a year ago.

But, we'd never be free from the virus until every last zed was gone, every sick animal died, and every survivor was vaccinated. We were lucky. We had a head start on a new life. Our small group was one of the first to receive vaccines because I was part of the delivery crews. We were free from the virus, but we still had zeds and "zabid" animals to deal with. Only when both those predators were gone, would we have a fighting chance.

Baby Ted Nugent kicked out his legs before settling back into his nap. The twins slept much of every day; evidently, newborns did a lot of that. The baby girl—who I'd already nicknamed Little Debbie—must've woken, because Vicki cooed, "Happy Easter, sweet Debra."

"We're almost there," Clutch said, and I looked outside.

Trees had replaced fields, and we passed a sign that read *Fox National Park, 3 miles*.

I leaned back against the headrest and took in a deep breath. Fox Park seemed a dream, and warmth suffused me at the idea of being back there. Out of everywhere we'd been in the last year, Fox Park was the place that held the most potential for being somewhere we could start a new life. We followed Griz's Humvee as it turned into the park.

New grass was fighting to sprout up through trodden ground. Regularly, a zed would be found lying on the ground, trampled by the herds and now freezer burned into a crusty-looking shape of something that had once been human.

"They sure got close to the park," I mused at the telltale signs of the herds.

"Yeah," Clutch said. "We were lucky to get out when we did."

I thought for a moment, back to the days of the outbreak, to Doyle's militia, to living on the river, and to living below ground in a silo. "You're right. We have been lucky."

"It's getting late," he said and picked up the handheld radio. "We'll stay at the old town hall for tonight if it's still secure. Tomorrow, we'll go through the park and assess if we can rebuild."

"Copy that," Griz's voice chimed in.

"Roger," Jase's voice came through.

"We'll be able to rebuild," I said confidently. "It's not like we need more than a cabin to start with. And, I can't imagine the herds managed to trample all of our gardens."

As we pulled up next to Griz's Humvee at the old Fox town hall, which had been the state park rangers' office before the outbreak, I looked for signs of danger but found none. "It doesn't look like the herds came into the park. They must've just stayed on the roads."

"My guess is that they were getting too clumsy for all these hills and trees," Clutch said. "I noticed their paths stayed on flat lands and only veered off when there was something that drew their attention."

"We weren't here to entice them," I said before stepping out of the Humvee and inhaling the woodsy air.

Jase joined me, with Buddy at his heels. Sometime while Clutch, Griz, and I had been at the capital, Jase and the self-sufficient dog had decided they'd make a good pair.

"It's good to be home," he said with a smile before his eyes widened. "Whoa. Check it out."

I followed his finger. My mouth dropped.

He twisted around. "Hali, get over here. You gotta see this."

Hali ran over and covered her mouth. "Oh my God."

Clutch stopped in front of the Humvee. "Is that...a deer?"

Sure enough, crossing the road was a young buck. It paused to look at us before continuing its journey into the trees.

"Yeah," I said breathlessly. "I assumed they'd all been killed."

"A deer," Hali said breathlessly. She turned and kissed Jase, giggled, and skipped toward the large cabin.

Jase watched her leave. After a pause, he made eye contact with Clutch and then me. "She's my girlfriend. I thought you guys should know."

Clutch belted out a laugh. "Everyone knew that."

"It was that obvious?" Jase asked.

"Yes," I said, biting back a laugh. "But, it feels good to say it, doesn't it."

The corners of his lips curled up. "Yeah. It does."

It took Clutch and Griz only a few minutes to make sure the large cabin was clear of any danger. Fortunately, it showed no signs of trespassers—human or zed. We had our sleeping bags out and dinner ready by the time Jase and Hali fed the twins with formula Marco had brought back from the big store back in Omaha.

While everyone sat around after we'd cleaned up, Clutch stood, took my hand, and led me upstairs. "Remember this room?"

I smiled and nodded. "It was the first time we had sex," I said bluntly. I'd almost said that it was the first time we'd made love, but it hadn't been like that at all. It had been only a couple months after the outbreak. We'd been stressed out, afraid, and in need of human contact. In some ways, things hadn't changed much. In other ways, things were completely different now.

He smiled. "Yeah."

We sat down on the floor, with me in Clutch's arms, and looked out the window. We didn't talk. We simply sat there and enjoyed the peaceful silence together.

It had taken one year for the zeds to destroy our world and the world to come back and destroy them. We still had work to do. Fortifying the park, flying missions, and avoiding sick animals—it wouldn't be easy. Not by a long run. I didn't even know if the few survivors who remained had what it took to survive as a species. But, we'd try.

Who knew what tomorrow would bring. Until then, I was content. We were safe in this building. We had seeds to plant and enough food and supplies to get us through the next couple of months. I kissed Clutch, and together, we watched the stars.

BONUS CONTENT

Cracked: A Deadland Short Story

Captain Tyler Masden's tale during the outbreak

I sat on the floor behind the sales counter, holding my rifle and staring blankly at the blood splatter and flecks of human flesh peppering my fatigues.

Jonesie scrambled back to my position. "Our six is still blocked, Maz, but there aren't as many zeds as before."

I looked up, watched him for a moment, and then squeezed his shoulder, "We'll get our window soon. Then we'll head out." I left off the part about the window I was waiting for would come by the way of some panicking civvie grabbing the zeds' attention with his screams and lead them away from our current location.

Two hours ago, we'd holed up in a coffee house on the edge of a strip mall, with nothing but a floor-to-ceiling pane of glass between us and a street full of the unstoppable undead out front. We should've kept moving before the herd doubled in size. I'd made a rookie mistake by leading my team here. We were sitting ducks. As soon as one zed homed in on us, we'd be butchered. Right now, I was counting on the coffee smells to camouflage us from the predators outside.

Gripping my handheld radio, I looked over the remnants of my platoon. *Three*...that was all that was left under my command out of the thirty-five troops I'd led into Des Moines twenty-eight hours ago to keep the infection from spreading outside the city.

We never stood a chance. Des Moines had already turned into zed city by the time we arrived to close off the highways. Within the first hour we'd been overrun. Since then, we'd been passing the time getting slaughtered and running for our lives.

The worst part was that not only did we have to watch our brothers-in-arms die once, when they were shredded by the infected, but we had to put a bullet through each of their heads when they awoke. Those we didn't get to in time were now bloodthirsty predators outside the coffee house window. Some were the men and women under my command. I'd led them to their deaths. And, by the look of things, they wouldn't be the last.

I pressed the transmit button on my handheld and tried to keep my voice low. "Third Platoon to Fox. What's the word on pickup?"

"All resources are still unavailable, but there's a guy pulling together a militia. A team has been sent to rendezvous point gamma-alpha-niner-three to pick you up. What's your status?" came the quick response from Camp Fox.

I pulled out my map, located which RP—rendezvous point—to head toward, and drew a circle around it. "We're getting eaten alive here. There are four of us still viable. But we're completely surrounded, and the zeds are going to sniff us out any minute."

A lengthy pause, then Lieutenant Colonel Lendt's voice came through the radio. *"Masden, all other units are either down, unable to get to your position, or unaccounted for. Plan B is officially in effect. Phoenix is being sent down from Minneapolis and will be there in eighty-five minutes, and they will not wait for you. You need to get the Third out of town and to the RP and fast."*

I set the timer on my watch and saw the rest of the Third do the same. "But, the RP is over six clicks from my current position."

"We are out of options. Do you understand what I'm saying, Captain?" Lendt asked.

"Understood, sir," I replied tightly. "But, we're caught in a FUBAR sit here."

"Believe me, if I had any choppers to send, I would. But I'm counting on you to get your asses out of there before Phoenix strikes. I know you can do it Captain. I need you back at Comp Fox before sunset. Out."

I slid the handheld into my vest and breathed deeply. Jonesie watched me with a tight jaw. Thompson had long since gone silent. He sat with his back against the wall, staring straight ahead. Hart, his head on his knees, had rubbed his temples red. All three faces bore the same expression. *This shit's fucked up.*

It was the same look I'd seen on the faces of the civvies I'd left on a roof of an office building, promising them that a helicopter would soon arrive. They didn't believe me, but we'd left them anyway. Help wasn't coming then.

Just like help wasn't coming now.

"You heard the Colonel," I said, keeping my voice just above a whisper. "Let's get the hell out of this shithole."

Hart motioned toward the big front window. "But we don't stand a chance out there. We'll never make it to the RP," he said, his voice raising an octave with every word.

"We can stay holed up here," I replied. "And in eighty minutes—if the zeds don't find us first—the Air Force is going to drop a shitload of H6s on our heads and blow us to kingdom come."

"We might be able to ride out the blast in here," Hart said.

I chortled. "Trust me, there's no riding out an H6 blast. If the initial explosion doesn't turn all your bones to powder, the following fire will barbecue you. And the matter isn't up for discussion. We crossed under I-80 already, which means we're on the north edge of town. We can make six clicks in eighty minutes."

Hart glared. "It might as well be six hundred clicks for how many zeds are out there."

"The matter is closed, Private," I growled out. "And, if you keep talking, we'll have biters here in no time."

I stared down Hart until he finally lowered his head. Hart was a fresh Army recruit, not even finished with basic training yet. Jonesie and I each had four years in the Guard. Thompson, a couple less. Not that branches mattered anymore. When the zed outbreak started, the military scrambled to pull together every able-bodied troop they could. Getting thrown into battle with new guys was bad enough. That Hart had seen right through me didn't make things any easier. I wasn't officer material, hell, I'd never planned on being one. I'd joined up to get college paid for. For fuck's sake, I was a weekend warrior who'd done more sandbagging than shooting. I'd never even seen action until yesterday.

I'd made lieutenant only three days ago. Two days ago, Lendt promoted me to captain. At how quickly the zeds were chewing up officers, I'd be a general by next week. It wouldn't matter that I'd just lost thirty-two troops under my command. They would keep throwing more troops from every branch at me until we ran out of troops to send to their deaths against an enemy that never stopped. How many had died under my command? Was it eighty now? No, more. *Eighty-six.*

"What's the plan, Maz?" Jonesie asked in a low voice, ever the calm one.

Pulled back to the current SNAFU, I swallowed. After being in a hot zone for over twenty-eight hours, I was mentally and physically exhausted. And now Jonesie—my closest friend—along with all that was left of the Third Platoon, was looking to me to save our collective ass.

"Take five—check your ammo and refill your canteens—and then we head out for the RP. We'll hoof it until the road opens up. Then we'll grab wheels," I finally said. "Thompson, open up some of those bags of ground coffee and run some water into them. It might help to mask our scent out there."

I'd lost five good men learning that little lesson. If it moved like a human, the zeds went after it. If it made noise like a human, the zeds went after it. If it smelled like a human, the zeds *really* went after it.

Thompson handed me a bag of soaked coffee grounds. I grabbed a clump and smeared the grounds across my vest, rubbing extra over a broad dark stain I'd acquired when Frankie bled out in my arms. The pungent smell of coffee grounds was a vast improvement from the stench of plague saturating the air and my clothes.

I climbed up on my knees, and raised my head just enough to peek over the counter and out the window. On the street, vehicles were mashed together, filling up every inch of open space in front of us. The lights on an ambulance still flashed, though they were growing dim. Even if we could make it through that obstacle course of twisted metal and mangled bodies, we'd never make it past the hundred or so zeds. We'd use up what little ammo we had left to clear out the herd. And who knew how many more the noise would draw out. Not to mention the fresh ones joining the bloody herd every minute.

I checked my ammo. Half a mag. What I wouldn't give for a .50 cal machine gun with unlimited ammo right about now.

After everyone finished checking their ammo and refilling their canteens with water bottles off the shelves, silence reverberated through the place for long seconds.

I shouldered my rifle and pulled out my knife. "Let's do this. Once we're outside, we're invisible until we get in a vehicle. No shots unless there's no other option. Got it?"

Yes, sir and *hooah* were my only response.

I took lead and crawled into the back room to the service door. I pushed aside the stack of boxes propped against the busted door and scanned outside through the window. Two zeds trudged near a dumpster. One had been a younger man wearing a nametag the same golden color as the coffee shop sign. The other, a middle-aged woman in business clothes, had been badly chewed upon.

I held up two fingers. "The alley looks wide open right now. Thompson, you take lead. Hart, you're with Thompson. Jonesie and I will take out the two tangos at the dumpster and will be right behind you. Whatever happens, do *not* draw attention. Got it?"

Jonesie gave a slight nod. With a glance and a returning nod from Thompson, I helped Jonesie open the door.

Thompson took the lead. On his way past me, Hart grumbled something under his breath, but I ignored him.

Jonesie stepped outside next. I hustled up behind the zed, pulled out my blade, and skewered its temple just as it turned its jaundiced eyes on me. It fell lifelessly to the ground. I turned to see Jonesie standing over a dead zed, pulling his knife free from its forehead. When no other zeds jumped out from behind the dumpster, we jogged to catch up with the rest of the Third.

At the end of the alley, Thompson flattened against a small outbuilding, and everyone followed suit. He peered around the edge of the building and snapped back. He held up the all-clear sign and then took off at a sprint.

We ran to catch up.

After several blocks, we slowed to a steady jog but continued this way for over forty minutes, weaving around cars, killing every stray zed that noticed us. My hand ached from gripping the knife. As far as I could see, the roads were still blocked every so often with wreckage. Nothing short of a Humvee would break through the mess, and the best vehicle we'd found so far was some hybrid car with the driver's side door wide open.

I decided to keep hoofing it. There were getting to be more trees and the stores had switched over to rows of houses. The number of zeds was decreasing, and we were moving faster. It wouldn't be much longer before the roads were open enough that we'd be able to grab anything and get out of town before Phoenix struck.

We no longer stopped at corners. We ran through shaded alleys, pausing to kill strays and stopping only at buildings and intersections to get our bearings.

We paused at a small detached garage. Thompson peeked around the corner. He hollered and fell back with a zed clinging onto him. He swung his rifle, and a quick burst of automatic gunfire broke the quiet like an alarm clock in the early morning.

"Goddammit, Thompson!" I hissed as Hart and I yanked the zed off him.

He climbed to his feet. "Sorry, Maz. Fuckin' zed got the jump on me."

With our stealth approach literally shot all to hell, another zed came running across the yard, leveling its empty gaze hungrily on us. My blade through its temple finished it off. Three more that had been busy chewing on something in a car turned our way.

I threw my arm forward. "*Run!*"

We took off, but every zed in a mile radius must've heard the gunfire and was closing in from every direction. As Thompson and Hart cleared a path in front of us, a pair came at me from the side. Freshly turned zeds were as fast and agile as humans, and these were as fresh as they come. I grabbed the first zed by its shirt and flung it to the side. It twisted around and lashed out at me. I jumped back and shoved a blade through its eye. The second zed pile-drove me into the ground, snapping its jaws at me. A few more gunshots and it slackened. I rolled it off me, flinging brown sludge off my flak vest.

"I'm empty!" Thompson yelled. I joined him and started firing into the wall of at least twenty zeds at the roadblock in front of us. With each zed that fell, three more climbed over it.

My rifle clicked on empty. I dropped it and pulled out my sidearm, keeping my knife ready in my other hand. The zeds came at us from every direction. Those still in buildings pounded on doors and windows.

"This way!" Jonesie yelled, jumping over a dead zed at his feet, and we all made a hard right to follow him onto someone's driveway. As we ran for the open gate to the fenced backyard, several zeds blocked our way.

A petite zed with long pink nails slashed at me. One quick shot to her head sent her down. More zeds were closing in every second. Rifle fire cut down the first wave of zeds behind us. I fired at every zed that came at us from the yard.

Something grabbed my foot, and I looked down to find a shot-up zed gnawing on my boot. I kicked it, trying to find anywhere to stand that wasn't littered with still writhing bodies.

"Agh, fuck!"

I looked over to see Hart knock down a zed that had gotten past me. He reached up and clutched a bloody ear. Then he snarled and raised his rifle. "Die, you mother fuckers!" Wild eyed, he laid down machine gun fire in a wide, manic arc. Zeds fell all around us.

My eyes widened. "No!" I barely ducked in time to miss Hart's panicked firing. Thompson wasn't so lucky. With a grunt, he fell to his knees, clutching his chest where blood was spurting out. His shoulders slumped and he fell face forward. The zeds, oblivious to the gunfire, went after the easy prey without any regard to getting shot.

Hart's rifle ran out of ammo. A quick glance from Jonesie, and I knew exactly what he was thinking. The instant the zeds closed in on Hart, we ran for the gate. His screams sliced my nerves, but there was nothing I could do to end his agony. Not that I would have. Thompson had been a good Guard. One of the best.

Jonesie and I shoved through the still-standing zeds at the open gate between the garage and house. I stabbed a long-haired zed just under its nose, going through its sinus cavity to get to its brain, and it tumbled backward, collapsing to the ground. Jonesie took out a pair of kids trying to chew through his pant leg.

I fired my last shot into a goliath blocking our way to the backyard. I used the Beretta as a hammer on a zed's nose as it lunged for me. We tumbled through the busted gate, leaving the herd to funnel in behind us.

The backyard was fully enclosed by a privacy fence so there were relatively few zeds back there. But zeds poured through after us. Jonesie ran around the large play set and I hurdled the sandbox. We hit the fence at the same time. I swung a leg up. Hands grabbed at me from behind but I managed to shove over the fence.

Jonesie and I landed hard into another backyard, this one also enclosed by a matching wood fence, and thankfully zed-free. I fell to a knee and pulled out my map and compass. It was damn near impossible to get bearings without any landmarks. I glanced up at Jonesie. "Did you catch the last street sign?"

He frowned. "It was numbered, I think. Maybe E 14th Street?"

I came to my feet. "The RP is north of town off 60th, so we've got to be close. It should be just northwest of us."

Jonesie looked at his watch. "We've got less than ten minutes. Not enough time."

Increasing growls and moaning from the other side told us we didn't have long. The fence behind us was already cracking and swaying under the waves of zeds pressing against it.

"It'll be enough," I said and ran to the wood gate. I opened it a crack and counted at least four zeds in the driveway. I shut the gate as quietly as I could, but as I clicked it closed, pounding from the other side vibrated the wood.

Jonesie rubbed his face. I motioned to the north side of the fence, and we shimmied over it and fell into the next yard. I rolled onto my feet in time to knock back a zed. It tripped and fell backward. I didn't stop to finish it. The loud sound of cracking wood signaled that the herd had made it into the yard where we'd stood seconds earlier. Jonesie and I took off running through the backyard and climbed the fence into the next.

As soon as we hit an alley, we took off at a sprint, no longer stopping to take out strays. We were zed magnets, pulling together quite a tail, but we kept running full out, searching for any viable vehicle but saw none. Sweat burned my eyes. My lungs were on fire.

Once we hit 60th, the sidewalk disappeared along with houses, and we ran side-by-side down the road toward the RP. My muscles shook, but I pushed through. Jonesie panted at my side, and what sounded like a stadium-full of pounding footsteps followed too closely behind us.

Lendt came through my radio. *"Third, sit rep. Fox to Third. Come in."* I didn't bother picking up. *"Masden, goddammit, pick up."* After several attempts, Lendt finally said, *"Phoenix will be there in two. You better have gotten your asses out there by now."*

The RP was well over a click away, though I could see the hill in the distance. We'd never get there in time. I could hear the zeds closing the distance behind us. Unlike us, the bastards never seemed to tire.

A small pickup truck shot through the intersection we were about to cross. Its tires squealed as it cranked to a stop in front of us. Unable to stop in time, I flattened into the side with a painful thud. Air flew from my lungs.

The driver, a young man in full camo, waved to the back of the blue truck. "I'm with the militia. Get in! Hurry!"

Holding my cramping stomach, I tumbled over the side and collapsed onto the bed. Jonesie landed on top of me and rolled clumsily off. Something rammed into the truck with a soft but solid thump, and I pulled myself up to find a zed clawing for my face.

Jonesie kicked its face, sending it back a couple feet. The driver stepped on the gas, and the truck lurched forward. Another zed that had been reaching for us spun around and disappeared behind the truck. Several zeds met the truck head-on, leaving behind flecks of flesh and brown blood on the hood and windshield.

Turning back around, I leaned against the back window and sucked air as the truck put distance between us and the zeds. Jonesie sprawled out on the bed, panting. "I can't believe it," he said between gasps. "You really pulled it off, Maz. I just may have to kiss you."

I kicked his leg. "Try it and I'm tossing your ass out the back." Though I was having a hard time believing it myself.

He chuckled before wiping sweat from his forehead. His smile fell. "That was some fucked up shit back there."

I stared at the shambling shapes growing smaller in the distance, each one seemed to bear the face of a troop from my platoon. "Yeah."

The driver slid open the back window. "Sorry it took me so long. I saw you guys from the hill, but had to take a couple detours to get to you."

"Nah. Your timing was great," I said. "You saved our asses back there, soldier."

"Just doing my job," he said. "And the name's Sean. I sell seed corn. I'm not a soldier. I just joined the militia this morning."

"Captain Tyler Masden with the Camp Fox National Guard," I said. "And this is Corporal Paul Jones."

Jonesie limply waved before draping his hand across his chest.

Sean nodded. "I'm just glad I saw you guys—"

"Talk later," I interrupted, watching a dozen evenly spaced white parachutes float down from the massive C-130. "You'd better step on it. Phoenix just got here."

Jonesie pulled himself up on an elbow. "Aw, hell."

We both stared as the parachutes floated peacefully toward the ground. When the first parachute disappeared somewhere downtown, I tensed and then lunged, flattening myself over Jonesie in the back of the truck.

An earthquake shook the ground. Each tremor sent us a few inches off the bed, only to land on the metal again with a painful thud. Hissing, I kept my head covered. Seconds later, the truck swayed as a gust of oven breeze and blistering dust shot over us. I gritted my teeth and held my breath against the tainted air. Shockwaves vibrated my teeth and bones.

Only after I was sure no more waves were coming, I rolled over and sat back up to see the city engulfed in black smoke.

"Holy shit," Jonesie muttered. "That should take care of the zeds."

"Yeah," I sighed. Except that, watching Des Moines burn, I didn't think of all the zeds the H6s incinerated. I only thought about the poor innocents I'd left back on that roof.

————

A tear ran down the cheek of the C130 pilot as she witnessed the destruction of a million lives. She hastily wiped her cheek with the back of her glove. She'd never imagined she'd be ordered to bomb her own country. Des Moines wasn't the first city that she'd burned, and it wouldn't be her last. Kansas City's payload was onboard and being prepped at that moment in back of the cargo hauler. Her orders would be complete after that, but after talking it over with her crew, she'd added one more drop to the list.

She'd lost radio contact with the St. Paul Air Reserve Station over twenty minutes ago when the base was overrun by zeds. It had taken her crew only a few seconds to make a pact. They'd hold back the last H6. Then, they'd fly back to the station and deliver the only mercy they could to their infected families and friends.

"God help us all," she whispered.

————

Looking out to the horizon with eyes that could no longer see, a soldier who was no longer alive crawled out from under the rubble of Des Moines. Flames licked at his tattered fatigues. The badge with the name "Pvt Jonathan Hart" could no longer be read under the blood and char. His ears were gone, burnt away in the blast. Pain registered but it was smothered by an insatiable need. As more joined him, only one thought remained.

Feed.

PERFECT: A DEADLAND SHORT STORY

Benji Hennessey's tale during the outbreak

Mom calls me Perfect, but all my friends call me Benji. She said I got more chrome-zomes than everyone else and so I'm special. When she'd first told me I had Down Syndrome, I was worried that kids wouldn't like me. But, other than a few jerks, no one picks on me because my eyes look funny or because I talk a different. Sometimes, I wish I was just like everyone else. But, most of the time I'm happy with who I am. I have lots of friends, and one day, I'm going to be an actor on TV. Maybe even in the movies.

Some of my classes are in a smaller room with kids who have a tough time learning like me. We were in there the day everyone went crazy. Mrs. D left the room to talk to someone, and when she came back, she was scared. She called our parents to come get us, and we all waited while she paced the room, talking about zombies. When we asked what zombies were, she said they were monsters. That made sense why she was afraid of them then. I was scared of monsters, too.

Mom was the first to arrive. She rushed through the door, grabbed my wrist and yanked me away.

I reached back for my bag. "But my homework—"

She didn't even slow down. "No time."

Mom worried me because she didn't stop to talk with Mrs. D. She *always* stopped to talk with Mr. D.

"Bye! See you Monday!" I called out over my shoulder as my mom pulled me through the doorway.

I wasn't the only kid leaving early. A few other parents were there, too, some with their kids, others heading into classrooms. Mom hurried us down the hallway lined with lockers. My mouth fell open, and I pointed to a woman leaning against a first-grader's locker. "Mom, she's hurt!"

Mom stopped, looked at the woman and then yanked me away. "She's sick."

I had to jog to keep up with Mom's longer steps. When we burst through the glass doors, outside was even crazier. Horns were honking and people were shouting. At the Home Depot next to my school, two men were locking people into the outdoor section behind big black gates. My heart pounded in my chest. It was so crazy that it didn't even seem real, so I sucked in a deep breath to make sure I wasn't dreaming.

It sure felt real. And it wasn't fun.

Mom led me to where she parked the car on the front lawn by the flagpole.

"Get in, Benji," she said in a rush. "We have to hurry."

I swallowed. This wasn't like Mom at all. She was always happy and chatty. I pushed up my glasses and climbed in. She'd locked the doors and gunned the engine before I even had my seatbelt fastened. I shivered even though I wasn't cold. "What's wrong, Mom?"

She glanced at me and gave me a half-smile, but it fell into a frown all too quickly. "I—I don't know yet. People are...they're...well, people are getting sick."

"Like the stomach flu? *Blegh.*" I hated the stomach flu almost as much as I hated the chicken pox.

"Something like th—"

Tires screeched, and I saw the blur of a car outside my window. Mom swerved onto the median and back onto the street. I held onto the dashboard. I snapped around to watch the other car drive away. "Did you see that? He's driving the wrong way."

Mom didn't say anything. Her eyes were wide and she was taking really deep breaths. She clenched the wheel so hard I could her white bones through her skin. I turned on the radio so she could listen to the country music like she always did when she drove. Voices came on instead. They must've been in between songs.

Mom turned off the radio. "Not today, sweetie."

She was acting weird, and it scared me. I squeezed my eyes shut and clenched my teeth and rode out the rest of the drive home in a nervous silence.

As we reached our driveway, the Jacobsens ran over to meet us. Mom hit the garage door opener button. "C'mon, c'mon, c'mon," she said, pounding her palm against the steering wheel with every word.

Mr. Jacobsen ran straight into the back of the car, and I jumped. "Whoa." When Mr. Jacobsen punched at our back window, I frowned. "Why is he so mad?"

"He's sick, sweetie."

Mrs. Jacobsen leaned against the hood on Mom's side of the car. Blood oozed from her neck, and she clawed at the windshield. I shrunk into my seat, trying to get away from both of them. "Mrs. Jacobsen looks sick, too."

"Yes. They're both very sick. And we have to stay away from them, or else we could get sick, too."

Mom gunned the engine, and the car lurched forward. As soon as we were in the garage, she hit the button. We both turned around and watched as the door descended—so slowly—as our neighbors approached. Mr. Jacobsen was the first through the door. The door stopped moving and the garage light flashed.

"Shit!" Mom hit the button again, but this time the door climbed, and she mumbled something as it opened all the way and she hit the button to descend again.

This time, Mrs. Jacobsen set off the sensor, and the door stopped.

"No," Mom whimpered and she repeated the process, but more neighbors were filtering into the garage, and some folks I didn't know. There were five, no six in the garage now.

"Look, there's Jackson," I said, pointing to the fourteen-year-old who lived four doors down. He walked right up to Mom's door and punched at the window. I jumped in my seat. Jackson wasn't smiling like he usually did. And his lips and teeth were covered with red.

"He's sick, so he's not your friend anymore, Benji."

"You mean he won't get better?" I asked. "They've got something like Gramma had?"

Mom shook her head. "It's not cancer. But it's bad like it." She lowered her head and didn't say anything else. The only sounds were all the people growling and banging on the car. I didn't like getting sick, but they must really hate this bug for how angry they were.

Mom's long hair covered her face, so I brushed the strands to the side to find her crying.

I wiped a tear away, but more kept coming. I hadn't seen her sad like that since Gramma died, and it made me sad. "Don't cry, Mom. It's okay. We won't get sick."

She took my hand and kissed it. She let go, grabbed her purse, and rummaged through it.

She pulled out a gun, and I my eyes grew wide. "Where'd you get *that*?"

"I need you to do something for me, and it's important you do exactly as I say. Can you do that?"

I pushed up my glasses and nodded.

"When I yell, 'run', I need you to hurry inside the house and lock the door behind you. Then I need you play your best game of hide-and-seek ever. I need you to find the very best hiding place in the world and don't make a sound. You can do that for me?"

I swallowed and nodded. "But you're coming, too. Right?"

"Of course." She gave me a small smile. "I've got a key. I'll come in as soon as I make sure no sick people try to get in the house."

"I'm scared. I don't want to be alone."

She pulled me into a long hug. "I'm always with you, Perfect."

She clicked something on the gun and held it on her lap. "Are you ready?"

I nodded again, and then clutched her to me. I tried to ignore all the sick people, but they were so loud. I finally pulled away, sniffled, and pushed up my glasses.

"You'll always be my Perfect." Still crying, she scowled at the people banging on our car. "Hold onto the door handle. When I yell, 'run', you run. Got it?"

My lips quivered. "O-okay."

"Roll down your window. Cover your ears. It's going to be loud, but you won't get hurt."

My fingers trembled but I did what she told me. Mom raised the gun and then a huge boom hurt my ears. My hands snapped over my ears. Mr. Jacobsen fell back, and Mom grabbed at me. I couldn't really hear her because there was some kind of loud siren going off in my ears, but I could see she was yelling.

"*Run!*"

I tensed, nodded, grabbed at the handle, shoved open the car door, and tripped over Mr. Jacobsen who reached out to me. I stumbled around him and toward the door to the house. Jackson ran at me, but Mom shot him, too. She stood outside the car now, and started shooting everyone near me, just like she was the Lone Ranger. I was watching her instead of where I was running, and I tripped going up the two steps, but caught the door handle and threw myself inside. I fell against the door, shoving it closed, and twisted the lock.

Panting, I raced around the house like a blind mouse, checking out my usual hiding spots like the closet and under my bed. Finally, I decided to hide in the basement and tucked in behind the furnace. That area had always been off-limits to me, so it had to be the best hiding place in the world. As I sat in the dark, brushing away cobwebs, I waited for Mom to come find me, just like she'd always done when we played hide-and-seek. I was careful to keep quiet. Mom would be so proud. This was my best hide-and-seek yet.

I heard more gunshots and a woman's screams, and then it got quiet. After a few minutes, I heard the garage door close, and I tensed. Mom would come inside soon and try to find me!

I was glad I wouldn't have to hide for much longer because I didn't like the basement. It was dark and damp and there were funny sounds in the basement. The furnace would growl and hum. Something else would kick on that sounded a little like the furnace, too. The phone rang upstairs but otherwise it was completely quiet upstairs. It was getting pretty scary, but I stayed hidden and waited for Mom, just like she'd told me.

When I'd gotten dressed for school this morning, Mom had said it was too cold for shorts, but she'd let me leave the house in my favorite pair, anyway. I should've listened to her. It was really cold on the concrete. It made my teeth chatter.

Mom still didn't come to find me.

I cried myself to sleep sometime after the sun went down and everything went black.

When I woke the next morning, I had to pee so bad. I crawled out from my hiding spot, with shivers running all the way into my deepest bones, and hustled up the steps, grabbing my crotch to keep from wetting myself. At the top of the stairs, I looked both ways before running for the bathroom. My eyes watered as I stood at the toilet and relieved myself.

Finished, I tiptoed down the hallway and into Mom's bedroom to find her bed still made. With a frown, I headed to the kitchen, but Mom didn't have breakfast ready. The TV wasn't even on yet. But I was too hungry to wait for Mom. I grabbed a box of cereal and ate straight out of the box, just like I'd seen Grampa do when I stayed with him.

The phone rang, and I jumped, dropping the box. Cereal flew everywhere, and I scrambled to sweep it into a pile. As I swept, I realized that it could be Mom on the phone and I rushed over and grabbed it.

"Hello?" I asked.

"Benji? Oh, thank God you're all right!"

My heart felt like it was going to burst with happiness. "Grampa! You'd never believe what happened. First, Mrs. D let us go home early. Then, Mom—"

"We'll talk about that later," Grampa cut in. "Let me speak with your mother, kiddo."

My bottom lip trembled, but I swore to myself that I wouldn't cry again. "Mom said she'd be right behind me, but she hasn't come home yet. She took out a gun and shot the neighbors in our garage because they were sick. She told me to run and hide."

"God, no, Anna. My girl..." Grampa drifted off, and it sounded like he was crying.

"I hid just like she told me," I said. "And I was really quiet."

"That's good, Benji. You did really good," Grampa said, but his voice cracked. "I just miss Anna, I mean, your mother."

"I miss Mom, too," I said softly. I wanted to go into the garage and check on Mom. But if she got sick, she wouldn't want me to get sick, too. And so I had to wait until she came inside.

Grampa wasn't talking so I munched on the cereal in my hand while I waited. It wasn't until after I wiped my hand on my shorts that he finally spoke. "I'm coming to pick you up, Benji. I need you to hide until I get there."

"Okay," I said, but I worried about how long I'd have to hide. Hide-and-seek wasn't fun anymore. Grampa lived far away. The car ride to his house took three hours each way. I took a deep breath. "Please hurry."

"Hang tight, Benji. This mess will be over in no time. I'll be there later today."

"Okay. Love you, Grampa."

"I love you, too, Benji," he said, his voice rough, and hung up.

I held the phone in my hand until the dial tone switched to beeping, then to nothing. I hung it up and picked it right back up again. I hit 1 on the speed dial. The phone rang, echoed by a ring that sounded like it was just on the other side of the door. Just because I couldn't Mom if she was sick, there was no reason I couldn't at least talk to her.

"Come on, Mom. Pick up," I said, cradling the phone against my ear.

She might be upset that I didn't stay quiet and hidden like she told me, but she'd understand. I hid *all* night.

A thump. The sound was raw and crude, not gentle like Mom. But, if it was Mom, why didn't she use her key to get in before she got sick?

The ringing finally stopped and I got her voicemail. I held my breath. Why didn't she answer?

She was too sick to even talk to me.

When the truth hit me, I looked at the phone in my shaky hand and hit 2 on speed dial.

Grampa answered on the first ring. "Hello?"

I was too scared to talk.

"Benji, is that you, kiddo? I'm just about to start driving your way."

I nodded.

"Is everything okay?" he asked.

"I think Mom's sick," I whispered, my words echoed by a pounding on the door. I gulped. "She sounds mad, and she wants inside."

Grampa cussed. "Can you hide?"

The thumping was so loud, but I could still hear the fear in Grampa's voice.

"I can, but," I sucked in a breath. "But, Mom always finds me."

"I need you to be strong, Benji. Hide where she can't get to you. I'm coming for you."

"Okay," I replied in a quiet voice and hung up the phone.

I shivered as I walked away from the pounding at the door and toward the cold, dark basement. At the top of the stairs, I stopped and my jaw slowly dropped. I turned around and hurried for the pantry instead. It wasn't a large pantry, nothing bigger than a tiny closet. But, I'd always been small for my age. I crawled onto a shelf, shoving canned goods against the wall, and tugged the door shut as quietly as possible.

I'd hidden in pantry once during a game of hide-and-seek. It was the only time Mom hadn't found me, and I'd won the game. But, I couldn't open the door from the inside and had gotten scared (I was just a kid back then). When Mom had finally found me, she scolded me for not calling out for her, and then she held me because I cried. After a week of night terrors, she put a door handle on the inside of the pantry. But I'd never hidden inside since.

Mom would never find me here.

After many minutes, there was a loud bang, like the door was slammed open. Someone was definitely inside, because I could hear clumsy stomping, things crashing to the floor, and angry grunting and moans. The voice sounded somewhat like Mom's but...different.

When something brushed against the pantry door, I hugged myself, clenched my eyes shut, and held my breath. *Please don't find me. Please don't find me.*

The next sound came from a bit farther away, like she was walking away from me. I tried to breathe quietly and slowly but it was hard. My heart was beating too fast. A ruckus erupted, the sound of pans banging together, and I bit my tongue to keep from giggling when I imagined Mom banging her head onto the pan rack hanging from the ceiling like she'd done so many times before. But this time, she didn't cuss and then apologize and chuckle like every time before. She didn't say anything at all except grunt.

She's sick.

My lower lip trembled as the shuffling sounds moved away from the kitchen. I bit my lip to keep from crying.

Over the next few hours she moved through the house, and I never made a sound. I was so hungry that I'd almost reached for a snack cake on the shelf above me, but I was afraid she'd hear and find me. My muscles felt weird from not moving, and I wanted to stretch out. After what felt like forever, the sounds neared my hiding place again and I heard her tumble down the two steps into the garage.

I let out a big breath.

I waited until I hadn't heard a thing for a really long time.

I slowly reached out for the door knob. A can rolled off the shelf and landed the floor with a thud, and I froze. I strained my ears, but I couldn't hear Mom.

I inched my hand to the door knob and turned it as slowly as I could. When light peeked through, I waited, then pushed it open. I jumped off the shelf and fell to the floor. Both my legs were fuzzy feeling, but I managed to get to my feet.

I ran over to the door and tried to close it, but it wouldn't stay closed. The wood was all splintered on the frame where it was supposed to lock. I grabbed a chair from the kitchen table and dragged it across the floor. The metal legs vibrated against the floor, so I pulled it faster and pushed it against the door, and I could hear movement in the garage.

I jogged over to the phone and punched 2 on speed dial. The phone rang and rang until it went to voicemail.

"I'm okay, Grampa," I said into the phone. "Mom is in the garage again. And I put a chair against the door."

Something banged against the door.

My eyes widened. "She's back! Got to go!" I hung up the phone just as the chair slammed into the wall, allowing the door to open partway.

Mom struggled to squeeze through the doorway, and she looked so sick I barely recognized her. Her skin looked look someone had colored her with a yellow magic marker. But much of her neck and face was covered with dried dark brown mud or something. Even her eyes were yellow as they zeroed in on me.

The chair between the door and wall kept the door closed just enough she couldn't get through. She reached out to me. Bites, gouges, and scratches covered her arm. It was like she was gesturing me to come to her, and I found my feet taking me closer. Only this time, as I drew closer, she growled and tried to claw at me.

I jumped back and bit back a sob. "Oh, Mom. I can't. You're sick," I muttered. Then I turned and ran.

I ran from the kitchen and down the hallway to the patio door. I heard a ruckus in the kitchen and footsteps behind me. I was too afraid to look back.

I slid the glass patio door open and jumped outside, slamming the door closed behind me just as Mom slammed into the glass. Some of the dark brown mud on her face smeared against the glass and she lunged again. I pumped my arms as ran across the patio and to the small storage shed in the backyard. I pulled up the wide door and looked inside.

In the corner sat my dusty bicycle. I was the only kid my age who still had training wheels. I'd quit riding last summer because I'd been too embarrassed to ride with the extra wheels.

I was still embarrassed, but I could pedal really fast, faster than I could run. I spun the bike around and climbed on. I nearly spun out on the concrete as I pedaled as fast as I could out of there.

Mom was slamming herself into the glass door, trying to get outside. Other people I didn't know (but couldn't be certain because they looked *really* sick) all started chasing me. They could run nearly as fast as I could ride, so I had to pedal faster than I'd ever pedaled before. A mean-looking man covered in brown stains reached out and tore off some streamers on my bike handlebar.

A bigger kid grabbed at my arm, and I nearly flew off the bike. It took me awhile to get my feet back on the pedals, and I kept pumping. One of my training wheels was wobbly after that and squeaked every time I leaned too far over.

After three blocks, I was finally putting distance between all the people in my neighborhood but new ones kept showing up from behind houses and cars. I had to swerve around sick people and crashed cars. The wobbly training wheel fell off, and I had to lean on the other wheel to keep from falling over.

My legs burned, but I kept pedaling. My chest hurt and I couldn't get enough air, but I kept pedaling. Sweat burned my eyes and kept making my glasses slide down my nose, but I never slowed down. I rode away from all the sick people until the houses started to spread out and fewer cars sat on the road. But, I didn't feel any safer until I passed the Wal-Mart on the edge of town. I finally slowed my pedaling when I passed the sign *Thank you for visiting Fox Hills, Midwest's Hidden Gem.*

This was the way to Grampa's house. I slowed down, but I didn't stop. I rode until the sun climbed all the way up into the sky. My other training wheel was getting wobbly. I kept hoping to see Grampa's truck, but I never saw anyone else on the road.

I gritted against the hurt inside and kept pedaling. I'd ride all the way to his house if I had to.

I was so thirsty. Hungry, too, but my stomach didn't hurt as much as my chest and legs. Both felt like I'd walked through fire, they burned so much. But I was afraid if I stopped, I'd never be able to get going again. And I'd never get to Grampa's house if I stopped.

I saw two sick people in a parked car not far from town. After that, I didn't see anyone, sick or otherwise.

My bike slid on loose gravel, and my other training wheel flew off. The bike tipped over. I was too tired to jump out of the way, and I cried out when my knee hit the hard pavement. Hissing through my teeth, I pulled myself out from under the bike and sat on my butt. I took off my glasses, wiped the sweat—and maybe a tear or two—from my eyes, and pushed my glasses back on. Sniffling, I picked out pebbles from my bleeding knee. It really, really hurt.

Mom would definitely put a band-aid on this. I hope I don't bleed to death.

After several minutes of watching my knee bleed and looking for sick people, I pushed myself to my feet. It was really hard because my knee throbbed, and my legs felt like they didn't have bones in them anymore. But I managed to get to my feet, and I started limping down the road. It was three hours to Grampa's house. I rode way longer than that already, so I should be there soon.

Walking was easier than riding, but it was slow. I don't know how many hours I walked, but the sun had gotten to get low in the sky, and my wet clothes were making me shiver. My mouth was dry and my head was starting to really hurt. I watched my feet drag over the pavement with every step. *Fifty-two, fifty-three.* Every time I hit one hundred, I started over because it was hard to think straight.

A loud engine sound made me lose count and I looked up. A long ways down the road were bright headlights heading right toward me.

As it drew closer, I saw it was a big green truck, with a man standing behind a big *something* on the back of the truck. I smiled and waved my hand. Maybe he'd seen Grampa!

"Zed! Ten o'clock!" the man shouted from the back of the truck.

"Hold your fire!" another man yelled as he ran around the front of the truck and toward me.

He was holding a gun, too, and it was a lot bigger than Mom's. He slowed as he approached as he looked me up and down. He was wearing green, just like the color of the truck.

"Hi," I said and rubbed my sore throat.

The turned back to his friends. "He's okay. He's not infected."

The man came down on a knee and held out an opened bottle of water. I grabbed it with more speed than I thought I could muster and chugged the water, though I spilled some by accident.

The man gave me a nice smile and handed me a candy bar. I liked him already.

"You're safe now," he said. "I'm Captain Tyler Masden with the National Guard at Camp Fox. You can call me Tyler."

He held out his hand, and I gave him my empty bottle.

"My name is Benji Hennessey, and I live at One-Fourteen Maple Street," I said as I tore into the candy bar, and then added, "But my mom got sick, so I had to leave."

Tyler gave a sad nod. "Sorry to hear that. There are a lot of people getting...sick lately." After a moment, he frowned. "How'd you get to be all the way out here?"

"I rode my bike, but then it broke, so then I walked."

Tyler whistled. "That's impressive. I bet you could use a ride."

"Yeah," I said with an eager nod and quickly added, "I have to find Grampa."

"And where's he?" Tyler asked.

"That way." I pointed. "Grampa lives three hours from my house."

"Three hours? That's an awfully long ways. It's getting late. How about I take you to Camp Fox for the night? There are no sick people there. How's that sound, Benji?"

"That sounds nice, but I can't," I replied. "I have to find Grampa. He's looking for me."

Tyler's lips tightened but he didn't seem angry. "Well, we'd better see if we can find him. Do you know your grandfather's phone number?"

"Two."

"Is that all?"

I frowned and then smacked my head. "Oh, no. You have to hit the tic-tac-toe button first."

Tyler smirked. "Well, maybe we'll try to find him another way."

"Hey, Maz, You're not going to believe this," the man said from the back of the truck. "The Camp reported that Lee's squad brought in a guy with the same last name a few hours ago. He said he was on his way to pick up his grandson named Benji, but he'd had a car accident on the way."

Tyler reached out his hand. "How about we get you to your grandfather, Benji?"

I put my hand into his and smiled. "I'd like that very much. It's been a bad day."

CDC Case Definition: Zombiism

Zombiism (*Marburgvirus Zonbistis*)
2013 Case Definition

CSTE Position Statement
19-ID-52

Clinical Description

Zonbistis is transmitted to humans by direct exposure to infected tissues. The disease is characterized by clinical death, congealed blood, jaundice, stiff gait, insatiable hunger, and severe violent propensities. Infected hosts display minimal brain functioning. To promote transmission, *Zonbistis* enhances activity in the hypothalamus, thus increasing the host's appetite and likelihood of biting, although the infected have shown less interest in eating, and the underlying reason has yet to be determined. The virus has proven extremely resilient and virulent, continually replenishing itself within its host. Only severe trauma to the host's brain stem or destruction of the virus through fire is believed to eradicate the virus in the host.

If exposed to the virus, infection rate is 99.998%. There is no known cure. Upon initial infection, *Zonbistis* will take over its host anywhere from seven minutes to three hours, depending on severity of initial infection, level of injuries, and the host's physical condition. At the point of the host's clinical death, the virus is considered to have taken over.

When first contracted, initial symptoms include acute or insidious onset of fever and one or more of the following: headache, sweating, diplopia, blurred vision, bulbar weakness, hypoxia and/or dyspnea, nausea, vomiting, and shock.

Laboratory Criteria for Diagnosis

Detection of *Zonbistis* spp. in clinical specimen or isolation of *Zonbistis* spp. from wound or ingestion.

Case Classification

Suspected: Symptoms suggestive of *Zonbistis*.

Probable: A clinically compatible case with presumptive laboratory results.

Confirmed: A clinically compatible case with confirmatory laboratory results.

Comments

The virus is believed to have originated in a genetically modified pesticide undergoing testing in Brazil. When the pesticide was combined with an organic cleaning agent, the silica-coated cells of the pesticide were shown to have mutated into *Zonbistis*.

Comparing Deadland to the Divine Comedy

Author's Note: Dante's Inferno

100 Days in Deadland is set in near-future Midwest America decimated by a zombie plague. In this truly unique story, our heroine, Cash, and her guide, Clutch, are forced on a journey through hell that echoes the one Dante and Virgil took in the "Inferno," the world-renowned first poem in Dante Alighieri's epic medieval tale, **The Divine Comedy**. In both tales, there are nine circles of hell that must be survived, and the thirty-four cantos of the "Inferno" are reflected in the thirty-four chapters of **100 Days in Deadland**...reimagined zombie apocalypse style.

100 Days in Deadland follows the pair of survivors, caught up in the sudden rush of the zombie plague, which begins on Thursday, the day before Good Friday. Once thrown into Dante's "Inferno", Cash and Clutch come across the three types of sinful beasts: the self-indulgent (zombies), the violent (survivors), and the malicious (Doyle, who represents Satan).

In each circle of hell, Cash and Clutch witness the same sins that Dante and Virgil had many centuries ago. However, where Dante often stood on the sidelines, Cash is thrown deep into the action. As Cash progresses through each circle of hell, she is changed by her environment. And, like Dante, Cash survives each circle by holding onto hope, having faith in her guide (Clutch, who represents the poet Virgil), and demonstrating unrelenting perseverance.

Like Dante's "Inferno," **100 Days in Deadland** is a story of the human condition, showing how our experiences change us. You will find violence, heartbreak, and tragedy. However, you will also find perseverance, compassion, and hope. Dante's "Inferno" also lays out four key components of every apocalyptical (and even every zombie) story: the end of the world as we know it, cause and effect of the human condition, perseverance, and—as shown in the poem's last line—enduring hope:

"It was from there that we emerged, to see—once more—the stars."

Symbolism to the "Inferno" is lush on nearly every page of **100 Days in Deadland**, from the obvious call-out, "Abandon all hope all ye who enter here" in chapter three to the subtlest hints, such as Cash shooting awake to the sound of a "thunderous" blast at the beginning of chapter four. The weather, such as the violent winds and storms starting in Lust (when Cash and Clutch come across the victim with pale lips at the corn bin, i.e. the "carnal tower"), echoes both the atmosphere of the "Inferno."

In chapter six, Cash ends up in a cafeteria full of hungry zeds, not much different from the sixth canto, which held tortured souls cursed with "insatiable hunger." In chapter seven, when Cash and Clutch arrive at the Pierson farm, they find money left on the table, a modest reminder of the Dante's message that money can't buy peace.

Doyle's camp represents Dis, the evil city in the Inferno that holds the darkest secrets and the most violent and treacherous sinners. Its true name is implied in chapter eight by the sign reading *Doyle's Iowa Surplus*, where only the capital letters are easily recognizable in the faded paint, foreshadowing that the camp will play a pivotal role in the final circle of Hell, where Cash must defeat Doyle.

In addition to Cash taking a journey parallel to that which Dante took, hundreds more echoes of Dante's "Inferno" can be found in **100 Days in Deadland**. But, the story you just read is not and never was meant to be a replacement for Dante's "Inferno." It is not designed to help you get an "A" in English if you read this novel instead of Dante Alighieri's epic poem. This story was meant to be an enjoyable read, which I hope is exactly how you found it.

Author's Note: Dante's Purgatorio

Loosely based on Dante Alighieri's "Purgatorio" (the second poem of the three-part *Divine Comedy)*, *Deadland's Harvest* covers the continuing journey of Cash and her guide, Clutch, through the zombie apocalypse. When this story begins, Cash (representing Dante) has gained experience and confidence from surviving the "Inferno" in *100 Days in Deadland,* and is better prepared to handle the deadly sins, of which she and others are found guilty. Since they are the *deadly* sins, there is plenty of death to be found in each section and chapter (paralleling the poem's cantos).

As with the first book in the *Deadland Saga, Deadland's Harvest* is a tale of suffering and spiritual growth and a continuation of the story of the human condition. As with "Purgatorio", each terrace purges a particular sin in an appropriate manner. At its heart, *Deadland's Harvest* is about penance. Cash and the Fox survivors cannot move on until the sin is recognized and acknowledged. There are implications to each deadly sin, portrayed by either survivors or zeds and often resulting in the deaths of innocents.

At the macro level, *Deadland's Harvest* is focused more inwardly than *100 Days in Deadland* and you'll see the main characters evolve in their own way. Cash, like Dante, begins to take accountability for her own life (and sins). Clutch (representing Virgil and later, Beatrice) continues as her guide, but their roles become more balanced through their journey as Clutch morphs from purely her guide to her love. It takes Clutch awhile to transition from the guise of Virgil to Beatrice. He must overcome his PTSD and injuries and open his heart to Cash. Only once he becomes Beatrice can he finally become the leader he needs to be. Similarly, Jase also morphs from a supporting character to a man in his own right by taking on the role of the great Statius.

While there are plenty of "Purgatorio" Easter eggs in this novel, I also intentionally broke from Dante Alighieri's storyline to stay true to the *Deadland Saga*. For example, this story does not start on Easter but instead starts exactly six months after Easter. For ease, I labeled the name of the first section "Purgatory" rather than the various levels of ante-purgatory.

I kept true to the themes and symbols in "Purgatorio" as much as possible. Here are just a few images you'll find similar between the two stories:

- In Purgatory, Clutch, Wes, and Cash hide from a herd of zeds (representing the penitent) traveling slowly, "like a flock of sheep." Later in Purgatory, Cash needs two keys to unlock their path to continue. In this case, one key opens the hangar, and the other starts the airplane.
- In Pride, Cash, like Dante, is guilty of the first deadly sin, which others have suffered for.
- In Wrath, black smoke erupts on the *Aurora* when the *Lady Amore* shoots flares at the barge.
- In Greed, the earth trembles as the herds arrive.
- In Gluttony, the starving zeds (again representing the penitent) surround the *Aurora*, which represents the fruit tree forever out of reach and surrounded by a river.
- In Lust, the Fox survivors are so desperately eager to be free from zeds, they set a fire that burns out of control and leads to their punishment. The survivors, representing the penitent, walk through flames as they struggle to escape the fire, the punishment for lack of self-restraint.

For the full list of Easter eggs, visit my website at www.rachelaukes.com.

Author's Note: Dante's Paradiso

Thank you for reading **Deadland Rising**, the final novel in the three-part **Deadland Saga**. Inspired by Dante Alighieri's **Divine Comedy**, the **Deadland Saga** takes the reader through a journey that echoes the one Dante took in the three poems that comprise the **Divine Comedy**.

In **Deadland Rising**, reminiscent of "Paradiso," Dante (represented by Cash) and Beatrice (represented by Clutch) discover redemption and salvation in the final part of their journey. Zeds play a smaller role as the survivors switch from running from sin (monsters) to rediscovering their humanity.

Like "Paradiso," this story covers virtues and how love can heal the worst of wounds. The thirty-three chapters reflect the thirty-three cantos of the poem, and Easter eggs can be found throughout **Deadland Rising**. Here are just a few items you'll find similar between the two stories:

- In Uncertainty, Cash and Clutch come across a nun (Piccarda Donati) and other historical people.
- In Ambition, they learn from Justinian, a Roman emperor and talented orator.
- In Prudence, they are surrounded by light (both sunlight and candlelight).
- Fires are an underlying theme of Fortitude.
- In Courage, they look from high (on the roof) over the wolves (of the capital).

• As with all three poems, all three novels end with "stars."

For the full list of over one hundred Easter eggs, visit my website at www.rachelaukes.com.

About the Author

Rachel Aukes is the award-winning author of over thirty novels, including *100 Days in Deadland*, which made Suspense Magazine's Best of the Year list. She is also a Wattpad Star, her stories having over seven million reads. When not writing, she can be found flying old airplanes over the Midwest countryside and catering to an exceptionally spoiled fifty-pound lapdog.

Join Rachel's spam-free newsletter to be the first to hear about new releases: www.rachelaukes.com/join

www.ingramcontent.com/pod-product-compliance
Lightning Source LLC
Chambersburg PA
CBHW070225200726
48293CB00005B/1468